THE DARK BL

Freda Warrington was born in Leicestershire and grew up in the beautiful Charnwood Forest area which inspired a feeling for atmosphere, nature, colour and fantasy. After training at Loughborough College of Art and Design, she worked in medical art, graphic design and illustration while writing novels in her spare time. She now lives in Derbyshire. Her first novel, *A Blackbird in Silver*, was published in 1986. Her first two vampire novels, *A Taste of Blood Wine* and *A Dance in Blood Velvet*, are available from Pan Books.

FREDA WARRINGTON

DARK BLOOD
OF
POPPIES

PAN BOOKS

First published 1995 by Macmillan Publishers

This edition published 1996 by Pan Books
an imprint of Macmillan Publishers Ltd
25 Eccleston Place, London SW1W 9NF
and Basingstoke

Associated companies throughout the world

ISBN 0 330 33850 1

1 3 5 7 9 8 6 4 2

A CIP catalogue record for this book is available from
the British Library

Typeset by CentraCet Limited, Cambridge
Printed and bound in Great Britain by
Mackays of Chatham plc, Chatham, Kent

This book is dedicated to our friends,
the Warringtons in California:
Freda, Ralph, Alisa and Danny, with love and thanks.

CONTENTS

IRELAND, 1704

On the night the vampires came, Sebastian Pierse was thinking of vengeance, grief, fire and blood. Perhaps it was his anguish that drew the vampires to him. He gripped his injured right arm but he hardly felt the pain, or the hot ichor running from the gash to mingle with the rain on the cobblestones. With sweat and rain running into his eyes, he put his head back and uttered a raw scream of rage and desolation.

The cry rang off the walls and was swallowed in the downpour. The courtyard was the heart of the magnificent house he had built for his wife Mary, but in darkness it was forbidding, a roofless prison.

He had worked for eight years to create the mansion and the deer park on the banks of the River Blackwater, the grandest house County Waterford had ever seen. He had dreamed of taking Mary out of the draughty tower house to begin their family in the residence they deserved. It was days from being finished. And now he was going to burn it to the ground.

He had been going to call it Mary Hall after her. Not now. They would never live in it now.

Nothing left but to reduce the dream to literal ash.

Sebastian stared at the rows of lightless windows above him. His overwrought mind played tricks; he thought he saw shapes moving across the panes and his nerves jumped. *Who's inside? Those shadows again!* No, only a wave of rain.

What will it take, he wondered savagely, to set this place afire? An English army would have been of some use now, Cromwell's or William's; adepts at the gutting of tower houses and castles. Where are they when they're needed? Can one man do it alone, with only peat and firewood to set it ablaze?

Yes, he told himself, and in his madness he believed it. I'll burn it, however long it takes.

But he could hardly move his arm. He was shivering. His shirt clung to him, the linen soaked with watered blood, the lace ruined. When Mary had told him the truth back at the old house, that primitive stone pile, he'd had no urge to punish her physically. Not even to seek out her lover and avenge himself with a sword-thrust. All he could think of was the house, symbol of his family's survival, the future. But in a few words his wife had turned the future to winter.

The child isn't yours, Sebastian.

The sight of her haunted him; her long skeins of wheat-coloured hair, the curve of her belly under the white chemise, her face blanched with hate and fear as she made the admission. Her hand reaching behind her for a pair of scissors, as if to defend herself, even though he'd never shown her violence in his life. But he'd left her and run out into the night, across the ploughed fields and the woods and the long slopes of the estate, as if running could excise the wild grief of betrayal.

The shadows had followed him; shapes cut from the night, seen from the corner of his eye. For years he'd been a self-contained man, experiencing no strong emotions – until tonight. Tonight he'd gone insane.

He had tripped and fallen on a rock, gashing his forearm. The cut went almost to the bone and the blood was still oozing, but he didn't care.

After all we did to keep our property out of the hands of the English! His ancestors were half-Welsh Anglo-Normans, Catholics who'd come to Ireland in the twelfth century and intermarried with the Irish until the English came to regard them as no better than Gaelic chieftains. But Sebastian's family had survived the numerous attempts to confiscate their lands.

My father and grandfather got the better of Elizabeth and Cromwell, he thought. *God forgive me, I even turned Prot-estant to outwit William of Orange. So much effort and sacrifice – only to find it was for nothing! But if I can have no descendants to inherit this house, I am damned if anyone else* shall have it. Not Mary, not my brothers, not some accursed Englishman.

He swayed, his vision blurring. Again he sensed figures around him, flat as shadows against the courtyard walls.

He had been seeing them all day, even before he discovered Mary's faithlessness.

He'd been seeing them for years. In the corners of his study, when he had read late into the night; flitting between tree-trunks when he rode out to see his tenant farmers; writhing on the freshly plastered walls of the mansion, after the artisans had gone and he was there alone.

Sebastian turned, trying to see them more clearly; to convince himself they weren't really there. He had to plant his feet wide apart to keep his balance, he was suddenly so dizzy. His heart began to beat harder. It was the eternal presence of the shadows over the years that had helped to make him into a brooding introvert, at ease only in his own company.

You are never here! Mary had cried. *Always cloistered in your own room, or out on the farms, or up at the new house with your architects and builders. I never see you!*

What defence was that against the crime of adultery?

The fire, he thought. Must do it now while I can still stand –

The black sky split open, and the rain became a deluge. Cursing, he ran across the courtyard, boots slipping on the cobbles, and reached the door to one of the cellars behind the kitchen. He was soaked to the skin, his breeches hanging heavily on him. There were logs and kindling in this cellar, he knew. Wait until the rain stops, he thought, lifting the latch and stumbling inside. Then I'll do it. And perhaps I'll die in the blaze.

The darkness inside the cellar was absolute, but he knew the shape of it. A long chamber with recesses for storage. A low, arched ceiling, curving down into the walls. Racks set ready for barrels of beer and wine. Just a store-room . . . but to Sebastian it had an atmosphere of intense menace, like an ancient torture chamber, silent but for the drip of water and the sobbing of its ghosts.

He sank down against a wall, cradling his right arm in his left. Even in despair, he didn't weep. He never wept.

Then someone shut the door. He heard the hinges creak, saw the strip of greyness narrow and vanish. Then there was the distinct sound of the bolts being fastened.

Sebastian scrambled to his feet. 'Who's there?' He said it in English and again in Gaelic, but there was no reply.

He started forwards, then heard a footstep between himself and the door. They were in the cellar with him, the shadows.

He was trembling as much with rage as with fear. That anyone dared to interfere with his revenge; that he'd been so foolish as to rush out without a sword or pistol at his side.

His arm was very bad. He hadn't realized. The bleeding had stopped, but he couldn't feel his hand at all.

'Sebastian,' a voice whispered. And it was a woman's voice, with the strangest accent he had ever heard.

'Who is it? Show yourself!'

He saw eyes in the dark. The shadows had eyes! He saw a tall shape, rimmed by the faintest gold aura.

And then a light appeared; a wash of candlelight, painting the walls ochre and throwing lurid shadows from the feet of three terrifying figures.

Sebastian couldn't breathe or move. Only the edge of his rage at Mary kept him from collapsing. Yet in that annihilating moment, he forgot all his human concerns; they fell away like rags in a blast of lightning from heaven.

They were not human. They were angels. Standing before him was a magnificent golden man with extraordinary eyes, deep yellow like a cat's. He seemed to shine.

'Sebastian,' he said. His voice was beautiful yet metallic, just as he'd always imagined an angel's voice to be. 'I am Simon. Don't be afraid. We have only come for your blood and your soul.'

And in blinding terror, he knew. This was a fallen angel, Lucifer robed in glory. And for the dreadful sin he'd committed, they were about to kill him and dispatch him to hell.

He crossed himself with his good hand. The golden man laughed. His gaze fastened on Sebastian's blood-stained sleeve and remained there, as if fascinated by the blood. 'What have you done to your arm?'

In panic Sebastian looked from side to side, and saw the other two clearly. One was an attenuated man with white skin and snow-white hair, gleaming with a silver light. The third one, holding the candle, was a woman. He had never seen anything like her before, not even in Dublin or London. Her skin was dark brown like a nut, her hair a waist-length fall of blue-black silk.

All three were intensely, inhumanly beautiful. They were dressed in robes of richly coloured satin, heavy with embroidered symbols. That didn't seem strange; he would not have expected angels to dress like gentlefolk or peasants. But they were too perfect, frozen in beauty like painted statues. And although they were lifeless they seemed unnaturally animated, so vital and full of fire that the humans they resembled seemed flabby sleepwalkers by comparison.

All Sebastian's irreligious cynicism evaporated.

'Is this punishment for what I did?' he breathed.

'What did you do?' said the one called Simon, amused.

'I renounced my religion. I became a Protestant, I betrayed my father and brothers. I know it was a sin but it was the only way I could claim the estate and keep it out of English hands!'

'This is nothing to do with that,' said Simon. He came closer as he spoke, but Sebastian would have backed into the others if he'd moved. 'God recognizes no sects. No, Sebastian, we haven't come to punish you. We have watched you for a long time.'

Simon placed his hands on Sebastian's shoulders. His eyes were new-minted sovereigns, spellbinding. Holding Sebastian's gaze, he lifted the injured arm, peeled back the wet sleeve and began to lick the wound. Sebastian, horrified, could do nothing to stop him.

'Why?' he whispered. 'What are you?' But as he spoke, he knew. Not angels or devils but the faerie folk, the old Irish gods who had existed for thousands of years before Christianity drove them out. The children of the goddess Danu . . .

'Vampires,' said the woman. She came up behind him and

put her arms round his slim waist. 'Immortals. *Others*. My name is Rasmila and our friend is Fyodor. Don't be afraid of us. Tell us what is wrong. Why are you here alone, in such pain?'

Hypnotized by her voice and by Simon's eyes, Sebastian felt that the world had imperceptibly shaded into another realm, and he began to speak.

'Tell me, how better could I show my love for my wife than by building her this house? But she says I never loved her. Ten years we've longed to have a child. When she told me she was with child at last I was so happy, I couldn't wait to bring her here to live like a queen as she deserved, to leave a great mansion for our descendants ... until I found out that the baby isn't mine. A servant told me she had taken a lover while she was staying in Dublin a few months since, that she'd done it because I couldn't give her children. So I asked her and she admitted it. She said it was my fault, that I was never with her, that she wanted to prove she wasn't barren. But I was working for her while she was acting the brood mare with another man! And now she loves him and I have no wife, no child, nothing. So I built the house for nothing. It must be demolished.'

'Poor Sebastian,' Rasmila said into his shoulder.

'But what are you thinking of?' said Fyodor, stroking his neck, regarding him with pitiless silver eyes. Their hands felt hot and cold, like the sun and like finest porcelain. 'Destroying this house is not revenge. Shedding blood is revenge!'

Simon lowered the arm from his lips, still cradling it. Sebastian looked at the torn, discoloured skin as if it did not belong to him. The pain had receded. 'Fyodor is right. This house is innocent; if you burn it down you only hurt yourself. But if you desire true revenge – we can give you that.'

'How?' Sebastian was shivering with awe – and now with a fearful excitement.

'Give yourself to us, and we'll empower you to do anything you desire,' said Rasmila.

'What's the price? My soul?'

'You think you possess a soul?' said Fyodor contemptuously. 'You are only a thought in God's head.'

'But His thoughts can live for ever.' Simon's large hand, with fingers like gold rods, hovered over his chest. Sebastian felt his life caught in a metal-cold balance.

'You were my choice,' said Rasmila. 'Mine. You are beautiful and perfect. We love you, Sebastian. Who do you love? Mary?'

'I love . . .' He could feel his knees, his whole being giving way. 'I love this house.'

Fyodor grinned. 'Then sweep your enemies from your path, and you'll be free!'

'Free?'

'To follow another path,' said Simon.

'I don't understand.'

'Give us your body and your blood, and in return we'll give you life eternal.'

'No,' he said weakly. 'No.' But he knew he was going to let them have their way. He was selling himself to the devil – but as he sank into it he was still half-resisting, thinking, God help me! Save me!

God remained mute.

'We are the wings of heaven,' whispered Rasmila. Her kohl-lined eyes ensorcelled him; her warm mouth met his, igniting all his nerves. As she began to make love to him, he couldn't resist, even with Simon and Fyodor watching. Didn't want to resist. He let her unlace his shirt and breeches, barely aware of his injured arm. He felt her fingers slide against his bare skin; he kissed the unreal flesh of her neck and breasts. Astonishment and desire took him in a flash-flood, all the frustration of his poisoned love for Mary. In an unholy dream he pushed her down on to the flagstones, running his hand along the firm thigh beneath her robe. Underneath she was softly, sweetly naked.

Oh, she was human. Oh God, she was.

He entered her urgently, oblivious to the fact that two deities, like gold and silver flames, bore witness. Perhaps he was failing some test, giving in to temptation, but he didn't care. The fire was everything. She clutched at him, kissing his throat, laughing and gasping encouragement, and he couldn't hold back.

The fire peaked, so complete and perfect that it was almost painful. The bliss made him sob. But it was over too soon. Then his whole body ached with coldness and the terror reclaimed him. His only impulse was to haul himself out of her arms, out of this madness.

She held him fast, seeming angry. Such strength, for a woman! He hadn't satisfied her but he didn't care, he only wanted to escape the eerily dispassionate ferocity with which she gripped him, her arms round his back, her legs locked round his.

The attack came from two directions at once, insidious as sword-cuts; no pain at first, only a sense of shock, of his skin being pinched and pulled harder and harder . . .

Rasmila was biting his throat. Her teeth had broken the flesh, the sensation plunging so deep through nerves and muscles that it seemed to needle his heart. And the pale one, Fyodor, was closing his mouth over the wound in his right arm. He did not lick at it as Simon had done; he reopened it savagely, sucking hard so the blood flowed again.

Sebastian began to choke for breath. He knew that this sick feeling and the buzzing in his head was the beginning of death. He must fight it but he couldn't. He was losing. Dying.

'Yes, you will die.' Simon's voice came down a great, echoing tunnel. 'But you will live again. You will be like us.'

A god. The thoughts whirled through him as he was jerked out of his body and into a burning, gold and purple firmament. *A milk-skinned betrayer with the jewelled eyes of a saint.*

When Sebastian returned to the old house, he found Mary fully dressed in her chamber, throwing clothes into a trunk. And her lover was with her; some thin-faced, English-educated Protestant he'd never seen before. He'd come to take Mary away. Cheek of the devil.

Seeing him, they both shrank away in terror, clutching each other. How cold and bare this stone chamber was, but Mary had forfeited the luxury of the new house. He wondered what he looked like; demonic, he imagined, his clothes ragged and blood-streaked, his face luminous with the light of un-death.

'There's nothing to be afraid of,' Mary told her lover. 'My husband's gentle, he won't lift a finger to us. Tell him I'm going with you!'

Sebastian killed the man before he opened his mouth. Tore his throat out with his fingernails, saying as he did so, 'I'd rather she'd had some Irish peasant under a hedgerow than you.'

Mary screamed. She tried to escape but he held her easily with one hand, even though she was a tall, strong woman. Even though his hand had been all but useless a few hours earlier. There was no sign of the wound, not even a scar on the flawless skin.

And Sebastian felt completely calm. Unmoved by her terror, unmoved even by the knowledge of her infidelity. It no longer seemed to matter. But her beauty moved him; she was still lovely, magnificent with her handsome face and luxuriant hair and the sweet rosy glow of her skin.

'All I wanted was to give you a son!' she cried.

'I would rather have had you, and no son.'

'I tried so hard to love you, but you didn't want me!'

'You are mistaken,' he said quietly. 'Let me show you how I wanted you.' And he bit her throat.

Then he wept. His tears flowed out with her blood; and all the passion he'd never realized he felt for her, all the passion he had neglected to show her, all of it was distilled in the crimson heart of that moment.

His love for her sated, he let her lifeless body slip to the floor. And the servants came running in, screaming, but he walked past them as if nothing had happened; walked into the darkness and vanished.

Afterwards, he stood on a hill with Simon, Rasmila and Fyodor, looking up at the stars. Nets of light webbed a clear deep sky; he'd never before seen with such clarity, never dreamed that such crystalline beauty was hidden from mortal

9

eyes. And he could see for miles; northwards to the River Suir, the towers of Cahir Castle, the Golden Vale of Tipperary and Cashel of the Kings; close at hand, his own estate, the stump of the stone tower where Mary lay dead, and the unnamed hall, a great, pristine mansion like a gold casket swathed in deep blue twilight. The River Blackwater flowing darkly past; the peaks of the Galtee and Knockmealdown mountains; and in between, the quilt of pasturelands and luxuriant woods, steeped in a thousand tints of green and violet and silver. Night colours he'd never seen before. The air was sweet and icy, like wine.

'And was your revenge satisfying?' Simon asked.

'It was meaningless,' said Sebastian.

Simon nodded as if he understood, but Fyodor said, 'To milk your enemies of their blood – meaningless?'

'I thought it would be a great, affecting tragedy, but it wasn't. The one thing that mattered . . .' He struggled to explain, as much to himself as to them. 'The only thing that mattered was the blood. I realized as I drank my wife's blood that no other affection, nothing that held me in life, can hold a corpse-light to that red passion.'

'Exactly,' Simon said intensely. 'And now you're free of your earthly bonds.'

'Free?' He looked at Simon; still awed by his gilded beauty, yet no longer afraid of it. 'What does that mean? I don't care about Mary. I don't care about the house or the estate or any of it. If the price of my revenge is to care about nothing but blood for all eternity, I might as well be dead. You three have done this to me, and I don't even know why! And I should be angry, but I'm not, because even that doesn't matter.'

Rasmila slipped her hand through his arm. 'Don't be angry. You will find other things to care about. What will you do now? Stay here, or leave?'

'What?' Sebastian looked at her in amazement. 'I thought you meant to take me with you.'

'Ah, no,' said Simon. 'We are immortals, not nursemaids. We've bestowed these glorious powers on you, but it is up to you to learn how to use them. I'm afraid you are on your own.'

For a moment, Sebastian felt the absolute terror of abandonment. 'You can't leave me now! Why have you done this to me?'

Rasmila replied, 'Once or twice in a century, we choose an individual whom we think worthy of receiving these gifts; power over humans, eternal life, a glimpse of heaven. You were my choice, Sebastian. You will be a wonderful immortal; don't let me down.'

With the terror subsiding, he realized he was glad. He did not want these divine, malevolent creatures around him for all time; more than ever, he wanted to be on his own.

'You want me to prove myself? Or rather, to prove to your comrades that you did not make a bad choice?'

'Of course,' she said stiffly, withdrawing her hands from his arm.

'Well, you can go to hell, all of you,' he said. He was becoming aware of the blood-thirst as a sprawling, red, uncontrollable entity; the coldness of his own heart as a terrifying wasteland. Nothing of paradise or any faerie realm. 'Hell. That is surely where you came from, is it not?'

They all looked at him with hard, cold eyes. They hadn't expected this ingratitude. He thought, perhaps they could kill me as easily as they made me, but if they do I don't much care. I'm not afraid of them and I never will be again.

'We did not transform you to win your love or your hatred,' Simon said sternly. 'Your feelings mean nothing to us. We are only God's messengers; this is God's way of testing you. You will learn that this existence is both a blessing and a curse. The pleasures of immortality have a severe price; to be alone for ever.'

'Good,' Sebastian said harshly. 'That's what I want. You have it the wrong way round, my friends; solitude is the blessing, blood-hunger the curse.'

Simon and Rasmila looked at one another; exquisite demons with eyes of flame, disappointed yet amused by his insolence.

And Sebastian decided that he would be the one to leave, before they had a chance to abandon him. The only way to show he was not their victim. He began to walk through the long grass, down the narrow road into the endless dark.

No one came after him, not even Rasmila.

He knew he had to leave Ireland. He felt the whole world opening up to him, although it was no longer the world he knew, but a dark twin of its daylight self. But before he left, he felt compelled to take a last look at his house.

How often had he walked through these cavernous rooms? The entrance hall and kitchens; above, the great saloon with its double row of long windows, the library, the drawing-rooms and dining-rooms, the bedchambers, the nursery; all silent, shadowy, empty. The scents of fresh paint, new timber and polish infused the air, as heady as mead. Most of the craftsmen's clutter had been cleared away and the rooms were naked, aching to be filled by carpets and furniture, paintings, books and ornaments. To receive the imprint of a family's personality.

He had walked through these rooms with pride and optimism; he'd run through them in anguished despair, cursing them as if Mary's infidelity were their fault. And now he haunted them in a quiet reverie, saying goodbye.

Someone will live here, he thought, but it will not be me. Some other family will shape these spaces to their own design and it won't meet with my approval, but . . .

A revelation. He still cared about the house after all. The human urge to destroy it had passed. He didn't even begrudge it to strangers.

A tightness in his chest, like the strange new blood-thirst, like euphoria. It doesn't matter! The house still belongs to me. It will always be mine in spirit, and whoever lives here will never feel at ease, because they'll know they are only tenants of an unseen landlord.

It is time to leave, he thought, but one day I shall come back.

They'd seduced him with the devil's promises, the old gods; ravaged him and flung him into this incomprehensible purgatory. He brooded bitterly as he walked away from his home, away from everything that had mattered . . . but in truth, he knew he'd wanted it. He'd invited it, drawing them to him with his love of solitude, the heat of his despair, his yearning for fire and revenge.

Sebastian was new-born, but he felt ancient. The vampires had only given him what he needed.

PART ONE

PART ONE

Man's daughter she is not, nor Angel's bride
beyond paradise's prolific marshes
waiting to be milked
the unicorn
carries her, Lilith, who already knows
the mysterious form of the mandrake root
and the golem that grows in the kernel. She knows
that jasper placed in henbane
causes a mortal sleep, drier and stranger
than the one fastening on Orpheus' back
that in the starred moray's vulva
there is a mermaid's embryo
in the tiger lily the latex
that will beget Amazons, and one hundred
female deities are waiting in the steeped firtree
in the shape of gold ducklings
another hundred female deities
will be nursed by unicorns and their blood
will be white to contagion, prescient to fire.

Rosanna Ombras
'The Song of Lilith'
Translated by Edgar Pauk

CHAPTER ONE

CRUEL ANGEL

Violette Lenoir, prima ballerina assoluta, was not proud of her ability to inspire terror.

Of course, it has its uses, she thought as she watched her *corps de ballet* daintily traversing the mirrored studio. I need their respect; without it, I'd have no authority. Perfection requires discipline.

Sometimes, though, she would go too far. If she involuntarily let her vampire nature slip through the human façade and really frightened some poor girl or boy, afterwards she would feel mortified. So she was always on her guard. It made her seem a ruthless taskmaster, never cheerful, never relaxed.

Violette was standing at the barre, supervising rehearsals for *Coppélia*. She was dressed like her dancers in practice clothes; leotard, skirt and tights of grey wool. She was not tall but she seemed so, being very slender and long-limbed. And she looked like Snow White, with her alabaster skin and black hair — confined at present in a loose bun on her neck — her claret mouth and large knowing eyes. Their colour was startling and changeable, sometimes deep blue, sometimes violet, like the iridescent wings of a butterfly.

As a human, she had been just as beautiful and had danced with equal grace, albeit with greater effort. She had always commanded respect, been renowned for her perfectionism and adored for her talent. Outwardly, nothing had changed.

No one has guessed, she thought. None of my dancers, musicians or staff, not even Geli, has any suspicion that a few months ago I became a vampire, or something worse ... No one knows what Charlotte and her friends did to me, that day they brought me into the Crystal Ring.

I can see it in my own eyes, she thought, catching a glimpse of herself in the mirror – but they can't. Or at least, they think the cold light there is just me playing the autocrat. They don't know *why* they are frightened of me. Thank goodness vampires cast reflections after all, or I really should be in trouble.

The ballet was still her life, and she couldn't give it up. If she was to go on working in the human world, it was vital that the truth remained her secret. Such a struggle, though, against the blood-thirst, the raging entity that dwelled in her soul. A perpetual strain to keep it in check.

While these thoughts wove across the back of her mind, she was watching the dancers with intense concentration. Their synchronization was still imperfect. One girl, Ute, whose technique was usually flawless, had been making mistakes all afternoon.

'No!' Violette snapped. The pianist came to an abrupt halt. 'We changed that step yesterday. Can't you remember anything? Like this!'

Moving to the centre of the studio, she demonstrated *en pointe*, her blocked shoes barely making a sound. The girls watched raptly, desperate not to fall short of Madame's expectations.

'Try again,' Violette said crisply.

She knew they were tired, but she felt no pity for them. Her own teachers had never shown her any. 'If you cannot stand hard work, leave,' was the advice she would give any dancer who had the audacity to complain. Harsh, but realistic.

This time, the *corps de ballet* was perfect . . . until Ute went wrong yet again on the simplest step.

Violette felt like shaking her, but she forcibly suppressed the urge. Such feelings were dangerous; letting them loose could unleash the floodgates of her vampire thirst. She must always hold herself like stone against her emotions.

'Ute!' Her voice made the mirrors ring. 'What is the matter with you? If this is the best you can do, perhaps you had better consider giving up your role to someone who can concentrate.'

The girl, thin and elfin with honey-coloured hair, looked at the floor. She was a fine dancer and should make a prima ballerina one day. But Violette could see that something was badly wrong today.

The long curve of Ute's neck held her attention. She asked more gently, 'What actually is the matter?'

Ute's reaction was to flee the studio in tears. The others shifted uneasily and looked knowingly at one another. Madame Lenoir had reduced them all to breaking point at one time or another. They were better dancers for it, but they never forgot the pain. Violette knew they half-hated her sometimes.

'Continue,' she said, and the long-suffering pianist began again.

Violette knew she pushed her dancers too hard. She had almost forgotten how it felt to battle with aching, stinging muscles, to dance on until she was almost blind with exhaustion. Since she had become un-human, she no longer needed to warm up before class; her limbs were always strong and supple, and she could have danced for days if she'd wished. And that made her impatient with human weakness, even though she knew she was being unfair.

Less than a year ago, she had been fighting a continual war against the arthritic disease that was slowly eroding her joints and locking her spine. Would I still have been dancing now, if it hadn't been for Charlotte? No, I would have been looking forward to life in a wheelchair. But the price I am paying . . .

When the rehearsal was over, she went to her office and found Ute outside, her face drawn and eyes bruised from crying. Violette took her inside, sat her down on a hard chair, and gave her a handkerchief. The lights, under blue shades, cast a cool harebell glow.

'I don't mean to upset you,' Violette began. 'Anyone can make mistakes. But it's only a few weeks until we sail for America and with two ballets to remember we can't afford to be less than perfect. You should understand by now why I have to be so strict.'

'Of course, Madame,' the girl whispered, her head bowed. 'It's not the discipline, I'm used to that.'

'What, then? Are you feeling ill?'

'No, Madame. It's my father, he . . . wants me to go home.

He's insisting I give up my career and go home to look after him.'

'Why? Is he sick?'

'No, he's in perfect health. He says he misses me. He doesn't think a girl should have a career, especially not on the stage. He never wanted me to come in the first place. Madame, I don't know what to do.'

'It's simple. Stay here.'

'But, Madame, you don't know him!' Sobbing again, Ute went on to explain all her father's arguments. Utterly ludicrous and selfish, they sounded to Violette. But the girl was weakening towards his demands. Her weakness made Violette furious rather than sympathetic.

She felt herself becoming Lilith, looking at the young dancer through cold and ageless eyes. Knowing that Ute must be brought face to face with her own stupidity. And Violette could not suppress the impulse, however much she wanted to.

'Are you mad?' Violette walked round her desk and gripped Ute's shoulder. The girl's head jerked up in shock. 'You would sacrifice a career as magnificent as yours will surely be, deprive the world of your talent, just to satisfy the whims of a selfish old man? What do you want to be, when you are sixty?'

'Madame?'

'Do you want to be an embittered old woman, living in obscurity in some Bavarian village – or do you want to be sitting behind this desk in my place?'

She saw the pulse jumping in Ute's neck. She felt it accelerating under her fingers. Caught the scent of her fear. And then she committed the sin. Gave in to Lilith's thirst.

That night, Violette stalked the deserted rooms in darkness, a creature condemned never to sleep. She was still in her practice clothes. Clawing at her arms like an abstracted Lady Macbeth, she stared into the darkness and felt stricken.

Her apartment above the studio was no longer a place of refuge and sleep. It had become merely somewhere to keep her possessions and change her clothes. Somewhere to be alone, yes, but she felt alone wherever she was, so it really made no difference. Her maid, Geli, must have noticed the change in her, and wondered why she no longer suffered aching backs or demanded ice-packs on her knees. Violette had made no attempt to explain, and Geli was too meek to ask.

Charlotte had insinuated herself into Violette's life without invitation. Unwelcome at first, she had soon become irresistible. A strange and lovely creature, sweetly old-fashioned, with her demure manners and a gorgeous wreath of tawny-bronze hair. Deceptive Charlotte; a demon who drank blood. And who, for all her promises of restraint, had eventually slaked her thirst from Violette's veins. It had seemed a violation, a betrayal of trust, but I encouraged her, Violette thought. I was as much to blame. And afterwards, we still couldn't leave each other alone.

Violette had not consented to becoming a vampire; not until the very last moment, at least. It was Charlotte who had insisted, forced it on her. Violette had fought, though not too hard, because somewhere in her soul she had known it was inevitable. Her fate, if such a thing existed. But she hadn't wanted it; she'd dreaded it.

Her dread had been a premonition. The condition of vampirism had proved hateful to her; the desire for blood agonizing, the bliss of sating it loathsome. But that wasn't the worst of it.

In the moment of transformation she'd become someone else. Someone who knew too much, whose talent was to corrupt and ruin and transmute.

That other being's name was Lilith.

Now Violette's life was one of conflict with her other-self. Violette fought for creativity, to keep her ballet together, to create beauty, and never to take a sip of blood from any member of her company.

Lilith's intentions were the opposite.

You cannot be a vampire and live like this, Lilith would whisper. *You cannot go against your instincts. Listen to me.* Oh, the seductive whisper in the night. *Listen, and you will know everything and be everything. Look into their pitiful souls and show them the truth!*

But Violette would not listen. She tried to turn away, but

when the thirst came on her she *was* Lilith. It was terrifying, exhilarating in a way, but still she hated it. At those times, to protect her precious dancers, she would leave the premises and wrestle with the hideous thirst outside, alone in the darkness.

Tonight, with the blood-thirst guiltily sated, her restlessness led her to the empty studio. On the expanse of polished floor, lit by long rhombuses of starlight fanning through the windows, she began to dance as if in meditation. She felt cold. This coldness had washed over her time and again today, as if someone were watching her.

She felt human presences around her in the building like motes of dust, sleeping. She sensed humans in the houses along the river bank, and across the river, where the domed and spired city of Salzburg slumbered. Sleeping mortals. Lilith's prey.

What can I do? she thought. How can I find a way to bear this?

Ute, too, lay in her little attic room, asleep or unconscious, perhaps restless with bad dreams. Violette would never forget the flat astonishment in her eyes, or the searing tang of her blood. She could only pray that the girl would forget. Ute had been dazed, stunned; her mind, unable to accept what had happened, would reject it.

I only drank a little, Violette told herself. The physical harm will pass — but what have I done to her mind, her emotions?

However strictly she treated her dancers, however aloof she appeared to be, the truth was that she cared passionately about them. Would have laid down her life for them.

When Violette-Lilith took a victim, it was not just to satisfy her thirst. There was a deeper compulsion. Her bite was transformative; it forced her victims to see themselves clearly, forced them to change. The results could be disastrous. And Violette hated bearing the responsibility, but Lilith would have her way.

Outside, the river flowed softly and the breeze, cold off the Alps, ruffled the forested hills.

Violette thought of leaving the world for a few hours and entering the Crystal Ring. But the other-realm of immortals was even colder and less comforting. There was no respite. Wherever she went, Lilith went with her.

So she danced slowly, her hair flowing loose over her shoulders.

Perhaps it would have been easier to bear if she'd known that Lilith existed only in her imagination. But others had acknowledged it. Three angelic vampires, calling themselves envoys of God, had captured her and delivered her to a human, a self-styled magus called Lancelyn, who'd had ambitions to tame and exploit her wild energies. He, too, had claimed to know her. He'd given her many titles; the Black Goddess, Sophia, Cybele; he had offered her some hope that she was not merely evil. We can empower each other, he'd said. Your darkness is the veil of Wisdom; let me lift it, let me become immortal through you. Then we will both find the truth.

She'd almost succumbed. In her despair, it seemed Lancelyn was the only one who could help. But at the end, his desires had been merely selfish. He wanted to possess her, to marry her and achieve magical communion through consummating the marriage.

And everyone wanted to control me, as if this force inside me is too terrifying to be let loose.

But Violette had always hated men, from her father onwards. Many had wanted her, several had dared to try, but she had never given in. She found their lusts repulsive. It was a matter of pride that she kept herself for ever alone and separate.

So Lilith had risen up and destroyed Lancelyn, before the violation, magical or not, took place.

I had to do it. But she wondered, could he have taught me anything? It seemed I was just on the edge of knowing. He was the only one who understood me, and now he's gone.

On the verge of indulging in self-pity, she briskly curbed the impulse. If anything helped her to cope, it was her long training in the self-discipline of ballet. She forced herself to think of nothing but the steps.

As she danced, she became aware of shadows solidifying around her, as if they were watching her, judging her.

The three angels again? She thought she'd broken their hold

over her and seen the last of them. Anger rose in her chest. Oh no, not again, she thought. You can't come back to haunt me again! Your power over me is gone. You no longer exist.

She began to dance wildly, as if to repel them, but they were closing in. And she experienced a sense of danger so extreme that it brought her to a halt.

Letting herself blend half into the Crystal Ring, she saw the intruders vividly for an instant. Five elongated demons, black and hard as jet, glittering dimly against the distorted cobweb walls. Vampires. In the other-realm, she too looked like them. Not her angelic persecutors, she realized with momentary relief . . . but who were they?

As Violette slipped back into the solid world, they came through with her, taking human form in the studio. Four men and one woman with radiant skin and the mesmeric stillness of snakes. Violette recognized only two of them; Charlotte's friend, china-faced blond Stefan and his mute twin, Niklas. Stefan had helped in Violette's transformation; she was not sure whether that made him her friend or her enemy.

Facing her, they gave minimal nods of greeting, as if to a respected opponent. Their eyes were guarded, impassive and accusing all at once, like those of a jury, and they exuded a thorned hostility that astonished her. Studying them, she felt intimidated, nervous, outraged.

'Violette?' Stefan said softly. He had the grace to look apologetic, at least. 'Please forgive the intrusion. My companions have something to say to you, but it won't take long. I don't think you've met Rachel – ' He indicated the woman, a tall, thin creature with hair like apricot flames. 'And this is John, and his companion Matthew.'

The two men were very similar; slight and pale, with long, dour faces and dark hair, cropped severely short. They had the unworldly look of holy men from mediaeval portraits, but they stared at her with suspicion and loathing. She thought, *witch finders*.

There was no courtesy in their invasion, so she showed them none in return. 'What do you want?' she demanded.

'Madame Lenoir,' said Rachel. Her polite tone was razor-edged. 'You may not know me, but you knew my closest friend. Her name was Katerina.'

A flash of ghastly memory. The metal screech of train wheels, sparks, blood smeared on a steel rail . . .

'You killed her,' said Rachel.

'I don't deny it,' Violette said thinly. 'But if I hadn't, she would have killed *my* dearest friend, Charlotte. Have you come for revenge?'

'No,' Rachel's face was like ice, translucent; her lips vividly scarlet. 'I only mention it so that you understand I am not seeking revenge. We want justice. We want you to do the right thing.'

'Which is what?'

'You must give up your ballet and your public appearances.'

Violette laughed with sheer astonishment. 'I beg your pardon? Why in the world should I do that?'

'You are breaking the laws,' Matthew said harshly. He was slightly smaller than John, and more belligerent.

'What laws?'

'The laws of God, of Satan, and of our nature.'

'Oh, do tell me about Satan!' Violette said, her anger rising.

'As vampires we are possessed by the devil,' said Matthew, clearly convinced of it. 'You must know this! We are being tormented for the sins we committed in life. As Satan's instruments we must serve and appease our master until it pleases God to release us – because, you must understand, even the Adversary is part of God's great plan. We submit in humility to our fate. But you, Lilith – you serve neither God nor Satan. You are outside. You are too arrogant, too dangerous.'

'Females of our kind are more deeply possessed than males. They have no humility, no sense of duty,' said John. His voice, though quiet, had a grating harshness. 'But you are the worst, Lilith. It is not our role to make lascivious displays of ourselves in public!'

'Immortals should vanish from mortal eyes and prey on them from the night,' said Matthew. 'You are not like us.'

'Of course I'm not like you,' Violette said contemptuously. 'You two haven't left the thirteenth century.'

Rachel said, 'You may think John and Matthew old-fashioned, but they have a point. Vampires are designed to be discreet creatures, yet every other person in the world seems to know your name. Your photograph appears in the newspapers. How long do you think you can sustain this charade? Someone's bound to notice that you are not growing older, and your nocturnal habits are a little strange. Some sharp-minded victim will recognize you.'

'None of this is any of your business.' She gazed at the golden-haired twins. 'Stefan, you don't agree with this, do you? I thought you were my friend!'

'I am,' he said softly. 'But I agree with them. You can't go on trying to live a human life.' His blue eyes had a shamefaced look, but he held her gaze steadily.

'It *is* our business,' Rachel said coolly. 'You could bring disaster on all of us, not just yourself. We're not infallible. You cannot go on flaunting yourself like this.'

'Can't I, Rachel?' Waves of rage rolled through her. Their impudence! 'Who are you, who precisely are you to come here uninvited and tell me how to behave? I don't believe you're frightened of being found out by humans. We can disappear; what can they do to us? No, it's something else.'

Rachel compressed her lips, as if she were struggling to keep the discussion civilized. 'You killed a vampire.'

Violette moved closer to her. 'Are you afraid of me?' She looked hard into each of their faces in turn. Their nervous responses both excited and alarmed her. Frightening them could well provoke them to attack her, and she was outnumbered – yet she couldn't stop. 'Do you think I am going to be another Kristian? Is that what this is about?'

'Kristian also broke the laws!' Matthew exclaimed. 'He, too, was arrogant! That was why he had to die!'

Rachel turned and glared at him, as if to quieten him. Then Violette knew for certain. They *were* afraid. So afraid that they wanted her dead. Even kind Stefan!

'How dare you assume I would want to emulate Kristian? Or that I have the remotest interest in any of you?' As she spoke,

Violette-Lilith was filled by a strange energy. How menacing, their hostile faces; how bitter it felt, to be so feared and hated! But her own fears and emotions were coalescing into a flame of ice.

'You must obey God's law,' said John.

Violette shivered. This talk of God made her ill. It brought back unwanted memories; dark shapes standing over her, the wings of cruel angels beating all around her.

'You want me to disappear, but what if I refuse?'

No one replied, but she sensed the weight of their combined wills weighing on her. They spoke for all vampires; even Karl, even Charlotte, and all those vampires she had never met but who knew of her existence, had felt her creation as a shiver of darkness through the fabric of the Crystal Ring. They all wanted her dead. But Lilith would not submit; she rose up like a great shadow in Violette's soul, ready to fight or flee.

Lilith did not need to ask why they hated her. Lilith knew.

'Well, you've made your request and my answer is no,' said Violette. 'Now if you would kindly leave . . .'

Matthew looked up at the ceiling, his face ghastly in the starlight. 'Sweet mortals, sleeping peacefully above us. Have you never partaken of their blood? You must have been tempted.'

She thought of Ute. Painful shame suffused her. 'I've sworn not to touch them,' she hissed.

'You can protect yourself, but you cannot protect them,' Matthew said softly.

'What?'

Stefan murmured, 'Matthew,' as if to silence him but it was too late, the threat had been uttered.

Violette felt her fury gathering, rising like a great glassy wave through a seashell rush of silence.

'I can take any threat to myself,' she said, 'but not to my company. No one threatens my people, *no one*.'

The wave of fury broke, crashed, exploded through her.

She lunged forward and seized Matthew by the throat. He tried to slip into the Crystal Ring but she went with him, dragged him back. His sombre expression flashed into hideous panic as she squeezed his neck, shook him, pierced the skin with her nails.

John, Rachel, Stefan and Niklas grabbed her. She threw them all off with one hand, heard them spinning across the floor, colliding with the mirrored walls. Lilith's strength seemed limitless.

Then she tightened her grip on Matthew's neck, snapped his spine, wrenched his jaw back and back until the skin ripped. Muscles and fibres tore, blood oozed like mulberries from the wound. She went on clawing at him until the vertebrae parted, the last of the fibres and the spinal cord stretched and finally broke with dull, moist popping sounds. And then she bent and drank blood from the stump of his neck.

The red fluid flowed through her like sexual pleasure. It made her tremble from head to foot. But the victim was dead.

Violette flung him aside in disgust. She was not sure at precisely what stage he had died; vampires clung to life like cockroaches. Lifting her head, she saw the others staring at her, their eyes glazed with horror. Stefan put his arms protectively around Niklas, as if he feared for his twin's life. But Niklas's eyes were incongruously blank, showing no reaction beyond a faint echo of Stefan's disbelief.

Then Violette realized what she'd done. Decapitated a vampire with her bare hands.

But Lilith hadn't finished.

She leapt up and went after Rachel next. The woman tried to flee but Violette was too fast. She seized the long hair, snagged her hand in the flamy skeins, and wound Rachel towards her. Biting into the white neck, she sucked hard. Scarlet light filled her. Rachel thrashed in helpless terror.

All the time, Violette had moved slowly and calmly, with the weightless grace of her art. It was not that she felt particularly strong. It was just that the others seemed as weak as children, as fragile as paper in her grasp.

John ran past her. Still feeding, she reached out easily and grabbed him. And as she did so, over Rachel's shoulder she saw

Stefan fleeing into the Crystal Ring. Dragging Niklas with him, he looked back over his shoulder with an expression of horror and regret – and then they vanished, as if the mirrors had swallowed them.

And if they hadn't fled she would have attacked them too, friends or not. Lilith had no pity.

Now she held Rachel and John together, one in each hand, writhing helplessly against her. Both were covered in their own blood, even though vampire blood was reluctant to flow freely. She hadn't bitten John, only ploughed his flesh with her fingers.

Then Violette found herself descending from fury into shock. As the fever subsided, she came out of it shaking, aghast at herself. Have I really been so violent? Dear God, it was so easy! I hardly even noticed what I was doing!

She shook her two captives. They were like sacks of flour in her hands.

'Now you will leave my property,' she said, her voice a blade of menace. 'And if you ever return, if you ever threaten any of my staff or any human associated with me, if I so much as see you anywhere near this place – you will think Matthew was quite lucky.' She raised her voice. 'Do you understand?'

'Yes,' Rachel gasped. Her face was wrought with primeval fear. The colour had fled her lips.

Then Violette flung her and John down, so that they landed across Matthew's body. 'Get out. And take that thing with you. Go on, take it!'

John's eyes lanced hers with venomous hatred. Now she'd slain his friend, as well as Rachel's. Now she had two mortal enemies. It would have been safer to decapitate them as well, but the killing frenzy had subsided. She couldn't do it.

'We can't take a corpse into the Ring,' Rachel whispered.

'Then leave by the back stairs. Just go!'

They obeyed. John hefted Matthew's body over his shoulder, his face a mask of blood and tears. Rachel took the head, a grisly burden. And with blank looks of fear, like two lurid demons carrying a soul to hell, they fled.

Violette listened to their soft footsteps descending, an outside door opening and closing. Their presences dwindled along the course of the river; she followed them in her mind until she could sense them no more.

She was alone. Silence settled like snow around her.

The light was static, like silver gauze. She wanted to weep, but couldn't. Her reflection showed, not a winged and clawed monster, but a young ballerina, composed, beautiful, and incapable of hurting a soul.

Violette went to the mirror and stared at the *doppelgänger*. Their fingers met and trailed across the glass; their faces had the same cool expression. The mirror held no answers.

'Help me,' she said to no one in particular. 'Help me.'

Her gaze moved to the pools and streaks of spilled blood on the floor. They glistened like the juice of berries, like jewels. She caught a succulent aroma. Oh God, the blood . . .

As if pulled by puppet-strings she felt herself kneeling, arching down to breathe the scent, to touch the blood with her tongue.

A movement made her freeze. A large black and white cat had strolled into the room and was inches from her, lapping experimentally at the same deep red stain. And Violette suddenly saw a vision of herself as a sinuous beast, half-serpent, half-wolf . . . and she leapt up in horror, panting for breath like a mortal.

'No,' she gasped, digging her nails hard into her own arms. 'No, I am not an animal!'

The cat lost interest in the blood and came to Violette, mewing and weaving around her legs as if nothing was wrong. Violette bent down and scratched the top of her pet's head. 'Magdi,' she whispered, her eyes unfocused, 'tell me it didn't happen.'

After a few minutes, Violette went into the dressing-room and filled a bucket with water and detergent. With the same diligence she applied to choreographing her ballets, she went down on her knees and set about scrubbing the bloodstains out of the smooth, varnished floor.

CHAPTER TWO

FRIENDS AND STRANGERS

On clear cold nights, when a full moon hung over the Swiss Alps, Karl and Charlotte often walked for hours through the magnificent peaks. In temperatures no human could endure, they climbed impossible slopes with ease. Anyone seeing them would have thought they were ghosts.

If there were compensations for the darkness of immortality, Charlotte reflected, this was among the greatest. To stand on the summit of a mountain, with the world rolling away in white silence below; Karl's arm around her, perfect understanding between them, their coats blowing in the icy wind.

Tonight she felt as if she were outside herself. Below the rock on which they stood was a straight two-hundred-foot drop, with a thick blanket of snow at the base. Irresistible. Detaching herself from Karl, she went to the very edge and hesitated for a moment, drunk with euphoria. Then she spread her arms, and dived into space.

The bitter air made a banshee wail in her ears. She felt weightless as she fell and completely at peace. This is what it means, to be mortal no longer.

She landed in deep soft snow, an ice-crust breaking beneath her. Plumes of white powder rose and blew away on the wind. The broken crust skittered away over a hard, gleaming surface, silver-blue starred with opals. She lay on her back, staring at the sky; the stars were so thick they were like snow crusted in the folds of black velvet. The moment seemed eternal.

There was another explosion of snow near by; Karl had jumped after her. Finding his feet, he came wading towards her.

'Charlotte!'

She accepted his hand and stood up, shaking the snow from her coat. The spark of anger in his eyes startled her.

'Have you gone mad?' he said, holding her elbows, staring hard at her. 'If you want to fly, go into the Crystal Ring. Don't attempt it on earth.'

She was taken aback by his fervour. 'I wanted to see how it felt to jump. I knew I couldn't kill myself.'

'No, but you might still have been badly hurt. Our flesh can tear and our bones can break. We heal but the pain is terrible.'

'I know.' She lowered her eyes. 'You're right. I'm sorry. But there's no harm done.'

He relented, and smiled ruefully. 'You must forgive me also, for being overprotective. Sometimes I still think of you as human.'

'Well, I'm not.'

The euphoria was still within her. He looked at her, shaking his head, more amused than annoyed. Her beautiful demon lover.

'Shall we go home?' he said.

On the path that wound down through the pine forest, they walked arm-in-arm like any innocent couple out for a stroll. Charlotte loved these moments when she could forget the blood-thirst, though it was never far from the surface. Simply bask in the pleasure of being alone with Karl.

They both sensed the presence before they saw her; a peasant woman from one of the alpine farms, heavily wrapped up against the cold, walking up the path towards them. Charlotte could smell animal blood on her. Probably she'd been up half the night helping a cow to calve, and was now looking forward to her warm bed.

In the three years that Karl and Charlotte had been together, they had always preferred to hunt separately, each feeling that the drinking of blood was too personal to be witnessed by anyone. Perhaps it was a form of denial. To hunt together would have been conscious collusion, a step too far across the borderline of evil.

Normally they would have let the woman pass by. Nothing

was different this evening, there was no reason for them not to let her go.

But something happened.

It was as if a dark, mutual need flowed between Karl and Charlotte. No word was spoken. They did not even look at each other. But as the woman reached them they stopped as one and blocked her path.

The woman almost leapt out of her skin. She was in her late twenties, fresh-faced and charming in her headscarf, shawl and long skirts. A benevolent soul. But Charlotte, seeing her through the frosted kaleidoscope of her hunger, perceived her only as prey; meaningful and precious as a sacrifice, but prey all the same. And Karl, his eyes like flames behind amber glass, shared the feeling. He did not look at all human in that moment.

The woman froze in terror as they moved around her. They weren't violent. As tender as siblings they closed in on her, embracing her with gentle hands; Charlotte feeding first, then holding her while Karl sank his wolf-teeth into the plump throat. Moving behind the victim Charlotte fed again, breaking the virgin skin on the other side of her neck.

Her hands met Karl's around the woman's hot body as they fed, so they clasped each other with the victim between them. The moment was eternal, primal, throbbing with heat and blood. Transcendent.

This was the first time they'd fed together like this. It was more than lust. It was a blood ritual, connecting them to the darkest side of their natures. Lifting them to wordless ecstasy . . . twining them in damnation.

Afterwards, they carried the woman to the edge of a village to be found; maybe to live, most likely to die. And then they went home without speaking a word.

There was nothing to say. They were both shocked to the soul, both swimming together in the same shadowy lake of passion. Moved, excited, afraid.

Home was an isolated black chalet poised high in a pine forest beneath the Alps, with the peaks of the Eiger, Mönch and Jungfrau floating on the horizon. Within, the rooms had a timeless, faded luxury. Persian rugs, muted floral wallpapers, elegant eighteenth-century furniture; a library lined from floor to ceiling with books, a music room, a kitchen that was used only by the peasant woman who climbed the steep hill to clean and dust the house twice a week. If she thought her employers strange, she was too well-paid to ask questions.

Vampires had few material needs – the only nourishment they required was blood, and they did not fall prey to disease – so they could have lived naked in graveyards, if they'd wished. Charlotte knew no one who did. They still preferred to live like humans. The trappings of ordinary life became a fascinating luxury to some; to others, a poignant connection to their lost humanity. In this, Charlotte and Karl were no different. Their house was an essential refuge.

In the drawing-room, after they'd taken off their coats, Charlotte forced Karl to look at her. It seemed he could hardly bear to do so. His exquisitely sculpted face, dark eyebrows giving bewitching intensity to his lovely eyes, soft full hair of darkest mahogany – black in shadow, red where the fire caught garnet lights on the strands – still almost stopped her heart with their beauty. But sometimes he scared her to death. Tonight had added another, irrevocable layer of darkness to their relationship.

'Now do you believe I'm not human?' she whispered.

Charlotte was lighting candles on a low table, each new flame adding a wash of light to her golden-pale skin. All around the room, candles burned, some warming oils to fill the air with fragrance. Ribbons of incense smoke rose through the light.

Karl watched her. They both remained silent. There was a poised sense of reverence between them, for what had gone before and what would surely follow.

The large drawing-room now had the look of a church prepared for a midnight service. This was a ritual in a way; dream-like, unplanned, but inevitable. Celebration or wake for the death of delusion.

Karl, seated on an upright chair, felt the familiar rich curves of the cello between his knees. Scents of old, varnished wood and rosin mingled with the spice of incense and sandalwood. He set the bow to the strings and began to draw out the deep warm notes. He played a nocturne in a minor key, mournful and evocative. Charlotte, arrested, blew out her match and closed her eyes. He saw her body tauten as if with sexual yearning, saw the tip of one fang indenting the rose-red curve of her lower lip.

The solitary line of music seemed to express everything that had passed between them that evening. The mad fall from the mountain, the mutual bliss of killing. How easy it was, he thought, when we hunted in private, to pretend that we were better than we really are. To pretend that our sensibilities are delicate and our self-control perfect. And then the thirst comes in a primitive rush and we fall on our prey like animals, not disgusted by what we are but worshipping it. And, oh God, it was so like making love. Devouring each other while that poor woman died between us.

As Karl played, Charlotte rose to her feet and began to dance. So hard, even now, to believe that she was a vampire and not still the sweet young woman he had first met. So hard to believe she had shared the kill with him! In a dress of cream, rose and gold lace she was slender and graceful, her upright back and neat square shoulders swathed by her waist-length hair. Candle-light threaded its warm brown depths with gold. Her hair was a shimmering wreath, framing a face that had not aged a day. She smiled at him as she danced, and she looked so carefree, so heart-breakingly pretty, that it was impossible to believe that blood had ever gushed over her flawless teeth.

Only her eyes had aged. The amethyst discs were layered like agate with experiences and sorrows that no mortal had ever had.

She was an element, a nymph, an enigma. Karl watched the flow of her hair, the subtle roundedness of her breasts, hips and thighs moving beneath the lace. He felt an intense longing to make love to her . . . but that could wait. They had all night.

The nocturne wound to its sombre end. Charlotte curtsied, her arms stretched behind her like wings.

'I'm not Violette,' she said apologetically.

'Thank God for that,' said Karl.

She came to him, and stroked his hair as if she were a little nervous of touching him. 'Do you still dislike her so much?'

'*Liebchen*, as I keep telling you, I don't dislike her. I only meant that I want to be with you, no one else. And I do not particularly want to talk about Violette.'

'But we must.'

'Why?'

'Well, we can't talk about—' She gestured at the window; the outside world, the forest, the shared feast. 'Can we?'

He folded his fingers round her hand. 'Not yet.'

'I think – I really feel – that Violette is going to be all right. As long as she goes on dancing there's hope . . .'

'That she won't destroy us?'

'That she'll hang on to her sanity. That she won't be unhappy.'

'And so she won't carry out the threat she made against us?' Karl said wearily.

'Dear, she wasn't herself—'

'But she said it. She threatened to take you away from me, and change us both into people we would not recognize. I can't forget that.' Karl wished he could just tell Charlotte to forget Violette, but it was Charlotte's obsession that had made the dancer into a vampire, and now she felt as endlessly responsible as a mother. 'However, I will not live under the shadow of any threat. I had enough of that with Kristian. We're free now. We had three self-styled "envoys of God", threatening to set up a leader in Kristian's place, but they failed, because vampires cannot be ruled. I refuse to fear Violette, or to let her frighten you.'

'I'm not afraid of her. I made her.' Charlotte knelt beside him, her face shining in the tremulous light. 'She's my mother, my daughter, my sister' – Karl was glad she did not add, 'my lover' – 'and I won't run away from her.'

'Of course not, but that doesn't mean she isn't dangerous. The last time I saw the "envoys", they warned me against her. I don't trust them, but I can't dismiss their warning . . .' A memory of the scene enveloped him. He felt the frost-burn of the *Weisskalt* and saw the three – angels or devils, they were something more than vampires – leaping like flowers of fire from the white snow into the black cauldron of space. Simon-Senoy, Fyodor-Sansenoy, Rasmila-Semangelof. Karl wondered what had become of them. 'We should be cautious, that's all.'

Her hand, rosy with another's blood, rested on his thigh. 'Yes, but we mustn't avoid her. We must go to her ballets, remain friendly with her. Don't you see, if we try to avoid her that will only make her more dangerous!'

She was anxious for his reaction. She knew that his antipathy towards Violette had deep and twisting roots, but for once he agreed with her. 'You're quite right, *liebling*. Safer to keep an eye on her, *nicht wahr?*'

Charlotte relaxed. 'It *will* be all right, Karl. Play for me again.'

This time she remained beside him, sitting on the carpet with her head resting against his thigh as he played. The strings were responsive under his fingers; he'd lost none of the touch he'd learned as a human, had lost only the need to strive and compete. The slow melody drew them both deeper into the lake of sensuality. Sharing a victim had generated a richer desire that they could sate only on each other. Each felt the moment drawing nearer through the music, the flow of scent and light; the unutterable joy of fulfilment and the sweet-sharp exchange of blood becoming deliciously, languorously inevitable.

Karl played the last note, and leaned down to kiss Charlotte. Her tongue touched his lips, parted his teeth; he tasted blood in the sweetness of her mouth.

'I always remember the first time you kissed me,' she whispered, her mouth close to his. 'Do you remember?'

'In the garden at Parkland Hall, on the bridge. And I had tried for so long not to give in.'

'And you told me that you were bound to hurt me—'

'But that night you came to my room anyway,' he said, his words running into hers. 'I knew that if we made love I might not be able to control the blood-thirst, but I couldn't stop.'

'Neither could I. I didn't care what happened to me, didn't care about my reputation or about anything. Even when you said you couldn't marry me. The secrecy was terrible. It almost broke my heart, knowing it couldn't last, but not knowing why.'

'I could hardly have told you I was a vampire.'

'I wish you had, instead of the way I did find out! But I don't regret it. The secrecy was delicious too, knowing we shared a secret that no one around us knew.'

'Your father would have wanted to kill me if he'd found out,' Karl said, smiling.

'And I thought David *had* killed you. God, I thought I'd never see you again. I don't know why I didn't die of a broken heart.'

'Because you're strong.'

'No ... because I couldn't bear to believe I wouldn't see you again, I thought if I just hung on long enough, I could will you back into existence.'

'In a way, you did. Ah, but I would not have put you through what happened for anything ...'

'But it was inevitable,' she said, 'from that moment on the bridge ...'

Their mouths touched, but a faint, unwelcome sense of intrusion made Karl draw away from her. He sat back in the chair, sighing.

'What is it?' she said anxiously.

'You are not concentrating,' he said. 'We have visitors.'

They were not so much visitors as a deputation, Charlotte observed, trying to be as effortlessly courteous as Karl appeared. Ilona, Karl's burgundy-haired daughter; blue-eyed, flippant Pierre, who was no one's friend; Stefan and his mute twin, Niklas. With them came two immortals whom Charlotte had heard of but never met; Rachel, a white, rarefied creature with scarlet hair, and a slender dark man who looked like a mediaeval cleric. His name was John.

Although Charlotte resented the interruption, she was always pleased to see Stefan. She greeted him with a kiss. He smiled, but his eyes, bright as cornflowers, avoided hers.

'What brings you here?' she asked.

'This is a little awkward,' he said softly, and moved back to Niklas's side. Both blond-haired and china-skinned, the only physical difference between them was that Niklas's irises were not blue but palest gold. His movements were echoes of Stefan's, as if he had no mind of his own but was Stefan's silent other-self.

'Don't be coy,' Ilona said sharply. 'They've come to talk about Violette.' As always she looked exquisite, as precise as a fashion-plate.

'What is there to say about her?' Charlotte was instantly defensive, but Karl quietly took the visitors' coats, not jumping to conclusions.

'You tell us,' said Ilona, 'what there is to say about Violette.' Without asking, she wound up the gramophone and put on a record. The thin, cheerful lilt of a jazz band made an incongruous background as the vampires seated themselves around the drawing-room. How awkward, Charlotte thought, that there were no social niceties with which she could ease the atmosphere; she could not even offer them a drink. Like birds of prey they settled and gazed unblinking from lovely, passionless eyes. All of them watching her.

Charlotte busied herself stoking the fire and lighting lamps; the shades were mosaics of stained glass held in leading, limpid, glowing. When she'd finished, Karl came to stand beside her by the fireplace. She was glad of his company. Rachel also remained on her feet, on the far side of the room by the balcony window. She seemed restless, and constantly put her hands to the sides of her neck.

'Do you really think it is fair,' Charlotte said, 'to discuss Violette when she is not here to speak for herself?'

'You wouldn't want her here,' said Rachel. 'Believe me, you wouldn't.'

'Why?' Charlotte glanced at Karl, suddenly chilled. Something's happened, she thought, but surely I would have known—

John, the hard-eyed stranger, said, 'Tell them, Rachel.'

Again she scratched at her throat. She seemed to have

difficulty speaking. 'A vampire who places herself in the public eye, who goes on dancing and lets herself remain a world-famous figure, is unnatural. We should exist as chameleons in the twilight. No human should know our faces or our real names. She's breaking that law.'

'There is no law,' Charlotte said impatiently. 'What does it matter what she does? No one will guess.'

'Someone might, if she reaches seventy or eighty without a line on her face,' Pierre said laconically. Neither he nor Ilona appeared to be taking this seriously; Rachel gave him a vicious glance.

'It's not just that,' she went on. 'There's something about her, something wrong. It's no secret that she believes herself to be Lilith, the Mother of Vampires; what that implies I'm not sure, but it's obvious she's half-mad and too powerful for her own good.'

Charlotte was furious, but her anger was fuelled by guilt. She knew Rachel was right, but couldn't accept it. 'You don't even know her! At least give her a chance before you condemn her.'

'Oh, we gave her a chance,' said Rachel. 'We went to see her to ask her very politely to stop dancing, to stay out of the way of both humans and vampires.'

'Well, I can imagine how she reacted to that!' Charlotte exclaimed. 'Who went to see her, exactly?'

Stefan answered uneasily, 'Niklas and myself, Rachel, John and Matthew.' He cautiously met Charlotte's eyes; she glared at him but he didn't look away.

'Ilona and Pierre, did you go too?'

They shook their heads. Ilona said, 'We're only here now because Stefan seemed to think it was so important.'

'Much ado about nothing,' Pierre added, 'but amusing.'

'Nothing?' Rachel's alabaster face lengthened. 'I tried to be fair, I set aside the fact that she murdered my friend Katerina—'

'Katerina could be very provoking,' Ilona put in. Charlotte could have strangled her for her flippancy, for saying such a thing in front of Karl, who had loved Katerina.

'I tried to be fair,' Rachel repeated, seeming close to breaking down, 'but she wouldn't listen to reason. John, you tell them. I can't.'

John leaned forward, his eyes black with hatred. Although he wore a modern suit, it hung on him like an inappropriate stage costume. 'Matthew's dead. She killed him. He was the dearest companion of my heart, and my only refuge from the madness of this century, and she slew him. She tore his head off with her hands.'

Charlotte gaped at him. Conjuring the scene in her mind, she was horrified. 'Why? What did he do?'

'He did nothing!' John flared. 'She flew into a rage and attacked him for no reason!'

Stefan added quietly, 'Actually, Matthew had suggested that unless she took our advice, her ballet might be in danger.'

'Oh God,' Charlotte sighed. 'He should have known better.'

'But they were only words!' Rachel said. 'There was no cause for her to use such violence. But the fact that she did proves my point. She's insane, she's capricious, and she doesn't care who she harms.' Again she rubbed at her neck, tangling long skeins of flame-red hair. 'She attacked me, too ... and I've lost myself, I don't know what to do. I'm so afraid.'

A long, heavy silence. Charlotte looked at Rachel in dismay, realizing that she was not merely agitated but in torment, and no one could offer her any help. *And Violette's done this*.

Controlling her emotions, she said, 'What exactly do you expect us to do?'

'You made her immortal,' said John.

'I didn't do it alone!' She glared at Stefan, willing him to come to her defence, but he only shook his head as if to say, *It's out of my hands*.

'It's no good appealing to him,' Ilona said tartly. 'He may have helped in the transformation, but we all know you initiated it. And the fact that Katerina also took part did not prevent Violette from slicing her head off.'

Charlotte couldn't look at Karl. 'She did it to save my life. And I can't know the truth about Matthew unless I hear her side of the story. Why are you trying to turn me against her?'

'We don't want another Kristian!' said Rachel.

'Don't be ridiculous!' As Charlotte spoke she had a ghastly memory of the way they'd banded together to assassinate Kristian. She felt Karl's hand on her shoulder and knew he was sharing her memories. God, if they were proposing a similar lynch-mob against Violette!

John said, 'We want to know why you transformed her.'

'What business is it of yours?' Charlotte said indignantly, but Karl's hand grew heavier.

'You might as well tell them,' said Karl. 'We have nothing to hide.'

'All right.' Charlotte composed herself, determined to outface them. 'It was my fault. She didn't want it, but I insisted; I can't justify it. As a human she was beautiful. I was drawn to her as if she were my sister, more than a sister. I didn't plan it – until she told me she had a disease that would stop her dancing within a few years. I couldn't bear her talent to be lost, or to see her grow old and bitter. Was I selfish? I wanted her to stay as she was, so I took her.' And now Karl's fingers were so tight that pain ran through her neck as if from the kiss of fangs.

'And then she went crazy,' said Pierre. 'Stefan's already told us. There's no point in denying it.'

Charlotte felt betrayed, to think that Stefan had told everyone about such an intimate and painful event.

'Which of you did *not* go mad in the first moment of realizing what you'd become?' Charlotte said. 'Who wasn't horrified by the blood-thirst, who didn't believe himself damned?'

'Damned, yes,' John said thinly, 'but none of us became Lilith, the queen of vampires.'

Charlotte said helplessly, 'I can't explain it. It's too complicated. I could theorize all night, but I can't *explain*.'

'When you made her,' said John, 'every vampire felt the darkening of the ether. Everyone knew when she came into being! She has sown a seed of darkness in the Crystal Ring that will destroy us all.'

Charlotte couldn't answer. She had noticed changes in the Crystal Ring but she couldn't talk about them, even to Karl. Couldn't admit it was happening.

'And what of you, Karl?' said John. 'Have you nothing to say?'

'Like Charlotte, I would prefer to reserve judgement until I have spoken to Violette,' Karl said, too diplomatically for Charlotte's liking. She wished he would defend her wholeheartedly. She couldn't blame him for his distrust of Violette, but she hated it, all the same. 'There's no denying that Violette may present a danger. However, I trust that you are proposing caution rather than assassination. We aren't extremists, and like Rachel we prefer an undisturbed existence. That's why we all opposed Kristian. We would do well to remember that we're all on the same side.'

'Of course we are!' said Stefan, but John's expression remained closed.

Charlotte had to make a stand. 'Look, it's my fault Violette was initiated, and I take full responsibility for her. You don't know her! Until you understand her reasons, don't you dare pass judgement on her. All she cares about is her dancing; why should she be remotely interested in any of you? If you don't pester her, she won't touch you. But if you go to her uttering threats, what do you expect? Just leave her in peace and you'll be safe. You have my word.'

'You must be very sure of your influence over her,' Rachel said acidly.

'But Matthew,' said John. 'An eye for an eye, the Bible says—'

'If you go anywhere near her—' Charlotte flared, losing control. Karl gently held her back.

'He wouldn't dare,' said Ilona.

'I support Charlotte,' Pierre broke in. 'The whole thing is ludicrous. What's become of us, that one neurotic fledgling sends us screaming for *maman*? Grow up and leave Violette alone.'

Charlotte ignored him. It had to be callous, sarcastic Pierre who came to her defence, not the ones she really cared about; Stefan and Karl.

'Do whatever you like,' Rachel said, her voice faint. She

leaned back against the windows, supernaturally white against the blackness. She was almost translucent, as if fading into the Crystal Ring. 'I want nothing more to do with Violette. I want . . .'

'Where are you going?' John cried, leaping up.

'I don't know. Away.'

And she vanished.

'It looks as if the case for the prosecution is collapsing,' said Charlotte, looking pointedly at Stefan. 'I think you had all better leave.' And Karl, expressionless, fetched their coats and distributed them without ceremony.

John left without a word, but the look he gave Charlotte was sourly threatening, almost deranged. He seemed entrenched in some ancient dogma of God and Satan, so far removed from her that the chasm could never be bridged. I don't know you, she thought. I don't care what you believe; just get out of my house and leave us alone!

Ilona, unperturbed, presented herself to Karl and he kissed her on the forehead. Charlotte had learned to read his feelings, even though he was so skilled at hiding them; his age-old sorrow at everything that had passed between him and his daughter, and the bitter-sweet love he felt for her.

Charlotte said, 'Ilona, you don't agree with them, do you?'

Ilona turned to her with a cool smile. 'Only one thing has ever frightened me, dear, and that is Violette. For some reason, the mere thought of her scares me to death. But I won't give in, I won't let her get away with it.'

The admission floored Charlotte. Before she could respond, Ilona had gone into the Crystal Ring. Pierre gave a sardonic bow, and followed her.

Stefan glanced at Charlotte, as if he were about to leave without saying anything. She said, 'Wait a moment.'

He came to her, Niklas a silent mirror-image at his side. His hair was a white-gold nimbus, his eyes angelic. A sheath of iced sweetness that would draw back to reveal hard white wolf-teeth to his victims. His was a teasing cruelty; he loved to steal affection before he stole blood.

'Are you angry with me?' Stefan said. 'H'm, silly question.'

'How could you do it? Turn against Violette, when you know what she is to me? God, you even helped to transform her!'

'Charlotte.' He gave her arm the lightest touch, then dropped his hand. 'I haven't turned against her. I only said what I believe.'

'And so did I.' She looked sideways at Karl. He was watching her, one side of his face lit by fire, the other side in shadow.

'You know my feelings,' said Karl. 'I don't trust Violette, but there are very few whom I do trust.'

'When I came into the Crystal Ring,' said Charlotte, 'I signed no agreement that said I had to answer to other immortals, did I?'

'We answer to no one.'

'Then why do I have to suffer crowds of them coming here and threatening my friend?'

'I was not threatening her,' said Stefan. 'I am truly concerned about her, and have been since the moment of her transformation, as you know perfectly well. If anything, I was trying to protect her. I went to her in friendship; unfortunately, the others had different ideas and things got out of hand. It was meant to be a friendly warning, because if she doesn't take herself out of the public eye and live a quiet life, she is going to make enemies far worse than John and Rachel.'

Karl was alone in the library, near dawn, when another unwelcome visitor came. Charlotte had gone out to rest in the Crystal Ring; they each needed a little time alone, if only to gather their thoughts. Karl was seated at a table, looking through a large volume of mythology, ostensibly to pass the time, though he found himself searching for references to Lilith, or symbolism that could be related to her. Now and then he made notes on a pad beside the book.

He was also thinking about Benedict and Lancelyn, two human occultists who had tried to control and use vampires against each other. While trying to limit the chaos they were creating, Karl had almost lost Charlotte to Violette. *I can* understand Charlotte's fascination with her, he thought regretfully, her magic and unapproachability . . . but I could see even then that Violette was something *other*. I tried to warn Charlotte, but I knew she wouldn't listen. And Violette came through the transformation in anguish.

I could have dismissed her conviction that she's Lilith as a delusion, if it hadn't been for the angels.

He'd assumed that Simon, Fyodor and Rasmila were vampires like himself until they had revealed themselves as dual beings, envoys of God whose purpose was to tame Lilith. So, he wondered, were they all suffering the same delusion? Lancelyn saw extraordinary qualities in Violette as well. He called her the Black Goddess, spoke of finding enlightenment through her. He would have made a formidable immortal, more knowledgeable and intelligent than Kristian, Karl reflected, but he overreached himself.

In defending herself against Lancelyn, Violette had left him languishing in madness. Saddened and disillusioned by his brother's fate, Benedict had wanted no more to do with the occult . . . but the angels?

In trying to fulfil Lancelyn's ambition they had been ruthless; they'd tortured Karl, almost killed Charlotte and Stefan. Yet when Lilith-Violette rejected their authority, they had fled.

Karl recalled his last meeting with them in the *Weisskalt*; the image haunted him. They had delivered a warning. If you do not deal with Lilith, she will ruin you . . .

Oh, Charlotte, I wish you had never met her, he thought. But perhaps you were being used by the Crystal Ring, Raqi'a, as Ben called it, used as an instrument of Violette's fate. That would make sense – if only I believed in such things.

An oil lamp burned on the edge of the table; beyond its glow, the library – a long room that led off the drawing-room – lay in shadow. Suddenly aware of an intrusion, Karl looked up and saw a tall, gilded figure appearing by the far window. His clothes were modern and ordinary, but his appearance was quite opposite. Light golden skin, a short, bright halo of hair, topaz eyes; a Grecian deity or a lion in human form.

After their encounter in the *Weisskalt*, Karl had neither

expected nor wanted to see him again. But the intruder was smiling as he approached with long, confident strides.

'Simon,' Karl said, sitting back in his chair and putting down his pen. 'I would thank you not to walk in unannounced.'

'My dear fellow, what sort of greeting is this? You surely didn't expect me to stand outside and knock on the door like a human?'

'It would have been a courtesy.'

'In that case, accept my apologies for violating your privacy,' Simon said with apparent sincerity. 'What are you writing?'

'Nothing that is any of your concern.'

Simon chuckled. 'Be careful what you write, Karl. It may come back to haunt you.'

'What do you want?' Karl could not forget that Simon had once taken pleasure in tormenting his friends. 'I hoped I'd seen the last of you.'

'I hoped so, too.' Simon gave him a cool look. He, in turn, had not forgotten that Karl had tried to kill him. 'But things change.'

'Where are your companions? I thought you were inseparable.'

Simon wandered over to a bookshelf and took out a book at random. 'After the matter of Lilith, we had differences of opinion and went our separate ways.'

'And I thought you had ascended to heaven.'

'There is no need for sarcasm, Karl.' He flicked through the book without interest, then pushed it back on to the shelf. Karl noticed that he seemed troubled, yet his presence was intimidating; dazzling and heartless, like the sun. 'No, we came back to earth.'

'In what sense?'

'In every sense, I suppose. When we failed with Lilith, God had no further use for us. We felt abandoned. Fyodor and Rasmila blamed me.'

'How unfair.' Karl rose, moved to the front of the table and leaned back against its edge. 'So, how much are you still the angel Senoy, and how much a mere vampire?'

Simon's eyes were downcast, brooding. 'I don't know. I

never thought it could happen. Can you imagine how it feels, having looked on the ineffable face of God, to be cut off from the light?'

Karl's objective curiosity got the better of him. 'To be honest, I can't. What exactly happened?'

He didn't expect a straight answer, but to his surprise, Simon seemed to be in a confiding mood. He spoke in a low voice, as if to himself. 'After we left you we floated above the *Weisskalt*, we flew into space towards the sun as if we were invincible . . . But it went wrong very suddenly. Perhaps we climbed too high, perhaps our euphoria made us overconfident. We started to feel the cold, we lost our way, the light blinded us. I had to take the others back to earth at once. Fyodor almost died. And we realized that God had forsaken us, in the blink of an eye. To teach us humility, I suppose.'

'That must have been quite devastating,' Karl said without inflexion. 'But before it happened, how did it feel to be an angel?'

'Perhaps "envoy" is the more accurate term.'

'Less romantic.'

Simon looked up. His eyes were glass orbs with the sun behind them; single-minded, pitiless, yet void in the most sinister way. 'How can I describe it? I always *knew*. The light spoke to me. We had powers, we knew so much that ordinary vampires did not; where to find individuals with special gifts such as Sebastian, Kristian or Lancelyn. I knew what to do. Make Kristian a vampire and he'll be a magnificent ruler. Watch over Lancelyn because he has a destiny. Even while we were asleep in the *Weisskalt* part of us remained sentient! Isn't that proof of God's existence?'

'I have no idea,' Karl said flatly.

'And when we woke and became whole again, we *knew* we were the angels whose task was to tame Lilith. It was what we *were*. I can't explain. But, Karl, it was glorious!'

'And suddenly it ended.'

Simon's expression became contemptuous. 'Rasmila and Fyodor were ready to accept it. They became dispirited, they were like lost souls – but they had no ambition to recover our status. All they could do was cling to me like children, as if I could make it all right again. I grew sick of it. I don't need them!'

'You're very callous,' said Karl.

'Am I? Are angels callous, even disempowered ones? I suppose I am. I need vampires around me—'

'As an audience? Lovers? Slaves? I suppose Rasmila and Fyodor were all of those.'

Simon's eyes shone like ice. 'I need to be at the heart of things! I can't bear to see everything falling apart.'

There was naked pain in his voice, but Karl could feel no sympathy. 'Go back to sleep in the *Weisskalt* then. Your suffering will be over.'

'Your attitude does you no credit. I did not come here for sympathy.'

'You're not receiving it. So, you've lost your friends and your power? I fail to see what I can do about this.'

'It's partly your fault, Karl. Have you no sense of duty?' Simon came closer; Karl wished he would keep his distance, but pride would not let him back away. 'I believe there's a task I must complete before God will let me back into the fold. He wants me to prove myself.'

Karl, who had no time for God, laughed. Simon's pupils contracted to points. 'You could have been my equal, Karl. Confronting the three of us in the *Weisskalt*, a situation that would destroy most other vampires, you showed only a kind of world-weary insolence. That reveals incredible strength! You could have been great. You killed Kristian and you almost killed me. Other vampires have seen this power in you and begged you to lead them! Yet you've thrown it away. Diminished yourself for the sake of a quiet life. Is this really what you want?'

Karl was watching Simon carefully, trying to judge whether he was likely to become violent. 'I've never been interested in the sort of power that Kristian or Lancelyn craved. I don't see it as diminishment, but either way, it hardly matters.'

'Ah. So you're still content for vampires to remain a leaderless rabble?'

Karl laughed. 'Quite so.'

'You find this a joke?' Simon said, raising his eyebrows. He walked in a slow loop round the table, glancing at Karl's notes as he passed. '"Myths of Babylonia and Assyria",' he read. 'How interesting. Lilith as wind-hag.'

His intrusiveness was becoming very irritating. 'I see,' said Karl. 'You have come here to find out where I stand on the question of leadership. But why?'

'Things are going wrong, Karl. The Crystal Ring is growing ever more hostile. You might say that heaven has turned its face against us – and all this is Lilith's doing! We needed to tame her but we failed. Without control, she creates chaos. We gave you a very clear warning that she would put you, Charlotte and your daughter in danger – yet you've done nothing!'

'Violette's only interest is in dancing. I don't think touring *Swan Lake* and *Coppélia* is going to destroy the world.' But Karl was thinking of the fearful vampires who'd wanted action taken against her. *She tore off Matthew's head with her hands.* He thought of the steel-calm way in which she'd dispatched Katerina under the wheels of a train.

'And you approve of that, do you? A vampire living among humans, flaunting herself in public.'

'God, I have heard enough of this for one evening,' Karl murmured. 'It's up to her.'

'But it isn't. You think she's harmless, but she'll ruin us all!'

Karl knew Violette was far from harmless. His and Charlotte's resolve to remain in friendly contact with her was in itself a subtle attempt at control.

'Vampires need unity,' Simon went on. 'While we remain fragmented we'll be unable to defend ourselves against her. We need a focus.'

'I hope you are not asking me to be this focus.'

Their eyes met. The look was a mutual challenge, the repulsion of powerful opposites. Then Simon's face changed, softening to an earnest expression of hope, reconciliation. 'Karl, don't let's argue. We had such a fight, you and I; the physical and mental torment you endured was tremendous. Yet you survived! I have great admiration for you. Can you accept my apologies? Can we let bygones be bygones?'

Karl stiffened. 'It is somewhat hard to forget that you almost starved me to death, then caused me to attack my own friends. All I can say is that you are a more tolerable person for not being drunk on power. If I were you, I'd leave it that way. Why do you suddenly want to be forgiven now?'

'You have such strength, Karl! Kristian's followers offered you leadership, even though you'd slain Kristian, because they saw qualities in you that you cannot even see for yourself!'

'I've already given you my answer. If you're so obsessed with this, why not do it yourself?'

'It's not my vocation.' Simon leaned close to him, his tone becoming passionate. 'God's role for me is not to be the king, but the kingmaker. That's what we did with Kristian, and almost succeeded with Lancelyn. I can't do it alone because I have to be needed; being needed is what gives me my power! I must succeed this time.'

Karl drew away. 'Ah. The puppet-master. Lancelyn empowered you by calling for your help, and now you want me to do the same, while I become your puppet?'

'It's not like that. When did we ever tell Kristian or Lancelyn what to do? I haven't even seen Sebastian since we created him. You can't accuse me of manipulation. It's not for myself; we need a leader for the benefit of vampire-kind!'

'Even though these would-be leaders have caused all our troubles?' Karl said acidly.

'So take on the role yourself and make it what you want!' Simon's expression turned scornful. 'I find you incredible, Karl. You do momentous things like murdering Kristian, creating Charlotte, protecting Lilith – and then you sit back and say you want a quiet life!'

'You make it sound as if I've earned it,' Karl said mordantly.

'If I go to someone else, you will be sorry.'

'Please tell me you are not considering Sebastian.'

Simon grinned viciously. 'Now wouldn't he make a leader to be reckoned with!'

'He'd be far worse than Kristian. At least Kristian had some kind of code of behaviour.'

'You had the choice, Karl.' He was still smiling, but Karl

sensed uncontrollable frustration seething beneath the gilded surface. Perhaps a trace of fear, too? 'One last chance to change your mind.'

'No. I won't be blackmailed. You would never find Sebastian anyway; even Kristian couldn't track him down, *Gott sei Dank*! No, I won't change my mind. I thought we would be friends when we first met,' Karl said, rather sadly. 'You reminded me of a human I once knew, a brave and decent man, a war hero. But you were a liar. You enjoyed tormenting us. You spoke of God's great purpose, yet you cared about nothing beyond getting your own way. You're no archangel and you never were. Don't talk to me about uniting or safeguarding vampire-kind, when you secretly despise us all.'

Simon glared at him. Karl saw dark crimson fires at the core of his golden eyes, the worm eating at the rose. Finally he said grimly, 'No, you're right; you would not make a suitable leader. You're weak, and love has blinded you to Lilith's evil. I should have known better than to try to reason with an atheist.'

'I'd sooner go to hell than bow to your cruel god,' Karl retorted coldly. 'I can quite see where Kristian got it from.'

'How can you not believe!' Simon cried with sudden fervour. He seemed to gather himself, as sleek as a tiger with imminent violence. I was right, Karl thought, he is on the edge of madness and he is dangerous – but I will never let him think he can intimidate me.

'You're not the first one I've met who claims to have spoken to God,' Karl said. 'It means nothing and it makes no difference.'

'But I will find my way back to Him, and your blind heresy will not stop me, friend-of-Lilith. Traitor.'

His hands rose threateningly, his fangs extended to their full length, but Karl held his ground. 'Don't, Simon,' he said quietly.

Simon ignored the command. Swift and savage, he lunged, struck Karl across the face to disorient him, seized his throat two-handed. Wedged back against the table, Karl could not dislodge him. Simon gripped him above his collarbone and under his chin, as if stretching Karl's throat between his hands.

And his staring eyes were like Niklas's; the iced-gold, terrible, mindless eyes of a *doppelgänger*.

A thought flashed through Karl's mind. If there is a god who creates angels like you, then we are damned, for certain.

He thrust his hands in prayer position up between Simon's arms and stabbed his fingers at those glorious eyes. Simon loosed his grip to defend himself; Karl kicked his legs from under him and dropped down on top of him, his hands clamping Simon's elbows to the floor, the tips of his canines touching the angelic neck. The flesh was peach-soft; real flesh, not ectoplasm.

Yet Karl did not bite down. Instead he pulled back. 'I don't want a single mouthful of your blood. I remember what happened when Rasmila so generously gave me hers. A trap to put me in your control.'

But Simon looked defeated, furious. Karl thought, he's lost his way and he's frightened of something, very frightened. And he'll never forgive Violette, or me.

'You'd better leave,' said Karl. 'If there is anything else you wish to discuss in a civilized fashion, by all means call again. But if you threaten me, or if you lay a finger on any of my friends, I'll bury you with Kristian.'

He rose to his feet, letting Simon stand up.

'You've made a great error of judgement,' Simon said, straightening his rumpled shirt, 'but then, I suppose you've had a lot of practice.' The vitriol in his eyes could have melted glass. 'If you think, after this, that I'd seek your opinion on anything – you flatter yourself, my dear fellow.' He pushed past Karl, looking back over his shoulder as he faded into the Crystal Ring. 'You're going to hell with Lilith, for certain.'

CHAPTER THREE

THE CLAWS OF THE OWL

Kristian was dead, but Schloss Holdenstein remained; an age-raddled pile of brown stone on a ridge above the River Rhine, crowned with a complexity of decaying roofs and turrets. Its silhouette against the creamy sky was indefinite, like some beast that shifted position in its sleep. Rocks and ancient trees crusted its flanks. The hillside below fell steeply to the river bank, fell again into the deep green mirror of the water.

No human authority ever came near the castle. Isolated in the winding, forested lushness of the Rhineland, it lived under its own laws.

It lived once, thought Cesare, but now it is dying.

Every day Cesare would wander the tortuous corridors of the castle, the cramped, windowless chambers, the staircases leading upwards and downwards at mad angles. Sadness pervaded every room. Sorrow and desolation breathed from the very walls. How empty, how drear this place has become without the presence of the master, Cesare thought. Deserted and slowly dying of grief.

And he would wander through the innermost network of rooms where Kristian had held court; the inner sanctum, and the large chamber where the ebony throne still stood. He imagined Kristian's presence everywhere, as if by remembering he could bring the master back to life. He dreamed and mourned, dry-eyed.

And then Cesare would return to his own cell, and meditate on the futility of his existence.

There were only a few vampires left in the Schloss now, but he might as well have been alone. They never spoke to each other. There was nothing to say.

When Kristian had first disappeared, Cesare and the other disciples had tried to carry on as normal. Two years they had waited, held together by the knowledge that Kristian *must* come back, that two years were only a fragment of a vampire's life. And then Karl had come to tell them that Kristian was dead.

Devastation – even though Cesare had already suspected the truth. And knowing they were lost without a leader, he had told Karl, 'You took us from him so you must take his place!'

Karl had refused. In his anguish, Cesare had tried to kill him; Karl had won the fight, almost severing Cesare's head.

After the wound had healed, Cesare had changed. He no longer cared about anything. If Kristian were not coming back, there was nothing to live for. And so he and the other vampires, the last remnants who could not face the world outside the castle, merely existed. Went out at night to drink blood; rested in the Crystal Ring; uttered hollow prayers to God; spent the rest of the time, all those interminable hours, huddled in their cells, thinking of nothing, questioning nothing. No one came or went. Nothing ever changed.

Another year had passed since then. It felt like twenty.

Cesare drifted through eternity in the absolute depths of depression and did not even know it. He was dead inside.

So when dawn found him one morning, sitting cross-legged on the stone flagstones with a book of Kristian's writings in his lap, he thought he was imagining the new presence he sensed entering the castle. His senses were numbed by years of despair. He felt the shadow brush his mind, felt it walking along the corridors towards his cell, ducking under the archway and standing before him . . . and still he dismissed it as a conjuration of his despair.

'Cesare,' said a raw, whispering voice.

He looked up. Saw a vampire in a shabby dark suit; colourless face, eyes pouched with grief, black hair standing on end. A sack dangled from his left hand.

It was a face Cesare knew, but had not seen for a hundred and fifty years. Impossible. He put the book aside and stood up, shaking the creases out of his robe. 'Who are you?'

'You know me, Cesare. You cannot have forgotten me!'

Cesare frowned. 'John?'

'Yes, I am John. You must help me!'

Memory; then an awakening of emotion, a thrust of black anger like a splinter in the cobweb greyness. 'But you are in the *Weisskalt*, Kristian put you there.'

'I woke up,' said John, his eyes glassy, maniacal. 'Kristian's death woke us and we escaped, we came back to life.'

'But you were Kristian's enemies, you and that bastard Matthew!' Cesare felt terrified by his own anger; it surged like vertigo, exhilarating and uncontrollable. He wasn't quite dead, after all. 'You attacked him!'

'And we were punished. Don't turn me away.'

And Cesare was so stunned to be thinking, feeling, talking, that however much he hated John, he wanted to keep him here. 'What do you want?'

'Someone has got to help me.' John lifted the sack, thrust his hand inside and grabbed something. He let the sack fall to the floor; in his hands he was cradling a severed head.

Cesare stared at the distorted features. The mouth and eyes drooped as if with sour pain. The skin around the neck stump was horribly ragged. 'What happened?'

Tears ran down John's face and his mouth worked, but he seemed incapable of answering. Finally he whispered, 'It's Matthew. Someone – she—' He shook his head, swallowed. 'I heard that Kristian could bring vampires back to life if he had the head. Do you know how to do it?'

Cesare pondered. Suddenly he'd forgotten his own misery; he had a decision to make, and that gave him a slender connection to life. 'Why should I? I loved Kristian, you hated him. We can't be friends.'

John visibly trembled. 'Please!'

And Cesare thought, how pleasing it is to have this creature at my mercy! 'Why did you hate Kristian? Tell me!'

'He was arrogant.' John spoke stiffly, hugging the repulsive head to his chest. 'He wouldn't see that vampires are the devil's possessions and we must submit to our punishment. Kristian dared to call on God's name without the intercession of the

Adversary! He claimed that we were blessed, not damned. Blasphemous arrogance—'

Cesare broke in impatiently, 'But if there is a devil, each of us *is* the devil. God has a use for us. We are not punished, but *punishing*; our purpose is to visit God's wrath on mankind! This isn't an evil purpose. It's a noble one. John, we believe the same thing at heart. The only difference is that Kristian's followers take pride in what they are.'

'Pride is a sin.'

'If you must believe you're evil, at least believe you have a place in the scheme of things.'

John gasped. His face lengthened and he looked up, like a saint seeing a vision of heaven. 'If I could only believe it!'

In that moment, Cesare no longer felt hostile towards him. He felt fatherly. John's sin was ignorance; something that could be cured, given time. Cesare went to him and put a hand on his shoulder. 'We can talk about it to our heart's content. It is so long since I had the chance of a theological argument!'

John looked sideways at him, his eyes wild with fear and hope. 'So you will help us?'

Cesare lifted the grotesque burden out of his arms as tenderly as if it were a baby. 'Come, I'll show you what to do, and you can do it yourself. The head must be immersed in blood every day. Fresh human blood.'

Vampires do not sleep and they do not dream, Violette had been told. What, then, were the nightmares that assailed her in the Crystal Ring?

Strange that although the place terrified her, it felt like home. She never wanted to go there yet she couldn't stop herself; eventually the masochistic fascination would overcome her, like dark sticky-sweet strings pulling at her mind and body. Easy as breathing, automatic as a heartbeat, was the side-step into the vampire realm. The world faded. Her own molecules seemed to melt and harden into a new shape, and she found herself in a wind-blown forest of shadows, under a sky of purple flame.

The sky drew her. She began to run, climbing a coil of cloud that frayed into nothingness under her thin, taloned hands. Black, her hands, the skin like that of a beaded lizard; each scale a flake of jet. She felt as thin and hard as a whip, weightless.

I wonder what my face looks like, she thought. If my body is so changed, is my face that of a demon, with eyes like red braziers? I can never see my own face here!

She let the thought go. She was all sensation, a dancer. Her hair writhed about her shoulders.

Leaving the lower levels behind she climbed into the sky, swept up by the currents. Not a true sky but a strange multi-layered dimension, a sphere of liquid glass.

Mountains sailed majestically in the void, but they were like reflections, insubstantial, dissolving to nothing at their roots. Their ebb and flow dizzied her. Tonight they were bruise-coloured, racing along like clouds on a mad wind, crimson light pouring down their sides like blood.

She thought she saw lightning, bleaching the void from indigo to palest amethyst. She seemed to hear thunder.

How cold it was. Desolate, vertiginous. All this sweeping emptiness, not a soul to be seen. So much beauty and energy wasted. The meaninglessness of it chilled her.

She struggled to climb above the storm, but the currents gripped her and flung her to and fro, a twig on the ocean. Part of her relished this. She stretched out on a cushion of air and closed her eyes, felt herself falling, rising, falling, rising. She was frozen to the bone, but it didn't matter.

In the Crystal Ring she could forget the thirst.

The trance came swiftly. Healing rest that gave immortals some respite from perpetual consciousness. At least, that was what it should have been – but to Violette it was a leering carnival of memories. Remain awake, and fight a bitter war against the thirst; sleep and face the visions. The choice crushed her between millstones and ground her flat.

At first she dreamed she was on stage, dancing, carefree. The little green cave of the stage was a self-contained world, limitless in its way; the audience, unseen in a black abyss beyond the blaze of lights, did not exist. This was her solace and her purpose. It was her addiction. It took away the pain and she could not do without it.

But three shadows waited in the wings.

She danced harder and faster but she could not drive them away. Her chest ached with exhaustion. She couldn't breathe. There were hands on her throat, a distorted male face glaring into hers.

Her father's face, his rasping voice. 'This black hair is from the devil, Vi. All women are blood-suckers. All women are from the devil.'

She could make no reply to this injustice. His belief infected her as his hands squeezed out her life . . . then suddenly he was torn away from her. She watched him being borne into the distance, still raging . . . the attendants were carrying him away, but the horror stayed inside her, a thrombus of insanity.

He metamorphosed into someone else as he receded. Another man whom she'd driven mad; not intentionally, never that. It seemed to happen without her willing it. And this one, this kind, irascible and obsessive goat called Lancelyn, had called her Goddess.

Goddess, devil . . . but no one could call her by her true name, no one could tell her the truth.

Her father, Lancelyn, Janacek and Adam; they all loomed over her, these men of power, covetous, possessive, lustful. She cowered and obeyed them, hating them, and then something inside her lashed out, a reptilian tongue of flame to scorch them and to free herself.

Can't I have freedom without destroying them? Why could they not love me without making me hate them?

Yet it could be no other way. They needed to control me but I am too strong. Too wicked.

The three shadows watched and smiled.

Violette stood by Janacek's grave and saw the woman watching her from the edge of the trees. Charlotte, demure in mourning black; a façade, as was her whole semblance of humanity. Clear, steady eyes under the brim of her hat.

Come to me, Violette. I can change you into what you were meant to be. I killed Janacek but I did it to free you!

Charlotte came out of the shadows to ensorcell Violette and draw her into the darkness, but Violette's soul was already darker than a vampire's. It was she who swallowed Charlotte whole.

She was dancing again, but struggling now. Her chest hurt. She could not feel the stage beneath the point of her toe; every time she took a step there was a sensation of collapse as if her leg had splintered. No pain. Yet she stumbled again and again. Looking down she saw that her feet had become claws. Callused, taloned claws like an owl's.

Violette shook herself out of the hallucination, shivering and trying to cry out. But she couldn't make a sound, and there was no one to hear her if she could.

Her panic dropped away as swiftly as it had struck. She was used to this now. The visitors were tormenting, but she had learned not to fight them.

The Crystal Ring flung her down the rolling flank of a cloud. God, she was cold. And the pain was still there in her throat and breastbone, a cruel hand squeezing and pulling. Taut fire, from mouth to heart to abdomen.

The thirst.

That was what had brought the nightmare of strangulation. It had brought her awake and now it forced her, resisting bitterly, down towards the earth.

Night closed over her. The Crystal Ring melted to nothing, and the mortal world blew in on a warm, assured breeze. Violette felt stone beneath her feet; looked down, and saw ordinary feet in button-strap shoes. Human form again. She stared at her calves in silk stockings, the dark-blue hem of her coat. The brim of her cloche hat half-concealed her eyes. She hoped that no one would recognize her.

How tempting to imagine a miracle; that the Crystal Ring did not exist, that her bad dreams, of being owl, serpent, Lilith, vampire, had never happened. But the thirst remained to mock the wish.

I want to feed, she thought.

She found herself near the Mirabell Palace, an iced cake set in formal gardens. She heard the soft dance of fountains. All around her stood elegant, square buildings of the eighteenth century, and beyond them, forested ridges rose against the midnight sky. A chamber orchestra was playing in a house near by; always music in Salzburg. Violette, outside everything, pictured the musicians embowered in the golden warmth of some salon, and her hunger leapt and almost choked her.

She began to walk towards the river.

Half-way across the bridge, she stopped and leaned on the parapet. People went by, glancing at her as they passed. She needed their blood but she held herself rigid against the stone post, staring out at the river, thinking, soon, but not that one . . . not him . . . not her.

Lights hung pear-shaped in the water. To her left, a hundred yards along the bank, stood the big pale-green mansion that housed the Ballet Janacek. One or two windows near the top of the building were still lit up. Not all the *corps de ballet* had gone to bed. Bad girls, she thought. We are soon to begin our American tour; you need your rest!

Amazing that she could think of anything beyond the hunger.

I won't feed tonight, she thought. Her lip stung, nipped between her teeth. I won't.

On her right was the old town, sheltered by the Mönchsberg ridge. She could see lovely colours, which no human could perceive, in the darkness. All the scintillating roofs, domes and spires of endless churches. She'd sought solace in them once, but what had they done to save her from this fate? And what would they do if she approached them now, but denounce her and revile her?

Her eyes, as she gazed on the beautiful churches, were cold.

Footsteps approaching again. Something about them was not right; the steps were slow, soft to the point of hesitancy, and yet very emphatic. The presence came on, but no heat and no human life-glow came with it.

It was a vampire walking towards her.

Her head turned in an unhurried arc. A tall man in a dark, expensive coat and a cashmere scarf stood regarding her with unapologetic frankness. He was good-looking, she supposed, in an insolent way; his hair, as much of it as she could see under

61

his hat, was brown and curly, his eyes blue and well-shaped but just a little too large and widely spaced. He had the look of a charming sadist.

He said in French, 'Madame Lenoir? I have been looking for you for a long time.'

'Well, you've found me.' Although she answered him in the same language, he detected her accent and switched to English.

'Forgive me, I'd assumed you were a compatriot.'

'English names don't go down well in the ballet world,' she said tartly, 'but we can talk in English, French, German; whatever you wish, assuming we have anything to talk about, which I doubt.'

His eyebrows lifted; he looked amused. 'Madame, I am Pierre Lescaut. No doubt you have heard of me.'

'Not that I can recall.' This was not true; Karl had spoken of his wayward friend on several occasions.

He responded to her dismissive manner with a smile. Removing his hat, he bowed extravagantly, then kissed her gloved hand before she could avoid it. 'Well, now you have. I am enchanted to meet you at last. I am a friend of Karl von Wultendorf; you know him, I take it?'

'Slightly.'

'I find it incredible that he would not have mentioned me.'

'Perhaps you are of less importance to him than you realize.'

Pierre's smile became a touch grim. He turned and leaned on the parapet beside her. He was too close and she wanted to draw back, but she refused to give ground to him. 'And you know Charlotte, Stefan, Niklas?' He sounded sarcastic. He must have known that Charlotte and Stefan had initiated her.

'Of course,' she said thinly.

'They are all talking about you – all except Niklas, of course, who has very little to say about anything.' He grinned, but his eyes were cruel, jeering. 'That is why I had to find you and satisfy my curiosity about the new immortal who is creating such interest. You know, you have not many friends, Madame Violette.'

That made her look hard at him, but she did not reply. He said, 'Might we stroll together? I think we should talk.'

She thought, why? I have nothing whatever to say to you. But she did not say it. She glanced back at the ballet's house, imagined an unscrupulous vampire such as Pierre preying on her darlings, and stood pinned by a rod of fury. Then she slipped her hand through his proffered arm and led him away in the opposite direction.

'Let's climb to the fortress,' she said. 'There is such a lovely view of the Alps from the other side of the ridge.'

It began to rain as they walked. The pavements shone. The steep, cobbled path that wound up between the trees towards the Fortress Hohensalzburg seemed to run with mercury.

Pierre held Violette's satin-sheathed hand in the crook of his elbow, congratulating himself. What superstitious fools had Kristian left behind? How could they be afraid of this lily?

Pierre thought he was falling in love. He actually felt protective towards her, when in the past he had never given a damn for protecting anyone but himself.

She was startling to look at, a goddess among mortals and vampires alike. The combination of pale skin and black hair was irresistible, like an exotic Beardsley drawing. Her large eyes, enhanced by the velvety strokes of her brows and lashes, were truly violet; not like Charlotte's, which tended towards amethyst-grey, but the deep luminous indigo of the Crystal Ring itself. She seemed both delicate and strong. Imperturbable – but hardly likely to perturb anyone else.

He said, 'I believe you need to feed, Madame.'

'You're observant.'

'I don't need to be. It's obvious from your pallor, your whole demeanour. I know this . . . tension. You should not leave it too long.'

Her face underwent a transformation. Her self-absorbed repose was chased out by rage; one long moment of it, blazing from her eyes. He almost recoiled from the pressure of their blue light, and the hardness of her mouth. 'Don't tell me,' she said, 'how to conduct myself.'

One glimpse, then the shutters folded down over her soul once more. Pierre exhaled. Shocked at first, he then experienced a *frisson* of excitement.

'I pity the poor human who runs into you in the forest, *chérie*.'

'Don't pity them,' she said tightly. 'I can control the thirst, if you can't.'

'Can you?'

'And I am not your *chérie*.'

'Forgive me, Madame. I did not mean my idle remarks to offend you. *Mon Dieu*, perhaps there is something in what they say after all.'

'What is it they say?'

They had reached the fortress. The walls stood dark and impenetrable against the sky; all around, the trees rustled in the darkness, alive with the patter of raindrops. The air smelled earthily sweet.

The gates were locked, but the Crystal Ring carried them swiftly through layers of wood and iron, and into a huge curved corridor that led steeply upwards. Ahead of them, behind the immense walls, the museum and the state rooms lay in darkness; the tourist guides and staff slumbered, a troop of Boy Scouts slept in the old barrack rooms. A succulent treat for later, Pierre mused. The few sentries who kept watch were oblivious to the vampires' passing.

'Well, certain immortals seem to believe you are mad, although who they are to judge, I have no idea,' said Pierre. 'They claim that you have ill intentions towards them. They say that you tore off a vampire's head with your naked hands and your dainty sharp nails, although I think they must have exaggerated; even Kristian never did such a thing. They seem to have a paranoid conviction that you are – how can I put it? Not quite a conventional vampire, if such a beast ever existed.'

'Who is saying these things?' Her refined English voice was colourless.

'Oh, everyone.'

'Stefan?'

They crossed a courtyard and descended a flight of steps to a terrace, bounded by a waist-high wall. The fortress rose up in all its masculine weight behind them; beyond the wall there was the valley, the sky and the mountains.

'Yes, Stefan, Karl, Rachel, Ilona, John. They all went to Karl and Charlotte's house yesterday evening, to tell Charlotte that she'd created a monster.'

'And you happened to be there too?'

'Only because Ilona insisted I go. And for Ilona to be concerned about anything is quite out of character. You have certainly stirred them up. But no one seems to wonder what has created this hysteria—'

'Except you.' Her voice was paper-thin and soft, and like paper it could cut without warning. 'And if they think I'm a monster, what do they intend to do about it?'

'No decision was reached.'

'Do they want to kill me?'

'Perhaps.'

She leaned on the wall, silent. Across the valley, the Alps pushed up from the earth's crust under a frosted white webbing. They were immense yet they seemed to float; millions of tons of rock, weightless as the earth itself was weightless in space. The sky was dark and clogged with clouds. Rain pattered down, but Violette seemed untouched by it.

Pierre watched her, fascinated and amused. She had a true ballerina's neck, long and slender. He studied the creamy curve of her throat – as much of it as her black fur collar revealed – and felt a perverse desire to kiss her there.

After a long time she asked, with evident difficulty, 'What did Charlotte say?'

A breath flickered in Pierre's throat, not quite a laugh. 'She agreed with them. Oh, she defended you with passion, but it was a case of, "the lady doth protest too much". She was in a panic, because in her heart she agreed with them.'

Violette bent her head. Her arms stiffened as she leaned on them. 'Even Charlotte,' she said under her breath. Then, turning to him, 'So, I have no friends in the world, then?'

Pierre shrugged, lifting his hands. 'It's a cruel world, isn't it?'

'This means nothing to me. I'd guessed it, anyway.'

He moved closed. 'Surely it means something. I came to warn you.'

'Why?' Seeing deep suspicion mingled with contempt in her expression, he felt wounded.

'I refused to believe what they said, Madame, until I could make up my own mind. Now I have met you, my opinion is that they are a bunch of hysterics. Clearly you are a gracious and gentle creature who would not dream of harbouring bad intentions towards anyone. *Ma chérie*, you won't even feed on humans until the need nearly kills you – will you?'

He ventured to put a hand on her shoulder. She looked at the hand, then at him. 'What are you doing?'

He placed his other hand over hers, where it rested on the wall. 'You have one friend.'

He leaned towards her. Couldn't resist her. Her scent was gorgeous, a mingling of floral perfume, of rosin dust and satin and wood polish from her studio. But no taint of blood. She hadn't fed for a long time, and now he could see how her flesh was drawn against the bones. He was shaking with the excitement of being near her, yet he couldn't understand himself. How could another vampire be as alluring to him as a human victim? He must remind himself that she wasn't human, and that he must not approach her with his usual gleeful confidence but with great delicacy.

'You, my friend?' she said. 'I don't think so.'

Her coldness dismayed him. 'But I have—'

'You have done nothing but mock me since we met. I've no idea what you are playing at, Monsieur Lescaut, but it is nothing kind. Nothing sincere.'

'I am not mocking you now.' His hand slid along her shoulder and rested on her spine, but he held himself back. Careful now. Use all your charm. 'Why did you walk up here with me, Violette, if you did not see something in me to your liking? We are not human, we don't have to pretend. We needn't waste any time . . .'

'What do you want?' She looked alarmed. That was good. It meant he'd got the upper hand.

'To kiss you.'

'Oh,' she said softly. 'So you want to kiss me, do you?' Oh God, yes, he thought, but she put a finger to his lips. Her whole manner changed; her aloofness vanished, and a seductive softness came to her mouth and eyes. 'Wait. Let me kiss you.'

This is not happening, he thought in an ecstasy of excitement. He smiled and closed his eyes. 'Whatever you say.'

Pierre knew he'd made a mistake, half a second after it was too late. Her hands slid softly over his shoulders. She leaned into him, her face questing towards his. Then, in a flash, her fingers became sprung traps, and her mouth slid along the edge of his jaw and fastened on his throat.

His eyes flew open. He gripped her wrists, couldn't shift her. Her fangs darted into him and he felt her stiffen and shudder from head to toe, felt the unvoiced release rumbling through her like the purr of a lioness.

Other vampires had fed on him before, it wasn't so bad, it could be quite pleasant. But this was hideous. The first taste of his blood seemed to madden her, and now she was unleashing all her pent-up hunger on him. She pushed him back across the wall, almost cracking his spine, and came down on top, tearing at his neck, sucking –

Helpless at first, Pierre began to struggle. It should have been divine, surrendering to her, but it was horrific. Nothing sensual about her. She was not like Ilona, beautiful, savage, but still womanly; she was elemental, covering him like the wings of a vast owl that hunted by night.

His instinctive escape to the Crystal Ring was blocked. She held him to this place of suffering. Pain ran molten from his throat to his spine and he thought, has she taken so much blood from me already?

He sensed the blind ecstasy that devoured her. How intimately he knew the power of the thirst. He knew that now she'd begun to satiate it, she would not be able to stop . . . And his own response, even through his agony, shamed him. A need he rarely felt because blood-thirst was everything to him, a need he despised as human; powerful sexual desire.

Suddenly the pain ceased and her face rose over his. Blood gleamed on her lips; her mouth and eyes were purple caves.

'Do you want to kiss me now, Pierre?' she said throatily. 'You think me some pliant doll you can first jeer at, then have just for the asking? My friend, are you, you bloody liar?'

The chill wave of her contempt quenched all desire. In sheer panic, he seized the moment to thrust his foot under her ankle to wrench her off balance. Then he was off the wall and away, pushing past her clawing limbs, taking long strides that brought him to his knees in the dust, his legs were so weak.

He staggered up and ran on.

He crossed the courtyard, ran down another open corridor, and found himself in a maze. There were high walls on all sides, running off at various angles, steps leading in three different directions. No sign of a way out. The fortress was vast and he had no idea of its layout.

He felt her following him. Strange faint sounds like wing-beats, claws scraping in the dust, an animal panting after its prey.

Pierre made another wild leap at the Crystal Ring, fell back like a bird with clipped wings. He could have wept. How has she taken so much strength from me in such a short time?

He ran into a dark archway. She was behind him, playing cat-and-mouse, laughing. His heart pounded and he turned clammy like some scared human.

She can take a vampire's head off with those little hands . . .

He broke a lock, burst into a tower room, and ran up flights of stairs to the top. Another door led out on to a roof; he opened it, thought of throwing himself off. A long fall down the outside of the fortress and down the ridge . . . the only escape, and it wouldn't kill him, but he hated heights. One of his inadmissible weaknesses.

Pierre could hear her climbing the stairs quite slowly after him. Why didn't she take a short cut through the Crystal Ring? To mock him, surely.

There were old weapons displayed on the walls for sightseers to look at. Pierre took down a spear and sat crouched in an alcove to wait for her.

Then his fear edged into anger. Are you the devil's pet, witch? he thought. This had happened to him too many times, a stronger vampire feeding on him, stealing his pride with his blood. Usually it had been Kristian, sometimes Karl. Perversely he hadn't minded that so much – but from a woman, it was insufferable.

An owl screeched, somewhere far away in the forest. Dull light fanned through a thickly leaded window and through the open door. She'd probably sense his presence, but if she didn't, if her senses were dampened by the blood – *my blood, you bitch* – she'd think he'd gone out on to the roof.

He watched the stairwell from which he'd just emerged, listening for her, suddenly realizing that he could no longer hear her, couldn't perceive her presence at all.

She's gone, he thought, shivering.

Then the hairs rose on his neck and his head whipped round. She wasn't in the stairwell but in the doorway on the roof, a silhouette in a dark-blue arch, moving towards him.

'I haven't finished with you,' she said.

She glanced dismissively at the spear, and came on.

Pierre wasn't giving her the chance to get near him. With a shout, he leapt up and charged at her, the iron tip aimed at her heart.

Momentarily startled, she hesitated. The tip passed between the long fur revers of her coat and made contact; he felt the thin material of her dress give, the flesh break, bone splintering. She gave a cry; he smelled blood, saw the dark stain growing between her breasts.

Fevered, he ran her right up against the opposite wall and pinned her there.

Her eyes were white orbs, her mouth open. Blood ran from her lips. She spoke, her voice bubbling through the fluid. 'A stake through the heart, Pierre? You should know you can't kill me like that.'

'Run away into the Crystal Ring, then, *chérie*,' he grated. 'I am going to kill you, one way or another.'

'For making you feel foolish?'

He stabbed and twisted the spear. 'They were right about you! You are insane, you're the thing that mortals daren't name!'

'Satan?'

'Cancer!'

He began to push the spike deeper, feeling horribly exhilarated, yet helpless. She was in pain but she wasn't dying. And why didn't she just step into the Ring? Was it the pain that stopped her, or was she mocking him further?

The metal slid deeper. It must have pierced her heart. She groaned, and her hands came up to grip the shaft, forcing it out of her body. Her gloves were wet and black with blood, yet her grip was solid. He pushed, she resisted. They struggled against each other, static, and all the time her gaze hung on his.

Mon Dieu, her expression! A blank, sightless look, as if some demon had possessed her, and all she could do was to look on aghast at its actions. Her horror infected him and he wanted to scream.

Suddenly she wrenched the spear out of her chest and lifted it with terrible strength, swinging Pierre clear off his feet. Taken by surprise, he couldn't let go. She swung him in an arc, rushing forward as she did so. He was borne backwards at speed, felt the window at his back, felt the impact as the leading burst and the glass shattered around him.

Then he was out in thin air. The maw of the valley tilted beneath him. Frantically he held on to the shaft of the weapon, his legs jerking as if for a purchase on nothingness. He had a glimpse of Violette's face above him, a white gargoyle, an ice-queen.

'Please—'

She let go of the spear. Cast it outwards, as if releasing a dove.

He fell, limbs flailing, down the high grim walls of the fortress, down into the trees, and onwards down the sheer side of the Mönchsberg ridge. The edges of rocks caught him cruelly, but still he fell.

A hard surface slammed into him. It seemed he went on falling, the momentum of his descent translated into shivering waves of agony. He slid down over a curved, ridged plane and came to rest in a niche, with saints looking down at him. Curving above him was the copper-salted cupola of a church. He'd landed on its roof.

Bones were broken, he knew. Ribs, an arm, his left leg in two places. He stared up at the clouds, at the louring presence of the fortress high above. Is she still up there, he thought, laughing at my distress?

Pierre knew he would be forced to lie here until his unnatural body began to heal itself. He wouldn't die, but after a while he began to wish he could. He wept with the pain.

God, what's she done to me? Something more than physical injury. Something worse than humiliation.

It seemed that a clawed creature with an owl's predatory eyes and a serpent's body swooped down, brushed him with dark feathers, covered him with a mantle of bitter darkness. Then it was gone.

Cesare found John sitting beside the sarcophagus, his head resting on his fists on the rim. He'd been sitting there for days. The stone coffin was half-filled by blood, a shiny purplish-maroon blanket through which Matthew's head showed like a death-mask.

Cesare found the abattoir stench that filled the chamber rich and sweet.

'Well?' he said.

'The same as yesterday, and the day before, and the day before that,' John answered dully. 'Nothing is happening.'

Cesare swept the blood away from Matthew's cheeks and studied the sunken, slate-blue skin. No sign of regeneration. If anything, it was beginning to decay.

He sighed. 'If there is no improvement by now, I'm afraid there's no hope.'

John's fists tightened, but his voice was quiet. 'Why isn't it working?'

'I don't know.' Cesare licked his bloodied hand clean; the blood was still warm. 'Perhaps Kristian had some magic we lack. Or it might be that the head had been severed too long. It's no good, John. Let Matthew go.'

He expected a display of denial and grief, but to his surprise John only whispered, 'Very well. Would you do one thing for me? Take Matthew's head out and bathe it. I can't bear to.'

'Of course.' Cesare scooped the head out of its clotted caul and took it to the side wall of the chamber, where there was a bowl of water on a wooden stand. He stood with his back to John, rinsing the strings of blood from the heavy, waxen head. It took time; the hair was matted solid.

As he worked, John said, 'I believe you.'

'About what?'

'We belong to God,' John said softly. 'I believe it.'

Cesare smiled. He was pleased – no, more than pleased; thrilled, vindicated! He had converted a lost soul. He'd done something useful. 'That is wonderful.'

'It's not your fault Matthew wouldn't return to life.'

'You are being very gracious about this,' said Cesare, drying the head on a square of sacking. 'I half-expected you to blame me, although I'm sure we did everything right. I thought you would be distraught. You're taking it very well, John; I'm impressed.'

'No, it's her fault,' John breathed.

'Who?'

'Lilith.'

The word struck Cesare like a whip. It plucked a discordant memory; flapping darkness, a brief scene from his own mortal life, centuries past; himself as a scared boy, his mother standing over him with a rod in her hand and the burning pain, tears, terror . . .

Cesare said nothing. He thought that if he heard no more, the darkness couldn't hurt him. But John went on quite calmly, 'Lilith, the Mother of Vampires. She killed Matthew, she stopped him being reborn. She is the Enemy, not Satan. She is going to destroy us all.'

Angered, Cesare wanted to make him stop. He span round,

only to find he couldn't speak; he could only stare at the thin figure sitting on the stool by the coffin.

John had pulled out half his hair, leaving his scalp a mosaic of welts and glistening red holes; and as he went on raving in the same calm, rational voice, he tore out a handful with every other word, as if to tear his grief out by its bloody roots.

CHAPTER FOUR

MOON IN VELVET

'Charlotte?'

The familiar, light voice still sent an eerie thrill through her. Charlotte turned and saw Violette in the doorway, dressed in ivory and silver; a dress of silk georgette, sewn with silver bugle beads.

Violette stepped out of the shadows and into the firelight. The dress shone but her face and arms were matt, velvety-white petals. Her hair was arranged in soot-black coils over her ears, under a beaded bandeau. All the poise of her profession was gathered, quiescent, in her slender form.

Charlotte had been reading, but she quickly put the book aside and stood up. 'Violette, how lovely to see you. How are you?'

'I . . .' The dancer fell silent on one syllable and stood gazing at the fire, seeming, Charlotte thought, not quite present. Sometimes she could kiss Violette in greeting, at other times she could not, and tonight was one of those times when Violette plainly did not want to be touched. Charlotte had no idea how to broach the subject of Matthew's death, or the visit they'd received from John and the others.

After a few moments Violette continued, 'I waited until Karl had gone out. I wanted to see you alone. Do you mind?'

'Of course I don't mind! I was going to come and see you, anyway. Please, sit down.'

'Thank you, but I won't.' Violette clasped her hands across her waist. 'I can't sit still. I should be helping the wardrobe mistress with the costumes for the tour but I couldn't stay there, I . . .'

Charlotte moved round to face her. Dear Lord, she thought,

how drawn she looks! She said, 'You haven't fed tonight, have you? How long has it been?'

'I fed last night,' Violette said shortly.

'Is it the same thing that's troubling you?' Charlotte spoke gently, but her heart was sinking. 'Are you still finding it so hard to hunt and feed?'

Violette said nothing. She looked desolate. Charlotte's gaze, travelling over her, was suddenly and shockingly arrested. 'What's that mark on your chest?'

'This?' Violette smiled humourlessly, and drew down the front of her dress to reveal the flesh between her breasts. Charlotte had only seen the tip of the scar she revealed; a ragged pearlescent star, its centre still flushed with purple. 'Isn't it wonderful, how fast we heal? Last night it was almost through to my spine.'

'Who did this?' Rage electrified her, and she was already mentally accusing John. To think that one of the fools who hated Violette had actually tried to kill her! 'Who was it? I'll tear them apart!'

'I think you would.' Violette looked mildly at her, then walked away through the arch into the library. As Charlotte followed her into the darkened room, she added, 'Something happened.'

'Tell me. You know you can tell me anything.'

Violette paused by the table, her head lowered. 'There was a girl called Ute,' she began, speaking so quietly that Charlotte could barely hear her. 'One of my *corps de ballet*, an excellent dancer, almost ready to become a soloist. She came to see me one evening. She had family problems; her father didn't want her to dance and was putting great pressure on her to go home. She was so upset, poor angel, and she came to me for advice. Wise counsel.' The ballerina hesitated, putting her hand to her breastbone as if the place were still sore. 'I am responsible for all my dancers, especially the girls. Some of them are very young and I have to be everything to them, parent, teacher, guardian. So Ute trusted me in her distress, and I . . . I hadn't tasted blood for three days.'

'Oh, Violette,' Charlotte sighed.

'It wasn't just the thirst. I wasn't sympathetic, I was furious with her for giving in to a selfish old man. I think I scared her out of her wits. And then I did it. And all the time I was sucking her blood and swooning with the pleasure of it, I loathed myself, utterly loathed myself. This thing that takes me over . . .'

'It's the thirst. If you would only drink when you first feel it, you wouldn't become so desperate that you lose control.'

'No, it has a name. This thing that takes me over is Lilith.' Charlotte said nothing. The pursuit of this subject never achieved anything. Violette flexed her shaking hands. 'I am her, but I don't know what she wants. *She* seems to know; I wish she'd let me in on the secret. I know she's driven. Driven, like me. We're just the same, so if I hate her I must hate myself—'

'What happened to the girl?' Charlotte broke in.

At one end of the library there was a small stained-glass window. Violette moved towards it. 'Ute lived. I wasn't crazy enough to kill her, the point isn't to kill them. Do you remember that other young woman I attacked, Benedict's wife, Holly? That my bite seemed to stop her caring about her husband, and stop her clinging to him? Well, something changed in Ute too, but not for the better. She didn't remember what I'd done to her, but she had nightmares. I watched her trying to sleep, her pale little face on the pillow.'

Charlotte recalled Rachel's inexpressible agitation and misery. Lilith's judgement, it seemed, did not discriminate between vampires and mortals.

'But she stayed with the ballet?'

'Of course not,' Violette said contemptuously. 'She ran home to her father, the first moment she could crawl out of bed. I suppose I can't blame her. Who'd stay with a madwoman like me? But how could Lilith—' Her voice was suddenly anguished. 'How could *I* do that to her, when she was in my care?'

The window was violet, with winter trees traced in lead, and a moon of thick white glass caught in the branches. Violette was an inky-haired shadow against it. She turned and opened the window, and the scene outside was just the same; the violet sky, the moon.

'They are out there,' said the dancer. 'Humans. Prey. All I have to do is leap over the sill and go out to them.'

'Yes,' Charlotte said without inflexion. 'That's all you have to do.'

Violette's hard white fingernails scraped at the sill like a bird's claws. She released a short breath. 'But I can't.'

Charlotte watched her guardedly, unable to bear the luminosity of her pain. She wanted to soothe Violette with a sheer surfeit of affection, but she couldn't move. She was afraid. 'Why not?'

'The same reason, always the same damned reason! This demon inside me . . .'

'Close the window,' said Charlotte.

'I'm not cold.'

'Close it anyway.'

'Do you think I'm about to start baying at the moon and growing hair on my palms?' Violette banged the window shut. 'Nothing would surprise me now.'

'But the moon does influence everything, even us. If you haven't noticed that you are more restless when the moon is full, you're not very observant.'

'Just tell me, Charlotte, what I am supposed to do. I swore that if I ever harmed one of my company, I should find some way to do away with myself.' She was staring down at her hands. 'It must be possible.' Suddenly she extended her right forefinger and drew the nail across the inside of her left wrist. A slit appeared, red as poppies.

Charlotte ran to her and seized her hands, prising them apart. 'Don't be so damned stupid!'

She met Violette's gaze. Close to, she did not seem even to resemble a human. She was a remote, unapproachable being. She looked as if she might seize Charlotte and drink from her veins without a moment's reflection; she had threatened to do so in the past. Charlotte had seen and heard enough to dread the consequences. Unwelcome transformation. Perhaps the death of her love for Karl – and his for her.

But she held her ground, and Violette did not touch her.

'I've told you the answer,' Charlotte said. 'Stop trying to resist the thirst.'

'I can't. You don't understand how it feels. I can't simply give in to Lilith. I can't bring myself to feed on just anyone, Charlotte. I feel compelled to choose my victims. And it's agony, choosing them. Whatever I do, whether I defy the hunger or obey it, it's a fight and it hurts.'

Growing braver now, Charlotte touched the scar between Violette's breasts, the tiny smooth beads on the dress indenting her fingertips. 'Why do you ask for advice when you won't listen to me? This scar; what sort of fight left you with such a terrible injury?'

A pause. 'You know Pierre Lescaut, don't you?'

'Yes, I know Pierre.' Understatement.

'He did it.'

'What?' Charlotte was mortified. After Pierre had been the only one to offer his support—! She couldn't grasp it.

'You might have told me,' said Violette, 'that a group of vampires came to you complaining that you'd created a homicidal lunatic and to discuss what ought to be done about me.'

Charlotte exhaled. 'I was going to.'

'But they came the night before last, didn't they? Why the delay?'

'I'm sorry. I really didn't know how to tell you. I hoped it would blow over, but I was going to come tonight—'

'Well, it's too late. Pierre got there first. He suggested that far from speaking in my defence, you supported them against me.'

'That's a lie!' Charlotte had not wanted a confrontation, but her mixed emotions got the better of her. 'I was always on your side, even after what they said about Matthew! Was it true? Did you kill him?'

Far from looking ashamed, Violette's expression hardened. Charlotte saw Lilith's soul burning like white flame behind the purplish-sapphire irises, and she recoiled.

'It was a warning,' Violette said grimly. 'No one threatens my ballet, no one. I told you, if I have become a danger to my own people, I shall kill *myself*.'

'And Pierre?' Charlotte almost lost her voice. Perhaps Violette had slain him, too; the thought made her realize, with a shock, that he meant more to her than she dared admit. 'What happened?'

As Violette related the story, without emotion, Charlotte broke away from her and leaned on the table. Pierre's behaviour left her incandescent with fury – but it appeared that Violette had become the aggressor. She could have defended herself without being so vindictive, Charlotte thought. Oh God, what have I brought into the Crystal Ring?

'The worst thing,' Violette finished, not much above a whisper, 'is that I felt nothing. I wasn't angry, I wasn't vengeful, I felt no pity or pleasure. I feasted on his blood, fought with him and thrust him through the window, and I didn't care about any of it.'

Charlotte was trying to form a response when Violette rushed at her. She was too shocked to defend herself as the dancer gripped her shoulders and pushed her back against the book-shelves. 'I didn't care!' Tears glittered on Violette's long black lashes, more a squeezing out of pain and frustration than of grief. 'Have you got some magic formula to make me care about anything, Charlotte?'

Violette jerked her forward and slammed her back again. Her mouth came down just above Charlotte's collarbone, burning. By reflex Charlotte tried to side-slip into the Crystal Ring, but Violette held her in place without effort. So strong. Charlotte closed her eyes, petrified. This is it, she thought. This is where she takes my blood and destroys my soul—

Stefan and the others are right. Violette is insane and a danger to us all. What am I doing, trying to protect her?

She felt the hard pressure of fangtips – then a sudden rush of cold air where the demanding mouth had been. Karl was there, gripping Violette's shoulders, his usually calm eyes ablaze.

He hadn't physically stopped her, Charlotte realized. Violette herself had stopped, when she felt his presence in the room.

'Get your hands off me,' she said softly.

'When you've let go of Charlotte,' he replied, his tone a

quiet coil of frost. 'Do you wonder that you are making so many enemies?'

Charlotte held her breath, certain that Violette would attack Karl instead. But the dancer lifted her hands and stepped lightly away, the blood-lust still etching her face. 'What's the matter?' Violette said poisonously. 'I only wanted to do what you've done repeatedly to her, even when she was an innocent human girl. The same violation, Karl. Do you think it's worse for me to do it? Double standards, or jealousy?'

Trembling, Charlotte peeled herself away from the bookshelf. The dancer seemed to strip all the vampiric power from her and reduce her to a defenceless state. She said, 'I think you'd better leave.'

Violette stayed where she was, still looking at Karl. 'This time, I stopped. But when the proper time comes, you will not be able to stop me. No one will.'

'Do you really think you can take Charlotte away from me?' Karl's expression became thoughtful, but his eyes were jewels of auburn fire, calculating. Charlotte hated the way they looked at each other.

'What do you think?' Violette almost smiled.

'That you would do it, not because you love her, but because you hate me,' Karl said levelly. 'Am I right? I can't read your mind, *gnädige Frau*.'

The ballerina's mouth lost its slight curve. 'Don't turn everything to yourself. You are afraid of me, aren't you? You're both afraid. I don't know why; I only prey on the weak.'

'I know,' Karl said. 'You only take infants whose parents have neglected to leave an amulet in the cot with the magic names; Senoy, Sansenoy, Semangelof.'

Violette gave him a bitter look. 'And the words, "Out, Lilith." Don't forget that.' She turned away from him, and her demeanour seemed to soften. 'God, oh God,' she murmured. Then she came back to Charlotte, rested both hands on her left shoulder, and kissed her cheek.

Charlotte tensed. Incredible to think that those gentle, expressive hands had recently done such violence; unbearable, when she recalled that, as a human, Violette had never hurt a soul.

Violette stroked her cheek as if to quiet her. 'I'm sorry, my dear. I didn't mean to hurt you. That's not why I wanted – not to hurt you – you understand, don't you?'

Charlotte nodded, her throat thick. She understood. The desire for blood dressed up as love, lust, affection; anything but cruelty. Yet, in the end, it could only be cruel. She still adored Violette. The fact that, at this moment, she couldn't stand the dancer touching her was in itself a quiet torment. 'We want to help you, but you're making it almost impossible. Don't you need any friends?'

'I need you,' Violette whispered. 'Don't desert me.'

Charlotte brought herself to clasp her wrist. The self-inflicted wound had already healed to a magenta line. 'I won't.'

'I want you to come with us on the American tour.'

'Why?'

So lovely, the cloudy-crystal face; powerful, fragile, compelling. 'I'm not sure I shall survive it without you.'

Charlotte knew Karl would not want to go. She felt his eyes on them, reserved and brooding. Putting Violette gently away from her, she said, 'We'll talk about it. Now, for God's sake, go and hunt. Find someone and just take them. Don't hesitate.'

'I think,' Violette said, to her relief, 'that I should perhaps do that.'

She vanished. The Crystal Ring, receiving her, hissed faintly like a column of snow-crystals vapouring. Charlotte was alone with Karl.

She found herself so shaken that all she wanted was to run into his arms. But a mixture of anger and shame held her back. She met his eyes, thinking, is he so sure that Violette attacked me? For all he knows, I invited the embrace. If he thinks that – can I in all honesty deny it?

But Karl only said, '*Liebchen*, are you all right?'

'No. No, I'm not.' She came forward, meaning to sit down at the table, but he intercepted her. One hand enfolded her waist, the other her head. She felt his long, delicate fingers sliding through her hair. Divine. She leaned her head against his shoulder. And it felt like a kind of self-betrayal, accepting comfort from a man who was about to say, 'I told you so.'

'I really thought she'd be happier, once she decided to stay with the ballet,' she said.

'Obviously she isn't.' Karl half-sat on the edge of the table, loosely holding her hands. 'You must admit now—'

'Oh, but it gets worse! Pierre went to talk to her last night, to warn her against the rest of us, apparently. I don't know why. He was just being Pierre, too clever for his own good. But he offended her so she attacked him. They had a dreadful fight, but he came off the worse. So yes, before you say anything, everyone was right. She's a threat. She feeds on other vampires, as Kristian did.'

Karl was quiet, his eyelids falling, lashes forming long dark crescents against his cheeks. 'Pierre always had a talent for doing the wrong thing. He always seems to survive. It is the sordid truth that some vampires prey on others to establish their power; in the end it's our only proof of superiority. Violette steals Pierre's strength with his blood, leaving him forever more subservient to her. That's what Kristian used to do.'

'But I don't think that's why she did it. You can't compare her to Kristian!'

'No. She is an anarchist, not a megalomaniac.'

'I suppose Pierre will come to you, whining about the injustice of it,' she said tightly. 'But you didn't see the wound he gave her! I'll never forgive him.'

'Even if he acted in self-defence?'

'You would defend him.'

'I'm defending no one,' Karl said calmly. 'But, *Liebling*, Pierre hasn't come, has he? I wonder why not . . . Kristian's bite was a crude demonstration of possessiveness and power; it had no lasting effect on the mind. Violette's is something else. That is why I fear her. Whoever she touches is never the same afterwards. If ever she has her way with you, you will be someone different – and you might no longer need me.'

Karl could admit, 'I fear her,' with unaffected honesty, and yet he had the steadiest nerves of anyone she'd ever met, an uncanny self-possession. She loved that, and envied it a little.

'And if she ever touches you, Karl—' Coldness flashed over her body and she dug her fingernails involuntarily into his hand.

'She won't. She said we can't stop her – but Kristian also thought himself invincible.'

She was watching him as he spoke. Her breath was arrested by the startling reminder of how easy it was to misread his expression. Serenity metamorphosing with the merest slide of shadow to ruthlessness . . . the memory that although he'd loved Kristian in a way, Karl had slain him without pity.

'Swear to me you'll never do anything to hurt her!'

Another change in his face; her vehemence had startled him. His eyes were solemn, questioning. 'Charlotte, how can I? God knows, I made enough promises in the past that I couldn't keep. I won't make another. I know you love her' – astonishing to hear him state it so easily, when she could never admit it to him – 'but do you imagine I could put her life before yours, before Ilona's or Stefan's? *Liebe Gott*, it doesn't bear thinking about. If she placed you in danger, I would have no choice.'

Charlotte felt the long waves of emotion crest and fall away within her, but the dilemma remained. 'Nor would I, if she threatened you,' she said. 'You know, dearest, don't you? I set you above everyone else, whatever the cost.'

'And it has proved expensive for you, beloved,' he said very softly. 'Almost more than conscience can afford.' He slid his fingers along her jaw, making her look at him. 'I can promise one thing; I'll never contemplate harming her, as long as she leaves us in peace.'

'And if someone else threatens her?'

'Then I would try to protect her – if she needs anyone's protection.'

Charlotte hugged him with the sheer relief of hearing him say this. He added, 'Well, I suppose we shall have to go to America with her. I still believe it is safer not to let her out of our sight for too long.'

'It will be nice to go,' she said. 'To get away from others of our kind for a while. God, what else can happen?'

'Ah.' Karl smiled ironically at her, his hands resting on her hips. 'Let me tell you about Simon.'

By the following night, Pierre had crawled down from the church roof and found a shrub-covered cleft between some rocks where he could curl up with his suffering.

He was a victim of the unfortunate fact that a vampire full of fresh blood would recover from his injuries fast; one who had been drained, as Pierre had, would find the healing process much longer and more painful. The searing pain in his chest and limbs immobilized him, but there was no escape into unconsciousness.

Sometimes he hallucinated, and was glad when the pain brought him, sobbing, out of it.

He hated Violette with violent passion. He had to survive, if only for the pleasure of vengeance.

On the third night, sheer hunger drove him out of his refuge against the agonized protests of his body. He hunted successfully. First a sour-faced, elderly woman, then a succulent pair of young lovers.

Pierre felt no better.

He felt the blood seeping into his unnatural cells like sap into a spring flower, filling each tiny sac, swelling them with life and growth. He began to heal so fast that he could feel his bones creaking as they fused.

Yet something was still wrong. The physical discomfort was receding, yet he felt dizzy and weak. He had terrifying fits in which he found himself clawing at his own body, running, choking for breath like a human; trying desperately to escape something that wasn't there.

He realized, to his own disgust, that these were attacks of fear.

Afterwards, he would be left exhausted, almost too weak to hunt – like a dying man losing his appetite. This alien condition only fed the fear.

He recovered his ability to enter the Crystal Ring quite soon, only to be seized by attacks of vertigo that drove him back to earth. There was something wrong with the Crystal Ring; an oppressive shadow above him that seemed to follow him everywhere. Afraid to hunt, afraid to enter the realm that had been his element for a century or more! He felt disgusted at himself.

He had never sought help from anyone, but he needed it now. Existing between hotels and the houses of his victims, he had no home of his own. To whom could he go? There was no Kristian, no comforting father-figure to relieve all his burdens with simplistic dogma. He couldn't go to Ilona or Karl in this state; God, the humiliation would be insufferable! If he went to Stefan, Karl would find out. And all Karl will say, Pierre thought bitterly, is, 'You brought this on yourself.' Sadistic bastard.

Kristian was gone, but Kristian's castle was still there. However bleak it might be, it was the only place that bore the faintest resemblance to a concept of 'home'. Almost unconsciously, Pierre began to head towards it, a wounded animal going to ground.

The green and golden meadows of Austria blended into those of Bavaria, Germany, the Rhineland. He wound his way through pine forests by day, passed through villages and towns by night like a driven ghost, oblivious to the charms of the painted and timbered houses around him.

Sometimes he ran, sometimes he fell and could not move. He would forget to feed, then wonder why he felt so weak, so hungry. His finely tailored clothes were crumpled and dirty, and if anyone saw him in daylight they would stop and stare. A tramp or a lunatic, he must be, this white-faced creature with maniacal blue eyes.

This was Violette's curse.

Reaching the Rhine, he turned and followed the wide iron-grey flow northwards past the Lorelei, where the banks rose high above the sinuous waters; and at last he saw Schloss Holdenstein, a cluster of brown turrets and tiled roofs standing high above the vineyards. An atoll of sterility amid an ocean of green life.

Afterwards, Pierre could not remember crossing the river,

nor climbing the hill to the Schloss. He must have entered the Crystal Ring involuntarily. One moment he was watching the rain churning the water, the next he was inside, lying face down, arms outstretched on the chill flagstones, clinging there like a bereft child to an indifferent mother.

Cruel twist. Of all the people who least deserved a mother's comfort . . .

'But it wasn't my fault,' he moaned under his breath. 'It wasn't my fault!'

Something moved in the rushlit corridor. Looking up, Pierre saw soft black sandals, the hem of a dark robe. Standing over him was a monkish figure of medium height, with a cherubic face, cropped fair hair, and pale grey eyes with pinpoint pupils.

'What has the storm blown in?' said the figure. 'Have you come back to us, Pierre?'

'Cesare,' Pierre groaned. He'd hated Cesare, Kristian's lap-dog, but in the abyss of his despair he reached up and tugged at the felted hem. 'You must help me.'

'Must we?' The bland face stared down in contemplation. Pierre half-expected the vampire to kick him and walk away. Instead, to his amazement, Cesare bent down and helped him to his feet. 'What has brought you to this, my friend?' he said into Pierre's face. He smelled of the castle; dust, damp, nothingness. 'Well, you're safe now. Come with me. We'll look after you.'

There was an odd possessiveness in the way Cesare held him tightly around the shoulders and led him deeper into the Schloss, but Pierre was past caring. He wanted to pour out the story, if only he could control his chattering breath.

Along the corridor he saw another vampire he knew; a Cinderella figure with straight dark gold hair and a broom in her thin hands. Maria, another of Kristian's unsmiling brood. Others were gathering to witness Pierre's arrival. There were only a few left now, but they had been Kristian's most devoted followers, and they lingered in Schloss Holdenstein like a sect awaiting the Second Coming.

No one ever came here now. Pierre supposed his arrival was quite an event.

Things were hazy for a time. Vampires in umber robes moved around him. Someone brought him a human to feed on; the small creature squawked and fought, but Pierre overpowered it without difficulty. Luscious blood, washing away all pain. The body was removed afterwards, and he hadn't even noticed whether it was male or female, an adult or a child. It didn't matter.

When his head cleared, he found that he had been placed on a couch in the centre of a bare stone chamber, lit by the naked flames of torches. How familiar it was. There was the tall black chair on the dais, where Kristian had used to hold court. Cesare stood near the chair, but he did not occupy it. The other vampires, about ten or eleven, were grouped around Pierre, watching him. Bleached faces, drab robes; no spark of recklessness or humour in any of them. Yet the juxtaposition pleased him; they could have been courtiers, attending a sick monarch.

Pierre felt stronger now. He felt safe from Violette, certain she could not breach these thick walls. Safe, he became more angry than afraid, and he had an expectant audience to play to.

'What happened to you?' said Cesare. 'You were babbling before we fed you. We couldn't understand.'

'Babbling?' Pierre was affronted by the image. He tried to sit up but fell back on to the cracked leather upholstery. Then the words started to tumble out. 'There's a new vampire, she was only created a few months ago, a madwoman called Violette. She has long black hair, black like a raven. Loveliest creature you could hope to see, but she's crazy, she tried to murder me—'

'Our father Kristian used to say that a woman's outer beauty was a sign of her inner decay,' said Cesare. 'It seems she has addled your mind also.'

'Yes, she has,' Pierre said savagely. He stretched out his hand. '*Regard*, how I'm shaking. This is what she's done to me!'

A wave of horror overcame him and his head rolled back. Through a yellow mist he heard the rustle of their robes, the murmur of concerned voices. When he opened his eyes, Cesare was standing over him.

'You say she is called Violette?' Cesare said, his pupils boring into Pierre's. Beside him, another vampire was leaning down; Pierre didn't recognize him at first, then suddenly realized it was John. He had changed drastically since their last meeting. A mediaeval-style robe like Cesare's had replaced his modern clothes, and his hair had gone; ripped out, it seemed, leaving his scalp a bald, livid mass of scars. His priest-like face was pulled into ugly lines by some hidden sickness of the soul.

Before Pierre could ask what had happened to him, John said, 'He's talking about Lilith.'

At the name, a look of dread transfigured Cesare's face; a kind of superstitious revulsion. 'Is it so?'

Pierre nodded mutely, his stomach clenching in alarm. 'She hasn't been here, has she?'

Cesare ignored the frantic question and turned to the others. 'Behold, the second one who has come here complaining of this Lilith!' he exclaimed.

'But what does it mean?' said a pretty male with yellow hair and black eyes.

'I don't know yet. But at least it has drawn us together, given us a reason to talk and think again.'

'You mean you know nothing about her?' said Pierre. 'You've never heard of Violette Lenoir? John, didn't you tell them?'

They all looked blankly at him, and John shook his ravaged head. 'She is only Lilith to me. This human persona she puts on is nothing, it has no reality to us.'

Pierre threw his hands up in exasperation. Now he recalled why he had despised them; how ghastly that he needed them now. 'When did you last leave the castle, Cesare? If you live like hermits here, it's no wonder you never see anything, never hear anything. You haven't a clue what goes on in the real world, have you?'

'Of course we leave the castle,' Cesare said thinly. 'We have to feed. But your so-called "real world" is one of shadows. It is nothing to us but sustenance. Kristian rightly taught us to despise it.'

'I remember. You only go out at night, like the ghosts of monks haunting graveyards. Very Gothic. And do you sip only your victim's life-auras, so they fall down in fear and never know what has taken their life? Or have you lapsed from Kristian's path? Do you allow yourself a little taste of their blood?'

Cesare was thin-lipped. 'Kristian was exceptional. Very few of us can aspire to such high standards of austerity. Tell us of this female, Pierre.'

'She's a well-known dancer in the human world. If you ever went out, you would have heard of her. She became a vampire because Charlotte – Karl's companion, you remember her?'

'I believe I saw her once,' Cesare said dismissively.

'Charlotte became obsessed with her, and brought her into the Crystal Ring. But she came out of it mad, and convinced she's some demon called Lilith. I don't know what her intentions are, but I do know she's out of her mind. She's only a few months through the veil and she's already killed two vampires and had a damned good attempt on me! You know who Lilith was meant to be?'

Another spasm passed across Cesare's rounded face. 'The Mother of Vampires. Kristian spoke of Lilith as God's instrument, His vessel. She was there at the beginning and she will appear again at the end, to destroy us, to drink her own children dry and cast us into the maw of hell . . .'

The hush that followed his words was charged with fear – and, if Pierre was not mistaken, a bizarre, hungry excitement. He closed his eyes, suddenly wishing he'd gone to Ilona after all; to have his fears ridiculed would have been comforting, but to have them taken seriously was shredding his last hold on reality.

'But we can defeat her, if we only hold true to our faith.' Cesare clasped Pierre's shoulder. 'You can help us, Pierre. Show us where to find her.'

The proposal filled Pierre with a rush of dread. 'No!' he cried, almost hysterical. 'No. I can't, I'm ill. You must let me stay here. Please.'

'Vampires don't suffer illness.'

Pierre loathed Cesare's condescending tone, but he'd put himself in the position of having to endure it. It didn't matter.

I believe in nothing, he thought. I don't care what any of it means, as long as I never see Violette again. I'll do anything for Cesare, sell myself to a man I've always despised, if it means gaining protection from the witch!

'The question is this,' Cesare went on. 'Is this Violette really Lilith, or is she only blaspheming? Either way, she must be dealt with. She has done unforgivable things to John, Matthew and you ... Of course you must stay here, my dear friend. And I think that you are perhaps right.'

'About what?'

'That I've kept myself cloistered here for too long.' Cesare's eyes were fixed on some non-existent point in space, his dread of the unknown becoming a quivering light of defiance. 'I've decided it's time I went out and reacquainted myself with the world.'

Charlotte and Karl still went their separate ways to feed, as if their mutual feast on the peasant woman had never happened. It remained an unnamed beast between them. On her own after Violette's visit, however, Charlotte did not begin to hunt at once. She travelled through the Crystal Ring to Vienna, in search of a friend.

She found him quite quickly. He was not at home but on his way there, strolling through one of Vienna's public gardens. She went ahead of him, and waited under a tree. He was alone, and had the melancholy, self-contained look she remembered. He was tall and slim with thick grey hair, his face still leanly attractive although he was approaching sixty. Josef.

When he was almost level with her, Charlotte stepped into his path. He stopped, turning white and raising one hand to his chest; for a moment, she thought the shock of her appearance had been too much. Then he breathed out heavily and smiled. His grey eyes, behind black-rimmed spectacles, gleamed with pleasure and regret.

He was in no danger from her. Josef was her only mortal friend.

'I always seem to startle you to death,' she said apologetically.

'Your choice of words is uncomfortably close to the truth,' he said. 'You never knock on my front door, like a normal visitor. But, my dear Charlotte—' He took her hand and kissed it, then held it warmly between his palms. 'Such a sweet death I would welcome.'

'No, you wouldn't.'

'Maybe not, but let me dream. Then you will not alarm me so much.' He tucked her hand through his arm, and they walked together. Lights from the street wove linden-green webs in the foliage.

'I don't mean to frighten you, Josef, really.'

'But you can't help it. It's in the nature of our relationship. I still see in you the little girl who was the daughter of my good friend, George Neville, yet here you are, a ghost.' In the *frisson* of silence that followed, a weft of knowledge flew between them. He saw her as she really was, an unholy creature in a human shell. When they'd met by chance the previous year, he'd recognized her, even though he hadn't seen her since she was a child. It was because she looked so like her mother; the same deep-lidded eyes, sombre mouth, warm brown hair that turned to gold leaf in the light. But behind the veil of feminine softness stood the hard truth of her nature; that she'd been drawn through death and now lived beyond it, watching humans with the radiant eyes of a goddess and the red tip of her tongue poised in hunger.

Josef had watched Charlotte end the life of his sister, Lisl. Lisl had been desperately ill, dying; he'd wanted her suffering to end. But Charlotte knew that the memory and the sadness would never leave him. There was no haze of romance to shield Josef from the horror of what Charlotte was. Taking his sister's life out of God's hands could have been a gift from hell as much as from heaven.

And yet he said softly. 'Such a dear and beautiful ghost, men would give their souls to be haunted by.'

'They say vampires can't befriend humans without causing disaster, but we keep trying. I've something to ask you, but your soul is safe, I promise.' They were passing through an arbour of honeysuckle, between beds of daffodils; for a moment

Charlotte's head was filled with the scent. The world seemed timeless and weightless, caught on that flowing saffron wave. 'It's a friend of mine. I told you I was worried about her, that time I came and asked what you knew about the legends of Lilith.'

'I remember. Your vampire friend, Lilith.'

'I'm still worried. She's so disturbed, I'm afraid she'll harm herself.'

'Don't vampires harm others? I don't see what I can do.'

'But you know the mythology, you know how to interpret it. You told me you'd studied psychology.'

'Charlotte, after I moved from the science of physics to that of the mind, I worked as a psychoanalyst for a short time, until I retired to look after Lisl. Yes, I study and I write, but I've had no practical experience for years.'

'You don't forget. If you could watch her, perhaps even talk to her if she'd permit it, you might gain some insight that would help!'

He turned away from her. His coat and scarf blew in a breeze; lights through the bushes made a silver mosaic around him. 'Charlotte, my friendship with you is one thing. But to give help to another . . . another of your kind, I don't know.'

'I know it's a lot to ask, but it means everything to me. I don't know what else to do.' He was shaking his head, troubled. Out of desperation she added, 'Josef . . . It's Violette Lenoir.'

His head came up and he looked at her in amazement. '*The* Lenoir – the ballerina? You wouldn't joke about such a thing, would you? Of course you wouldn't.'

'It goes without saying that you mustn't tell anyone.'

'Who would believe me? But I have seen her dance many times –' He waved vaguely in the direction of the theatres. 'And now you tell me she's—'

'Disturbed. Unhappy.' Charlotte said quietly. 'Perhaps it would help you to understand if I tried to explain something about us. What if I told you that what you would call the "collective unconscious" can be perceived as a real place by vampires?'

'Can it?' He looked at her sceptically.

'Well, there is an other-world that only we can enter. Some call it the mind of God; they believe passionately in God, and use it as justification for the wicked acts that our nature forces us to commit. But I believe it's the subconscious of mankind. Not just their unconscious but the electrical impulses of their conscious thought-waves and dream-waves. Energy is matter, matter is energy, after all. It's a question of perception. Vampires can perceive thought-impulses as matter, an ethereal double of this world; and I mean ethereal as in *ether*, a crystal-structured medium through which we can move like fish through water—'

'Charlotte, stop!' he exclaimed. 'This sounds almost scientific, but—'

'I was a scientist,' she said tightly. 'I didn't just make my father cups of tea all day. I understood and participated in what he was doing.'

'Forgive me. I didn't mean to sound condescending. It is rather hard to conceive of such a place, that's all.' He took her arm and they walked on through the garden, very slowly.

'I know, but suspend belief for me, won't you? I'm telling you the truth. We call this other-world the Crystal Ring, or Raqi'a—'

'Ah, I know that word,' said Josef. 'The "firmament".'

'And it creates vampires. If a human is taken into it on the point of death by three other vampires, he or she becomes a vampire too.'

'Rebirth,' said Josef thoughtfully, 'not from the energy of the real world but from the energy of the collective mind. Is that what you're saying?'

'Yes. I've no proof. It's what I feel to be true.'

'But then ... Why vampires? Why not – oh, anything the human mind can conjure? Monsters, dream lovers, figures from mythology? Archetypes, as we Jungians say.'

She laughed. 'But we are monsters and dream lovers, Josef. And what else is Lilith but a mythical figure? But we must be vampires, we couldn't be anything else, because we represent the very extremity of human fears and hopes.'

'The fear of death and the hope of eternal life,' said Josef, nodding. 'Yes, you are almost making sense!'

'Thank you,' she said sarcastically. 'But you've left one out; the fear of the dead coming back to life and feeding on the living. Isn't that the deepest terror of all? The breaking of nature's laws. We can never be fully defined scientifically, because the laws of physics, chemistry and biology break down around us. We come from the lawless realm of dreams.'

Josef was quiet for a while. 'So vampires have theories and theologies,' he said. 'Amazing.'

'And we argue about them as much as humans do.'

He was fascinated now. She saw the glow in his face. 'Let me propose a theory,' he said. 'Archetypes are motifs that crop us everywhere. Lilith appears in every mythology under many names; a primordial image. It sounds to me as if Violette has absorbed an archetype from the Crystal Ring that has a particular significance and resonance for her. It may be a complex; that is, a fragment of the psyche that's broken away due to some traumatic influence.'

'I'd say she's had enough of those in her life,' Charlotte murmured. 'So if she thinks she's wicked and destructive, she separates that part of herself and calls it Lilith?'

'It is possible. In the voices heard by the pathologically insane, the complex can take on its own ego character. Does Lilith talk to her?'

'I don't know,' she said. The words *pathologically insane* went on reverberating. 'I've never asked.' She caught his coat sleeve. 'Oh, but you've convinced me you have something to offer her. I don't know what else to do. We are vampires, but we are still – well, human, in a way. If I can only persuade her to talk to you—'

'I'm not sure.' Josef looked at the ground. His hands were in his pockets, his shoulders hunched. 'I'm tempted; it would be fascinating. But if she refuses to talk to me, it would be useless.'

'But surely you could learn something just by observing her for a length of time? Don't turn me down flat! Wait; before you answer, I want to offer you something in return. The Ballet Janacek is going to America at the beginning of summer. Karl and I are going too; we're patrons, of a sort. There's a spare berth on the ship, it wouldn't cost you anything to come with us.'

His face softened, and he smiled. 'Why would I want to go to America?'

'The tour opens in Boston.'

'Ah.' His ragged eyebrows rose.

'I've seen the photographs of your niece Roberta on your desk. You often mention her. You said she lives in Boston, and you haven't seen her for years.'

'Oh,' he said, moisture coming into his eyes. 'Oh, this is quite a bribe.'

'Well, wouldn't you like to see her?'

'My little Roberta, I called her Robyn, with a "why", because she was always asking questions.'

'And wouldn't she love to see her uncle? All you have to do in return is help Violette. I thought it would make you happy.'

His face was tender, lined with old sorrows. 'Extraordinary, that a vampire should care for the happiness of a mere mortal.'

She shrugged. 'Most don't. Please say yes.'

He was trying to look grave, but he could not keep the look of joy from his expression. 'Yes, I'll come. Dear God, I am going to see my Robyn! Thank you.' He bent and kissed her cheek. A kiss of friendship – yet his lips remained there, warm, almost fervid. She had to bite down on the sudden, treacherous thirst; time to end the meeting before it went too far.

In that instant she knew that the words she'd spoken earlier had already come true. *Vampires cannot befriend humans without causing disaster.* Josef wanted Charlotte as a lover, even though he could not have her, and that was keeping him from ever finding someone else.

She had never taken his blood, never would. But still she was insidiously picking his soul apart.

CHAPTER FIVE

ANGELS FALLING

Sebastian avoided other vampires, as he had done for decades. There was nothing about them he desired or needed; he wanted the citadel of night entirely to himself.

He loved America for its sheer size and grandeur. Forests, lakes and mountains where he might track a single victim across a vast stretch of wilderness. Cities, seething with the rich and the poor of all nations, where he could pass from slum to glittering skyscraper like a chameleon. And very few vampires on this vast continent to offer him competition.

Sebastian had the ability to go unnoticed by humans, when he chose. He could leave them without memory of his face or voice, with only a feeling of unease, of having been brushed by the shadow-wings of the underworld. He could also pass unseen by other vampires; a rare gift. Immortals usually sensed each other's presence, yet they never seemed to notice Sebastian unless he was actually in sight. This meant he could vanish long before they realized he was near by; it gave him a sense of uniqueness, of superiority.

It was two hundred and twenty-three years since Simon and his companions had drawn Sebastian into the dark womb of vampirism. He hadn't seen them since. Not that he wanted to; but sometimes he would wonder why they'd chosen him. It was as if they'd visited a gratuitous curse on him, then withdrawn to their own realm afterwards, laughing at his fate. The fair folk, it seemed, had a grim sense of humour.

You will make a wonderful immortal, Rasmila had said, and in a way she'd been right. Sebastian had known from the very first instant of transformation that he was an orphan in the darkness. He found it purgatory, and yet it was his only possible fate, the natural extension of his solitary, dark character. He relished his own pain and the evil he visited on others. In shaping the darkness to his own design, his revenge against the faithless Mary had been only the beginning.

How very faint and far away that seemed now. Meaningless, as he'd told Simon afterwards. What was it all for, anyway? he had sometimes wondered. I didn't love Mary as I sucked out her life. I hated her. I only loved the blood. And yet, on a deeper level, it had not been meaningless at all but the profound sealing of his vampire nature.

After he had taken a last look at the house – Blackwater Hall, as the eventual owners had christened it – he'd taken ship to America, and had not returned to Ireland for many years. He would happily have put a million miles between himself and the old country; he wanted no more of its shadowy magic, its religions and superstitions, the wars and the endless struggle just to hold on to his birthright. In the early years of his new existence he had been savage, bitter and self-absorbed. But as time passed he discovered that vampires, although un-dead, were not frozen in one mood for ever; the bitterness passed, the blood-thirst and the fear of eternity came under his control. And then he began to think of the house again.

Eventually, some sixty years after he'd left Ireland, curiosity had drawn him back. He discovered that the scandal of the Pierse who had murdered his wife and her lover, then vanished, was local legend; a folk-tale told by old men in their cups. The estate, having passed to the Crown, had been awarded to some Protestant family in gratitude for their loyal service to William of Orange, all as Sebastian had expected. He felt no resentment. He simply wanted to see what the family were like, how they kept the place. Blackwater Hall; he liked the name. It implied that the house belonged to the river and the land, not to some self-important nobleman. Indeed, the family were pleasant enough people, fair to their tenants, less arrogant than they might have been. Sebastian approved of the way they looked after his demesne.

And yet he owed it to the house and to himself to haunt them a little; to frighten the old men, to feed on the young, strong ones. To turn a capable wife into a crazed neurotic, to seduce a virgin and ruin her for marriage, to kill a first-born son here, a beloved small daughter there. Just to darken their lives once in a while, as the generations came and went. Although America remained his hunting ground, every few years he would return to Ireland for old times' sake, and listen with pleasure when people said, 'That Blackwater Hall is haunted; it's cursed the family are!' And he would slip silently into the house and torment the hapless inhabitants a little more.

Sebastian had finally driven out the last of them in the 1860s. The house had stood empty ever since, a state of affairs that gave him immense satisfaction. At last he had the place to himself when he paid his visits.

Most of the time, however, he did not dwell on the past. He lived in the moment, drinking impressions and sensations as if they were blood. Tonight he was in New York, moving soundlessly through the soft sparkle of lights in search of human heat, noise, the shimmer of music and laughter. How the New World had changed since he'd first set foot here! The age of jazz. It had all mushroomed since the Great War; skyscrapers soaring up everywhere, motor cars with their long bonnets and wire-rimmed wheels crawling nose to tail through the streets. Dirt and fumes, noise and energy. The electric mood of criminality engendered by Prohibition, a law that was enticing more people than ever before to indulge in the forbidden fruit of alcohol. Wild music, outrageous clothes, a new cult of youth. And yet there was still a romance about it, a kind of innocence.

Sebastian neither liked nor hated the changes. He drifted through the streets with the indefinable sense of ennui that had possessed him for months, years. He felt like an observer from another time, distanced from the world yet connected to it by the cord of ravenous thirst.

Losing himself in the crowds who were walking to and from parties, shows and cabarets, he watched the women, with their furs and diamonds and sleek, shiny hair; sensed them watching him as he passed by, captivated by the treacherous beauty of a vampire. Later, he would meet one who would invite him home; the only difficulty was in choosing between them . . .

And he suddenly realized that he was bored.

It was all too easy to take a victim whenever he wanted; they would meet and part (if the victim survived) as strangers. Years since he'd indulged in the extended pleasure of cultivating a relationship, cruelly teasing and torturing his lover for months before the final, fatal betrayal.

He thought, is it possible that I have let myself become too isolated? When a vampire possesses too much power, there are no longer any challenges and he must go to greater and greater lengths to find pleasure.

Lost in reflection, he paused outside a theatre to watch the people streaming out. Yellow light spilled over the sidewalk. Sebastian walked between the white marble pillars of the frontage to look at posters in glass cases, advertising future shows. Musicals, plays, operas, concerts.

Could these human entertainments relieve my weariness of spirit for a while? he thought. And then I'd slake this thirst on some lovely woman from the audience ... or one of the performers, even better.

But I've done it a hundred times before. Is there anything new?

Then a particular photograph caught his eye. The poster beside it announced that a European company called the Ballet Janacek would be performing *Swan Lake* and *Coppélia* at the Manhattan Opera House, but it was the face in pearly shades of grey that captivated him. 'Prima ballerina assoluta Violette Lenoir, the greatest dancer of our time,' he read. Long hands folded over her breastbone, a divinely curved neck, white feathers clasping a face of exquisite, fairy-tale beauty.

Sebastian smiled. Now, to indulge the pleasures of seduction and treachery with this goddess would be a game worth playing!

But it was a month before the ballet came to New York and he couldn't wait, he wanted to see her now. He looked at the list of cities and dates, and saw that the tour opened in Boston a fortnight earlier.

Yes, he thought, I'll go to Boston. He had always had affection for the city, with its sophistication and wealth and restraint. He felt at home there, among all those Irish exiles; he always felt such empathy with them as he drank their blood, as though they had the smoky richness of the past and the endless depths of old stories in their veins.

A voice said over his shoulder, 'Beautiful, isn't she?'

Sebastian had had no sense of a human approaching him; rather, it felt like a shadow, a dimensionless entity behind him. Annoyed at himself for daydreaming, he swung round to see who'd invaded his reverie. And found himself staring into the lion-golden eyes of Simon.

Simon was leaning against a pillar, arms folded, smiling; a tall, blond figure in a beige mackintosh. There was a faint shimmer about him, but he was not the terrifying, angelic figure Sebastian remembered from their first encounter. Sebastian was shocked and not remotely pleased to see him.

'Well, Sebastian, it has been quite a time,' said the apparition. 'I suppose you thought you would never see me again.'

'I haven't been holding my breath, I can assure you,' Sebastian said, looking coldly at him. 'I thought you were dead; there was a rumour that Kristian had destroyed his creators.'

The angel-demon only smiled at his hostility. 'We slept in the *Weisskalt* for a time, that's all. Now I am back.'

'Without your companions?'

'Fyodor, Rasmila and I had a slight difference of opinion. I work alone now.'

'How did you find me?' Sebastian asked. He was inwardly furious that another vampire had tracked him down. 'Even Kristian could never find me.'

'You have quite a reputation for being elusive, my dear friend,' said Simon. 'But don't forget that I created you; that means there's an insoluble link between us.'

'A shame you didn't stay in the *Weisskalt*, then,' Sebastian murmured. He was aware of the human noise and energy bustling all around him, but he and Simon existed in a separate world, a glass bubble. 'Why now, after two centuries? What do you want?'

'Only to talk,' Simon said, shrugging. 'You haven't changed a bit. Still the suspicious misanthropist.'

Sebastian gave a sarcastic laugh. 'So, you don't approve of

Rasmila's choice? You prefer men of Kristian's calibre. I gather he was your choice; Kristian, that well-known philanthropic saint.'

Simon's smile vanished. 'You knew him, then, despite your taste for solitude?'

'Yes, I had the misfortune to meet Kristian.' Sebastian exhaled. 'I once went to the continent in the 1850s. I met a vampire called Ilona; she wanted to take me to Schloss Holdenstein and like a fool I went, out of idle curiosity. What I saw there confirmed all my prejudices against other vampires. A despot, tyrannizing his followers in the name of God. It disgusted me. How could beings like you and I, strong and deathless, bring themselves to kiss and flatter such a tyrant out of cowardice?

'Yet I understood, in a way. When you transformed me, you flung me to the dark, the unknown, maybe to Satan. Some vampires must find it intolerable. So Kristian could maintain a hold over them by saying, "I am ordained by God!" They were prisoners of their fears; they preferred to cling to a self-appointed prophet than to face the dark on their own.'

'It's all very well to speak of them with such contempt,' said Simon, 'but don't underestimate Kristian's sheer strength. Didn't he try to win you to his fold?'

'Oh he tried,' Sebastian said grimly. 'He treated me like a king from another country when I first arrived; he must have thought it was a gift from God, the challenge of winning over an immortal of equal strength to himself. It deteriorated by degrees from flattery and persuasion to arguments, threats and violence. Finally he tried to put me in the *Weisskalt* but I escaped and never went back. He tried to find me and failed. I suppose he must have given up in the end. But I'll tell you this, Simon; I could have killed him, if I'd chosen. I could have taken his place.'

He thought Simon would be angry to hear that his protégé was not infallible. Instead, a strange look of intentness infused Simon's face. 'Why didn't you?'

'Because I didn't care. Their power struggles and passions were too human; an irrelevance that merely corrupts the purity of a vampire's true nature.'

Simon gasped and shook his head. 'What a beautiful sentiment!' he exclaimed.

'Besides which, some other vampires tried to involve me in a conspiracy against Kristian. They saw my strength and wanted me to kill him. I refused; why should I do their dirty work for them? I let Kristian live, because his followers *deserved* him. Karl was the worst. He hated me for not helping, and hated me more because he thought I was corrupting his daughter.'

Simon laughed. 'Were you?'

'I was only encouraging Ilona to indulge the depravity that came naturally to her. But she was as deeply entwined with Kristian as the rest.' Sebastian spoke with disgust. 'No, the whole episode only convinced me that I want nothing to do with them. I had no desire to go back.'

'But your house in Ireland; you go back there, don't you? Why don't you reclaim it, and make it your own?'

Sebastian looked coldly at him, wondering how Simon knew so much. Oh, for perfect privacy! 'I've no need to reclaim it, because it was never taken from me. It can't be; it's as if it exists partly in the Crystal Ring, a spiritual house that transcends its earthly form. Do you understand? It's mine in spirit, so the deeds to its fabric are irrelevant.'

'Yes, I understand.' And Simon was looking very warmly at Sebastian now. 'And I believe Rasmila chose well in you, after all.'

'Did she?' All Sebastian wanted was to end the conversation and leave. Simon's presence was too vivid, oppressive. 'Does it matter?'

'Oh, yes. It does. I bring news, dear fellow, in case you didn't already know. Kristian is dead.'

Sebastian, who had barely thought of Kristian for seventy years, experienced a twinge of delight. 'He is? How splendid. Are you heart-broken?'

'Don't attribute human emotions to me, however flippantly,' Simon replied, unmoved. 'Karl killed him. I punished Karl, then forgave him; it's in the past now. The point is that vampires are without a leader.'

Sebastian sighed, and leaned back against the theatre wall. 'I don't know why you're telling me this. I couldn't be less interested.'

'You should be. Like Karl, you think you're above it, but you're not. There is a new immortal at large who is too dangerous to be allowed her freedom, and everyone will be affected if she isn't stopped. *Even you.* It's not right for such a small but powerful number of creatures as vampires to be divided against each other.' Simon came to him and placed a hand on his arm. Sebastian endured the touch with annoyance. Simon still possessed an intimidating presence, and his eyes were like a bird of prey's, magnetic. 'You have magnificent qualities, Sebastian. It takes a century or more for a vampire to grow into his full strength but you are more than ready now. Come home with me, take control of your immortal kin, and unite them against the danger!'

Simon seemed to expect him to be flattered and over-whelmed; all Sebastian felt was cynical dismay. He breathed the warm night air and stared out at the surging life in the street, the shadowy towers rising towards heaven with a thousand tiny lights shining in their windows. He loved this solitude. He thought of Boston, he thought of human blood and the cruel game he was planning. To exchange that for the cold company of other vampires was laughable. 'Why not do it yourself?'

'It's not my role. Angels may give counsel to men but they don't come to earth and rule men. I can't be God's servant *and* a leader. Someone must choose the leaders under God's will because, frankly, they cannot be trusted to choose themselves.'

'I see,' Sebastian said evenly. 'Well, it's a generous offer but I have to refuse.'

Searing anger lit Simon's eyes. 'Why?'

Sebastian felt dark emotions rising towards the surface. 'You, a supernatural creature from whom I seem to have no secrets, should know that I've always loved being alone. I loved it so much that it destroyed my marriage. Why do you expect me to have changed?'

Simon drew away, looking sideways at him. 'It's not a question of what you want. We gave you the gift of immortal-ity, and now I offer you a chance to use your gifts. You would make such a leader, Sebastian, wise, strong, beautiful as an angel. What harm have I ever done you? All I offer you is *power.*'

'I know,' Sebastian said softly, 'but I don't want it. You never asked what *I* wanted.'

Simon laughed, seeming exasperated. 'Do you think the Virgin Mary ever complained to the Archangel, "You didn't ask what *I* wanted"? This is the most supreme egotism! Don't you understand that you have been chosen by God? You can't refuse!'

'I don't believe in your god.'

'Do you believe in the devil, then?'

'I believe in the older gods,' Sebastian said darkly, 'and I fear them, but I won't bow down to them – especially not to one who doesn't even recognize himself for what he is. You came from nowhere and thrust this existence on me; now you think you can appear after two hundred and twenty-three years and expect me to welcome you like my saviour? Go to hell, Simon. Sort out this mess yourself. I won't be used.'

The gilded face hardened. 'You sound so like Karl!'

Sebastian read a great deal into the oblique insult. 'So, you asked him before you came to me, and he also refused?' He laughed, but Simon said nothing. Sebastian leaned close to him, fired by the thrill of defying his all-powerful creator. 'Is that why you transformed me? Insurance? I was second in line, in case the mighty Kristian was assassinated? Or forty-seventh in line, for all I know.'

Simon stared past him, as if all the troubles of the world were on his shoulders. And Sebastian felt nothing for him; no sympathy, no interest, no desire to help. Nothing. 'No,' Simon answered. 'Even God's plans go awry; that's the penalty we pay for the gift of free will. All we wanted was to create strong, beautiful immortals worthy to serve God!'

'So what will you do to me if I refuse?'

'Don't refuse.'

'I already have. You might be able to kill me – but dead or alive, I'll never do your will. You brought me into this, Simon. At least have the decency to leave me alone!'

Although Simon didn't visibly move, a shudder of anguished emotion seemed to pass through him from head to foot. Then it vanished and he was the serene, burnished god again. Pressing his fingers to the glass that encased the photograph of Violette Lenoir, he said, 'Very well, have your way.' His voice was ice-crisp and dangerous. 'Enjoy the ballet. But afterwards, think again about what I've said – then decide whether I am right or wrong.'

When Simon left New York, he was in a state of despair. Although he'd entertained the possibility that Sebastian might refuse, when it came to it, he could not accept that his powers of persuasion had failed so miserably. Not once now, but twice. And there was no one else worthy of the task.

I have to do something, find someone, he thought as he soared through the Crystal Ring. I must appoint the saviour; only then will God let me back into His circle!

He couldn't admit it to himself, but he was in a state of panic. His powers were collapsing; he felt like a creature of spun sugar, left out in the rain. Yes, he could still impersonate the golden seraph to vampires like Karl and Sebastian, but inside he was falling to pieces – and they knew. Secretly, they knew.

Even the journey from America to Europe was an expression of his weakness. At one time – when the trinity had been complete – he could have made the journey through the Ring in a few hours, without stopping to feed. Now he found it laborious. He had to work his way up through Canada, slipping into the real world now and then to sate his thirst. By the time he reached Greenland, he was so chilled by the Ring's embrace that the snowy wasteland – so like the *Weisskalt* – seemed warm by contrast.

He rested again in Iceland. Having sucked the blood and the life-auras from a farmer and his daughter – quite the prettiest girl he had ever seen, such a waste – he climbed a glacier and sat in the white silence, praying. Below the glacier's rim there was a brown wasteland, boulder-strewn and veined by dry rivers; to the south, the black cone of a volcano stood on the horizon, and to the north lay the Arctic Ocean, heart-stoppingly blue. But the stark beauty passed him by.

We made a mistake, we let Lilith escape, Lord. Now we're being punished, and rightly so. I understand. I must tame her, I know – but how? Who is to help me? Why are Karl and Sebastian so blind to the dangers? Oh, they will be sorry on the day of judgement but that is of no consolation to me now. Yes, Lilith is the Enemy, and until immortals return to your fold, Lord, and unite in your name to revile her, she will visit your punishment on them. And I'm the only one who can see it. The only one!

Simon had deliberately not told Sebastian who Violette Lenoir was. The fastest way to discourage Sebastian from doing anything was to suggest that he should do it, as he'd learned to his cost. If he had said, 'She is your enemy!' Sebastian would not have gone within a hundred miles of her. His only hope now was that when Sebastian saw her he would guess, and understand what Simon had been asking.

A thin hope. Dear God, if you would offer me a mandate to take power, I'd do it! But I can't. I need someone like Lancelyn to need me. Without them I can't mediate, I can't act.

Alone, I am nothing. Lord, have mercy.

The Lord, however, remained dumb. Not the kind God in which humans put their faith, but a demanding, heartless, punishing God. He had no mercy, not even for his angel Senoy.

They dropped softly down from heaven to land on the snow-crusted ice in front of Simon; a white shape and a black shape. Fyodor and Ramila.

He glared at them, ice-crystals stinging his eyes. They'd let him down and he wanted nothing more to do with them, but they would keep following him with their soft, pleading eyes.

'Simon!' Rasmila cried, falling to her knees in the snow beside him. 'What are you doing here? Where have you been? You look so pale!'

'Go away,' said Simon.

'No,' Fyodor said fiercely. 'Not after it has taken us so long to find you.'

They were dressed in thin clothes in which a human would have frozen to death, Fyodor in a shirt and trousers, Rasmila in a midnight-blue sari. The garments were ragged with wear, but vampires were oblivious to the cold; or rather, they felt it, but because it could not harm them it had no bite. Their long hair was wild and they looked mad, demonic, and incredibly beautiful.

'I have asked you many times to stop following me,' Simon said coldly. He hid his inner turmoil behind the mask of aureate confidence.

'But we won't,' Rasmila said stubbornly. 'We'll follow you until you give in.' She kept grasping at his hands, despite his efforts to shake her off. 'Simon, please! You can't abandon us after we've been together all these years!'

'But I can and I have.' Her pleading made him furious.

'Do you love someone else? Is it Karl?'

'I love only God!'

'What god?' Fyodor exclaimed. 'Weren't we deluding our-selves when we thought we were angels?'

'No, never,' said Simon.

Fyodor gripped Simon's shoulder and shook him. 'Give up this idea of being God's envoy! It's over. Come with us and be happy to be a vampire; to suck out human blood, to glory in your own savagery and power. Isn't that enough?'

But Rasmila cried, 'No, it's not over! Let us come with you! If we were all together again the power would come back!'

'No,' Simon said grimly. 'It won't.'

'What can we do to prove our love?'

'Nothing. I don't care.'

'But you must care!' Rasmila clung to him, but he endured her embrace like a rock, feeling no emotion but irritation. 'Don't you remember how we first became angels?' Her voice dropped, becoming softly melodic. 'Fifteen hundred years ago we were all lost souls, we wandered through the world feeding on blood, with no memory of how this curse had come upon us, each thinking ourselves alone. And then we met, the three of us, and we fell in love, we loved each other so deeply we could never bear to be apart . . .'

'I never loved you,' Simon said callously, but Rasmila would not be deflected.

'You don't mean it! For a thousand years we needed no one else. It was always the three of us, no one else . . . and then the light began to speak to you, do you remember? The light of heaven, the eye of God in the Crystal Ring. It told us what to do. It came to us through you, Simon, and you said, "God has chosen us to do His will." And we kept watch on other immortals. We saw that they needed guidance. And God told us to keep watch on humans and choose the ones worthy to enter the Crystal Ring. And the light and the power were so beautiful, weren't they? When we were together. Three in one. Waiting for Lilith to appear on earth so that we could fulfil our purpose and bind her to God . . . It can be the same again, Simon. Senoy. I am still Semangelof.'

'No, you're not,' Simon said woodenly. 'You let me down, both of you! You weren't strong enough to hold Lilith. You were vessels for the light but you were too fragile; you broke and the light spilled out.'

'And we can't be repaired?' Fyodor said bitterly. 'Was it the will of God that drove us to create other vampires – or was it boredom, Simon? Immortality and love were never enough for you. Too dull to be the same for ever, so you had to metamorphose into something more important, you had to have others to feed your importance—'

'Stop it. I've heard enough of this nonsense.'

'And then you grew bored with us!' Fyodor cried. 'Well, forgive us for being constant in our love! But you, you hate yourself for being imperfect, so you blame us. And, damn you, I still need you!'

A spear of ice went through Simon's heart. 'All that matters is destroying Lilith before she destroys us. Don't you understand? If we don't control her we will not be *here* to love or hate each other! You can't help, so leave me alone.'

'I wish we'd stayed in the *Weisskalt* for ever,' Fyodor murmured grimly.

'We can help. We'll prove it,' Rasmila moaned. 'Only don't send us away, we can't bear it.'

Infuriated, Simon tried to prise them off, but they hung on his neck, weeping. And then he did something he had never done before. He attacked them physically. Tore Rasmila off his neck, hit her so hard she span away across the ice; bit a great hole in Fyodor's neck and flung him aside. And yet they went on reaching out to him like wounded children, weeping bitter tears of rejection; and still Simon felt nothing, nothing to the frigid core of his soul.

Pierre was nothing if not a realist; he hadn't expected anyone to come looking for him. It came as a shock when Ilona arrived at Schloss Holdenstein. She was dressed as always in the depths of fashion; a coat of maroon velvet and black fur, scarlet dress dripping with beads, rubies and red gold flashing on her wrists and encircling her hair. She was incongruous within the death-soaked walls, an affront to the sombre memory of Kristian – so Cesare would have thought, but he, fortunately, was absent.

Pierre tried to react to her arrival with his usual world-weary flippancy, but he made a poor attempt at it. Fear had gnawed holes in his composure, and now, as she appeared in his dank, rushlit chamber, he suffered an unravelling sensation. It felt suspiciously like a desire to hold on to Ilona and cry his eyes out.

'It's taken me an age to find you,' she snapped. 'What the devil are you doing here?'

'Exactly what there is to do here,' he replied, trying to match her sharpness. 'Nothing.'

Ilona saw straight through him. 'What's wrong with you, Pierre?' She moved closer, her perfect face a map of shrewdness. 'You were in none of your usual haunts. I couldn't believe I'd actually find you here, but I had a strange feeling . . . and here you are! Have you lost your mind? You always hated it here!'

'What do you want?' He was irritated now. Everything irritated him, since Violette's attack.

'There have been rumours,' she said, walking round the room and glancing with disgust at the sparse, crude furniture, 'about you and a certain ballerina . . .'

'Rumours? The bitch tried to kill me!'

'Shame she didn't do the job properly,' Ilona said crisply. 'So you ran *here*? To *Cesare*?'

'Not to Cesare.' She aggravated him, but he almost enjoyed the familiar joust; rage was easier to cope with than fear. 'He doesn't own this place. I had to go somewhere.'

'To hide?'

'You didn't see her! She was crazed! She—'

'I've met her. She *is* crazy, but really, Pierre, she is only a slip of a thing. How did she reduce you to this state? You don't look fit to scare the birds out of the fields.'

Pierre lacked the strength to answer. He sank down on to the bench where he'd been sitting before she arrived, trying to read some meaningless religious tract that Kristian had left behind. Ilona stared at him with rancid contempt, but it rolled off him. He simply did not care. She said, 'Where is Cesare, by the way?'

Her tone was softer, quizzical, as if she were really shocked by Pierre's appearance. 'He went out to look for Violette. He's been gone for days, so perhaps she's slaughtered him too.'

'You told him about her?'

He shrugged. 'Yes, everything. Why not?'

'Well, he won't find her. She's gone to America. Karl and Charlotte have gone too, to keep her out of mischief, I think.'

'Good luck to them,' Pierre whispered. 'She should be kept out of trouble. Permanently.'

She sat down beside him, her velvet-brown eyes fastening vampire-like on his. 'Do you really think so?'

'Do you?'

She did not answer. He wondered if Ilona, cruelly cavalier as she was with human life, had it in her to kill another vampire . . . then he remembered Kristian, and closed his eyes. We are both capable, he thought. But not alone. The thought of even approaching Violette made him shiver with horror.

Ilona asked, 'What does Cesare say?'

'He's been quite agitated, especially as John got here before me.'

Ilona pulled a face. 'I know. I saw him on my way in. What has he done to himself? He could star in *Nosferatu*.'

'He's sick. They're all sick here. And Cesare wants to launch a one-man crusade against Lilith.'

'He wouldn't dare set himself against the Mother of Vampires, would he?'

'Oh, he had an answer for that,' said Pierre. 'Lilith is the mother who will devour her children at the end of time, unless the sons of God stand firm against her, or something.'

'Aha. Of course. Matricide. I can just see Cesare as someone who hated his mother and would like to murder her symbolically.'

At her words, Pierre felt as if his whole body were yellowing, wilting. Remembering a conversation with Karl. *I was not like you, Karl, wanting to stay human for love. I was greedy for what Kristian offered me. After he'd transformed me, and I was desperate with the thirst, he took me to his coach . . . and there inside was my mother. My first victim, my mother . . . I fed on her without a qualm. The silly witch had already made herself a martyr for me, so what better way to go than to give me her last drop of blood too?* Oh, how flippantly he'd uttered those sentiments! Now they haunted him. What he felt was not so much long-delayed guilt as a twisting pain that seemed to have been imposed on him from outside. By Violette-Lilith.

'Are you listening to me?' said Ilona.

'Yes,' he said savagely. 'Could you do it, feast on your own mother?'

'I don't know,' she said in a strange, thin tone. 'I never knew her. Kristian had her murdered when I was a few months old, so that he could take Karl away. So I have absolutely no feelings about mothers, though I have often felt like strangling my father. I once thought I would like to be a mother, but what's the use of it, when your children turn on you?'

For some reason her words filled him with creeping dread. 'You sound like Violette. Stop it.'

'My God, she has really got to you, hasn't she?' Ilona touched his shoulder. 'Poor Pierre. You so badly wanted to be evil and heartless and gloriously wicked like Sebastian, but you just haven't got it in you.'

'Oh, yes, him,' Pierre said, stung. 'I should like to see how *Sebastian* gets on with her. She'd tear him to shreds.'

'Why didn't you come to me, instead of baring what there is of your soul to Cesare?'

'Oh, and thrown myself on your sweet sympathy? I think not. Why the hell does it matter?'

'Because Ceasre's deranged, and so's John. Couldn't you leave this band of half-wits alone to fester in their ignorance? Why stir them up? We have enough troubles without them blundering out into the world as well.'

'Cesare's harmless. He's a fool. He's actually been quite nice to me.'

'Well, I can't see him joining forces with Stefan; they hate each other,' said Ilona. 'John, maybe. Otherwise the opposition to Lilith seems to have collapsed. Everyone she touches falls apart. Matthew's dead, Rachel's vanished, and here are you cowering in this pit—'

'Don't be kind to me, Ilona. Gloat a little.'

'You used to like me to tease you.'

'I've lost my sense of humour.'

'I'm not surprised, in this place.' She stroked his cheek. 'Good God, you're freezing! Come out with me and hunt.'

'No, Ilona . . .'

'You need blood.'

Pierre shrank back, shaking his head. 'I can't leave the castle.'

'Why can't you? Do you need a note from Cesare? I see no shackles, the door isn't locked.'

The words came out of him, crackling like the skeletons of dry leaves. 'I can't, because I'm frightened.'

Ilona stood up, looking down at him with disgust. 'You make me sick, Pierre. I thought you were like me, but you're just a coward. No one can hurt us! She humiliated you, that's all. That's what you can't face, *nicht wahr*? Ooh, bruised pride.'

When he did not reply, her face darkened. 'I shall tell you what I am going to do. I'm going to America, not with Karl but on a later sailing, so they won't know I'm there. And I am going to prove, to myself and to everyone else, that she is nothing to be afraid of. This talk of killing her is exactly the same as hiding from her; it gives that madam power and status she doesn't deserve.'

'Be careful,' he said, with a touch of his old mockery. 'Stefan told me she has a grudge against you.'

'Oh, that. She claims I attacked and mutilated her father, years ago, and my attack drove him out of his mind. So I am indirectly responsible for all the family problems that sent *her* mad. Have you ever heard such nonsense? She has no proof that I ever met her damned father, but if I did, he should have been grateful that I didn't kill him. Men,' Ilona spat. 'Boys!'

She vanished abruptly into the other-realm, but not before Pierre had seen the look in her eyes. For all her brave words, Ilona was as terrified of Violette as anyone. And that made him want to huddle around his own fear and cry out to her not to leave him alone.

As the ship slid through the waters of the Atlantic, Charlotte reflected that it was a relief to be among strangers, journeying to a new land. No other vampires – apart from Violette – to come between her and Karl. Kristian, Katerina, Andreas, Ilona, Pierre, even Stefan and Niklas, had all tried to weaken the bonds between Karl and Charlotte in one way or another. It was good to leave it all behind.

Neither she nor Karl had been to America before. The physicality of the journey was important to her. Karl had told her that travelling through the Crystal Ring would have been impractical. A long, exhausting journey through the Ring with few sources of blood would put them at risk of starvation, and of becoming too weak to escape back to earth; Charlotte had broken impatiently into his explanation. 'But it doesn't matter. I don't *want* to go through the Crystal Ring. We're going to another continent, the New World. I need to experience the journey in earthly reality and time, otherwise it wouldn't – it simply wouldn't seem real. I need to know it's *real*. I want to be aware of every second of the journey.'

All the same, she had nearly swallowed her words at the beginning. Charlotte had grown used to skimming from one place to another through the unearthly paths of the Ring; she was aghast to discover how infinitesimally, almost unbearably slow the liner's progress seemed. It made her feel agitated, impatient to dive into the Ring and fly ahead. But after a few days she grew attuned to the gentle pace, and relished it. It was what she needed, to absorb the steady onward surge of the ship through the waves, the daily rhythm of life in this elegant, self-contained community. It heightened her anticipation of the unknown, exciting new land to an exquisite degree.

She hadn't yet told Karl that Josef would be on board. It was a delicate subject. The liner was so large she could probably have avoided Josef from one end of the voyage to the other – but she did not want to be dishonest with Karl. I'll tell him soon, she kept promising herself.

She and Karl fed discreetly and sparingly on the other passengers, leaving members of the ballet company strictly alone. There was a minor outbreak of an illness causing lassitude and fever, but no deaths.

Violette, meanwhile, was barely seen throughout the voyage. She remained in her suite, attended only by her maid, Geli, who was used to her odd behaviour and seemed to attribute it to Madame's artistic temperament. She appeared twice a day to supervise a ballet class – essential to keep the dancers on peak form – then retired again. Even Charlotte barely spoke to her. She knew that Violette's turmoil over taking blood was exacerbated by the confines of the ship, and that she was half-starving herself as a result. She also knew that Violette was spending too much time in the Crystal Ring, trying to escape the relentless pressure of her existence. Nothing Charlotte said made any difference. Eventually Violette lost patience and refused to see her at all.

The talk among the passengers was of the legendary Madame Lenoir. Greatly excited at the prospect of seeing her in the flesh, they were to be disappointed. Charlotte had given up hope of Josef even glimpsing her before they reached New York.

Some months ago, Charlotte had told Karl about Josef. A friend of my father, she'd said; we met by chance and he recognized me. I tried to pretend that he'd made a mistake but he saw through me ... She had even admitted that Josef knew she was a vampire. Karl had always warned her against making human friends, so she had been nervous of his reaction, but, to her surprise, he'd been quite sanguine about it. She found it touching that he still trusted her, even after her relationship with Violette.

For Karl to be confronted by Josef in person, however, was a more difficult matter. If she'd told him before the ship sailed, Karl might have persuaded her to leave Josef behind. So she had waited until it was a *fait accompli*.

No use in delaying the moment any longer, though. On the second night, at a cocktail party in a large mirrored state room that was rocking gently beneath them, she took Karl to meet Josef.

Josef greeted her warmly and kissed her hand, his kind face suffused with pleasure. If Karl was at all disconcerted by this show of affection, he did not betray it. Smiling to hide her apprehension, Charlotte retrieved her hand. 'Josef, may I introduce Karl Alexander von Wultendorf. Karl, this is Josef Stern.'

The men's reaction to each other was formal and guarded, and they exchanged pleasantries with polite insouciance. Watching them together, Charlotte's head swam. Both tall, lean and elegant in evening dress, they could almost have been father and son.

She only wished they liked each other; they clearly didn't. Karl hadn't been told why Josef was here, so nothing of importance could be discussed; instead a neutral conversation about the ship and the vagaries of travelling concealed an ice-edged game. Josef, less adept at hiding his feelings, obviously resented Karl's presence and his claim on Charlotte. He also knew Karl's true nature, which made the exchange even more difficult for him. And Karl, aware that this stranger knew the secret, was also wary. He would not stoop to expressing dislike for someone, but she sensed his antipathy, saw the iced-blood light in his eyes.

No one else, if they'd joined the conversation, would have guessed anything was wrong. When Charlotte ended the exchange, finding some excuse to take Karl away, the two men parted with impeccable courtesy, like old friends.

Then Karl took Charlotte's arm, led her through the crowd and up on to the deck. The wind off the ocean was damp and chill; no one else was braving the night air.

'So tell me, *Liebling*,' Karl said lightly, 'what is Josef doing here?'

'I should have told you.'

'Ah, so it is not a coincidence.' His eyes pierced her, drily reproachful.

'No. I invited him.' She looked sideways at him, nervous of his reaction. 'I thought he might be of some help to Violette.'

Karl rarely showed any immortal arrogance – the assumption that humans had nothing to teach vampires – but she sensed a touch of it in him now. 'In what way?'

'He was a scientist, that's how he knew my father, but he's also worked in psychology and he's familiar with the Hebrew writings on Lilith.'

'And this qualifies him to psychoanalyse Violette? I wish him luck.'

'What else can we try? He might, just might perceive something that will help her!' Charlotte wished she did not feel so defensive. 'Also he has a niece in Boston; it was the perfect opportunity for him to visit her.'

'You are very considerate.'

'Are you jealous?' she said, suddenly amused.

Almost a smile on the beautiful, beloved face that rose like a moon of death over his victims. 'Charlotte, the man is in love with you.'

'I know,' she said, with a minimal lift of her shoulders. 'But he knows we can only be friends. He accepts it.'

'A mortal friend,' he said gravely, 'who knows what we are.'

'I hope this is not going to turn into another lecture about the dangers of making human friends.'

'No lecture. Have I not left you to learn by experience?'

The remark was subtly barbed. Her friendship with Violette

had proved disastrous. 'You can be such a bastard, Karl, without even trying.'

'Not to you, beloved.' His tone softened. 'I wish you had told me of this plan, that is all.'

'I meant to. But I knew you'd warn me against it, and of course you're right, I know perfectly well. I shouldn't have involved him. I should never have let him see what I am . . . I don't know why I did. He seemed able to accept it without being horrified, that's all.'

Karl was leaning on the ship's rail, arms folded, his eyelids veiling the seductive light of his eyes. 'And it means so much to you, to be accepted by one mortal.'

'Of course it does.' She laid her hands on his sleeve. 'Did you never need a human to accept you?'

'Only you.' He raked one hand gently down her back; the spider-touch on her skin made her shiver, as it always did, like the very first time he had touched her.

'He isn't my secret lover, Karl. Perhaps he would like to be – but he isn't.'

'I know. But my concern is really for him. Anything that can help Violette is to be welcomed, but how is she likely to react when you present her with a psychiatrist?'

'She'll be furious with me. That's why we have to handle it extremely carefully.'

'Quite,' said Karl, 'because Josef is the one who will suffer if Violette reacts badly. By bringing him among us, you've put him in great danger.'

She exhaled. 'I know. But I've warned him, and I'll protect him.'

'I hope so.' His long white fingers pressed into her shoulder; the fingers of a musician, precise and strong, seeking perfection in his art. 'For his sake.'

In the hour before dawn, after Charlotte had fed, she stood alone at the rail, the cold salt spray on her lips echoing the hot salt of blood. As she watched the rise and fall of the waves, she found herself thinking about her family. Just those few words, 'He was a friend of my father,' led her along a thread of memories. She remembered her father, a gruff and imposing figure in his shapeless tweed jacket; a man with the modern mind of a scientist and the heart of a Victorian. She recalled the quiet, happy times they had spent in his laboratory, Charlotte assisting his experiments as he teased out the secrets of the atom; trying to bring order to his brilliant flights of thought. The laboratory had been her refuge from the outside world, which had seemed so terrifying. She and her father had been close but they had been unable to communicate; he couldn't bear to lose his favourite daughter to a man, and especially not to Karl. He had thrown them out of the house. Charlotte had gone back once, to try to explain, only to be rejected again. (How could anyone explain why they'd become a vampire?) Hurt, she'd hurt her father in turn, and she could never forgive herself for it. Immortal detachment could not always keep her from wondering how he was. His health had never been good . . . but she couldn't bring herself to pursue that line of anxiety.

At least I didn't leave him quite alone, she thought. He has Anne, David and Maddy. Her brother David and her friend Anne were married, and had gone to manage Parkland Hall estate for her Aunt Elizabeth. How had their lives changed? Anne had been her best friend, supportive until Charlotte had knowingly gone several steps too far with Karl. She and Anne had parted, not quite enemies, but no longer friends. Charlotte had never fully come to terms with the loss. She often thought, did it mean as much to Anne?

David, kind and protective as he'd always been, had never understood at all. How could he? He'd seen Karl attack his friend, Edward, who had suffered a mental breakdown as a result. David also believed that Karl had killed their sister Fleur and her husband. He had never accepted that the killer had actually been Ilona. In a way it was irrelevant. The ultimate responsibility for vampires infiltrating the Neville family was Karl's – as he would be the first to admit.

Hardest of all to think of Fleur. Yet it all seemed so far in the past.

And then there was Madeleine, Charlotte's younger sister. She had had such confidence in herself, all the poise Charlotte lacked, until Karl had come into their lives. Thinking herself in love with him, she could not accept that he preferred Charlotte. But then disillusion, horror and the loss of Fleur had shaken her to the core. She was strong, though, Charlotte thought, stronger than me. She will have survived. I would just like to know—

No. Stop this.

A year ago, David had tried to find her. He'd sent a private detective after them; Charlotte had seen through him immediately, taken his blood and clouded his memory so that he could not report back to David. But the knowledge that David could not let go caused her incredible pain. *The price of being with Karl was to leave my human life behind completely*, she had told herself. *Oh God, why can't you let go . . . and why can't I?*

But I must, and I have. To think of them is futile. They have no idea where I am, and I hope they've stopped caring. I'm dead to them, and they to me.

This is where I belong. Leaving the old life behind. Travelling to New York, Boston, a new world. She watched the grey-green waves rising and falling, drawing the ship slowly on towards the horizon; let her imagination flow forward in time to envision the mist-grey bowl of the harbour, towers rising through the haze, and the great oxide-green statue in all her grace, the flame of liberty making its eternal promise.

The real world came as a massive shock to Cesare.

With every step he took away from Schloss Holdenstein, he became more aware of his own defencelessness and naïvety. All his vampire life he had sheltered within the monumental black temple of Kristian's wings, seeing nothing but Kristian's glory, drinking his philosophy, viewing the world with his narrowness. And after the master's death he had remained behind the blind walls of the castle. Merely existing . . . half-believing that one day Kristian must return, or that *something* must happen, otherwise his eternal life had no point.

For nearly two centuries Cesare had seen the world only by twilight or starlight. He had seen his victims only as prey, lacking any inner life or rights of their own. He knew nothing of world events, politics, wars, the ebb and flow of nations. He was unaware that fashions had changed, that the car had begun to take over from the horse, that women were questing towards equality with men.

Even without Kristian, he had been at peace in the austere shell of his existence. His despondency had been a constant state, not a disturbing passion. He'd lived a monk's life. His mind had become a small, cramped thing, a walnut shell sealed round nothingness.

But the shell was cracking.

Venturing from the security of the castle was like walking on red-hot knives. An umbilical cord stretched and stretched behind him. How the sunlight dazzled. How strange the people looked in the light, mingling with each other and quite oblivious to him. He was used to being his victim's universe, the last thing they saw as he sucked out their life. How he hated to be ignored! Yet he bore it, forcing himself to do the very things he'd always abhorred; to observe and learn.

A strange and dreadful feeling was budding inside him. *Fear.* He experienced his ignorance as a great, shaming veil between him and the new-gleaming world.

He knew Violette lived in Salzburg, but he did not go there at once. He did not want to face her without an armoury of knowledge and confidence. Instead he travelled down through Switzerland and into Italy, once his native land. Everywhere he went, people took him for a priest and called him Father. Cesare liked that. It restored his sense of self.

The world itself dismayed him. Everywhere he went he found decadence, promiscuity, weak and faltering governments, people with no direction and no philosophy. The idea of Communism also disgusted him, with its vain concepts of equality. A new order was sorely needed, among mortals and immortals alike.

But how little I know, he thought. How much I have missed! These little admissions jabbed through the hard coating of complacency, burningly painful. And one day, not far from his birthplace in northern Italy, they overcame him. He broke down before the altar of a tiny village chapel and wept, dashing his head again and again on the flagstones.

Kristian is gone. He is never coming back!

And who is there to carry on after him? No one but me!

A life-sized crucifixion, crudely carved and brown with age, hung above the altar. A faith he'd forsaken long ago to follow the true saviour, Kristian; a soft human belief that sentimental-ized weakness and pity. But now it seemed to represent something else. The rigid arms nailed to the cross were Kristian's arms, the agonized face under its diadem of thorns an expression of Kristian's own anguish at his betrayal.

Yet Cesare knew this was an illusion, a lie. *Kristian, the truth is you let us down!* Blasphemy.

In his grief, Cesare leapt up on to the figure and clung to it, tearing at its shoulder with his fangs. There was no one there to witness the bizarre scene. The wood splintered, tearing his tongue and lips; the taste of sap and old paint filled his mouth, foul as bile. Yet he went on and on in his frenzy, clinging to Kristian and punishing him at the same time. Tearing apart the lie that was no better than the human lie of Christ.

At last the black and silver storm in his skull overcame him, and he fell. As Cesare lay on the flagstones, God spoke to him in the form of a thundering, nightmarish vision. He saw a blond child, lying curled up under the wrath of a witch, a vast, ragged figure with wings and claws, wild black hair completely cover-ing her face. She was beating the boy with a rod, lashing and lashing into the tiny tender body with sadistic glee. Her hair and rags flapped in a gale from hell.

And Cesare knew she was both the child's mother and the universal mother, the goddess of destruction, the devil's bride, the Enemy. He heard the annihilating hiss of her voice. *I made you all and I shall destroy you all!*

Terror overwhelmed him. We aren't yours to destroy, we're God's! He wept with compassion for the tiny golden child, but he couldn't move. And he knew that the child was an angel. One of God's immortal children. And it must not, it could not die!

Then, in the distance, he saw a bright gold figure with white wings springing from his shoulders, a flaming sword in his hand, flames for hair. And Cesare saw himself at a door, with a key in his hand. And he understood.

I must open the door to God's army. Let them through and they will slay the witch mother and save the sweet child of immortality!

And he knew that the child, also, was himself.

The vision ended and he rose to his knees, gasping with the frenzied mingling of terror, and injustice, and hope. He laughed and cried. 'Forgive me, Father,' he said, clasping his hands. 'I doubted you, but now I understand. Kristian died to test me. Use me, Father, let me be your sword in the war against the Enemy!'

Presently, when he'd managed to compose himself, Cesare walked out into the sunlight. As he emerged, he saw lines and lines of soldiers marching past him along the dusty, bright road. And he thought it was the most beautiful sight he had ever seen; the light filtering through the green leaves, washing like golden balm over these brisk rows of disciplined, sharply idealistic, strong young men.

Cesare felt like a seed washed clean by spring rain. He felt new-born.

Now, he thought, I am ready to face Lilith.

He arrived at the Ballet Janacek's house in Salzburg by night and entered, feeling all-powerful and slightly disdainful, as if this act of stealth were below him. With heaven on his side, Violette could not touch him; the prospect of confronting her filled him with the grim fire of excitement.

But the house, save for a sleeping caretaker, was deserted. Cesare's disappointment was overwhelming. His first reaction was that Violette had deliberately, spitefully thwarted him; then he felt somewhat calmer, relieved. He thought of feeding on the caretaker as a small act of revenge, but a letter lying on a desk distracted him. It concerned the ballet's forthcoming tour of America; he deduced from it that they would not be back until autumn.

But this is excellent, he thought. It gives me time to think, to plan!

Cesare did not leave at once. His new interest in the world led him to explore store-rooms and offices, kitchens and rehearsal rooms. He lingered in the empty dance studio, ascended to the private apartments.

There were photographs of Violette throughout the house, on walls and desks. Other dancers, too, but hers was the face that held him. Blanched skin and huge dark eyes, black feathers clasping her head; even in monochrome she was as perfect as a moonstone. 'Odile, 1926,' the caption read. Cesare had no idea who Odile was. A witch, clearly.

Here she was again, in loose white chiffon, her hair unbound, 'Giselle, 1925.' A glacial sylph under a mantle of soot-black hair, with eyes like the Crystal Ring. Cesare stared and stared at the images, trembling. Through those terrible eyes her soul lanced straight into his, and he recognized her.

Oh yes, she was the witch of his vision.

She was the Enemy.

She represented everything Kristian had fought against, an affront to God. Alien, impure, uncontrollable, irreverent, wicked. She would bring degradation and death.

He backed away, transported by the pure fire of hatred. Then he knew. Pierrre and John had spoken the truth. Lilith was real and she was at large in the world, more terrible than even John had suspected.

'And you're mine,' Cesare whispered to the frozen face. 'Mine to deal with.'

Leaving the house, he raced back to Schloss Holdenstein through the Crystal Ring as if winged. No good to wallow in despondency, hoping in vain for Kristian's resurrection, he thought; I must do God's work in my own way. Destroy the Enemy and create a new order.

He thought of what he'd seen in Italy, the strong and joyous young men in uniform, and his heart filled with delight. But they were only humans, he thought. I am immortal, the Chosen of God. I have a battle to fight, a golden world to create – and never again, as I build the new empire, shall I walk in someone else's shadow.

He'd stolen a small, framed photograph. As soon as he reached the castle, he drew it from a pocket in his robe and gazed on the insolent face of chaos. Violette was in a daring, tight-fitting costume of glittering jet scales, as if she'd tried to take on the appearance of a vampire in the Crystal Ring. The caption read, 'The Serpent, *Dans le Jardin*, 1926.'

'If you think you are going to slaughter the children of God,' he whispered, 'you are very wrong, Lilith.'

He smashed the glass with his knuckles. His blood smeared the dancer's image, dripping slowly over her throat and breasts, obliterating her eyes.

CHAPTER SIX

APPEASEMENT

In her elegant house on Beacon Hill, Roberta Stafford lay beneath her lover, expertly coaxing his excitement to a peak while her thoughts wandered elsewhere. His back felt hairy, damp and crêpy with age, but she never let her distaste show. She was an accomplished actress. Thankfully, because he was not young, his demands were modest.

At last he convulsed, grunted, and rolled aside with his wrist flung across his flushed forehead. Roberta — Robyn to a favoured few — immediately threw back the covers to let the cool air on to her body.

'Wonderful, wonderful,' he said. 'I must remind myself of why I'm keeping you in luxury more often.'

Robyn laughed, stroking his cheek. 'Whenever you like, Harold. I'm always here.'

'Was it wonderful for you, my dear?'

'As ever,' she said ambiguously. He reached for her but she evaded him and got out of bed. She went to the window and reached between the curtains of creamy lace to open the window. It was a golden afternoon. When she turned round, Harold was out of bed and beginning to dress. She regarded the doughy folds of his skin, his paunch ballooning over his sparrow legs, his heavy jowls and sparse grey hair, with a kind of affectionate tolerance. Harold wasn't so bad. His love-making might be inept but it was financially rewarding. After all, he was no worse than any other man she'd had, and he was the only one among them she did not actively despise.

'So, I hear you finally threw him over,' said Harold, tying his shoelaces.

'Who?'

'Your young beau . . . Russell Booth?'

'Oh, him,' Still naked, Robyn helped him to fasten his collar and his gold cufflinks. 'He wasn't my beau. He was getting altogether too serious. I had to end it.'

'Word is you broke his heart.'

'He'll get over it.'

'Word is you also broke *him*.'

'He must have thought I was worth it. He had a damned good time in the process. He's got a rich daddy, he'll be all right.' She sat down at her dressing-table and began to brush her thick, waist-length hair.

'He's not the only one with a rich daddy, is he?' Harold came and leaned on the back of her chair; the respectable businessman in his old-fashioned suit and wire-rimmed spectacles. 'You're a tough woman, Robyn.'

'You don't mind, do you?' Robyn glimpsed her own reflection; eyes soft and mischievous, her face glowing, her smile fresh and without artifice. She might be uncomfortably close to forty, but she could still be taken for twenty-seven. 'He knew the conditions, and so do you. No wedding bells, no exclusive rights.'

'Oh, I'm not jealous, my dear. You can have as many boyfriends as you like, as long as you don't throw me over for any of them.'

'I couldn't afford to, don't worry.' In fact, she had money of her own, but she preferred to spend Harold's. She turned her head and kissed the back of his hand. The white hairs were dry against her lips.

'Well, I have to go,' he said. 'But I got you a present.'

Robyn gave a soft laugh, pleased. He always brought her an offering, even when he only came to rant about his problems and drink her Bourbon – which, of course, his money had illicitly bought.

His hands slipped under her hair and attached a sparkling band round her neck. A diamond choker. 'Just a little something,' he said. His 'little somethings' were always worth a fortune.

'I suppose this means you bought your wife a present too.'

'Oh, sure,' he said, 'but yours cost more. Actually, the diamonds are a kind of peace offering. I really wanted to take you to the ballet, but my wife wants to go, so I have to take her instead. I'm sorry.'

'Oh, never mind,' Robyn said, utterly indifferent. 'You're very sweet. Did you think I'd be angry? Have I ever been angry with you?'

'Never. Why d'you think I keep coming round? You're the nicest natured woman I've ever met.'

He patted her on the shoulder and left.

When he'd gone, Robyn took off the choker and let it drop on to the dressing-table. The tiny hard gems clicked as they folded on to the polished wood. Her depression lasted only a few seconds. Then she pulled herself out of it, rang for her maid to run her bath, and began to gather her hair into a coil at the nape of her neck.

Her hair was the only thing about herself she admired. Heavy, thick and glossy, a deep glowing brown threaded with the most gorgeous colours of autumn, she sometimes regarded it as a separate entity that by some freak of fate had attached itself to her. Her hair wove the power that attracted men to her. And she was pretty, she knew, though she was unimpressed by that; scores of women in Boston were prettier, and younger, and she could see the subtle ravages of maturity in her strong-featured face. Her allure came from a deeper level. She had a quality of repose, of warmth and tolerance. Men felt they could talk to her, that she'd welcome them, faults and all, in a way that other women could not. At the same time they found her mysterious. The combination seemed to be irresistible. Robyn did not waste time analysing her appeal, she simply took full advantage of it.

Some men only wanted sex; they were fun, because she could pick apart their egos with exquisite subtlety, dragging the process out over months until their own insecurity made them impotent. But the best ones were those who fell in love and begged her to marry them. Those she could destroy utterly, especially if she had got them to leave their wives before she rejected them.

There had been two or three a year, not droves, but each one had been a work of art. She was very selective. She chose only the men who had the most to lose. And it was particularly satisfying to follow her vocation in Boston, that most puritanical and stratified of societies.

For each man who fell, there was another to replace him. She could have drawn up a waiting list. They never learned. Her reputation was known, but they always thought it would not happen to them, that they'd be the one to change her. That was her weapon; she let each one believe it when she said, 'You are different to all the others. I never loved until I met you.'

Some of them she had quite liked, superficially. But deep inside, she despised their schoolboyish infatuations, their arrogance, their obsession with their prowess in bed. They deserved punishment.

Sometimes she hated her existence, but mostly she drifted through it with the same placid optimism that drew her lovers into the trap.

The Irish maid, Mary, came in and said the bath was ready. Robyn slid into the perfumed envelope of water and lay in contemplation of the grey marble tiling, which was dewed and beaded with steam. She felt pleasantly tired, soothed by the sound through the open door of Mary tidying the bedroom.

Her housekeeper, Alice – who was more companion than servant – came into the bathroom through wreaths of steam. 'Would you like your back washed, madam?' she asked, calling her 'madam' with a kind of affectionate insolence. Robyn sat forward, enjoying the feel of the soapy sponge on her back. Alice's hands were firm and soothing, like those of a masseuse. She was the same age as Robyn but looked older, her round, kind face still handsome in a cloud of dark hair. Over the years that she'd kept house for Robyn, they had grown very close. Robyn saw her as her only friend, an ally against the world.

'Would you like to go to the ballet, Alice?' she asked. 'There's a company here from Europe, you probably saw it in the *Evening Transcript*. Harold was talking about it, too.'

Alice paused in her task. Streams of hot water coursed

delectably down Robyn's spine. 'The ballet, h'm? Yes, I'd love to, but surely some gentleman—'

'To hell with them,' Robyn said decisively. 'Harold wanted to take me, but of course he can't be seen with me in public.'

'Well, if you've no one else,' Alice said darkly, rising to her feet. She was unimpressed by any favours that Robyn offered, knowing they could be withdrawn without notice. And yet her cynicism was tempered by warmth. Her devotion to Robyn was absolute, so well-worn that it encompassed all her foibles without surprise or condemnation. 'I'll have to send Mary for some fresh towels, madam.'

While Alice was out of the room, Robyn heard the doorbell ring. She cursed. There was a long pause, then Alice returned with an armful of white towels.

'There's a gentleman caller for you, madam.' Alice seemed to be suppressing a smile.

'Oh, damn. I'm tired,' Robyn sighed. Then she thought of her heart-broken youth. 'It's not Russell, is it? Tell him to go away.'

'No, it isn't. He asked me not to say who it was.'

'Oh, God, tell me it's not my father!'

'No. It's someone you will want to see, I promise.'

Robyn rose from the water, creamy-skinned and long-limbed, and let Alice wrap her in the cloudy softness of a towel. 'I hate mysteries. All right, tell him to wait, then come back and help me do something with my hair.'

Robyn took her time, unable to think of a man she would actually be pleased to see. On entering the parlour, she almost did not recognize the tall, slight man who rose hastily to his feet to greet her. It was years since she'd seen him; how grey his thick, unruly hair had turned! But the kind, chiselled face behind the black-rimmed spectacles was the same.

She flung herself into his arms, laughing. 'Uncle Josef!'

He hugged and kissed her with a delicacy that verged on awkwardness. They had met only three times; once when she was a child and Josef had visited her family, once when her parents had taken her to Europe. The last time had been after her wedding, seventeen years ago. Such a long time. But they had always kept in touch.

'Forgive me for not announcing myself,' he said. 'I wanted to surprise you.'

'Oh, you certainly did that!'

'My little Robyn.' He held her at arm's length, his grey eyes flickering over her. 'You look so lovely. Glowing.'

'So do you, Uncle.' She laughed again in amazement. 'But you're in Vienna! Whatever are you doing in Boston?'

'It's a long story. I have a friend who was travelling to America and asked me to come with her.'

'Who is she? Come on, do tell.'

He looked away, seeming embarrassed. 'It's not what it sounds like. She really is just a friend. She was travelling with the Ballet Janacek and there was a spare berth . . .'

Robyn shook her head, amused, and went to open the french door to the terrace. The ivory nets fluttered like bridal veils in the breeze. 'Do you believe in coincidence? I was just talking to Alice about going to see them. Now I've heard them mentioned twice in one afternoon. That must mean something, mustn't it? Do sit down. Alice is asking Mary to bring us some tea.'

But Josef followed her to the door and stepped out on to the terrace. A flight of steps led down to a tiny walled garden filled with shrubs and ferns, honeysuckle spilling over the walls, plants in terracotta tubs, a lemon tree in the centre of a handkerchief lawn.

'Where are you staying?' she asked.

'At a rather grand hotel on Tremont Street. Oh, I'm not here to impose on you, don't worry.'

'I never thought you were, dear.'

'But this is a lovely house,' he said.

'Thank you,' she said, smiling. She added silently, and so good to have it to myself since being widowed. Robyn was very proud of her home, one of a row of town houses that stepped gently up the hill of Chestnut Street. Built of soft red brick, it had long, leaded windows with white paintwork and black shutters, black railings tipped with gold, and a flight of steps running up to the front door. Inside was a hall with a polished floor and large Chinese vases; one flight of stairs led down to the kitchen and breakfast room on the ground floor, another, carpeted in pale green, led up to the main bedrooms where she and Alice slept. The smaller bedrooms on the top floor were empty except for Mary's. Robyn had decorated the whole house with the same light touch; dark polished wood, luxurious pale fabrics and a few carefully chosen antiques. The parlour was her favourite, a double room that ran the length of the house; all cream and ivory with touches of gold. Visitors always told her how elegant and friendly the house was, how much at home they felt there.

'Well, there's plenty of room with just Alice, Mary and me here,' she said. 'A married couple come and help too, but they don't live in. Mrs Wilkes does the cooking, Mr Wilkes is my chauffeur, gardener and so on. They're very sweet.'

'You are not lonely, then?' he said.

'No, not lonely.'

'It's so wonderful to see you,' he said with feeling. 'The last time was—'

'My honeymoon in Europe,' she said flatly. 'Seventeen years ago? My God.'

He looked at her ruefully. 'You don't write as often as I do.'

'I'm sorry. I'm a dreadful letter-writer. But I send photographs every Christmas, don't I?'

'And they are all framed on my desk.'

'And I wrote several times last year, after Auntie Lisl died. I was so sorry, I know how much you loved her.'

A look of pain went across his face, arrowing deep inside him before it vanished. 'She was terribly ill. Her death was a release.'

'So now you're all alone . . . or are you?'

'All alone,' he said resignedly.

'I don't know how you have escaped all the women who must have fallen in love with you over the years.'

'Because I could never make a choice. I knew myself well enough not to make a particular woman unhappy by marrying her. Well, now I have grown up enough to be tired of being a bachelor, I find it's too late. There is someone, but she doesn't love me, and so . . .' He shrugged.

'She must be mad.'

'I am quite happy,' he said, 'apart from missing you.'

He held her hands loosely, and they looked at each other, taking in every detail, every new line, every sadness. He meant far more to her than her own father did. 'Have you seen Mom?'

'Yes, I've seen her. I felt I should, out of courtesy.' A shadow across his face, a slight tightening of his voice. He did not get on with her parents, even though Robyn's mother was his sister.

'Then I'm surprised you're here,' she said lightly. 'They've quite disowned me, and I'm sure they told you why.'

The shadow deepened, but he sounded more sad than disapproving. 'Robyn, it did not come as a surprise; your letters give away more than you probably realize. But are you really happy, living like this?'

'How would you like me to live?' The anger that sprang into her voice shocked her; she thought she had it under control. 'The way my parents wanted me to live, married to a respectable Bostonian, happy ever after? So much for that!'

Josef looked startled and concerned. She turned away from him; he reached out to touch her arm. 'Do you miss your husband so much? I thought you seemed unhappy with him, but I know it's hard being alone.'

'Miss him?' she gasped. Josef didn't know the whole truth. No one did, except Alice – and her mother, but she had refused to listen. Robyn stopped on a held breath, and she wanted to tell Josef, *I danced on his grave*, pour out every bitter detail – but a movement inside the room stopped her. 'Here's Mary with the tea,' she said, quietly letting the breath and the anger go.

On the threshold, with the fluttering nets curtaining the interior, he caught her elbow. 'My dear, I didn't mean to upset you. I spoke only out of concern. If I've offended you, I'm sorry.'

'You haven't offended me,' she said. 'My God, who am I to

take offence at anything? Really, I'm quite all right. My life is under control.'

'Robyn,' he said, fixing her with compassionate grey eyes, 'you do not have to justify yourself to me. I'm not your father. I have only one demand to make of you.'

'Which is . . .'

'That you do me the honour of coming to see *Swan Lake* with me.'

The dancer in white and silver was an avatar of perfection.

In the enraptured eyes of her audience, Violette Lenoir's art and genius made her more than human. Amid the painted sets, the music and the lavish costumes, she was in her true place; an enchanted higher world, an aquarium of light within the boundaries of the stage.

Only a few in the audience knew Violette's true nature. Strip her of her satin and tulle, feathers and grease-paint, and she would still glow like porcelain and ebony. The stage was camouflage. Take her out of context, and her otherness would shine like a torch for those who had eyes to see.

It was the first night of *Swan Lake* in Boston. Charlotte watched from the darkness of a box with Karl beside her, drinking Violette's magic.

As Odette, the dancer was all innocence and flowing delicacy, radiating a passionate warmth she never showed in real life. The ballet was still the only medium through which she could express herself. But it was only as Odile – Odette's evil counterpart – that she was truly in character. She did not have to act, she didn't even have to try. She became a frightening entity, a pillar of glacial fire contained by the luscious blackness of her jewelled and feathered costume. Her power and the daring fluidity of her dancing were stunning.

In the darkness, Karl reached out and took Charlotte's hand.

It will be all right, Charlotte told herself. As long as Violette goes on dancing, it will be all right.

The story wound to its poignant climax. Violette danced her

encores, while the audience showered her with flowers and applause. When the house lights came up, Karl said, to Charlotte's surprise, 'I think we should go and see her, don't you?'

She agreed, with a dart of apprehension. How ridiculous to be afraid of Violette! But she couldn't help it. The dancer had barely spoken to her since leaving Europe. Images of Violette tracing a red line across her wrist with her nail ... seizing Charlotte, poising fang tips on her throat, confronting Karl with twisted pain and anger in her eyes ... Her morbid isolation throughout the journey.

As they moved through the foyer, the scent of the crowd – rank and sweet on a thousand notes – woke her thirst. The pressing desire no longer came as a shock; she drew it into herself like a breath, and the prospect of sating it later – outside, in some dark place where there was no one to see – was exciting.

Nothing obvious marked Karl and Charlotte out as predators. Someone who looked for too long might see that they were almost too perfect in the soft radiance of their beauty to be human. But fascination would dazzle the onlooker against the truth, and he'd never see that their allure was a jewelled and poisoned trap.

At the stage door, a doorman tried to stop them. Charlotte smiled at him until his eyes clouded and he let them through. Dancers, musicians and scene-shifters milled around them in the brick corridor. The American accents of the theatre staff, their exuberance, the differences of their clothes and manners – all struck Charlotte as fresh and strange, reminding her that she was no longer in Europe. Even the lowliest errand boy had a cockiness that could have been taken for impertinence, if it hadn't been tempered by such good humour. They were all startlingly friendly, greeting her and Karl as they passed. The ballet company members were more aloof, acknowledging Charlotte only because they knew her as an enigmatic patron of the Ballet Janacek. She returned their greetings absently, her eyes fixed on the door of the prima ballerina's dressing-room.

'Come in,' Violette called before Charlotte had knocked.

Exchanging a look of ironic unease with Karl, she opened the door.

The dancer, seated at her dressing-table, was wearing a cream satin gown and her hair was still coiled around her head. The cold cream she'd used to remove her make-up gave her skin a glassy shine, a thin glaze over the crystalline vampiric surface.

As they entered, she stood up and greeted them with real warmth in her eyes. 'I'm so glad you came. I wasn't sure you would. Did you enjoy it? Didn't they love us?' And she clasped both Charlotte's and Karl's hands, laughing.

After their recent encounters, Charlotte was taken aback. She had so rarely seen Violette in anything but distress that to see her in this innocent glow of happiness was astounding. Karl, uniquely, seemed lost for words. 'I told you *Swan Lake* was the one to do,' Charlotte said, relaxing a little.

'And you were right. Ballet Janacek, the toast of Europe; soon to be the toast of America.' Turning back to the mirror, she began to unpin her luxuriant hair. It unravelled into a mass of untidy fronds around her shoulders. 'I noticed a man in the front row tonight,' she said lightly. 'Grey-haired, quite handsome, staring and staring at me, more as if he were analysing my performance than enjoying it. Have you any idea who it could have been?'

Shocked at Violette's perceptiveness, Charlotte did not know whether to lie or to admit the truth. After all, it might not actually have been Josef. She decided on a diplomatic evasion. 'A reporter, probably.'

'Perhaps, but he was on the ship with us. He never saw me, but I saw him. It was the way he looked at me tonight ... there was a woman with him, brunette, very striking.' The veneer of euphoria, Charlotte noticed sadly, was extremely thin. Violette's eyes in the mirror were haunted. 'I'm sure it doesn't matter.'

'Well, if you see him again, point him out and I'll tell you whether or not I know him,' said Charlotte. Karl's face was immobile, but for the merest flicker of his eyes. She was grateful to him for changing the subject.

He said, 'If they'd seen you tonight, even your opponents would be convinced that it would be a tragedy if you were to stop dancing. You must go on, Violette, if it's what you want.'

'It is.' She turned to them, her joy resurfacing. 'Mortal or immortal, it is the only thing that matters to me. It's still my life. At least that hasn't changed. I know that if Charlotte hadn't transformed me, I would still be waking up half-crippled by stiffness every morning, and wondering how long I could stay out of a wheelchair. Instead I can dance for ever, as if my shoes are possessed by the devil. If I have been a little wild at times . . . well, I bear no grudges.'

Karl kissed her hand; a token of truce, a mere courtesy. But when the dancer came to Charlotte and hugged her, there was a terrible electricity between the two women. Charlotte, who had often wished Violette would be less sparing with shows of affection, wanted to escape the embrace.

'The good people of Boston are giving a party in our honour,' she said into Charlotte's ear. 'I hope you'll come. You know how I hate these affairs.'

'Of course we will. We're always here if you need us.'

'Oh, I do,' she said with sudden intensity. The tip of a fang grazed Charlotte's earlobe. 'You and Karl. I need you.'

Sebastian had looked forward to *Swan Lake* with keen anticipation. Boston struck him as fresh and tranquil after New York; he decided that he would like to stay here for a while. And by the end of the week, the ballerina would be his.

He viewed the imminent game, not with glee, but with sombre passion, rather as if it was his duty to his dark vampire nature. How else should the devil behave?

It will put paid to her dancing, of course, he thought as he took his seat in the theatre. It could destroy the company; and by the time I've finished with her – after a few months, depending on how amusing I find her – she will of course die. What a waste. But how glorious, to extinguish such a light!

Sebastian loved needless tragedies. They moved him unutterably.

He settled down in the back row to await Odette's appearance; but within seconds of her bewitching entrance, he was sitting forward in astonished horror. The ballerina in white net and swansdown was a vampire!

The pearly glow of her skin, the lustre of her eyes and the fluidity of her dancing; everything gave her away. Sebastian was appalled. Recalling his encounter with Simon in New York, he thought, did Simon know about her? He certainly knew that if he'd told me, I would never have come to see her.

Sebastian almost left the theatre immediately, but suppressed the impulse and forced himself to watch, nails digging into the plush arms of his seat.

Violette Lenoir. A slender-limbed weaver of enchantment; he wondered if her rapt audience had the faintest idea of what they were worshipping! Of course not. If she'd been human he would have found her captivating. Instead she stirred nothing in him, beyond a detached appreciation of her skill. He saw her for what she was, a savage, heartless creature of ice. Like him. But to brazen it out before a human public!

It is one way of attracting prey, he thought cynically. Well, if I cannot feed on the fruit of her veins, I'll find someone else; another dancer, perhaps, less famous but lusciously human.

He sighed. It would not be the same. The cloud of desolation was descending again.

But did Simon want me to discover that Lenoir is one of us? With what purpose? Why did he suggest I reconsider what he'd said after I'd seen her? If it was an attempt to manipulate me, he should know it won't work. I have no interest in my 'kind' and I refuse to rule or be ruled. How much more plainly could I have stated it?

There were two other vampires in the audience, he noted with distaste. He couldn't see them, and had no idea who they were; he could only feel their presences, like two cool gems amid a sea of sweltering humans.

He left half an hour before the performance ended, not wanting to risk meeting them face to face. The foyer, all rose marble and gold leaf, was quiet; the street outside, with its tall brownstone and Victorian buildings, was gently busy, patterned by the moving lights of cars. With his hands in his pockets, Sebastian began to walk towards the Public Garden. Boston's heart, the garden and the common; green land between the old town and the wealth of Beacon Hill.

The late spring air was warm, but he found no pleasure in it. He was so deep in meditation that he hardly noticed the warning sign; a glass dagger pricking his mind, so sharp that it could slide right through without him feeling a thing—

Suddenly alert, he looked ahead to locate the source of the vampire's presence, but it was too late. The woman had seen him; she was standing on the sidewalk, smiling. Waiting for him. He couldn't avoid her now.

She wore a coat of black figured velvet and fur, jet beads twinkling on her ears, her dark fire-tinged hair frozen in a precise curve around the pale heart of her face. And she was watching him with the cruelly humorous disdain he remembered from Kristian's castle, seventy years ago.

'Sebastian!' she said, her eyes shining. She hadn't lost her charming Austrian accent. 'This is the most wonderful surprise!'

'Ilona.' He inclined his head to her, polite but cold.

'Is that the best you can do? After all these years!' Without waiting for an invitation, she pressed close to him and clasped her hands behind his neck. With an inward sigh he relented and embraced her, pressing his lips to her cold skin.

'How did you know I was here?' he said.

'I didn't. Don't flatter yourself into thinking I crossed the ocean to look for *you*; I did not. I saw you in the theatre, but you were too busy staring at Violette to notice me. I have a little advantage. Like you, I seem to have an almost invisible aura. A glass needle, my father calls me; you don't know I'm there until I'm right under your skin.'

Ilona slid her hand through his arm, and he found himself walking with her across the road and along Boylston Street towards the Public Garden. He was not pleased to see her, but he could not shake her off without resorting to violence, and at present he lacked the will even to argue with her. It really didn't matter.

'I had a feeling you would leave early,' she went on, 'so I came out and waited for you.'

'So, are you here with the other three?' he asked. 'The enchanting Lenoir and her companions ... I'm afraid I didn't stop to see who they were.'

'One of them is Karl.'

'I might have known,' Sebastian said resignedly. They entered an undulating green space, shadowed by trees. On the lake a few yards away, the swan boats were moored for the night. 'It goes without saying I have no wish to see him.'

'His companion is Charlotte, some human he took up with about three or four years ago. She's a nice little immortal, but too soft for her own good.'

'Ilona,' he said, 'I am really not that interested.'

'You haven't changed, have you?' she said with relish. 'Still the loner, and the fastidious vampire-hater. You even used to make love to me as if you hated me.'

'Wasn't that the way you preferred it?' he said acidly.

Laughing, she leaned back against a wide tree-trunk. Sebastian reflected that their relationship had held few rewards. Vampires were equals; they couldn't be ensorcelled or tortured. Yet he realized that he still found her extremely attractive. He stood close to her, one hand resting on the trunk above her shoulder.

'I'm not with the others,' she said. 'They don't know I'm here. And they certainly don't know *you* are here.' A hint of slyness came into her voice; she liked to feel superior. Such similarities had drawn Sebastian and Ilona together, though they had done their utmost to tear each other apart during their brief, fierce liaison.

'Ah, I remember,' he murmured. '*You* are the main reason I prefer to be on my own.'

'You really know how to hurt a girl,' she said in a satirical New York accent. Then, in a rush of intense feeling, she said, 'But of course, you don't know! Everything's changed. Kristian's dead!'

'Aren't you the bearer of glad tidings,' he said coolly. He wasn't about to tell her that he already knew.

'Perhaps, but some think Violette might be worse.'

Simon's words again. *There is a new immortal at large who is too dangerous to be allowed her freedom.* 'Violette?' He felt his patience and his interest vaporizing. Was this another attempt to involve him in vampire affairs? 'If you have something to say to me, Ilona, just say it.'

She blinked, uncomprehending. 'Not content with humans? You want to kill the art of conversation as well?'

'I have already had Simon plaguing me with cryptic remarks about doom and destruction. Get it over with. Tell me about Violette.'

'Charlotte transformed her. Couldn't leave her alone. She looks harmless enough on stage, doesn't she? But a number of vampires are busy working themselves into a frenzy of terror over her, for reasons I wouldn't like to speculate on. She's certainly crazy. She has two immortal heads on her belt already; more, for all I know.'

Sebastian did not want to hear this. He couldn't have cared less about Violette, as long as she left him alone. 'What's your opinion, Ilona? I can't believe you're frightened of her. You're like me; you don't really care, do you?'

She shrugged. 'She doesn't like me, but she has never done anything about it. But she attacked an acquaintance of mine, and the effect it had on him was quite alarming.'

'In what way?'

'It reduced him to a trembling heap, afraid even to set foot outside the dubious sanctuary of Schloss Holdenstein. Pierre is a coward but only in the sense that he prefers an easy life; if anything, he has a positive taste for being abused and humiliated. So tell me; what power does Violette possess, to dismember his personality in a way that even Kristian could not?'

Despite his indifference, Sebastian felt unease pass over him like crow's wings. Anger stirred coldly in its wake. 'I have no idea, and as I said, I do not care. I don't want to hear about the petty infighting between you and your kind.'

'*My* kind?' Ilona glared at him. 'Dear God, do you really think yourself so superior to the rest of us?'

'Not superior. Separate. And that is the way I prefer to remain.'

The rage in her face cooled to disdain. 'Have it your own way. No one missed you when you left Schloss Holdenstein; why should we need you now?' Her mouth, a perfect plum-red bow, curved into a smile that said firmly, *you cannot hurt me*. She was as lovely as a flower, but his desire for her was passionless, purely physical. 'There is something else. You must have noticed changes in the Crystal Ring. Doesn't it seem darker, stormier? Hostile, as if it doesn't really want us any more . . .'

Her tone chilled him. She was mocking the fear, but inside he sensed that she was genuinely terrified.

'I rather like it,' he said.

'You would. Well, there is a rumour that it's Lilith's fault. Her presence has warped the Ring. She could be our doom, they say, unless we—'

Sebastian broke in, 'You called her Lilith.'

'Did I? It's what she calls herself; I told you she's crazy.'

The name stirred some inky stratum within him. A formless shape raised its head, dissipated, vanished. 'But you don't believe this nonsense?'

'I can't stand hysteria,' Ilona said, sliding her arms under his coat and round his waist. 'I'm here to prove it *isn't* true. And you; what are you doing here? Playing games with some human?'

'You remember me. How touching.' He kissed her; her mouth opened beneath his, warm and eager. Then she drew back and smiled, stroking his cheek.

'Confess,' she said. 'You look as miserable as sin. You're bored, aren't you? Let's forget all this. I'm going to take you to a party.'

He rested his hands on her shoulders. His need to be alone was proving stronger than his lust for her. 'Will Karl and the others be there?'

'Of course. It's in the ballet's honour.'

'Where?'

'Some house on Commonwealth Avenue—'

'Good. I shall avoid Commonwealth Avenue like the plague.'

She frowned. 'Why? they needn't see you; they won't see me. And there will be humans there, an ocean of fascinating strangers to choose from.' She pressed her slender body against him, her mouth invitingly curved. 'As we're both at a loose end, I thought we could amuse ourselves together, as we used to.'

'Well, you thought wrong,' he said icily. 'I don't want to be with vampires, Ilona. I don't want to see Karl or hear another word about Violette. I hate vampires, Ilona — and that includes you.'

She glowered venomously at him, her head tilted to one side. 'You arrogant bastard!' she said. And she showed the tips of her fangs.

Sebastian's hands tightened on her shoulders. His mouth fell to her throat, his lupine teeth springing through her flesh. As her jewel-like blood liquefied in his mouth, Ilona yelped, tried to struggle, then clung to him, groaning with mingled pleasure and pain. But after a few seconds, realizing that he was not going to stop, that he was doing this not in desire but in a simple reminder of his strength, she began to fight again.

Sebastian was not angry. It was only the bleak, lightless vista within him, demanding its solitude. Its autocracy.

He took a last swallow of her burning blood and withdrew, leaving Ilona more indignant than hurt. She began to say something but he pushed her away, slamming her back into the tree so hard that she gasped and fell to her hands and knees on the tree roots. Oblivious to her curses he left her there, and walked softly away into the darkness.

CHAPTER SEVEN

HOUSE OF THORNED VINES

Charlotte's father, a philosopher and scientist, had used to say that the microcosm contained the macrocosm: that if they could understand the physics of the atom, they would understand the universe itself. And this theory, Charlotte thought, also held true for social gatherings. Several times in her life a party had become a central event, a small universe complete in itself, its relationships and emotions forced in a hot-house of artificial contact.

As a human she had hated these events. There had been some secret to their enjoyment that she couldn't unlock. But tonight, as she and Karl entered the mansion where the party was being held, the prospect of the evening ahead excited her. They would move among unsuspecting humans, who would be captivated without knowing why; they would have innocent conversations with mortals while acutely aware of the blood beating beneath their fresh, unbroken skin. And Charlotte would think, all I have to do is say the word and you would go anywhere with me and gladly permit an embrace that might end your life . . . Yet she would spare them. Most of them, at least. Such an electrifying pleasure.

Karl met her eyes, and she saw her anticipation echoed there. Almost a shock to know that he shared her passions, that his gentlemanly detachment was a mask. She could never fully accept it, because their unity of feeling was only a step away from the sharing of the feast: wondrous, horrific, forbidden.

The party was being held after the first performance of *Swan Lake*, the only night that suited the ballet's schedule. Karl and

Charlotte were introduced to the host, an imposing patriarch named James Wilberforce Booth; a patron of the arts and a major figure in Boston, Violette had said. Then they entered the ballroom, a grandiose hall of gleaming white marble, sparkling with mirrors and chandeliers. It was already crowded, the dancers mingling with wealthy socialites. French doors stood open to the garden, releasing columns of light to the darkness.

'I like this city,' said Charlotte. 'It feels familiar, and yet it is so different.'

'I love the subtlety of the differences,' Karl said softly. 'Their accents, the way they dress and move. These old Bostonians pride themselves on being of English stock yet they are now completely American. Here we are in this little aristocratic fortress, but we could walk outside and enter a different world: Irish, Italian, Chinese. Every community re-creating itself. And there is such energy here.' He sounded rapt, as if he were contemplating that energy as seething human heat, life and blood. 'This land seems full of possibilities that have died in Europe. They are not jaded by the weight of history.'

'When we walked down by the harbour,' Charlotte murmured, 'I imagined I could see the immigrants walking off the ships through the sea fog. Like ghosts, full of hope.' She was almost talking to herself now. 'Everything is so different and exciting, yet it feels . . . almost like home.'

The gleam of fascination in Karl's eyes reaffirmed her knowledge that vampires thirsted for much more than blood. She'd seen that look when he'd approached her father, eager to become involved with his scientific work. However often Karl warned her against befriending humans, the truth was that the mortal world intrigued him.

As they made their way through the guests, he asked, 'Did you invite Josef?'

'Of course,' Charlotte answered. 'Tonight's the ideal time for him to meet Violette. She was in no state to see anyone during the voyage, but now she's happier, she might be more receptive.'

'And have you told her about Josef?'

Charlotte sighed. 'No. I'll say he's a friend, that's all. I hope he'll learn something from talking to her. I don't like subterfuge, but if I tell her the truth – I can just imagine how she'd react!'

Karl shook his head. 'You do like playing with fire, *Liebchen*, don't you?'

'I can't see either of them, anyway. Violette's bound to be late.'

'If she comes at all,' said Karl.

'Oh, she will. She has a strong sense of duty towards her admirers.'

'True,' he said. 'She is never ungracious to strangers; only to her friends.'

Charlotte pretended she had not heard this barbed remark. Glancing towards the doors for some sign of Violette's arrival, she saw Josef with an attractive woman on his arm. She caught his eye and he came over to her, introducing his companion as his niece, Roberta Stafford.

'Call me Robyn,' she said. 'Josef gave me the name; that's why I like it.' And she smiled affectionately at her uncle.

Charlotte liked her immediately. She seemed friendly, mischievous and irreverent; quite unlike the staid matrons who made up a large proportion of the guests.

'I hope you won't find us all as dull and proper as our hosts,' Robyn said, looking pointedly at Mr Booth senior and his sons, two rigid, unsmiling men in their twenties. 'No liquor in the fruit cup, no champagne; you must think we're hideously uncivilized.'

'Isn't prohibition meant to be a civilizing influence?' Karl said ironically.

'The effect is exactly the opposite, if you ask me,' said Robyn. 'Oh, liquor can be had if you can pay for it. But the Booths are teetotallers. If they can't enjoy themselves, they're darned if anyone else is going to!'

'I hope we're allowed to dance,' said Karl.

'Oh, sure; dance, smoke, anything.' She touched Karl's arm conspiratorially. 'Just as long as you don't look as if you're *enjoying* it!'

While Karl was speaking to Robyn with his usual charm,

Charlotte watched keenly for her reaction. His effect on women could be devasting; Charlotte herself had fallen heavily, after all. But Robyn, it seemed, was too worldly – or perhaps too cynical – to be so easily stricken. Her manner was relaxed; friendly, not flirtatious. Only a flicker of her eyes betrayed a slight bemusement.

She doesn't know what we are, Charlotte thought. I knew Josef wouldn't tell her. She senses an indefinable strangeness about us, has no idea what it is.

Josef was the one who reacted. As Robyn touched Karl's arm, and Karl laughed with her, Charlotte saw Josef turning white. She knew he was suddenly seeing Karl as predator, Robyn as prey. Taking his niece's arm in mid-conversation, Josef stammered an excuse and steered her away.

'A shame,' Karl sighed. 'This is one of the disadvantages of Josef knowing what we are. Even if I told him I had no intention of touching her, he wouldn't believe me.'

'Never in a million years,' Charlotte said wryly, 'because you were tempted, weren't you? And so was I.'

The image of the shared feast blazed between them like blood-red flame; and when their hands touched, it was like lightning. But no one around them suspected anything.

Despite what Sebastian had said to Ilona, he found himself walking along the broad, imposing Commonwealth Avenue until he found a grand red-brick house alive with light and music. 'The City of Boston welcomes the Ballet Janacek' announced a banner draped above the open front door.

Although he had genuinely had no intention of coming here, the idea of the party had drawn him like an oasis in the parched plain of his boredom. A sea of fascinating strangers, as Ilona had promised. Arriving early, before any vampires or even the dancers were in evidence, he was able to circulate freely for a time. He watched the women, listened to their chatter and felt their warm moist hands on his. In New York he had been intrigued by the angular beauty of the flappers, their unstructured, revealing dresses and the undignified exuberance of their dances. The ladies of Boston and their débutante daughters were more conservative, but the differences captivated him. He took in the subdued brilliance of their jewels and beaded gowns like an observer from another age.

As always, Sebastian felt like a foreign visitor among them, unsure of the customs, but he liked the feeling. That was as it should be. And how easily women fell for a mysterious stranger.

Presently the dancers began to arrive, and the women and men rushed to them in a fawning flock. Although Sebastian didn't want to be seen, even by Ilona, he had no intention of leaving. He would enjoy the party from the outside, from its secret corridors and recesses.

Leaving the ballroom, he went to explore the lavish rooms of the mansion, stepping in and out of the Crystal Ring to avoid being seen. He could tolerate crowds for only a certain length of time, and sometimes he wanted solitude more than he wanted blood.

On an upper floor, however, his attention was caught by a lone human presence at the end of a corridor, shedding its heat on to his skin. Curiosity drew him. He opened a door and found a young man sitting in a study, in darkness.

Sebastian closed the door behind him and walked across to the leather couch on which the man sat. Faint light from the window sheened the expensive dark furniture, the man's hunched shoulders and thick, light brown hair.

He was quite handsome, Sebastian noted, and very unhappy. There was a gold cigarette case at his feet, cigarettes scattered on the rug.

'Are you not in the mood for a party?' Sebastian asked softly.

The man looked up, resentful at being disturbed but too sunk in depression really to care. His collar and tie were undone, and he gripped a glass of gin on his knee. You would never guess, Sebastian thought, that drink is meant to be illegal. 'I tried but I – I couldn't face it. Someone turned up who I didn't want to . . . I know I ought to show my face for my father's sake but I can't. I'm no good to anyone, I guess. My brothers said it would cheer me up, but . . .'

'The contrast between their happiness and your sorrow is unbearable.'

The man uttered a huge sigh. His face was flushed, his eyes lifeless. His accent was pure Harvard. 'Yes, unbearable. You put that well.'

Sebastian bent down, gathered the spilled cigarettes into the case, and handed it back to the young man. 'Thanks. Clumsy, my hands were shaking. I couldn't be bothered to pick them up.'

'Shall I light one for you?' the vampire asked.

'I'd appreciate it.' Sebastian obliged; the man sucked deeply and blew out clouds of reeking smoke. 'Thanks. You?'

Sebastian declined. He sat on the rolled arm of the couch and looked down at the bowed head. 'Would it help to talk about your troubles?'

'Did my father send you up here to persuade me out?'

Sebastian had seen the mustachioed patriarch greeting guests in the ballroom, flanked by his wife and two humourless sons. This wretched creature, he guessed, must be the black sheep. 'No, but I'm sure he's concerned about you.'

'Concerned, hell. You won't tell him about this, will you?' He held up the glass. 'He thinks liquor is the devil's work.'

'It will remain our secret,' said Sebastian. He thought of a false name and said, 'I'm John Waterford.'

'Russell Booth.' They shook hands. The young man named Russell took a loud swallow of his drink and stared at nothing, his eyes glazed. Then he said, 'It's a woman, what else?'

'And she let you down.'

'That's an understatement. Bitch! No, no, I can't call her that. I loved her. She was older than me, quite a bit older, but it didn't matter to me. I wanted to marry her. My mother and father and brothers were dead against it. Said she'd been married before, as if that mattered. Said she had a reputation, but I wouldn't listen, I thought she'd be different with me. God, I worshipped her. I really thought she loved me. The clothes I bought her, jewels, a car. I even made business investments for her.'

'Ah. That sounds like a bad idea.'

'Sure, she took me for a fool. I think she would've hung on to me for as long as my money lasted, if I hadn't found out she was seeing someone else. I mean, not just one; she had a string of 'em. Not just anyone. She can pick and choose, and she only picks on rich men.' He laughed bitterly, then seemed on the edge of tears. 'I make her sound like a whore, but she's not. I can't explain. You'd understand if you met her; men'd just die for her . . .'

'So, has she ruined you?'

'Oh, the money doesn't matter. Father isn't speaking to me, but he'll come round. I loved her, that's the problem. When I found out about the other men, I went crazy at her. You know what she did? She laughed. I still can't believe it! After everything, she *laughed*, called me an idiot, said I'd got what I deserved. It's what she does for a living, see; she bleeds rich men dry, and if she can break their hearts in the process, that makes her even happier. My brothers tried to warn me, she's done it countless times. What she likes best is to take young men – fools like me – and ruin them for any other woman.'

'She sounds perfectly charming, and not particularly unusual,' Sebastian remarked. In fact, he was becoming interested.

'She's one on her own, I'm telling you. But the worst thing, the very worst thing is this.' He struggled to force the words out. 'She's here. She turned up tonight and my father couldn't do a damned thing about it because she's the ballet's guest, not ours. She knows what she's done, she knows my family hate her, and yet she walks in with her head in the air, laughing at us!'

'What a nerve,' Sebastian said admiringly. 'So that's why you're hiding up here?'

'I saw her but she didn't see me. I couldn't bear it. To face her and know she despises me—!'

Sebastian shook his head. 'You should have faced her, to show you don't care.'

'But I do care! I still love her.' Russell looked up at him with hollow, desperate eyes. 'I can't stop. But I hate her too, I want to kill her for what she's done! Kill her, then myself.'

'Very romantic.'

'If you think this is funny, you can just—'

'Please, my friend.' Sebastian took the man's drunkenly clenched fist and pushed it gently away. 'I feel for your pain. But you are making yourself into her victim, when you should be forgetting this sentimental nonsense of love and thinking of cold-blooded revenge.'

Russell stared at Sebastian, jerked out of his self-absorption. Then he slumped. 'I can't. I've got no will left to do anything. It's pathetic but I'm beyond it.'

'I was suggesting that perhaps I could do it for you.'

'You?' another flash of life, tinged with alarm. 'What the hell d'you mean?'

'I could do to her what she has done to you. Give her a taste of her own poison.'

The man's eyes were huge, his mouth slack with astonishment. Sebastian smiled. And the man saw, with ghastly vividness, that it was not an empty promise. Terror sobered him. 'No. No. I couldn't do that to her.'

'Describe her and tell me her name.'

'No, no—'

'Why not? How else will she ever understand what she has done to you, unless she suffers it herself?'

Russell hesitated, trembling. Through his instinctive desire to protect his ex-lover, there shone an unholy light of excitement. 'OK,' he whispered quickly. 'Her name is Roberta Stafford and she lives on Chestnut Street. You'll know her when you see her; she's plain *beautiful* with brown hair like all the colours of fall. Her friends call her Robyn, with a "y".' He caught his breath, as if to suck back the information he'd spilled out, shocked at himself.

'I shall look forward to meeting her,' Sebastian said, thinking, however did I miss her? His hand slid up over the man's shoulder and on to the damp skin of his neck. 'Don't worry, you've done the right thing.'

'Yes. Yes, but—'

'She deserves it.'

'Yes. She deserves it! But—' There was desperate anxiety in his eyes. He had obviously realized on a subconscious level that

Sebastian was worse than dangerous; that he was evil. 'You won't hurt her, will you? Physically, I mean.'

'No more than this.' Sliding down on to the couch with snake-like ease, Sebastian covered the strong young body with his own and felt his fangs spring down and through the tender skin.

'What – what is this—?' One feeble, terrified protest, then surrender. Sebastian was already drinking the hot, pulsating blood, absorbing with all his senses the ambience of smoke and stale alcohol, of sorrow and bitter despair.

I don't suppose they'll find the body until after the party, Sebastian thought; but when they do, they'll think the poor creature drank himself to death.

Robyn was happy tonight. She'd been content on her uncle's arm as they had moved through the auditorium to take their seats for *Swan Lake*; nothing to prove, no one to impress. The ballet had delighted her, taking her quite out of herself. As for her guilty conscience about letting Alice down, she'd assuaged it by buying Alice tickets for *Coppélia* on a different night.

Leaving the theatre afterwards, she had seen Harold with his wife in the crowd. Robyn amused herself by catching his eye, making as if to acknowledge him, then turning the gesture into something else. How satisfying it had been to see his eyes bulge in sudden terror, the blood engorging his face. She heard his wife – a formidable matriarch – exclaiming in annoyance as Harold, for no apparent reason, steered her abruptly at a right angle.

'Someone you know?' Josef asked shrewdly.

Robyn was laughing. 'Not officially.'

But Harold, thankfully, was not at the party afterwards. For all his wealth, he had not gained admission to the inner circle. Although Robyn was unimpressed by the status that money or talent conferred, she found the idea of mingling with the dancers oddly thrilling. On stage, they had seemed too ethereal to be quite human . . . particularly Violette Lenoir.

'This is wonderful,' she'd whispered to Josef as they had first entered the ballroom.

'Very impressive,' said Josef, looking around.

'No, not the room. James Wilberforce Booth has three sons; Russell, Victor and William. I had an affair with Russell, and his family loathe me. I dropped him a couple of weeks ago and now I'm a complete pariah in their eyes. Watch them looking daggers at me! I shouldn't be here, but there isn't a damn thing they can do about it.'

'Oh, Robyn,' her uncle said sadly. The bland, icy eyes of Victor and William were already pouring venom in her direction, she noticed with glee. 'Don't you mind them glaring at you like that?'

'No, I love it. They're the ones tearing themselves apart, not me.'

'But what happens if you bump into Russell?'

'What if I do? I might just lead him on and dump him all over again. Don't look at me like that! I am joking.'

'Are you?' said Josef, shaking his head in disapprobation. But she didn't mind; he loved her too much to condemn her.

Russell, however, did not appear, and the Booth family studiously ignored her. It was beneath their dignity to make a scene. Robyn secretly felt relieved. At least she was left in peace to enjoy the evening.

There were a number of people here whom she knew. Some, regarding her as a woman who caused scandals in the most strait-laced of societies, consistently shunned her, but she didn't care. There were plenty of others – mainly younger ones – who were prepared to overlook her reputation for two simple reasons: she had the status bestowed by wealth, and she was good company. People seemed to find a sweetness in her that made it impossible for them to believe the worst.

Until Josef's friends appeared, the evening was light and pleasant; the moment Josef took her to meet them, the atmosphere changed. She received a complex influx of impressions; that the strangers were a strikingly attractive couple, and that Josef clearly adored Charlotte. The daughter of an old friend, he'd said, but the excuse was transparent. So, Robyn thought, this is the mystery woman! How sad that he loves her without hope, and has to suffer seeing her arm-in-arm with her lover. Josef's plight touched her; her usual indifference melted. And she read their stances and gestures like an adept; Charlotte was obviously fond of Josef, even attracted to him, but she was wound up in an unassailable bond with the man at her side. While Karl and Josef quietly resented each other.

But the interlaced impressions went deeper. Karl and Charlotte were not merely beautiful but curiously *vivid*. Certainly they were breathtaking to look at; Charlotte's solemn face and violet eyes, nested in a wreath of gold-frosted hair, her arms pale and slender against the russet velvet of her dress. And Karl . . . she wondered if he were one of the male dancers. He had that slender strength and grace, a dark presence that was quiet and yet overwhelming. But more than that . . . It was as if the ballroom and everyone in it were sketched in watercolour, while these two were painted in the rich detail of oils. They had a luminosity to them, a beauty and depth more extreme than reality.

Unnerving, somehow. Accustomed to finding herself the centre of attention, for once Robyn felt invisible. All her attention was gathered on them. She made light-hearted conversation, giving nothing away, but she was aware of her mood shifting and darkening.

Perhaps Josef sensed it too. He ended the exchange so abruptly that Robyn was too taken aback to protest as he led her away. He'd gone very pale.

'What's wrong, dear?' she said. 'Aren't you feeling well?'

'No, no, I'm quite all right. But we can't keep them all evening, they have to circulate.'

Robyn decided not to challenge him. There were too many people around, introductions to be made, one conversation spilling over into the next. The dancers, mostly female, were recognizable among the other guests. Bohemian and distinctly European in appearance, poised in their movements. A wealth of human beauty. Robyn felt languorously enchanted, almost as if she were hallucinating; seeing through a crystal haze that laid blurred strings of diamonds on mirror frames, silver gauze over the whole room. Everyone seemed to move as slowly as swimmers through a flooded temple, their pearlescent flesh adorned with silk and jewels. And through this uncanny light, she kept watch on Karl and Charlotte from a distance.

Together or apart, they were always exchanging glances as if passing dark telepathic messages. Always observing others, too, like spies. Emotionally they were wrapped around each other like two red-flowered vines. When they spoke to strangers, their expressions were friendly but unreadable. With each other, though, their faces became radiant, expressive, sensual, conveying a hundred thoughts without words. Karl's long dark lashes lowered as he spoke softly to Charlotte, her sombre expression igniting into sunlit charm as she smiled. Such exquisite responsiveness.

And watching them, Robyn felt a burning sense of distress. Oh Lord, not jealousy. She despised romantic love as the lie of all time; it cut her, to be reminded that it was not a lie for everyone. Even if it isn't for ever, she thought ironically. Yes, I know it looks as if it's already endured for years, but there's always something that might break it. Oh, but to feel that passion, if only for a month, a year, a day! If I could be seventeen again and unbruised . . .

A sudden rise in the level of conversation nudged her back to reality. There was a flurry of excitement that turned everyone's head, then a swelling wave of applause. The prima ballerina assoluta had arrived at last.

Like worker bees around the queen, everyone in the room seemed to be clustering around Violette Lenoir. Minutes passed before Robyn could even see her.

Then she glimpsed a small woman, a water spirit in ashes-of-roses silk and silver lace, lilies in her coiled black hair. On stage she had projected a magnificent and commanding presence; in life she looked softer, more delicate, and wholly a star. A weird shiver went through Robyn's nerves; a shocking recognition of another creature like Karl and Charlotte, etching itself on her inner mind with alarming significance.

Robyn was amazed at herself. Nothing had impressed or moved her like this for years. What was causing these delusions?

Too much fruit cup, she thought drily. She felt Josef's hand on her elbow; he too was looking at Violette, and seemed more troubled than ever.

'Well, there she is at last,' Robyn said cheerfully. 'The star of the show. Do I get to meet her too?'

'No, I—' Josef took out a handkerchief and patted at beads of sweat on his forehead. 'I don't think so.'

'Uncle, are you sure you're not ill? Do you want me to take you home?'

'No, but I think you should go now.' He tucked the handkerchief neatly away. His voice was low, full of concern.

'Go home? Whatever for? I'm enjoying myself.'

'Some of the people here . . . they are not so nice.'

She laughed gently, imitating his Viennese accent. 'Oh, Uncle, what makes you think I'm so nice?'

'I mean it. They may be . . . dangerous.'

'Are ballet dancers more dangerous than ordinary folk? What are they going to do, pirouette us to death?'

'I'm serious, Robyn.' He looked embarrassed and worried. 'I shouldn't have brought you here.'

'Why not?'

'I – never mind. I just shouldn't. I didn't think.'

'Well, if you won't explain, I'm certainly not going home. Don't worry about me. I can take care of myself.'

His face seemed to close up with resignation. If he refuses to explain, she thought, he can hardly expect me to understand! And then an autumn-coloured figure glided to his side as if from nowhere; Charlotte.

'May I steal your uncle for a while?' Even her voice was lovely, Robyn noticed, with its unassuming English delicacy. She gave Robyn a look of genuine warmth. 'Do you mind?'

'Of course not. Go ahead.' Robyn answered with a smile. She watched them walk away together, the golden-brown head tilted towards Josef's shoulder.

A moment later, a man she knew – one of her hopeful admirers – cornered her, but others joined them so she was able to excuse herself and move slowly round the edge of the dance floor towards the beckoning peace of the garden.

What's the matter with everyone tonight? she wondered. Me, especially. I need some air.

Heads turned as she passed but she took no notice. They were dream figures; this was a dream. Not unpleasant, this swimming sense of unreality; it was almost euphoria, mingled with a restlessness she'd never felt before. And ... and yes, a twinge of jealousy that Josef alone was privileged to meet Violette Lenoir.

Why? she thought abstractedly. *Some of the people here ... they are not so nice. They may be dangerous.* How in heaven's name am I supposed to take that?

As Charlotte led Josef towards the corner where Violette was holding court, he said, 'Won't she be suspicious of your motive for introducing me to her?'

'Oh, probably,' Charlotte replied. 'She misses nothing. But I won't let her hurt you, Josef, believe me. Just talk about the weather or the ballet, anything, but observe her and tell me what you think. And be careful what you say to me, because we have very sharp hearing.'

She could see by his drawn expression that he had serious misgivings. 'Really, I don't know that I will be of any use—'

'Neither do I. It's just a feeling, that you might see *something* we've missed that might help us to understand her.'

'Ah. There is a name for this exercise,' he said.

'Yes?'

'It's called clutching at straws.'

Violette was sitting in an alcove between marble pillars, embowered by green ferns, receiving a stream of admirers. They were allowed to sit with her for a little while, then they must move on; everyone was polite, Charlotte noticed, and no one tried to monopolize her. Violette was leaning forward in her chair, elbows resting on the arms, hands folded loosely in her lap, her ankles crossed. A concealing posture, although she looked quite relaxed as she spoke to a middle-aged man and his wife.

'Our daughter just loves the ballet,' the wife was saying. 'We wondered, Madame, if you would be so gracious as to see her dance, tell us if she has any future? You must be dreadfully busy, I know—'

'It's no trouble,' Violette said kindly. 'Bring her to the theatre tomorrow afternoon.' And the couple fluttered and gushed in gratitude.

Charlotte knew that Violette had once hated this attention, the unavoidable by-product of her talent, but her transformation had given her this at least; she could endure it, because it no longer mattered. Easy for an immortal to act the gracious goddess – and Violette was nothing if not an actress.

There were too many people wanting to talk to her; impossible for Charlotte to introduce Josef. Instead, she and Karl found him a chair, and they seated themselves at the edge of the group.

Looking round to make sure that Josef was comfortable, she saw that he'd turned paler than ever. He removed his spectacles, polished them, and replaced them on the long blade of his nose. 'What is it?' she said. She glanced at Karl, but his face was impassive.

Josef replied very quietly, 'It's like the first time I saw you, Charlotte; I mean, the first time I realized what you are.' He glanced uneasily at Karl. 'Having once recognized it, I can hardly fail to see the signs in others. It is disturbing, to put it mildly. But she is . . . oh God, more than beautiful. Divine and terrifying. What else could Lilith be?'

He spoke in a barely audible whisper, but the word was a soft hiss. *Lilith.* And as he spoke it, Violette looked up, her gaze travelling past her immediate companions and locking on to Charlotte's. Eyes dark with lethal anger, she rose from her chair in one graceful undulation. 'If you would excuse me for a few moments . . .' she said lightly to her admirers.

Then she came straight towards Charlotte, Karl and Josef, like a serpent poised to strike. Josef's hands tightened on the arms of his chair. Violette fixed Charlotte with an all-seeing, contemptuous stare, as if to demand, *How dare you bring some human to stare at me as if I were a specimen to be dissected?* Then her glance flicked away. She glided past them and vanished into the crowd.

Josef wilted with relief. Charlotte touched his arm, aware that she, too, had been rigid from head to foot.

'Charlotte?' Karl said softly.

'Damn it,' she said. 'I should know Violette well enough by now! Why does she still make me feel like this?'

'I'd say you have every reason to be afraid,' Josef said heavily. 'I can't explain, but she terrified me on a level than even you have never touched. What I can make of this, without actually speaking to her, I don't know . . .'

'We should not have involved you, Josef,' Karl said, his voice low. 'This is not for a human to deal with.'

'Karl's right,' said Charlotte. 'I'm sorry.'

'No, no.' He waved his hand dismissively, and his colour began to return. 'I don't give up so easily.'

'I'll go to Violette.' Charlotte made to stand up, but Karl's hand pinioned her arm.

'Don't,' he said. 'You know how unpredictable she is. Leave her; she'll come to you soon enough.'

She gave in. 'Josef, I think you should go back to the hotel.'

'Nonsense. I'm perfectly all right.' Josef looked gravely at her. 'I am not concerned for myself; it's Robyn I'm thinking of. I was a fool to bring her here.' His glance flicked to Karl and back.

Charlotte saw the look, and sighed inwardly. 'Robyn is not in danger,' she said firmly. 'Don't worry about her. You're safe, and so is she, I assure you.'

Robyn was pleasantly surprised to find the garden almost deserted; there was a group of men smoking in the verandah, a few couples on the terrace, but no one took any notice of her as she passed. How lovely to be alone in the night, with the scent of honeysuckle and orange blossom floating around her. Passing a couple who were pressed into a wedge of shadow between an ivy-covered tree and a wall, she started a little, not seeing them until the last moment. A man's back, a mass of dark hair; a woman's hands, like pale sea anemones against his evening jacket. She could not see their faces. For a moment she thought it was Karl and Charlotte again – but no, she'd left them inside with Josef. Only a courting couple, wrapped up in each other. She passed by quickly, pretending she hadn't seen them.

She found a tree to hide her from the house and leaned against it, feeling the bark imprinting her bare back. I must shake off this foolish mood. Why is Josef being so mysterious about his friends?

'I guess he'll tell me in his own good time,' she murmured aloud. She stretched, breathed in the sweet air, exhaled.

A voice in the darkness said, 'Will he tell you? Men never tell women anything. It's their last weapon against us, keeping us in the dark.'

Robyn jumped, her heart pattering. An English voice, delicate as ice-feathers, cutting as a sliver of crystal. Holding herself steady, she called softly, 'Who is that? How do you know so much?'

There was a movement, subtle as leaves fluttering, and Robyn saw the woman framed in a trellis arch, outlined by scattered light from the house and the stars. The figure of a dancer, lily-perfect; her ashes-of-roses dress a dewed cobweb, her hair witch-black. Robyn could not see her face. 'I'll tell you what I know,' said the dancer, 'if you will tell me.'

Detaching herself from the tree, Robyn hesitated, then went towards her. 'Sure, would you like to hear some stories?' Robyn said, an incredible excitement and pain fountaining inside her; none of it betrayed by her casual tone.

'Oh, yes. Tell me,' said Violette, holding out a hand – the hand that had earlier described Odette's grief and Odile's malevolence so eloquently – as if in welcome.

And that was how their conversation began, without preliminaries, without awkwardness. There were no social barriers in the darkness. They met as two women who shared an instinctive empathy.

'I'm Violette,' said the dancer.

'I know who you are, Madame.'

'You have the advantage over me, then,' Violette said strangely. She slipped her hand through Robyn's arm; how deliciously soft their flesh felt, pressed together. 'Even I do not know who I am. But you will please call me Violette.'

Robyn realized that not all stars relished the continual attention they received. 'I'm Robyn.'

'I'm pleased to meet you, Robyn.'

'You found it a little crowded inside?'

'Too hot, too crowded. I need to get away sometimes.'

'Away from their eyes,' said Robyn. They walked side-by-side along paved paths, between neat rows of trellis hung with roses, honeysuckle and vines. At intervals there were octagonal arbours, neatly clipped bay trees in tubs, pollarded fruit trees. Robyn was slightly above average height, but she felt clumsily large beside the petite dancer.

'Thirsty eyes,' Violette agreed. 'They have eyes like vampires, even the women, though the men are the worst. It's so tiring, trying to satisfy the demands they make. The social demands, I mean.'

'What about their other demands?' Robyn said boldly. 'Or don't they dare?'

'A few have tried.' The dancer's tone was chilly. 'Not many. But I want to hear about you, Robyn. Tell me—' She spun round in front of her suddenly, took both her hands and pulled her along as if dancing. Robyn saw her eyes; expressive blue-violet jewels caged by black lashes and arched blackbrows. Hypnotic with light and life, yet strangely hard, as if they dammed a vast and ruthless soul.

Violette led her to a wooden bench under a cavern of trailing Virginia creeper. Robyn felt drugged, dream-laden. She was acutely aware that she was in the company of a virtual goddess, at a loss to understand why the ballerina had chosen her company to the exclusion of all others – but rather than making her feel awkward, it only enhanced the weird thrill of their encounter. So easy to talk to Violette, as she'd never talked to anyone before, not even Alice. Impossible not to tell her. Violette unwound the story from her like silk.

'It was my father's fault,' Robyn began. 'He hates me – or isn't capable of loving me, at least. He must have been capable of love once, when he met my mom. He met her on a trip to Europe, in Vienna, married her there and brought her back to Boston. Unfortunately, he didn't realize she was Jewish until it was too late – or rather, he realized, but he didn't understand that marrying an outsider was going to prevent him from being everything he wanted to be in society. He should've known, but he was young, hot-headed. That's the problem; not that she was Jewish, but that she was an outsider, not a girl from the right Boston family. No connections, no status. So he had to work extra hard to achieve his ambitions, and it left him a little bitter because he was very ambitious; wanted to be the richest, most important man in town. To him, his children were nothing but . . . How can I put it? Commodities.' She leaned back on the ivy-covered wall as she spoke, feeling the tender leaves crushed against her skin. Aware of Violette's cool radiance close beside her. 'Wasn't so hard for my brothers; all they had to do was succeed in business. But my sisters and me . . . well, we were all pretty, and that made us valuable. So he sold us.'

'Sold—?' Violette sat forward, her face intent. Robyn was amazed to have said something that shocked her.

'You know, business deals. He gave us away as a kind of favour. It was, "Clinch this deal and your son can have my beautiful, rich daughter." That's how I came to marry Samuel James Stafford.'

'And you had no say in the matter?'

'You don't know my dad. He always gets his own way. I was young and scared of him, and Mom always took his side. So I decided to make the best of it, convinced myself I loved Samuel. I believe I actually did, in my naïvety. He was handsome in a cold, Harvard sort of way, and he was completely obsessed by me. Wouldn't take no for an answer. So everything was fine,' she said sarcastically. Violette leaned towards her, holding Robyn's bare arms, and something eerie and inexplicable happened. Her eyes captured Robyn's, magnificently luminous. And it seemed they entered another place together, where no one else existed, and Robyn's whole life was unreeling in a whispering necklace of images.

Her husband's jealousy and cruelty, suppressed for the few weeks of their honeymoon, then slowly unleashed. His verbal bullying, the sexual degradation that escalated to outright brutality. His bouts of drunkenness, the beatings from which she barely emerged alive. And then, webbing her into the sticky prison of deceit, his apologies, his endless resolutions to reform, his pathetic declarations of love . . . and the cycle began again.

'I could do nothing. No one would have believed me; I would only have brought disgrace on my family if I'd tried to end the marriage. It would have wrecked one of my father's most important business connections. And that was the truly horrible thing,' she whispered, her wrists now resting on Violette's shoulder, their faces close together. 'That my father and Samuel's father had sold me into this, because they both knew what Samuel was like before he married me. *They knew.* And I was a slab of drugged meat to tame the hyena, to keep him from ruining his family's reputation and business. They knew, these men, they all knew. What could I do against their silent conspiracies, their handshakes and deals, when a daughter or a wife is just a thing to be bought and sold?'

Tears of rage running down her cheeks. The wind rustling the ivy like rain, as she described the years of bitter pain. 'I conceived five times and I miscarried five times. Three of those were because he'd hit me or knocked me downstairs, the others out of sheer despair. After the fifth, I never conceived again. So he decided I must be the devil because I was barren.

'I had eight years of hell, and then heaven smiled on me. The bastard died of a heart attack.

'When we came home from the funeral, my housekeeper Alice and I locked the doors. I tore off my widow's weeds and we danced and shouted and laughed like a pair of mad witches until we could dance no more. And then . . . I set about taking my revenge.'

'Against the men you hated.'

'Against all men. Couldn't do much about my own dad because it would've hurt Mom, but I got *Samuel's* father; I seduced him, ruined his marriage and his business within a year. And then the others. Young and old. I decided that no man was ever going to use his bullying weakness to trick me again. Never.'

'Do you hate them all?' Violette spoke with a kind of urging hunger in her voice that startled Robyn, bringing her part-way out of the trance.

'Not *en masse*,' she said thoughtfully. 'Some of them have good hearts. Harold's not so bad, too old to be any real trouble. And my uncle, and Wilkes, my driver. H'm, that's three; can't think of anyone else.'

She smiled wryly, but the dancer's face remained intense, almost livid. Unnerving for all its beauty.

'So you don't believe in love?'

'Do you?' said Robyn. 'Here I am, talking about myself all night, not giving you a chance. Why do I get the feeling that you feel the same, that things have been just as bad for you?'

'Not quite as bad, because instinct made me keep them at arm's length before they got the chains on me – but bad enough,' Violette murmured. Her hand slid over Robyn's shoulder, down her upper arm, then retraced its path. How cool her touch was, how sensuous. 'We both knew, the moment we saw each other, didn't we? Like knows like. The same bitterness, the same suffering, even though we've lived our lives thousands of miles apart.'

I can't believe she's telling me this, Robyn thought, electrified. 'It's a pretty common experience.'

'I know,' said the dancer. 'I see it everywhere, this hideous weakness that makes men into monsters and women into victims – and the other way round, as well. And it enrages me. No, I don't trust love, even when I see a couple doting on one another. What are they trying to hide?'

'Who are they trying to fool?' Robyn added, thinking of Karl and Charlotte.

'But have you ever wondered,' Violette said, her voice softening, 'how it would be with a woman instead?'

Now things are getting out of hand, Robyn thought. But at the same time she was seized by the subversive thrill of trying something new and forbidden. 'Oh, Lord,' she said, embarrassed. 'Thought about it, I guess, but never—'

The dancer leaned in and pressed her lips to Robyn's. The kiss was cool, dry, brief – and it completely unravelled her. 'Never?' Another kiss. 'Never at all?' Another, another. Robyn was shaking. This was awful and yet it was tantalizing . . . why not a woman, after all . . . no one, male or female, could resist Violette . . . Her hands crept up around Violette's shoulders, slid into her luxuriant hair. Yet she was scared to go further, worried that Violette was not sincere, and that if she betrayed any feelings the dancer would pull away and mock her.

Violette's mouth met hers, parted her lips and teeth. Her tongue felt shockingly hot. What Robyn felt was not exactly sexual, for she had suppressed those feelings in herself for too long. It was a generalized heat, rippling waves of sensation flowing over her skin, an almost unbearable sensuality flowing from Violette's fingertips, her lips, every point at which their bodies touched . . . a red excitement building in the core of her spine . . . yes, sexual after all, but frightening, a frightening pressure.

Violette was pushing her back against the wall, her kisses travelling over Robyn's cheeks and jaw, growing more and more fervent. She felt trapped. She tried to loosen the dancer's grip, to convey that this was too much, too soon – she'd expected gentility, shouldn't women be gentle with each other? – but Violette was too strong. As she pressed Robyn down, her passion seemed to have become single-minded, self-centred, blind. Like a rapist.

'No, don't. Stop it, please stop,' Robyn tried to say, but Violette's hand was on her windpipe and she could not speak. Choking.

'You deserve it,' Violette murmured. Her lips slid hotly down Robyn's throat, came to rest on a throbbing vessel just above her collarbone. 'Yes, you deserve it.'

Teeth nipped the skin, making her nerves leap with pain. She shivered with violent fear, yet something within her was yearning outwards, surrendering to this dark entity. Yes . . . do it . . .

Cool air rushed between them. Violette pulled away, and all the pressure vanished. She was looking across the garden, as if she'd heard something; then she turned back to Robyn, and pressed one hand lightly between her breasts. 'But not yet,' she said, eyes glazed. 'Please excuse me.' She stood up coolly, as if nothing at all had happened, and slipped away into the darkness, leaving Robyn confused, breathless, bereft. Quite unable to move.

As she sat there, almost in a state of catatonia, she saw the distant silhouette of a woman on the edge of the terrace, light spinning a golden web in the edges of her hair. And she heard Charlotte call out softly, imbuing a single word with concern, warning and rebuke.

'Violette!'

After Sebastian left his victim cooling in the study, he had a decision to make. He was eager to meet the unique Mrs Stafford, but if he rejoined the party he was bound to be recognized by Karl and the others. They might not *sense* him as such, but once they saw him they'd know. He wasn't afraid of a confrontation; he simply couldn't be bothered with it.

So Sebastian decided to delay the moment. No hurry, after all. He haunted the edge of the gathering by keeping to the terrace and the gardens, moving in and out of the Crystal Ring, listening to conversations. It didn't take him long to work out which one was Robyn, although he couldn't get a clear view of her face; there was only one chestnut-haired woman with any kind of presence about her. The anticipation of seeing her clearly was tormenting.

He knew she would be beautiful. It went without saying. Unusual beauty, perhaps. Someone special, a worthy substitute for Violette.

Those other vampires had better not make a claim on Robyn, he thought. If they try, that *would* be a confrontation I'd relish.

As he watched her from a distance through the french doors, his thirst stirred. So warm and alive she looked, the exact opposite of Violette; laughing, confident, seductive in her small gleaming world. The centre of attention.

Ah, the first glimpse of her face! A surprise, as he'd anticipated. Not a fragile or simpering beauty, this. Her features were emphatic; a strong nose and chin, soft brown eyes that narrowed mischievously when she laughed, a mobile, deep-red mouth. She looked warm, kind and poised; a strong character. People accepted her despite her prejudices, he realized, because they liked her. And she was lovely. A shaft of creamy fire, tipped by the chestnut jewel of her hair.

His disappointment over the ballerina was dust.

Sebastian wanted Robyn fiercely, but he would not go inside to her. He'd wait, here in the stirring shadows and the balm of the air, at one with the night that was the twin of his own soul; dispassionate, brooding, limitless, silent.

'So, you came after all?' said Ilona's voice from the shadows a few feet away.

He looked round, saw her leaning against an ivy-covered wall. His earlier attack appeared not to have damaged her composure, although her eyes had an icier glitter than before. Again he cursed himself for letting her catch him unawares.

'I had a feeling you wouldn't be able to resist it,' said Ilona. 'I'm glad I met you now; I was just growing bored. So, here we are, both hiding out here because we don't want to be seen. A little pathetic, isn't it?'

Sebastian looked stonily at her, folding his arms. 'You're free to leave,' he said.

She frowned. 'Are you still going to be a swine to me?'

Sebastian could feel a human approaching; he pushed Ilona back against the wall, behind a tree. 'I can think of no reason for you to pester me like this,' he said, 'unless I broke your heart when I left Schloss Holdenstein. Is that it?'

'Don't flatter yourself,' she whispered. 'I enjoy getting on your nerves, that's all.'

'You always did.'

The human was passing them now. They pressed back into the darkness, faces hidden, like lovers. But Sebastian knew it was Robyn. He caught her perfume; jasmine, rain-soaked flowers, the secret heat of her body, and the calescent pull of her blood . . .

Part of him hated Ilona for keeping him away from her, but in another way, he didn't mind. There was plenty of time. This interlude only served to sharpen his anticipation. And in this desire for Robyn he held Ilona tightly, feeling her stiffen and gasp with pleasure.

She said softly, 'Don't be nasty to me, Sebastian, or I'll tell Karl you're here. You wouldn't want that, would you?'

'Oh, and what could Karl do about it?'

'Well, he has interests in certain humans here and he knows what you're like; he'd want to protect them from you, which would rather cramp your style. And you don't want to tangle with Violette, believe me.'

'She's nothing,' he said. 'But you don't want Karl to know you're here, either, do you? The threat works both ways.'

She shrugged. 'No, it doesn't. He'll notice me soon enough. It doesn't matter to me as much as it matters to you.'

Ilona reads me too well, he thought with an inward sigh. 'And if I'm nice to you, dearest?'

She smiled at his mordant tone. 'No one will ever know you were here. Our little secret.'

'Well, I suppose you have a point,' he said, warming towards her more out of increasing lust than friendship. Aggravating as she was, her body felt firm and lithe against his. 'We're too alike to tell tales on one another.'

'That's it,' she breathed. 'Don't spoil my fun and I won't spoil yours.' Her mouth glistened dark red, succulent as a fruit; her hands moved warmly over his chest, tantalizing him. All at once, her presence did not seem nearly so unwelcome. 'I think we should go somewhere quieter for a little while, don't you?'

And if Sebastian was aware that Robyn had met another woman in the darkness, it made no more impression on him than the flutter of leaves.

When Violette reappeared from the garden, Charlotte took her arm and steered her into the verandah, a cool square room with marble benches and potted ferns. The light and heat of the party shimmered beyond the pillars, but here it was deserted, cool and dark as water. 'How could you, Violette?' she exclaimed. 'If I hadn't called you just then, you would have fed on her, wouldn't you?'

Violette jerked her arm from Charlotte's grasp, her eyes glacial. 'I find you incredible. After the months you have spent pleading with me to give in to the thirst, you interrupt me and lose your temper with me for finding a victim! How dare you?'

Charlotte felt furious, but Violette was so wintry that she despaired of reaching her.

'I dared to stop you,' Charlotte said, 'because you were about to attack someone I promised would be safe.'

'Do you really imagine you have some responsibility to single out individuals to protect? That is a lie.'

'No, it isn't! Anyone else, Violette – do whatever you like – but not Josef, and not Robyn! He's my friend, and she's his niece.'

'I know. I saw them together.'

'But you didn't care?'

The lapis eyes widened, star-flecked. 'Why this human friend, Charlotte? I told you I saw him on the ship, and again at the ballet with Robyn beside him, and you wouldn't admit you knew him! Who is he? And then you bring him here to stare at me, like a doctor deciding whether or not to lock me up. Why?'

Charlotte looked down, embarrassed. Nothing escaped Violette. 'Because that's what he is, in a way.'

'What?' The frost in her eyes turned to flame.

'He's made studies of ancient mythology and its relationship to the psyche. I hoped that if we could understand why you think you are Lilith, it might help you. I wanted to tell you but I didn't because I knew you'd refuse to see him.'

'So instead you lie to me and try to sneak him into my company—'

'I'm sorry. But this is precisely why I did it. I knew you'd react like this.'

The last words, spoken quickly, seemed to defuse Violette's rage. She laughed, but her face was colourless. 'What do you expect? How many times do I have to tell you to stop trying to help me? You're as bad as the others, who just want to burn me at the stake! Anything to deny what I am — but at least my enemies are honest about it!'

Charlotte turned away and sat down on a bench, one hand clasping her bowed head. She did not know what to say. 'Is that why you were going to attack Robyn — to punish me?'

'For God's sake. You should know me better than that! It had absolutely nothing to do with you or Josef.'

Charlotte looked up. The sight of Violette, a birch–pallid figure contrasted by the depthless sooty blackness of her hair, stirred her deeply, as it always did. 'Why, then?'

'Because I saw in her a web of pain and mistakes. Her whole soul is webbed down by bitterness and malice . . . and I wanted to tear it all out.'

Charlotte was still angry, and disinclined to listen. Her patience with Violette was wearing thin. 'This is just the thirst, Violette. It will find any tortuous route to trick you into satisfying it.'

'No. I keep telling you, I can see into people. I don't want to, I bloody well hate it! But when I see someone like Robyn, I have this urge . . . to tear her with my teeth. To suck out the poison, to make her see what a fool she's being.' A long pause. A dark Crystal Ring demon seemed to shine like a skeleton through the delicate fabric of Violette's body, as if she'd become translucent. The impression horrified Charlotte, left her strengthless and depressed. Violette said lightly, 'Obviously we're wasting each other's time with this conversation. Let's go back to the party.'

'Will you speak to Josef? Give him a chance, at least.'

'No, I won't,' Violette said imperiously. 'And I'd thank you to drop the subject. Don't ever try such a trick again! Now, come on. Karl will wonder where you are.'

For once, Charlotte had no inclination to prolong the argument. 'Yes, you're right,' she said coldly. She stood up, not wanting to look at Violette, nor to touch her. But as they walked towards the ballroom, the dancer stroked her arm with sharp fingernails.

'You didn't stop me feeding on Robyn; if the moment had been right, I would have done it there and then. I'll do it eventually. And when the time comes, Charlotte, I'll do it to you.'

Robyn was recovering a little, beginning to rationalize what had happened so that her mind could encompass it and dismiss it. A woman made a pass at me! Why am I so surprised? After all, I have a shrewd idea of why Alice never married and why she's so devoted to me, although she'd be mortified if she knew I'd guessed, poor puritan soul ... No, but it was the blatancy of it, and the fact of who she is. *Violette Lenoir!*

She stretched out her feet, leaning back into the ivy. I need a drink, she thought, a real one. I'll go back inside and find Josef in a minute ... but she remained where she was for at least fifteen minutes. God, what a strange evening!

I think I was willing to let her seduce me.

A sinking sensation, almost an ache, went through her at the thought. I've never thought of women in that way but, God, I'm so sick of men, anything would be better. Anything to put out this fire.

But I had the feeling that Violette didn't really want me. She wanted me to want *her*, just so she could reject and humiliate me. Was that the game she was playing?

Robyn's heart hardened. So, the great dancer has problems, has she? Well, Madame, you can just leave me out of them.

Bitterly amused, quite herself again, she rose and began to walk back towards the house. A tunnel of climbing roses led to a central pergola with a little fountain dancing in the centre. On the far side, blocking the path she wanted to take, stood a man she had never seen before.

She stopped, annoyed. It would look so obvious to retrace her steps. Besides, if he were a gentleman, he'd step aside and let her pass.

'Good evening,' she said, walking towards him.

'Good evening,' he responded. But he did not move, so she had to stop awkwardly in front of him.

'Excuse me, please.'

He only looked at her, eyes half-veiled. He was a little under six feet, no more than five inches taller than her – yet he seemed to be looking down on her from a great height. In the shadows, she could hardly see anything of his face. Only the hint of a firmly defined chin, an unsmiling, sculptural mouth, those disdainfully lowered lids. Dark, thick hair. Elegant bearing . . . another of the dancers?

Then the feeling hit her again, setting all her nerves aflame. He was too vivid, too overpowering. *This man was another like Karl and Charlotte and Violette.* But this encounter hit her the hardest, as if the others throughout the evening had only served to oversensitize her.

'Would you mind letting me past?' she said tightly.

'Forgive me, madam, but are you Mrs Roberta Stafford?' The voice was quiet, its strength coiled up; the accent very soft, with the faintest hint of Boston Irish. A neutral voice, belonging to a creature that blended with shadows.

'Yes, I am,' she said guardedly.

'I've been looking for you.'

'Well, I've been at the party all evening; I can't think why you didn't see me—'

He cut across her. 'I've brought some news. Bad news.'

Chilled, she felt a rush of irrational dread. 'What is it?'

'I regret to tell you that your ex-lover, Russell Booth, is dead. He took his own life, Mrs Stafford. He killed himself because of you.'

The garden tipped and slanted away beneath her.

When she came back to herself, she was on a wooden seat, still inside the pergola, with the stranger sitting beside her. He was holding her arm and his fingers felt like cold satin. 'Are you all right?' he asked.

'I never usually faint,' she said, drawing deep breaths. 'I don't know why . . .' It hadn't been the news itself. It had been his gentle, dark voice. It had been the stab of guilt, as if Death himself had come to point an accusing finger at her and say, *You killed him.*

'It's the shock,' he said. He was so sombre. A spirit from the shadow-world, unreal, yet as electrifying as the sun.

She pressed her fingers to her head, and reason began to reassert itself. 'Wait a minute,' she said. 'He couldn't possibly be dead. He lives here. If he had committed suicide, I hardly think his family would be holding a party, do you?'

'Perhaps they don't know how depressed he is. How much he is drinking. Because of you. Because you came here tonight.'

'So he isn't dead.'

'If he isn't dead, it's no thanks to you,' said the soft voice from hell. 'If he is – you must bear the responsibility.'

'This is crazy. Would you help me inside, please?' she said sharply. Perhaps if she could see him in electric light, with other people around – but he didn't move. She started to shiver. The silent, detached presence of death, faceless in his dark hood . . . she felt herself fading again, blood rushing sickly to her stomach. *I cannot be having this conversation with my own conscience because I don't possess one.*

Collecting herself, she said, 'Mr—' He volunteered no name, so she went on angrily, 'Sir, I'm terribly sorry to hear about Russell's problems, but I don't know why you've made a special effort to tell me. My friendship with him ended some weeks ago and I haven't been contact with him since. You have absolutely no right to make such insinuations!'

'I stated a fact. In his eyes, your callous usage of him has destroyed him.'

'How do you know?' She sat forward, gripping the edge of the seat. She was going to run for it, if her legs would bear her. 'Who precisely are you?'

'Only the messenger, Mrs Stafford.'

She could see through him. He was transparent. She could see the bench and the climbing roses through him!

Her head swam. Gasping, she shut her eyes.

When she opened them again, she was alone. Air stirred softly in the space where he'd been; ghost, figment of inchoate madness, or truly a hand from limbo groping for revenge.

Impossible.

Robyn stood up. Walking very briskly, as fast as she could without actually running, she gained the columned verandah. Great squares of blond light swam in her vision like a mirage. On the steps she missed her footing, and collapsed into Karl's arms.

CHAPTER EIGHT

PRAYERS AND CONFESSIONS

Cesare found John sitting at a table in his cell, his bald, scarred head bent over a book. Pierre was there too, slumped on a pallet as if he had lost all interest in living.

'The world in which you were living is a terrible place,' Cesare said gravely from the doorway. 'A sewer.'

'What?' Pierre looked up, his face skull-hollow and waxen. Candlelight gleamed horribly on its starved planes. His eyes were wetly bulging orbs, and his unwashed hair straggled in matted curls. Cesare regarded him with a mixture of pity and irritation.

'A sewer,' he repeated, 'infested by vermin who squabble without dignity to survive, who mate and breed without discrimination, maim and kill each other for entertainment and who worship depravity. And who think that in return for a stab of remorse and a prayer of repentance, God will forgive them.'

'This is news?' Pierre said wearily.

Cesare felt a touch of rage at his insolence, but he suppressed it. A leader must tolerate the petty faults of his followers, he thought. And his heart was full of emotion from everything he'd seen in the outside world. Brooding on it, he experienced dismay, frustration and sorrow, mingled with the thrill of ambition. *I can and I will do something about it!*

The sight of these two victims of Lilith suddenly filled him with sympathy rather than contempt. John, no longer the dapper, self-contained monk, was becoming demented and monstrous in appearance. His scalp would have healed and his hair grown back if he'd wished it; instead, he deliberately chose to make himself ugly, as if in penance. On the corner of the table sat Matthew's head, like a grisly candle welded there by its own wax. It was beginning to dessicate a little, the lips drawn back from the teeth in a ghastly grin, the fangs hanging loosely at their full length. Vampire flesh, it seemed, did not decay messily like that of humans, but turned slowly to dust. Yet John could not let his friend go.

To Cesare, this symbolized the way vampires would cling to the past unless he – the new prophet, dare he think it? – could turn their thoughts to the future.

'And you, Pierre,' Cesare murmured, walking to the pallet and looking down at him. 'Once so bold and cruel; now you cower here, afraid of your own shadow. It's pitiful.'

'Whose fault is that?' Pierre snarled. 'Yes, I'm scared!' He waved a hand at John. 'I spend time with vampires I hate, rather than be alone. I despise myself for it, but I can't help it. Violette's crippled me.' His eyes grew wilder, and his hands trembled like netted doves. 'I daren't go into the Crystal Ring because she's there; I see her eyes in the clouds, and her hair like a great black shadow above me. The strangling knot of her hair. Why am I so afraid? Why, why?'

He lurched forward and clung pleadingly to the front of Cesare's robe, but Cesare eased him gently back on to the pallet. 'Because she is the Enemy. I wasn't criticizing you, my brother. Don't be ashamed of your weakness; you have faced the greatest threat there is.'

'I have?' Pierre looked marginally less ashamed.

John, meanwhile, only stared at Cesare from dead eyes. He was speaking less and less as the days passed.

'When I look at you two and Matthew, I know this is only the beginning of her evil work,' said Cesare. 'I believe that the darkness of the Crystal Ring is Lilith's shadow falling between us and God. I believe it is her fault that we could not bring Matthew back to life.'

At that, John's eyes flared with a poisonous light, but he said nothing.

'Perhaps it was Kristian who protected us from her before,' Cesare went on, passion coming into his voice, 'but Kristian is gone, and we have to protect ourselves. But the Almighty has revealed His purpose to me; I am the one chosen to unleash the forces of heaven against her.'

Far from seeming impressed by this statement, Pierre groaned, '*Mon Dieu*,' and covered his face with his hands, muttering to himself.

'What are you saying?' Cesare snapped. He gripped Pierre's shoulder; Pierre tensed, his nerves apparently in rags. 'I can't hear you.'

One blue eye blazed up at him from the tangle of hair and fingers. In it, Cesare saw the cynical spirit of the atheist. Pierre, though, seemed to think better of arguing. 'Nothing, nothing. I don't care what you do. Dress this up as a religious crusade if that's the way you see it – only please, please, get rid of that damned woman! I see her in the corners when the candles go out. *Please*.'

Cesare let go, and smoothed the crumpled material of Pierre's shirt as if petting a dog. It was pleasing to see Pierre with all the blasphemous insolence knocked out of him. Very gratifying. Like a bud, a tiny change that heralded a brighter future.

'I'll crush her as I'd crush a wasp.' Cesare dropped a rounded hand on to Pierre's in benediction. 'Come and pray with me, my brothers. We should all pray together.'

Pierre shrank away, shaking his head.

'John?' Cesare held out his hand.

The other vampire rose without a word and came to Cesare, pausing only to glance back at Matthew's head. Pierre, too, stared at it with a horrified expression, as if to say, don't leave me alone with that thing! But as John and Cesare left, Pierre did not follow.

'Let him be,' said Cesare. 'I'll make a believer of him eventually.'

Cesare led John to Kristian's inner sanctum, the private cell tucked beside the meeting chamber which contained the ebony throne. Closing the outer and inner doors, he knelt down on the bare stone floor, pushing John down opposite him. This is now my sanctum, not Kristian's, he thought.

'Concentrate,' he whispered. 'Let your mind flow outwards

to God. This is our prayer for guidance; more than a prayer, a call to God's intercessors. A summoning!'

The chamber was lightless, but the vampire acuity, Cesare could see the red scabs of John's skull throbbing vividly, the raddled hollows of his face. 'This is blasphemy,' John whispered. 'We have no right to call on God's name. We'll be struck down for our presumption!'

'Are you still clinging to your old ways? You must find some pride in yourself, some courage! Listen; I never used to think for myself.' As Cesare spoke, tears began to flow down his cheeks. 'Kristian died to force us to think for ourselves! And I'm so happy.'

'Happy? When we're in hell? No, God has sent Lilith to finally destroy us all. We must submit ourselves to His will, not demand help!'

Cesare looked into the baleful eyes; he leaned forward and grasped John's shoulders. 'No, you're wrong! Very well; let this prayer be the proof. If the angels come and strike us down, then you'll be proved right. But if they answer us and help us, then you'll know that I am right! Do you agree?'

The swollen skull dropped in acquiescence.

'Good. Pray with me.'

Cesare let his vampire sight dim until the darkness was absolute. He drifted a little into the Crystal Ring, hovering between the two realms. As he did so, the flags beneath him seemed to soften, holding him like an ant in molasses. The sanctum became featureless, like the inside of an egg, flushing from black to deepest purple.

Cesare clasped his hands and began to pray silently. Very far above, he felt a cold black energy gathering, feeding him.

He thought, I could begin a new religion here and now. Kristian could be the vampires' Christ; the prophet murdered by his enemies only to live again. But there has been no resurrection . . .

He began to tremble. In truth, Cesare no longer wanted Kristian to be reborn. His own ego was growing too vigorously to tolerate the competition.

He chastised himself for such blasphemy.

A compromise, he thought, bowing his head. I will call on God to send a sign. If Kristian appears, I'll submit to His will and establish the Church of Kristian. But if not – dear Lord, send me guidance!

He thought of his vision in the chapel, when he'd seen the angel with the white wings and hair like flame. Yes, send me a holy messenger, a guardian angel. I am here only to do your will.

His lips began to move.

'Almighty God, Lord of All, Creator and Destroyer, hear me. In the name of Kristian our Father, I beg for guidance. I am thy servant, thy messenger, a thought in thy great mind. I beg thee, send forth thy thoughts as envoys to do thy will in the world . . .'

Something was happening. The purple glow flushed to gold above him.

'Oh, Kristian, beloved Father, send thy spirit to me, tell me how best to continue thy work. Appear, appear in God's name.'

The aureate light swelled to a sphere, and Cesare's heart swelled with it. John groaned, and began to tremble violently.

'God has heard us!' Cesare cried. John moaned loudly in terror and keeled over, face down, arms outstretched.

The light birthed a shape, a long glowing figure that dropped down to hover before Cesare's wondering eyes. A force pulsed from it, icily bright as God's wings. The force pushed Cesare out of the Ring and fully into the sanctum.

Inky air enfolded him but the figure was still there, its brightness filling the chamber. All detail was blurred by the yellow–diamond light.

Cesare pressed his hands to his chest. He was overawed, but it seemed crucial to address this spectral being as an equal.

'Kristian?' he whispered, half in dread.

'No, not Kristian,' said a voice within the light. 'I am your guide, your holy messenger, your sword of flame.'

Amazement and wonder flooded through Cesare. 'God be praised! Speak, being, tell us who you are!'

'My name is Simon.' The light dissipated to reveal, nor an angel, but a strongly built, blond man in modern clothes; a white shirt, fawn-coloured trousers. But his eyes contained the sun, and he was as golden as Cesare was colourless. 'Though I have sometimes been called Senoy.'

And to Cesare's astonishment – for neither he nor John were accustomed to displays of physical affection – this glowing creature gathered them both in his arms and hugged them hard to his chest.

'God be praised, indeed,' Simon-Senoy whispered, biting into Cesare's neck.

Simon had felt the call as he wandered aimlessly through the Crystal Ring, brooding on his losses and failures.

To be needed, he was thinking, that's the essence.

Fyodor and Rasmila keep begging me to take them back but they're children, they need a nursemaid, not a soldier of God. And Sebastian never needed me, which hurts, but perhaps it's as well; he is one on his own and I need a pair in order to re-create the magic trinity.

Yes. The alchemy of three.

He thought of Karl again.

I need . . .

He floated in silence, wrapped in violet clouds, webbed by the lines of magnetism that shimmered in translucent rainbow ribbons all around him. He watched the knot of darkness far above him, perceiving it as a hole through which all the energy and beauty of the Ring was slowly leaking away.

Panic and despair flashed through him, and were gone. His frigid tranquillity returned.

And then he felt the pull. The magnetic lines tautened and thrummed like harp strings. The ether shuddered with sound-waves. He felt his skin turn hot, and looking at his hands he saw that they were glowing, as they had used to when he was God's envoy.

Simon gasped, and stared at his hands. God, dear God, can it be? Thank you, thank you!

He felt his power returning. Not all of it, no great blaze of ineffable light; just enough to prove that he was still an angel,

that someone on earth needed him and had therefore empowered him.

And he fell with the pull, diving and swooping towards the
source as if winged; heard the touching words of prayer, bathed
in them as if in a rain of honey; slipped softly to earth to face
the ones who had summoned him.

And it was partly an act, his manifestation, for his new-born
strength was still fragile; but it was enough to convince them
that he was the answer to their prayers. A sword of God to slay
Lilith.

Because someone had finally realized what Lilith was, seen
the need to destroy her, called for Simon's help at last! And he
was so grateful that he could not help but embrace them in his
joy.

When Simon stood back to look at them at last, he was not
particularly enraptured by what he saw; a mouse-blond choirboy
with a visionary light in his eyes, and a mutilated little man who
resembled some mediaeval woodcut of Satan. No beauty here.
But there was *something*, a feeling of inchoate power that Simon
found incredibly exciting. So he hugged them and bit their
throats and swallowed their blood in ecstatic greeting.

Because it was better than nothing. It was a start, at least.

The day after the party, Robyn walked down to the Public
Garden and sat under the willows by the lagoon. The gold-leaf
dome of the State House glinted distantly through the trees,
bright against an overcast sky. She wished the sun would come
out; the weather was so capricious in early June, and could
change from chilly to hot in an hour. But the park was always
green and lush and enveloping; the dogwoods laden with
blossom, the leaves of the purple beeches and the maidenhair
trees shimmering all around her.

Robyn watched the swan boats circling endlessly around the
small lake. Round and round they went in slow, genteel
procession, each with a man at the stern pedalling stoically
between the wings of a carved white swan, families seated in

rows on the benches, children throwing bread to the ducks. She stared at the boats until she almost hypnotized herself.

She was alone. She'd put off Harold, invitations to lunch, everything, saying she felt unwell. It wasn't a lie. She was in a state of shock. All she wanted was to be on her own to think.

When Karl had caught her on the terrace, she'd put on a show of light-heartedness to disguise the state she was in; oh, how foolish of me to miss the step, no harm done, how lucky you were there ... But he'd known there was something wrong. She could see it in his eyes. God, Karl's eyes ... too much like the eyes of the stranger in the garden for comfort. He and Charlotte had been solicitous, rather as if they feared she'd been in some kind of danger. Robyn, however, had said nothing about Violette or the stranger. None of their business, really. She only wondered why they were so concerned.

Josef hadn't seemed himself, either; preoccupied, he had insisted on leaving the party early. So Robyn had asked Wilkes to drive him back to his hotel, but Josef wouldn't say what was wrong; only that he was tired.

Now she wished that she had dispensed with social niceties and asked Karl and Charlotte directly, 'What exactly is going on here?'

At the time, though, it had been impossible. Their magnetism had struck her harder than ever. Karl was lovely; it pained her to admit it, but it was true. So why, when he and Charlotte had been so charming and kind, had she felt so uneasy with them?

Having seen Josef safely to his room, she'd gone home and to bed. No chance of sleeping, though. In the middle of the night, she'd gone into Alice's room and woken her up.

'I think I met a ghost last night,' Robyn had said. 'Or if not a ghost, I don't know what you'd call him. An angel of death, maybe. He told me that Russell was going to commit suicide over me. Or already had.'

Alice had sat up in bed, only half-awake. 'You woke me up to tell me this?'

'Didn't you hear what I said?' And she told her bemused companion everything.

'But, madam, if he had killed himself, they would hardly have been holding a party, would they?'

Robyn exhaled, all the tension leaving her. 'That's what I said. I know what it was; his goddamned brothers playing some kind of sick joke on me. Funny thing is, I never took any of that family for having a sense of humour.'

Later, while Robyn had been eating breakfast, Alice had gone out to visit a friend. She'd returned within minutes, looking stunned.

'I just met the housekeeper from the house next door to the Booths. She told me that the family found Russell dead in his study first thing this morning . . .'

Now Robyn sat by the lake, her stomach in a cold knot. The young man's death, however tragic, didn't really touch her heart, but the eeriness of last night's encounter persisted.

Maybe I imagined him after all. Some sort of ghastly premonition.

It was only a few minutes' walk from the Public Garden to Josef's hotel on Tremont Street, but she didn't feel like seeing anyone. She had a feeling that even if she asked him outright, 'Who are your strange friends?' he wouldn't give a straight answer.

As she sat there, watching people enjoying themselves on the boats, she became aware of a shadow in the corner of her eye. He appeared as suddenly as he had vanished; a dark figure in a black overcoat, his face pale against the material. He was standing beside the bench, hands in his pockets, silent as the air.

Robyn looked at him in a mixture of shock and relief. Her heart was pounding. *So I didn't imagine him, and he wasn't a ghost!*

'Good afternoon, Mrs Stafford,' he said, not looking at her.

'Good afternoon — I'm afraid I don't recall you telling me your name,' she said, with all the poise she could gather. She would not let him see he'd unsettled her; she would not give any man that power.

'I am Sebastian Pierse,' he said, 'and I owe you an apology.'

His words, spoken in a low, contrite tone, took her aback. She studied his profile and saw a high, curved cheekbone, well-shaped nose and jaw, long black lashes. Features a sculptor might have moulded with idealistic fingers – but they told her nothing about his character. The distant look in his eyes could have been arrogance, yet she felt it was not. It was something subtler and darker.

She said, 'Yes, I think perhaps you do.'

But he only stood there, watching the swan boats drift by, as if he were transfixed. Eventually she said, 'Why don't you sit down, Mr Pierse?'

'Because I like to wait until I have been invited.' He walked round to the empty space beside her, inclining his head to her as he turned; a movement as effortless as the dancer's, with all everyday awkwardness planed away. As he sat down and half-turned towards her with one arm on the back of the bench, she saw him clearly for the first time.

'It was unforgivable of me to have approached you without warning,' he said. Her eyes flicked discreetly over him. Difficult to tell his age; he could have been anything between twenty-five and forty, and a world away from the brash, scrubbed good looks of American men who were considered handsome. His was an old-world beauty, chiselled but not polished, the fair skin radiant with a particularly Celtic translucency. Despite his pallor, though, he seemed all shadows. His hair – darkest brown, soft, formless and too long – shaded his forehead. Dense black eyebrows and lashes gave his eyes an alluring depth. The irises were hazel-green; shaded woodland pools. Shadows etched his cheeks and lips.

'You must understand,' he went on, 'I was upset about my friend's death. That is no excuse—'

'No, it isn't,' Robyn said coolly. 'You were extremely rude, and I most certainly did not deserve the insinuations you made.'

'I know. I'm sorry.' The lulling timbre of his voice inclined her to forgive him.

'Was he already dead when you came to me?'

'Yes.'

'How did you know before anyone else?'

'Others knew,' he said. 'They didn't want to distress the party guests by announcing it, I imagine.'

This statement did not quite ring true to Robyn, but she had no grounds to accuse him of lying. She asked, 'Did you know Russell very well?'

'As I said, he was a friend. I know nothing about you, Mrs Stafford, except what he told me.'

'And what did he tell you?'

'That without you, he had no reason to live.'

His head was turned slightly away from her, but he was looking sideways into her eyes; aware of her, but inwardly distracted. Certainly not attempting to flirt with her. She felt both irritated and intrigued.

He was quite beautiful, in his understated way, like a creature of another race, another time. Not unlike Karl ... different, but with the same ability to confuse and captivate—

Oh, no, she told herself firmly. He won't get me like that. I'm immune.

'Look, Mr Pierse, I know you're upset by Russell's death. So am I. I was fond of him' – half-truths slid out with equal ease – 'but our relationship had no future. He was so young. I was hardly his parents' ideal daughter-in-law; it would have ruined his life if we'd married. I had to end it, for his sake. I knew he was upset but I thought he'd get over it; I never thought he'd go to such lengths.'

Sebastian sat forward, looking straight at her. 'Would you have acted any differently, if you'd known how desperate he was?'

'Why should I?' A smile iced her lips. 'His threatening suicide would have made our liaison no more feasible. I have a distinct aversion to emotional blackmail.'

'Quite so. All the same ...' As he spoke, she received the impression that Sebastian Pierse actually did not give a damn about his so-called 'friend'. She thought, *who the hell are you?* 'All the same, I can quite see why he felt as he did.'

This remark took her completely by surprise. It wasn't that she was unused to such compliments; it was that she hadn't expected it from someone who seemed so aloof. 'I beg your pardon?'

'Now I've compounded the sin,' he said. 'Mrs Stafford, would you consider forgiving me over dinner?'

His lovely eyes were suddenly all over her, absorbing her. Robyn felt a dart of triumph. It seemed she'd misread him. He was no phantom, only a man, and he was falling for her after all, so predictably, like all the others.

In that moment, an intention uncoiled delightfully inside her, like the tongue of a snake. I've got him, she thought. And he thinks it's so easy. But I'll have him, and I'll make him suffer, and I'll make him pay for thinking he can manipulate me.

'I don't know that I should. I hardly know you.'

'All friendships have to begin somewhere. Please,' he said with endearing sincerity, 'let me make amends.'

'Well ... all right.' She spoke with careful indifference, letting her eyelids fall. Then she looked up, with that innocent, enticing look that made idiots of most males. 'If you really think we have anything to discuss.'

'As long as we've laid Russell to rest, we can begin again with anything in the world.' He sounded positively tender. 'Anything you desire.'

Alone in his hotel room, Josef felt at home. The solitude of a plain, comfortable room, a lamp pooling yellow light on the desk, an open book; all pleasantly familiar. It was late, but it was his habit to read long into the night. He sat in his shirt-sleeves, reading about the long-haired demoness of the night, Lilith.

And he felt certain that Charlotte would visit him tonight.

He had not seen her since the previous night at the party, when she'd admitted that Violette had been talking to Robyn in the garden.

'Nothing happened,' Charlotte had said, trying desperately to reassure him. 'And I've told Violette to leave her alone.'

'Will she do as you say?'

'Yes. She has no reason to attack Robyn or you, she doesn't take victims indiscriminately. Robyn isn't in danger.'

But Josef was not reassured. It had been so close! To think of

Robyn in the darkness with that vampiress, all unsuspecting . . . it chilled him to the bone. While Charlotte had tried to reassure him, the fact that she was clearly mortified only underlined how dangerous she felt Violette to be.

His neck ached. He pinched the skin between his eyebrows. *If anything happens to Robyn, if Karl or Violette touch her, it will be my fault! God, how did I get into this?*

Everything in the literature he'd gathered portrayed Lilith as an uncontrollable, negative force. The dark side of the psyche. How could a creature as wild as Lilith be contained, except by destruction? The word of God or a stake through the heart. And Josef, despite everything, still believed in God and the opposing power of evil.

He was waiting for Charlotte to arrive, so that he could express his fears and make sure of keeping his niece out of danger. She always arrived soundlessly from nowhere; he should be used to it by now, but it was still a shock when the moment came. The spidery realization that he was no longer alone.

He could feel her standing behind him, a presence more tangible than a ghost. He caught the faintest scent of perfume, the barely audible tread of a shoe on the carpet.

Without looking round, he drew in a controlled breath and released the tension that had gathered in his shoulders. *I'm not nervous,* he reminded himself. *I will be nonchalant.*

'*Guten Abend*, my dear,' he said warmly. 'I hoped you would come.'

'I'll bet you did.'

The voice was not Charlotte's. It was low, sharply accented, and cutting as glass.

He twisted round, one arm gripping the back of his chair. The slight figure standing at the foot of the bed was Charlotte's opposite. A bright young creature fresh from a party, she could have been, dressed in sparkling black and crimson, but her face belied that impression. It was a bleached heart framed by short hair under a black, feathered bandeau, beauty deformed by the livid hunger that blackened her eyes. Dark red roses, the same colour as her hair, trailing over the shoulder of her dress, seemed suggestive of congealed blood and sweetly musky decay.

He'd never seen her before, but she reminded him of Karl. Did Karl have a sister, another member of the dark clan?

Gripping the chair to steady his trembling hands, he said, 'Can I be of some assistance, Frau——?'

'Oh, you are cool, aren't you, Herr Stern?' She came towards him, and before he could stand up, she had somehow twined herself around him and was sitting on his knee. Her hands caged his neck, thumbs on his windpipe. God, how cold she was! When Charlotte had touched him her hands had sometimes felt warm, sometimes cool, but this creature felt like iced wax.

And she seemed heavy for someone so slender, her thighs like stone bars across his. A demanding weight, leeching his warmth.

'What is this?' Josef whispered.

'I think you know, vampire-lover.' Her smile was a parody of tenderness. She pulled off his spectacles and threw them on to the desk. Because she was so close to him, her face seemed to come into clearer focus and he sat staring at her in flat terror and fascination. So flawless, the skin, so radiant. The eyes, drowsily luminous and dark as blood-drops . . . pupils widening, sucking at him. And her mouth, full and softly glistening. When she spoke, he glimpsed her teeth and the red tip of her tongue. 'I thought you were a little old for Charlotte . . . but no.' Her fingers travelled over his cheeks and forehead, burning him with trails of frost, and raked through his hair. 'You are very attractive, old man, like a magus with your silver hair and troubled eyes. You've seen a lot of life, haven't you? Too much. And now you're tired. So tired.'

She was hypnotizing him, he knew, but he couldn't stop her. A dream state fell on him, but the edges meshed into nightmare. He wanted to move but his body was anchored.

Suddenly she twisted round and slammed her hand down on the book, so hard that he jumped.

'What do you know about her?' the vampire demanded. One moment seductress, the next interrogator.

'Who?'

'Lilith, of course. Otherwise known as our mad genius Violette.'

'Only what is in the book. Take it, read it for yourself.'

She turned back to him, enveloping him again. 'Well, it doesn't matter. You'll tell me eventually, if there's anything to tell. Do you love Charlotte?'

He couldn't hold back the truth. 'Yes.'

'And does she do this to you?' With her left hand, the vampire began to break the buttons from his shirt, slicing through the thread with her fingernail. And now her hand was exploring his ribs, sliding down over his lean abdomen, stealing the warmth in its path. Her lips touched his cheek, travelling in light kisses towards his mouth.

Josef's hands came forward to grasp her hips. He couldn't help it. He felt heat building in his loins. Fear flowed through him with the sourness of regret as he realized what a fool he'd been, welcoming Charlotte into his life to prove his open-mindedness; to say, 'See how courageous and knowing I am, not like the superstitious fools all around us!' Because, even though Charlotte had always been gentle and kind to him, she was still a vampire. She had to restrain her hungers to spare him. And this fiend who now devoured him was the dark side of the same coin. She was the danger he'd refused to acknowledge.

And still he welcomed the pressure of her lips on his as their mouths parted in a mutual 'O' of lust, their tongues meeting, tasting—

She tasted of blood.

Ending the kiss, she whispered into his ear, her breath making him shiver. 'You want me, don't you?'

Josef nodded, eyes closed, mouth awash with fear and desire.

'On the bed or here on the chair?' Her matter-of-fact crudeness was in itself a mockery of human behaviour.

Drugged now by the aching need for release, he tried to say, 'The bed,' to maintain at least that semblance of decorum, but before he could speak she swung one leg across to straddle him, her dress ruching around her thighs. Her hands worked at his trouser buttons. Then she slid forward and he felt the naked heat of her, pressing hard against his engorged flesh.

He groaned. The ache and the heaviness of blood were unbearable.

'You want me,' she whispered into his neck, 'even though you know what will happen.' And she laughed, a ripple of malice.

'Why are you doing this?'

'Because Charlotte values you. It pleases me to destroy what others value.' As she spoke she lifted herself on to him, sheathing him in her moist, tight flesh. She wasn't cold there but hot, burning. The pulsing rhythm began and his head fell back. Couldn't see, couldn't think. Only this excruciating ecstasy, building and building, thrusting up through webs of terror.

Josef felt her tear his shirt off his shoulders. Her nails ripped slits in his chest, drawing blood. The blood ran down; she licked it away. Then she began to bite him, again and again, bruising him but not breaking the skin; pausing now and then to lap at the nail wounds.

He cried out with pain. Heavy agony twisting tighter—

His climax was like an artery bursting. He felt as if he were pouring blood inside her. Turning dizzy, he slumped back, trying to push her away with strengthless hands. He couldn't breathe.

But he was lost under the fervid bud of her mouth, as it nipped and bruised its way towards his neck. She was like a lush jungle vine entwining him, a flesh-consuming, purple-tongued flower scented with musk and blood.

'Well, that was not your best effort, was it?' Her voice shuddered with her own excitement. His eyes came open and met her gaze. Her pupils were sightless with deadly thirst, her mouth open and the canine teeth lengthening as he watched. They locked into place with a ghastly faint *click*. 'Relax,' she said sarcastically. 'I'm not going to kill you.'

Let it end. Why does she hesitate?

In a final peak of horror, he knew that it was not his throat she wanted. Instead she slid off his lap and knelt between his feet. 'You should have remembered,' she hissed, 'to attend to my pleasure before your own. One chance only.'

The vermilion mouth with its ivory daggers came lancing down. Blackness exploded around him like the wings of a thousand crows.

Violette haunted the alley behind the hotel as if she were a stray cat at the kitchen door. She felt restless to the point of distress. The thirst again, the damned thirst.

Three hours ago, she had been a swan queen commanding a stage. Now here she was, huddled in a black coat and a concealing deep-crowned hat, pacing the backstreets like a vagrant alcoholic.

That's what I am, she thought. An addict.

If the audience could only see me now.

I'll have to do it. Take a human. I could go to Robyn . . . no, no, not yet. It will have to be a stranger.

Or I could resist it. Not do it at all . . . until my control breaks and I take someone at random, oh yes, my male principal perhaps, or another of my poor girls! No. She bit her lip and the tang of her own blood tormented her beyond endurance.

Do I have to go through this every night, *every* night to the end of the world? Why can't I be like Karl and Charlotte? Just – do it.

Or . . . or feed on other vampires. It isn't the same and it isn't enough – but it's better than nothing, better than this agony.

She looked up at the long rows of windows. Most were dark, but a few showed strips of light between the curtains. She knew which room Josef was in.

Violette had been furious with Charlotte for bringing Josef, a mortal, to study her like a zoologist cataloguing a new species. But later, her anger had faded.

What do I know, after all? I feel Lilith inside me like the raging cruelty of nature. The lioness bearing down the weakest quarry. The cuckoo pushing babies from the nest. Nestlings left to die like little children caught in wars. And through her I remember things that could not possibly have happened. I remember them like dreams with gaping holes where the cold gales of the Crystal Ring rush through.

I know nothing about who I really am. But perhaps Josef does know. Perhaps he has a wisdom like Lancelyn ... and even though Lilith's instinct is to mock and tear up the wisdom of men, I think that I should for once swallow her pride and ask for help.

She knew that Charlotte and Karl were not far away. They had been out to hunt and were returning to the hotel; she could sense them, faint but clear, drawing steadily closer. A few minutes before they arrived; she had time to see Josef. Not to harm him. Only to talk.

She entered the Crystal Ring and floated through the steel-grey layers that were the kitchens, the foyer, stairs and corridors. The humans she passed were shimmering hairpins of fire, oblivious to her.

As she approached Josef's room, she knew something was wrong. There was a warping of the atmosphere, a heat haze of fear and excitement. As she reached the door, the scent of shed blood uncoiled to torment her and her thirst responded, drawing her fangs to their full length against her will.

Someone has reached Josef before me!

The door dissolved, letting her through. As she snapped into the real world, she saw them; the human on the chair, his head back, hair dishevelled, face contorted – and the vampire straddling him. She was dressed in blood-colours, her hair like dark blood, red stains drying on her hands.

Ilona. Violette heard her own father's voice from years past, *'She was a Lamia ... hair the colour of blood ...'* Remembered the horrible mutilation that he'd exposed to her time and again in his pathetic madness, the mutilation that in the end had helped to destroy not only his life, but her mother's and her own. At the time, she'd thought her father was out of his mind. It was only through meeting Charlotte, years later, that she came to understand that he hadn't been mad, that he had really been the victim of a vampire. And that his attacker had been Ilona.

As Ilona slid off Josef's knee and lowered her savage mouth towards his groin, Violette was already swooping down on her. In an ecstasy of rage, she seized Ilona and ripped her bodily off her victim.

Josef slumped to the floor, unconscious.

Ilona twisted round, eyes blazing, to see who'd thwarted her. 'Oh, you!' she spat. Her hands whipped out in attack, but Violette was faster. Catching Ilona's wrists, she pulled the woman towards her, regardless of her furious struggling.

Ilona did not even try to escape into the Crystal Ring. It seemed she preferred to fight. But Violette would only have gone with her if she'd tried; no one could escape the wings and claws of Lilith, not even Karl's daughter.

Violette's hunger was urgent, but Ilona, too, needed to satisfy the thirst she'd been about to unleash on her victim. Suddenly she jerked a hand free and seized Violette's hair, pulling hard to keep the dancer's mouth away from her throat. They were both strong, both ruthless. There was even a thread of sadistic delight in their conflict.

Violette broke Ilona's grip and her mouth clamped to Ilona's neck as if magnetized. How sweet the firm body felt against hers, taut with emotion. Need overwhelmed Violette and she sank her fangs. Ilona went rigid. The blood was dense, a little sour but in a delicious way, like crisp apples. Pleasure throbbed through Violette from throat to loins.

Relief. Release, at last.

Ilona was spitting imprecations in her ear. 'You – bloody – witch!'

And she broke free with an explosion of strength. From the corner of her eye, Violette saw Josef on the floor, huddled up and groaning. There was blood all over his shoulders and torn shirt, human blood, which she still needed, despite the draught she'd taken from Ilona's veins. And the need, which she loathed, incensed her beyond reason.

'What did you call me?' Violette said thinly. She advanced on Ilona who was backing away, her face feral.

'You heard.' Ilona clawed at the wound in her throat. 'How dare you touch me!'

'How dare you hurt *him*?' Violette pointed at Josef. 'He was mine.'

Ilona dodged the lash of her hands. 'What is this, a new rule that we must put our names down for victims? Are you making the rules now, Madame?'

Ilona was fast, but Violette surpassed her. She grabbed the bony shoulders and began to bite Ilona hard, anywhere she could reach; face, neck, shoulders, arms. Ilona shrank away, mad with pain, defending now instead of attacking. Violette flung her down and pinned her to the floor, spattering the carpet with blood. 'This isn't for Josef. It's for my father.'

The impudent face glared into hers, indignation thrusting through her pain. 'Not your bloody father again! Haven't you got over it yet? For God's sake, you're a vampire now! You would do the same thing to him yourself!'

Violette gripped her arm and jerked her back on to her feet. For the first time, Ilona began to look truly scared. 'Look to yourself, before you talk of fathers. I can see into your heart, Ilona, though I've no wish to look into such a foul pit.'

And she struck Ilona's face, hard. Ilona reeled away but Violette followed her, striking her again and again. 'Why don't you fly away into the Crystal Ring?'

'I can't, damn you! Stop it, leave me alone!'

But Violette-Lilith, caught up in the dark ritual of vengeance, could not stop. She pursued Ilona round and round the room in a cruel dance, blows becoming slashes. She tore Ilona's dress and broke her long necklaces, scattering beads everywhere, and gouged wounds all over her back and chest. When Ilona's cries turned from protestations to pleas for mercy, Violette finally ran her up against the wardrobe and held her there, nails sinking deep into the flesh of her arms.

'You bastard, you bitch,' Ilona gasped, almost beyond speech. 'Pierre was right. I'll never forget this.'

'No, you won't. You hated Karl for making you into a vampire; do you want your existence to end now? Because I can do it, I can snap your spine and take your charming head off, and it will all be over. So, do you want to die?'

'No. No.' Blank terror in her face.

'How surprising.' And Violette opened her mouth on Ilona's soft neck, sucking and tasting the skin. Thrusting her fangs slow and deep into a vein she drew hard, working her tongue to increase the flow and keep the wound from healing too fast.

She was drifting away on the shadowy flow. This victory was quite empty, actually. It meant nothing at all. There was something above her she couldn't quite grasp, a mass of darkness floating in the Crystal Ring that also seemed to be a house with blind windows and locked doors . . .

The hands falling on her shoulders came as a massive sensory shock. Someone lifted her, tearing her off her prey as she'd torn Ilona off Josef. She'd been too deep in trance to sense the danger, and for a moment she could do nothing to defend herself. The hands, transmitting rage as deep as her own had been, were dragging her back and turning her round, pincer-hard in her flesh.

And she found herself looking into Karl's face. His anger, cold and ferocious, was terrifying; she'd never seen such a look in his eyes before. In her vulnerable state, Violette feared him; and for that, she hated him.

'Leave my daughter alone,' Karl said quietly.

Charlotte was behind Karl, staring at Violette. She looked shaken, but said nothing. Instead she went to Josef and dropped to her knees beside him, her gilded-bronze head bent in concern; more like a daughter than a vampire.

Ilona was leaning back against the wardrobe, her face lime-white. Ragged wounds oozed all over her shoulders and arms. Her sweet neck, bent to one side, was jewelled with blood.

'The protective father,' Violette said wearily. Her brief fear evaporated, and Lilith's sour rage stirred again.

His fingers tightened. 'What have you done to her?'

'Ask her what she was going to do to Josef.'

'As if you care about him,' Karl said grimly. He seemed very controlled; although he looked furious, Violette felt in no physical danger from him.

So it was to her astonished horror that he bared his fangs without warning and lunged at her throat.

Charlotte cried, 'Karl, don't!'

Violette sprang to life, broke Karl's grip and thrust him away. Lilith's strength again; she knocked him half-way across the room. There was a moment of stasis, black and distorted. Violette surveyed them through a glass pane of alienation. Karl, holding on to the chair that had arrested his fall; Charlotte, hovering a few feet away, not knowing which of them to protect. Poor Charlotte, she thought, having to watch her loved ones trying to destroy each other. Ilona, struggling like a broken-winged bird; and Josef, curled around his anguish and shame. How wretched it all seemed. How ghastly.

Even Karl is not physically stronger than Lilith, she thought. Perhaps no one is. And this gives me no pleasure at all. It is meaningless.

Half of her wanted to flee, to leave them to this tortuous drama; but because it meant nothing, she stayed, held by their unearthly stares like a moth in torch-beams.

Then Karl circled her, as if giving a wide berth to a snake, and gathered Ilona in his arms. Violette heard her whisper, 'Get off me!' and the remark brought a cold smile to his lips.

But Ilona lacked the physical strength to resist Karl's embrace. As he put an arm under her shoulders to hold her up, Charlotte spoke with remarkable self-possession. 'You'd better take her out of here, Karl. I'll look after Josef.'

'And Violette?' No inflexion in his voice, but he gave Violette a look of wintry contempt she would never forget. All her own emotions withered to grey stillness. She loathed herself.

'And Violette,' Charlotte said firmly. 'She won't hurt me.'

Charlotte was so angry both with Violette and Ilona that she could barely speak as she helped Josef into bed. He stumbled as he went, clutching his torn clothes around him with both hands. His face was white. He would not meet her eyes.

'Are you all right?' Charlotte asked gently.

'Yes. Yes. She took no blood.' Lying back on the pillow, Josef closed his eyes, pain ploughing his forehead. 'Not much, at least.'

'I'll send for a doctor,' she said, looking at the scratches and wounds all over his chest. The punctures made by a vampire's fangs healed quickly, but Ilona had made most of these with her nails.

'No!' he exclaimed. 'No doctor, please.'

'But some of these might need stitching.'

'And how in God's name am I going to explain how I got them?' He shuddered. 'She – she did not – Violette stopped her before she – before it was any worse – Oh, my dear, I am so sorry.'

'Whatever for?' Seeing his distress, however, and knowing Ilona's habits, she could guess what had happened. Dismay washed through her. Ilona liked to seduce, then to drink; and although Charlotte could not rationally hold Josef to blame, she couldn't suppress a touch of disappointment at him for not resisting. She'd idealized him, but he was only human. 'No, it's my fault, Josef. I should never have put you in this danger. I meant you no harm, but one vampire draws others.' She tried to touch his forehead, but he jerked away.

'Don't touch me,' he said.

'Why not?'

'Because I'm too ashamed of what happened,' he said hoarsely. 'Too ashamed.'

'Do you want me to send for Robyn?'

'No! Don't say a word to her, she must never know!'

'But you must have these wounds dressed, and if you won't have the doctor or Robyn, there's only me.'

He turned away from her, folding up around his pain. 'I know you mean well, but leave me alone, please.'

Sighing, Charlotte left him and went to Violette. The dancer was sitting in an armchair, legs crossed, one foot pointing and flexing in the air. Extraordinary that she would switch from violence to repose so quickly.

'Is it true?' Charlotte said. 'Did you save Josef from Ilona?'

The vivid blue-violet eyes came into focus. She seemed more than ever a stranger. 'I was saving my father,' she said.

Charlotte caught her breath. She'd thought that Ilona had only intended to take Josef's blood. God, she thought, I should have known! 'You mean she—'

'I caught her about to do what she did to my father, yes. The same mutilation. I had a crazed idea that if I saved Josef I'd somehow save my own father. As if I could turn back time and prevent the trauma that ruined our lives. That's why I went crazy with her.'

'Were you going to kill her?'

'I was tempted.' Violette opened her long, expressive hands. 'I threatened her.'

Charlotte put her hands to her face. 'Oh God, Karl would have despised you for all time!'

'I think he does, anyway. I don't suppose he'll ever forgive me, but I don't really care.'

'Don't you?' Charlotte flared. 'I can't bear this. You're both impossible! You don't give a damn for the effect this has on *me*!' When Violette made no reply, she continued less heatedly, 'He wanted to help you. Now you've made two more enemies, Karl and Ilona, when you might have had two friends.'

'Oh, should I just have left Ilona to it?' Violette said frostily. 'Can you not understand the reason for my anger?'

'Of course, but Ilona is still Karl's daughter! He wasn't going to stand by and say, "She deserves it." God knows, it's hard to feel any sympathy for her – but how can I feel any for you, when I witnessed what you were doing to her? And if you and Karl go on fighting, it will kill me.'

The lovely eyes widened. 'Tell *him*.'

'I'm telling you. I know that even Karl has no power over you. So if you ever do anything to hurt him—'

'He attacked me, Charlotte! I wouldn't kill him, for your sake – and how could I really harm him otherwise?'

'You change people.'

'Anything I've done to Ilona can only be an improvement, then.'

There was a silence. Violette turned away. She was beautiful in the half-light, the quintessential ballerina in black. Charlotte still worshipped her, even while she felt like strangling her. And feared her, always.

'What were you doing here, anyway? Hoping to destroy Josef, whose only crime was to trust me?'

Violette's eyes and voice softened. She looked down. 'I came to talk to him. To see if he really could tell me . . . what I am.'

'Leave me alone. Leave me alone!' Ilona repeated the words fiercely as Karl helped her along the corridor to his and Charlotte's suite. But she uttered the words as if saying a rosary, and she was trembling and boneless in his arms.

A short man with round glasses emerged from a room, stopped and stared at them. Karl cursed; he'd wanted no witnesses to his daughter's distress. He met the man's eyes; the man gazed back mindlessly for a moment. Then a change, a dreadful realization, came over the man's face. Turning white, he gagged as if his heart had stopped, and stumbled back into his room. And Karl gained the door of the suite with no further intrusions.

Vampires often fed on one another. It was an act that could express anything from love to domination. It could be a divine exchange or a savage violation. It seemed to Karl, though, that Ilona had been brought to this state by something more than blood-loss.

In the room, he let her down on to the bed and she sat on the edge, arms folded tautly across her knees, her face set. Karl put no lights on. The room seemed cavernous in darkness, his daughter's arms and shoulders rimmed by a fragile pearly glow. Karl found a towelling bathrobe and draped it round her. Her wounds, though ghastly, were healing fast.

Despite the state she was in, he felt sudden anger. Decades of pain they'd caused each other. Always, always this implacable conflict between them. Every time he thought it was over, it flared up again.

He sat down beside her, drawing his anger down to a cold thread. 'Why didn't you let us know you were here?' he asked, falling into the *Wienerisch* dialect of the last century; a language they seldom used these days, even with each other. A rare intimacy. 'Why are you always doing this?'

'Doing what?' Her words escaped through a knot of pain.

'Following us. Saying nothing. Destroying people just to hurt us.'

She scraped her teeth, fangs retracted, over her lower lip. 'You know why.'

Karl placed his hand on her cheek and made her face him. He tested the texture of her cheek with a light stroke of his thumb, looked into her eyes. All her cruel spirit seemed quenched; he saw fear, confusion, fleeting thoughts dwindling to points of fire in an abyss. The revelation shook him. He hated what she'd become after he'd transformed her – but seeing her like this was almost worse.

'Did she take much blood?'

'Enough, thank you, *Herr Doktor*,' she said. He offered her his wrist; she stared at the tender flesh, then turned her head aside. 'I don't want yours.'

'But you need it.'

'Not from you. Why don't you just—'

'Leave you?' He spoke coolly. She could not know the depth of pain she inflicted by refusing his help. One whip-cut on another, down the years. 'No. Not until you tell me what Violette has done to you.'

'Isn't it obvious?' she snapped.

'I mean mentally.'

Ilona shuddered. Her arms shook like white ropes under some dreadful tension. 'You know why I have to torment you.' Her self-control seemed to give way under a great weight of water. Karl realized, almost with horror, that he had never seen her cry since she'd been a child. Never, until now. As she leaned into him, pressing her forehead into his shoulder, he held her as if she were a stranger. As if some terrible contagion would soak into him with her tears. 'You took my life from me. I wanted my husband, I wanted my child. You took them away from me. You even took Kristian away! You wanted me to be a vampire, so that is exactly what I became.'

'But, Ilona,' he said gently, after a moment, 'you had no child.'

'But I would have done. I was pregnant when you took me

away. The transformation killed it, of course. *You* killed it.' And as she spoke she collapsed against him, sobs convulsing her like dying breaths. Karl's hand played absently with her hair. He felt numb, the revelation a distant thorn-prick.

'You never told me.' His voice was hollow.

'I never meant to. I told Charlotte once, to explain why I hated you so much, and made her swear not to tell you.'

'Charlotte knew?' The thorn-prick became an ache. He gripped her arm. 'Why didn't you tell me before I took you?'

'How could I? I didn't know what you were going to do, until it was too late. What difference would it have made?'

'I don't know,' he said truthfully. 'I don't know.'

'None, because you were too wrapped up in what you wanted to consider my wishes.'

'It's true.' The ache reached his throat and eyes. He could hardly speak. 'I was only thinking of myself. I wanted you with me for ever, not growing old with some mortal man.'

'Yes, jealousy, too; you think I didn't know? You didn't just kill the child I was expecting, but all the potential children. Our descendants. You didn't ask, you didn't give me a *choice*!'

'I know,' he whispered. Ilona had never spoken so openly before. He'd longed for her to confide in him; now she was doing so, he found he could hardly bear to listen.

'And my husband; after I became a vampire, I went back and killed him. You didn't know that either, did you? I sucked him dry, because it seemed the only thing to do. Strangle my mortal connections, cut them dead so I didn't keep wanting to go back. I can't remember what he looked like, actually.'

'God, Ilona . . .'

'But none of this occurred to you, and even if it had, you would have taken me anyway.'

'Not if I'd known it would still cause you such pain a century later.'

'But it doesn't.' Her voice was thin, chilling. 'Don't you understand? That's why I'm crying, because I feel nothing. I can't feel!'

Karl's grief hardened. It wasn't sympathy Ilona needed; she never had. 'If that's true, why do you still want to punish me? I am not very good at being a martyr to guilt, however bad a father I have been.'

'Did I spring fully armed from your head?' she cried. 'Because you never talk about my mother, never!'

'Would you want me to? When I told you that Kristian had had your mother killed, you fawned on Kristian all the more, knowing I'd hate it. There's nothing to say about our mortal lives, Ilona.'

Her sobs ebbed away. She lay across him as if she'd disgorged all her strength. Her arms were like spilled milk. 'I'm not weeping for my mortal life, father. I'm weeping because I swore I'd never tell you these things, and now I've broken my oath. It's the humiliation. This is what Violette has done to me.'

Karl lifted her up and cradled her against his side. Ilona's slender body fitted sweetly along his chest and shoulder. And for once she neither teased him nor reviled him, but simply rested there.

'I was wrong to make you a vampire,' Karl said. 'But if I hadn't, you would be dead by now. Perhaps your great-granddaughter would be here with me instead. Would you really have preferred that?'

She gave him a poisoned look. 'Oh, I am a consummate hypocrite. You know how I feel about you. Don't humiliate me even more by forcing it out of me. You *know*.'

'Why is it humiliating to admit you love me? Why does it almost kill you to weep in front of me, or to admit that I have hurt you? For the love of God, I was your father. You once said we can't retain human relationships, but I don't agree. If you cannot trust me, who else is there? But that is why you feel compelled to torment me, isn't it? Because you know you are safe to do so.'

Karl expected a violent denial. To his surprise, her only reaction was a shaky laugh. 'You frightened me once,' she said. 'The time Kristian brought you back to life and you found that I'd come back to him, even after the way he'd treated me. You looked straight through me and it was the first time I felt you had stopped caring. Oh, I would hate it if you didn't care.'

'And do you think my patience is infinite?'

'No, but I know you would always save me if I were in danger, as you did tonight. You even went to the *Weisskalt* to save me!'

'So we understand each other, then,' he said gently.

Ilona raised a hand to stroke his neck. The hand pulled off his tie, undid the collar of his shirt. Like a cat she slid her cheek over his ribs and collarbone, nuzzled into his throat, then bit him. Her canines were so swift, so sharp, that Karl felt barely any pain. He let her drink, cradling her, his head tipping back a little, eyelids lowered, lips parted. Not breathing. And as he looked down on her raptly bent head, he saw a vision of a baby's head, with a mop of the same plum-dark hair, suckling contentedly at her mother's breast. And this grotesque parody represented exactly what they were; a reversal of nature.

When Ilona raised her head, her brown eyes had turned molten, like a sated lover. Her fingers pressed into his neck, warm satin; the robe and the torn dress fell away from her milky shoulders. It took Karl all his will not to feast on her in turn.

'I'm going back to Europe,' she announced. 'I wanted to prove Pierre wrong about Violette – only to discover that he was right. She has got to be stopped.'

Karl's mood darkened. Violette had become an insoluble problem. Much as he distrusted her, he did not want to see her harmed, if only for Charlotte's sake. She seemed indestructible; even a band of vampire assassins might not touch her. But, he thought, how long can I stand by while she attacks people like Pierre and Ilona? How long before she turns on Charlotte?

'It will only create more trouble,' he said. 'More grief.'

'So? I have to prove to her that she hasn't changed me, that she can't turn me into a gibbering wreck like Pierre.' Ilona seemed her normal self again; Karl did not know whether to be pleased or dismayed. 'Behaving vilely and destructively, tearing apart everyone she comes across – that, my beloved Karl, is my job.'

Sebastian knew that Roberta Stafford lived on Beacon Hill, in Chestnut Street. To discover her actual address had been simple;

after they'd parted in the Public Garden, he'd secretly followed her home.

Tomorrow night he would take her out to dinner, like the gentleman suitor he played so well; but tonight he haunted the street outside her house as his true self, a malevolent predator in the darkness. It pleased him to spy on his prey in her natural setting.

Leaning against the trunk of a tree, Sebastian felt rain begin to patter softly down through the leaves. The drops wove webs of light from the lamps, glistened on the beaten-pewter surface of the road. A lovely street, he thought, with its cobbled sidewalks, its gas lamps and rows of red-brick houses stepping gracefully up the hill. So quiet, folded discreetly on its riches like a hen on the nest. The lindens, maples and maidenhairs that lined the sidewalks were so lush that it was hard to see the buildings at all through the mass of leaves. No two houses were alike; each had its own architectural details, its individual ornaments. Roberta's was particularly charming; four storeys high, with tall windows framed by white woodwork and black shutters. A narrow front garden behind black railings, vines smothering the lower brickwork, wisteria twining around the arched doorway. The railings were topped with gold leaf, the steps whitewashed. The home of a rich widow, perhaps, utterly respectable.

And yet, defying propriety, this extraordinary woman lived like a courtesan in the grand old style. A touch of admiration firmed Sebastian's mouth. He was intrigued, despite his world-weariness. He wanted to savour this. Wanted to catch an illicit glimpse of his victim.

He found a way round the row of houses, along an alley and into her tiny walled garden. Kitchens on the ground floor; a flight of steps up to a terrace, where lights shone in the parlour. The thick lace curtains were ideal to shield a vampire from sight, even if he pressed right up against the glass. Four people in the room; a puffy-faced businessman, a middle-aged woman with dark hair, a maid who was on her feet holding a tray, and Roberta herself. A cosy, happy gathering; even the maid was joining in the talk and laughter.

Roberta was facing away from the window. Sebastian could see only her head and shoulders over the back of her chair; a sleek, brown coil on the nape of her neck, the curves and angles of her shoulders as sensuous as sculpture under the thin straps of her dress ... and her neck, peach-soft and delicately downed with gold, pleading for the touch of his fingers and lips.

The anticipation was exquisite.

None of them saw his face; half in shadow under a mass of dark hair, lace-patterns icing one high cheekbone and moulding the sharp line of his jaw, catching one point of light in a darkly introspective eye. They did not sense him watching them, still as a portrait; they did not see him withdraw and vanish. But he had learned enough for now.

The business type was called Harold and seemed to be one of her lovers. How many does she have? he wondered. The two women were her maids, Mary and Alice. Roberta had treated them with astonishing warmth, as if they were more friends than servants. Obviously they were very loyal.

Interesting, all this, Sebastian thought. He already knew that his victim-to-be was very far from being the hard, cold *Belle Dame sans Merci* whom Russell Booth had led him to expect. She was kind to her servants. She was ordinary. Hidden, then, the real poison of her heart.

He almost began to smile, but his pleasure hardened at once into black thirst. Too much sadness in the past to feel any joy now. He was not a gloating killer. He obeyed the grim urges of his nature, and in obeying them became their master; his passion for blood was bleak, ruthless and absolute.

Tomorrow. And even then he would not take her immediately, because he had learned that her uncle was travelling with the ballet, and that he knew Karl. So he could not fulfil his plan until the uncle and the vampires had left town. No trouble; he would have taken his time anyway. It had been a risk to tell her his real name, but then, a little risk only spiced his anticipation.

So hard to wait, so tantalizing.

As Sebastian walked down Spruce Street towards the Common, he met an Irish housemaid with autumn hair like Robyn's. Did she feel safe alone, so late at night? he asked her, effortlessly imitating her brogue. Charmed, she smiled and blushed. Quite safe, sir. I'm only after visiting a friend. But, he said, will you let me walk you home?

She let him, and they talked about Ireland as they went. As always Sebastian felt the strange conflicts of memory inside him. Savage pain no longer . . . it had all been resolved long ago. But there was still something, the dark green pull of the old land and the house.

The Irish girl trusted him, and was flirting shamelessly. She led him to the back of a big house on Marlborough Street; more old Bostonian wealth and grandeur. In the shadow of the kitchen door, they stood looking at each other like young lovers who were not quite sure how to procede.

'Well, good night, sir,' she said, looking at him expectantly.

He kissed her. 'I'm superstitious,' he said. 'I won't come in until I'm invited.'

Her eyes were huge, dew-soft. He had not mesmerized her into this. 'Would you like to . . .' she whispered.

They crept along corridors and up the back stairs to her attic room. As soon as the door closed he pulled her to him, scaring her a little. His hands travelled over the cheap material of her coat, ripping off the buttons in his excitement. She was compliant, not as inexperienced as a good Catholic girl should have been. If they were really frightened or unwilling, which was rare, he would content himself with their blood. Sebastian was not a rapist – only of their veins, at least.

But she responded eagerly as he pushed her down on to the small, lumpy bed, tearing away her skirt and undergarments. He loved physical passion, enjoyed it to the roots of his being, but always with a kind of grim detachment. She tried to kiss him but he turned his face away; that was not the intimacy he wanted. She was wriggling beneath him, fighting a little, gasping for breath.

'Slow down,' she said, voice high and faint. 'What's the hurry? Please, slow down!'

But he could not. He didn't care about her. All that mattered was the blind urgency as he thrust himself into her warm moist flesh, the shuddering build up of fire.

How he loved this. Sometimes the blood itself was not enough. Blood was the necessity, not sex – but to take it like this, in full, aching possession, gave feeding an edge of unparalleled rapture.

His fangs entered her neck and the hot ichor surged into his mouth. Flame now in his throat and loins, sharpening, one feeding on the other with every swallow, with every thrust . . .

He was only half-aware of his victim's mingled pleasure and pain. Pinioned under him, she couldn't even cry out. She was only a vessel, a source of the rubescent heat building and building within him. He raked his hands through her hair and dug his fingers into her skull, imagining . . .

Imagining that she was Roberta.

'Roberta,' he murmured through the blood. '*Roberta.*'

And his climax was a surge of lava that went on and on, flowing up from his loins to his heart as the blood flowed down to drench the searing thirst . . . on until it slowed to a trickle of pleasure, and the girl's body lay cooling beneath him.

Once it was over, Sebastian wanted to escape as quickly as possible. Leaving the house through the Crystal Ring, he walked away as if nothing had happened. He strolled down to the Charles River and stood looking across the dark water towards Cambridge. Anyone seeing him would have thought he looked too thoughtful, too genteel to harm a soul. He was satiated, at peace; a little depressed, perhaps, but nothing to cause pain.

The wide flow of the river filled him with its tranquillity, troubled only by the faintest rippling of new hunger; the desire not to take a substitute, but to seduce and drain and possess the one who really mattered.

CHAPTER NINE

RED LIKE THE ROSE

'Where's Ilona?' Charlotte demanded. She switched on the lights as she entered the suite, but Karl was there alone. He was standing at the window, looking out at the street. Outside, she glimpsed the flow of traffic crawling between tall Victorian buildings, a flicker of lights on the darkness; heard trolley cars rattling, motor horns, drunken voices singing in the distance. American cities never slept, it seemed.

'She's gone,' he said.

'Oh, has she?' Charlotte couldn't hide her anger. 'She must have known I wanted to tear her limb from limb.'

Karl turned to her. His shirt was undone, his skin pale as if he needed to feed. His eyes were quite cold. 'Don't you think Ilona has suffered enough at Violette's hands? What reason have you to vent your anger on her?'

Charlotte gaped at him in disbelief. 'She attacked Josef and nearly maimed him for life! What more reason do I need?'

Karl's impartiality seemed to have deserted him. 'But you took this risk when you brought Josef with us.'

'So it's not Ilona's fault? Karl, I know she's your daughter but I can't believe you're taking her side. You can't condone her attacking Josef!'

'But you can condone Violette's behaviour?'

His hostility floored her. In his eerie beauty, with his soft, deeply coloured hair and his compelling eyes, Karl always wielded a heart-stopping power over her. But to see that beauty glazed with something of Kristian's bane frightened her.

'Violette was protecting Josef,' she said.

'Simple restraint would have sufficed. To attack Ilona with

such viciousness was uncalled-for, I could even say wicked; and yet, Charlotte, you still insist that Violette is merely misunderstood? What will it take to make you admit that she is evil and that nothing will change her?'

'Evil?' Charlotte, trembling and enraged, took a few steps back towards the door. They had never quarrelled like this before. She'd never known Karl to be so implacable. Often she'd wished he would not be so good-natured and reasonable; she took back the wish now. 'Ilona deserved it! Violette only reacted as she did because—'

'I don't want to hear it.'

'You tried to feed on Violette,' Charlotte said in a low voice. Her own words, and the inimical light in Karl's eyes were filling her with dread, but she couldn't stop. 'You attacked her. I can't believe you did it! I'm not sure I can forgive you.'

'Can't you?' Karl smiled thinly. 'Still so distasteful, to be reminded that I am not always a perfect gentleman?'

She turned away. Furious with him, but hating the feeling. Hating it.

'Charlotte,' he said, starting to come after her. She made for the door, but Karl was too fast, and caught her before she reached it. Then he held her hard, his chin on her hair, his body moulded to hers from chest to thigh. 'We must stop this.'

'How?' she whispered. 'I've never known you to take sides before.'

'I know. I loathe it. But I told you I couldn't stand aside if Violette threatened anyone I loved. Even for your sake, I couldn't hold back—'

'And Violette would probably have killed you, Karl, not the other way round,' she said bitterly. 'And it's killing *me* to see you at each other's throats. Literally. What am I supposed to do?'

'To begin with,' he said, his mouth near her ear, 'we must not quarrel about it.'

She sighed, still aggrieved, but unable to disentangle herself from his seductive embrace. 'Why not?'

'Because it is precisely what Ilona and Violette would want, is it not?' he said. 'Imagine how it would delight them, to know that they'd driven us apart.'

And Karl's arms were now so tight around her that she couldn't draw breath. Almost desperate, his embrace. Charlotte gave in, and they held each other in the pure relief of reconciliation, but she was thinking, how close we've come to letting this tear us apart! The terror of losing Karl is too painful to bear ... So, maybe Violette's right. I should submit myself to her, let her bite cure the addiction, my fatal dependency on Karl's love. Take this merciless fear away.

When Robyn went to see Josef at his hotel, late the next morning, she found him in bed with the covers drawn up to his chin.

He hadn't responded to her knock; she had had to get a porter to unlock the door. As she approached the bed, she felt her heart rising into her throat in fear that he was unconscious or dead. He looked grey.

But his eyes were open, gleaming dully.

'What are you doing here, child?' He sounded weary, as if he had no wish to see her.

'You were meant to call on me today, don't you remember?' she said cheerfully. 'When you didn't come or send a message, I was worried. Whatever is the matter?'

'Nothing,' he said, breathing out heavily.

'Come on, you can't fool me. What is it? Aches, pains, fever? Have you seen a doctor?'

She made to touch his forehead, and was shocked when he jerked away. His brow contracted with irritation. 'Don't touch me.'

'Why not?' She sank down on the edge of the bed beside him, puzzled and alarmed. 'I've never seen you like this before. What is it?'

'I told you, nothing. Headache. One of my headaches. Please leave me.'

He wasn't telling the truth, she was sure. The sheet gripped around his throat was a concealment. 'Have you seen someone about these headaches?'

'*Liebe Gott*,' he whispered. 'I tell you. I just need to rest. Would you please go so I can?'

'If you insist. But what is it, Uncle, really?' She put her hand on his, felt him flinch. 'You can tell me.'

He gave her a long, candid look. An awful intelligence swam in his eyes. Regret, guilt, some unspoken sin. Then he said, 'There are vampires . . .'

'Vampires?'

'They suck your blood but they take your mind as well.'

Robyn made a worrying deduction from this. 'Uncle, are you in trouble? Someone extorting money from you?'

He seemed to recollect himself. 'No, my dear, nothing like that. I'm rambling, I think I have a slight fever.'

'Well, that's it then,' she said briskly.

'What?'

'You're obviously in no fit state to move today, but first thing tomorrow you're coming to stay with me. No arguments, now. If you don't co-operate, I'll get nasty; I'll send Mother round with chicken soup.'

'Not that.' He tried to smile.

'Have you eaten? I'll ask room service to bring you something, and I'll come back again this evening and see how you are.'

'There's no need.' He patted her hand, but his appreciation of her kindness was a dry shadow. 'Charlotte is looking after me.'

Light from the corridor fanned into the darkened room; Robyn looked up and saw Charlotte in the doorway, a silhouette rimmed with wheaten light. Robyn stood up and went towards her, the weirdest feeling of unease filtering through her, as if the air were full of sinister secrets.

'Do you know what's wrong with him?' Robyn said, rather sharply.

'A slight chill, that's all,' said Charlotte. Her violet eyes looked so innocent. 'We're looking after him. There's no need to worry.'

'Nevertheless,' Robyn said firmly, 'I'll see Josef this evening, and tomorrow I'm taking him home.'

'I thought you were not coming,' said Sebastian.

'I am rather late,' Robyn said without apology. He stood up to meet her as she approached. The simple luxury of the restaurant – marble pillars, potted ferns, a figured red carpet – seemed a faded backdrop to Sebastian's dark and vivid presence. Dressed in black, he looked very old-fashioned, yet he seemed to get away with it. His offhand disregard for fashion was rather charming.

An attentive waiter took her coat the moment she slipped it off her shoulders. 'I've just been to see my uncle at his hotel,' she continued as they were shown to their table. 'I called on him this morning and he wasn't well, so I thought I'd drop in again.'

'Nothing serious, I hope.' They sat down, separated by white linen and silver, candlesticks and flowers. Voices murmured around them. In the centre of the restaurant, a pianist was playing a white grand piano.

'I don't think so.' For a moment she was preoccupied. She was concerned about Josef and had no appetite; she almost did not want to be here. Then she recollected herself and shone her full attention on her companion. 'I found him in bed with the covers up to his chin. He claimed it was only a headache, but he was acting oddly. He wouldn't talk and didn't want me to stay.'

Sebastian looked amused. 'Are you sure there were no shapes in the bed that should not have been there? The chambermaid, perhaps?'

Robyn laughed, despite herself. 'He's no angel, my uncle. Maybe that's why he understands me. Anyway, he seemed better tonight, but he still wouldn't talk. Sat there looking as if he had the weight of the world on his shoulders, but he wouldn't tell me why. We almost had an argument about it. That's why I'm late.'

'Did you think I would not wait?

His eyes, under the dark combs of his lashes, woke a disorientation in her that she didn't like. 'Oh, no,' she said with cool sweetness. 'I thought you'd wait.'

'And you will not brood about your uncle all evening?'

'It's absolutely not in my nature to brood,' she said.

'Nor in mine.' And there was the merest flash in his expression of something that disturbed her, an echo of his manifestation at the Booths' party. Gone.

Robyn took tea with her meal. Wine was prohibited, which was doing nothing for the restaurant trade, she reflected; and nothing for her state of mind. She would have appreciated a drink to relax her – but with Sebastian, perhaps it was better to stay fully alert.

Afterwards, she found she had almost no recollection of what they'd talked about. They talked easily; inconsequential chat about Boston, the weather, the charms of New England, the theatre, something or other. One thing was certain; they never once mentioned her deceased lover, Russell. The first taste of lobster awoke her appetite and she thoroughly enjoyed the food; perhaps that was why she never noticed Sebastian actually eating.

By the end of the meal, he was still a mystery to her. Obviously he liked her; he seemed happy enough in her company. Yet he seemed detached, friendly in an unaffected way, making no attempt to charm or impress her.

She liked that. It was refreshing. It saved her from having to parry the syrupy clichés of seduction, which most men seemed to think she must find irresistible. She could just be her good-natured, if slightly acidic, self.

'May I escort you home?' he said, as their coats were brought and doors held open for them. He always sounds, she thought, as if he's parodying polite behaviour.

'You may.' Perhaps he's like me, Robyn thought. He lives in society but he despises it.

From the restaurant near the harbour, they walked arm-in-arm past Faneuil Hall and the market, and across the Common towards Beacon Hill. Little lights shone in the trees, and the paths were darkly inviting. The evening had taken on a strange atmosphere the moment they'd met; a quiet electricity that made everything shimmer. Unreal, too real. Dreamy excitement that threatened to break into nightmare. Sebastian was so unusual, his presence almost too intense for her; beautiful, different, one moment warm, the next a thousand miles away.

Robyn was not at all sure she liked him. Not that it mattered. She never allowed herself to become emotionally attached to her victims.

He might induce another kind of dependence in a more vulnerable woman, though; a wanton addiction, like opium. Robyn felt repelled at the thought. This was not going to be easy . . . but the challenge was preferable to boredom.

He said, 'You know, Mrs Stafford, you are not at all what I would have expected.'

At that, she began to laugh. She tried to stifle it, but couldn't.

'What is it?' he said.

'It's just that they always say that. I'd taken you for being a bit different.'

For a second, she had the impression that he'd turned completely hostile. Lights moved over his face as if over ice. Again she felt an echo of the dread that she'd experienced in the garden; but when he spoke, his voice was warm and slightly satirical. It seemed she'd been mistaken again. 'Who are they, who always say it?'

'Men. They've always heard about me, you see, like you had. They seem to expect some red-taloned houri, Cleopatra with a poisoned dagger. It's a bit of a shock when they find out I'm just . . . ordinary. Then they say what you said.'

'Well, I am sorry to be so predictable, but I would hardly call you ordinary.'

'I don't like to ask what you would call me.' She looked at him, aware of the radiance of her own smile lifting and lighting her face. Her smile had power; she saw him respond. 'However, I have a suggestion.'

'Yes?'

'You can call me Robyn.'

She had not been concentrating on their route. Without thinking, she had let Sebastian lead the way to the top of the

Common, across Beacon Street and along Charles; and she was stunned when he took the correct turning into Chestnut Street and headed straight and sure to her house.

She hesitated on the doorstep, shivering a little. 'I don't remember telling you where I lived.'

'You didn't,' he said. 'I was following you.'

With one hand curved around a railing, he stood looking at her. He was lean and dark, his hair swept untidily back from his milk-crystal face, eyes gleaming. He looked as if he would be quite happy to be on his way, a night-hunting cat. He made no attempt to kiss her, nor did he seem inclined to.

This was the moment at which Robyn always had to make a decision. With the ones who were too eager, who would keep after her like dogs panting for her favours, it was best to play hard to get. Reducing them to a fever of unrequited passion was the way to manipulate them. But with difficult men, the ones who played it cool and gave the impression they were not much bothered if they never saw her again, it paid to go for the kill. Show them what they'd be missing if they lost her. The velvet snare; worked every time.

It was obvious that Sebastian belonged in the second category. She was about to invite him in when he took the decision out of her hands, leaving her partly annoyed and partly relieved.

'I hope I shall see you again,' he said. And he kissed her hand, and walked away through the leaf-laced shadows of Chestnut Street.

Whatever had ailed Josef, he seemed to recover quickly once Robyn had collected him from the hotel and settled him in her house. It gave her maternal side a rare outing, to fuss over him. Although Josef insisted that he was quite well and had no need to be cosseted, his protests were half-hearted. He seemed glad of her attentiveness, as if he'd been on the edge of danger and felt safe here.

He stubbornly refused to discuss the true nature of his illness, however. Robyn didn't press him. He remained subdued and reluctant to be touched, as if some part of his spirit had atrophied. Restless too; he went out often, and she suspected he was visiting his strange friends, Karl and Charlotte.

'Why don't you invite them here?' she asked on the third morning, as they sat companionably in the parlour after breakfast.

A flash of alarm on his face. His answer was a pure evasion. 'Oh, they are very busy, and of course the ballet will be leaving Boston the day after tomorrow . . .'

'They can't be *that* busy, surely. What exactly do they do?'

'Well, they are . . . Madame Lenoir's business partners. Patrons of the ballet. I can ask them, but I very much doubt—'

'Uncle, stop. If you don't want to bring them here, that's your business; don't make excuses. Kind of a shame, though,' she said, watching his expression. 'I'd like to have met them again. And Violette.'

'Violette?' he said, flinching.

'Yes, why not? Although I suppose she really is too busy and important to take tea with the likes of me,' Robyn said ironically. 'So, the ballet leaves in a couple of days?'

'Yes, a week in New York, four days in Philadelphia and so on; it's an exhausting schedule,' said Josef.

'But what are you going to do, dear? Are you going with them, staying here, or what?'

He folded his hands, and gazed at the fire-screen and dried flowers that stood in the grate. 'I don't know. I only came with them so that I could see you. I think I shall stay here a few more days, do a little sightseeing, perhaps go to New York, and then sail back to Europe. If it is all right for me to stay? I can always go back to the hotel.'

'Nonsense,' she said, thinking, how tired he sounds. 'You can stay here as long as you like.'

'A few days only, I promise,' he said, looking at her over his glasses. Much as she loved his company, she was secretly glad that he would be leaving soon. His presence had forced her to suspend her usual lifestyle. She could not in all decency receive Harold while Josef was here, nor cultivate prospective admirers – nor see Sebastian.

In fact, Sebastian had not attempted to contact her since their dinner date a few days ago. Hadn't even sent flowers. Robyn had an uneasy feeling that she would never hear from him again. His silence both disappointed and offended her; Robyn had to be the one to end liaisons, and she couldn't tolerate being treated so casually.

'You mustn't go until you're in a fit state to travel,' she said firmly.

Josef breathed out as if heartsore. Instead of brushing off her concern, he spoke kindly. 'Robyn, I owe you an explanation for my behaviour.'

'You don't, dear. Whatever's troubling you – well, I'm here to help, but if it's private you're under no obligation to tell me anything.' She spoke sincerely, mentally crossing her fingers that he would confide in her.

'The night I was ill . . .' he began, folding his hands. 'Well, I was rather ashamed of the whole affair, but it was brought about by . . . a difficult situation.' He's choosing his words too carefully, Robyn thought. 'Charlotte invited me on the tour because she was concerned about Madame Lenoir's state of mind.'

'Oh!' Robyn was shocked, then a recent memory unwound.

'You understand, it's a delicate matter; I could hardly walk around telling people that Madame is . . .'

'Crazy?'

'Must you be so outspoken?'

'So, you came along as her personal psychologist?'

'Not exactly.'

'I'm not that surprised, to be honest. I was talking to her at the party. She was very strange.' Recollection of the scene brought a wistful smile to Robyn's lips, a shiver that was almost thrilling. 'I'd say that lady has problems . . . but talented people are often crazy, aren't they?'

'I would not dream of passing such judgement on her,' Josef said, rather sharply. 'The point is that it was done behind Madame Lenoir's back, and when she found out she objected strongly and refused to talk to me. So there is no point in me going with the ballet. It has all been very embarrassing, combined with the fact that I . . . I have great affection for Charlotte, therefore Karl and I are not what you would call friends.'

'And he's not someone I'd want as an enemy,' she said quietly.

He gave her a quick, keen glance. 'Why do you say that?'

Robyn shrugged. 'He struck me as having an exceptional personality, that's all. A sweetheart – unless you cross him.'

'Yes, well.' Josef exhaled. 'The day you came to the hotel, I was rather the worse for trying to drown my sorrows the night before. I couldn't tell you because I was ashamed. That's all. Foolish old man.'

He looked up, anxious for her to believe him. Actually she didn't, but she had to take his story at face value. After all, what could he possibly be hiding?

'Are you telling me that I've been pampering you because you had a hangover?' She was pleased that her teasing drew a smile from him at last.

'Can you forgive me?' He leaned forward. 'But tell me, what happened when you met Madame at the party?'

'Not much,' Robyn said offhandedly. 'I was in the garden and she appeared from nowhere and started talking to me. I ended up telling her things I wouldn't normally dream of telling anyone; I don't know why. She seemed to understand, and she was . . . fascinating, really. And then . . . well, I think she tried to make a pass at me.'

'A pass?' Josef tried to sound impartial, but he turned red. 'Are you sure it was not – not, er, an attack of some kind?'

'Attack?' She was amazed. 'Why would a ballerina go around attacking people? Oh, no, it was sexual,' she said, not sparing his blushes. 'You know, kisses, touches. I was so stunned I couldn't stop her. Almost scary in a way . . .' Memories again; Violette's lips hotly branding her neck, the soft-breathing night air, the sensation that some unearthly creature, half-bird and half-serpent, was possessing her . . . Robyn shook herself. 'But I don't know how serious she was because she suddenly stopped and walked off, just left me there. Very weird.' A thought struck her. 'Is this why everyone's concerned about her? Uncle, I don't have to remind you that having sapphic tendencies is not a form of mental illness? Or do I?'

His silver eyebrows jerked up. 'Not at all. I hadn't even thought about it.'

'Most men prefer not to think about such things, but they happen, all the same. I wasn't shocked. I'm very broad-minded.'

'Tolerant Robyn,' he said, his voice softening. 'Well, some might not agree with you, but I can assure you I do. No, her problems are . . .' Evasions again. 'Creative ones. To do with her art. She, er, works too hard for her own good.'

'Stop struggling, dear,' Robyn sighed. 'If you can't tell me, just say so. I don't expect you to divulge professional secrets.'

'I'm sorry. It's very delicate. Anyway, it's academic now, since she won't see me.'

No more was said about the touchy subject of the dancer. They spent a pleasant morning together and were discussing the best place to go for lunch, when the doorbell rang.

Mary came in to announce the visitor. 'Ma'am, there's a lady to see Mr Stern. Madame Violette Lenoir.'

Robyn saw her uncle's face turn the colour of wet ash.

'I hope you don't mind me coming to see you,' Violette said. She felt nervous; ridiculous, but she couldn't help it. The maid had shown them into a morning-room on the ground floor while Robyn stayed upstairs to allow Violette and Josef to talk alone. It was a small, light room which contained a writing bureau, bookshelves, two armchairs, a towering rubber plant. Josef was an ambiguous figure in Violette's eyes. Slender, stooping a little as if he felt he were too tall, he seemed a silver-haired sage, full of wisdom. He was not Janacek, not a manipulative bully; just a kind man with a weakness for women. And she also could not help comparing him favourably with the self-styled magus Lancelyn, whose robust over-confidence and goatish sexuality had repelled her.

Josef, however, was clearly very uncomfortable, even embarrassed, in her presence. She'd caught him in the most compromising position imaginable with Ilona. And then he'd witnessed the fight between them; part of it, at least. He'd regained consciousness and must have seen Violette's wild assault on Ilona.

'I've had time to think,' she said. 'I've decided that I ought to hear whatever you can tell me about Lilith.'

'Madame, I am honoured. Shall we sit down?'

They settled themselves in the leather armchairs, a few feet apart with a rug between them. She had refused the maid's offer to take her coat and hat; irrational, but they felt like a layer of protection between her and an intrusive world. She said, 'There was another man who claimed to know my secrets. His name was Lancelyn. He tried to help me but he went too far and I destroyed him. He's insane now; he might even be dead, I don't know.'

'Is this a warning?' Josef asked gravely. 'You cannot expect me to speak freely if I am afraid of what you might do if I offend you.'

'No, I want the truth,' she said. 'I appreciate your taking a risk for my sake. I regret not listening to Lancelyn, but he should regret the way he mistreated me. Don't be afraid of me. I've only come to talk to you. That was why I came to your room before – to talk, not to harm you! You must appreciate that it is extremely difficult for me to admit that I need your help. It puts me completely at your mercy.'

He appeared to relax, just a little. 'All I ask is that no harm comes to my niece.'

'It's understood.'

Josef cleared his throat. She felt just as if she were in a psychiatrist's office. 'Lilith is a figure who occurs in most mythologies, under different names, usually as a wind-hag. For instance, in Sumer she was Lil, a storm spirit, while the Semites of Mesopotamia called her Lilith, a night demon who lays hold of sleeping men and women and causes erotic dreams. In Syria she became a succubus and a child-killing witch, but she is best known from Jewish holy books, the Zohar and the Talmud, as the first wife of Adam.'

Memories flared in Violette's mind. They were unpleasant

but she gave herself up to them, letting Josef's voice soothe her. She said, 'Yes, I was in the Garden, a disgustingly fecund garden crawling with life ... the man lies over me, he won't accept me as his equal, he tries to force me but I won't let him. I call on the secret name of God and I flee to the desert. God sends three angels after me but I won't go back with them.'

'Their names?' Josef sounded intent, fascinated.

'Senoy, Sansenoy, Semangelof. I had never heard those names until the moment of my transformation. The knowledge came from inside me, not from books.'

'Well, there are various stories of Lilith's origins which may sound archaic and strange to us now. The Zohar says that the Left, the side of Darkness, "flamed forth with its full power, and from this fiery flame came forth the female moonlike essence". Two great lights arose, the Sun and the Moon, but they quarrelled about their power and God settled the dispute by diminishing the Moon and sending her to rule over the lower orders. The dominion of day belongs to the male and night to the female.'

'And the female is dark,' Violette murmured. 'She belongs to the night, she has been diminished and from that comes her anger . . .'

'And gives birth to the evil that is Lilith.'

Perhaps Josef had used the word without thinking, but her tormented mind latched on to it. 'Evil.'

'But the Zohar teaches that knowledge of her is essential to self-development,' Josef said hurriedly. 'It speaks of two inter-twined shoots, red like the rose, male and female. The male is Samael the devil, the female contained in him is Lilith. The female is always contained within the male, as God contains the Shekinah—'

'The pair above and the pair below.' She already knew the words. The images that they conjured were not memories but dream-shadows, indefinable and threatening. 'Samael of the dark side and his female, Lilith; the Serpent, the Woman of Harlotry.'

'Do you really need me to tell you anything?' said Josef.

'Yes; I don't always know it until you say it, but everything you say, I recognize. I can feel the weight of these men's writings, holding me down. Go on.'

Josef's words, too, weighed on her like chains. 'Cast out of heaven, she becomes the bride of the devil. In psychological terms, you could say that men experience her as the witch who seduces then kills—' He struggled for a moment – remembering Ilona, Violette thought – then recovered himself. 'Or as the succubus, or the mother who kills her own young. And to women she is the dark side of the self which desires to be joined to the devil.'

The essence of evil, she thought, shuddering. No redeeming feature. 'She was the first Eve,' said Violette. 'The demoness who was usurped by the second Eve. And the second Eve was good until the first, Lilith the Serpent, corrupted her.'

'Yes, the Serpent is often identified with her. Mediaeval woodcuts show the Serpent with Lilith's face, whispering in Eve's ear. Then the Zohar says that after the Fall, God brought Lilith from the depths of the sea and set her to punish the children of men.'

'Like Kristian,' she breathed. 'An instrument to wreak God's vengeance on mortals. That's what he believed vampires were, and perhaps he was right. Lilith, mother of vampires and the lash of God.' Sudden rage seized her and she sat forward. 'Who is He, this punishing God, who so hates His own children? Is this what you believe?'

Josef flinched, the colour leaving his face. He seemed to think she would attack him, and she was close to it; but she mastered herself and sank back.

Josef breathed out raggedly. 'The God I believe in is a gentler being, but my opinions about this are irrelevant. It's what you believe that matters.'

'You call it belief, I experience it as reality. Lilith is inside me. She hates men for their so-called "wisdom" and their rejection of her; she hates women for their child-like clinging to men. She hates life, she loves the pure sterility of the desert.'

Josef put in, 'She chooses to create art rather than nurture a husband and children?'

Anger again – how dare he judge her? – but she controlled

it. 'She sees into people's souls, sees their foolishness and wants to tear it out ... My conscious self wants her to reveal herself fully to me but I daren't let her. All I know of her and everything I hear of her tells me she's evil. She is the destructive storm, the hag of death. I can't tell where I end and Lilith begins any more, I can't live with her energy and this continual dark fire throbbing like a tribal dance inside me. No escape unless I end my own life – or others end it for me. Perhaps that's what I'm trying to do, drive someone else to kill me. Karl, Ilona, John, Rachel, even Charlotte – but the harder I try the more I frighten them, and their fear makes Lilith insane with rage.' Her voice fell. 'She is going to do something terrible if she doesn't stop.'

Josef was quiet for a minute, thinking. He seemed very much the psychoanalyst now; one who kept asking questions, nodding, but never giving any answers. Her despair deepened. 'In a sense,' he said, 'you could see Lilith as God's equal, in that her rejection of the angels creates an impasse between the upper and lower powers. She is the counterbalance to God's goodness and maleness. In Jungian terms you could describe her as God's anima, his dark, avenging female side.'

'Oh, good,' said Violette. 'Now we know something about the men who wrote about her, but we know nothing about Lilith herself.'

Another pause. 'Tell me, did you have any foreshadowing of this before you became ... a vampire?'

'Yes. All my life. My father taught me that women are intrinsically wicked. He said I destroyed him; I tore my mother open when I was born, so she would never sleep with him again, and that drove him to other women. One of those women was Ilona. She didn't kill him, but the physical mutilation she gave him drove him out of his mind. I believe you understand.'

Josef groaned softly, tried to turn it into a cough. She sensed his shuddering horror at the fate he had narrowly avoided. And she thought, men are so vulnerable, really. Can't I feel even a little pity?

'He said I killed my mother,' she went on. 'He said I was

from the devil and he blamed everything on me. Ridiculous, I know. But now I am like Ilona, a Lamia like her, so who is to say he was wrong? Perhaps he foresaw it. All my life, the three angels were waiting for me; three shadows, waiting for Lilith to come into full possession of me. I tried to obey them! I tried to repent of the darkness and walk into the light but Lilith wouldn't let me. Charlotte insists there is no God ... so why do I have these memories? Other people's memories, maybe, or the visions of the men who wrote the Zohar ... therefore I'm mad, but what exactly does my madness *mean*? I still reason and think and suffer. It may not be real to anyone else but it's real to *me*.'

'You could say that Lilith represents the side of woman that refuses to obey,' said Josef. 'She chooses flight and the wilderness, rather than the safety of obedience to God.'

'Outcast.'

'There are darknesses that must be cast out in order for society to function,' Josef said gravely. 'If all women behaved as Lilith does, there would be chaos. You want me to tell you that Lilith is redeemable, that she is not completely of the darkness, but I can't. Perhaps her feelings are understandable but that does not make them excusable. You must come to terms with this or you'll never recover.'

'Recover?' His answer incensed her. 'You are male; wise, pure and spiritual, created in God's image. Lilith is female; bestial, unclean and destructive. Whatever modern ideas you profess to have, that's what you feel in your heart, isn't it?'

'Not at all.' She sensed that he was struggling now. He had said nothing she wanted to hear. He had only confirmed her fears, made it all worse. He forged on, 'I see mythological figures as psychological archetypes. I can only theorize, but I believe that Lilith − as you interpret her − is a complex, a psychic fragment that has splintered off and behaves as if it has a separate and complete personality of its own. You have perhaps absorbed the primordial image of Lilith from Raqi'a and projected upon it the side of your personality that you find unacceptable. You can't live with it, so you divorce it from your other persona, the ballerina, and name it Lilith. But you are battling and capitulating to your own shadow. If you are to become whole, to achieve individuation, you must accept this. Call Lilith into yourself and face her; it's the only way you will vanquish her.'

'Oh, to vanquish this blood-thirst would be a fine trick!' she hissed. Josef shifted uneasily, looking dismayed and anxious. 'So, you maintain that it's all in my mind? How do you explain the fact that the three angels who came after me were real, physical entities? Ask Charlotte, ask Karl. Explain how Lancelyn knew what I was without being told. You can't, can you?' She stood up, ready to leave.

'No, I can't.' He rubbed at his forehead. 'I'm afraid I haven't handled this very well. Please, Madame, don't go. We've barely scratched the surface. It might take hours, days of talking even to begin to understand it.'

'No,' she said, donning the mask of the courteous ballerina. 'I've heard enough to know it would never work. Thank you very much for seeing me, Herr Stern, thank you for trying; but you've only confirmed what I already suspected. I am damned.'

Robyn had curled up with a book, trying to forget that the dancer was in the house, trying to ignore the thrilling unease she felt. Insatiably curious, she longed to eavesdrop on their conversation, but her conscience would not let her do it. Irrational to fear for Josef's safety — what could the petite ballerina possibly do to harm him? — yet she could not help linking Violette to his illness and his disturbed state of mind.

Half-an-hour passed. Then a strange sensation made her look up. Violette Lenoir was standing by Robyn's armchair as if she'd materialized from nowhere.

Robyn started so violently that she dropped her book. She laughed, trying to make a joke of it. 'No wonder you're renowned for your light step, Madame.'

She made to stand up, but to her surprise, Violette knelt down beside her and put a hand on her arm. 'Don't get up. You weren't so formal when we met in the garden.'

Robyn, always at ease with men, did not know how to react

to this woman. Her presence was uncannily affecting. She wore a black cloche hat, glossed with feathers and jet beads. Under its deep crown her face was a lily, its translucency accentuated by the darkness of her lashes and brows. Her irises, deepest blue-violet, were as startling as kingfishers.

'Where's my uncle?'

'I told him I wanted to speak to you alone, so he stayed downstairs. You know we're leaving soon; I came to say goodbye.'

'Oh.' Robyn's mouth went dry. She remembered how Violette had embraced her, the strength of her fingers, her mouth, gentle at first, then suddenly demanding. The thrilling terror of it. Now she felt as jumpy as a thirteen-year-old girl. 'Would you like some tea, Madame?'

'No, nothing, thank you. And I keep telling you to call me Violette. Don't say anything until you've listened to me.' Her demeanour, Robyn saw, had changed from their meeting. She seemed softer, more vulnerable, even anxious. 'There are certain things of which I can't speak. Dangers. Your uncle is aware of them and he has been afraid for your safety.'

'What are you talking about?'

The briefest hesitation. 'Oh, ballet company politics. Jealousies. Conflicts.'

'What on earth has that to do with me?'

'I asked you to listen, Robyn. Please. This is hard for me. It's almost impossible, actually.' Violette's hand, gloved in black leather, grew heavier on her arm. 'I frightened you in the garden. I didn't mean to; it's something I can't always control. But the strangest thing is that I have found myself completely unable to stop thinking about you since.'

Robyn, taken aback, managed to suppress any sound she might have made.

'The last thing I want is for any harm to come to you,' Violette went on. 'Your uncle may be worried about you, but I would find it unbearable if you were to be hurt.'

'What is it?' Robyn exclaimed. 'Do you have a jealous admirer who wants to murder me?'

Violette exhaled, seeming at a loss. 'I wish I could be more explicit but I can't. I simply wanted to say that I'm sorry I frightened you; I didn't realize how badly I'd behaved until afterwards. And if I'd known how I was going to feel, I would never have acted so callously. I suppose it's too late to say this now. I hardly know you, yet I feel I can tell you . . .'

'You can. Anything.'

'Then don't be too hard on me. Don't even reply, if you don't wish to. Because I have never in my life made a confession like this to anyone; I never thought I would need to. I love Charlotte but she's too much like me, her passions are like ice-thorns and she's only ever torn me apart. But when I saw you . . . I saw someone with all the warmth and strength I lack, someone who could perhaps heal me. How I despised love, until I met you! But I'm not asking anything of you, Robyn. I simply wanted to tell you. You make me feel human, and I've never felt human before.'

'Oh, my God,' Robyn said softly.

Violette looked steadily at her. Her presence uncoiled all Robyn's certainty about the world. Her other-wordly allure would have captured anyone. It came to Robyn that if she so chose, Violette could seduce her into doing anything; but she held back, respecting Robyn's choice.

To be wanted by this goddess was too dazzling to bear.

'Are you horrified?' said Violette. 'I don't blame you. Please don't be polite. Don't say, "I'm terribly flattered but I prefer men," or any of that. I just want you to remember that you were the first person I've ever felt I could love, and probably the last.'

She began to stand up, but Robyn caught her hand and said, 'Don't go.'

An incredible wave of excitement was rolling through her. She saw a way to leave everything behind, to shed her tawdry life like a snakeskin; Harold, the endless string of victim-lovers, the bitter scars, the hollow tedium of waiting for Sebastian to call. All of it. Replace it with an affection that was new and tender and clean.

'Violette,' she said, her voice shaking, 'what if I said I was not horrified? Quite the opposite, actually. If I said that I want to come with you when you leave . . .'

Violette went paler, if that were possible. She looked dumb-struck, and Robyn realized that this was the last reaction she had expected. She had spoken in the certainty of rejection. Finding acceptance, she was utterly bewildered.

Tears brimmed in her eyes. And the tears, Robyn saw, were tinged faintly with red.

'Oh, Robyn, no. It would be impossible.'

'Are you worried about people talking? No one need know. Don't you need a "personal assistant" or whatever?'

'It's not that. God, I'd love to, but I'd destroy you.'

'I'm not so easy to live with, either. Ask my house-keeper.'

She spoke lightly, but Violette did not smile. The white and indigo light of her eyes, rimmed with red crystal, suddenly glared with annihilating menace, arctic ice steeped in blood. 'No, I mean it. I would destroy you.'

Violette dropped her gaze. Robyn's heart began to beat again. She felt angry, bereft and cheated. 'So after all that, you're turning me down?' Robyn said, voice hardening. 'Good grief, what *do* you want?'

'I'm sorry,' Violette whispered. 'I had no idea you would – No, it's impossible.'

'If you leave here now, we'll never see each other again, will we?'

'I doubt it.'

'I don't understand!'

'Forgive me.' Violette leaned down and pressed her lips to Robyn's. She was trembling. Robyn thought she was about to break down, but when she slid her hands on to the dancer's slim shoulders, Violette immediately pulled away. 'Please for-give me. I'll never forget you.'

'Likewise,' Robyn said stiffly. She watched as Violette let herself out. 'Goodbye, good luck and—'

Go to hell! she added silently, her jaw clenched, her whole body rigid with emotion. Where the gloved hand had touched her arm, her skin tingled and burned.

★

'What did she want?' Robyn and Josef said in unison, as he came back into the parlour. Then they laughed, but their mirth was uneasy. Violette's shadow hung between them.

He said, 'Have you been crying?'

'I'm just being silly,' she said, sniffing. 'So, what happened? You go first.'

'Oh, nothing.' Josef said, stroking her hair. 'Well, not quite nothing. She decided to talk to me after all, but ... I don't think I said what she wanted to hear. I wish I knew what she *does* want.'

'You and me both!'

'Why, what did she say to you?'

Robyn tried to make light of it. 'She made declarations of undying love, would you believe. I must have gone clean out of my mind for a few minutes, because I asked her to take me away with her.'

Josef's face dropped in horror, and he actually bent down and shook her. 'Dear God, you mustn't go!'

His reaction took her aback. 'Why not?'

'Because—' He straightened up, pushing a hand through his hair, leaving it more untidy than before.

'Come on, Uncle, tell me.'

'She is someone around whom I believe it is not healthy to spend a great deal of time. She's very demanding. Can't you imagine what sort of personality it takes to train and discipline all those dancers? You would lose your own self to her.'

'You make her sound like a vampire.'

'Robyn, please—'

'It's all right, I'm not going. She wouldn't let me, and you know why? She said almost what you've just said, that she'd destroy me. Sounded as if she was trying to protect me from her.'

Josef sank on to a sofa, holding his head in relief.

'But it would have been fascinating!' Robyn said. 'I could have written a book about her! "My life with a mad genius".'

'Don't joke about it.' He settled his spectacles on his nose and regained his composure. 'Well, it's almost over; once the ballet's left town you'll be—' She thought he started to say the word, 'safe'. 'I'll be on my way and you won't have unexpected guests disturbing your peace. Your life can return to normal.'

'Won't that be fun,' Robyn said drily. All she felt at the prospect was immense depression. 'Without people like Charlotte, Karl and Violette around, I think I shall just die of boredom.'

'It's you, Cesare,' said the angel, Simon. 'You are the one chosen to lead us against the Enemy.'

They clasped hands, and in the gloom of the inner sanctum, yellow light flared in their palms and knifed between their entwined fingers. Power. Cesare looked into Simon's wondrous eyes, and laughed. They laughed together, intoxicated by hope.

They had talked endlessly since Simon had arrived. Cesare longed to ask, were you ever human? Can I, too, achieve angelic status? But it was too soon, too presumptuous to ask questions of such a perfect being.

John did not laugh or speak, but it was enough that he was with them, an essential part of the triumvirate.

'Join us,' Cesare said, and John came silently to complete the circle. Where John's hands met Cesare's and Simon's the glow was blackish-bronze; but it was power, all the same. A bullish strength, like earth, like iron.

'You understand,' said Simon. His irises were tiger's-eye discs overflowing with ethereal light; to Cesare he was a seraph, whose emotions burned too bright and cold for humans to bear. His face was gold ice, yet strangely ravenous. Immortal hunger. 'I came to you because you understand. Lilith is the Enemy, and you know, as Kristian did, that God is not the forgiving being of men's fantasy. He visits vampires as a plague on mankind; might He not also visit a plague on straying vampires?'

'And we must warn them,' said Cesare. 'Bring them back to the true path!'

'Yes!' Simon said fervently. 'We're in perfect agreement. And you will be a worthy successor to Kristian. My beloved lost son Kristian.'

Cesare gasped. 'You – *you* were one of Kristian's creators?'

His mind could hardly encompass the knowledge. This was a day of wonders.

Simon inclined his head modestly. 'I have created certain vampires in my time; Kristian was the finest, sadly missed. But he's gone, so I've come back to earth to help you bind Lilith in hell where she belongs. And it's your role to unite and lead us. Are you ready?'

Cesare listened in awe and dazzling excitement. 'But can I make the others believe me when I tell them how dangerous Lilith is? Can I make them accept me as leader?'

'You can and you will. Am I not your mandate from God? Come, it's time.'

Cesare nodded, squaring his shoulders. 'I'm ready,' he said.

He led the way into the meeting chamber, where he'd asked the other vampires to assemble. They were waiting sullenly, only a few now, ten or eleven; not in a group, but each standing alone. Only Maria, perfect child, was looking at Cesare with respect. The others, including Pierre, reminded him of unearthed moles, blinking resentfully at the daylight.

To address them, Cesare stood near the throne dais, but not on it. John and Simon flanked him. And in a low-key, almost conversational tone, Cesare began to talk.

He told them of his journey through the outside world, its depravity and corruption; he spoke of Kristian, of the death and resurrection of hope. He held up the photograph of Lilith in its frame of broken glass and dried blood. 'This is our Enemy,' he said.

Did they believe him?

Not at first. They didn't care at first, but he went on, and as he spoke he discovered the gifts of an orator. He brought John forward, and John showed them Matthew's head. Cesare summoned the wretched Pierre, and with his arm round Pierre's shoulders, spoke eloquently of Lilith's cruelty.

'This is what she'll do to us all if she is not stopped! This is only the beginning of her reign!'

Cesare's voice rose. Passion swelled from his throat as he described the darkness growing in the Crystal Ring. 'We've all seen it, all felt it. We can't deny it! And it's Lilith's fault. She will be the death of us.'

The vampires had drifted into a tighter group. Now they were paying attention. Now they were afraid.

'You know the story of Noah; that God in his rage destroyed the whole human race, saving only a chosen few. Well, Lilith is the flood. She has been sent to punish vampires for turning their faces against Kristian and against God. She is the Dark Mother who consumes her own children.'

His audience listened with parted lips and staring eyes. The atmosphere turned as stiff as winter.

'But there's hope. Schloss Holdenstein can be our Ark, and we the chosen few – if we stay together.' Tears began to flow from Cesare's eyes as he walked among them, overcome with emotion. 'You know I loved Kristian faithfully; I never turned against him, unlike some. When I asked Karl to be our leader I did it with our best interests at heart. I made a mistake. But I've learned a lot since then. I offer myself as your leader, if you will have me. Your leader and your servant.'

How bright were their eyes now, how beautiful the faces that regarded him from the hoods of their robes! Like young priests and young widows.

'You all loved Kristian too,' he said. 'That's why you stayed. And it has been very hard to bear eternity without him. So I prayed to Almighty God and He answered; He sent us Simon, His envoy, Kristian's creator. And Simon is God's assurance that I am destined to lead you against the Enemy. I will be a soldier-priest whose only purpose is to destroy Lilith and lead vampire-kind back to their holy estate. At my side stand God's weapons, the sword of flame and the hammer of God; my beloved comrades, Simon and John.'

And suddenly the owl-bright eyes all around him were full of tears, and they began to smother Cesare with embraces, laying their hands on him in supplication and love. Yes, lead us, Cesare. We want you. Save us! We'll do anything, anything.

No apathy in their faces now. He'd brought them back to life!

'We'll draw other vampires here to share in the truth and the light,' he said, 'as many as possible, all the vampires in the world if we can. But any who will not come, and any who shelter Lilith – they are our enemies.'

And Cesare was shocked at the harsh assertiveness of his own voice. Where had it come from? From God, of course! He moved among his followers in a state of near-ecstasy, feeling that he was haloed in golden light, that his feet were winged.

It could become addictive, this adoration.

And Simon looked on beatifically, thinking, do you think you are safe, Violette, in your little world of human adulation? Do you imagine that the theatres in which you escape reality are any less fragile than eggshells?

He wondered where Rasmila and Fyodor were now. If they come looking for me again, perhaps I'll make them stay and serve Cesare. How hard are they prepared to work, to win me back? He smiled cruelly to himself. Would they bring Lilith to me in chains?

Their passion is there to be used, as is that of Cesare and John. I'll use them all in God's service.

Yes, let Cesare stoke the furnaces of their hearts, that I might feed on their energy. I need all the light I can consume to burn away the shadow between myself and God—

The thought of Lilith made Simon freeze briefly, like a mouse under an owl's shadow. But the dark wings passed over, and his inner sun shone again.

You'll do for now, Cesare. You'll do for as long as you feed me with the light of your vision.

PART TWO

Use both your hands to hold me
Tight! Tighter than you should
My heart is coldest steel
But my body's flesh and blood,
Walking hand in hand with silver,
Close as gold to kiss,
Only lovers left alive
And they're swallowed in the mist.

I'm your Sword of Light
Won't you be mine tonight?
I'm your Sword of Light tonight
Going to scorch you deep inside
Make you glad to be alive
Because I'm your Sword of Light.

Wrap tight your cloak around me
And I'll whisper close my dreams.
My home is such a long way
And I'm older than I seem.
I've come a long way
With the good news;
See you need my help.
But don't ask me to be your guide
I'm a stranger here myself.

I'm your Sword of Light . . .

Horslips
'Sword of Light'

CHAPTER TEN

SWORD OF LIGHT

'I went to see Josef after all,' Violette said, as they sat on the train that was taking the company to New York. A week at the Manhattan Opera House, then on to Hartford, Philadelphia, Baltimore and the Southern States.

'What happened?' Charlotte asked. She already knew; Josef had told her when she'd gone to wish him *bon voyage*, but this was the first time she'd heard it from Violette herself. They were alone in the compartment.

'Nothing.' Violette stared listlessly at the landscape rushing past. 'He told me things I didn't want to hear. Things that frightened me, because I already knew them.'

'And then?'

'And then I thanked him, and left. What else? Do you think I attacked him?'

'Of course not,' Charlotte said sadly. 'So, it was no use?'

'Lilith is an aspect of my personality, he implied, which I must learn to accept and control; some hope of that.'

'But isn't it even partly true?'

'Perhaps. He was very kind, and I know you had my best interests at heart when you brought him, but he couldn't help. No one can, as I keep telling you. Except . . .' She fell silent, as if dwelling on something else.

'Except what?'

A pause. Then she spoke, very low. 'It was his niece. I suppose I may as well tell you.'

'Robyn?' Charlotte said anxiously. 'I did ask you not to—'

'I don't know what possessed me; I've always been on my own, it's Lilith's nature to be alone. But when I saw her . . . Oh, I love you, Charlotte, but you are a beautiful golden ice-crystal. You began our relationship by scaring the life out of me, and it's all gone downhill from there. But Robyn is human, soft and warm, so warm. And she's innocent of all this. She's the only person I've ever seen who was capable of making me act completely against my nature. Alarming, isn't it?'

'Violette, you can't.' She gripped the dancer's arm. 'You'd kill her. Vampires and humans can't—'

'Do you think I haven't realized that?' Violette said coldly. 'Did it ever stop you – with Karl or with me?'

'God,' Charlotte breathed. 'Don't, don't—'

'What?'

'Don't do to her what I did to you! Don't drag another human into this. This obsession, it's lethal.'

'What's wrong? Are you jealous?' She spoke with a touch of Lilith's sharpness. Charlotte couldn't answer. 'Well, don't worry. She wanted to come with us, but I said no. I told her how I felt, but that nothing could ever come of it.' Violette turned her head away and leaned her forehead against the window, her face opaline.

After a few moments, Charlotte asked softly, 'Why?'

'Because I knew it was all an illusion, what I felt. I knew what would happen, if I let her come. So I ended it before it began.'

She was expressionless, but Charlotte felt the wave of emotion she was suppressing. Pure heart-break.

'Oh, Violette,' Charlotte said, shaken. 'I've never had the strength to resist my passions like that.'

'Not strength. Just realism. And you and Josef should be happy at least, because all the vampires have left Boston and Robyn's perfectly safe again.'

The day after Josef left, Sebastian came to Robyn's house. It was just as if he'd been waiting for her uncle to leave.

He came in the evening, finding her alone; Robyn had been planning a quiet evening with just Alice for company. He invited her for dinner but she'd already eaten; she offered him a drink and he accepted, and they sat in chairs on either side of the fire-grate, while Alice withdrew to her own room – somewhat ungraciously, Robyn thought – to do some sewing.

Robyn tried to make conversation, but there was a terrible tension between them. Sebastian's dark presence and his bewitching eyes assailed her physically, like heat. And she thought, why are we delaying the moment? This is what I wanted, anyway, to seduce him.

Eventually Sebastian said, 'I don't know why we are wasting so much time talking.'

'Neither do I,' she said. She stood and held out her hand to him. He accepted the invitation; as he rose from his chair and put his drink aside, she noticed that the glass was still brim-full.

The bedroom, all heavy cream lace, was pale gold in the lamplight. Robyn had designed it very carefully to look luxurious, pure and inviting. Rose petals, with an underlying note of musk, perfumed the air. They had said nothing to each other as they climbed the stairs. There seemed no point. But still Sebastian made no attempt to touch her. Was he feigning indifference, or merely going with her out of idle curiosity?

'I won't be long. Make yourself comfortable,' she said as she went into the bathroom.

Sex itself meant nothing to her. It had done once, in the earliest days of her marriage, when she'd imagined herself happy. Betrayal had murdered her physical desires. Now she would never allow them to reawaken.

She undressed and put on a robe of oyster satin. When she emerged he was already in bed, his hair almost black against the big pale cloud of the pillow, one bare arm a shadow on top of the cover. There were fine dark hairs on his forearms, she noticed, but his chest was statue-smooth and as beautifully moulded.

Robyn felt businesslike as she went to the bed and let her robe slide to the floor. The tiniest spurt of apprehension went through her, as it might through an experienced swimmer who dislikes the first chill kiss of the water; then, nothing.

She needed this passionless clarity in order to put on the act that men so loved. She was like Violette, in a way; she prided herself on her choreography. Her emotions went into the art, not the act.

The bed was soft, dew-clean and enveloping as she eased herself into it, Sebastian holding up the covers for her. She always kept her setting perfect. How else could a jewel be shown off to its best advantage? Her house, the extension of her self, was almost as seductive to her lovers as her body.

'You know, I thought you would take more persuasion than this,' he said. His fingers touched her cheekbone. She felt her heart jump into a harder rhythm.

'I'm not open to persuasion,' she replied. 'Either I will or I won't.' She stroked his breastbone with her fingernails. 'I decide.'

'So I met with your approval?' He was half-smiling. His perpetual faint contempt of everything increased her determination to conquer him.

'Obviously.' She reached behind her head and took out the single comb that held her hair in place. Waves brown as autumn spilled over her shoulders. She was not sure the trick would work on him, so the change in his face was as much startling as gratifying. The mocking aloofness vanished. He became sombre, rapt.

'Your hair,' he murmured. His fingers moved in and out of the long strands; coral in anemone fronds. Smiling, she moved towards him, her hands travelling slowly over the firm chest, down the long flat abdomen, teasing and coaxing. Her mouth followed in a down-curving trail of kisses. She made circles and S-shapes with her tongue. To her surprise she found herself almost enjoying her work; she had never had such an aesthetically pleasing body before, so lean and silken, almost luminous, like the angelic form of a changeling.

All men, in her experience, were amazed by a woman taking the initiative; presumably their wives just lay there, which was hardly surprising in most cases. Amazed, then brainlessly drunk on it.

Yet as she reached the sable curls between his thighs, he caught her chin and stopped her.

'No,' he said, 'wait.' He drew her up so they lay face to face. 'Let me make love to you.'

'If you prefer.'

'It's only courtesy.' He was playing with her hair again. 'All you have to do is respond, however you wish.'

She maintained her inviting smile, but her heart sank a little. She preferred to be active and in control. At least this way, if he couldn't wait, it was unlikely to last long.

Sebastian was in no hurry, however. It wasn't that he was unaroused, quite the opposite. Rather, he possessed self-control. He began to caress her as she'd caressed him, and she looked up with just a touch of dismay, thinking, oh God, he is one of those who like to go on all night.

He paused, one cool hand enfolding the globe of her left breast. 'I can see through you, Robyn. You do this for a living, do you not? You don't really want to be here.'

She snatched a breath to retort, but he pressed a fingertip to her lips. 'Never mind,' he said. 'Indulge me. I don't want to hear any pretend moaning. Just relax. Trust me . . . as if I were a friend.'

His eyes were undeniably beautiful. Perfectly shaped and so clear, two woodland pools speckled with diamonds of light under the long lashes. Such a lovely colour, the irises, soft green edging into brown. Almost feminine. Eyes to die for.

Robyn sank back into the pillows in languorous resignation. Why not relax? she thought. Let him do what he wants. Float away.

She closed her eyes. His hands wove patterns over her arms, shoulders and breasts, absorbing heat from her as they worked. It was incredibly soothing. A warm feeling woke under her heart, a sort of fluttering ache. And she realized that she'd been suppressing it for hours.

Instead of kneading her with frantic hands, as other men did, his touch was heart-rendingly gentle. When his lips touched her collarbone, she stiffened with pleasure, suppressing any sound lest he think she was faking it. His mouth alighted here and there on her face, not meeting her lips until she was ready, more than ready for the kiss.

As her mouth opened under his, thirsting for the hot pressure and the taste of him, he slid one hand over her stomach and thighs. How gorgeous his hand felt. The warm ache flared and spread, tingling down the insides of her legs to her toes.

Now he pulled her on to her side, slipping one long leg between hers. Close as velvet, this intimacy, yet still he did not enter her. He was teasing her. And she was shaking now with the effort of denying her own arousal.

The yearning became sweetly agonizing. Oh God, he knows exactly what he's doing, she thought. How can he – this is cruelty, he can't do this to me!

But her head fell back and she groaned. He was not going to enter her until she became so desperate that she made him . . .

The sensations sharpened, deepened. He was inside her at last. She could have cried at his gentleness, the incredible sensuality of his flesh all around her and in her. To do this to me when I won't find any release . . . he'll finish and roll off happy and just leave me . . .

But instead of pushing blindly after his own pleasure, Sebastian found hers; found the exact place and drew her expertly along the mercuric path.

She clung fiercely to him, rocking with him, willing him not to stop. The barriers she'd set in place for years melted, curled away, vaporized. Flames fluttered through her, feathers, chains of red jewels, building towards the single point of fire. She couldn't stop now, couldn't even think. And suddenly, violently, the fire broke.

The sensation was so powerful that it was close to pain. It was an opening, a surrender, the honeyed stab of absolute release. The waves of it pulsed on and on, stealing her voice and her soul, stranding her in blackness. But it was a warm, satiny blackness filled with red stars.

'No one,' she gasped. 'No one has ever—'

She lay drained, unable to move. Sweat sheened her limp body. And her lover, the stranger, looked down at her with pleasure and affection.

'Well?' he said.

'How did you do that?' she exclaimed.

'You sound a little angry with me. Was it such a terrible shock?'

He moved gently inside her as he spoke, waking tiny flames of pleasure. She wanted to kiss him savagely, to possess him for ever; and for making her feel like that, she hated him. Then he began to withdraw from her. With a cry of protest she clasped him, saying, 'Don't.'

But he withdrew and lay on his side, leaving her empty. 'Oh, you like me now?' he said, teasing. He stroked her hips; she arched towards his touch.

'What do you think?' she whispered.

'And your other lovers have never given you such pleasure? Is that not part of the bargain?'

She didn't answer. I shouldn't have given myself away, she thought bitterly; should have pretended it happens all the time. He went on, 'Most men are selfish fools, anyway.'

'Oh, tell me.'

'But all it takes is a little consideration.' He caressed her cheek, smiling, she thought, with self-satisfaction as if he were proud to have stolen her composure. But he was so lovely. She was drowning too deep in sensuality to fight him.

Her hand slid down to his thighs and grasped the satiny penis, still erect and slick with her fluids. He seemed to have gained a terrible power over her, by holding back while she'd lost control. 'But what about you?' she said, coaxing him towards her.

'Why are you so impatient?' The dark amusement on his face tantalized her, like glints of light in a forest. 'We have all night, surely?'

And again he held back and began to kiss her with tormenting delicacy. Her kissed her forehead, cheeks, nose. His lips printed her jawline and neck with heat, sending cold and hot waves over her. He seemed to love her throat more than any other part of her, though he lavished attention everywhere. Worshipping her. His divine touch pulled her down into the whirlpool again.

The bed became a secret other-world in which it no longer mattered that Sebastian was winning the battle. Here was safety.

No one would know if she gave herself up to him in the sweet darkness.

Her body opened up to his in sheer relief and the wild feelings took her again. She danced with chains of stars in the womb of night. Again the red claws of joy pierced her and she writhed against the spasms as they impaled her, lifted her up and threw her out into the universe.

Her eyes came open with the wonder of it. She saw Sebastian's face poised above hers, not amused now but intent, his eyes blank with lust. She wanted him to share her fulfilment, even though the look distanced her, even scared her a little. She gripped his buttocks, thrusting hard against him. 'Yes.'

Then he spoke, and his voice shocked her. He sounded different, not lost in passion but as steel-hard as a knife. 'Is this what you wanted, Robyn?' he said savagely. 'To find out . . . to find out how your victims feel?'

A moment of primal terror. She went rigid, but all was swamped in chaos and she couldn't even think, let alone escape. His head dropped so she could see only the mass of dark hair shimmering. And then he groaned and cried out, 'Oh God. *Robyn.*'

She wanted to hold him through the convulsion, his rapture provoking a last, aching response in her – but the echo of his hard words stopped her. Maybe he didn't mean anything—

The thought was only half-born when it happened. He seemed to undulate, his head rearing over her then swooping down to her neck. An incredible pain flared in her throat. Dull at first, like a wasp sting it grew in intensity, throbbing, stinging, pulling.

He was biting her. Choking her. She heard him swallowing, felt her veins leaping and her heartbeat thundering in her head. A dim but overwhelming horror filled her.

He's drinking my blood!

It wasn't pleasant, not a bizarre heightening of their love-making. It was vile. Her hands tingled and her ears buzzed with blood-loss. And she was pinioned under him, even her thoughts held under swirling water.

Knowledge crowded in, not in words but in fleeting images. That she'd been tricked. That he was taking revenge for Russell's death. But this wasn't fair! Frustrated rage. You'll pay for this, Sebastian, you'll pay!

She believed it until she realized that she was dying.

No panic. Just slipping away.

Seeing their eyes and their spell-woven hair all around her. Sebastian. Charlotte. Karl. Violette. Was this their horrible secret? No, oh God, impossible, *no* . . .

Robyn wasn't dead yet. Something nudged her back to consciousness, and she realized that Sebastian was no longer drinking. His teeth were still in her neck, two hard rods impaling her, but he seemed to pause with the faintest shudder, the faintest sigh against her skin, raising gooseflesh all over her body. Then he released her. The fangs slipped out of the wounds. The pain receded.

As he lifted his head, mouth still open, she glimpsed the sharp canines; worse, she saw them retract until she thought she must have imagined their sharpness and length. Blood glossed his tongue and lips. Sickened, she wanted nothing but to escape him.

He held her down. Their bodies were still joined . . . how terrible the betrayal seemed then. But his face!

Not the cruel, triumphant expression Robyn had expected; instead he looked as she felt. Confused, stricken, angry.

All at once she found her breath. 'You bastard!' she exploded. How weak her rage sounded. She craved words that would wound him like bullets, but none existed.

'What did you expect, beautiful child?' His face lifted into more composed lines, and mockery shadowed his mouth – but she sensed an effort behind it. 'If you play in the forest, you are going to meet a wolf.'

Her anger gathered strength, and she made a violent effort to push him off. 'You bastard.' She spoke forcefully now. Her only desire was to get him out of the house, but without rousing the household or putting her servants at risk. 'Get off me! Get out!'

She hit him impotently; a foolish thing to do, but instead of retaliating he slid lithely out of bed. His face turned icy-cold as he gathered his clothes.

'I have no wish to stay, believe me,' he said.

He dressed swiftly. Rage stung her eyes as she watched him. The cheating beauty of the devil, he possessed. And she hated him, hated him.

'Now get the hell out of my house before I call the police.'

And he was gone. He simply vanished where he stood.

Robyn flung a pillow through the space where he'd been, as if to exorcize him. It bounced off the edge of the dressing-table and fell to the floor with a *flump*.

She meant to get up, to go and wash, perhaps to fetch a hot drink to calm herself. To soothe her uncontrollable shivering.

'You don't frighten me!' she said aloud.

Then she found she was too weak to move.

Then the chill wind rushed in and blew out her anger, followed by the fever and the nightmares.

Cesare walked with Simon and John through a pine forest on the banks of the Rhine; the tree-trunks dark pillars in a navy-blue night. Cesare felt at peace. It seemed only right that an angel had come to him. Confident of his convictions, Cesare felt that he walked on starlit air with his warrior-comrades of gold and iron in place beside him.

And now he dared to ask Simon the question, 'Were you ever human?'

'Once,' Simon answered. 'Thousands of years ago. The centuries wear us thin, until we become glass vessels for the light of heaven to shine through.'

'So a vampire such as myself *could* become an envoy of God!' Cesare exclaimed.

Simon sounded sad, rather weary. 'You might not wish it. It can be a great trial.'

'But not a burden, surely?'

'It is never a burden to serve God,' Simon agreed.

'But there are not enough of us to serve God,' Cesare said

thoughtfully. 'It isn't enough to bring existing vampires into the fold. We need new blood, a new race.' He became more animated as he spoke, sensed the other two gazing at him. He'd caught their imaginations. Even Simon hadn't conceived of this. 'New vampires who are not tainted by all the old—'

Cesare stopped suddenly. There was a figure walking towards them through the trees, from the direction of the castle. A female with the bearing of a princess in a cape of umber fur, jewels and feathers in her hair. He did not recognize her until she came right up to them and greeted them with her usual acidic smile.

Ilona.

'What's going on here?' she said. 'I've been talking to Pierre; he told me to come and find you three. I've just come back from America because I—'

A shadow came into her eyes, and she hesitated. Cesare had always disliked her, with her aura of insolence and wanton femininity. He held her eyes, impressing his new-found power upon her. 'Go on,' he said.

Her eyes flicked to Simon, John, and back to Cesare. 'I've been the victim of Violette. She almost tore me to pieces. I've come to say that everyone is right, she's dangerous.'

Much as he disliked her, Cesare was thrilled. More ammunition! 'So you fled here for sanctuary!'

'Sanctuary?' Ilona tilted her head in disgust. 'Hardly. Yes, Violette attacked me but I'm still on my feet. And now I want to show her that whatever she's done to the rest of you, she can't destroy *me*. I'm not such a fool as to tackle her alone, however. Pierre tells me you're banding together against her, so anything I can do to help – I am at your disposal.'

Cesare wanted her help, but he didn't want *her*. She was too arrogant; she needed to be taught some humility. 'Lilith must have brought you down harder than you realize,' he said softly, 'for you to offer us help instead of hindrance. Go and find Maria. She'll give you some more suitable clothing and instruct you in a few simple duties.'

Ilona's smile remained perfectly steady. 'It must be rather galling,' she said sweetly, 'to be fifth best.'

'What do you mean by that?' said Cesare.

'I'm glad to see Simon has found someone at last, even if he is scraping the bottom of the barrel. He lost Kristian and Lancelyn, and surely you know, Cesare, that he has recently been begging both Karl and Sebastian to take this position before you? He only came to you because they turned him down. Maybe he asked others, I don't know. It seems he's just as much a loser as you are. Still, I suppose that for you, fifth best is quite an achievement.'

And Ilona turned and walked away, her head in the air, a blood-coloured spider-queen retreating from her prey.

Stricken, Cesare watched her go. His incredulous rage was so extreme that it paralysed him. The sharpest of weapons, her words had slid unnoticed through his defences, causing no pain until it was too late.

And that is Lilith's power, he thought. The power of women. To take everything from you with a single lie.

He turned slowly to Simon, and found his voice. 'Is it true? You asked a dozen others before you heard my call?'

Simon, for all his golden self-assurance, seemed distinctly embarrassed. 'Only two—'

'Then you lied to me!'

'No! What lie have I told you? Yes, I asked Karl and Sebastian, but you must understand that this is God's role for me, to choose immortals who possess qualities of leadership. And I've made mistakes. I admit it, because only God is perfect! I went to them before I knew about you. A ruler must have the desire to rule; Karl and Sebastian both lack it. But you, Cesare, you have vision, and that is the single most important quality a leader could possibly possess. You were not my first choice, I admit it freely – but you are the best.'

Simon's mint-gold eyes were mesmeric with his need to be believed. Cesare, somewhat reassured by this answer, said stiffly, 'We need all the help we can muster, but I won't tolerate Ilona's insolence. She represents the very anarchy we're fighting against.'

'I'll go after her,' said Simon. 'She'll behave, don't worry.'

As Cesare watched the athletic figure of Simon striding away through the trees, he turned to John and said softly, 'I don't trust him.'

John stared at him from blood-rimmed eyes set in a grim, hawkish face. He'll be outraged, Cesare thought; how can I say such a thing about an angel of God?

But John only said, 'It's good not to trust. Never trust anyone.'

Another revelation. 'I think Simon needs me as much as I need him,' Cesare murmured. 'I think I could become stronger than him.'

Afraid of saying too much, Cesare kept the remainder of his thoughts to himself. To create a new race of vampires, yes ... Ones who would not look at me with the jaundiced eyes of those who think I am inferior to Kristian and Karl and Sebastian. Ones who would worship *me* for myself alone. Yes, to create new ones ...

And then, to destroy the old.

Simon caught up with Ilona and placed a firm arm around her resisting shoulders. Although he was quietly furious with her for nearly wrecking the delicate balance between him and Cesare, he was determined to hide the anger and be the essence of sweetness. They walked slowly along the hillside, a forested slope dropping towards the dark mirror-plane of the river.

'What's going on, Simon?' she demanded.

'Obvious, isn't it?'

'So, Cesare's the latest victim of your games? A little gold dust on your skin and hair and oh, you must be an angel. You don't fool me.'

Simon found her impertinence amusing. 'Don't underestimate him. He's not as stupid as you think.'

'No one could be,' Ilona said tartly. 'You weren't too happy at my mentioning Karl and Sebastian, were you? Most amusing to hear you scrambling for excuses as I walked away. "Not the first, but the best"? Really, who but an idiot would fall for that?'

Simon remained unprovoked. 'Where did you see Sebastian?' he asked casually.

'In Boston. He's such a virtuoso; Karl, Charlotte and Violette were there at the same time – sometimes virtually in the same room – yet they never noticed him. But I did. And after Violette attacked me I almost went running to Sebastian for help.'

'What stopped you?'

'I know what he's like,' Ilona said with a touch of bitterness. 'He hates his own kind, as you doubtless know. He'd have told me to go to hell – despite the fact he was making love to me the previous night – and I loathe being spoken to like that, Simon dear.'

Simon caressed her cheek. 'I wouldn't dream of it. It's a shame you *didn't* go to Sebastian, though. However he reacted, it might have made him stop and think about Lilith, after all.'

'Surely you can manage without Sebastian's help?'

'Of course,' Simon replied lightly, but he was thinking, perhaps we can't; we need every single strong immortal there is. 'I'm glad you came to us – but if you want our help, you must stop upsetting Cesare here and now. This is a warning, not a suggestion.'

Her mouth pursed dismissively.

'What's more important to you,' Simon asked, 'your pride, or defeating Violette?'

'Defeating Violette.'

'Then you must learn to co-operate. You won't be consigned to sweeping floors with Maria, believe me; we'll find a far more meaningful use of your talents. Cesare has vision; wouldn't you like to play a part in creating a beautiful new race of vampires?'

'Like John?'

Simon shook his head. 'Our kind should be beautiful. It pains me to see John making himself deliberately grotesque – but he must deal with his anger as he will. Even he has vision of a kind. You could share it if . . .'

Ilona smiled, a baleful light glinting in her eyes. She is ludicrously attractive, Simon thought, this daughter of Karl's

... 'Don't worry,' she said. 'If it means getting the better of Violette, I'll swallow rivers of pride as if they were blood.'

Robyn felt the life flowing out of her throat; relived it again and again. She burned and shivered. Her eyes bulged in their sockets, blood-rimmed ... she saw a ghost-face, *his* face, grinning down at her through the darkness. Her hands fluttered like pinned moths.

The bed was awash with blood. She lay drowning in her own life-blood. She saw her own breath bubbling up towards the thick, slopping red surface; she flailed in the blood, retching and panicking, struggling to thrust her face into the air—

Yellow lights came swerving towards her, terrifying. Alice and Mary were rushing into the room, staring down at her, their faces hideous with horror. They looked like crones, like funeral mourners.

They dropped their lamps and they screamed, screamed.

Robyn woke.

With a silent *snap* the world returned to normal. Morning light glowed through the thick lace curtains. The room looked tranquil and friendly. And although the bed was rumpled from love-making and from her restless dreams, there was no blood. No blood.

She got up, found her robe and slipped it on as she went to the dressing-table. Dizzy. No strength in her limbs.

Her face in the mirror looked drained, with blue crescents under her eyes, a grim set to her usually mobile mouth. And on the right-hand side of her neck was a bruise, jewelled by two faint, pinkish moons.

Is that all? she thought, probing the place with her fingertips. It felt sore. Nothing serious. Hardly noticeable, really. Almost healed.

She sat there for a long time, staring at her reflection, fingers moving lightly over the wound. There was a slight crusting of dried blood just below it, another on her cheek like the imprint of lips. Did he kiss me after he fed on me? she thought. I can't remember.

She scraped away the dried blood with a fingernail. Soon all the physical evidence would have vanished.

The real damage, she thought, is inside me.

She was not sure how she knew this. It was an instinctive knowledge, a dark infection that he'd left swirling inside her. Yet she felt numb.

Why didn't he kill me? I thought he was going to; I think he meant to. I don't know why he stopped.

I don't think he'll come back.

She leaned her forearms on the edge of the dressing-table, dropping her head on to them with a huge sigh. She did not feel afraid now, only depressed, betrayed, humiliated to the very centre of her being.

Mary came in with the tea, which made everything seem quite ordinary. But when Mary saw her mistress's face, she looked shocked. 'Ma'am, you don't look at all well, if you don't mind me saying so. I think you should be after getting back into bed.'

'I think so, too.' Robyn smiled, but it was an immense effort to speak at all. 'Run me a bath and change the sheets, there's a dear, then I'll have a lie-in.'

Robyn's lie-in was to last four days.

Alice was continually at her side through the days of her illness. She insisted on calling the doctor, who was brisk and unsympathetic. He concluded that Robyn was anaemic, and she thought, tell me something I don't know.

Yet Robyn couldn't describe precisely what was wrong. Lassitude, a dreaminess in which there seemed no point to anything. Nightmares of blood and betrayal; in her febrile slumber, every kind face she'd ever known turned on her, every friend was revealed as a vampire. Alice and Mary, Josef, Harold, Violette . . . Violette.

She dreamed in glaring, fiery colours that she was copulating with devils, or with priests who turned into demons. She would wake up suffocating. Then she would lie awake, too languid either to weep or feel angry. Simply brooding on Sebastian. Remembering his dark, deceptive beauty. His hands on her body. The soaring sexual fire he'd awakened ... she'd never forgive him for that, either.

She couldn't forget. Thoughts of him obsessed her.

It was not for ever, though. On the third day, she began to feel better, more like her usual self, though still strange as if half-drunk. Perhaps that was why she spoke so unguardedly to Alice.

Alice had removed her lunch tray, looking approvingly at the empty plates; there was nothing wrong with Robyn's appetite. She fussed with the pillows so Robyn was sitting up comfortably, then sat down beside her. The room was full of flowers from Harold and a couple of would-be admirers, but there had been no word from Sebastian.

'The night you were taken ill,' Alice said, 'did your gentleman friend stay the night?'

'Part of it,' Robyn sighed. 'I told you his name.'

'Well, Mr Pierse hasn't called to see you since.'

'I know.'

'I wondered ... Did he hurt you in some way?' Robyn didn't answer. Alice went on, 'Only you looked so ill that first morning. I noticed a little mark on your neck, and you've been so ...'

'Out of my mind,' Robyn said softly. 'I think that's what I am.'

'Don't you tell me it's none of my business, madam! I'm here to protect you, not just to wait on you hand and foot.'

'I wasn't going to, you sarcastic beast. Yes, he hurt me.' Without emotion, Robyn told Alice everything.

The housekeeper turned her face away as if in denial, but her eyes, swivelling into the corners to hold Robyn's gaze, had a chiding look.

'You know, it doesn't matter if you don't believe me,' Robyn said. 'I can hardly believe it myself. I was attacked by a vampire who seemed to know everything about me ... and I'll tell you what it was. It was unfair.'

Alice blinked. 'That's quite an understatement.'

Suddenly Robyn felt a flare of anger, the first sign that she was still alive. 'No, I mean it. *I* am the one who takes revenge. What the hell right did he have to come here and usurp that privilege? Did he think he could leave me too scared ever to approach a man again, in case I met another like him? Well, he's wrong. I won't give him the victory!'

'Madam . . .'

Robyn subsided, smiling grimly at herself. 'So, do you think I've lost my mind?'

'I think,' said Alice, unmoved, 'that maybe you should see the doctor again.'

'You don't believe me,' Robyn said, with perverse satisfaction. 'No doctor can help, don't you see? But it's all right. I'm feeling so much better I do believe I'll get up tomorrow. To think that I expected to be bored when Violette and her friends left town . . .'

Karl reflected that he and Charlotte had experienced some of their most exquisitely happy moments during the Ballet Janacek's tour. The endless activity allowed even the minds of immortals to rise above the grimmer questions of their existence and float on the shining surface. As the tour took them from Richmond, New Orleans, Houston, Dallas and Wichita to San Francisco and other cities en route, Violette seemed completely fulfilled. Endless travelling, rehearsing and performing filled her days, enabling her to forget her conflicts with Lilith and with other immortals, at least for a time. While there was no love lost between her and Karl, he was glad that she seemed at peace.

With that anxiety eased, he and Charlotte took advantage of every opportunity to explore a new land. They walked in deserts, ascended purple and white-veiled mountains, watched great waterfalls cascading under the moon. They trod the length of the Grand Canyon between its soaring red walls, made love in glorious wildernesses of rivers and giant redwoods. They captivated strangers and sipped their blood without guilt, feeding together as they had on the peasant woman in the Alps, as if all restraint had been magically lifted.

Their truce held; they were able to speak of Ilona and Violette without rancour. Both Karl and Charlotte found it unbearable to quarrel. But Karl sometimes wondered, are we clinging together a little too fiercely? Conceding too much influence to the forces that threaten us?

Yet it was a wondrous time. Like angels treading a virgin land, they experienced the full beauty and mystery of their strength.

'I don't want to go home,' said Charlotte as they walked along a cliff edge on the Pacific, the world all burned-gold and azure.

'Don't say that,' Karl replied. 'Wishes come true in the most unfortunate way, sometimes.' He took her hand, and led her into the Crystal Ring.

He watched their joined hands as they made the transition, saw their pale flesh turn darkly iridescent, like black opal, like colours swirling on oil. The change never ceased to amaze him.

They ran together, almost flew, until they found a bluish, rippling path to lead them to the higher levels. It was as if they'd shed their earthly forms to reveal their true natures; slim, ink-dark demons, their hair and clothes turned to glittering webs. Often when they were in this form, they desired each other violently, for a reason Karl did not fully understand. Only that their vampire beauty was pared to its feral essence.

Now, though, Karl led Charlotte upwards until coldness began to prick their skin. He didn't tell her that he was searching for something. The Ring above America was still the firmament he knew; the same wild skyscape threaded with auroral arcs of magnetism, same unearthly colours and weird atmosphere. The differences were subtle, localized, ever-changing. And the overlying note of hostility, which grew ever more noticeable, was also present. The realm of mankind's subconscious was a single, primordial mass, it seemed.

The bronze hills rolling through the lower layers of the ether were as wild as ocean waves, and the electric blues of the void had darkened to bruised shades of violet.

'Raqi'a used to seem so tranquil when you first brought me here,' Charlotte said, hanging on to his arms as the currents tried to tear them apart. 'Now it's always stormy. What's happening?'

'I wish I knew, beloved.' They climbed the side of a vast chasm that dwarfed the Grand Canyon. Nothing was solid here, but they were almost weightless, like water-flies skimming the surface of a liquid. Below them, the earth was hidden in shawls of purple-black shadow; above, veils of cloud diffused the fierce distant light of the *Weisskalt*. And between the upper and lower layers, insubstantial mountains hung as if reflected in a shimmering, glassy medium.

Karl looked up, and saw what he had been seeking. He folded his arm around her shoulder and pointed upwards. 'There,' he said. 'Tell me what you see.'

'I know,' Charlotte whispered. 'It's here, too. It's everywhere we go.'

Amid the ever-moving skyscape, there was one great, raven mass that seemed to remain in the same place while the ghost-mountains rolled around its skirts. The sight of it, as always, filled him with dread.

'Describe it,' he insisted.

'Every time I enter the Ring it's there, a huge black shadow, floating at just that height. Wherever I go, it's always there. As if it can be seen from anywhere, like the moon from earth. Yet it always seems close, as if it follows us . . .'

'Yes,' Karl said. 'Everyone has seen it, but no one talks about it. Not even us.'

Charlotte stared at him, and he saw fear in her eyes. 'Because we're afraid of it.'

'And we think that if we don't mention it, it will go away. But it won't. It's growing.'

'But what is it?' she asked.

'I have no idea. I only know that it's dangerous.'

'And so cold,' Charlotte breathed. 'But you're right, we must explore it, not run away. Isn't that why you brought me here now?'

The structure reared above them, like a fortress of obsidian. It was a concretion that had no place in the Ring. A tumour. Karl, despite his horror of it, was fascinated. It seemed to be increasing in size, drawing everything towards itself, accruing its mass from the wispy arms of ether that spiralled slowly inwards.

They were climbing towards it. It wasn't so far away that they couldn't reach it, after all. Charlotte was moving ahead of Karl, her scientist's curiosity, as usual, overcoming her sense of self-preservation; a quality in her that Karl both loved and regretted. 'Be careful,' he said.

'But I must know what it is!'

The object became a black wall spreading across the sky in front of them. Charlotte stretched out her right hand. 'Don't!' Karl cried, but it was too late. She had touched it.

Holding her, he felt the impact, a glacier crashing through his nerves. The shock flung them apart. Charlotte was spiralling back to earth like a winged seed.

Karl caught her, slowed their descent until they landed feet-first on a lower layer. But Charlotte seemed barely aware that she had fallen, certainly not shaken by it; she was staring at her fingers.

'It was solid,' she gasped. '*Solid*. How can it be? If all the Ring turned to black rock it would be dead to us, we could never come here again, and then how would we rest, how would we travel or vanish or ... Oh God, would we cease to exist?'

'Charlotte, don't,' Karl said softly. All the same questions had passed through his own mind. Is the Crystal Ring dying, or turning against us, or both? No, it's unthinkable!

He guided her downwards until the world snapped into reality around them, and they were in human form again, standing on a cliff with the Pacific Ocean glimmering darkest cobalt below them.

'Hush,' he said, clasping her hands. '*Liebling*, don't be afraid.'

'I'm not afraid, I'm all right,' she said, still staring at her hand. He held her, pressing her hands to his chest. Her fingertips were frozen. 'But what's causing this change? How can something solid exist in Raqi'a?'

'I wish I had an answer.'

'It means something. Some event must have precipitated it.'

'Kristian's death?' Karl said thoughtfully. 'The creation of

Lilith? Or her breaking of the angels' power over her, or my placing a dangerous Book in the *Weisskalt* for safe-keeping, or our scorn of God—'

'Karl!' she exclaimed. 'Why is it our fault?'

'It probably isn't.'

'Then don't take everything on to yourself.' She ran her hand over his cheek and through his hair. He looked into eyes of violet crystal, lit with ravenous curiosity, fear, courage, and an elusive edge that resisted definition; all the qualities that had drawn Karl irresistibly to her. Charlotte seemed at once wholly self-assured and fragile. Unbearable ever to argue with her or to be cold to her, even where Ilona and Violette were concerned. 'But what are we going to do?'

'I don't think there is anything we can do, *Liebling*. I have a feeling that the truth will reveal itself to us in time . . . before it's too late, I hope.'

'But it's all connected,' she said, eyes widening with anxiety. 'And if this is because of Lilith – then it's *my* fault. I made her. How can I live with causing this darkness?'

CHAPTER ELEVEN

SILVER, CLOSE AS GOLD

'I shall get up tomorrow,' Robyn had said, but first there was the night to endure.

She lay half-sleeping and half-waking, a little delirious. The moon shone through the curtains, a white coin dappling the room with lace patterns. The bed in which she lay seemed expansive, a snowy plain frozen under a moon in another world. She thought the floor was a river that she must cross or die. Hallucinations.

She saw a thin dark figure against the moon and the lace curtains. Her blood began to pulse through her head, slow and heavy.

'Alice?'

No reply. It seemed she lay there for an aeon with the faceless silhouette gazing down at her. Whether it was male or female or even human, she could not tell. She felt pitifully vulnerable.

In a spurt of panic she cried, 'Alice!', or dreamed she did; there was no answering call, no sound of her companion scrambling from her own bed to rush to Robyn's aid. And she knew that no one was going to help her.

The figure came closer. Robyn was confused. For a moment it seemed that this black creature was a bird of prey hovering, Odile in black feathers, the death crone in her most beguiling livery. *Violette*, she mouthed, but her voice failed.

When the shape moved again, it changed. Not Violette; too tall, too masculine. Still no light on its face, but now she recognized the shape of the hair and shoulders.

'What do you want?' she hissed.

There was a chair by the bed, in which Alice had been sitting to keep her company. The intruder pulled it back and sat down. His nonchalance was as infuriating as it was unnerving. Just for an instant, as he seated himself, she saw his profile against the moonlight; the sharp beauty of nose and jaw, one dark soft eye turned obliquely towards her.

He crossed his ankles, rested his left elbow on the arm of the chair and his chin on his hand, and sat gazing at her.

'*What the hell do you want?*' she said. She was angry now, breathing fast.

'I wanted to see you again,' Sebastian replied.

Robyn groped for the lamp on her bedside table, clicked it on. The bulb burned, flickered, and failed with a *tink*. For one second, captured as if by a photographer's flash, she'd seen his face, the long, pale wrists and hands, the candid, heartless eyes. He wasn't smiling. The serious set of his lips alarmed her far more deeply than his usual mockery.

'Well, now you've seen me,' she snapped. Oh God, she thought, hold on to yourself. Don't let him see how scared you are.

'I can see you quite clearly without the light on,' said the soft voice.

'Who let you in?'

'No one. I let myself in. Vampires do that, you know.'

She was unconsciously fingering her throat, trying to gather the collar of her nightdress around it as a fragile shield. 'Oh, I love the way you just sit there and admit it! Is this it, then? You've come back to take the blood you didn't steal before?'

He reached out with his right hand and caught her wrist before she could evade him. He was so fast. He'd got her before she even thought of moving. Shock electrified her.

'If I wanted to,' he said, 'there's nothing you could do to stop me. Scream and fight all you like. If anyone comes to help you, they won't stop me either; they could get rather badly hurt, actually, and I'm sure you would not be wanting that. Oh, Robyn, you're trembling.'

He pressed her fingers and let her go. She snatched the hand away and cradled it against her chest, like an abused kitten. It felt ice-cold and numb. But her loins contracted and tingled with the memory of his body against hers.

'Of course I'm trembling. Wouldn't you, if you thought you were about to die? But I suppose you wouldn't know what it feels like, since you only pick on victims who are too weak to fight back!'

He was silent for a time. His silence made her feel more wretched than ever. Defying him was futile, like defying a thunderstorm.

Eventually he said, 'Now I know why I came back.'

'Why? Why are you doing this to me?'

'I could have killed you, my dear. I meant to, I meant to drain all your lovely blood . . . but I stopped. Why did I spare your life, do you think?'

'To prolong the torture? Do you know I've hardly left this bed since you were here? I've had such fevers and nightmares as you wouldn't believe. I think I'm still dreaming now. But I suppose you're happy to hear this.'

'No. It is just an unfortunate side-effect for those we leave alive. Our bite causes madness, to one degree or another.' Then he added, unbelievably, 'I'm sorry.'

'What?'

'It gives me no pleasure at all to see you suffering.' Another pause, in which she gazed at the silhouette, not knowing what to make of his words. He dropped his hands to his knees, leaning towards her. 'Do you want me to leave?'

'I – I don't know.'

'I haven't come to prey on you. I only want to talk. I give you my word, though you may be disinclined to believe me . . .'

Yet Robyn found she did believe him. And even if he'd said he wanted her blood again, her answer would have been the same. 'No, I don't want you to leave.'

'Why not?'

'I'm curious to know what someone – some *thing* – like you could possibly want to talk about.'

'God, you're a hard one, aren't you?' said the vampire. 'I spared your life, and I don't know why. I've never done it before. And you want me to stay; even knowing what I am, you want me to stay . . . and *you* don't know why. This is an interesting situation that requires some discussion, does it not?'

Robyn had drawn herself into a sitting position against the headboard and was staring at him, chilled. 'Do you always kill your victims?'

He shrugged. 'I take what I want. If it kills them, that is their affair. What I mean is that I do not usually force myself to stop before my thirst is satisfied.'

'And do you always make love to them first?'

'No, of course not. It would be far too much trouble. The blood is essential, sex only a distraction – though, it has to be said, an excruciatingly pleasurable one. I do it quite often, I suppose . . . but no, not always.'

'I think,' she said, her throat in spasm, 'that you are an utter fiend.'

'And what about you, Robyn? I gather you have a nice line in making men lose their heads over you. Are you any better than me?'

'I don't kill people.'

'Just drive them to suicide.'

'I don't rape them, either.'

'Nor do I, my angel. I've never taken anyone who wasn't willing. And if I'm in a generous frame of mind, I ensure they experience so much pleasure that they're willing to die for me anyway. Isn't it so?'

'Ah yes, that,' she said bitterly. She resented him for forcing her to taste the forbidden drug of rapture. And there was a conflict raging inside her; how could she accept him as a vampire, un-dead, impossible mysterious demon – yet still speak to him as if he were a man? But she knew the answer. Her veil of scepticism had been eroded by contact with Violette, Karl and Charlotte without her even realizing it. And Sebastian, in attacking her, had torn down what was left of the curtain, leaving her in the raw light of knowledge. And this knowledge revealed, also, that these were reasoning creatures. Ones who appreciated the weight of their own actions. Her mouth dry, she said, 'So you – your kind – like to seduce before they attack, do they? Make the victim a willing participant, share the guilt. Subtle.'

'You don't hate me for giving you pleasure, surely?' he said.

'But I do. Manipulator, as well as fiend.'

'And have you not manipulated me?'

'How?'

'It's against my will that I'm here now,' said Sebastian. 'I didn't mean to come back. I'm not so happy about that, either, but, well . . .'

She looked at the shadow-figure, sitting motionless with his hands lying along the arms of the chair, a patriarch in a Gothic throne. He looked solitary, tormented, lethal. Not a man she could just dismiss like one of her lovers. A vampire haloed by the moon.

And yet so nearly human. A creature she could engage in battle, mind to mind.

She asked suddenly, 'How did you come to be like this? Are you very old?'

'Not old enough. Too many questions, beautiful child. Only don't expect me to faint at the sight of a priest, or to catch fire in the sun. Can I see you again, when you're feeling better?'

He could be so charming, when he chose. It was almost touching, the way he asked permission, as if he needed it. A wave of fatal excitement rose in her throat, capsizing all common sense.

'Can you make love to me without . . .' Her fingernails grazed the place where he'd bitten her.

'It's extremely hard not to.'

'Then it will happen again.'

'Every time.'

'And will it kill me?'

'Eventually,' he said very softly, 'if we don't stop.' He stood up and leaned over her. 'Well? Knowing this, do you still want to see me?'

And knowing it was suicidal, Robyn said, 'Maybe once.'

The vampire bent to kiss her. She stiffened; her terror was instinctive. But his mouth only met hers in the gentlest kiss, warmly tantalizing. His hair brushed her cheeks. She slid her arms round his neck to draw him down to her, only to find herself embracing the air.

After Sebastian had gone – vanished – Robyn turned on her side and lay staring at nothing, curled up like a child. But after a while she fell asleep and slept soundly, undisturbed by fever or by dreams.

In the morning, she woke feeling well, and suffused by manic excitement as if she'd offered to do some insane and exhilarating stunt, like flying on the wing of a biplane.

I'm going to see him again. He's not going to kill me, or even harm me. I'm going to get the better of him! What a challenge; to outwit him, not a mere man, but an actual devil!

Will he come tonight? A warm tremor of desire went through her. She danced around the room.

Then she noticed how late it was, and wondered why Mary hadn't come in with the tea.

Putting on a dressing-gown, Robyn went into the corridor and saw that the door to Alice's room was still closed. Softly opening it, she found the room in darkness, the curtains closed.

'Alice?'

She looked down at the figure in the bed, and cried out.

Now she knew why no one had heeded her cry in the night, why no one had come to her this morning. From Alice's room, she ran upstairs to the maid's bedroom, her heart pounding and her mouth sticky with fear.

Like Alice, Mary lay unconscious, pallid, breathing with shallow, laboured sighs. And on her throat, too, were the fading crescent-scars of Sebastian's fangs.

Cesare's plan was taking shape swiftly. Now, when he addressed his followers in the meeting chamber, he did so from the dais, with one hand resting on Kristian's ebony chair. And no one suggested that he was presuming too much.

There was much to do before Violette returned from America. The day of her return in the autumn loomed in Cesare's mind like doomsday. 'When Lilith comes,' was a phrase he used often when talking to his flock, and it always sent a wave of thrilling terror over them, as if they'd been caught in the backdraught of Satan's wings.

Cesare felt happy, fulfilled. Vampires had been arriving at Schloss Holdenstein unbidden, alarmed by rumours, or by the growing knot of blackness in the Crystal Ring, or by some instinctive knowledge of Lilith that had come rippling through the ether. His little band numbered twenty now, and more would come, he knew. They know they're in peril, he thought, they are afraid, and they're coming to *me* for help!

Further proof, as if he needed it, that Cesare's leadership was ordained by God.

Even Ilona had been tamed by the need to survive. Cesare was paradoxically grateful for her attempt to make mischief; it had revealed Simon as less than perfect, thus forcing Cesare to be more self-reliant – and determined to prove himself. The trinity was powerful – Cesare saw Simon, John and himself as fire, earth and air – but Cesare was careful to keep an edge of distance, of control. John was right, he thought. I can trust only myself.

Everything was going well. More vampires were joining the crusade, and Ilona was beginning the work she did so well. But in secret, Cesare's happiness was tainted by attacks of doubt.

Despite Simon's assurance, 'You were not the first but you are the best,' Cesare could not get Sebastian out of his mind. He remembered Sebastian's single visit to Holdenstein in the last century; recalled a vampire even more evil and wayward than Karl, who'd dared to challenge Kristian. Cesare hated the thought that Simon had chosen such a rogue to take power. And such arrogance, to have turned Simon down!

Cesare despised Sebastian – but he couldn't forget him. Sebastian had become a shadow in his mind that would have to be forcibly exorcized.

And then there was Lilith herself.

In moments of clarity, when the crusading fervour retreated and he felt a little depressed, Cesare would sit alone in the inner sanctum and dredge through his deepest fears. I'm bringing my army together by uniting them in terror and hatred of the Enemy – but what do I really know of her? How can I send them against her, when I haven't even faced her myself?

Am I a coward?

No, no! He clenched fists on his thighs, but the words went on shivering through his mind, a nightmare litany; *when Lilith comes, when Lilith comes* . . .

And he looked up to heaven and thought, how can I send my flock against her if I have not first confronted her myself? I must prove my courage. I must prove that I need the machinery of an army against her, that I'm not merely acting out of cowardice.

I must face her alone. Just once.

He called John and Simon in and asked, with a trace of desperation, 'How *can* we destroy her?'

'I don't think she can be destroyed,' said Simon, 'but she can be hurt. Ask yourself what would hurt her most.'

Because Cesare could not conceive of vampires caring for humans, he couldn't answer; but John said, 'To destroy her ballet. She killed Matthew because he threatened her dancers.'

And Cesare was suddenly full of excitement and ideas.

'We can't touch her yet, but we can strip everything from around her,' Simon said. 'Take away her ballet, take away those who would shelter her; leave her alone, exposed.'

'Alone and threatened, she'll be at her most dangerous,' Cesare said, shuddering. Sometimes he still felt the ache of long-faded scars on his back, recalled too vividly the gut-loosening terror of his childhood . . .

'Yes, but also at her most vulnerable.' Simon's gilded face showed no sign of fear. 'When she comes home, we'll give a little while to lull her suspicions—'

'And then,' Cesare breathed, 'and then we'll welcome her home.'

Every Sunday, Robyn went to Trinity, the Episcopal church in Copley Square. It was part of her pose, to make herself appear more acceptable to Boston society; what could they say about a woman who attended church and did charity work? The word 'hypocrite' sprang to mind, but she didn't really care.

She wasn't religious, but she liked the church building. She loved its Romanesque solidity, the arches, turrets and pointed roofs. The interior, all dark wood with a wealth of painting and decoration, had a feeling of warmth. She liked to sit in the gloom and study the glorious LaFarge and Burne-Jones windows. Simply to flood her senses with their stormy purples, apple-greens and electric peacock blues was spirituality enough for her.

But this Sunday she prayed.

Please, God, let Alice and Mary get better.

Please forgive me. Let them get better and I'll never fall again.

To tease Robyn, Sebastian did not return to her house for a few days; to tease her, and to tantalize himself. Meanwhile he enjoyed the city on his own; the separate worlds of wealth and poverty, the churches, the burial grounds where he could seize a victim between the gravestones and the trees after the true spirit of his nature. From the grand bow-fronted houses of the Back Bay and Mount Vernon Street to the tenements of the North End, he would hunt invisibly and indiscriminately in the night; and then he would walk along the harbour, staring past the ships and ferries to the black-sapphire water. Clearing his mind of it all.

Yet everywhere he went, he imagined Robyn beside him, sharing the silver beauty of the night, her form outlined by moonlight . . . imagined himself leaning down and driving his fangs into the tender flesh of her neck.

The worst thing she could do to me, he thought ironically, is to have left home and vanished without trace by the time I decide to go back for her. And she might do it to spite me . . . but I doubt it.

One evening he crossed the Charles River to explore Cambridge and amuse himself among the students and intellectuals. It was there, as he wandered through the tree-filled squares and stately buildings of Harvard University, that he suddenly realized he was being followed.

Strangest sensation of dimensionless entities watching him; like the time Simon had found him in New York.

And then, with a stab of cold, human alarm, he saw them; two glimmering figures, one pale, one dark.

If Simon could find me, why not Fyodor and Rasmila? he thought. But why, why?

For a moment he was back at Blackwater Hall, two hundred years falling away with the rain that streamed over his icy skin . . .

He took a step forward. The black shape resolved itself into a lamp-post, the white one into a sliver of light falling between two buildings. And Sebastian stood aghast at himself for falling prey to his own imagination.

He felt shaken, to his own disgust. Again he found himself thinking of Simon and Ilona – and of Violette. He loathed these intrusions. It infuriated him that every time he drove them out, they crept back.

His gaze swept up, past the pillared front of a library, past the shimmering leaves of elms and beeches, to the night sky beyond.

'If you interfere with my existence,' he said softly to Simon, Violette, anyone; perhaps to the demon in his own soul, 'you will regret it.'

The sensation of being followed vanished, but it left him feeling empty, distressed, thirsty for something more than blood.

That feeling drove him back to Robyn's house.

He stood on the terrace in her garden, watching her in her parlour. A glowing cream and golden jewel-box of safety. She was alone for once; she looked so innocent, curled up with a book like a little girl, yet he thought she seemed uneasy. She kept breaking off to sigh and gaze at nothing.

Sebastian watched her for a long time without moving. Second nature for a vampire just to watch as if turned to stone, never tiring of the object that fascinated him . . . as Simon had watched him.

Thinking of other vampires had left a sourness in his mouth. He needed Robyn now to wash the taste away.

Presently she put her book aside and walked round the room, adjusting an ornament here, a picture there. She sensed something, he could tell. And at last she came towards the french doors.

As she opened them to the night, he moved away through the Crystal Ring. When she saw him at last, he was standing in the centre of the small lawn, by the lemon tree.

He saw her start, felt a wave of nervous heat radiate from her. Then she came down the steps and straight towards him, demanding in a loud whisper, 'What the hell are you doing here?'

In a pyjama suit of ivory silk, with her hair brushed loose over her shoulders, she looked astonishing. Lustrous eyes wide with anger, one hand clasping the jacket at her throat, a bloom of blood in her cheeks. He could have fallen on her. When he said nothing, she grew angrier. 'Have you been watching me?'

'Naturally,' he said softly. 'It pleases me greatly to look at you. Do you mind?'

'Yes, I mind. You're damned right I mind!'

Then he realized that he'd underestimated how angry she actually was. She was alight with rage. It shook him a little to see her like this.

'I was waiting for you to come out to me,' he said, smiling.

'Why the hell couldn't you knock on the front door like a normal man? You know, telephone first or leave a card. It's been driving me mad, wondering whether you were coming back or not, wondering *when*, you goddamned—'

'You said you wanted to see me.' His tone was cool, and he knew how he appeared to her; pale, too still, his eyes hypnotic but unfeeling. He enjoyed his power to frighten her – yet he was intrigued by the way she refused to be cowed, attacking him like a fiery russet sea breaking itself on a spire of white rock.

'That was before I found what you really are!'

'I thought it was obvious—'

'I'm talking about what you did to Mary and Alice!' she cried. 'I found them after you'd gone. You went in to them – how dare you, how *dare* you do that to them!'

Sebastian allowed himself to look amused. Robyn looked ready to kill him. 'You have no cause to be jealous,' he said.

'What?' She caught her breath in disbelief. '*Jealous?*'

'I didn't stop to make love to them first. It would have taken far too long.'

Her mouth dropped, eyes opening wide. He continued, 'I am joking, my dear; I have no carnal designs on your servants. But blood is blood. It is the one thing I absolutely must have.'

She glared speechlessly at him. 'You invited me to come back,' he said, 'knowing what I am.'

'Don't you dare try to blame this on me!' She'd backed away from him, but now she came forward, pointing a finger at him. 'If you ever touch Alice or Mary or any of my other staff again, I'll—'

'What?'

Her voice fell to a quieter note. 'I'll certainly never see you again. I don't see what you can do about that, unless you kill me – and that would kind of defeat your object, wouldn't it?'

Sebastian exhaled softly. She was right, and she'd won a small victory. 'I don't want to kill you, and it would be no pleasure to force you. And I would mind very much if you refused to see me. You look cold, Robyn. Aren't you going to invite me inside?'

'Oh, you need an invitation now?' She studied him, her eyes glittering, then she relented. 'All right. Come in.'

He followed her, watching her hair swaying against her upright back, the way the soft jacket hinted at the rich curves of her hips. He turned to close the french door, but Robyn went to a lace-covered table and picked up a small object, closing it in her hand so he couldn't see it.

'Where are Alice and Mary?' he asked.

'Mary's in the kitchen. Alice has gone to a concert with some friends.'

Sebastian spread his hands. 'So, no harm done.'

'That's a matter of opinion.' She turned to him, leaning

against the table. 'They were both in bed for a day; not as sick as I was, but bad enough. I don't think Mary remembers what happened, although she jumps at every little noise. But Alice . . . I'm sure Alice knows what you did. She won't talk about it, but I can see it in her eyes. I don't know what I'm doing, letting you in here.' Her head drooping, she pressed a fist to her forehead. 'I really don't know what I'm doing.'

Sebastian went to her. Her head jerked up; she looked dishevelled, flushed, wholly irresistible. He could see why so many men had lost their heads over her; almost shaming, that he wasn't immune. He wanted to touch her, but sensed she would only shake him off.

'Robyn . . .'

'Does this mean anything to you?' She opened her fist. Pressed into her palm was a silver crucifix on a chain.

He regarded it, unmoved. 'No. Does it mean anything to you?'

She bit the side of her lip. The gesture was so unconsciously erotic that it was all he could do not to seize her. 'My mother's Jewish and my father's a Unitarian and I'm a cynic. And a sinner. So I guess it ought to mean something, but it doesn't.'

'But you go to church.'

'So?' Another flash of anger. 'Have you been following me?'

He shrugged, leaving her to guess. 'Well, I was once a Catholic, severely lapsed, so there you are,' he said lightly.

'Oh, well.' She let the chain slide through her fingers. 'I wanted to see if you would scream and leap through windows, like in *Dracula*.'

'I can do that, if you'd find it entertaining.' Sebastian was looking at her more softly now. Her fear of him was fading. 'But not in response to a piece of metal.'

He allowed himself the luxury of touching her then. He rested his left hand on her shoulder and rolled strands of her brown hair between his fingers. She did not flinch.

'You were trying to protect yourself. I don't blame you for that,' he said gently, 'but you can't.'

A dull pain, laced with tenderness, fleeted across her face.

She pressed her cheek to his hand, swallowing hard, as if she wanted to stop herself, but couldn't.

'I think we should go up to my room,' she said, 'don't you?'

They dived through a lake of flame and smoky light, joined from mouth to loins. Smoke and light that had turned liquid, transmuted to wine and honey. No bed beneath them, nothing of earth to constrain them. Sebastian felt that he'd transported Robyn to the Crystal Ring and they fell through the clouds for ever, entwined.

It was even more glorious than the first time. They knew each other now but there was more to learn. And this time, to his delight, Robyn did not fight her feelings but absorbed him, craving sensation, passion, release. His body slid over hers on the sweat that oozed from her human pores; he loved the moist heat, the saltiness, all her natural scents. Her eyes were half-closed, her throat taut with her netted breath, her fingers kneading his back, nails scratching him; her limbs and breasts heavy against him as they rolled over and over, striving to consume each other.

Robyn climaxed beneath him, blood rising in her face, her heart clamouring against his chest. All through him, he could feel and hear her heart. Folding her elbows behind his neck she clung to him, rocking, almost weeping.

And now he must follow her into the mindless light. Every sensation was an almost unbearable pleasure, a lightning flicker on the edge. *Robyn . . . ah, God . . . I cannot believe . . . I am lost in you now . . .*

He saw her eyelids lift, her expression change. Eyes ringed white with anxiety, she whispered, 'You don't have to – you don't have to feed, this time . . . do you?' He couldn't answer. It was too late. 'Sebastian?'

White heat swept over him. Through it, he became dimly aware that she was resisting him; trying to push him away, to keep his mouth from her neck. But he couldn't stop. And when she realized that she couldn't prevent it, she began to fight in earnest, squirming and hitting out and gasping.

Somehow she deflected him and his fangs sank into her shoulder instead. A taste of blood, not enough. He bit her again, again, found a thick vein at last. Sucking hard, he quivered with the bliss of it, while all the time she went on struggling beneath him.

Stop now, said a subconscious voice. *If you want this to happen again, you must stop now!*

One deep, delicious draught of her blood had to be enough.

The pleasure passed its red peak and ebbed away, leaving him weak with satiation. He rolled to one side, oblivious now to Robyn's distress. So he was shocked when she delivered a powerful slap across the side of his head.

'You *bastard*!'

He caught her arm, without effort, to prevent a second blow. She wormed away from him and sat against the headboard, clasping a pillow, her knees drawn up and ankles crossed. Scarlet threads ran over her collarbone, matting strands of her hair.

'I asked you not to. I told you to stop!'

'And I told you before that I couldn't.'

Robyn, trembling with the aftershock, began to cry. She looked so lovely, curled up under the burnished veil of hair, that he wanted her again. But he would not, could not feel remorse.

'It hurts,' she said angrily. 'It feels horrible.'

Sebastian left the bed, brought a flannel and a glass of water from the bathroom. She stared at him as if she hadn't expected him to reappear. Giving her the glass, he sat beside her and began gently to bathe the wounds he had made.

'Look, Robyn,' he said softly. 'They're healing. They are only faint marks now. Hardly there at all.'

'Don't you have the remotest idea of what it feels like?' she said bitterly.

'Of course I have. It's when they take all your blood, *all* of it, that you want to be worrying. How do you think I became like this?'

She froze. He watched the enticing rise and fall of her larynx as the mouthful of water trickled down her throat. 'Oh God, is it going to happen to me?'

'No, it isn't. We're not infectious like the smallpox.'

'But you still bring death by degrees.' Calmer now, she regarded him through narrowed eyes. 'What's *your* bed like, I wonder? Black, with a white lining?'

'No, no, I don't sleep in a coffin and I am not going to turn to dust if I'm still here when the sun comes up. Now, tell me – ' he pressed his hand to her cheek, 'do you feel as bad as you did the first time?'

'No. Just a little dizzy. I'm all right.'

'Because I stopped, Robyn.'

Her eyes flashed open. 'What if a time comes when you can't stop?'

'We both take that risk.'

'No, *I* take it.'

'By your own choice.' He lay beside her, pulling her down towards him. 'I won't force myself on you.'

'I just wish you could make love to me without taking my blood,' she whispered. 'Is it too much to ask? Oh God, it is, isn't it?'

He pressed his lips to her warm, downy forearm, linked her arms around his neck, and kissed her. She glowered dully at him, then gave a heartfelt groan and pressed herself against his long, lean body. He entered her again and she gave herself up to him, liquefying.

'Listen to me,' he said into her ear. Her breath was a warm cloud on his neck. 'Don't fight me. Relax, then it won't hurt. I promise I won't take much.'

They they were on fire, melting, hurled outwards and falling like comets through space . . . and when the moment came, his mouth slid gently over the contours of her throat. Finding the place, he bit into her with swift tenderness.

This time she only stiffened beneath him. Then her breath ran out in a sigh and she lay unresisting but not passive; participating, simply in the way that she rested her cheek on his hair and stroked his shoulder, while her emotions informed her whole body with fugitive radiance.

He kept his word, though it wasn't easy.

'Was it so terrible?' he asked afterwards.

She rubbed her thumb over his lips, and looked at her own blood smeared on her thumb-tip. Then she unconsciously sucked it clean. 'Not quite so terrible,' she said faintly. 'It was rather like floating.' She almost smiled, but her eyes were drowsy and distracted.

Sebastian lay back, cradling her against his cheek and stroking her hair. He was not at all eager to hear what she was thinking. He just wanted to hold her.

As he did so, an inner voice began to speak in horrified amazement. What the devil am I doing, showing a mortal this tenderness? Have I gone mad? Humans are below us, they are like animals, their sufferings are transient and meaningless ... and yet, I feel compelled to be careful because I do not want her to die.

The feeling was almost one of panic. But he controlled it, telling himself firmly, of course I'm not mad. It's purely expedient, using any means to keep her alive and pliant so that I can prolong my own pleasure. That is all.

Have I quite deceived you yet, my Robyn?

When the ship sailed from New York, bound for Hamburg, Charlotte was sorry to leave. The tour had been successful beyond Violette's fondest dreams. The Ballet Janacek had been fêted across the continent. Most importantly of all, Violette had appeared happy.

Throughout the tour, she had been kind to her dancers, gracious to the press, and had not said a word to Charlotte of her usual concerns. Charlotte suspected that Violette had taken her advice at last; that she was obeying the thirst instead of fighting it, and going out each night to feed as swiftly and neatly as a cat, in order to devote all her thought and energy to the ballet.

She will do that for her art, Charlotte thought, but not for herself.

Sadly, the idyll had to end. Crowds of well-wishers lined the quay as they sailed, cheering and waving and throwing flowers. They saw Violette as a living legend, already an immortal. None of them, thought Charlotte, possesses the faintest idea of what their darling Lenoir is really like.

Home drew them now like a current sucking them across a mist-veiled sea. Charlotte was aware of her own mood darkening, and she sensed the same thing happening to Karl. There would be no more wanton sharing of prey on their own side of the Atlantic.

Violette took to her cabin again, and would see no one but Geli. Charlotte began to despair. But one evening, as she stood alone at the rail, watching the calm green sea shimmering under a glorious sunset, Violette softly joined her.

'Something's waiting for us at home,' Violette said. 'I don't know what it is ... but something bad. Don't you feel it too?'

'Yes,' Charlotte admitted. 'But we have to go back. If we try to stay away and ignore it, we'll only make it worse.'

Violette fell quiet. Other guests were strolling on the deck, elegant in evening dress. A few glanced at Violette, but were kind enough to respect her privacy.

Charlotte said gently, 'While we were on the West Coast, Karl and I went into the Crystal Ring . . .'

'You go there every day.'

'I mean that we went to look at the – the darkness there; to study it, instead of denying it—'

'Stop,' said Violette. Her face was white glass; Charlotte heard the rail creak under the pressure of her fingers. 'I don't want to hear about it.'

'Don't you want to know what happened?'

'You're still alive, aren't you? How bad could it have been?'

'Bad enough.'

'And do you think it's my fault?' Violette glared frigidly at her. 'Some physical manifestation of my inner sickness, is that it?'

Charlotte exhaled, and rested a hand on Violette's shoulder. 'Of course not. But it won't go away on its own. You won't talk about anything.'

The dancer looked away. 'And you and Karl never stop. What good does it do? I can't talk about it; please, Charlotte, leave it alone. I don't even want to think about these things when I get home. All I want is to start work on a new ballet.'

'Immediately?'

'Yes, why not. I know what I must do next. A ballet about Lilith.'

Charlotte was dubious. 'It could be a risk.'

'After *Dans le Jardin*? Yes, I know. Please don't remind me of that disaster. No, I think I've learned by my mistakes. This will be different; the themes won't be so blatant, and I won't use modern music or experimental sets. It will be dressed up as an old-fashioned, tragic fairy-tale. Another *Giselle*. It will be beautiful. But I've got to do it, Charlotte. It's trying to claw its way out of me.'

'What's the story?'

Violette brightened, seeming glad of her interest. 'There will be Adam and Eve again, but this time the Serpent is a woman, Lilith. I'll give them different names, of course. A young man has a passionate affair with a dark spirit of the forest, but when the time comes for him to marry, he chooses an innocent, compliant young girl as his bride. Rejected, Lilith curses them. She torments the wife and tries to seduce the man; she murders their children and brings about their downfall—'

'It sounds very dark.'

'No, no, it will work. It will be beautiful and tragic!' Violette said fervently.

'Do you really see yourself in such a negative light?'

Violette met her gaze. 'You know I do. That's why I need to explore it. Josef told me to face what's inside me, after all.'

'How does it end?'

'I don't know. I really don't know. But I need Ute to dance the woman; if only I hadn't driven her back to her bloody father!' She looked at Charlotte, suddenly thoughtful. 'I suppose you wouldn't consider—'

'I couldn't. I can't dance.'

'Yes, you can. I've seen you.'

'But it's cheating, isn't it?' Charlotte said, her head on one side. 'I can only do it because vampires can imitate humans, not because I have trained for years. It wouldn't be right.'

'And Karl can't spare you.' Violette sounded more sad than bitter. 'No, you must go back to Switzerland. It's not fair of me to keep you in Salzburg. I'll find someone else.'

'But don't make it too dark. Have the children kidnapped, not murdered, so there can be a happy reunion!'

Violette smiled. 'I wish you would write the story for me. All the steps are in my head. I'm going to start rehearsing the ballet without even the remotest idea of how to end it.'

Charlotte thought, and does acting out your life save you from having to live it? But she didn't say it. Planning the new project made Violette calmer, at least.

'You won't dance because you're not human,' Violette said presently. 'Do you ever wish you were human again?'

'I think of it, but in all honesty I wouldn't go back,' said Charlotte. 'Would you?'

'I never felt human, even when I was, so perhaps it wouldn't be as different as I imagine. It's just that I met someone who made me feel there was hope, and I had to leave her behind. You know, I wish I hadn't been so noble.' Pain darted across Violette's face; a longing for something that Charlotte could not provide. 'Do you think it's possible to cross the Atlantic and back in a night, through the Crystal Ring? Should I go back now, before we're too far away? If only I could see Robyn one last time . . .'

'You could probably do anything, dear, but I shouldn't,' Charlotte said gravely. 'Leave her alone. What possible good will a vampire lover do her?'

'It's only an idle wish. At least I know Robyn is safe; she'll never know what she escaped! I think it's only that I wanted to escape into *her*, into a warm, comforting human, because I'm frightened.'

Her face perfect as snow between raven wings of hair, Violette looked anything but vulnerable.

'Of what?'

'Myself, of course. I'm not afraid *for* myself. I know nothing can really hurt me. I'm terrified of my capacity for destruction. I can hold Lilith in check for a time; you have no idea how hard I worked to ensure nothing went wrong on the tour.'

'I think I can guess.' Charlotte stroked her arm.

'Well, I can control her for a time, but she will have her way in the end. And I don't know what is going to happen,' her voice fell to a whisper, 'when we get home.'

CHAPTER TWELVE

SHADOW DANCE

Robyn had expected Sebastian to leave before dawn, so she was startled when she woke from a deep sleep to find him still beside her. It was daylight, nearly eight o'clock. Half-asleep, her eyelids and her whole body leaden, she began to sit up.

'Don't move,' Sebastian said. 'I like to look at you. So lovely to watch you sleeping.'

But Robyn was thinking of Mary and Alice, one of whom was about to come in with the tea. She rarely let her 'gentlemen callers' stay the night. The last thing she wanted was for either of her servants to be confronted by their vampire attacker.

Too late; she'd barely sat up when the door opened.

It was Alice. Seeing Sebastian, she dropped the tray. As it hit the carpet with a dull crash of metal and china, a rattle came from Alice's throat like an aborted scream. She turned and fled the room.

'You'd better go,' Robyn said, feeling cold towards Sebastian in the aftermath of too-heavy sleep. 'Go on, get dressed!'

'Why?' I thought that was a housekeeper, not an outraged mother.'

His beauty threatened to captivate her, the leaf-green eyes and soft darkness of his hair making her want to eat him alive, but she resisted. His flippancy was merely annoying. 'She's also my companion. She's scared to death of you! I happen to care more about her feelings than yours – so get out.' She climbed out of bed, putting on her dressing-gown and tying the cord.

'Without even a bath or a cup of tea?'

'Don't be facetious,' she snapped. Grabbing a hairbrush, she turned to the dressing-table mirror and stared at her reflection. The colour in her cheeks was high but otherwise her skin looked drained. She fingered the healed marks where the vampire had attacked her, on one shoulder and on both sides of her neck. Where he'd fed from her the second time, there was a bruise and two tell-tale streaks of dried blood. Alice must have seen them.

Sebastian's face appeared in the mirror behind her. His long hands folded over her shoulders. Robyn knew she was acting insanely, letting him sleep with her and feed from her veins; thank the Lord he does have a reflection, she thought drily, or I might just lose my mind completely. He said, 'Are you regretting last night?'

'I'm regretting the whole thing.'

'Don't.' He pressed his mouth to the side of her neck. She jumped violently, but he only kissed her there. How hot and silken his lips were, making her tingle with the echoes of their love-making. How carnal it seemed, in the judgemental light of day. Almost bestial. 'When shall I see you again?'

'I don't know,' she said, savagely brushing her hair. 'How soon do you want to come to my funeral?'

'A few days,' he said ambiguously, and turned away.

She heard him dressing. Eventually she swung round to say, 'Don't go yet,' only to find that he had already gone.

Alice was in her room along the corridor, staring out of the window. Outside, Robyn glimpsed the roofs of Beacon Hill, sea-mist condensing on the humid air, treetops flying a gorgeous array of colours.

'It's OK, Alice, he's gone,' she said.

Alice turned, looking pale but very severe, like one of the prim Episcopalian women she claimed to despise. 'Just what in God's name do you think you're about, letting that creature into your bed?'

'Are you all right?' Robyn asked meekly.

'Never mind me, just answer the question!'

'I notice you assume I invited him, not that he forced his way in.'

'I know you, madam. No man ever makes you do anything you don't want to – not even him. How can you let this happen, knowing what he is? It's obscene!'

Finding Alice outraged rather than cowering in terror, Robyn's concern mutated into irony. 'There's one good thing about it. At least you believe he's a vampire, instead of thinking I made the whole thing up.'

Alice flinched, and her hand flew by reflex to her throat. 'I don't know what I believe! I only know – he did something terrible to me. I can't stop seeing his face . . .' The faint lines on her rounded face deepened. 'A stranger's face leaning over me in the middle of the night. His mouth open, the terrible sharp teeth . . . And it was agony, like being stabbed with knives, and there was nothing I could do to protect myself. And then seeing my own blood on those teeth . . . But the worst thing was the helplessness. An ordinary man I could have stabbed with my scissors, maybe . . . but his eyes paralysed me. If I was scared, how do you think poor Mary must have felt? It was obscene. All I know is he's mad. Evil. So for you to be sleeping with him – that's evil too, madam, just plain *evil*.'

Alice's passion rendered Robyn speechless for several seconds. When she managed to answer, her voice was husky with shame. 'Look, Alice, I'm sorry. I made him give his word that he'd never touch you or Mary again. I know you're afraid of him, with good reason, but it's all right. You're safe now.'

There wasn't much conviction in her words. In truth, she had no control over Sebastian and had no idea how far she could trust him.

'Even if we're safe, what about you? There was blood all over you!'

'Don't exaggerate.' Robyn lowered her gaze.

'It was obvious what he'd been doing! And you *let* him?'

Robyn gave a single nod. 'In a sense.'

'For the love of God, are you trying to kill yourself, or what *are* you trying to do?'

Robyn took a deep breath. 'I'm being stupid, I know, but—'

'Stupid? Suicidal! What *is* he? I mean, we know he has a taste for blood, but what actually *is* he? You don't know, do you? Yet you're being completely reckless! Why, for heaven's sake? *Why?*'

'Because—' She paused, trying to find the words. 'Because he's a wonderful lover.' She touched her friend's shoulder, but Alice remained stony. 'He's the most wonderful, the *only* wonderful lover I've ever had.' She hung on the throbbing edge of memory. All the searing, impossible pleasure that had gone on and on until she was a wrung-out rag, breathless . . . the frightening struggle against his blood-thirst, then the reluctant surrender . . . Unspeakably strange feeling. Lying there, breathing lightly, his fangs impaling her, she'd become aware that the pain was bearable; still a dreadful piercing clamp on her throat, but with an evocative and diamond-sharp integrity of its own. She'd floated, sinking down on waves of faintness which were hallucinatory yet not unpleasant. So weird, to be feeding him as an extension of their sexual bliss. A bond between them. A cruel, unequal, unhealthy bond . . . yet a bond, all the same.

'I can't just give him up,' Robyn said. 'And I rather hate him for that.'

Alice's face opened up with surprise. 'Hate him?'

'Yes, you know, for getting under my defences. I've got to figure out some way of taking revenge, because he's got no reputation to lose and couldn't give a damn about money. I need to think of something else but it's hard . . . so until I do, I'm going to enjoy myself with him, use him the way he thinks he's using me.'

'You're crazy. You've got to stop.' Alice seized Robyn and actually shook her, as if she were a little girl. 'Don't you realize he's probably murdered people?' Her voice fell. 'There was a housemaid found dead in a house in Marlborough Street, a young man dragged out of the river . . .'

'That's speculation,' Robyn said, but cold gooseflesh ran all over her.

'He should be gaoled. He should hang. I'm going to tell someone.'

'Who are you going to tell?' Robyn cried. 'No one will believe you. Don't tell anyone, Alice, please. Don't interfere.'

Alice's face, usually serene, was hard with determination. 'Hasn't it occurred to you that you have responsibilities to the people in this household? Not just to Mary and Mr and Mrs

Wilkes, but to *yourself*. What would we do, if anything happened to you? How do you think I'd feel? How would your Uncle Josef feel?'

'Stop it!' Robyn lifted her hands in exasperation; her mother's gesture. She had to shut her mind to this wild vista. 'Stop worrying. Nothing is going to happen to me.'

Idyllic as the tour of America had been, Karl found it pleasant to return home. He absorbed the familiarity of their surroundings as he and Charlotte climbed the steep hill towards their chalet; the crisp whiteness of the mountains against the sky, the air like cold wine infused with scents of peat and pine.

It was also a delight to be alone with Charlotte. Violette had returned to Salzburg with her company, neither she nor Charlotte expressing any wish to stay together. Karl was glad.

But as he and Charlotte reached their door, they paused and looked at each other.

'There's someone inside,' said Charlotte.

Entering Raqi'a, they melted through doors and walls and swiftly reached the drawing-room. There was a fire in the grate, and two blond figures lounging on the sofa. Stefan was sitting up, Niklas lying down with his head on his twin's lap, while Stefan absently stroked his hair.

Seeing Karl and Charlotte, Stefan pushed Niklas aside and shot to his feet. Niklas rose beside him like an ironic mime, a delayed reflection.

'I've been waiting forever for you!' Stefan exclaimed. 'I couldn't find out exactly when you were meant to come home.'

Throwing her coat on a chair, Charlotte said, 'What's wrong?'

It was rare for anything to perturb Stefan, but Karl saw anxiety in the cornflower-bright eyes. 'We had a visit in London from Cesare and a couple of his underlings. He's changed, Karl. He thinks he's Kristian and he's starting to act the part.'

Karl's heart sank. He thought, could we not have had a few minutes' peace before this began? 'What happened?'

'He said he was summoning all vampires to Schloss Holdenstein. He has something very important and very exciting to tell us; a crusade to save us all from Lilith. But here's the rub; anyone who refuses to come will be considered an enemy, a minion of Lilith.' Stefan began to pace slowly around the room, trailing his hand across Niklas's shoulder as he passed him. Karl had rarely seen him so agitated; angry, in fact.

'Surely he didn't frighten you?' Karl asked.

'Oh, but he did!' Stefan exclaimed. He looked at Charlotte. 'You didn't know Cesare in the old days, but he used to be so quiet he might as well have been part of the furniture—'

'He would make excellent firewood,' Karl said darkly.

'I can't explain it,' Stefan said, 'but he's acquired a power he never had before. He threatened us, and he meant it.'

'But you don't like Violette anyway,' said Charlotte, with a hint of resentment. 'How could he think you were on her side?'

'I don't *dislike* her,' Stefan said, walking to the fireplace and back. 'She makes me uneasy, but that's beside the point. The thing is this, and I beg you to take me seriously, Karl; Cesare's dangerous, and he's on the march. And I've had enough. Kristian, Simon, Lilith, Lancelyn – how much more must we suffer before they leave us in peace?'

'I know,' said Karl. 'I feel the same. I had a feeling we'd have to deal with someone like Cesare before long . . .'

'Well, *you* can deal with him,' said Stefan. 'You're on your own.'

Karl looked hard at him, and Stefan stopped pacing. 'I don't wish to fight with anyone,' said Karl, 'but if it becomes necessary – are you saying that you won't help us?'

'That's exactly what I'm saying. Cesare's gathering an army. He'll become an immortal dictator and it will be "Follow me or die". And we can't stop it, Karl, without creating an army of our own. What's the alternative? If we plunge in and fight him, we'll almost certainly be killed. No, thank you. I came to warn you – and to say goodbye.'

'No!' Charlotte exclaimed. 'Where will you go?'

'That would be telling. I really wouldn't like to think of Cesare torturing my hiding place out of you.'

And Stefan's vivid eyes burned straight into Karl's. Difficult ever to be angry with Stefan, but Karl felt let down. 'So, you're disappearing?'

Stefan went to Niklas's side and put an arm around his shoulders. Niklas went on staring into space with a faint smile and vacant, gold-glass eyes. 'Correct. We're running away. Call me a coward, call me all the names under the sun; water off a duck's back. It's not for myself, it's for Niklas. He may be a vampire, but he hasn't the wit to protect himself. If it came to a physical confrontation, all my energy would be taken up in protecting him, which would make the exercise pointless. The last time, I almost got killed; what would Niklas have done without me? I can't live without him, nor he without me. I don't want to be a fugitive, but I have no choice.'

Karl sighed. Stefan's decision dismayed him, but he couldn't argue with it. 'Do what you think best. We'll miss you.'

'You'd be wise to come with us.'

'Perhaps.' Karl met Charlotte's eyes. 'But we must stay.'

'Then be careful. I don't deserve such understanding friends,' Stefan said quietly, 'and I don't want to lose them.'

He clasped Karl's hand, and hugged him; then he went to Charlotte, and kissed her on the cheeks and lips, almost with the passion of a lover. Charlotte was trying not to cry.

'I'll write,' said Stefan. He placed his arm round Niklas and they vanished into the Ring.

Charlotte stared at Karl, her eyes alight with sadness and rage. 'If Cesare thinks Lilith's so dangerous that he has to raise an army against her, he must be an imbecile!'

'Without question,' Karl said heavily. 'But I'll have to go to Schloss Holdenstein and find out what is happening for myself.'

'On your own?'

Karl usually suppressed the desire to be overprotective towards Charlotte, but for once his sense of foreboding got the better of him.

'This time, *Liebling*, if you don't mind.'

And he spoke so gently that she couldn't refuse.

★

Karl had never considered himself an idealist. What possible ideals could a vampire hold, who had wantonly forsaken all morality? Yet now, as he climbed the rugged slope to Schloss Holdenstein, he realized that he had envisioned a Utopia of a kind.

He had imagined a world in which, with Kristian dead, each vampire would be free to determine his or her own destiny, codes of behaviour, relationships. They would dissolve into anonymity among their human prey. No vampire would interfere in another's existence; after all, why should they even want to?

Now he understood, with a heavy heart, how misplaced his optimism had been.

Something worse in Kristian's place ... not a precisely defined opponent, but something complex, fugitive and ever-shifting.

Violette – or Cesare?

In the castle's dank corridors, Karl walked softly, gauging the vampire presences around him. And ... he hesitated, curious ... humans?

He went on, down into the windowless heart of the castle, where Kristian had once held court. The atmosphere had always been stifling, heavy with blood and death, but now there was also a feverish note.

Karl wanted to see Pierre. He also needed to know if Ilona had come here after she had left Boston so abruptly; anything could have happened during his months spent in America.

As he followed a winding corridor that led between a network of cells, Cesare, with horrible inevitability, stepped out to meet him. Karl halted, resigned. He hadn't really expected to reach his friends unchallenged.

Stefan was right, Cesare had changed. Not physically; he remained a pallid, deceptively boyish figure with his drab robe and mousy colouring. But there was light in his eyes, a new energy and confidence in his bearing.

Karl anticipated hostility, but to his surprise, Cesare grinned and clasped Karl's right hand. 'Karl, how wonderful to see you. Have you come home?'

Does he really imagine I ever thought of this as home? Karl thought, regarding the pale-eyed figure with contempt. He'd had the chance to kill Cesare once; he wished now that he'd taken it.

Karl withdrew his hand. 'I have come only to see my friends.'

'Be my guest,' Cesare said, sweeping his hand as if to usher him along the corridor.

'Thank you,' Karl inclined his head with icy courtesy, 'but I don't believe I need your permission.'

He walked straight past Cesare into the warren of rooms that lay around the inner sanctum, where he sensed Pierre's presence.

A cell, reached through a doorless archway; flames flickering, stonework blackened by years of candle- and torch-smoke. A table, a few ancient chairs, and a wooden pallet on which Pierre lay, entwined with a human; a well-built male with fair hair. The male was naked but for a cloth around his loins.

At the table sat a grotesque vampire whose bald skull was a mass of scar tissue. It took Karl a moment to realize that this was John, and that the severed head perched on the table's corner was Matthew's. Karl experienced a surge of horror and pity that shook him.

John sat writing with a feathered quill, ignoring the proceedings, but Ilona, perched on a stool, was watching raptly. Her knees were crossed and she was leaning forward, her sharp chin resting on her hand. Her dress was a dark plum colour, like her hair, like the blood that escaped Pierre's lips to streak his victim's shoulders and chest.

Karl caught the scent of it, and the musky-salty human smell that lured vampires with the promise of satiation. He responded, despite himself. His fangs slid half out of their sockets with the pressure of desire.

Ilona turned to look at him, lips tightening into a smile. 'Father! Join us, why don't you,' she said. 'Pierre, leave some for Karl.' Her eyes were sultry from feeding, but something about her had changed, Karl observed. Nothing definable. A sort of dullness of spirit. He recalled, with a stab of pain, how she'd wept on his shoulder and fed from his throat; and the thought fleeted through him, all this hideous misery has been caused by Violette . . .

'Thank you, I shall refrain,' Karl said, although he could have fallen on the man's throat. As Cesare moved into the doorway beside him, Karl again sensed the feverishness that seemed to pervade the whole castle. 'Cesare, are you not aware of how unwise it can be to kill victims in your own domain? The castle has enough ghosts already.'

Nothing, it seemed, could dent Cesare's good humour. 'We do not kill them, and they are not victims.'

'We have to bring Pierre's supper to him because he still won't leave the castle,' Ilona added. 'You wouldn't want him to starve, would you?'

Pierre appeared oblivious to them. His eyes were closed, his mouth clamped to the man's neck, his hands locked around the broad, naked shoulders. The man was conscious, rigid in the deathly embrace. Muscles stood out in taut curves along his arms. His hands wagged in the air, the thick fingers splayed. His groans could have been of agony or rapture.

'I wouldn't be so confident that his victim is not going to die,' said Karl. He leaned against the corner of the archway, folding his arms. 'No one, not even Kristian himself, could ever tell Pierre what to do. No power on earth could make him cease feeding before he has finished.'

'Pierre,' Cesare said lightly, moving towards the pallet. 'Enough now. We must not damage him.'

To Karl's astonishment, Pierre obeyed. He dropped the man, pushed himself away and knelt on the end of the pallet. He looked dishevelled, as if he hadn't combed his hair or changed his clothes for weeks. Ichor dripped from his lips, and his expression was fearful.

Karl was so shocked that he felt tears spring to his eyes.

'How long has he been like this?'

'Months,' said Ilona. 'Since before you went to America. He improves a little, then he slides back.'

The human had curled up on his side, groaning. Ignoring him, Karl went to Pierre. 'My friend,' he said gently, 'what has happened to you?'

'I told you,' said Ilona. 'Violette.'

Pierre rubbed his hand across his mouth, smearing the blood. 'Nothing's wrong. Leave me the hell alone!'

'Violette seems to be happening to everyone,' Ilona remarked.

'She appears to be dangerous to whose who cross her,' Karl said neutrally.

Ilona's face tightened with indignation. 'I didn't cross her, Father. I was taking a victim. Isn't there an honour among vampires that forbids us from interfering with another vampire's kill?'

'She's dangerous to all of us,' said Cesare. 'I hope you haven't come here to defend her, Karl.'

'I came, as I said, to see Pierre and my daughter.'

'Is there hope for you, then?' Cesare's cheerful expression did not slip. 'Can we persuade you to our cause?'

The question was semi-rhetorical, so Karl didn't reply – but he sensed an underlying insistence. An answer would be demanded eventually. Karl found the change in Cesare alarming. No longer a mere acolyte, waiting passively for Kristian's second coming, he had found his own path at last. Cesare's inner light gave him a simple, translucent beauty; and this quality had the power to draw others to him. To dazzle them subtly, Karl thought, so they never notice they've been blinded.

A sound, a new tendril of warmth, made Karl turn round, his hand on Pierre's shoulder. Two more humans entered the cell, strong young men dressed in brown robes, barefoot, both fair. They bowed to Cesare, then went to the young man on the pallet.

'Take him away, wash and feed him,' Cesare said. The men helped Pierre's victim to stand and dressed him in a robe like their own. He swayed, but he was clear-eyed and smiling faintly. Facing Cesare, he gave a sharp, deep nod of respect. There was nothing short of adoration in his eyes.

'Master,' he said, trembling pride in his voice.

Cesare touched his cheek, and the man – big and powerful enough to break Cesare in two, had they both been mortal –

looked as if he might faint with delight. 'Go and rest. You have earned it.'

Karl watched with a mild sense of revulsion.

'Be a gentleman, Cesare,' came Pierre's hoarse voice. 'Offer Karl a drink.'

Cesare's face tightened slightly, but his tone remained gracious. 'Let me not withhold refreshment from you.' He gestured towards the two who had just entered. 'Take which-ever you wish.'

Karl wanted nothing from Cesare, but as he studied them, curiosity overcame him. Fresh-faced men in their early twenties, in the very prime of their strength, who stared back at him with full intelligence, with respect and eagerness to please. Even Kristian had never kept humans in the castle like this. The strong rush of blood through their bodies drew him powerfully. It crossed his mind that this might be a trap of some kind, but he dismissed it. He thought, Cesare hasn't grown that devious – yet.

He approached one of the men. He was as tall as Karl and much broader, with short-cropped hair and a tanned, freckled face. Sinews stood out in his wide neck, muscles moved under his smooth skin, as if he were tensing himself for military inspection. No visible fear.

Karl moved slowly, watching him. What do you see as I approach you? Do you understand what I am going to do?

Karl placed his hands on the shoulders, feeling their muscular thickness through the loose-woven material of the robe. Per-spiration broke out on the man's upper lip. As Karl felt his tension increasing, he breathed the heat with a fascination that verged on trance, thinking, *you see my marble face and my dark eyes and you know what I am, yet you do not flinch* . . .

Karl struck. The blood hit him like a wave. He felt the hot clasp of flesh round his fangs, salt and fire in his mouth, the seductive softening of the victim's body against his own. How animal, this pleasure. Utterly sovereign.

A vampire could wrestle with his conscience for all time, but it would never be more than a shadow-dance obliterated by the throbbing reality of the kill.

The first surge over, Karl began to distance himself, letting the flow of blood slacken, taking slower and more sparing draughts until at last he could bring himself to stop. Amazingly, the man showed no signs of weakening. He remained rigid, as if he'd trained himself to withstand the assault. It was Karl who, half-swooning with pleasure, had to lean on him for a few seconds; one elbow draped over the man's shoulder, face against his collarbone. The momentary loss of control reminded him of why he usually hunted alone; why he never cared to feed in front of anyone, particularly Ilona.

Regaining control, Karl drew back. The man dipped his head towards Karl's hand, like a cat questing for his owner's touch, then seemed to recollect himself and stood to attention once more. Karl studied him, trying to read his eyes. All he saw there was the self-negating obedience of the soldier . . . and looking at the other two, he saw exactly the same expression.

'Who are you?' Karl asked softly.

'That's enough.' Cesare's voice was a gunshot. 'Brothers, you are dismissed!'

Repeating the ritual bow, the three men left. Karl felt a kind of bemused horror, even while he floated on the rim of the crimson afterglow.

'What is this? Are you keeping captive prey now, like dairy cattle?'

'Only the finest,' Ilona said quietly. 'Not cows, but magnificent bulls, actually.'

Cesare cut across her. 'We have nothing to explain to you unless you come to us wholeheartedly and give yourself to the service of God.'

Karl faced him, making his own expression unreadable. Recalling Stefan's fear, he felt angry that Stefan and Niklas had been driven out of their home by this creature. 'Why would you want me? You know what I did to Kristian; I made no secret of it.'

'But I forgive you, Karl.' Cesare's eyes glowed like a saint's, pearl and crystal. He opened his hands and clasped Karl's upper arms; Karl found the touch distastefully over-familiar, but he endured it. 'There are many here who rebelled against Kristian, besides Pierre, Ilona and John. More come every day. There are even vampires who came out of the *Weisskalt* when Kristian died, came back to life to help me. The past is forgotten. God has instructed me to unite all vampires against the Enemy. If you come to us you will be saved – but if you stay out in the darkness you will be friendless, an outcast for Lilith to devour.'

'Is this what you are telling everyone?'

'It's the truth,' said Cesare. 'You're not a fool, Karl. You do not need me to tell you how dangerous she is, do you?'

Karl couldn't reply. He went on denying Violette's nature, but Cesare's simple words cut straight to the core of his fears.

He said, 'There were two vampires named Rachel and Malik. Are they here?'

'No,' said Cesare, 'not yet.'

'And what of Simon, Rasmila and Fyodor?'

Cesare gave no answer. 'Well, Karl? Are you with us or against us?'

'I did not come here to take sides,' Karl said evenly. 'I would like to speak to Pierre alone.'

'Impossible.' Karl heard spines prickling through the fur of Cesare's voice. 'If you cannot give me a clear statement of your intentions, you had better leave until you've had time to think.'

Ilona slipped to Karl's side. 'Do as he says, Father. It's really not worth arguing with him.'

Ignoring them, Karl went back to Pierre. Cesare followed insistently. 'You will leave now and you need not come back until—'

He touched Karl's arm. Karl turned, furious, shaking him off. 'Don't lay hands on me. How long did it take your throat to heal, after the last time you tried?'

'I was weak then. I am strong now. This is your last warning.'

Cesare's conviction gave him a stunning air of authority. He generated an aura that was not merely charismatic but dangerous. But after all Karl had endured to win his freedom, he could never bring himself to submit. Everything he had seen grieved him deeply.

'Well, I'm going,' Ilona said impatiently. 'Karl, if you've any sense, you'll come with me.' The Crystal Ring received her, and she vanished.

Karl turned to Pierre, who was now leaning against the wall, his long legs drawn up under him. 'Pierre, I wish you'd come with us. It distresses me to see you like this.'

'Why are you so solicitous, suddenly?' said Pierre. 'I've always done my best to make your life unpleasant; I hope you are not about to reward me with some nauseatingly sentimental speech about friendship.'

'Call it curiosity, then,' Karl said patiently. 'Tell me what happened. Come away with me and talk to me.'

The curly brown head drooped. 'Really, there's no point. I can't leave, and I've nothing to tell you. Do as Cesare says. Get out.'

Cesare was watching, his smile a strand of wire. Then John rose, walked from behind his table and stood glowering at Karl. And here, Karl saw, was Cesare's real strength. A brutish power, glowing like hot iron from the gargoyle face and minotaur's shoulders. It was as if John's once neat, slender form had been reforged in hell.

It was the horror of it, rather than the implied threat, that Karl found terrifying. A nebulous thought, *the Crystal Ring can do this to any of us, through Lilith* . . .

This impasse could only lead to a fight, if Karl stayed, and he had no taste for the indignity of physical violence. Wisest to leave. He felt defeated – but at least, he thought, I can catch up with Ilona before she's too far away.

'As you wish,' Karl said sardonically. 'I shall certainly consider what you've said.'

Returning Cesare's gelid stared with a smile, Karl stepped into the Ring and went to look for his daughter.

The *Bierkeller* was a sweltering mass of bodies, noise and laughter, stewing in smoke and lager-yellow light. Werner was already drunk, but not too drunk to be brought up short, almost sobered, by the sight of an incredible-looking woman sitting alone. Instantly he wanted her, and he began to tremble at the thought.

He'd just walked away from his student friends in disgust, sick of trying to argue politics with them; frustrated at their shallowness, their refusal to listen. Intellectuals, they fancied themselves; they hadn't an idea between them. It broke Werner's young heart to see what was happening to Germany. They'd been crushed by the Treaty of Versailles, lands and rights unjustly confiscated; inflation running wild, while incompetent bureaucrats floundered and squabbled. Werner couldn't bear to see his mother working herself to death just to put a loaf of bread on the table. He was idealistic; he wanted something better for his ruined country . . . wanted something more out of life. He needed a purpose. Drunkenness gave him the illusion of knowing all the answers; but he knew it was an illusion, and that only made him want to drown his frustration in more beer . . . or in a woman's arms.

He wished he was not still a virgin, at eighteen. Girls liked him, but his mother had instilled him with the fear of God and he always backed off at the last minute. But he'd had enough of his own timidity, his friends' taunts. He was ready now, but he felt so awkward. This angel couldn't possibly want him, or even notice.

She'd seen him! Werner froze, unable to believe his luck when she gestured with an unlighted cigarette. Her stare was a magnet. As he wove his way towards her around lakes of spilled beer and damp sawdust, the cacophony of voices and music seemed to recede.

'May – may I join you, *Fräulein*?'

She nodded at the empty stool opposite, leaned forward for him to light her cigarette. He ordered drinks, but noticed that she didn't touch the red wine she'd asked for. And her cigarette in its long holder was merely an accessory; she only mouthed the smoke before expelling it again. Her beauty was extraordinary, beauty to reduce a man to slack-jawed imbecility.

Over her shoulder, Werner saw his friends – five-flushed, raucous youths sitting a few tables away – giving him jealous looks and making crudely suggestive signals. He ignored them.

Werner was shaking. He hoped she could not smell his sweat.

Her name, she said, was Ilona. While they talked about nothing in particular, he could not take his eyes off her mouth. Deepest red, like her dress and her hair, her lips were dark blooms against her shell-pale skin. She was a contrast to the florid *Fräuleins* he knew, his sisters' friends; while they were attractive enough in a merry, rosy way, this woman was as quiet and sure as an arrow.

'Are you from Austria?' he asked.

'Vienna,' she replied. 'A long time ago.'

'I recognized the accent!' he said triumphantly. 'You know, you should be in a beautiful hotel with marble pillars and ferns, not this pigsty. You're too beautiful for this.'

'Aren't we all? In our own minds, at least.'

Ilona, he decided, was strange. She wouldn't flirt as girls often did, responding easily to his good looks. Instead she was caustic and distant. Wonderful, though. It never crossed Werner's uncluttered mind that he might secure her services for money. He behaved as if making an heroic effort to seduce a movie star.

As they went on talking he found that she was drawing out of him all his frustrations and dreams, listening as if he were the only man in the room – not shouting him down as his so-called friends always did. 'And how would you change things?' she asked. 'What would *you* do?'

Her interest intoxicated him. 'We need a leader, a good, strong leader, to kick this country's backside and give us a future. Otherwise we're lost. Lost. I want my mother to have a beautiful house and servants, my sisters to marry successful men. I want to give my children, if I ever have them, something to look forward to. We Germans need our *pride* back!' Ilona listened, leaning forward on the table, her chin resting on the diamond-circled stems of her forearms, her eyes like black tulips. He stared at her mouth, entranced by the delicate veining on the dark-red fruit, the tips of her teeth. He was slurring his words, couldn't help it. God in heaven, I have to have her or die!

Werner was in full flow when, to his devastation, they were

interrupted. A man appeared out of the crowd and sat beside Ilona without a word of explanation. Werner was furious. He would have hit the man, if he hadn't been too drunk.

The intruder gave him the briefest glance, then turned to Ilona as if Werner did not exist.

'What are you doing?' he said.

His tone was gentle, lightly quizzical. Ilona seemed annoyed. 'What does it look like? I don't know what you want, Karl, but I wish you'd go away.'

'You asked me to follow you.'

'To get you out of Holdenstein before Cesare lost his temper, that's all. I've really nothing to say to you. I said it all in Boston, I believe.'

Werner witnessed this exchange, feeling outraged but powerless. If this swine ruins my chance with her—! Suddenly he felt the hairs prickling on the back of his neck, for no apparent reason. It was only through observing the man that he realized just how extraordinary Ilona was – because Karl was the same. Luminous, elegant, darkly mesmeric.

That was why he couldn't find his voice to protest.

'I disagree,' said Karl. 'I'm sure you have a great deal to tell me.'

'I've told you far too much already.'

'What does it matter?' Karl placed a hand on her upper arm in a blatant show of affection. Werner was in despair. 'What has Violette done to you, to make you work for Cesare? I thought you despised him.'

'I do,' Ilona said crisply. 'I think he's a shit. But when it comes to Violette, I happen to believe he's right.'

Werner, hearing the words without understanding or caring what they meant, was rising unsteadily to his feet. 'Get lost, *mein Herr*. The lady is with me.' He lunged at the intruder across the table, his fist raised – only for the woman to catch his wrist in mid-air.

It was as if he'd hit a wall. He sat down again in shock. How could such a slender little hand be so strong? 'Don't,' she said, pressing his hand down on to the rough wood. Her fingernails pricked his skin, as if to hold him there, tantalizing him.

Karl's only reaction was a faint look of disdain. Werner thought, who the hell does he think he is?

'He's perfect, isn't he?' Ilona said to Karl. 'Young, strong, idealistic, handsome, a little naïve. I have a very good eye for them.'

'And Cesare wants them for Pierre?' Karl's eyebrows lifted.

'What else?' Ilona said smoothly.

'You tell me.'

'What do you want me to do? Are you going to follow me about trying to save me from myself, dear? Do you want to protect this young man from me? I don't think he would thank you for depriving him of my company.'

'Do what you will.' Karl stood up as he spoke. 'I've never interfered in your affairs. But I hate to see you being used.'

'I'm not! How dare you—'

'You *are* being used. I never thought you'd allow it to happen.' Karl inclined his head to her with cool politeness, and walked away. Werner tried to watch him, but after a few seconds he'd vanished among the revellers as if he'd never been there.

The woman was distracted for a moment, her face hard. Werner was so distressed at this exquisite creature being almost within his grasp, only to be torn away, he forgot his manners.

'Who was he?' he demanded possessively. 'Your husband? Your brother?'

Her attention swung back to his face. 'No,' she snapped. 'He's my father.'

'You mean your priest?' She started to laugh at this, and he added defensively, 'Well, he was hardly older than you!'

She was laughing uproariously now. 'No, he really is my father.'

An obvious lie. Werner, agitated and aroused, had no idea how to master the situation. 'But what was he saying to you, what did it mean?'

'Nothing. Forget it.' As she looked into his eyes, he felt something dimming and slipping away inside his mind. Suddenly he couldn't remember a word of her conversation with the stranger, nor why it had seemed so urgent that he challenge her about it. His train of thought evaporated. Her eyes were so softly moist, and she was still laughing . . .

'Can I share the joke?' he said, clasping her hand.

'One day. Don't look so worried. You are a dear boy.' She tilted her face enticingly towards his, and suddenly, with an immense rush of excitement, he knew that everything was all right. He was aching to taste her mouth, her neck, her breasts . . . to leave boyhood behind.

She seemed to know, and to be offering everything. 'Now, are you ready to take me home?'

While Charlotte was alone, she tried not to worry about Karl. Tried not to resent him for going without her.

Cesare, another Kristian? She couldn't bear to believe it. But to have frightened Stefan, she thought, it must be true . . .

She went out to hunt, taking her time so that it wouldn't seem so long until Karl came back. Lost herself for a while in the river of fire and rubies that reminded her, with such overwhelming intensity, just how far she had come from being human.

When she arrived home, a couple of hours after midnight, she realized there was someone in the house. A whispering, unseen presence, a column of dust.

'Stefan?'

She struck a match, lit an oil lamp and replaced the stained-glass shade. In the dragonfly scatter of aquamarine and crimson light, she saw the tall shape hovering. Gold dust. Then it materialized fully and gazed at her with terrifying eyes. Cat's eyes of pale gold flame.

Charlotte pressed back against the sideboard, catching her breath as if she were mortal. She took in the bright hair and handsome face of a gilded statue from Greek legend. And when it came to her who he was, as if she could ever have forgotten, her fear surged.

'Don't look at me with such horror,' said Simon. 'I've come to talk to you.'

'Karl will be back soon,' she managed to say.

'Not too soon, I hope.' Simon smiled. 'I came to see you, Charlotte. Won't you invite me to sit down?'

'Can I stop you?'

'Don't be unfriendly.' He went to the sofa uninvited, but Charlotte stayed on her feet. Somehow she managed to gather herself into a semblance of poise.

'Why not?' she said. 'The last time I saw you, you made strenuous efforts to kill Karl and most of our friends. Why should I be pleased to see you?'

The fallen angel only shook his head. He looked breathtaking, she had to admit; and the worst thing was that he reminded her of her brother, David, appearing to possess the same openness and decency – even if, in Simon's case, it was a lie.

'Yes, we had such a fight, didn't we?' he said shamelessly. 'Especially Karl and I. The physical and mental torment you each endured was tremendous – and yet you survived. I have every admiration for you. So, can you accept my apologies? Can we let bygones be bygones, as humans say?'

Charlotte gaped at him. 'You came to apologize? It's rather hard to forget that you almost starved Karl to death then made him attack me and Stefan. And as for what you did to Violette—'

There was no contrition in his handsome face. 'Charlotte, my dear, it wasn't personal. We did what was necessary.'

'Cruel to be kind?' She lit more lamps. Jewel colours flared and overlapped, but they could not exorcize this demon.

'Quite. You look so lovely in your tawny silk and lace; you and Karl are both so beautiful. You could have such power if you came with me.'

She took a few steps towards him, as if she were on a tightrope.

'Came with you?'

His eyes seemed all colours of the rainbow. 'Yes, as lovers, friends, helpers, everything.'

She swallowed. 'What happened to Fyodor and Rasmila?'

'We parted, as I'm sure Karl told you. And doubtless you know also that I have joined Cesare and John at Schloss Holdenstein, but . . .'

She hadn't known, but she could believe it. Anxiety con-
stricted her throat as her imagination seized on dreadful images;
Karl arriving at the castle, Simon and Cesare ambushing him
. . . but she pushed the feeling away, because if she started
pleading to know where Karl was, it would only give Simon
more power over her.

'What's wrong?' she said. 'Aren't they good enough for you?'

'Oh, they are very good and very useful, but they could
never be *lovers*. They're immortal monks, with as much sensuality as straw. I need something warmer. I need you.'

'Why?' she whispered. She felt as if she were falling towards
his eyes, but she couldn't believe it was happening.

'You know Violette is our enemy. You may not admit it but
you know.' His words made her shiver. 'We must join forces
against her. I know Karl refused me before, but I'm giving you
a second chance. Be part of the future or . . .'

'Or what? Are you threatening us?'

'I don't need to. If you cling to Lilith, *she* will destroy you.'
He extended a hand. 'Come and sit with me, Charlotte.'

She resisted, but she found her own body betraying her,
trying to pull her towards him with threads of desire.

'I don't believe you're an angel,' she said, one inch away
from the reach of his fingers. 'To imagine that God and his
angels have nothing more important to think about than the
affairs of men – or vampires – is a childish construct. But it must
be one of the strongest thought-currents in the Crystal Ring,
and that's why you've been infected by it.'

'No, you're wrong.' Simon looked irritated, which pleased
her. 'If it happened to you – you'd know.'

'Perhaps it's safer not to let it happen, then. Otherwise you
forget who you are. You lose your sanity. You become just a
cipher for the Crystal Ring – or for God, if you insist.'

Without warning, Simon caught her hand and pulled her
towards him. She couldn't break free. 'You are too clever,
Charlotte.' With a swift movement, he turned her round and
dragged her on to his lap. 'Too analytical.'

He gripped her arms; their faces were very close now. His
eyes entranced her and she felt herself turning molten gold with

desire. His lips parted, and she ached to taste the beauty of him . . .

Suddenly she realized what was happening, and she jerked back, petrified. She was about to be willingly unfaithful to Karl—

Not willingly.

'Don't pull away,' said Simon, his hands tightening. 'Who will be hurt? Immortals are above earthly rules. And when Karl knows you want me, he will come to me too. And you do want me, don't you? Lilith is death but I am life . . .'

Charlotte felt her face flushing with stolen blood. She knew Simon was much stronger than her; if she went into Raqi'a he'd follow, and if she tried to struggle he would hurt her. And the dreadful thing was that she didn't want to struggle. There was nothing to do but relax, and slide her arms round his neck, and open her mouth to a kiss that was fiery sweet and as honeyed as blood.

CHAPTER THIRTEEN

THE CLARET-COLOURED VEIL

In Sebastian's absence, Robyn did her best to carry on as normal. She was determined not to let him rule her life. The thought of languishing in fever and love-sickness between his visits was abhorrent.

So she attended the usual charity and social functions, lunched with friends, drove down to Cape Cod with Alice in the hope that the sea would work some calming magic on her.

She continued to receive Harold, whenever he felt like calling on her, as if nothing had happened. But she put off a couple of prospective lovers, no longer interested in them. There was now only one man whom she wished to pleasure, torment and ruin ... The temptation of an impossible challenge.

Kneeling astride Harold, labouring to bring him to his brief little spasm, she recalled why she had used to find sex so depressing. Fortunately she didn't have to try too hard with him. He never seemed to mind what mood she was in, never chided her. But afterwards, as he entwined his sweating body around hers, he said, 'You got someone new, h'm?'

'Maybe.'

'I can tell. It's like you're not here.'

'Sorry.'

'I hope you're not falling in love with him.'

She tried to smile, but her mouth was uncooperative. 'I left that nonsense behind at school.'

'You're never past it, believe me,' he mumbled.

'I'll always be here for you, Harold dear.'

But he was very worried. Robyn wondered what she had given away.

While she was on her own, she thought about Josef and his relationship with Violette, Karl and Charlotte. Does he know what they are? He must, of course! That would explain why he was so evasive, and all the strange remarks he made. 'Some of these people are not so nice,' indeed!

And that time I found him sick and in bed, hugging the covers around him. Hangover, hell! Which one of them—

She rubbed her forehead as if trying to press out her frown. It was useless to worry about Josef now. She didn't know whether he was still in New York or on his way home. And even if she could pick up the telephone and speak to him this minute, what could she say? Warning him to be careful was only telling him what he already knew. Then he'd wonder how *she* knew . . . and she felt strongly that Sebastian must remain her secret.

There's so much I'd like to ask you, Josef, she thought. But you'd never tell me unless I explained why I wanted to know, and I can't.

She tried not to dwell on Sebastian, any more than she'd waste mental energy on any other man, but sometimes she found herself at a loose end, wandering through the house as if searching for something. Often, while engaged in some everyday activity, she would suddenly turn cold with an intense feeling of being watched. After a time, the sensation became continuous, as if his eyes were always on her.

Infuriating that he could do this to her. Infuriating, also, that she found it so arousing. She found herself always performing for a ghost audience; always moving, dressing, undressing as if Sebastian could see her.

And thinking, *When are you going to come to me again?*

'It would be perfect,' Simon breathed, his cheek pressed to Charlotte's as he held her on his lap. 'You and I and Karl. You can't refuse me, because you know . . .'

He kissed her again and Charlotte let him, aching. She had

only one chance to stop Simon, she knew. Only one chance to control herself.

Even through the rushing drumbeat of desire she knew what to do; even with his whirlpool eyes sucking her down, his hands plucking at the buttons of her dress along her spine. She must seem to give in. Relax completely against him, like a warm and helpless nestling in his lap, so he didn't suspect . . .

Whilst her mouth moved feverishly over his lips and cheeks, the centre of her mind remained aloof, apprehensive but calculating. Assuming victory, Simon closed his eyes and sighed with yearning. And Charlotte seized the moment; drew back her lips and struck.

How strong and thick his neck seemed, like oak! She feared her fangs would break like brittle needles against it – no, they were through the flesh, but now she couldn't find a vessel to fasten on to and his fingers were closing on her arms . . .

Her teeth broke through a vein wall at last and blood burst into her mouth. It tasted strange, like red wine turned to vinegar; too strong but she couldn't stop now. It was the only way to weaken him.

'Not yet,' Simon whispered, trying quite gently to pull her off. She thought, he hasn't guessed I'm attacking him, he doesn't think I'd dare! She sank her fangs deeper, burying her face in his neck, drawing hard to drink as deeply as possible before he realized.

She was shaking with trepidation, even through the bliss of feeding. If he stops me before I've taken enough he'll punish me and I don't even know if Simon can be weakened like other vampires.

'Don't,' he said. 'Charlotte, enough!'

He understood. She felt him go rigid, his desire swamped by rage. He began to resist her, his hands clenching so tight on her upper arms that she thought the bones would break.

Pain lanced her. Simon's strength was terrible – but so was Charlotte's. She was stealing it from him with every mouthful of thick, sour blood. And even he could not break the purchase of her fangs in his flesh.

He loosed her arms, and she felt his hands creeping around

her throat. Vampires could live without breathing so she knew he couldn't strangle her, yet the pressure still awoke the primeval terror of choking. Charlotte felt the constriction tightening until she was straining to force the tiniest trickle of blood down her throat . . . tightening until it seemed his fingers would break through her flesh and crush her spine.

She could no longer swallow. Agony filled her skull, but she went on sucking at the wound, the blood escaping from her lips to bubble over her chin and his hands.

Just as the pain threatened to overcome her, the pressure eased. To her astonishment, Simon's hands went limp and slid to his sides, his head tipping back as if he were in a swoon. Charlotte paused. If he was faking surrender to trick her, she couldn't risk showing mercy. She drank again, wincing as she pushed the blood past her bruised windpipe.

Her pain dwindled. Red incandescence filled her, while Simon became as boneless as a fainting human beneath her. Oh, his collapse was real; she even sensed a kind of masochistic pleasure in it.

'So beautiful,' he sighed very faintly. 'I could die for you . . .'

She was only sipping now, but too caught up in the divine rhythm to stop. After a few seconds, she felt Simon's hands caressing her back . . . and she sensed, also, a very dark and definite presence in the room, watching them.

Karl.

With a stab of dismay, she wondered, what does he see? That I'm defending myself against Simon – or making love to him? Because even I don't know.

Even in her panic she couldn't stop . . . not at once. It took a great effort to wrench her lupine teeth from the flesh with which they'd almost fused. Blood ran from her open mouth and stained Simon's collar. He was too weak now to prevent her escape. As she slithered off his lap, his arms fell away and he made no attempt to keep her there.

There was purplish-red blood all over his hands and on her dress.

Charlotte fled to Karl, mortified. His face, bewitchingly shadowed, revealed only a grave suspension of judgement as he looked from her to Simon, who was lolling against the sofa-back as if someone had stabbed him where he sat. His golden skin had turned flatly beige, all its radiance lost.

Karl's arm went round Charlotte, but before she could say anything, Simon pushed himself to his feet and walked shakily towards them, making a magnificent attempt to recover his poise.

To Charlotte's embarrassment, Simon kissed her hand and gazed meaningfully into her eyes. 'Was it as pleasurable for you as it was for me?' he asked silkily. She'd expected fury, but this was worse. Simon looked at Karl and nodded, 'As they say in the parlance of these times, your wife, my dear fellow, is a jolly good sport.'

Karl merely looked at him, his expression frigid.

With that, Simon left; not through the Crystal Ring, but through the door. Charlotte let out a long sigh of relief and despair.

'What happened?' Karl asked coolly. With long, delicate fingers he brushed the drying blood from around her lips.

Charlotte told him everything, even how close she'd come to letting Simon seduce her. 'He wasn't violent, he was just *persuasive*. God, I'm so sorry. I don't know what he did to me. The only way I could stop him was to feed on him. And I don't think he'll give up, I think he'll come back when he's recovered his strength, because he says he wants you, too.'

As she spoke, blood-heat suffused her face. To her own shame, she still felt intensely aroused and unable to hide it. She pressed herself to Karl's body, feeling that she must melt into him from head to foot.

'Karl . . .'

Rather than pushing her away, Karl responded with a kind of helplessness, as if his sovereign compulsion was to please her. And this transition from unassailable detachment to passion she found irresistible. Always had.

Later, as they rested on the bedcovers with the first glint of dawn turning their limbs to pearl, Karl said, 'I hope you were not thinking of Simon.'

'I hope you weren't, either,' she said reproachfully.

Karl smiled, but his half-veiled eyes had a look of sorrow and preoccupation. '*Liebchen*, do you think you have no power to hurt me?'

'I think,' she said, looking down at their entwined fingers, 'that I don't like myself, therefore I sometimes can't understand how you could possibly love me.'

'If you believe my love for you to be so fragile, will that drive you away to someone else? Violette, Josef, Stefan – even Simon? That's what I fear. Why do they all love you, if you are so unlovable?'

'I only want you, Karl,' she whispered. 'You know I'd die without you; it's frightening but it's the truth. Simon tried to tempt me away from you but he never could.'

'All the same, Simon is dangerous,' said Karl. Their faces were very close together on the pillow. 'Why does he want us both, do you think?'

'To take the place of Fyodor and Rasmila?'

'Or because he thinks we are stronger than John and Cesare. It follows that he wants us on his side because he's afraid of us.'

The thought gave Charlotte, who had often felt powerless, a thrill of excitement. 'You refused him,' she said, 'but he can't give up with you, Karl; I think he was trying to get to you through me. But I won!'

Karl breathed out softly, looking grave. '*Liebling* . . .'

'What is it?'

'Rasmila once played a similar game with me. I was starving and she gave me her blood, convinced me there was love or at least friendship between us. But her blood put me in her power for a time. Took away my conscience and will-power . . .'

Charlotte sat up, aghast. 'You think that's what Simon's done to me? God, no, you're wrong!'

'I hope so,' said Karl.

Remembering the magnetic evil in Simon's dazzling eyes, she shuddered, hugging her knees to her chest. She thought, I wouldn't put it past him to have set some kind of trap for me.

'Look at me,' she said, turning to Karl and stroking his cheekbone. 'Can you see anything wrong? Because if you can, I'll go away, I won't stay and risk betraying or hurting you.'

Karl's face, in its paleness and darkness, was lovelier to her than Simon's sun-bright beauty could ever be; his eyes, honey-brown crystal, infinitely more alluring. 'Don't leave me.' His voice was gentle, but the words were a command.

Her voice raw, she said, 'But can you kiss me, and lie beside me, and hunt with me . . . without trusting me?'

The woman, Ilona, took Werner to a cheap hotel. Once inside the room, she turned into a vampire.

Werner had never anticipated such pain, such pleasure, such fear. He'd dreamed of making love to her, but even his most lurid imaginings bore no resemblance to reality. Ilona lifted him out of himself, rendered him helpless as if he were staked out for slaughter, and led him into visions that no fever could have wrought.

She ravaged and hypnotized him. She dragged him through paradise and left him beached on the other side, gasping for air, his body throbbing with a score of puncture wounds, blood streaking his nerveless limbs.

Afterwards, she sat above him like a cat, licking her lips. Huge, passionless, intent eyes. A cat from a mouse's point of view.

He wanted her again. Wanted her for ever.

He told her, and she smiled.

'You're very good,' she said. 'For a virgin, you were perfectly incredible.'

He hadn't admitted that; his pride was dented. 'What makes you think—'

'It doesn't matter. Just be thankful you didn't disappoint me – because you would have found out the hard way if you had.' She rocked with heartless mirth.

Werner began to shiver, his teeth chattering. He seemed to see her through claret-coloured glass.

'But if you want more, if you want this for ever, you must come with me and do everything I say.'

'Anything.' He was losing consciousness now, pawing at her for help, for love.

'And when I say for ever – what was your name?'

'Werner.'

'When I say it, Werner, I do mean *for ever.*'

His thoughts closed up to a point, vanished. There was a long interval of oblivion; it seemed endless but a few times he bobbed almost to the surface of awareness, just enough to gain the impression that he was being carried, that there were soft-footed figures like monks all around him. Sensory delusions. Then blackness again.

When he came back to himself, he saw, through a haze of candlelight flickering on dank walls, that he was in a dungeon, lying supine on the floor.

Awareness woke before emotion, and for a few minutes he could only stare at the stone walls and the barred iron door. Then it struck him; *God Almighty, this is real!*

Panic ripped through him. He tried to sit up, only for an iron hammer to begin pounding behind his eyes. He collapsed again, moaning. Why am I here, why am I so weak?

'Ilona? Where are you? Let me out of here!'

'She can't hear you,' said the dry voice of a spider.

The cell was full of shadows, which filled Werner with the same unreasoning but overwhelming dread as the shadows in the corners of his room had done during childhood. Dread fulfilled, as a long, thin swathe of blackness detached itself and came towards him.

Bony hands, with fingers like steel and nails like thorns, grasped him. A ghastly face, all hooked lines of cruelty, glared down. Werner caught the butcher's shop stench of blood and stared in horror at the creature's naked, red-raw scalp and its pointed teeth.

'She delivered you to us,' said the demon. 'Do you fear God, Werner? Do you fear God?'

Werner thought he was in hell. He thought he was being punished by some mad demon-priest for the sin of fornication.

He was jerked into a sitting position, and saw the vampire's fangs lengthening, as Ilona's had. He writhed in uncontrollable fear. 'Let me go!'

'We cannot let you go because you have not repented. Do you fear God? Do you fear—'

'Yes, yes,' Werner cried, but the vampire went on repeating the phrase, its voice rising to a frantic shout, its shark-like mouth moving closer to Werner's face, red tongue wobbling.

'—God? *Do you fear God? Do you fear God?*'

Werner began to scream. He wet himself. And then, shaking in the vampire's claws as if in a fit, he began to sob and cry unashamedly for his mother.

Outside the cell, Simon stood with Cesare, listening to the terrified screams of their latest recruit. Cesare stood with his arms folded, nodding a little, seeming well content with the situation. Simon felt nothing; no pity, no satisfaction.

'This Werner is a fine boy,' said Cesare. 'Ilona has chosen well again.'

'I told you she'd have her uses,' Simon said tonelessly. His encounter with Charlotte had left him so despondent that he had no wish to listen to Cesare's banalities. Important, though, to maintain the angelic mask. His frantic draining of three victims had somewhat restored his strength, but he still felt listless, frustrated.

The cries were growing fainter but more desperate.

'A mother's boy,' Cesare said sneeringly. 'Well, John will swiftly knock that out of him. The more completely John breaks them, the easier they are to reshape. Twenty so far; how many more, do you think, before we begin the transformations?'

'As many as you wish,' Simon said, trying not to sound indifferent. 'But we must keep the number controllable. A round thirty, to begin with, rather than an army of thousands.'

'Of course. I believe in moderation.' Cesare looked sideways at Simon, irises slipping like fish to the corners of his eyes. 'The thousands will follow in good time. They will not merely form an immortal army against Lilith; they are for the world *after* Lilith.'

'The bright new day,' Simon murmured.

'Quite so.' Cesare's face shone with a softly radiant smile. 'By the way, Simon, we do need to talk about the question of transformation. The choice of immortals and the order of initiation is crucial—'

'Don't worry about it,' Simon said with a show of angelic authority. 'We'll discuss it later. All will be well.'

Cesare looked reassured. With a brief nod, Simon walked away, the human's distressed sobs dwindling but never completely fading from his hearing. An irritating noise, like a constantly whining dog. Even when Simon reached a small chamber at the top of the castle, he could still hear it.

He thought, What you don't understand, Cesare, is that unless we seduce Charlotte, Karl and even Sebastian to our cause, your dreams may never be realized. A few vampires may slip through our fingers and it won't matter; but they are the crucial ones, the ones who aid Lilith by refusing to aid us.

So close I came to winning Charlotte over . . . The memory of her fangs piercing his neck burned Simon as much with ecstasy as humiliation. The fact that she outwitted me, Simon thought, only proves me right. With her on Lilith's side, an army of green fledgeling vampires will fall like grass to a scythe . . .

Grey light, falling through a narrow window, rippled suddenly. Simon looked up. They were here again, his rejected lovers, Fyodor and Rasmila. Waifs, too pathetic to be desirable.

This time, however, they didn't rush to Simon to cling round his neck. Instead they greeted him with formal bows, self-controlled and dignified.

'We have given you time to consider,' Rasmila said. 'If you tell us again that you hate us and no longer want us, then we will accept you at your word. You'll never see us again. But if there is some way in which we can prove our love, you have only to speak . . .'

She did not look very hopeful. Fyodor's thin face had the set look of a man who had resigned himself to the gallows. Yet their dignity touched Simon. Or perhaps his union with Cesare and John had stopped him from blaming them so bitterly for past failures.

'Well, I can make no promises,' he said thoughtfully. 'But there are certain matters in which you may be of some use.'

Their faces lit up. They gasped, 'Simon!' but he turned his back on them, to shut out their expressions of gratitude and incredulous delight. In the depths of the castle, Werner's sobbing turned to the whimpering of an abandoned child.

Five days passed before Sebastian went to Robyn's house again. When he arrived one evening, he found to his disappointment that she wasn't there. The house was deserted.

Sebastian entered and wandered through the rooms in darkness, imagining her in each setting, looking at silver-framed photographs standing on lace runners on her polished sideboards. A group of pretty young women in wide-brimmed hats, laughing in an open-topped car; Robyn and her sisters? A formal Edwardian couple; Mummy and Daddy, no doubt. A very young Robyn, wearing a cowboy hat, on a horse. A lean-faced, intelligent-looking man arm-in-arm with two women; there was a caption on this one. 'Mummy, Josef and Lisl, 1902.'

No photographs of the dead husband, no happy wedding scenes.

All her possessions looked expensive, beautifully made, perfect in their context. Ornaments, vases of fresh flowers, creamy lace on dark wood. He breathed her lingering scent, imagining her here in the parlour, climbing these stairs, brushing her hair at this dressing-table, stretching out on the bed ... her tall and voluptuous body snow-dappled by moonlight.

I wish you had been at home tonight, Robyn, he thought.

Yet he did not wait for her. A pensive mood had fallen on him and actually to see her now would have destroyed the magic of haunting the empty house. It was as if Robyn, not he, were the ghost.

Sebastian was reminded of another house that he had loved. He felt it calling powerfully to him now, though it lay across an ocean. Houses. He felt more affinity with them than he ever had with humans or vampires.

But the thought of Blackwater Hall reminded him of Simon,

and then of Ilona and the others. He cursed silently. Am I lingering here, he thought, solely to avoid their inevitable intrusion into my life? Maybe. What of it? I don't want them, but I do want Robyn.

When he left, he did not return for another four days. He decided to punish Robyn a little, for not being there precisely when he'd needed her.

Every time there was a knock at the door, Robyn's heart would leap and drum in her throat. It was never him, of course. When had he ever bothered to announce his arrival?

Tonight – ten days since she had last seen Sebastian – she jumped in predictable reflex to the sound, then scolded her nerves into submission. Let Mary answer it, she thought. If it's anyone but Harold, I'll play the gracious hostess for fifteen minutes then make some excuse to get rid of them.

Mary came in and announced two names which sent a faint chill of apprehension through her. 'Victor Booth and William Booth to see you, ma'am.'

Russell's brothers. The last people in the world she wanted to see, but propriety demanded that she face them.

'Show them in,' Robyn said resignedly.

Two young men, with close-cropped brown hair, came in with their hats in their hands. 'Mary, take their coats,' she said, but the older one held up his hand.

'There's no need, ma'am. We won't be staying long. I'm William Booth and this is my brother, Victor.'

'Yes, I remember you. It's a pleasure to see you,' she lied. 'How may I help?'

The two men were of average height, thickset, as serious as detectives. No friendliness about them; neither attempted to shake her hand. Their fleshy, shiny faces called to mind a third, more handsome face.

'You remember Russell Booth?' said William. He seemed to be the dominant one. 'He was our brother, Mrs Stafford.'

Their eyes were like gun-metal, accusing. Robyn knew she was in trouble, but her defensive armour slid into place, an invisible glaze. 'I know. I was terribly sorry to hear about his death. Won't you have a drink?'

'We don't drink, ma'am,' said Victor. His voice was weaker than his brother's, with a strangled note that people must love to imitate behind his back. 'Neither did Russell, until he met you. Then it seems like he drank himself to death.'

She had a ghastly feeling of *déjà vu*; Sebastian approaching her in the garden, insinuating that she was Russell's murderer. But how could Sebastian have any connection with these men? It seemed preposterous.

'I'm afraid I'm not sure what you're implying, if anything.' She spoke without hostility, as if they were having a friendly conversation.

'I think it's clear enough,' said Victor. He was less sure of himself than William. She could take advantage of that.

'Are you suggesting that I had something to do with his death?' she said in soft amazement. She didn't confront them but moved away, while they stayed by the door. Harder to hit a moving target, she thought. 'That's unfair. I was very fond of your brother. He was a real gentleman; the best. We saw each other for a while but he was much too young . . .' She was on the far side of the room, her back to them.

'Too young to die,' said William. 'Too young to kill himself over a woman like you. Don't act the innocent, Mrs Stafford. We know all about you. There aren't many folk in this town who don't, from what we've heard.'

'What do you want?' she said sharply.

'We want you out of Boston. We want recompense, or we'll smear your reputation all over any town where you try to settle.'

Robyn gave no sign that she'd heard them. She pretended to be lost in thought, one hand playing with the slide that held her hair coiled on the back of her head. The slide came free. Sweeping her hair to one side so that it all hung over her right shoulder, she was about to turn and face them, only to be arrested by the familiar sensation that Sebastian was near by.

Disregarding it, she turned, her eyes downcast. 'Do you really think it was my fault?' she said, affecting quiet distress. 'I knew he was upset but I thought he'd get over it. I never realized . . . God, I should never forgive myself!' She swayed and caught the back of the sofa. Victor started towards her, thinking – as she'd intended – that she was going to faint. 'I'm all right,' she said, as he hovered, now looking more confused than stern. 'What could I do, except end our relationship? All right, I should never have let it begin, I admit that. But what was the alternative to ending it? I don't think your family would have approved of him marrying me, do you?'

She was a faultless, unaffected actress. Victor was half hers already, so it was William, on whom she now focused. 'If I was the cause of his troubles, I'm sorry. You look like fair men. I'm sure you can't think it's right to make such accusations against a widow on her own, particularly when they are based purely on rumour. You don't actually know anything about me, do you?'

Even William was looking a trace less sure of himself. She wasn't the hard-faced witch they'd expected, so they didn't know how to procede. Give me a few more moments, she thought, and they'll be eating out of my hand – or drinking Bourbon out of my lead-crystal glasses, miserable abstainers.

Now she would ask them again to sit down, and she would ask questions about Russell, perhaps cry a little. Favour one brother, create jealousy, divide them against one another. To play this game with two at once, what fun!

'Please, make yourselves comfortable,' she began. 'Whatever you want me to do, let's talk about it first. You don't object, do you?'

'No, ma'am,' William said reluctantly.

As he spoke, there was a footstep in the hall – no sound of the front door opening had preceded it – and Sebastian appeared in the doorway. He was wearing a dark overcoat and looked forbidding, every inch a creature of subtly malevolent strength.

The brothers, still on their feet, stared at him.

'You had better be leaving now, gentlemen,' said Sebastian. His soft tone was a promise of violence. 'If it takes two grown men to intimidate one woman, I think you should be crawling back under your stones while you can still walk. And if you ever come near Mrs Stafford again, you'll be reunited with your brother sooner than you hoped.'

Robyn could only stand and watch, incredulous, as William belligerently confronted the vampire. Victor joined him. 'I don't know who you are, sir, but this is none of your goddamned—'

Sebastian's hand shot out and alighted on William's throat. He appeared to exert no pressure. All he did was to fix them with his dark gleaming eyes, but both men stared back as if he'd produced a gun. William went grey.

'Out,' said Sebastian.

And they jammed their hats on their heads and hurried away, as if they couldn't escape the house fast enough.

Sebastian turned to Robyn with a look of amusement. 'Well, that was easy,' he said.

Robyn exploded, 'How dare you!'

'How dare I – what?' He seemed stunned by her reaction.

'Interfere in my life!' She felt so livid that she could have attacked him. 'You had absolutely no right to do that!'

'Beautiful child, they were threatening you. They deserved to have the fear of hell put into them, gutless pigs.'

'I was coping with them perfectly well on my own, thank you! I didn't ask for your help and I don't need it. They came here hating me and they would have left thinking what a warm, wonderful and wronged person I was. Given time I could have sent them both the same way as their precious baby brother.'

'To the grave?'

'To the bottle! I happen to remember Russell telling me that the reason they're both teetotallers is that Victor used to be an alcoholic. It would have been my pleasure to make him lapse. I love corrupting evangelists.'

Sebastian was gazing at her wonderingly, shaking his head. 'You really have an evil streak, don't you?' He came to her, leaned on the sofa-back beside her, and stroked her arm. 'I thoroughly approve of you.'

'I don't need your approval.' She folded her arms defensively. 'I'm nothing like you.'

'Yes, you are. You're exactly like me.'

'Go to hell.'

Without visible reaction, Sebastian turned side-on to her and gazed at the floor. 'So, these men,' he said. 'Would you have gone to bed with them?'

'If necessary.'

'It's a good thing I got here in time, then, is it not? And while we are on the subject, I want you to stop seeing that little old rich man who is always here.'

'Harold Charrington?'

'Whoever he is – and although he's old enough to be your father, I assume he's *not* your father, unless you're even more corrupt than I thought you were – I want you to stop seeing him.'

Robyn gaped at him. 'You are absolutely unbelievable.'

'Well?'

'You don't come near me for days on end – then you just walk in and make these ridiculous demands! What gives you the right? And why the hell are you so possessive, all of a sudden?'

Sebastian went quiet. His change of mood alarmed her. 'I want you to myself, Robyn. I don't want other men to be with you when I am not.' His eyes were very enticing, and his possessiveness made her feel weirdly agitated. At the same time, she thought, he could kill me. Just seize me and kill me, if I say something he doesn't like. To go on defying him was coldly thrilling.

'You're asking too much. I don't change my life for anyone. And I won't stop seeing Harold; he needs me, I enjoy his money, and he's the only man I don't actively hate.'

'Are you saying that you hate me?'

'Of course I hate you,' she answered harshly. 'What did you think?'

He grinned. He began to laugh.

'What's the joke?' she said, infuriated.

'The joke is this, my dear. The "brothers grim" came seeking vengeance on you, when actually it was I who killed your young lover.'

The floor seemed to sink under her. The sensation was one of dull horror, but not surprise. 'How?'

'I met him at the party the Booths held for the ballet. He was hiding in his room and drinking himself into a stupor because you'd had the affrontery to turn up. We were never friends; it was the first and last time we met. A young man alone, very drunk because the *Dame aux Camélias* had broken his heart, and needing a shoulder to weep on. Unfortunately for him, he chose mine. And I came looking for you afterwards, because his description of you so intrigued me. By the way, he didn't exaggerate.'

She was stepping away from him, mouth open with pain, denial. 'You sat and sympathized with him – then you killed him?' He nodded. 'God, I can just imagine it! And then you came hunting me?' She remembered Sebastian's silhouette in the arbour, like a dark dream. 'And you had the nerve to come and tell me Russell's death was *my* fault!'

'Ah, but I get such pleasure from telling lies and being cruel. Don't you?'

'So his death wasn't my fault after all.' Her fingers danced over the back of the sofa as she moved away towards the fireplace. 'He didn't kill himself over me!'

'And that's all you really care about, isn't it?' said Sebastian. 'So don't stare at me with those great eyes like saucers. Haven't I made you happy?'

'Get out,' she said.

'Now, Robyn—'

'I mean it.' She raised a hand, pointing at the door. 'I want you out of here now. Don't come back, don't ever come near my house again!'

It was possibly the bravest thing she had ever done, though she felt far from brave. She saw a flash of feral rage in his eyes, blinding as the sun, and she began to shake in fear of her life.

Then the look vanished. The vampire shrugged, as if it didn't really matter after all. 'If it's what you want, beautiful child, I'll bid you good-night – and goodbye.'

He made a sweeping bow, and vanished. She started violently; this trick never ceased to astonish her to the core. Unable to believe he'd really gone, she went out into the hall, but there was no sign of him.

Robyn returned to the parlour, and walked round and round the room in nebulous distress. She was in shock. She hurt all over, inside and out. What's wrong with me? Why did I tell him to go, if it wasn't what I wanted? But it *was*. I can't stand him, I hate him. I can't stand what he's done to me. I'm right to end it now, before it's too late!

She heard the front door open. Every nerve in her body jerked; but it was Alice who came in, Alice standing in the doorway, her brown coat and hat dewed with rain.

Robyn ran to her.

'What is it, what is it?' Alice said, hugging her, a loving mother soothing her child. Robyn told her.

'So he's gone for good?' Wild hope fractured Alice's voice. 'We're out of danger? Oh Lord, I hope so, I pray so!' Robyn couldn't reply; guilt silenced her. Even knowing how terrified Alice and Mary had been, the peril she'd placed them in by seeing Sebastian, she hadn't let it stop her. 'Oh, don't be upset, dearest. You did the right thing. Just be thankful it's over.'

It was not over, Robyn knew.

Robyn couldn't eat, couldn't sleep. Even knowing what Sebastian was, and the vile things he had done, and the danger he'd placed her in – still she craved him.

No logic in this, she thought. What's he done to me, to induce this infatuation? It's quite disgusting. I won't give in to it.

But to fight with him, to insult and torment and tear at each other – all of that was preferable to being without him.

Next afternoon, after a sleepless night and a miserable day, she went out alone and walked around the town until dusk. I'm not looking for him, she told herself. I need to clear my mind, that's all.

Should I employ a vampire hunter to track him down? I'm sure Uncle Josef must know one. If we stake him in his lair, will it free me from the curse? Good grief, what nonsense all of that is.

She walked through the wealthy areas of Beacon Hill and Back Bay. The tall houses with their bowed fronts seemed to grin at her in the gloom. She glanced into their lighted windows, seeing cosy family worlds from which she was forever excluded. She didn't want them, anyway. Their cosiness was an illusion; she knew the callous husbands, cruel parents, spoilt sons and petulant daughters who warred behind the façades. But those worlds looked warm and she was cold, even in her thick red coat.

Wandering down Beacon Street and into the Public Garden, she sat on her favourite bench by the lagoon. Squirrels scampered towards her, rising expectantly on their haunches; so dear, their bright eyes and tufted ears, but she had no food to keep them around her. Instead she watched the ducks on the water. The summer colours were just beginning to turn; the beeches tipped with burnished bronze, the elms glowing, the maidenhairs edging towards gold. Time to go home, she told herself. But she remained there, huddled up in her coat, dejected. Her life, she realized, had no point at all.

And then he was there, standing beside her, hands in his pockets and his collar drawn up as if he were cold; his presence as natural, as ordinary, as that of any human passer-by.

'So here you are,' he said.

'I'm often here.' She didn't look at him, but she saw his black coat from the corner of her eye. 'It's my favourite place to sit.'

'I know. Did you hope I'd remember?'

'It might have been at the back of my mind.' She spoke quietly, all anger burned out, feeling only relief that he'd found her.

'If it was, I'm glad,' he said.

'Glad that I'm stupid?'

'Robyn.' The vampire sat down, only a few inches from her. 'Robyn, Robyn.'

'Were you looking for me – after everything I said?'

'At least I respected your command not to come to the house. I don't believe you placed any restriction on meeting in the park.' He sighed faintly. 'It's hopeless, really, isn't it?'

Somehow his arms slid around her. She let him hold her, her gloved hands presently finding their way around his waist. The feel of his body through layers of material, his uncanny aura, the dark beauty of him, all filled the void. She wanted this soothing, seductive embrace. Needed it.

'Hopeless trying to keep away from each other,' he said.

She let the moment wash over her. There will be no foolish admissions, no angry words, she promised herself. Just this. A quiet relief, almost like sleep.

His fingertips moulding her chin, he looked at her. His expression was soft, concerned, sombre; woodland light and lovely shadows. He can't really care for me, she thought. The look seemed unaffected, but he was an actor, like her.

'You're a bad girl,' he said.

'Am I?'

'Yes. You haven't been eating properly, have you? I won't have you wasting away. Come along now, I'm taking you for dinner.'

He stood up, pulling her with him. Not resisting, she gave a quiet laugh. 'But who is going to be dinner; me?'

'Funny.'

'Shall I have steak tartare, to keep up my strength?'

They went to the same restaurant on the waterfront where they'd gone the first time. This time Sebastian made no pretence at all of eating. He simply sat and smiled at Robyn while she worked her way through four courses, and finished them all. She had been quite weak from hunger without realizing it. They hardly spoke. There seemed no need; the silent communication between them was continuous, a sort of candid resignation to fate, edged with black irony. They were absolutely at ease with each other. And both of them were thinking, what the hell is going to happen now?

Afterwards, they walked arm-in-arm through the old town, in their element amid the graceful buildings that had helped to shape history. When passers-by glanced at them, Robyn felt a delicious sense of conspiracy, reprehensible though it was; *you don't know what Sebastian is but I do!*

'What does it feel like,' she asked as they walked through pools of gaslight, 'to drink blood?'

'Tell me what it feels like to drink brandy, or to make love,' he said. 'You can't.'

'Better than sex?'

The corners of his mouth rose enigmatically. 'Different.'

'But how does it feel to know that they can't stop you?'

'Extremely exciting,' he said candidly.

She shivered. 'And it gives you special pleasure . . . to kill?'

'Now I never said that.' He spoke quite sharply. 'We have to feed. Killing, murder, whatever you wish to call it, is not my object. I have no interest in it. The blood, the bliss of drinking, is what matters. If the source of blood dies, it gives me no pleasure, I assure you.' He added, in case she should be in any doubt, 'No pain, either.'

'No guilt.'

'Why should I feel guilty? Do you feel guilty about the bloody steak you just consumed?'

'Don't tell me your victims are no more than cattle to you,' Robyn said acidly. 'I don't play mind-games with a bullock before I eat a slice of it. I don't go to bed with it, either.'

'Where's your sense of adventure?'

She ignored his flippancy. 'Well, have I been merely food to you?'

'You know you haven't.' His tone became low and tender. 'You know you mean much more to me than that.'

'I don't know anything of the sort.'

'Let me walk you home, anyway.'

They walked very slowly across the Common, where little white lights glittered in the webbing of leaves and branches. Crowds were coming out of the theatres in Tremont Street, behind them. But the Common and the night, the dome of the State House rising like a golden moon beyond the trees, belonged to them.

'I meant what I said,' Robyn continued. 'I won't be ordered about and I won't change my life for you.'

'And I meant what I said.' He spoke with alarming fervour. 'I want you to myself.'

'What's made you so possessive?'

He pulled her round so she was forced to stop and face him. His pale hand moved over the fabric of her hat, along her cheek, and came to rest on her left shoulder. He looked human, full of conflicts; tenderness, determination, cruelty, indecision. His great dark eyes shone with wonder and acid humour. 'What would you say,' he asked, 'if I told you I was in love with you?'

'I would say you're a liar.'

He laughed. 'Oh, you're cruel. Very sensible, though. Vampires can't love. But I want to see you, I need to see you. Do you believe that?'

'Yes.'

'And do you feel the same?'

'I feel,' Robyn said quietly, 'that I don't trust you.'

'Not at all?'

'Not the merest fraction.'

A silence. They walked on. Her hands were linked through his left arm, her head resting on his shoulder. Now and then his right hand would move across to clasp her hands in the crook of his elbow.

'Will you invite me in tonight?'

'Not tonight,' she replied, though she wanted him desperately. 'I don't see why I should let you satisfy yourself then disappear for days.'

'You're quite right. I was not going to accept if you had asked, anyway.'

'Oh, sure.'

'It's the truth. Because if I did not disappear, if I was here every night – however much we both wanted it – it would not be long before I lost you.'

In his face, webbed with shadows cast by the streetlights through the trees, she saw a terrible look that froze her. A look from a bleak place of bare hills, of ice-winds blowing between dark standing stones. She'd thought it impossible ever to feel any sympathy for him, but somehow her sympathy slipped its leash.

'My God, you're lonely,' she said. 'You're really lonely, aren't you?'

'Oh yes. The myth of the lonely vampire.' He kissed her cheek with cold lips, the chilling look still on his face, self-mockery blackening his voice. 'Who can resist it?'

Sebastian brought Robyn an armful of red roses, so dark they were almost black. He brought them to the front door. It was Mary's night off, so it was Alice who, unfortunately, had opened the door to him.

As Sebastian presented the roses in the parlour, Robyn was very aware of Alice standing in the doorway, staring hard at her mistress. Her face was waxen, her eyes brimming with horrified questions. *What is he doing here? You said it was over! You promised!*

Robyn hurried over to her. 'Would you put these in water, please?' Her voice fell. 'Alice, don't look at me like that. It's all right. Just leave us alone.'

Alice gave the bouquet a look of contempt. 'Deal with them yourself, madam. I won't touch anything of his.'

She walked out, very dignified, and went upstairs to her room. As soon as she'd gone, Robyn bundled Alice's feelings into a closet in her mind, and slammed the door.

'I don't think your companion likes me,' Sebastian said ruefully. And then he and Robyn fell on each other as if they were starving. His coat fell, the roses fell. He began to unbutton her dress, nipping her neck, his teeth seeming to grow sharper until he drew blood.

'No, no, not here,' she said, fighting him off. 'Come upstairs.'

Their coupling was brief, ferocious, sharp as rose-thorns. He bit her just as she reached the peak of bliss, so she felt the pain and the pleasure together. It was like being drawn down a silvery, glittering strand of wire. A thorned wire, dripping poison and narcotic crimson flowers.

When it subsided, they broke apart, gasping. And then they held each other and wept.

Summer became Fall, turning New England to flame. Robyn and Sebastian drove out to the mountains of New Hampshire and Vermont to see the rolling waves of apricot and gold, of bronze and toffee-brown and limpid yellow; preternatural tints of scarlet and darkest maple-red, dazzling all the senses.

Once Robyn said, 'You like this, don't you?' as if she could hardly believe that a vampire should retain any appreciation of nature.

Then it was Christmas, which meant nothing to Sebastian and very little to Robyn, as far as he could tell. She paid a short visit to her family and returned to tell him that the gathering had been polite but strained. Meaningless. She was glad it was over.

Snow fell, wrapping Boston in luminous softness. The city glittered by day and glowed by night, as if it had drifted backwards into another, more idyllic time.

Sebastian loved the chilly New England winter, the rain and snow and the cold sea-scented wind. They reminded him of Ireland. He was not at home here, had never been at home anywhere ... except at that house on the banks of the Blackwater in County Waterford.

He would have gone back there now, if it had not been for Robyn, holding him like a magnet in this prim old-fashioned town. He had been visiting her for months now, once a week or more often if he could bear to see her without touching her – or at least without taking more than a few sips of her precious blood. Sometimes, her cheeks as pale as magnolia petals, she would beg him not to feed on her that night; sometimes he would acquiesce, at others he would just take her anyway, leaving her furious, or silently hating him, or languid and tender ...

It was always different. One night they would tear at each other with hatred, the next with passion. That was why he couldn't leave her alone.

Every day he would think about her, and decide, I'll kill her soon. I've teased her enough. It's time to leave. Yet when the moment came, he could never do it. He made excuses to himself; I'll wait until I'm tired of her, so sated on her that she is no more than a husk to me. Or: she isn't quite enough in love with me yet. There's still that suspicion in her eyes. When she lets her guard down and trusts me completely – that's the time to strike.

But now, with the snow falling in great clotted flakes past the windows, they lay twined in her bed, warm as nestlings in down. The taste of her blood was lush in his mouth; the scents of her hair, her perfume, her skin, the natural musk of her body, all filled his senses. Her eyes were half-closed, sultry with pleasure. She hadn't tried to resist tonight. When he'd pierced the vein, she'd clutched at him, as if thrusting herself deeper on to the pain, trying to find a way to love it. And in the afterglow, she seemed content.

'Now, you are not finding it so terrible, are you?' he asked, gently teasing her.

She was happy, unguarded. 'If you must know . . .' She stretched, the warm weight of her breasts sliding over his ribs. 'I find myself wanting it. Like a sort of masochistic addiction. Rather a dangerous addiction to develop, isn't it?'

'Do you still hate me for it? That must be an addiction in itself, hating men. Have you found us all such monsters?'

'Of course. What else? My father, my husband . . .' and the words began to flow out of her, the story of her miserable marriage, how her injured soul hardened, scarred over by rage to become a pearl of cold vengefulness. And he spoke too, his words weaving through hers, of a love that turned to wormwood and the revenge he took.

'Her name was Mary, like your little maid. Her hair was fair too, and my Mary was beautiful, a tall fine woman. But we'd been married a long time and there were no children, and I badly wanted a child to inherit the estate or it would all have been for nothing.'

'You're talking about a time when you were human, aren't you?' The wonder in her voice drew him on, soporific as fireglow to a storyteller.

'I'm talking about the end of the seventeenth century, beautiful one. About a country where religion is more real than life, so real that people will persecute and kill each other in the name of merciful God. My family were Catholics, one of the old Norman families who came to Ireland in 1170; as Irish as the natives within a few years. We fought for centuries to keep our property out of English hands. But when William III conquered us in 1690, they brought in laws forbidding Catholics from holding public office or bequeathing an estate to an eldest son. So my father and my older brothers fled to France – but I stayed, and I did a very terrible thing. I became a Protestant, which under the laws entitled me to claim the estate. Do you understand? I betrayed my religion, my family and my people, in order to get my hands on my father's demesne.'

'So you had no principles in those days, either,' said Robyn.

'I had ambitions. It didn't mean much to me to change religion; it was only cosmetic, because I was never really religious. My Catholicism was more a thing of instinct than belief; not clear-cut, rather a feeling that there was a sinister dark meaning behind the surface, that the Virgin Mary and Christ were not what they seemed, that the saints were really the old gods . . . But the point is that it didn't matter, all I cared about was keeping the estate. But understand, it wasn't greed that moved me, it was passion. I loved that place so much I couldn't bear to give it up, even for the sake of family loyalty. No, I have never cared much for people. I loved Mary; I think she loved me . . . but I took her love for granted, I thought that to build a grand house for her was enough to prove my love. When she fell pregnant I was beside myself with joy, I thought that now we would be the perfect family in the magnificent new house. But the child wasn't mine. She said I was never there, that I didn't love her and couldn't give her children, so she'd turned to someone else and now she loved him, not me.' Amazing that he could speak of it without pain.

'What did you do?'

'I think . . . I think I meant to kill myself.'

Robyn was shocked. 'I can't imagine you contemplating that!'

'But I was human then, different. I was distraught. It had all been taken from me, wife and child, so there was no future and no point in the new house. It was a shell, mocking me. I meant to burn it down. What I would do after, I had no idea. Maybe I meant to die in the fire. But someone stopped me. They say Irish Catholicism is only one step away from paganism, that the faerie folk were never destroyed, only assimilated into the new faith and given the names of saints so the people could still worship without heresy. That was what I believed, without knowing it. They never went away, they only vanished into sea and stone, tree and sky. And that night, as I set about destroying my future, three of them came along and destroyed it for me. Three ancient gods with burnished skins and writhing hair and terrible golden eyes. They took me and made me into what I am.'

'Why?'

Difficult to answer, Sebastian thought. 'They saw the qualities of a perfect vampire in me, and it's hard to say they were wrong, isn't it? But there was an interesting thing about them, something not right, which was this; *they didn't know what they were.* I saw them as gods in themselves, but they spoke as if they were sent by the Old Testament God who is surely much younger than them, a deity to whom the devil was not enemy but servant, thus making vampires the legitimate tormentors of mankind.'

'What a very interesting point of view,' said Robyn, her eyes widening.

'At the time, theology was the last thing on my mind. I hated them for what they did, and blessed them too; they'd freed me from all mortal weakness and conscience, so rather than destroying my own house I went after my enemies instead. I killed Mary's lover, and then I showed Mary how much I really loved her by draining her blood until she died. And it was very easy, Robyn. I relished it. Because she no longer mattered, you see? Mortal passions no longer mattered to me. And then I left Ireland, because there was nothing there for me. The house still draws me back sometimes ... but only the house, nothing else.'

'So you don't feel anything now? You just pretend . . . as I do?'

They were both saying far too much. Suddenly their eyes met in a flash of mutual panic, and the slow recoil began.

'Oh, I feel, dear Robyn.'

'Yes. You hate women and I hate men, yet here we are together . . .'

'But I have an advantage over you,' he said drily, 'because I hate men too. I despise them all, male, female, human, vampire.'

'You care for me, though, don't you?' The gleam in her eye was imperious, not pleading. 'You spared my life. You protected me from Russell's horrible brothers. You can't stay away.'

'Don't you love me?' he said. 'Just a little?'

'I'd never tell you, even if I did.'

'So you do.'

'Are you waiting for me to say yes, so you can seize the moment to destroy me?' The gleam hardened to a diamond sparkle; tears or anger, he couldn't tell. 'Oh, I can see through you, Sebastian.'

'Because it's exactly what you would do yourself.' He was irritated that she outguessed him, but he didn't show it. 'Only you must remember that I have every advantage over you. You can't ruin my reputation, because I don't possess one. You can't break my heart. There's nothing you can do against me physically. But you, Robyn; you live or die at my whim. I only have to threaten your precious maids to put you in a fit of panic. But really, to break your heart, all I have to do is leave you.'

Her face was sullen, her lower lip a red plum which demanded to be kissed and bitten. But when he tried, she turned her face aside, so his mouth met the smooth warmth of her cheek. 'If you order me to go now,' he murmured, 'I might not come back.'

'Are you really so arrogant as to believe that I'm not still using you for my pleasure, as you're using me?' she retorted. She was sleek and composed, not visibly upset at all. An act.

'You say there's nothing I can do against you, no way to protect myself. Well, you may be right . . . but there is Violette.'

The name took him aback, like a blinding flash of light on a dark mirror. 'Violette,' he repeated neutrally.

'The dancer. Did you think I didn't know she was a vampire? Don't tell me *you* didn't know!'

'Of course I knew.' Startled, he failed to hide it, and had to suffer her gloating delight.

'But you didn't know that she was here before you.' Robyn's grin blossomed into a cruel laugh. 'You're not my first would-be vampire lover, you know. She didn't play games with me. She wanted me. She said that if ever I needed her help for any reason, just to let her know. I can get in touch with her very easily, Sebastian.'

He remembered the night of the party; Robyn drifting past him in the garden . . . and another presence which he hadn't registered because Ilona had distracted him. Violette! If only I'd known! Inwardly cursing both Ilona and the ballerina with equal vehemence, he said, 'You're lying.'

'I couldn't have made this up, believe me. Are you afraid of her? Because something tells me she's as strong as you. One telegram . . . oh, you'd have plenty of time to kill me before I even send it, but if you do – she'll know. She'll find out and she'll come after you. Maybe she'll bring her friends.'

Sebastian, thrown completely off-guard, found himself unable to reply. He was furious at his own helplessness. What Robyn said about Violette was true, she was almost certainly stronger than him. Now am I going to regret not listening to Simon?

'Very clever,' he said at last. 'So now we're equal. But do you want her or me?'

Her eyes darkened. 'You,' she said. 'Without the threats.'

Terrible feeling in his heart, like a trapped raven. 'Too late, my love.' He stared down at her, letting the icy poison of his soul infuse his face. She blanched. Terror stiffened her face and she strained to avoid him, but he felt no tenderness.

'Did you really think I ever felt anything but contempt for you?' he said.

He left her side without a kiss, dressed quickly and stepped into the Crystal Ring. Robyn, wide-eyed with shock, uttered not one word of protest.

Sebastian had had to leave before the fatal web of love ensnared him for ever. This time he had no intention of ever going back.

The demon-vampire, John, kept a severed head in the dungeon. Night and day, it grinned down at Werner from the sill of a narrow embrasure.

And each lightless day, John would come in and torment Werner; feed on him, physically torture him, mock him. And when Werner was a draggled heap of nightmares on the flagstones, John would lecture him for hours about God.

Werner's terror, John insisted, was a form of rebellion. Weeping for mercy showed a lack of acceptance. 'Until you have shed your fear,' said John, 'you will not be worthy to serve the great Leader.'

Werner didn't know what John meant. He had no idea what was expected of him, or why he was being held prisoner. He was ill, and starving, and all he wanted was to go home to his mother. *John asks me to repent and I've repented a thousand times but still he won't say what he wants* . . .

Then one day, it happened. Werner woke up and found that his fear had gone. Washed up on the edge of insanity, he had no further to go. He was crushed, empty, blank. He anticipated nothing but death.

The cell door opened and the gargoyle face glared down at him for a time. Werner waited indifferently for the torment to begin. 'If it is God's will,' he murmured, 'I submit myself to the will of the Lord . . .'

Yet nothing happened. Past caring, Werner drifted into sleep, only to wake again, with a start, to blinding light.

Only lamplight, but it hurt his eyes like the sun. Squinting, he made out a group of men standing around him, immeasurably tall, with radiance splashing over their firm flesh and bright hair. Teutonic gods, they seemed. Werner stared, one hand flung across his forehead.

One of them, brighter than the rest, seemed to fill the cell with glory. *Lucifer*, came the thought into Werner's fractured brain. *Fallen angel, Star of the Morning*.

Yet the heart of the gathering was a small figure who leaned down and took Werner's hand. He seemed as clear as a diamond. A neat, saintly man with the world's future in his ice-grey eyes.

Not human – but not like John. Werner was transfixed; his impression was that this man had passed through an esoteric veil to a higher plane from which he looked down sagely at the petty turmoil of earth. As Werner lay there, hopeless, open to anything, this figure's absolute certainty of purpose lanced straight to the vacant core of his soul.

'Poor child,' said the saint. 'How you've suffered. But it's over. Are you ready to come to us with a pure heart and give yourself to the service of God?'

Werner's empty heart filled suddenly with hope. He was so grateful for a little kindness that he would have given his life for this man. Leader. *Saviour.*

He reached out, his mouth opening with a yearning he'd never known before. *Give me this now, take me up into your world, save my soul!*

'Patience,' said the leader, reading his thoughts. He lifted Werner to his feet and kissed him on both cheeks. 'These men will take you with them, bathe and feed you. They are your friends; they have all been through the darkest night, as you have, and they will help you to understand that it is necessary to hammer iron in order to forge it. You will learn to serve, as your comrades are learning. There is a long way to go. But when you have proved worthy, you will be elevated to our ranks. Do you understand?'

Werner understood completely. He could hardly breathe for the wonder of it. Not merely to serve them but to join them!

The leader's gentleness healed all his wounds. He realized that Ilona had not abducted him but rescued him from the world's banality, delivered him to a place of pure vision. This leader, with his clear-sighted strength, was the saviour of whom Werner had always dreamed!

There was a future after all. The love he felt radiating from these glorious beings utterly eclipsed what he'd felt for Ilona and even his love for his mother. What could ever compare? Overcome, he began to weep.

I have entered Valhalla.

Falling to his knees, he kissed the saviour's hands. 'I am your servant, my lord, my king. I pledge you my life.'

'Your pledge is accepted.' The leader's voice was the sweetest blessing.

All around him, the young men who shared Werner's dreams smiled in approval.

CHAPTER FOURTEEN

FIREBIRD

From the moment she first conceived of the new ballet, Violette became obsessed by it. It blossomed within her day by day, so that in rehearsal she would be explaining to her dancers what she wanted of them even as it came into her head. She didn't tell them the truth behind the story; the characters were simply Siegfried, Anna and Lila, with assorted peasants and spirits of the forest.

Her instinct had been right; the ballet was destined to be as magnificent and moving as any of the greats. The whole Company knew. Elated from their success in America, they generated an atmosphere of feverish enthusiasm that Violette found electrifying. When she commissioned music for the project, the composer responded as if inspired by angels.

She called the ballet, *Witch and Maiden*.

Yet there was an element missing. How to end it . . .

Charlotte and Karl had gone home to Switzerland after their return from America. Violette found it easier to be alone. She missed Charlotte, but at least she was not continually reminded of the darker side of her nature. Some days she could almost convince herself she was human . . . until the thirst began.

One night, though, Charlotte came to see her. They met in the studio, where oblongs of light fell through the windows to ripple on floor and ceiling; snow light from the mountains, glass-green reflections from the River Salzach. The glow was soft, many-layered, infinitely lovely to the eyes of vampires.

'You're in danger,' said Charlotte. She was leaning against the barre, her dress of bronze silk and lace washed by the light. 'Almost everyone you've upset has gone to Schloss Holdenstein, and Cesare's elected himself their leader. They want revenge.'

Violette was unmoved by the news. She felt only a stirring of depression, like dead leaves in a graveyard. 'How have I upset Cesare? I don't know him.'

'But he knows of you. He's a fanatic; it probably wasn't difficult for them to convince him that you're the Antichrist.'

'Who, Pierre and Ilona?'

'Yes, and John. Simon's with them, too.'

'Simon.' She felt a wave of something too dull to be fear. 'And Stefan? Rachel?'

'No, Stefan's gone into hiding to protect Niklas. No one's seen Rachel at all. I hardly know her so I can't speak for her. But as for the others, I'm afraid they're planning to attack you.'

Violette smiled. 'Do you think they'd dare?'

'Don't underestimate them. The Crystal Ring can give us strange powers.' Charlotte looked steadily at her, her grey-violet eyes candid. 'It can take them away, too. We shouldn't take anything for granted.'

'Well, thank you for the warning.'

'I'm serious. Simon came to us and tried his hardest to persuade Karl and me on to their side. Perhaps he succeeded, I don't know.'

'What do you mean?' Violette felt suddenly anxious, despite herself.

'I drank his blood. Karl fears it may have put me in his power.'

'Any symptoms?'

Charlotte shook her head. 'But how can I know? Something might happen without me being aware of it, or able to stop myself.'

'You mean you might go for my throat? I don't think you'd win.' Violette moved away towards the windows. 'I don't want to hurt you. I don't want to hurt any of them; it's what Lilith does when she feels threatened . . . I won't harm them as long as they stay out of my way!'

'Well, I can't persuade them to do that. They're very frightened of you. They seem to think you've been sent by God to destroy them.'

'Perhaps I have,' Violette said softly. Turning, she saw

concern glittering in Charlotte's eyes. 'Are you sure you know what you're doing, defending me?'

'Yes. I brought you into this, and I love you. If they kill you, they can take me too.'

'And Karl?'

Charlotte didn't answer. 'I'd better go.'

'Yes, go, Charlotte. I appreciate the warning, but I don't want to hear about it. All I want is to dance.'

And Charlotte vanished, without a kiss, looking desperately sad. Violette was on the verge of going after her, but restrained herself. I have no room for sentiment. I must think about the end of this ballet, nothing else!

Alone, however, Violette couldn't get the conversation out of her mind. Images of violence plagued her. She remembered their terrified faces as she plunged fangs and nails into their flesh; Matthew, Pierre, Rachel, Ilona . . .

She needed to escape. Melting through Raqi'a, she left Salzburg behind and went towards the Alps. Once she was safely away from the town she returned to the real world and walked for hours, oblivious to the cold. No, rather she needed the coldness and wildness of the mountains. The bitter wind wailing through the peaks blew ice needles into her face, chilling her from head to foot. Numbing the pain.

She hadn't wanted to stay in the Crystal Ring. It was too tormentingly abstract, sinister, full of mysteries and accusations. No, the clean harshness of nature was the place to seek Lilith, to catch the black tips of her wings and bring her down.

What are you? Violette cried.

I am night, said Lilith. I am blackthorn winter and the death of dreams. I am madness and cruelty and fever, I am disobedience and disappointment and disease. I am the laughter of demons and the tears of God and the bride of the devil. I am all your worst fears.

You are many things, said Violette. You are a demon lover and a storm spirit and a night hag. You exist in every mythology. You have always been there.

Always, Lilith agreed. And I have a special affinity for blood. But why? What are you?

Look closer. Look harder. You're looking but you can't see me.

Violette tried. A great curtain of ink flowed across her mind. It was like groping for the end of the ballet; searching for Lilith and searching for the ending were the same thing! But she couldn't see it. She was looking at nothingness. What she'd taken to be Lilith was only a dead end, a wall of blackness. The real Lilith moved somewhere behind the wall but Violette couldn't reach her, couldn't grasp the truth.

Why can't I find you?

I am a Black Virgin in a shrine, Lilith informed her. I am a black stone in the earth. I am the end of all things.

But who are you?

I am you, said Lilith.

Then why can't I remember? Violette cried. How can I know I'm you, yet not understand?

Because, said Violette-Lilith, you are talking to yourself.

Violette crouched beside a rock in her thin lavender dress, the ice-storm battering her, and screamed out her hoarse anguish.

No one heard. The storm and the mountains ignored her.

After a time she stood up, entered the Crystal Ring, and surged away along the rolls of liquid cloud towards the south.

Again she'd denied herself blood, though she knew it was foolish. The thirst unhinged her. Her mind was full of the flapping of raven feathers, the maddening enigma of Lilith. Black because she is veiled . . .

Violette thought of Lancelyn, the arrogant human mage who'd tried to unveil her. He'd called her the Black Goddess, bringer of wisdom, madness or death to those who penetrate her.

He'd been so certain of finding wisdom; Violette had brought him madness. Perhaps death, too; she didn't know, didn't care. She'd destroyed him for his arrogance, yet the memory still needled her. What if he'd been about to unveil Lilith's mystery? It's obvious I can't unveil myself. It might have been my only chance. If I'd swallowed my pride, let him make an altar of me – perhaps it would have brought light to us both!

But I kept the veil closed. I was too afraid. I was, I am, terrified.

And it wasn't what Lilith wanted. She must always have her own way.

Lilith was pulling her towards another horizon now.

Violette couldn't forget the time that Rachel and the others had come to her; that terrible sense of being hated, purely for existing. She remembered the rage that had swept through her, Lilith's rage. She'd killed Matthew, actually killed another immortal . . . and she'd bitten into Rachel's long, thin neck and swallowed her fierce blood.

How could they ever forgive or forget?

Violette felt the pressure of hatred building up against her. At this moment she could sense it in the Crystal Ring, where every shiver of the ether seemed to express a human nightmare or the thread of a vampire's tortuous thoughts. Sometimes she could almost catch the wavelength of individual personalities. It had happened before, Lilith's preternatural power latching on to and leading her to an individual, even though Violette herself had no idea where to find them.

She was thinking of Rachel now; a victim of Lilith who had simply disappeared. So many questions Violette needed to ask . . . How to find her, though?

Lilith is guiding me, she thought. I mustn't fight. Let go . . .

She was a dark rag tossed on a sea of blue-black waves with coppery crests. Crimson light dripped endlessly down the sides of chasms above her.

The fragile energy of thought-waves, so Charlotte says. And every vampire is part of Raqi'a, so we must each leave a vibration, a trace of our existence here . . . She recalled an analogy that Charlotte-as-scientist had once made. 'Imagine the Crystal Ring as a cloud chamber. If human thoughts are the water vapour, then vampires are the atomic particles. Chains of bubbles form in our wake to mark our path.'

The other-realm flowed inside Violette-Lilith, became indivisible from her.

She saw a tall man with skin like burnished coal, walking across a parched golden plain. A single African, walking under a vast sky, watched by lionesses ... and she knew he was a vampire.

And that was where Rachel was. Africa.

A long journey, but Violette couldn't turn back. She climbed very high, almost to the *Weisskalt*, and travelled so fast that she terrified herself. Perhaps I could do it, she thought, travel to America in a night.

She found them at dawn, just as the sun was bleaching the hem of night. Insects sang in the grass. There was a single white tree on the plain, and beneath it she found Rachel and the African sitting cross-legged, like travellers sharing stories. They wore loose white garments, hardly more than strips of material to deflect the sun. Rachel's hair was an orange flame against the whiteness.

'Good morning, Rachel,' said Violette.

The woman started as if she'd seen a ghost; it was hardly possible for her to turn any paler, yet she did. The man merely looked up as if nothing could surprise him. He was thin, muscular, incredibly tall; he would have towered over them, if he'd stood up.

'Oh, my God,' said Rachel.

'Not exactly. Try the other side.' Violette knelt down, facing them. A snake slithered away from under her knees, but it didn't horrify her; it was her sibling. 'Won't you introduce me to your companion?'

Rachel recovered her composure and became cool, tense, very self-controlled. 'You might know him by the name Malik.'

'Malik. I've heard of you, yes, though we never met. One of the immortals who came back from the *Weisskalt* after Kristian died. One of the few who haven't threatened me.'

She studied his long, sombre face, his velvety eyes. He looked back serenely; she thought, maybe he doesn't speak English. But eventually he replied, 'I have no reason to threaten you, Lilith.' His voice was bass-deep, soothing. 'You are no threat to me.'

A suspended moment. A hot wind sprang up, rustling the grass. 'Am I not? Do you mean that if we fought, you'd win?'

'No,' he said. 'I mean that I have no reason to fear your bite. And you have no desire to attack me.'

She gazed at him, trying to perceive what he meant. And she realized that he'd spoken the truth. He raised no anger in her whatsoever. Why was he different?

She looked at his companion. 'You're a long way from home, Rachel.'

'But Malik isn't. This whole continent is his home, the savannah, the desert, the jungle. He hates what we think of as "civilization".'

'And what about you? Was it necessary to come so far to escape me?'

'At first. I was frightened.'

'Is that why you aren't with the others?'

'What others?'

'All those who are so terrified of me that they're planning to kill me.'

'I don't want to kill you!' said Rachel. 'I thought I'd be terrified if ever I saw you again – but I'm not.'

Rachel had changed, Violette observed. She'd lost some of her acerbity and aloofness. 'I'm not here to frighten you. I don't want anything. I only came to see what had happened to you.'

'You cared, after all?' Rachel's tension softened. 'I thought you might be another Kristian, but you're not. Malik and I are the same. We loathe Kristian and his kind, with their claustrophobic idea of "love" and their mania for power. I came here because I was afraid, but I stayed because I belong here.' She almost smiled, her mouth as red as her hair. 'I want this solitude now. The power to walk these great plains without fear of any hunter, whether they wield claws or spears.'

'When did you discover this?'

Rachel raised a long-fingered hand to her collarbone and fingered the luminous skin. 'When you drank my blood. You stopped me dead like a wall and made me see that in making demands on you, I was behaving like Kristian. Don't you realize, Violette, that you can't merely feed? You change people.'

'I know,' Violette whispered. 'Not always for the better.'

'Not always for the worse.' Rachel suddenly leaned forward, placed her hands on Violette's arms, and kissed her full on the mouth. 'I'm not your enemy. Not now.' Violette felt a flickering snake's tongue of desire, a poignant echo of Robyn's presence. Lovely moment.

Rachel sat back on her heels again and leaned on Malik's shoulder. They were gazing intently at her; Malik's face like ebony, Rachel's white as limestone. And Violette was suddenly afraid.

'You two see something in me that I can't see for myself. What is it?'

'Darkness and evil are not the same thing,' said Malik. 'When you see, you will know far more than I can tell you; but I do know that you must find the truth for yourself, or you will not believe it.'

'You're right. I wouldn't believe it.'

Rachel asked, 'Will you take Malik's blood, too?'

Violette looked at the tempting skin of his throat, so black it was dusted with blueness. His calm eyes were telling her something, whispering words she could not quite hear. *Dive down into the layers of darkness beyond the veil, let in the lovely silver light* . . . Her slow heartbeat quickened, and she had to look away. 'No,' she said.

'Why not?'

'Because Malik does not need to change.'

Violette had expected to meet an enemy and instead found – dare she think it? – two friends. Not quite friends, but two who at least didn't hate her.

She raced northwards through Raqi'a, not feeling the cold or seeing the skyscape.

Could I have persuaded them to come home and fight for me? I doubt it. They didn't want it, and neither did I. I suppose I could draw an army of adoring followers to me if I chose, throw them against Cesare's and watch them slaughtering each other like some gloating goddess of war.

That's why I drive them away. Because they'd love me so easily if I let them . . . and I'd destroy them. Cesare and Simon are right about me, so right, and that's why I must face my enemies alone.

Violette wished she could have stayed in Africa under the burning sky. Or in the desert, Lilith's wilderness where she'd once been whole, before the angels came to impose God's will on her. Impossible, of course. Chains drew her home. And if I'd stayed, she thought, I might have grown to envy Rachel's and Malik's love, another triangle from which I am excluded. But what right have I to envy anyone, when I despise love and all its lies?

She knew that even the comfort she'd sought in Robyn was an illusion. Yes, she wanted to come with me, and it broke my heart to reject her, but all she saw in me was a means of escape. She would never have loved me because her deepest desires are only for men.

Violette thought of Charlotte, who was less sure, but who loved Karl more than her own life.

I don't know how I can bear to see Charlotte again without seizing her and piercing her divine throat, riding out all this frustration on a carnal wave of blood.

Again she pictured Robyn, and thought of Malik's black eyes, telling her to follow her instinct. And the ache of missing Robyn, of being unable to finish the ballet, and of fighting Lilith's thirst, were all one.

Before she knew it she was changing direction. The magnetic lines drew her like gold threads, westwards above the Atlantic. She felt that she could travel for ever without rest or blood.

It will be night again before I arrive, then another day to return, she thought. I will have been away for two days or more, by the time I get home. Two days of rehearsal lost. And my girls will be worried.

But it would be worth it, she thought, to catch one glimpse of Robyn's face. If only I could find an answer there.

★

Robyn felt cool, strong and in control. She fooled herself that the feeling would last, and it did, for almost five minutes after Sebastian had left. Then the glaze cracked, and she broke down.

It was like bereavement. It was like falling, this hideous feeling of being gouged hollow, torn to shreds and hurled out to flap along the cold wind. She curled up, head between her elbows, hands folded over her head. The effort of not crying was agony.

Come back, come back. What are we doing, why must it be like this?

Morning came. The day dragged and died. The night was eternal. And then it all began again, and again.

Robyn did her best to carry on, but the spirit had gone out of her. Alice fussed, the doctor came and went, Harold brought flowers and chocolates and diamonds; nothing mattered. She didn't want to eat, or talk, or sleep, or think. Somehow she forced herself to do these things, but the effort was exhausting.

She found herself thinking of Violette.

He's punishing me for threatening him with Violette. For how long? Oh, Sebastian, come back so I can live again!

But he did not.

One night, three weeks later, she dreamed of Violette.

The dancer came to her at night, pale as lilies in the moonlight, black hair loose around her shoulders. She wore a floating garment and seemed to walk *en pointe* out of nowhere. She stood looking down at Robyn, then stretched out her long slender hand to stroke Robyn's cheekbone. Robyn saw her clearly, though she knew it was a dream.

'Don't be afraid,' Violette said, and she wasn't. 'I want you and I want your blood so much that I could die ... What would you say? Would you die for me too?'

Robyn couldn't speak, but when their eyes met, it seemed that Violette looked straight into her and saw all her secrets.

'You love someone else; is that it? But they have left you in pain.' Violette spoke softly, but a spasm crossed her face. 'Well, they could never in a million years love you as I do. Do I need to tell you? When I left you I thought the feeling would go away, but it hasn't. Why didn't I seize the chance? I can't bear to see you suffering at the hands of some callous lover, and I could end it, dearest. I could make you forget everyone and be mine for ever.'

'Do it,' Robyn tried to say. She was unsure whether she'd actually spoken. 'Take away the pain.'

Nothing ever changes, Violette thought, looking down at Robyn's beloved face, her lustrous brown hair spread on the pillow, the lace collar of her nightdress cupping her chin. I still love her. She's like the only house in the wilderness, the only fire in winter.

But I can't do it. I come this far and stop, because I want her to stay as she is, whole and warm, not broken by Lilith's savage caresses.

Violette was trembling. She wished she hadn't come after all.

I love you but I can never have you.

Any more than Charlotte could have me, or Karl could have Charlotte, without turning us into monsters. And if Robyn became a vampire she would no longer be Robyn, and as my human lover she'd go mad and die.

So I must leave her. Even if some bastard breaks her heart, she must heal in her own way, live her natural life.

But love and desire were drawing her towards Robyn's drowsy, sweet-scented warmth. Lilith's fingertips touched the lace collar, and Lilith whispered, *Why hesitate? Just take her. She needs it.*

The night Sebastian finally surrendered and went to Robyn, he found that someone had arrived before him.

From the darkness of the bathroom, with the door open a sliver, he saw Violette standing by Robyn's bed. He watched them from a lake of darkest loathing and disbelief. Knowing, now, that he should have taken Robyn's invocation of Violette more seriously.

The dancer was wearing a smoky lavender dress with ragged points falling to her ankles, long wide sleeves, a design of poppies sewn in darkly shining plum beads. She looked exquisite; Sebastian desired her, hated her.

She appeared not to sense Sebastian's presence, even with her ancient gifts. But he saw a subtle power coiled inside her, as he had when he'd seen her on stage. An unpredictable, edge-of-chaos power, like that of a snake, a storm, a scorpion.

Something familiar.

'I could make you forget everyone and be mine for ever,' she was saying. Seeing her rapt face, her seashell hand gliding over Robyn's form, Sebastian found himself overwhelmed by jealousy. It made him tremble. He'd never experienced such profound emotion, until he saw Violette with Robyn.

And Robyn, although her eyes were glazed as if she were asleep, whispered, 'Do it. Take away the pain.'

Violette's hand hovered on Robyn's throat. Any moment now she would pull down the high collar and see the pinprick scars of another vampire's fangs.

She's mine, Sebastian thought grimly. Only I may satisfy myself from her veins. No one else.

He was poised to cross the room, to seize Violette and drag her away, when she suddenly looked up, eyes wide, all hair-trigger alertness like a bird. Not staring at Sebastian, though, but at an alcove to the right of the bathroom door. And for a split second, he felt the flicker of a presence there.

A ghost?

Another vampire?

Anger transformed Violette's face. She turned and was gone in a dusting of mauve stars. The other presence also dissipated, leaving Sebastian to wonder if it had been real. But, he thought, *something* scared her away and it was not me.

Sebastian came out into the room and looked down at Robyn, who only sighed and turned over. She was asleep. She'd seen nothing.

Then he sprang into the Crystal Ring after Violette.

In a labyrinth of tilted walls and weird perspectives, he couldn't see her at first. Again he imagined there was another vampire somewhere above him, but it was faint, a mirage. As he climbed to a higher level – his transmuted body hard, slender and flexuous – he caught sight of her; a clipping of black thread against the flank of a cloud-hill. She was fast! Sebastian ran like a cheetah to catch up with her, his clawed feet catching and slipping in the strange substance of the Ring as if in liquid ice. As he came closer he saw how beautiful she was, even in her altered form. A serpentine yet feminine shape, gloved in black leather and black jewels which threw sparks of red, purple, silver.

And there was someone else following her, a greyish figure some way ahead of Sebastian. But all Sebastian's attention was gathered on Violette.

Intent on her, he experienced a shift of perception and thought suddenly, I know her!

Samael and Lilith . . . the devil and his bride. In the depths of his consciousness, the inky sediment stirred and took on amorphous shapes against a swirling bank of smoke and fire. Serpents dancing to a drumbeat.

They were memories that could not exist, funnelling backwards beyond the moment of his birth; unclear and nebulous, but memories all the same, as if his life had had no definite beginning.

I've always been here. The devil. And so has she.

I know her.

Robyn forgotten, he soared after her. Violette never looked back, neither at him nor at the greyish figure between them.

Eventually, though, Violette appeared to tire. She dropped out of the Crystal Ring over Canada, and Sebastian followed to find himself in a pine forest. Snow lay thick over the ground and trees; the world was luminous and bitterly cold.

He'd lost her again. Pulled by her aura, he ran, half in and half out of the Crystal Ring, stumbling in thigh-deep snow. Then he reached a clearing and stopped dead in the edge of the trees, arrested.

She was there, on the far side of the clearing. In the centre stood a human, a big, bearded man like a giant in his thick furs, hat and boots. There was a rifle in his hand, a dog as big as a pony beside him. A few yards away, firelight shone in the windows of a log cabin; no one else inside, Sebastian noted. This was a hunter who worked alone.

The man was staring at Violette as if his eyes would spring from his head. Where had she come from, in the depths of winter, a delicate snow-skinned woman dressed in nothing more substantial than a layer of silk?

Everything was stark, silvery, pure black on pure white.

'Are you all right, ma'am?' said the hunter. He clasped the gun, as if he'd seen such apparitions before, and had to shoot them. 'You'd better come into the—'

But Violette was already on her way towards him, one hand outstretched. She ran lightly over the snow as if over a stage. The dog barked once, jumped into the air from all fours, and fled. The gun fell from the man's palsied hands. And the dancer leapt on to him like a cat, burrowing between his furs and beard to feed savagely as if famished; and the giant could do nothing to stop this slender-boned female from clinging round his neck and draining his life away.

Sebastian watched, enraptured. The dog was barking frantically from a safe distance behind him. As the victim sank to his knees and Violette went with him, still feeding, Sebastian became aware that the third vampire was also half-hidden among the pines, observing.

Violette dropped the corpse and stood up as if dazed, her eyes blank, lips blood-red. As she stood there, the other vampire emerged from the forest and went towards her.

A cherubic young man, Sebastian saw, in a drab robe; physically unprepossessing, yet charismatic with self-assurance. Someone Sebastian had not seen for seventy years. Cesare.

The dog emerged and began to snuffle at his master's corpse, whining in distress and incomprehension. Violette disregarded the animal. Glaring at Cesare, she asked icily, 'What is this? Why are you following me?'

Her eyes, white and indigo, were demented. Sebastian knew she was lethal. Nothing to do with Simon's and Ilona's hints; he *remembered*. And the memories, so vague and yet so intense, were tormenting.

She must have seen him, even though she showed no sign of acknowledgement or recognition. Sebastian wasn't afraid of her. He felt they were equals, he despised her for daring to go near

Robyn – but for the present, he was willing to be entertained by Cesare's imminent humiliation.

The witch waited in the snow, purple as dead blood, pale as the *Weisskalt*, black as oblivion. The dark trees framed her.

Cesare felt as if he were climbing a mountain. She seemed so far away. He felt like a mortal confronting Satan, a tiny child doing battle with its monstrous mother.

He was so terrified that he felt elated. He knew God would protect him. God had given him the gift of prescience.

Cesare had vowed to confront Lilith before he asked his followers to do the same. It was a test he'd set himself; to perceive the resonance of her path through the Crystal Ring, to find and follow her, even when her caprice had led her across an ocean. Impossible journey, but he'd done it, proved himself Simon's equal.

Now all that remained was to prove that he dared to confront the Enemy. If he survived, he'd have the right to ask anything of his flock. If he survived.

He was puzzled by the presence of the dark vampire. A friend of Lilith's? I'll remember your face, he thought, remember that you were here with her. Will you still worship her on judgement day?

But the dark one meant nothing. Only Lilith mattered. She filled Cesare's world with the wings and claws and writhing hair of his nightmares.

Although Cesare could see that Lilith was beautiful, he felt no desire for her. His was a celibate nature, like Kristian's. The human weakness for sex, he believed, had no place in immortal lives.

But Cesare decided that one day, he would rape her. Not in lust, but as a token of his victory over darkness. That would make the act acceptable in God's eyes.

'Madame, my name is Cesare,' he said politely. 'No doubt you have heard of me.'

'Cesare, the great leader,' she said in a curiously flat tone. He hadn't expected her to be impressed, and she wasn't, it seemed.

'The leader of the good fight against you,' he said, direct as an evangelist. 'Your existence is contrary to the good of vampire-kind, Madame. You have harmed many of my friends. Your acts cannot be forgiven. I came to you to give you notice that my purpose under God's will is to rid the earth of you and your kind.'

I've done it, Cesare thought in jubilation. Faced her in the flesh. Now no one can ever call me a coward! And whoever her friend is, at least he'll serve as a witness.

Lilith frowned at him as if irritated. There were shadows round her eyes, and her fangs were at their full length.

'Who do you think you are?' she said, like a teacher to an annoying child. 'Isn't it a little pathetic to gather a castleful of crusaders to protect yourself against one woman? I don't want to hurt you, but I will, if you and your friend don't leave me alone.'

Cesare was in a turmoil of fear and triumph. He felt she was trying to seduce him into worshipping her with her searchlight eyes; he thanked God for making him pure and strong. He felt in mortal danger and he felt invincible, all at once. But his voice was clear and steady. 'Any threat you make, you will regret. Your dominion over the earth will soon be over.'

'My dominion,' she said frostily, 'is over one quite small company of dancers. And you are out of your mind.'

Cesare thought he heard the stranger laugh.

'Don't take this as a warning,' said Cesare. 'Heed the warning at home.'

Giving him the briefest glance of puzzlement and contempt, Violette leapt into the Ring, seeming to elongate as she disappeared. Euphoric with his own sense of power, Cesare followed. He had to have the last word.

But unseen hands clasped his arms, violently jerking him back to earth . . .

Sebastian saw Violette melt into the snow-light, saw Cesare start after her. Swooping after Cesare, Sebastian seized him and dragged him down like a netted bird.

'What in God's name—' Cesare cried as they fell heavily in the snow. 'How dare you lay hands on me? What are you doing?'

'Saving your life,' said Sebastian. 'Are you blind? She was close to tearing your head off.' He climbed to his feet and shook the clotted crystals off his coat. Near by, the dog still snuffed at the dead hunter, crying.

'Who are you?' Cesare said indignantly. 'One of Lilith's minions?'

'I am no one's minion. She must have thought I was with you. You have a bad memory.'

Rising to his feet, Cesare studied him, and was enlightened. 'Sebastian.'

'Correct.'

'You were Kristian's enemy! So, are you friend or enemy of Lilith?'

Sebastian remembered Cesare as being doggedly submissive and unremarkable. The vampire who stood before him now was a different creature, varnished by a silvery glow of authority.

'I heard how you behaved towards Simon,' Cesare went on with feeling. 'You're being a fool, refusing to help us. Don't you know she will slaughter all those who don't turn to God under my guidance? You must come to us. You must!'

Sebastian was taken aback by Cesare's fervour – and by his apparent concern for Sebastian's soul. But his thoughts were taking a darker turn.

'Why would Lilith come to America to take a victim, do you think?' Sebastian asked, putting an arm round Cesare's shoulder.

Cesare looked displeased by the gesture, but tolerated it. 'Only because that particular human had some meaning for her. I can't conceive of it myself, but I know there are vampires who develop affection for their prey, unnatural as it is.'

'So would you consider disposing of the female in order to distress Violette?'

'I'd consider anything, but there are many mortals closer to her, easier for us to reach. This human is probably irrelevant . . . but might I ask why *you* were there?'

'Following Violette, like you,' Sebastian answered glibly. 'I

349

hunt in Boston; I don't care for competition. I think I'll dispose of that female anyway, just to be sure.'

'So you have no love for Lilith!' Cesare's eyes shone.

'None,' Sebastian said emphatically.

'Then come with me, join us!'

'One day, perhaps.' Sebastian had no intention of doing so, but he had no wish to start an interminable argument with Cesare. *If ever I have to destroy Violette,* he thought, *it will be over Robyn; nothing else, no cosmic idealism.* And all that concerned him now was Robyn's safety. 'You had better go home and hope Lilith isn't lying in wait for you.'

Cesare moved away, shrugging off Sebastian's arm. 'Come to us soon,' he said ominously. 'If you don't, you'll regret it.'

'Cesare,' Sebastian said with a chilly smile, 'I have a message for Simon. Just one word. Samael.' He hoped Simon would drive himself mad, trying to work out what it meant.

'I'll tell him,' said Cesare, frowning.

He was gone; Sebastian was alone. Sighing, he stared up at the clotted sky; full of quiet rage at the intruders, and with horror at the knowledge that they had both trespassed on Robyn's domain.

As he took a last look at the clearing before entering the Crystal Ring, the dog swung up its large head and snarled, as if deciding, *here is my master's killer!* It came racing towards him, muscular body bunched and wolf-teeth dripping saliva.

With a single punch to its skull, Sebastian killed it.

By the time he arrived back at Robyn's house, just before dawn, Sebastian felt a searing thirst for blood. It was anger at Violette and Cesare. It was fear. *To think that they were here and might have killed her. To think that Violette might seduce Robyn away from me, or Cesare might see her as a pawn to be used against Violette!*

He'd been calm before. Now he was shaking.

I have to take her away before those other vampires come back.

Sebastian stared at Robyn's troubled face, her hair richly

tangled on the pillow, and he felt he was half out of his mind. He was angry with her, too. I must have her, he thought. Must keep her. Punish her.

He put his hands to his head. Fragmenting.

The other-realm crystallized around him and he walked straight through the wall, into the corridor. The walls leaned strangely around him, and the stairs to the top floor led up at an odd angle, the treads little compressed bars of light.

Warmth and thirst drew him. He mounted the stairs, melted through a door, and entered the maid's room. A neat, pretty room; flowered chintz, a brass bedstead gleaming in the lamplight.

Mary, it appeared, had just got up. She was sitting with her back to the door and brushing her hair in preparation for the day. She was in a loose white nightdress, her head to one side, all her hair hanging down in a wheat-coloured veil with the light shining through it. As she brushed she hummed softly to herself, dreaming the private dreams of which her mistress knew nothing.

Something alerted her and she turned, blue eyes wide, her hair floating with static. An ordinary face; pretty enough. Nothing to compare with the magnificence of that other Mary, the one who'd betrayed him, but it didn't matter. She was alluring enough, gilded by the heat-shimmer of his appetite.

Sebastian went quickly to her, knelt beside her and put a finger to her lips. He'd tasted her blood before but this time he wanted more, wanted everything. She was frightened at first, but one deep look and her pupils fogged and expanded with excitement.

'Shall we turn down the lamp?' he said.

The light shrank, shadows flowed in. Mary began to unbutton her nightdress, her eyes locked sightlessly on his, the tip of her tongue poised between her teeth.

He bent to kiss her breasts, and his blood gelled.

He couldn't bring himself to do it.

Enraged at himself, he pulled her wrists behind her back and bit into her throat, sharp and brutal. She made no sound. But even her blood tasted flat in his mouth. It wasn't what he wanted. Holding the girl away from him, he pierced her eyes with his, drawing the memory out of her. Then he flung her aside on to the bed.

A footstep outside. A column of warmth.

Then the door flew open, and a harpy came rushing at him, hair streaming, nightdress billowing, eyes wild. A dull line of steel swept down towards his head. He moved only just in time to avoid the blow, which caught his raised arm instead with a sickening pain.

He twisted the poker out of Robyn's hand and held her wrist. Her other hand catapulted up and delivered a hard blow to the side of his head before he could restrain her. She struggled, her face murderous.

'You *do* feel pain!' she exclaimed, gasping for breath.

'Of course. You almost broke my arm; I hope you're happy.'

'What the hell are you doing in here? You promised not to touch Mary, how *dare* you—'

The maid was curled up on the bed, unconscious. 'And you, with Violette,' he whispered. 'You were going to give in to her, weren't you?'

She went rigid. 'But that was a dream.'

'No, love, she was really here. I heard what you said to her. So I was going to take Mary and—'

'My God, you're so vindictive! You think you're gloriously evil but really it's so petty, it's mean-minded nastiness—'

'What you say is probably true.' He was holding her very close now, their breath mingling as they fought. Yet his hands were so light on her arms that she could easily have escaped, if she'd wanted to. 'I wanted to punish you, yes, and I felt vindictive – but I couldn't do it, Robyn. I've barely touched the girl. I didn't want her. And I could slaughter you for that.'

'For what?'

'For making me want no one but you. For souring all my other victims. For changing my nature.'

She stiffened, apprehension in her eyes. She thought he was going to attack her. 'What do you expect me to do about it?'

He embraced her suddenly, inflamed by her heat and scent through the satin sheath. He kissed her cheek, held her earlobe between his teeth, nipped gently at her neck. She shivered. 'I told you,' he said. 'I want you.'

She put her hand to her cheek where he'd kissed her, then touched the skin beneath his eyes. Moisture shone on her fingertips. 'Good Lord,' she said faintly, 'you're crying. Where did you learn that? You think you're winning, but you're not going to destroy me! How many more times do you plan to do this? Come back here swearing devotion, then desert me again?'

'You did miss me, then.'

A shudder. 'It was unbearable. You've no pity at all.'

'Have *you*? Robyn, I won't do it again. Come away with me.'

'Where to?' she gasped.

'Back to Ireland.'

'I can't. I can't possibly.' She was soft in his arms now, her desire for him – dare he think, her love? – melting through all the defences of anger, self-preservation, common sense. 'Do we have to talk about this now? Come out of here, let's go down to my room before I die.'

Violette wanted to cut Cesare and the stranger out of her mind and burn them, but she couldn't. They haunted her thoughts, all through the dreary journey home. Who was he, that dark and silent man with Cesare? I felt I'd seen him before but I know I haven't.

She thought of the hunter in the forest. Shivered with the echo of an all-obliterating hunger that had caused her to fall on him and drain him dry.

He was the first victim I've ever killed. Or was he? I can't remember. But he called Lilith's judgement upon himself; if I'd been a human woman, lost in the forest, he would have raped me and kept me to breed and cook his meals and all the time thought he was being kind. Such a man is fit only to keep a dog.

All the same, she felt sorry for the dog.

Hours in the Crystal Ring had tired Violette. She was travelling more slowly now, and she felt as heavy as marble, a foreign body in the firmament. The currents buffeted her cruelly. Daylight in the world, and so the ghost-sun, the eye of God, shone also in the Ring, high above the *Weisskalt* where it couldn't be seen; only its light deepening through layer on layer of azure.

As she descended, terror seized her, so sudden that she floundered and almost fell to earth. A dark current had caught her. It was drawing her inexorably towards its heart; a massive concretion in the fabric of the skyscape, a blackness, shifting and shimmering, now a many-towered fortress on a vast plug of rock, now a mountain ringed by ancient trees. A cliff, a wall, a prison. A house groaning under the weight of a million crimes, tortures, murders . . .

She knew what it was now. She'd seen it in Malik's eyes. It was the darkness of Lilith, the wall that lay between her and the blinding truth.

The wings of the death crone.

She twisted away from it and fell, arms across her face. She couldn't stand it. And as she fell, an unbearable thought screamed through her.

This cancer in the Crystal Ring is because of me.

It is me. It's Lilith. And I believe Cesare's speaking the absolute truth when he says I must be destroyed before I destroy everyone else. And I am being used by this uncaring fiend of a God . . . and like Lilith I shall never accept it!

She fell back to earth a few miles from Salzburg and walked the rest of the way, to calm herself. She'd been in the Crystal Ring all day. It was night again, and the winter air was like iron.

She thought of Cesare and his companion, the dark vampire who had said nothing, only laughed. Of the two, the dark one had disturbed her more. Had he been in Robyn's bedroom too? She hadn't sensed him there. She had fled, simply to draw Cesare away from Robyn. Just as well, perhaps, that she'd been forced to leave so abruptly.

And Robyn. How close I came this time . . . still knowing it was wrong! I should thank Cesare for stopping me in time, she thought. I won't go to her again.

She was in the town now. The river slid past on her left, the tall, elegant buildings on her right. The home of Ballet Janacek appeared in the distance, just a strip narrowed by perspective, its windows like rows of needles. As she drew closer, a strange sensation hit her. Unpleasant as the tingle of heat on frozen hands ... the presence of two humans, darting away behind the house, out of her sight.

Violette ran the rest of the way to the house. A smell washed out to meet her.

Smoke.

Heed the warning at home.

The milky-green building towered over her, its windows black mirrors, but she felt heat flickering inside, and smelled smoke, acrid like burning hair. Racing round the corner to a side entrance, she found the door ajar, the lock forced.

The fire was in the costume store.

A stench of paraffin, mingling with the fumes of burning wood and material. The heat struck her in an intense, fluttering wave, matching the horror and outrage that possessed her. *Who would do this to us?*

Flames danced between hampers, catching and running, silhouetting a costumed tailor's dummy for a second before catching the stiff layers of net; transforming Odile into a blazing Firebird.

CHAPTER FIFTEEN

AVATAR

Flames leapt, hungry to strip the bones of the old building. Upstairs, Violette's dancers and staff, more precious to her than her own life, slumbered. She was the line between their life and death . . .

Buckets of sand and water stood in the corridor; she'd never thought she would have to use them. Lifting the first two, she was already shouting at the top of her voice to wake the caretaker, who slept on the ground floor.

'Herr Ehlers! Fire! *Herr Ehlers!*'

Hefting the buckets inside the store-room, she slammed the door, shutting herself in with the fire. The walls and ceiling were as black as a coal seam; a great bubble of hot gas teetered towards the ceiling where it burst into flames with a soft *whump*. Sheets of fire rolled through the air and the smoke was thick with ash and carbon, but it couldn't touch Violette. Her unnatural body would not suffocate or burn. She faced it in a kind of paralysed horror, as if witnessing a fatal accident about to happen to someone else.

It took seconds to hurl the contents of the buckets on the worst of the fire. Not enough. The flames shied under the onslaught, flared up elsewhere.

Rather than open the door and unleash the heat, she entered Raqi'a briefly to slip back into the corridor. She risked someone seeing, but it didn't matter.

'Fire!' she yelled. '*Fire!*'

A vampire's voice at full volume, she discovered, was extremely piercing. The elderly caretaker and his wife came shuffling down the corridor through a cloud of smoke, trying to drag on their dressing-gowns as they came.

'Madame!' Ehlers cried, turning white. 'What are you doing? You must go outside immediately!'

'Call the fire brigade!' she snapped. Then she was past the couple, running upstairs towards her own apartment, shouting for Geli.

The maid was just opening the door as Violette reached the top of the stairs. She looked astonished to see Madame reappearing as abruptly as she had vanished. Geli held a hand to her mouth and her eyes began to water from the smoke.

'Don't just stand there!' said Violette. 'Go down the back stairs and out of the kitchen door. Hurry!'

The fifteen girls who formed her *corps de ballet*, and the ballet mistress who looked after them, lived in the attic rooms. Violette woke those who hadn't already heard the commotion, accounted for them all, ushered them downstairs and outside to safety. It was done in minutes. The girls coughed and clung to each other; some were crying, others staring in amazement at the apricot lights flickering in the windows, the smoke and ash whirling out into the night.

Minutes, Violette thought, as she heard the fire wagons trundling along the road by the river, bells ringing, galloping hoofs striking the cobblestones. If I had not come home at that precise moment they could all have died. The fire would have roared up through the wooden floors. But if I'd been earlier . . .

Now the shock and the rage hit her like a wall of heat.

If I'd been earlier, I would have prevented it, she thought grimly. I would have caught the scum who started the fire and torn out their throats. If I hadn't gone away selfishly to see Rachel and Robyn it would never have happened. And all the time Cesare was taunting me with his foolish speeches, he must have known, *known*, that this was happening!

The fire brigade was taking too long. Losing patience, she rushed back into the building. Behind her, the girls screamed and the caretaker yelled at her to come back, but no one could stop her. The inferno engulfed her, but she was an ice-statue that couldn't melt.

Under the crackling of the fire, she heard a tiny voice crying, crying.

A commotion outside. Figures loomed outside the store-room and water came jetting through the doors and windows. And Violette, meanwhile, began very methodically to smother the fire with her hands and feet. It was the swiftest, most desperate dance she had ever choreographed.

Her own dress caught light and blossomed into fire around her. Violette screamed. The heat seared her, she was terrified. She beat frantically at herself to put it out while the material fragmented and floated away and the heat seemed to scorch her bones – yet, when she'd conquered it, she found her flesh undamaged; carbon-blackened, but whole and creamily perfect underneath. The fear fled, but she hated this, the stench and the wanton destruction, the stupidity of it and the waste.

Tears made trails down her sooty cheeks.

The firemen knew she'd come back in. She could hear them shouting for her. Now I've given everyone a heart attack, on top of this, she thought. Water rushed in and drenched her, soaking the tatters of her clothes; the fire surrendered, leaving the costume store in saturated ruin.

The little voice grew louder. Something black and white darted out from under a sink, where the fire hadn't reached, and leapt into her arms. A terrified and bedraggled cat.

'Which of your nine lives was that, Magdi?' Violette whispered. 'And which of mine?'

Water was still showering in. Two firemen came stepping over the debris towards her; seeing her, they looked shocked, relieved, and then very businesslike. She was smeared with soot and all but naked.

'Come outside, Madame,' said one, putting his coat around her shoulders.

She relented, and let herself be led away. As she emerged from the house, with the fireman's coat on and the cat in her arms, the large crowd that had gathered in the street gave a huge cheer.

Suddenly she found herself surrounded by her dancers, who touched and embraced her as they would never normally have dared. 'Madame, you should not have gone back in! What if you had been burned, your face, your lovely hands? You might have died! How could you risk yourself like that? So brave!'

Brave, Violette thought, as she extricated herself from their arms in order to escape the throb of their blood. If only they knew.

The fire brigade had taken charge. Violette and the others huddled together outside, surrounded by people from the neighbouring houses, watching the men pumping water from the river to drench the flames. The horses which drew the wagons waited patiently.

The garish light had died. Sluggish wisps of smoke and steam carried a black stench into the air. Geli leaned on Violette's shoulder and cried, but Violette was numb.

The fire chief, who had an old-fashioned moustache and whiskers, wanted words with Violette. She gave Magdi to Geli, and went with him to the back of one of the wagons.

'You ought to see a doctor, Madame. The smoke is more dangerous than the flames.'

'I held my breath,' she said truthfully. 'I'm perfectly all right.'

He looked sceptical. 'All the same, you must have a check-up.' He was furious, but trying to be fair. 'It was extremely foolhardy of you to have gone back into the building. It's a miracle you didn't die. Didn't it cross your mind you were putting my men's lives at risk?'

'I'm sorry,' she said, gazing unblinking into his eyes, willing him not to question her any more. 'I'm really terribly sorry. But it's my ballet.'

He cleared his throat. 'I do appreciate your feelings, Madame. And your prompt action on discovering the fire undoubtedly saved your girls' lives.'

'Is it safe to go back inside now?'

'It's out of the question,' he said severely. 'The damage will have to be assessed. If there's structural damage—' He shook his head.

'Thank you,' Violette said, and walked away.

All around her, the neighbours were generously offering the girls beds for the night, or what was left of it. Such kind people,

THE DARK BLOOD OF POPPIES

Violette thought. But once she had calmed her girls down and ensured that they all had somewhere to sleep, she changed into a borrowed dress and coat and slipped away to be on her own. Chill air, a violet dawn slipping under the edge of night. The ashes of anger in her mouth.

Cesare, you damnable cowardly pig.

Attack me, if you must. I can look after myself. But my dancers can't and you knew it, you bastard, you knew it!

And I know I can't protect the ballet alone. It almost kills me to ask for help but for their sake I must do it.

Violette struggled through the Crystal Ring as if through treacle, she was so exhausted. It was turbulent, the dreamscape flowing like indigo rags across a purplish-sapphire void. She didn't climb high enough to see the dark knot in the Ring's fabric, but she could feel it above her, a black moon trying to pull her into its orbit, a black sun radiating death, not life.

Karl and Charlotte were not at home when she arrived. She paced restlessly around their drawing-room in the gloom, until the glimmer through the balcony windows turned to blue. And at last they appeared from the Crystal Ring, and stared at her, astonished.

'What's happened?' Charlotte cried, rushing to her. Violette had had a perfunctory wash at a neighbour's house, but the fire stench clung to her.

'I hate asking you for anything,' Violette said, clasping her hands, 'but I need your help now. We've had a fire. No one was hurt; I got them out in time, but it was pure luck. How can I possible tell them the fire was my fault? I made the enemies who are attacking us.'

'You are sure it wasn't an accident?' said Karl. He moved across the room behind Charlotte, regarding Violette without friendship. There was never any kindness in his face when he looked at her; not that she expected any. Each resented the other's hold over Charlotte, and always would.

'No, Cesare did it. I met him; he virtually admitted it, only I didn't understand what he meant at the time.' She told them about her journey to America. 'And I sensed two people running away from the house just as I arrived. Humans, not vampires. So he hadn't even got the guts to start the fire himself!'

And suddenly she could not speak. Hurt rage. Terror of what might have been.

'Violette,' Charlotte said, hugging her.

'Unless it was you, Charlotte, under Simon's power.'

'No!' Charlotte cried, aghast. 'How can you even suggest it?'

Violette had no idea what was making her behave so vilely to her only friend, but she couldn't seem to stop. 'You were the one who told me – I'm sorry. I'm upset. You think I have no feelings but if anything happened to my dancers I should die!'

She turned her face into Charlotte's shoulder. Charlotte said gently, 'It's all right. We'll help. It goes without saying.'

Karl said nothing, but at least he didn't object. Violette was relieved – but feeling grateful to him only made her resent him more.

'Cesare knows he can't touch me – but he can threaten and destroy everyone around me. And that gives him complete power over me. I suppose that's what he wants. Maybe he didn't mean to kill my dancers, only to upset me; a warning, he said.'

A silence. Then Karl said, 'He may be trying to provoke you into attacking him.'

'He's making a very good job of it!'

'So you must not take the bait.'

'I suppose Pierre, John and Simon condoned his actions,' Violette said acidly. 'And Ilona, Karl. What I want to ask is this; why can't they fight their own battles? I never meant to make enemies of them – but their weakness is precisely why I despise them so much!'

When she looked at them, their shocked expressions took her aback. Do I sound so bitter? 'Forgive me,' she said. 'I'm talking about your daughter, Karl. I suppose you have every reason to be on Cesare's side.'

'I am on the side of common sense,' he replied, with characteristic restraint. His voice and eyes, though, were glass.

'Even if it is an army of one. Charlotte, will you go back to Salzburg with Violette? I am going to Holdenstein to have a word with Cesare.'

'The damage doesn't look that bad,' Charlotte said. 'Will you go on with *Witch and Maiden*?'

Violette couldn't reply. How sad the house looked in the revealing light of day, the milky-green rendering blackened by smoke, the lower windows on the left-hand side boarded up. Perhaps it can be repaired, she thought . . . and then, will we have to make it a fortress?

'I don't know,' she said bleakly. 'I don't know if it's worth it . . .'

Then, to Violette's surprise, she saw a woman outside the front door, dithering as if she didn't know whether to go or stay.

'That's Ute!' exclaimed Violette, walking briskly ahead of Charlotte to meet her.

Ute was on the doorstep, a suitcase in her hand, looking distressed. Seeing Violette, a look of panic came into her eyes. 'Madame, I want to come back,' she said in a rush. 'But no one answered, and I could see there's been a fire, and I didn't know what to do. Is there still – is there still a Ballet Janacek?'

'Yes, there is,' Violette said firmly.

'Then will you have me back, please?'

Violette could see no mark on the ballerina's neck, no trace of bad memories in her expression. Yet the attack had effected some subtle change in her, all the same. 'What about your father?' she said coolly.

'I decided to defy him. All the time you were in America I cried myself to sleep every night, thinking of what I was missing. I had time to think about what you said . . . and suddenly, a few days ago, I discovered I wasn't afraid of him any more.' Her eyes were large with hope. 'Madame, is it too late?'

'It all depends on how much condition you've lost.'

'I practised in secret every day!'

'Good. I have a role for you but you've missed a lot of rehearsal time,' Violette said brusquely. Ute's face was radiant, but Violette couldn't afford to show the emotion she felt; if she did she would break down, or worse, express it disastrously as blood-thirst.

'Madame, thank you; I don't know what to say – but where—'

'We'll find you a hotel for now. Things will be difficult for a time; we need to find alternative accommodation and a rehearsal room until the building is repaired – but we will come back. *Witch and Maiden* will be performed as scheduled.'

Violette glanced sideways to see Charlotte's brilliant smile mirroring Ute's. 'One thing,' Violette murmured, 'just one thing has gone right today. Ute, I never gave your room away.'

'Tell me the truth, Pierre,' said Karl. 'Cesare is not bringing young men here solely for your benefit, is he?'

'Like bringing grapes to an invalid?' Pierre was sitting at a roughly hewn table, reading by candlelight. In shirt-sleeves and grey trousers, he looked clean, at least. He seemed better, but the shadow of fear lingered in his eyes. 'Well guessed, Karl. If he was doing it for my benefit, he'd bring women. Actually, he'd bring Violette, on a spit, with an apple in her mouth.'

'You seem more like your usual self, at least.'

'Sorry to disappoint you.'

Karl sat on the bench beside him. 'What is he doing with these humans?'

'I can't tell you. I'm not allowed to talk about it.'

'I shall have to make some more guesses, then. I know Ilona is going out and recruiting them.'

'Of course,' Pierre said sarcastically. 'Young, strong, heterosexual men are what he wants.'

'As slaves, worshippers, an army?'

Pierre shook his head, looking away. 'Stop this, Karl. He'll hear us.'

'Are you afraid of him? I'm not.'

'You don't have to live here.'

'Neither do you.'

Pierre sighed. 'Leave it alone, *mon brave*. It's nothing to do with you. What happened to your policy of non-interference?'

'I simply want answers. Cesare feels even more threatened by Violette than you do, does he not? So threatened that he's forming an army against her. And sending human agents to terrorize her by setting fire to her property.'

'I know nothing about that.' Pierre hung his head, but Karl grabbed his collar with one fine, powerful hand and dragged the vampire round to face him. Pierre's eyes fluttered with anger and alarm.

'Answer me.'

'Why didn't you kill him when you had the chance?' Pierre burst out. 'You let him live, so whose fault is it that he runs amok?'

'Well, he's a fool if he thinks an army of human devotees can protect him from Lilith,' said Karl.

He released the collar. Pierre put his head in his hands and groaned. 'Oh, Karl, Karl. Use your imagination.'

Candlelight gleamed on Pierre's brown curls, on the pallid fingers entwined through them. Karl released a gentle, horrified breath. '*Liebe Gott*. He means to transform them?'

Pierre gave a single nod, not looking at him.

'All of them?' Karl was aghast. Right or wrong, he believed in preserving the exclusivity of vampires, both for their own benefit and that of mankind. The creation of even one vampire could not be undertaken without the gravest consideration. His own pain, Charlotte's and Ilona's suffering, Katerina's death, Kristian's megalomania and Violette's madness ... all proved that the creation of a single vampire could be a disaster.

'A few at first, but there could be hundreds by the time he's finished. Maybe thousands.' Pierre sounded offhand, but he was shaking.

'Do you approve of this?'

'Of course not, but what can I do about it?'

'The earth can't support that many of us. What the hell is he trying to do?'

'Destroy Lilith, exterminate his enemies, conquer the world,'

Pierre said with a sneer. 'Just the usual. Cesare's an evangelist now. Kristian liked to keep his little dark empire cloistered here; Cesare wants to take it to the masses. Imagine it, a race of supermen, of golden immortals, eager to do his will. What heady nourishment to the ego! The inferior mass of humanity to be kept as cattle, of course. Us and them, to the extreme.'

A nightmare, Karl thought. Hell on earth. 'Has he started transforming them yet?'

'No, he's training them first, not just dropping them in it. He's learned by Kristian's mistakes. John breaks them, then Cesare becomes their golden saviour. A few have proved unsuitable, so—' Pierre drew a fingernail across his throat.

'And he's only using men?'

Pierre shrugged. 'He doesn't like women, does he? He thinks they're useless, except as tools to further his cause.'

'He's got to be stopped, obviously,' said Karl.

'I've told you too much.'

'Then leave here with me now!'

'I'm a lost cause, my friend. It's nothing to me.'

Karl stood up, put his arm round Pierre's shoulder and leaned down, his mouth near Pierre's cheek. 'If you don't face whatever it is Violette has done to you, you are going to die. Is that what you want?'

Pierre shrugged again.

'Where is Cesare?'

'Probably in Kristian's rooms. He's usually there.' Pierre looked up suddenly. 'Don't—'

'What?'

'Take any stupid risks.'

Karl whispered so softly that no vampire could have over-heard, 'I won't, my friend. I'm going to do what I should have done before, that's all.'

He found Cesare in the inner sanctum, as Pierre had suggested. There were humans guarding the door, humans flanking the simple, carved chair in which Cesare sat. None of them tried to stop Karl. Cesare simply watched as he approached, as if he'd carefully arranged himself in this relaxed posture. Obviously he knew I was here, Karl thought wearily.

'I trust you had an interesting conversation with Pierre,' said Cesare.

'I'm surprised you have to ask. I'm sure you heard every word.' Karl ignored the handsome, bovine attendants.

Cesare's smile was a portrait of benign wisdom. 'If I did, I had no reason to stop it. Pierre may have told you a lot, and you may have guessed the rest, but the extent of your knowledge is irrelevant. There's nothing you can do to stop us.'

That's true, Karl thought, if I don't abandon my vow not to interfere. At this moment, however, it seemed perfectly desirable to kill Cesare. Whatever he felt for Violette, he couldn't countenance the intimidation of innocent humans. It stank of Kristian's methods. Blackmail.

Killing another vampire wasn't easy. To drain the enemy then behead him was the most straightforward method. Karl had found it nearly impossible to kill Kristian because he'd been too strong physically. But Cesare was weaker than Karl; an easy target, really. And no other vampires close at hand to help him.

'You must realize that to create vampires in large numbers is an obscene notion,' said Karl.

Cesare's expression was obdurate and condescending. 'You condemn us only because you don't understand. If I could make you see! Spend some time with us, Karl. You'd come to realize how wonderful—'

Karl sprang, swift as light, and pinned Cesare's wrists to the arms of the chair. Cesare seemed paralysed. His head strained backwards, his eyes flicking back and forth under half-closed lids. Something struck Karl's back, hot hands clawed at his arms, but he ignored them. Only humans, trying to protect their master. He nipped Cesare's smooth pale neck, feeling distaste. The priest-vampire's robe smelled musty, like the castle, but the blood in his veins was red enough, like gelatinous firelight.

'Violette is not the devil,' Karl whispered through the blood, 'and you will leave her alone.'

Cesare tried to escape into the Ring, but was too slow. Karl went with him, still feeding, and pulled him back into the solid world.

Something changed. Karl sensed it even through his blood-frenzy. A radiance in the corner of his eye, a new presence that had not merely entered the room but filled it.

Without warning, Karl was wrenched off his prey and flung aside. He hit the flagstones with Cesare's scream filling his ears; his fangs must have torn the tender flesh as they ripped free. Karl landed on his back to find himself looking up at a splendid immortal with golden hair and lion-coloured eyes, to whom Cesare seemed a colourless sibling.

Simon. Angel, demon, envoy of God, deceiver. And beside him, John; a scarred red bull of a man.

Karl made to climb to his feet, only for Simon and John to lunge at him and hold him down. He struggled fiercely for a few moments, but John's strength was bizarre, as if there were a massive weight behind it. While John held Karl down, Simon caught Karl's throat and exerted vicious pressure, as if he were capable of digging his fingers deep into Karl's flesh, snapping vessels and tendons, crushing his spine . . . calmly removing his head with one hand.

No point in entering Raqi'a. They would only follow. Simon smiled into Karl's eyes, and Karl experienced a fear that he hadn't known since Kristian's death.

'You won last time. Now it's my turn, Karl.' Simon's nose was an inch from his. 'Circumstances have changed. I was once as weak as you, but now I'm stronger. Don't delude yourself; Cesare's right, you really *can't* stop us. And if you have any sense you'll join us, you and the lovely, obliging Charlotte. You must both be my lovers because you are too wise to be my enemies . . . aren't you?'

His eyes were amulets, burning into Karl's. Karl felt the rush of a terrible philosophy, a monumental change that could not be averted. Soul-destroying to accept it, but he knew now. He closed his eyes, eyebrows drawn down with despair. *They really cannot be stopped.*

Simon slid his hand over Karl's collarbone and under his shirt. Then he struck. Sharp pain pierced Karl's veins. He felt his vitality flowing out into Simon's mouth, while the angel-demon pressed himself hard to Karl's body along its length, pressing him flat to the floor.

Over Simon's shoulder, Karl saw Cesare smiling down, his face smoothly composed once more. He resembled a boyish monk, his hair a crisp halo.

'You can't leave us now, Karl,' said Cesare. 'You're ours.'

Karl was floating; a euphoria of weakness, embedded in a mesh of pain. Simon finished at last and raised his head, his mouth crimson, his eyes sultry flames. His body shuddered against Karl's, like that of a fulfilled lover.

'Oh, Karl.' Simon smiled. 'I have wanted to do that for such a long time.'

Charlotte was alone in Violette's apartment above the studio, arranging bowls of white roses in the hope of sweetening the air. It was a room of silver-greys, muted lavender and ashes-of-roses tints; soft, luxurious, melancholy – and tainted by the bitter-sour smell of dead fire.

The blaze had not reached the upper floors. Violette had wanted to return to her apartment, so they had, the damage to the building being of no danger to vampires. The fire chief would never know.

At this moment, Violette was downstairs, convincing the police and the fire brigade, as only she could, that the fire had been caused by an electrical fault.

And Violette was a heroine of a new kind for the newspapers. 'Brave Ballerina Fights Fire to Save 18 Lives – and Cat,' exclaimed the evening papers, launching into incredulous hyperbole. Charlotte had had to protect Violette from reporters all day. The blood of three of them now sang sweetly through her veins.

But she was waiting impatiently for Karl to arrive. She tried to resist looking at the clock, but her anxiety was increasing. What could have kept him so long at Schloss Holdenstein? He can look after himself, nothing happened last time . . . yet the thought of the place chilled her. I still feel it's dangerous even though Kristian is dead, she thought, stripping leaves from a rose stem and stabbing it into the bowl. A thorn pricked her finger. A drop of blood oozed out. She looked at the perfect red drop on the pearl whiteness of her skin, then absently licked it away. A tiny fork of lightning struck her tongue; strange, disturbing, that even the taste of her own blood could electrify her.

I should have gone with Karl, she thought. If only Stefan had stayed, he could have helped protect Violette. I know Stefan doesn't approve of her but he would have done it for me. God, I hate it when Karl insists on doing these things alone! But he's always been the same.

She watched the tiny puncture in her finger heal and vanish.

An unsettling feeling crept over her; she sensed that she was no longer alone in the apartment. There was someone, some cold, unnatural presence, in one of the other rooms ... something waiting behind a bedroom door. Waiting for her or for Violette?

Charlotte went to the panelled white door and turned the handle softly. The presence was radiant but very cold, and eerily familiar.

She opened the door quickly and halted in the doorway, transfixed.

The being in the room was white, seemingly cauled in an opalescent light through which she could see no clear features. Far from threatening her, it was lying half on the carpet and half on the bed, as if it had fallen there and could not get up.

Seeing her, it stretched out a glowing arm and said, 'Help me.' A heavy accent, perhaps Russian. 'Help me.'

A trap? Charlotte went cautiously towards it, all her senses poised. She knew this creature but it couldn't be ... Trying to peer through the glare, she made out the vague lines of a narrow face and long wisps of silver-white hair.

'Who are you?' she said.

The hand reached for her, but she stepped back.

'Fyodor,' said the hoarse voice. 'You know me, Charlotte-friend-of-Lilith.'

So it *was* him! She remained out of reach, suspicious. Fyodor, lover of Simon, enemy of Violette.

'Help me,' he said again. 'I am so weak. It's taken all my strength to find you.'

Reluctantly, she gave him her hand. She was ready to meet treachery, but he only leaned on her, dragged himself to his feet, and collapsed on to the bed. His glow faded, as if sucked back into his body and contained there, making his flesh so luminous that hers seemed golden-pink by contrast. His white shirt and cream-coloured flannels were not much better than rags. He looked bloodless and emaciated, a blue-veined albino ravaged by cocaine addiction. She remembered the cruel, sharp countenance as being full of arrogant mirth, but now it seemed deadened by suffering.

'What do you want?' she said, staring down at him.

'To talk to you. You created Lilith, so you must take heed.'

'Are your companions with you?' she said harshly. 'Are you planning to kidnap Violette again? Why in the name of God can't you leave her in peace?'

Fyodor held up his hands. 'I am alone. The trinity is broken. You could drain my blood, break my neck and throw me to the hounds of hell, Charlotte, if you wished. Since Simon left us I seem to have no strength . . .'

She sat down on the bed, folding her arms. 'Do you expect sympathy? My God, I should take you to Violette so you can kiss her feet and beg forgiveness for the way you treated her!'

Rage glinted in Fyodor's eyes, a silver lash. 'Love is blind,' he said. 'You are in love with a serpent, but a serpent can't feel love, it can only bite. You know we were only doing God's will!'

'When you half-killed us and coerced Violette into nearly being raped by Lancelyn – you were doing God's will?' Charlotte said bitterly. 'What a charming god you serve.'

His head tipped listlessly to one side. 'I'm inclined to agree. That so-charming God abandoned us. You are so young, Charlotte, a baby in vampire terms, but Simon, Rasmila and I – we are very old. The older we grow, the closer to the Crystal Ring we become, too confident of our powers. That's when the Ring seizes us and moulds us to its own designs. We become what it wants: angels, devils, gods. And when it's finished with us, it spits us out. It has a use for Simon again. No use for me.'

'Oh God,' Charlotte breathed. A frantic energy filled her; and at the core, a revelation. 'That's what I've always believed! God didn't make the Crystal Ring, it's the Ring that makes gods! And you've just found this out, haven't you? You've lost your faith!'

His silvery face creased with exhaustion and pain. 'Punishment. It hit Simon the hardest. I could have accepted it, just to be the cruel vampire again, no reason for my existence beyond the caprices of nature. But Simon can't let go. He must have influence and control, but he can't get it through Rasmila and me so he leaves us and fastens on someone new—'

'Cesare,' said Charlotte. 'I know.'

Fyodor sneered. 'Cesare isn't enough for him. Simon needs me but he won't admit it.' He touched her thigh; the touch tingled with a strange energy. 'I must make him see. I don't care about Lilith or Cesare. I want Simon back, that is all. I want Simon.'

Charlotte moved out of his reach, almost laughing. Lovesick, this poor creature. Simply lovesick. 'What on earth do you expect me to do about it?'

Fyodor sat up, long milky strands of hair hanging down to his lap. He was rather feminine, not the exuberant creature she remembered. Frail, androgynous. He said viciously, 'You're keeping him from me, you and Karl!'

'No, we're not,' she said. 'I've given Simon no encouragement. He's trying to use us, that's all. It isn't love. I don't want him, I think he's evil!'

She thought, now I've offended him, instead of reassuring him. But Fyodor showed no reaction. 'He gave you his blood,' he said quietly. 'Did that not make you adore him?'

'No. I wish he *would* take you back and leave us alone.'

Fyodor gasped and seized her hand, making her jump. 'Then come and fetch Karl!'

Silvery waves of fear were suddenly running all over her body. 'What?'

'They're holding Karl at Schloss Holdenstein. I want him gone.'

Charlotte was on her feet, distraught. 'Why didn't you tell

me as soon as you arrived?' she cried. 'Why did you waste so much time?'

She was out of the apartment and running down the stairs, not waiting for an answer. The stink of singed timber rose from the lower floors. At the top of the second flight, she saw Violette running up to meet her, as if she'd heard Charlotte cry out.

Charlotte seized her wrist and dragged her back up to the apartment, only to find that Fyodor had vanished.

'He was here,' Charlotte said. 'Fyodor. He said they're keeping Karl prisoner at Holdenstein. We've got to get him out!'

Violette looked unmoved, her face bone-china. 'No, Charlotte. It's a trap, don't you see?'

'What if it is? If Karl's in danger, I have to go to him, I can't sit here waiting! Will you come with me?'

She was ready to step into Raqi'a that second, but Violette said, 'No.'

Charlotte stared at her, incredulous. 'You're refusing to help Karl, after all he's done for you? He went there for your sake!'

'It's a trap,' Violette repeated, 'and if you have any sense, you won't go either.'

But Charlotte, floored by this betrayal, was seeing Violette in a starkly ugly light. 'I can't believe you can be so callous. I know you and Karl don't get on, but what does it matter? After everything we've tried to do for you, and received nothing but threats in return! Maybe Cesare and the others are right about you, and I'm the one who's been blind, not them.'

She couldn't look at Violette any more, couldn't bear her glacial eyes or her heartless words. Furious, bereaved, but dry-eyed, Charlotte turned away and arrowed into the Crystal Ring.

John had wanted to lock Karl in a cell and torture him, but Simon, disgusted by the idea, wouldn't hear of it.

'You don't know Karl as I do,' Simon said. 'He's not one of

your ox-headed young men. We will win him only by affection and reason, not by cruelty.'

Yet it was torment of a sort, Simon supposed, to treat Karl as they did. After Simon had drained his blood, they took him to the meeting chamber and sat him in a chair, with John on hand to restrain him if he tried to escape. And they kept him there for hours in a state of starvation.

Nothing worse to a vampire than blood-deprivation. Karl obviously knew he was too weak to flee into the Crystal Ring, didn't even try; he bore the ordeal with amazing composure. Simon was impressed.

Torchlight made the stone walls appear to be bathed in sweat. John, the gaoler, stood broodingly beside Karl's chair; Cesare paced up and down in front of him, expounding his beliefs with a force that would have had any mortal on his knees in obeisance. Simon, meanwhile, leaned on the other side of the chair and watched Karl.

The bliss of stealing Karl's blood had only whetted his passion. Simon was in love. He knew now the mystery that had made them all love Karl, even Kristian; he knew why Kristian had lost all sense of self-preservation where Karl was concerned. The mystery was distilled in Karl's beauty; the face of a poet, a lambency seen in paintings but rarely in life, dark amber eyes like fire captured within the shadows of his brows and long lashes. He was like a panther, caged yet losing not one mote of dignity.

Oh, why did you refuse me? Simon thought. What a leader you would have made! Cesare will do, his vision makes up for his lack of everything else – oh, but you with Cesare's vision, Karl! What a combination that would be. Perhaps will be yet, if you ever forgive me and let me into your soul . . . I am truly sorry for the pain I've caused you, but I couldn't, can't help it.

Simon's fingers played along the wood, a hair's breadth from Karl's arm. Karl ignored him.

Then Cesare had the humans brought in. They were beautiful too, in their own way, with their tanned skins and shining eyes. Their tans were fading. It would be a long time before they saw the sun again.

Simon felt Karl tense as the mortals were paraded before him in small groups, then led out again. Simon's own fangs ached and his body yearned towards their moist heat; how much worse it must be for Karl! But Karl showed no other sign of his extreme thirst; his face remained immobile.

'Are they not magnificent?' Cesare said. 'What glorious immortals they will make! You don't begrudge them eternal life, surely?'

'They will turn against you,' said Karl, 'as Kristian's children turned against him.'

'Never,' said Cesare, 'because I rely not on the random hope of love, but the sure foundation of discipline. They are already mine, through life, death and eternity.'

'Are they to have no thoughts of their own?' Karl's voice was steady, but taut with the undertow of thirst.

'What thoughts could they have, that are any better than mine?' Cesare asked reasonably. 'This misguided obsession with freedom leads to depravity and anarchy, the dark path to Lilith's domain.'

'They will begin to grow old if you don't transform them soon.'

'The time of their transformation is mine to decide.' Cesare looked reprovingly at Simon. 'You haven't weakened him enough. He still thinks he will gain some advantage by discovering our plans. It wouldn't matter, Karl, if I could tell you the time of transformation to the minute; you won't stop it.'

'And it will not matter if you keep me sitting here for a hundred years,' Karl said flatly. 'You will never persuade me to your cause.'

'Will this not persuade you?' More of the men came in, bowed, walked away. Delicious blood-heat wafted from them. 'Or this?' Another group. 'Or this?'

Two vampires came in, marching between them an exquisite young woman with dishevelled russet hair. She was afire with indignation. Charlotte.

That made Karl react, Simon noted with satisfaction.

★

When Charlotte saw Karl seated between John and Simon, his face carved to the bone by blood-loss, she broke free of her captors and ran towards him. But John stepped forward and stopped her. It was like hitting an iron gate.

His grotesque appearance shocked her; his hands on her arms were reptilian, strong as a machine. But it was the emanation of his soul that horrified her; there was nothing in his eyes but a conflagration, a circle of hell.

She could have leapt back into Raqi'a. No one had attacked her when she'd arrived; the robed vampires with their too-tranquil eyes had simply asked her to come to Cesare, as if they'd been expecting her. But her own escape would not help Karl.

She glanced around for Fyodor, couldn't see him. *Was he sent by Simon to trick me here, or did he come to me of his own accord? It hardly mattered. The result was the same.*

'Karl, are you all right?' she said anxiously.

'You shouldn't have come, Charlotte.' Karl sounded despairing. He glared at Simon, who let him stand up and come to her.

'I couldn't just leave you here!'

'But now they're holding us both prisoner. What does that achieve?' He stroked her arms lightly, his expression as sombre as death. And Charlotte knew, as if she'd never fully believed it before, that she and Karl were not invulnerable; that Cesare's powers were real, and that the movement being generated within Holdenstein's walls would roll onwards like an iron-wheeled monolith.

'It achieves this,' Simon said, waving John away. 'Time for you both to think. Time to see that if you don't join us, you're going to die. What's keeping you away? Pride? An outmoded human affectation, surely. A vampire's greatest priority is survival. And then there is love.'

Simon came close to them, rested a hand on Karl's shoulder and stroked Charlotte's cheek. She wanted to feel repelled, but didn't. She felt soporific. On the edge of surrender again.

She wondered if Cesare was jealous, like Fyodor.

'Did my blood call to yours, after all?' Simon asked, smiling.

'No. Your white-haired friend came and told me Karl wasn't being allowed to leave.'

'As he was meant to, even if he thought he was acting for himself.'

'Let Karl go! I'll do anything, I'll put myself in his place—'

'But we want you both. And now we've got you.' Simon's tone became gentle, appealing. 'I am not imposing unthinkable conditions on you. You won't be separated or treated as slaves. We'll all be together, you'll be treated as gods by the followers, as are Cesare and myself. All we ask is that you listen. Is it really so wonderful to be out in the cold with only Lilith for company, when you could be with us, warm and loved and safe?'

Charlotte pressed the heel of her hand to her forehead, recalling Violette's callous refusal to help rescue Karl.

'What is it, *Liebling*?' Karl asked, but she shook her head.

'Nothing. All of this.' But she thought, maybe Simon's right. Violette's a monster, I've always known it. She doesn't give a damn about me or Karl. Why go on defending her, when we'll be killed for our pains, and she won't even care?

Charlotte said, 'May I speak to Karl alone for a moment?'

'As you wish,' Cesare said graciously.

She and Karl went to a corner near Kristian's ebony throne. She put her mouth to his ear, whispering so faintly that even Simon's sharp ears wouldn't hear.

'What if we pretend to do what Simon wants? Pretend we're on his side, then seduce him away from Cesare.'

'No,' said Karl.

'It could be our only chance. Win some time and set them against each other!'

Karl hugged her as she felt his breath against her ear. 'And you're probably right, but I can't do it. Yes, it worked with Kristian; I pretended to love him in order to betray him – and that is why I can't do it again. It leaves a sickness in the soul that would make us feel no better than Simon. I can't, Charlotte. And I couldn't bear to watch you do it either.'

Charlotte squeezed her eyes shut. She felt ashamed even for suggesting it. 'Either we prostitute ourselves, or we die.'

'Not yet,' he whispered. 'We're too precious to Simon for

him to dispose of us so easily. If we must stay here, at least we can try to subvert others to our cause—'

'Enough,' came Cesare's sharp voice. 'How went the fire, Charlotte?'

'Nobody died,' she said, turning to face him. 'Hard luck.'

'I did not mean anyone to die. It was a warning, as Violette knows full well.'

'What else will you do to her?'

'Anything, everything. Whatever it takes. Simon says she cannot be destroyed. But I say she must and will be contained. And one day she will wither and die of self-loathing; she is bound to.'

Charlotte took a breath. 'Look, you know we can't escape, and Simon said we'd be treated civilly. Couldn't you let Karl feed?'

'I could,' said Cesare. He was silver-clean and sterile, as absolute as tyranny. 'But not until he's expressed some contrition and willingness to co-operate.'

Charlotte looked at Karl. He was in anguish, she could tell, though he was hiding it. He looked sadly at her as if to say, *You know me better than that.*

'This is inhuman!' she cried on a wave of helpless rage. Simon broke into delighted laughter.

'No, it's very simple,' Cesare said serenely. 'You can be tortured until Karl gives in, and he can be tortured until you give in. It's no trouble to John; it's his vocation. Or you could just give in, which would be less fun for John but easier for the rest of us.'

Karl embraced Charlotte protectively, his face in her hair. 'Leave, while you can,' he said.

'Not without you!'

Simon came and took Charlotte's hand. Karl glared icily at him, but as Simon began to draw Charlotte away, John seized Karl. They were both bundled back to the centre of the chamber, where Cesare stood near the chair. Charlotte was aware of Karl struggling, but there was nothing he could do to prevent Simon putting his fangs to her neck.

'It's over,' Simon murmured. 'You're angry now, but you'll

come to terms with it. It will be wonderful. We'll be angels together, Charlotte; oh yes, it is going to happen to you . . .' Simon's fangs felt like the tips of two icicles on her throat. 'Am I not as beautiful as Karl? Can you love me?'

'A jar of poison wrapped in beautiful paper looks like a desirable present,' she said. 'But it's still a jar of poison.'

His arms tightened savagely. She closed her eyes, waiting for Simon to strike, but the pain didn't come. She felt him freeze; then his mouth left her throat, and he looked up.

Charlotte felt the air tremble and the temperature drop.

It began like a wind groaning around the castle walls. And then it was like wings. Ten thousand ravens' wings, beating at the air unseen.

She was caught in a polar flow of dread, as if all Kristian's victims had stepped out of the walls to take revenge.

Everyone was looking around the room and at each other, eyes glazed with alarm; Cesare, John, Simon, Karl, the two vampires – strangers, male and female – who'd brought Charlotte in. There were cries from other parts of the Schloss. More vampires and humans came running in through the arched doorways, as if to beseech their leader for reassurance.

The walls shook. The air was displaced as if by some vast primeval beast with ribbed wings, black and leathery and pocked with stars. Night fell. Someone screamed.

When the sweaty torchlight resurfaced, the female vampire and one of the human males lay dead. The vampire's head had been severed, still in its hood. The male's blood had sprayed everywhere.

And Lilith was in the room.

Charlotte's heart flew in loops. Mortals and vampires were crying out hysterically and clinging to each other, while Cesare ran across the chamber towards the ebony throne on its shallow dais, stumbling as if he were about to expire with fury and fear.

The terror Violette inspired was something tangible and external, outside even Violette, like sound-waves shuddering through a gelid medium. Charlotte experienced it, yet it didn't touch her. She was inexplicably part of it.

And Violette followed us after all. What else matters?

Simon and John were still holding tightly on to Charlotte and Karl. Simon's strength was far greater than Charlotte's, John's unmeasurable.

Violette faced Cesare, her jet hair tangled with static and her eyes blue comets. Cesare clung to the back of the throne, as if it were a shield. When he found his voice, though, it was extraordinarily loud and commanding. 'Surrender yourself to us,' he said, pointing to Karl and Charlotte, 'or your friends will suffer.'

Violette blinked at him. Then she moved so fast that Charlotte hardly saw her, but somehow she was on the dais and had grabbed Cesare by the throat. His attempts to shake her off were pathetic. His eyes bulged, huge grey pearls.

'On the other hand,' said Violette, 'Let my friends go or Cesare dies. Perhaps you'd like him to die, I don't know.' She squeezed. Blood oozed between her fingers.

'Do as she says!' Cesare rasped. 'Let them go!'

Karl and Charlotte were thrown suddenly together.

Lilith's wings seemed to fill the chamber. She gathered Karl and Charlotte against her, and swept them into the Crystal Ring.

They had each tried to destroy the other, each tried to win, or at least to end the affair. Hopeless. Robyn and Sebastian remained fastened on each other like starving succubi, gorging darkly on sensuality. A horrible and wondrous feeling, like opium addiction, wanton and irresistible.

'I'll take you away from here,' he whispered sometimes, but she only laughed.

Sebastian was beginning to despair of persuading Robyn to leave Boston. He wanted to tear her loose from the chains of her past, her responsibilities, her lovers. 'No, this is my home, I belong here, I like it. Why should I want to move?' she would say, as if clinging by her fingernails to all that was left of her identity. As if she thought she had a choice.

He couldn't admit, 'Other vampires know where you live. I must protect you. Keep you to myself.'

If persuasion wouldn't work, it followed that he must force her to leave. Place her in a position, he thought in stony calculation, where she can't refuse.

One evening, after Robyn had said, 'I can't see you tonight, don't come to the house,' Sebastian went anyway. He melted in through the locked french window, and found Harold Charrington, dressed up for an evening out, sitting in the parlour on his own. He was in an armchair by the fire, smoking a cigar and looking thoroughly at home.

Harold hadn't seen how he'd got in. As Sebastian approached him, though, he didn't jump, didn't turn a hair. He merely looked the vampire over with a knowing, worldly air that Sebastian found infuriating.

'So, you're the one,' said Harold. 'The other man, the young lover. Pleased to make your acquaintance, sir.'

He rose briefly to shake Sebastian's hand, and sank back into the chair. Sebastian thought, how can she let those hairy, veined hands touch her? 'And you, sir, must be Mrs Stafford's grandfather.'

Harold laughed, unoffended. 'I may be well struck in years – but she ain't thrown me over for you, has she?'

Despising him, Sebastian sat down opposite. 'Well, now, I'm glad to have this opportunity to tell you to stop seeing her.'

Harold laughed harder.

'I'm quite serious,' Sebastian added.

The old man was shaking his head in amusement. 'Sure you are. When you get to my age, you learn a lot of tolerance. I know that to keep her, I've got to tolerate all her other admirers, too. You'll learn.' He chuckled. 'You'll learn.'

Sebastian stared at him, feeling the waves of his musty body-heat, the ticking of his arteries. That was the answer, of course.

Harold threw the stub of his cigar into the fire. 'I guess one of us had better leave. Wouldn't want to embarrass the lady.' He looked pointedly at Sebastian, then at the door. His employees, Sebastian thought, must be terrified of him.

Sebastian stood up. 'Allow me to point out something first.'

He beckoned; Harold rose, puzzled, the top of his head barely level with Sebastian's chin.

Sebastian seized him. Harold cried out. His spectacles fell to the floor.

'Wouldn't it be terribly embarrassing for your widow,' the vampire said, mimicking his educated accent, 'if you were to be found dead in the house of your mistress?'

Harold gaped like a flat-fish.

The vampire struck, feeding swiftly and neatly. The old man's blood was thick with potential clots; his heart thundered, stumbled, exploded long before blood-loss alone would have killed him. When Sebastian dropped him back into the chair, he looked for all the world as if he had expired there. His expression was oddly indignant, his lips blue as slate.

Sebastian replaced the spectacles on Harold's nose and left, very quietly, the way he had entered.

'I'm ready, dear,' Robyn said, walking into the parlour in her cream satin, with pearls in her hair; virginal, a little old-fashioned, just as Harold liked her. But Harold failed to leap to his feet. She saw his head lolling to one side and she thought, I took so long he's fallen asleep—

She saw the colour of his face. Saw the two tiny marks in his throat, only because she knew to look for them.

'Mary,' she said, her voice steady but threatening to crack. She fumbled her way backwards to the door, and called again. 'Mary, get the doctor, will you?'

Robyn managed to keep very calm throughout the doctor's visit, but inside she was in turmoil. 'He didn't look well when he arrived,' she lied.

The doctor failed to notice the marks. They were flea-bites, not gaping wounds. 'Looks like a heart attack,' he said grimly, frowning at Robyn. He knew Harold's wife. He disapproved of 'goings-on'. 'Happens to men of his age, especially if they overindulge their . . . appetites.'

'Could you please arrange for him to be taken away?' Robyn

said sweetly. 'He's not my husband, you see. He really shouldn't be here; I think you understand.'

Once the body had been removed and the grumpy doctor had left, Robyn sank down on a sofa with her head in her hands. Mary ran away to make tea, but Alice stood over Robyn like a prison wardress.

'Well, you've got to see sense now,' said Alice.

Robyn looked up, aggravated. 'What are you talking about? It was a heart attack.'

'But you and I know damned well what really happened!' Alice shouted. 'Now will you listen to me about that devil? He almost killed me and Mary; now he's really murdered someone. He's killing you, slowly. What will it take to make you stop?'

'Leave me alone,' was all Robyn could say. 'You're giving me a headache!'

She went to her room and lay awake, waiting for Sebastian, but he never came.

The next day Robyn was very calm and controlled. Yes, like someone walking a tightrope over a fire-pit, she thought.

She hoped with all her soul that Harold's death would be quietly forgotten, but she knew she couldn't be that lucky. The following days were a muted crescendo of chaos. Harold Charrington had been an eminent member of the business community, and the fact that he'd expired in his mistress's house could not be kept secret. Scandal broke and spread through the puritanical layers of Boston high society.

Robyn tried to brazen it out, but inside she was withering in a succession of embarrassing horrors. Reporters haunted her doorstep; friends failed to call; the church congregation shunned her and she was asked – discreetly, of course – to leave. It was the same everywhere she went. The hand on the elbow, the obsequious whisper, 'Madam, your, er, presence is causing a little, er, embarrassment so if you wouldn't mind . . . I'm sure you appreciate . . .'

Jesus, I hate all this! she would shriek in the privacy of her bedroom.

One ghastly afternoon, Harold's widow arrived, hysterical and baying for her blood.

Thankfully, Robyn was not obliged to confront her; Alice and Mr Wilkes saw the wretched woman off. But Robyn was being forced to become a recluse, and she couldn't tolerate it. Next it'll be the Beacon Hill Civic Association demanding that I clean up the neighbourhood by moving out.

I don't blame them, really.

I blame myself. But most of all I blame you, Sebastian, you bastard.

Sebastian hadn't appeared – as if, Robyn thought, he is only too aware of the trouble he's caused. He must have realized that I was fond of Harold. In fact, she missed Harold more than she would have believed possible; she even wept for him, once.

On the fifth morning after the death, she slept late and came downstairs to find her parlour full of people. Mary, Mr and Mrs Wilkes, the doctor, two police officers and a minister from Trinity. At the centre, radiating the grim resolve of a woman who'd had more than she could take, was Alice.

'I've told them, madam,' Alice said as Robyn halted in the doorway.

'Told them – what?' Her eyes raked over the grim faces of authority. She felt horribly exposed before them.

'That I believe Mr Charrington was murdered – and the name of the man I think was responsible, Sebastian Pierse.'

Robyn gaped at her. This was so hideous she almost laughed. And she felt betrayed.

'Why is the minister here? Have you also told them that you believe Sebastian to be a vampire?'

A stirring among them. Mary hung her head; only the clergyman looked unmoved, so Robyn knew that Alice *had* told him, if not the others. Robyn addressed the officials. 'I'm sorry you've had a wasted journey, but my companion has not been well lately. She sometimes has . . . ideas which are only partly connected to reality.'

Alice glared back stonily. Now the betrayal was mutual. 'I'm doing this to protect *you*, madam. I won't stand by and watch him destroying you!'

One of the police officers cleared his throat uncomfortably. 'We'd like to hear your side of the story, ma'am.'

'I can assure you, officer, no one is destroying me,' Robyn said firmly. She sounded calm, Alice the hysterical one. 'As the doctor will tell you, Mr Charrington suffered a heart attack, which was very unfortunate, but not uncommon for a man of his age. I'm grateful to you for taking so much trouble, but I don't want to waste any more of your time, so if you wouldn't mind—'

'I'm sorry, ma'am,' said the officer. 'It's not that easy. This is a very serious allegation which has to be pursued until we're satisfied there were no suspicious circumstances.'

'What can I say to reassure you? Sebastian Pierse is an acquaintance of mine, but he didn't know Mr Charrington and had no connection whatsoever to him. On the night of Mr Charrington's death, I only left him alone in the parlour for a few minutes while I went to get ready. The doors were locked, no one could have come in or out; there was certainly no sign of anyone having broken in. And when Mr Charrington first arrived, I had noticed that he looked unwell.'

The doctor nodded. 'Mrs Stafford did say that.'

Alice's eyes were blazing with the silent accusation, *Liar!*

'Well, then, what would you say to the allegation that Mr Pierse had on one occasion assaulted both your housekeeper and your maid in their beds?'

Robyn shook her head, 'I would find it quite incredible. Mr Pierse is a gentleman. If he were ever here that late at night, I can assure you that he was with me. Mary, do you recall Mr Pierse ever entering your bedroom?'

Mr and Mrs Wilkes sat in silence, their chins drawn in with puritan denial of what they were hearing. The maid's face was a mask of tension and bewilderment. 'No, ma'am, I don't.'

Robyn looked pointedly at the policemen, her eyebrows raised. 'I hope this has helped to clear things up.'

'Not really,' the officer said heavily. 'There may have to be a post-mortem, and we will need to question Mr Pierse. If you could tell us where to find him—'

'I'm afraid I can't.'

'It isn't in your interests to withhold information, ma'am.'

These words sent fear and indignation slithering through her. She felt that they were looking on her as a criminal, even though she had not been accused of anything. 'I would if I could, but I don't have his address.'

A pause; disapproval hung heavy in the room. She felt she would never be happy here again, as if she'd been invaded, raped under her own roof. 'You were seeing a man,' said the second policeman, 'without even knowing his address or circumstances?'

'He's a visitor from Ireland,' she said quickly. 'I should check the hotels if I were you.'

The officers rose from their chairs. 'You will be sure to notify us immediately if you see him, won't you, ma'am?'

'Of course, officer,' Robyn said graciously. 'If there's anything else I can do—'

'Don't plan any vacations. We may need to speak to you and your housekeeper again.'

Mary saw the policemen and the doctor out, to Robyn's immense relief. Her head ached. She sank down on the arm of a chair, rubbing her forehead, but she could not turn her wrath on Alice; the Wilkeses and the minister were still there.

'Mrs Stafford,' the minister began in a voice of oak and honey, 'I am only here to help you. If there is anything you wish to talk about, anything at all—'

'There isn't, thank you.'

'None of us is perfect, you know. We are all faced with temptation and 'it is only human to give in once in a while. Satan has all manner of tricks to make us think it's all right, even though we know in our hearts that it isn't. But God is merciful. You are a church-goer, Mrs Stafford. You know the church is there to help you, not to punish—'

Robyn jumped to her feet, feeling homicidal. 'I came to church last Sunday and was asked to leave. I don't think there's any more to say on the subject. So if you would excuse me?'

The minister left, looking grave and rather shamefaced. No sooner had he gone than Mr and Mrs Wilkes came up to her and announced their intention to resign.

'You've been very good to us, ma'am,' said the cook. 'But under the circumstances – I'm sure you understand – we're sorry, but—'

'I'm sorry, too,' Robyn sighed. 'Talk to Alice about it. I have a severe headache and I need to rest.'

With that, she left the room, barely glancing at the stunned Alice. In her bedroom, she sat down at her dressing-table, temples resting on her fists, trembling with emotion. After a few minutes, the door opened, and Alice came in, her face grim as thunder.

'You made me look a fool downstairs, madam.'

'And you made me look like an accomplice to murder!' Robyn flared. 'How dare you, how *dare* you drag the police into this! Have you gone completely crazy?'

'But I did it because that – that creature really is a murderer!' Alice struck the edge of the dressing-table, scattering perfume bottles like skittles. Robyn had never seen her so angry. 'I'm trying to save you from him and from yourself. But you, God help you, are trying to protect him! That *makes* you an accomplice to murder. So tell me, which of us is crazy?'

'Get out,' Robyn grated. 'If you want to lose your job, your home and your generous salary – you are going the right way about it.'

'You ungrateful b—' Alice closed her lips on the last word. Eyes brimming with acid, she marched out.

Robyn dropped her head on to her arms, utterly drained. She was too depressed even to cry. Why am I doing this? she thought. I know Alice is right, and that's why I'm so mad. Why am I protecting Sebastian and attacking Alice, when all of this is Sebastian's fault?

She sat without moving for an hour or so. Mary brought a tray of coffee, set it down with trembling hands, and left without a word. Robyn roused herself to drink the coffee, stirred far too much sugar into it, winced at the cloying sweetness. But she needed it to ease her shock.

That was when Sebastian appeared. She saw a dark movement in the corner of her eye and stood up to face him, livid.

'Have you got the remotest idea what you've done to me?'

'What is it?' He moved like a shadow towards her, beautiful, gentle, self-assured, infinitely more real than the dry judge and jury she'd encountered downstairs. 'The idiots in your parlour? For the love of heaven, Robyn, how can you be letting the likes of them upset you?'

'They want to question you about a murder. The minister wants to save my soul. They know about you.'

Sebastian shrugged. 'I'm a very jealous lover, child. You know that. I told you months ago to stop seeing Harold. You didn't really care about him, did you?'

Her head ached to the bone. 'Not as much as I should. I suppose that makes me no better than you.'

'Those policemen are no problem to us. They could all have heart attacks, you know.'

'Don't you dare! You don't understand how bad this is! They're only one step from saying that I murdered Harold myself – and there are lots of people in this town who would like to see me in gaol. Even if they can't prove anything, there's the scandal, the newspapers. I've got away with a lot over the years because women like me and men can't leave me alone – but even personal charm wears thin when it's just too embarrassing to be acquainted with me!'

'You're certainly a realist.'

'Damn right I am. But I'm damned if I'm going to let them drive me out of my home or my city. No, I won't let them win. I'm going to face it out.'

'Why?' He pulled her down on to the foot of the bed, his big dark eyes on her face. 'Just come away with me, Robyn.'

'That would be admitting defeat.'

'If you come away with me, no harm will come to Alice and the others.'

'You mean, if I don't, some harm *will* come to them? That's blackmail.'

'That's as maybe. They can't touch me, they can't even prove I exist; you're the one who will suffer, and I would have to protect you from it. But leave with me now, and they'll be safe, and it will all just fade away and be forgotten.'

Robyn exhaled. For all her fighting words, she was surrendering. She simply lacked the energy to face the day-to-day battle; the police, the church, the war with Alice, ostracism by society. Her crusade against the male gender had turned sour. There was only one man left now against whom she could aim all her need for revenge. Only one whose defeat would really mean something; this creature of darkness who had all but ruined her life.

'All right. You've got your way at last,' she said. 'Why do I feel I'm being taken away by the King of Elfland?'

He smiled. 'Pack your suitcase, and I'll come for you after dark. Let me show you what it is . . . to disappear.'

CHAPTER SIXTEEN

A GHOST AMONG GHOSTS

Winter had drifted down on Salzburg, an ermine cloak pricked by the black of church spires and treetops. The blue-steel clouds pressed down. And then the icy gales blew down off the Alps, whipping the world to pearl-grey nothingness.

Through the storm, Lilith brought them safely home.

Karl's skin was almost as whitely translucent as Fyodor's as Charlotte helped him to a sofa in Violette's apartment. There she gave him her wrist to drink from, and he was so famished that he didn't even try to refuse. Bitter-sweet, it felt, to cradle his head and kiss his dark, red-sheened hair, to be clamped to him by the pain, his need pulling at all her veins, pulling her into himself.

Violette paced behind them, as if she were restless to be somewhere else. 'I don't want thanks,' she said, her tone businesslike. 'I don't want to discuss it.'

Nothing's changed, Charlotte thought sadly. She rescues us but there is no reconciliation, no outpouring of emotion. She won't even talk about it! 'But why did you save us?' Charlotte asked; moved, exasperated.

'How could I not?' Violette exclaimed, as if that were a sufficient explanation. 'Do you still think I have any reason to fear Cesare? I could have snapped his neck. And if he comes near my ballet again – I will. God help me, I will.'

Charlotte gently stopped Karl feeding before he weakened her. He let her go without protest and sat back, clasping her hand to his chest.

'Cesare's strength lies in Simon and John,' Karl said. 'He

would be nothing without them. But Cesare's zeal is what holds them together. What kind of immortals his human followers will make I dread to think. I don't think they will be ... ordinary.'

Charlotte said, 'You mean the Crystal Ring will do something strange to them, as it did to Simon and—' She was going to say, 'Violette,' but thought better of it—'and John?'

'Possibly. Or their fanaticism may give them a strength we can't imagine. The pure power of will. Perhaps it comes to the same thing. All I suggest, Violette, is that you don't take it for granted that you are untouchable.'

Violette stood still. Charlotte glimpsed her inner pain, transient as a rainbow on oil. 'The time will come, I know,' Violette said quietly. 'Until then I *must* be left alone to complete *Witch and Maiden*. I'll protect you, if you will help me protect my dancers against that fiend and his henchmen. But I must produce one last ballet!'

Violette walked out, refusing to talk any more. Then Charlotte took Karl outside in the snow-storm to hunt. Almost no one abroad, no one to see them in the whirling gloom; but on the mountain-ridge behind the house, a few yards from the walls of a monastery, they met a novice monk of eighteen or so.

Charlotte let Karl take the prey alone, watching with tears of desire in her eyes. But after a time, unable to stop herself, she clamped her lips to the other side of the boy's throat. She and Karl held each other through a crimson storm while the boy died between them.

All through it, Violette's words hung in her mind.

One last ballet.

Afterwards, Karl fell to his knees on the snow as if in despair. Charlotte knelt beside him, her head on his shoulder; both of them shuddering with the sensual aftermath and with stark awareness of what they'd done. No need to speak. And the snow had made of the corpse an amorphous cocoon.

As they walked back to the house, Karl said, 'Well, this has taught us our limitations, at least. Violette may be able to defy Cesare, but you and I cannot.'

He seemed his normal self again. Charlotte felt inexpressibly relieved. In a way she had loved the exquisite tenderness of caring for him, but to see him so vulnerable terrified her. 'Will Cesare and Simon leave us alone, out of fear of Violette?' she asked. 'Or will it make them angrier?'

'As Violette said, the time will come,' he sighed.

'What did she mean, "one last ballet"?'

Karl only shook his head. 'If we could only vanish and live quietly as Stefan and Rachel are doing . . .'

'I wish we could, too,' Charlotte sighed. 'But we won't.'

'We take life to live,' Karl said ironically, 'yet we still have some principle of protecting life against tyranny. Who can fathom us? Well, we are not allowed to thank Violette, but . . .' He took Charlotte's hand and kissed the inside of her wrist where the marks of his fangs were fading.

'*Liebchen*,' he said softly. 'Thank you.'

When the blizzards abated, the sun appeared as a pale yolk in the blue eggshell of the sky and the town glittered under a crust of sugar. Children skated on the river. Enthusiastic tourists, muffled against the cold, were everywhere.

Karl watched them with pleasure, with a very detached, dual appreciation of them as objects of fascination and as potential prey. How lovely, the Austrian winter.

Violette had ensured that all traces of the fire were obliterated as swiftly as possible. Builders and carpenters worked flat out for Madame Lenoir, and were generously rewarded. A damaged ceiling, floor and window were replaced, the walls scrubbed clean and repainted, inside and out. New doors with stronger locks, new fire escapes and alarms were installed. Extra seamstresses were taken on to replace the destroyed costumes. Then Violette had brought the *corps de ballet* back to their rooms, and continued rehearsals for *Witch and Maiden* as if nothing had happened. The fire, she told everyone, was an accident.

But the flat acrid smell of burning lingered, and the atmosphere, Karl noticed, had changed. Joyful innocence had gone. Everyone was serious, loyal, and driven.

In the studio, the dancers wore woollen leggings and took greater care to warm up before rehearsal. Violette wanted no pulled muscles, if the ballet was to open in the early spring.

Karl and Charlotte had little to do but watch over the household while Violette was otherwise occupied; to cast their senses wide for human or vampire intruders. But no one came; Karl thought Fyodor might return to complain of Simon's heartlessness, but he did not. Whether Cesare was too frightened to attack, or simply trying to make Violette complacent, Karl was unsure.

Karl had lived too long to fall prey to anything as human as boredom; but all the same, he wished he was not bound here by a sense of duty. *If only I could leave Cesare to his games, take Charlotte far away where he can't reach us, forget it all!*

But for Charlotte's sake, for the sake of a houseful of humans whose art meant more to him than did their lives, Karl stayed.

'There is only one way to end *Witch and Maiden*,' Violette told them one day. 'Anna and Siegfried trick Lila. Pretending to make up their quarrel, they invite her into their cottage, where she is trapped and killed. Children reunited with mother; everyone lives happily ever after. And a glorious death scene, of course.'

'I'm sure it will be wonderful,' Charlotte said, but she gave Karl a dubious look.

Later, as Karl and Charlotte walked through the wind-sculpted white streets towards the old town, Karl said, 'The ballet is about Lilith, is it not? Lila is the witch and outcast, which is what Violette feels herself to be.'

'That's what she told me,' said Charlotte.

'Well, then you can read her fate in the ending she has chosen.'

Charlotte looked sideways at him, eyes large with anxiety. 'In what way?'

'She is not going to fight Cesare and Simon. She doesn't want to win. She wants, or she thinks she deserves, to die. The last ballet, the blaze of glory, then . . .'

Charlotte did not reply. She said nothing at all for a very long time. 'And an enemy trapped by a pretence of love,' she whispered eventually. Worst betrayal of all. Ghosts of Kristian and Katerina flickered between them. 'Does she fear that from us?'

'Yes, she fears it. I think that's why she sometimes tries so hard to push us into it. Prophecy fulfilled.'

Another silence. Then Charlotte asked softly, 'Why is she like this? Oh, Josef's explanation was plausible enough but it doesn't ring true. There's something more.' She caught Karl's arm. 'How did Lilith and Simon become as they are? Could it happen to us – if we let it?'

'*Liebling*, don't.'

'Perhaps it's already happened, and we're just playing out some role for the Crystal Ring.'

'Or are we playing a role, simply in being vampires?' Karl said thoughtfully. 'No, I don't accept it. Saying our free will is an illusion is like saying Simon's God, Kristian's God, exists. It negates all our attempts to be independent. Leaves us no will to fight . . .'

And in the bright crisp day he felt darkness; the crushing machinery of fanaticism whispering towards them, like the dark tumour in the Crystal Ring. There are ways to flee, or surrender, or die, Karl thought; but no way to win.

As Ireland's lush hills, soft as cloaks, rose around her, Robyn's recurring thought was, what am I doing here?

Sebastian's arm was round her, but she was cold. He'd insisted on making the last stage of the journey on foot and she had never before felt so invaded by the elements. Wind, mist, drizzle; at least it hadn't snowed, yet. Dusk was fading through a low, thick layer of cloud. The landscape seemed saturated, brooding, mystically silent.

He'd travelled with her on the Atlantic crossing from Boston to Cobh harbour near Cork. Somehow she hadn't expected that; she'd gained the impression that he had a way of moving invisibly through some mysterious ether. He had often disappeared on the voyage, and she had known that he was feeding on the blood of some poor passenger or crew member. The number of unexplained illnesses had been alarming.

It had disturbed her terribly. When he came to her, she would know what he'd been doing, yet there was no clue in his appearance or his manner. He would look composed, elegant in his mildly Bohemian way, with the same candid, affectionate light in his eyes. Perhaps a faint flush of colour in his cheeks. And Robyn couldn't resist him, even though she knew. More than disturbing, it had almost unhinged her at times.

They had travelled on false documents, which Sebastian had obtained with no apparent difficulty. Robyn was now an Irish Bostonian called Maeve O'Neill. Vampires, it seemed, could seduce whatever they needed out of humans; blood, money or forgeries. Now no one could trace them ... not a comforting thought, Robyn reflected.

Everything had to be done secretly. 'After we disembark at Cobh,' Sebastian had said, 'no one must see us together, no one must know where we're going. I shall disappear. Go and have something to eat, then at four o'clock hire a car to take you to Lismore in County Waterford. It will be dark by the time you arrive. I'll meet you there.'

'Where, exactly?'

'I'll find you,' he said, smiling.

Uneasy, she did as he said. At Cobh harbour she went to a garage and found a garrulous, obliging driver only too willing to chauffeur her anywhere she wished. Then she ate lunch, and passed the time until four by wandering along the waterfront, gazing at the charming houses and the silver-grey cathedral that dominated the town.

She had expected Ireland to feel like home, but it was a foreign country, she thought as the car carried her along a narrow road to nowhere. No leaves on the trees, but the pasturelands were a rich saturated green, the air like iced honey. They passed low, whitewashed cottages; she saw old men leaning on half-doors to watch the motor car go by, saw a face in a window that was no bigger than a handkerchief.

Time and again they had to stop for other traffic. Seven

horsemen, three bright carts drawn by donkeys, four gigs, a herd of cattle; everyone had all the time in the world. And once, Robyn saw a girl in long skirts, carrying a baby in a shawl. She carried herself like a princess, not a peasant.

In the distance, the mountains were grape-blue against a vast sky.

The driver kept up a running commentary all the way, but Robyn was trying to listen to something else. Music in an eerie key, emanating from the earth, the landscape, the endless road.

Then they turned a corner and she saw a great castle poised on a forested rock. It floated on darkness like the moon on a cloud, remote, enigmatic, silvered by the last of the light. Its flanks fell, fold on fold, into the black-sapphire depths of a river.

'What is that?' Robyn gasped.

'The Castle of Lismore.'

'Let me out here.'

'Are ye sure? Is it not the town you're wanting?'

'No, here. I'm being met. It's all right.' And she gave him a large amount of money, enough to make his eyes stretch. 'A little extra, to tell no one you brought me here.'

The driver nodded and tipped his cap knowingly. She trusted him.

The car had barely turned and driven away, leaving her on the roadside by a wooded shoulder of rock, when Sebastian appeared beside her. She was relieved, and scared. It had taken two hours to travel thirty miles.

'It's a long walk, but there's no other way for me to get you to Blackwater Hall without anyone knowing. It's easy for me to come and go, but not for you.'

'I must be out of my mind,' she murmured. 'I'm alone with a vampire, and no one in the world has the remotest idea of where I've gone.'

Sebastian did not reply.

He took her round the castle, over a bridge to the far side of the river, and into a dew-drenched field. The ground rose slowly. Robyn was soon out of breath, but Sebastian seemed disinclined to let her rest. He led her through a copse studded with rocks and treacherous hollows; she could barely see a thing, but he guided her without difficulty. They walked for three hours. Beyond, the moon peeped through the clouds and the landscape changed subtly. Its contours were mellower, sure sign of man's intervention. There were sweeps of grass, magnificent lone trees, copses, a lake and river gleaming like milk in the vaporous gloom.

'We're on the estate now,' said Sebastian. He sounded excited. 'You'll see the house in a moment.'

Must be something quite wonderful, Robyn thought. They came round the skirt of a hill and there it stood; a great mansion, broodingly desolate and ugly. Three storeys, with tall imposing windows, a pillared portico that soared from top to bottom of the frontage. The walls were mottled and crumbling, as if the place were shedding its skin with age. The windows, fogged like cataracts with dirt, stared indifferently at long-neglected gardens and stables.

Robyn couldn't speak for disappointment. What a hideous pile! Just as well she didn't put this thought into words. Sebastian was clearly enraptured.

'Was this your home?'

'I never lived in it,' he said, 'and I don't legally own it. After I left – vanished, as far as the authorities were concerned, and undoubtedly wanted for murdering my wife and her lover – it was confiscated and given to some English Protestant family. But I built it. I still feel it's mine. It *is* mine.'

He led her across the weed-infested drive, round a wing of the house and through an archway. There were carriage houses and store-rooms on either side. The arch gave on to a courtyard overlooked by rows of grim windows; Sebastian led her across to a small door of thick, aged wood. 'The house hasn't been lived in since 1864. The present owner is an eccentric bachelor who's never lived in it. Too much for him, I suppose; or too many ghost stories. He lives in a cottage in the nearest village and never comes here. They were all strange, that family.'

He lifted the latch and the door swung open. Inside was a huge kitchen, grim as a mausoleum, with floor-to-ceiling cupboards, a black range, a cracked sink full of debris; fallen plaster, broken glass, leaves, rust, cobwebs.

'It's colder in here than outside,' she said, hugging herself.

He turned away with a faint look of disapproval. 'No one has touched this place for over sixty years. When the last inhabitant died, they just locked it up and left it.' He went to the kitchen table, fitted candles to a candelabra, and lit them with matches from his pocket. 'I shall have to get some oil for the lamps,' he said. 'I forget humans need light, because we don't. But we find it pleasant.'

She followed him, shivering, through a narrow passageway. 'How often do you come here?'

'Once a year, once every ten years, as the whim takes me.'

'But you think of it as your home?'

He glanced at her with a wry smile. The light gave his face a sinister, inner illumination. 'I'm the ghost, dear. I was the reason the family moved out.'

They emerged into a square hallway, with a stairwell looming up into the shadows. As Sebastian led her up the first flight, candlelight threw a spectral glow over dust-covered banisters, wooden panelling, portraits in thick gold frames on discoloured walls. On the half-landing, the light gleamed on the treacly wood of twin double doors. Sebastian opened the left-hand door and ushered Robyn into the room beyond.

A cold and cavernous space around her; then he raised the lamp to reveal a room of eerie grandeur. A ceiling of carved and painted plaster, two storeys high. An impressive fireplace surmounted by a coat of arms at the far end; two rows of long windows along the right-hand wall, one above the other, the lower ones hung with dusty red velvet curtains. Faded rugs on bare floorboards. A full-sized billiard table, covered with a sheet, glass cases and glass-fronted cupboards everywhere, full of posed dead animals. One, on a table directly in front of her, contained a huge crocodile skull. All along the walls were the antlered heads of stags, staring out with black marble eyes. And countless dark portraits of ancestors, also fixing their painted gazes on hers.

'This is the saloon,' said Sebastian. Placing the candelabra on a table, he looked around, seemingly oblivious to Robyn. She walked slowly through the great room, both fascinated and repulsed by this surfeit of taxidermy. Case after case of finches, owls, birds of prey and gulls lined the walls; and then mammals, reptiles, amphibians of every description. Astonished, she forgot everything else. Then she came upon the butterflies. Even in the half-darkness they glowed with preternatural intensity, sulphur-yellow, electric blue, iridescent green ... faerie creatures pinned in rows.

She opened the drawer of a cabinet and found scores of monstrous beetles attached to cards.

'Sebastian.'

He didn't seem to hear her. He was brushing dust from the top of a display case on a small table. The dust, though thick, was only a surface covering, nothing to compare with the grime of the kitchen. And it struck her that this place had not been completely neglected for sixty years. Someone had looked after it.

She slowly circled the room, finding some new treasure in every cabinet; shells, minerals, fossils, birds' eggs. The journey was haunted, grotesque, filled with the whispering of all the unknown lives on the walls above her; shadows shimmering, a thousand eyes watching from the darkness. And the vampire in black, his face lit from below by insubstantial flames, his pale hands resting on the dark glass; expressionless, aloof, his lowered eyelids forming two black crescents against the fine skin. Death in repose.

When she came to his side, she looked through the glass that he'd cleaned and saw hundreds of ancient coins lying on bottle-green velvet.

'Who brought all this here? Not you?'

Sebastian was contemplative, as if he thought he was alone; perhaps he wished he was.

'Not me. The family were all eccentric. The last one to live here was an obsessive collector.'

'So all these things were left here when he died?'

He nodded. 'And after his heirs deserted, I decided to look after the place a little.'

He began to walk away, Robyn followed. He looked completely at home here. She could imagine him in sombre

Victorian clothes, or in an eighteenth-century tailcoat, white lace at his wrists, drifting from room to room; the solitary lord of the manor, eternally in possession, while the other inhabitants had been mere tenants — and knew it. She imagined their insecurity, their paranoia. A woman's voice, low and frightened. *He was there again in the library, Father. I didn't see him but I felt him. This house is so cold. It hates us!*

Now Robyn was the one who felt utterly out of place.

Another double door led to a drawing-room, which was insistently golden; wallpaper, frames, curtains, the scrolled woodwork of chairs, all were gold. Sebastian pulled off dust-sheets to reveal chairs lush with needlepoint roses, tapestry stools and firescreens. Too many ornaments; clocks, statuettes, stuffed birds under glass domes, black onyx elephants. More glass cases filled with shining semi-precious stones. More paint-ings, huge mirrors rimmed with gilt.

'It is just as it was left by the family,' Sebastian told her. 'I rarely move anything.'

He led her through a library; floor-to-ceiling shelves of books, a fireplace flanked by two *chaises-longues*, paintings of horses on the walls. Beyond it lay a boudoir, a room too small for the height of its ceiling; it was meant to be cosy but she found it ugly, with its green wallpaper mouldering and falling away, its green velvet hangings turning grey with age. But there were Chinese cabinets full of porcelain which must have been priceless.

'The house is not as I would have had it,' Sebastian mur-mured, 'but now it is as it is, it would be sacrilege to change it.'

He led her in a circuit of the first floor, along grim corridors, bypassing certain rooms. 'Servants' bedrooms,' he said. 'I do what little I can to preserve the living-rooms, but I cannot attend to everything.'

The circuit took them through a grand dining-room with marble pillars, a smaller breakfast room, and back to the saloon. Everywhere, the same decaying grandeur. The house smelled of damp and mildew, emanating a dank chill that was slowly soaking through to her bones.

She would rather have gone back to the gilded drawing-room, which at least had some semblance of homeliness, but Sebastian seemed to favour the saloon. Standing in front of the fireplace, he faced Robyn and pulled her hair out of its pins so that it fell loose over her shoulders. 'There are old clothes here, too. I hate modern clothes. I will find something for you to wear, a tight waist and long skirts . . .'

Her throat was dry. She looked up into his eyes, which glowed intently under the soft darkness of his hair. His hands moulded her shoulders. 'To make it harder for me to run away?'

A shadow touched his brow. 'Why would you be wanting to run away?'

She disregarded the question. 'It's quite . . . extraordinary here.'

'I'm glad you think so.' He glanced at the wedding-cake ceiling. 'By the way, I would suggest that you don't go upstairs for the time being.'

'Why not? Will I find the skeletons of the other women you've brought here?' A black joke, but as she spoke it did not seem remotely funny. Fear clenched a fist round her throat. No joke, no joke at all. Sebastian could tell any lie, assume any disguise.

He seemed distracted. He did not really react to the remark, and his gaze only glanced off her before returning to the room. 'You are the first and only person I have ever brought here,' he said softly. 'If you want to go up, you can. I have done no work upstairs, so you will find it damp, dirty and generally unpleasant. That is all.'

'Worse than down here?'

She had realized that the easiest way to offend him was to insult the house. He responded icily, 'I appreciate that this is not the luxury you are used to.'

She was a little afraid, and then she was furious. 'Do you intend us to stay here?'

He opened his hands, let them fall away from her shoulders. 'Yes.'

'How do you expect me to live? Is there any food here?'

'Of course not. I have no need of it.'

'Well, I can't live on air, nor on—' She couldn't say the word, 'blood'. 'Is there a village near by?'

'Four miles away. But you can't be seen coming and going, and you can't ask tradesmen to call because you are not meant to be here.'

'Otherwise you'd be happy for me to walk eight miles to fetch the milk, is that it?' she gasped. 'For pity's sake, Sebastian, there is no water!'

'There's a well in the garden.'

'You're not listening. There is no functioning plumbing *at all*, is there? Human beings have certain inconvenient requirements, in case you'd forgotten. You may have dispensed with them, but I haven't!'

He looked straight at her. 'Then find a suitable receptacle, and acquire the habit of feeding the roses. I really don't care what arrangements you make.'

Robyn was close to hitting him. 'Why do we have to stay here at all? You could take me to a hotel!'

'But I love this house.'

'What does that make me? Another ornament for your collection? You could have me stuffed and put in one of those cases, all your problems solved!'

He turned away from her. 'I'm tempted.' His callousness stabbed her. 'You don't have to stay, Robyn. Leave. Straight down the drive, turn right; the villagers will point you in the direction of Cork.'

'I'm tired,' she said. 'My feet hurt. I'm cold. If you can't say anything helpful, at least let me make a fire. Don't tell me; we can't have a fire because someone might see the smoke?'

He exhaled. 'I always have a fire. If anyone comes . . . well, it wouldn't be the first time. I simply put their minds at rest and send them away.' His tone was lightly sinister. 'Didn't you wonder why there is a pile of logs on the hearth?'

She hadn't noticed. 'If they're not too damp to light.' She went down on her haunches, pushed her coat sleeves back, and picked up a log. Dust blackened her hands. 'The least you can do is help me! Are those newspapers to light it?'

Sebastian crouched down beside her, very close. He took her

face between his hands and kissed her. 'Beloved child, I'm only teasing you. I can't resist it. But you're right, I am a fool; I had forgotten that humans don't live on . . . air. Will you forgive me?'

'Will you bring me something to eat?'

A faint sigh. 'Of course. I don't want you to leave. Forgive me.'

He crumpled up brittle sheets of old newspaper – the headlines were all about Lloyd George's treaty with Ireland – and piled logs on top. Damp or not, the wood caught light magically for him. Sparks flew, scarlet light danced. And at last, at last, she felt warmth brush her palms. Unfastening her coat, she knelt on the hearthrug and watched the fire blossoming.

Sebastian knelt beside her. Sliding his arm under her hair, he kissed her again, deeply and tenderly, his tongue tasting hers and lighting the nerves all through her body; simply went on kissing her until she turned fluid, like mercury.

'Well?' he said, after a time.

'You're forgiven,' she said, 'conditionally.'

He stood up, lifting her with him. 'Depending on my future good behaviour? Stay here and keep warm while I'm gone. I have been many things but never a grocery boy.'

'But it's the middle of the night!'

'So? I don't want anyone to see me. I'll take what we need and leave the money; they'll think the faerie folk have been a-visiting. Now, what would please you?'

'I'll make a list,' she said grimly.

While Sebastian was away, she sat huddled on the edge of the hearth, aware of the age and immensity of the mansion around her. She longed for her cosy home in Boston. Perfect madness to come here.

I've never been the same, not since the first time he . . . she rubbed at her neck, where many wounds had opened and healed. Do I love him? Is this what it feels like? Am I sitting in this godforsaken hole for love?

Half an hour passed. She was bored and uneasy, an unpleasant combination. She tried to sleep but couldn't; too many dead eyes staring at her. Everywhere she looked, birds, mammals, humans, all dead, all staring in accusation.

I wonder what Alice is doing? Hope she's forgiven me for leaving with just a brief note to say, 'Sorry.' Hope I left them enough money.

She stood up, wrapped the coat around herself, and went to explore. Going out on to the half-landing, she mounted the stairs, the candelabra in her hand. The treads, covered by a worn carpet, creaked alarmingly under her feet; rosy-cheeked, wooden-looking children in eighteenth-century dress stared at her from the paintings. They looked like little adults.

One flight up, she found a gallery that overlooked the saloon. Dust, moonlight, a different view of the estate. How bleak the landscape looked. On either side of the saloon were the bedrooms. Four-poster beds draped in rotting fabrics, wallpaper curling off the walls, more paintings, priceless furniture, an obscenity of neglect. One room contained no bed, only an oblong shape covered by a dustsheet. A huge coffin? She lifted the corner of the sheet. Nothing more sinister than a packing case. On the far side of the saloon, she found a four-room apartment that was a treasure trove of junk: more glass cupboards full of shells and stones, stag's heads on the wall and lying on the bed among framed prints, boxes full of tools, books, toys and military regalia. It looked as if nothing had ever been thrown away.

Apart from the master bedrooms at the front, the top floor was disappointing. Narrow, dilapidated corridors with paint and plaster flaking off the walls. Servants' or children's rooms, some empty, some filled with dark drifts of clutter, all unspeakably depressing in their starkness. Their windows overlooked the courtyard, around which the house formed a square. The flagstones were overgrown with moss. The mottled walls could have been those of a prison.

Don't go upstairs, indeed! He must have known that his words were guaranteed to awake her curiosity. *Don't open the box, Pandora.*

Then she found the nursery, tucked in the farthest corner. A large room, barely touched by the moonbeams through the single big window. No echo of childish joy; it was cheerless, grey, haunted. Naked floorboards on which several generations' worth of toys were shored up against discoloured, peeling walls. Robyn picked her way slowly through the room, looking at rusty prams, doll's houses as aged and neglected as the room that contained them, a rocking horse on massive green rockers, waiting in vain for a small rider. She touched its grimy mane, saw that its legs and neat Arabian head were riddled with woodworm. Dolls lay among wooden guns and toy soldiers like eyeless babies.

This house was haunted. Desolate with loss and regret.

Robyn suddenly began to weep, unable to help herself. She wept for the children who no longer filled this place with life; she mourned the children she had never borne, because God had seen fit to tear them prematurely out of her. No, it was my husband who destroyed them ... or maybe I did it myself to spite him, because I couldn't bring myself to perpetuate his flesh and his ego.

She sobbed unrestrainedly. Desolation everywhere.

If Sebastian had been my husband instead, could I have happily given him my sons and daughters?

In response, she felt a rending, sexual warmth spread through her abdomen. She fell to her knees. Oh God, so I do love him. Oh God, oh hell.

She put the candelabra down and leaned on the rocking horse's foreleg, her breath quietening. A foolish spasm. Over now.

In the heaped darkness that lay in the corner to her left, something moved.

Robyn jerked backwards, her hands flying out to the floor behind her. A scream rose into her throat and caught there, fluttering.

Seeing things, I must be—

It moved again.

She leapt to her feet, all her nerves screaming with the urge to flee. Yet she was frozen. The thing that unfolded and groped towards her was human-shaped. A glossy black head. Slender dark limbs.

It looked up, and she saw black irises ringed with white.

Robyn wanted to run, and couldn't. Running would not make it go away. Her instinct was to keep the thing in sight, but she dared not even bend down to pick up her source of light. Very slowly, she began to back away towards the door.

The apparition stretched out its hands towards her. The terrible eyes glared through her, past her. Then it spoke, and the sound of its voice made her suck in her breath with fear.

It said, 'You have forgotten us.'

Backing away, Robyn collided with something soft behind her. An arm came round and gripped her across her chest; her heart almost failed, and she cried out. She could feel her pulse running mouse-quick against the pressure.

A second later she realized that it was Sebastian who held her. Ambivalent feelings assailed her. Was he trying to protect her – or had he lured her here to throw her to this demon?

The first feeling won. She swivelled in his arms and clung to him. In that instant, she realized that the apparition had not been addressing her, but Sebastian.

'I have not forgotten you,' he said.

Robyn forced herself to look round. Now she saw that the creature was female, brown-skinned, naked but for a mass of blue-black hair. And she had that unearthly vampire glow about her! Yet she seemed more vulnerable than malevolent, huddling among the debris, and now stretching her hands imploringly towards Sebastian.

'What is she?' Robyn whispered.

His arms were firm and protective around her. She felt his breath on her neck as he answered with a soft sigh, 'One of my ancient gods.'

Charlotte was not happy with the situation; the feeling that the Ballet Janacek's headquarters had become a fortress, the constant tension between Violette and Karl, the unpredictable, threatening existence of Schloss Holdenstein. But things could be worse, she thought. We might have been prisoners of Cesare or we might have been dead. At least we're alive and free – for now.

In imagining that the immediate future was settled, she had forgotten to allow for life's routine caprices.

She was with Karl in Violette's sitting-room one morning when the dancer, whom she thought had gone to supervise the *corps de ballet*'s practice, came back in. There was a cream envelope in her hand.

'I was just speaking to the secretary in the office,' said Violette, 'and she gave me this; a letter addressed to a Mrs Charlotte Neville-Millward. Would that be you?'

Charlotte was so shocked that she sat down on the arm of a chair, unable to speak. Karl's eyes followed her, darkening with concern and a hint of dismay.

'I gather it is,' Violette said crisply, handing her the envelope. 'I thought your name was Alexander, but ... I suppose we are all pretending to be someone we are not.' She cast a glance at Karl. 'Well, I'm sure it is none of my business, so if you will excuse me ...'

She left, closing the door quietly behind her. Charlotte stared at the firm, neat handwriting on the envelope and the British stamp. *Mrs Charlotte Neville-Millward, c/o Ballet Janacek, Salzburg, Österreich.* 'Who could possibly have known I was here?'

'Do you recognize the writing?' Karl asked, looking over her shoulder.

'I think so. It looks like Anne's.'

'She has certainly taken no chances with your surname.'

She opened the envelope with apprehension. My family are trying to find me again, she thought in dismay. They still can't give up.

My dear Charlotte,

With no other clue to your whereabouts, I am writing to the Ballet in the faint hope that this letter may be forwarded to you. It is clear that you want no further contact with us. I'm sure that's for the best. However, if I owe anything to the years of our friendship, it is to tell you this. Your father is dying. If you still care, if your goodbyes were not as final as they seemed, you may wish to come home.

Yours sincerely,

Anne Neville.

The abrupt style was utterly alien to the Anne she remembered.

She thrust the letter at Karl and waited for him to read it. The shock of it washed over her very slowly, like some vast invisible horror descending from outside. Not my father, she thought. It's impossible, he must go on for ever. *Not my father*.

Karl said something. She looked up in a trance. 'Will you go?' he repeated.

'How can I? I can't possibly leave with things as they are. And you'll tell me not to.'

'I would advise you against it, with all my heart.' As Karl spoke, she had a vivid image of him in her father's house; his lethal charisma, radiant against the comfortable banality of everything else. Inevitable, her seduction. 'Vampires should not care, yet we still do. Caring baits the trap for us. Our loved ones change. They grow old and infirm and they die, leaving us behind. And because we haven't been part of the process, we can't accept it. They won't be the same, Charlotte. They won't know you. What can you do, except cause them more pain?'

'Would it be selfish of me to go to my father? Then why did Anne write to me?'

'A sense of duty.'

'But what if he's asked for me? How can I not go?' Sudden anguish, like the iron pain of a heart attack. 'I said such bitter things when I left, and so did he. Yet it never crossed my mind, when I left, that I would actually never see him again, that I'd *never* have the chance to resolve it.'

Karl's fine-boned hand rested on hers. 'Life consists of unresolved pain.'

'But I've been offered a chance! I don't expect forgiveness from any of them, it doesn't matter what they think of me. Just to be with him . . . but I can't leave here now, it's impossible.'

'Charlotte,' he said gravely, 'if you want to go, you must. It's

407

your decision. I can watch over Violette. I'm sure nothing is going to happen; but if it does, I would rather you were out of harm's way.'

'And you know I'd rather be with you.'

'Unfortunately, you can't be in two places at once,' he said drily, 'unless you happen to have a *doppelgänger*.'

'I've got to go to him, Karl,' she said. 'I'm sorry.'

'You owe me no apology, *Liebchen*.' He stroked her hair, and she leaned into him. 'Go swiftly, come back safely; that's all I ask.'

'God, I wish you could come with me, just so that they could see—'

'That I'm not the devil? But by their standards, I am. It would do no good. They think we both belong to the devil, Charlotte, so be very, very gentle with them.'

Telling Violette, though, was harder than she'd anticipated. Charlotte caught her alone in her dressing-room after the morning rehearsal. She thought the dancer would be unmoved, but to Charlotte's dismay, she looked panic-stricken.

'No, you can't go!' Violette exclaimed.

'It's only for a few days.'

'Or weeks, or months.'

'No. It's my *father*, Violette. I must go.'

'But what will I be without you?'

'What do you mean? You don't need me that much!'

'Don't you know?' Violette caressed Charlotte's shoulders and arms. She looked exquisite, her hair a soft silken mass, ruffled from dancing; but she was Lilith, seductive and terrifying. Suddenly she kissed Charlotte full on the mouth, a lingering, sensual kiss, charged with all her yearning. Then she clung to Charlotte, trembling from head to foot. 'Where do you think my strength came from to save you from Cesare? It came from *you*. Without you I'd be lost!'

Stunned, Charlotte could only hold her, but Violette was a creature of thorns, impossible to comfort. 'A few days,' Charlotte promised helplessly, and fled before she gave in.

★

Robyn watched the goddess kneeling among the discarded toys. She was naked, her legs splayed, a midnight rain of hair covering her shoulders. Against the cluttered greyness of her setting she was a polished, nut-brown icon.

'Is this why you told me not to come upstairs?' Robyn said. 'How many others are there?'

Sebastian spoke quietly into her ear. 'Robyn, I had no idea she was here. I have not seen her for more than two hundred and twenty years.'

Putting her gently aside, he went towards the creature. He was now dressed exactly as she had pictured him; dark tailored cloth, white lace. Her heart jumped. She pressed herself to the door frame and watched in bewilderment.

'What do you want?' said Sebastian.

The woman's eyes were white crescents, tipped up towards him. 'You have even forgotten my name, Sebastian.'

'No, I haven't.' He crouched down in front of her. 'You are Rasmila.'

She nodded. 'Though I have had other names.'

'Haven't we all?' he murmured. 'So, why after all this time—'

Her hand shot out to rest on his collarbone; he gripped her wrist, and Robyn thought, he's afraid of her! 'I have been waiting for you; I know you always come back here. I have nowhere else to go, no one to help me.'

'I've seen Simon. He told me you'd fallen out. He wanted to use me, as if I were just a wind-up doll you'd set in motion all that time ago, but I told him no. I had nothing to offer him. I have no interest in others of my kind. I have nothing to offer you, either, and I don't want you here.'

'You can't deny what you are!' the woman cried, shaking him. However alien she seemed, there was despair in her imploring eyes, her submissive posture.

'I never asked you and your friends to do this to me.'

'But you wanted it.' She rose up on her knees and pressed her lips to Sebastian's. He didn't try to stop her. Robyn's jaw dropped. The kiss lingered, knifing her like sudden treachery. 'We gave you the gift; now you must help us in turn! Our power is diminished—'

Sebastian pushed her away and stood up. 'I don't care. Kindly leave my house.'

Rasmila sank down again, head bowed. 'I won't go until you have listened to me.'

'Rot here, then.'

Ushering Robyn out of the nursery, he shut the door and led her downstairs to the saloon.

'Who is she?' Robyn demanded.

'I told you, one of the vampires who made me.'

'Why wouldn't you listen to her?'

'It was their choice to transform me; I am not in debt to them, and I don't care what problems they've brought upon themselves.' He threw logs on to the fire as he spoke, stabbed at them with a poker, seeming furious.

'But she seemed to be in distress,' Robyn said cautiously. 'Can't vampires suffer?'

'We can. But she was more than—' He stopped, apparently deciding not to elaborate.

'So you have no compassion for her?'

'She's not an orphan in the storm. God, it's a miracle she didn't attack you! It's lack of blood that makes us weak.'

'So you think she was just hungry? I don't think so.'

'She is not my concern! I want her to leave.' He held out his hand to her. 'Come on, you need to rest.'

Robyn was eaten up with curiosity, but he refused to answer her questions. She did not feel the slightest bit tired, but as soon as she sat down on the couch that Sebastian had pulled up to the fireplace in the saloon, she fell asleep.

She was woken by Sebastian's hand on her arm. 'Leave me alone, I've only just closed my eyes,' she grumbled.

'No, you closed your eyes about eight hours ago,' he said, 'and we have work to do.'

Robyn only believed it when she saw the light in the windows. Full daylight merely made the room look bleak and grey, revealing every mote of dust, every moth-hole. Cold and dispirited, she shook herself awake.

'Is Rasmila still . . .'

'I'm afraid so,' he said. 'Never mind. Come on.'

Together they drew water from the well in the garden behind the stables, carried containers into the kitchen, and cleaned an old tin bath. Sebastian even managed to light the range. She wondered if he would have been so industrious if he had not been trying to ignore Rasmila's presence.

Robyn heated water, scoured some cooking pots, plates and cutlery. The cupboards were overflowing with china. She could almost feel the ghosts of maids, cooks and footmen moving around her . . . and she cursed at having to do this menial work for herself.

I have a hundred thousand dollars' worth of diamonds in my suitcase, and here I am . . .

At least she was able to make herself a pot of coffee. She sat and drank cup after cup, with cream and sugar, while she made toast over the fire. Half an hour of heaven. It was the first time she'd felt warm since the previous night.

She stared around the cavernous room. A thousand pairs of eyes stared back. *This place was designed for vampires,* she thought. *I can't live here!*

Sebastian, in shirt-sleeves – a voluminous old-fashioned shirt in which he looked irresistible – had placed the bath in front of the fire and was filling it with buckets of hot water. 'If you love this house so much, why don't you buy it back legally? Then we could restore it. If I want coffee I like to ring for Mary, not break my back for three hours.'

Sebastian looked coldly at her, as if she'd uttered heresy. Again she felt like a trespasser. And she hated him for it, as he sometimes seemed to hate her. 'Your bath, madame,' he said acidly.

She undressed quickly and stepped into the deliciously hot water. To her surprise, Sebastian knelt beside the bath and began to wash her, as if she were a little girl. His hands felt wonderful, sliding all over her body on a layer of soap. He seemed enraptured by the way her limbs gleamed through the lather, by the flash of firelight on her glassy-wet skin. His long, green-brown eyes were contemplative under half-lowered lids.

'Do you really hate it here?' he asked.

'It's – magnificent. It's not what I'm used to, that's all.'

'Be patient.'

He helped her out of the bath, wrapped her in a towel and held her. She found it madly arousing, to be all but naked while he was clothed. But when she began to respond and to kiss him, he held her away from him and smiled. 'Later.'

She looked up, thinking of Rasmila. 'Is it because—'

'We have more work to do to make you comfortable.'

Refusing to put on any heavy, ice-cold Victorian garment that had lain in a chest for sixty years, Robyn dressed in the warmest clothes she had brought, a skirt, sweater and cardigan of russet wool. While she made another attempt to render the kitchen usable, Sebastian fetched more water and chopped logs. At least there was plenty of timber on the estate. He'd also brought a supply of candles, matches and oil from the village.

While he was outside, Robyn found she loathed being in the house on her own. The shadows seemed to move. It was so drear. She could not stop thinking about Rasmila, brooding in the ghastly ruins of the nursery.

It was dark by the time they finished. Robyn, finding the library the least unfriendly room, had lit a fire there. Now she was glad to collapse on to a *chaise-longue* in front of the fireplace. Sebastian leaned on the rolled back, his hands folded.

'Is she still here?' said Robyn, glancing at the ceiling.

'Yes.' He sighed.

'It's making me uncomfortable.'

'I don't want her here any more than you do.'

'So do something about it! At least find out what she wants!'

He was silent, pressing his fingertips together. God, Robyn thought, he's still such an enigma! 'Very well,' he said. 'Stay here. I'll go and use a little persuasion.'

When he'd gone, Robyn fetched her coat, which she'd left on the billiard table in the saloon. Returning to the library, she wrapped herself up and settled into her nest of warmth to wait for Sebastian.

Why did I let myself in for this? Alice, I wish I'd stayed home with you . . .

Her thoughts sank into the red glow behind her eyelids. She fell asleep.

'So, Rasmila,' said Sebastian, 'I almost did not recognize you when I first saw you. Such a long time.'

'Your memory is very bad,' said the figure in the shadows.

'My memory is perfect. I hardly saw you when you transformed me, if you recall. It was dark, and you all three had a glow about you that made it hard to look straight at you. I thought you were gods. Beautiful pagan spirits. You, Simon, and the pale one . . .'

'Fyodor,' she said. She was kneeling just as he'd left her. A statue. He'd felt almost nothing for Simon, but the emotions Rasmila aroused in him were both painful and incomprehensible.

'And where are they now?'

'Our trinity was broken. We served our purpose as angels to guide Lilith; when she rejected us, our power was gone.'

'I've seen her,' he said darkly, thinking of her leaning over Robyn's bed. 'Violette Lenoir.' He absently rested his hand on the rocking horse's head. Everything looked grey, even to his light-gathering eyes. Slate-grey, brown-grey, decaying in the musty air.

'We tried to be guides,' Rasmila continued. Her accented voice, very calm and precise, conveyed her sense of loss more powerfully than histrionics could have done. 'We tried to guide you, but you'd have none of us; we tried to guide Kristian, but he was betrayed by love.'

'I heard. Tragic.'

'And Lilith, who should never have been created, and Lancelyn, who overreached his powers.'

'A catalogue of misjudgements.'

She spread her hands, palms facing upwards on her knees. He saw the triangle of black hair gleaming between her thighs, the plum-coloured folds of skin, and his memories suddenly flowed and burned.

'And Simon blamed Fyodor and me and cast us aside – but he still needs us, if only he would admit it!'

'So, are you no longer a goddess?'

'I never was. I am a vampire. I have existed for over a thousand years. I have carried God's messages to and from earth . . . but God is now blind and deaf to me.'

'And Simon?'

She paused. 'If Simon, too, remains blind and deaf to me for ever . . . that would be even harder to bear.'

Sebastian smiled. 'So, what do you expect me to do about it?'

'Help me. I am afraid.'

'You? You came to me clothed in the night, like Kali.'

She bowed her head right down to the floor, trailing her arms behind her. Her hair was a raven shawl across the shoals of broken toys and dismembered dolls. He watched her, enthralled despite himself.

'You are too proud,' she said. 'You refuse to acknowledge any vampire but yourself. You wish you were the only one, but you are not! You must accept this.'

'Why?'

'If Lilith has not touched your life already, she will.'

Sebastian could not answer that. Images of the dancer and Robyn in the garden, heads close together, whispering the secrets from which men were excluded; the dancer hovering by Robyn's bed in all her icy, silk-veiled beauty. Robyn threatening him with Violette! Ilona, Simon and now Rasmila with that name on their lips, affecting to despise her while their terror of her was painfully naked.

'Simon and Lilith are both dangerous,' Rasmila went on. 'They will try to destroy each other.'

'So leave them to it! Isn't that what you want?'

She raised her chin and glared at him. He leaned down to her. She hesitated, then accepted his outstretched hand, letting him lift her to her feet.

'All of this is Lilith's fault! She sundered us from Simon, and without God's guidance he is like her; too headstrong. They will disrupt the Crystal Ring. It has already begun, Lilith has already caused great damage. Have you not noticed?'

The hostile storminess of the Ring, the knot of darkness that Sebastian had seen but tried to disregard ... 'Yes, I've noticed.' Unwilling to listen to her, he was nevertheless enthralled by her satiny flesh, radiant in its darkness as if brushed by sapphire dust. 'What do you expect me to do about it?'

'Help us against Lilith. Help us show Simon that he cannot defeat her without us!' She pressed closer to him. 'We created you for the benefit of immortal-kind. Why do you refuse to understand?'

'I do understand. I refuse to be used, that's all.'

'We made you! We never choose at random.'

'You chose badly, all the same.'

'You are betraying us,' she said, stroking his cheek. 'You are running away from your responsibilities.'

'I have none. I'm not in your debt.'

She slid one leg round the outside of his. 'Don't you remember how it was when we transformed you?'

He remembered. The darkness of the cellar. Three fallen angels, capturing his soul and delivering him into a state of un-death ... and in the darkness, a woman, whose face he could hardly see, drawing him to her. Naked beneath her robe. Blind lust possessing him as she enveloped him ... the absolute, abandoned sweetness of it, making him forget Mary and all that had gone before.

It was happening again. He saw her mouth and eyes shining as she unfastened buttons one-handed and pulled at his clothes. Her legs were round his waist, supple as a temple-dancer's. Weightless, she impaled herself on him and he thrust to meet her, sinking down on to the floor with her entwined around him.

The aching compulsion of it was almost painful. He gasped with wonder. The room was alight with jewels; jewels danced along his veins.

Rasmila clawed at him, uttering a single, soul-deep cry. Sebastian dropped his head into her shoulder. The sharp, soundless explosion convulsed him.

Tearing into her throat now. Streams of light on his tongue. The pleasure less focused but more intense, rushing him from sensual to unearthly rapture, taking him so far beyond himself that he needed the pain of Rasmila's bite to bring him back.

The divine exchange of blood. Something Robyn could not give him. He drew hard on her, merciless, but every drop he took, she stole back; neither could win. Sated and in equilibrium, they ceased and lay still, smiling a little at each other.

But he felt bleak. She was not Robyn.

'Now my blood is in you,' Rasmila said. 'You can't deny me.'

'You don't know me,' he said pleasantly, refastening his disarrayed shirt and breeches.

'My insight is not lost.' She sat up. 'You have given me something after all; your blood, your strength.'

Rising to her feet, she was magnificent against the window. A deity, Hindu or Celtic, there was no division; Kali and Cailleach were the same goddess.

'I hope you're suitably grateful.' He stood up beside her, brushing dust from his clothes.

'You will become involved, whether you wish it or not,' she said. Her expression was sweet, and as strong as steel. 'And so will your lover.'

'This is nothing to do with Robyn,' he said grimly.

'But it will be, if you turn your back. Are we enemies?' Rasmila touched his cheek.

'No.'

'No. I came to warn you, not threaten you. I am not Simon, I am not demanding leadership or great acts of heroism from you. Only friendship. A little help to protect vampire-kind from the madness of Lilith. I am going to find Fyodor now; we have been apart too long. Help us and we will help you in turn.'

'I don't think I need any help from you.'

Her serene face showed amusement. 'But if you change your mind, call me and I will hear. My blood will hear you.'

She moved away from him, seeming an emotionless icon. She's colder than me, Sebastian thought. In a swathe of smoky-quartz stars, she went into the Ring, and he was alone.

He stood among the detritus of long-vanished childhoods,

unmoved by it because he was part of it, a ghost among ghosts. Now I need to hunt, he thought, I need a human struggling in my arms and the hot blood . . . and then I need the solitude of the Crystal Ring.

Robyn was in his mind, but she was an abstract image, not a breathing reality.

'Do they feed on each other's energy, Karl, Charlotte and Lilith, as we do?' Cesare asked. His eyes were red, like those of a man who had been working frantically for days and nights. His face shone like mother-of-pearl with a sweaty madness. 'If she were separated from them, would she be made weaker?'

'Possibly,' said Simon. The triumvirate was in the sanctum, bathed in the oily light of a lamp. Simon was looking on Cesare with despair. If you were Karl, he thought, you would be rational, not crazed; and if John were Charlotte, then we might have a constructive contribution in place of baleful silence. 'I felt the power between her and Charlotte—'

'There is nothing to do with Karl and Charlotte but kill them,' said Cesare. 'An execution for the good of the majority.'

Seeing the glitter in his eyes, Simon thought, would you extend the threat to me, when you eventually see that behind my smiling mask, I actually hate you?

But Cesare's been badly scared and he's on edge. We all are. It took all our energy to calm the disciples and to hammer their fear into rage. John, poor devil, has merely sunk even deeper into his need for ugliness and violence.

'But killing them won't destroy Lilith,' Simon said wearily. 'We've seen her strength. It's a wonder she did not decapitate you there and then, Cesare, when she knew what you'd attempted to do—'

'You urged me to do it. "Kill the humans she loves," you said. "Imagine their flesh boiling, their bones cracking. We are fire from God; take her ballet away and Lilith will be nothing but a cloud of wailing anger!" But her damnable ballet is still intact, while two of my flock are dead at her hands!'

'I hope you are not insinuating that it is my fault,' said Simon.

'We made her angry; was that not the point? In that, we succeeded admirably.'

Cesare lowered his head, seeming to collect himself. 'Simon, forgive me, I do not mean to rail at you. But we must bring the transformations forward; I need my army! And Lilith made the men afraid. I cannot afford to lose them to their mortal fears!'

'The transformation is a simple matter,' Simon said. 'It can be done whenever you wish, all in one day, all in an hour. But really, Karl and the new immortals are irrelevant. Important, yes, but not central.'

'What, precisely, is central?' Cesare asked icily. 'It seems that, for all my efforts, I have failed to answer the question of Lilith to your satisfaction.'

'On the contrary, you have already given me the answer.'

'Have I?'

'Sebastian's message,' said Simon. 'One word. Samael.'

'But what does it mean?' How desperate Cesare looked, like a saint aching for a vision of God.

'It means that only one vampire is capable of destroying Lilith. And that vampire is Sebastian. He's like her, her equal and opposite, do you understand?'

Cesare exhaled. 'Who refuses to co-operate.'

'But who thinks, perhaps, that he can use this knowledge to manipulate us. Well, let him think he can do so. All that is required is for Sebastian and Lilith to hate each other, and to meet.'

Simon had expected Cesare to be impressed, but the leader only folded his arms and said scornfully, 'How on earth could you hope to effect that?'

'It is already in hand. Rasmila is assisting.'

'Rasmila, who has no thought in her head but you?'

'Exactly. She will do anything for me.'

'But I have met Sebastian. As I told you, he and Lilith had no interest in each other. He has no interest in anything but himself. No, Simon, forget him!' And Cesare gazed fervently at Simon with the passion that had won his disciples to him. 'He's like Karl, an unreliable, useless subversive. Such men are powerless because they throw power away! But we three understand it. Simon, if you and I and John lack the strength to defeat Lilith ourselves, what are we worth?'

Simon examined his gold-tinged hands. There is such a gulf between us, he thought. Yet there is a lot in what Cesare says. 'If only Charlotte and Violette were not joined at the hip,' he murmured. 'If only Charlotte would leave her . . . and come to me.'

Cesare seemed not to hear him. As if possessed, he lunged forward and shook Simon, his eyes burning white. 'What if Samael and Lilith came together and created something *worse*?'

One sound disturbed Robyn's sleep; the breathless, echoing cry of a woman in pain – or extreme pleasure. Her eyes snapped open. She stared at the embers of the fire, slept again.

When she woke properly, it was light. The fire had gone out and her coat had fallen to the floor. Numb with cold, she ached all over from sleeping in one position.

For a moment, she had no idea where she was. She saw a huge window framing a cloudy sky, reflected in the mirror above the fireplace. Painted horses gazed blandly from the walls above the high bookshelves. The spines of thousands of books in faded reds, blues and browns towered around her, intimidating her with the dusty weight of their age. Oh, this place, she thought, feeling sick at heart.

She sat up stiffly, swearing.

'Your language doesn't improve,' said a voice.

She twisted round and saw Sebastian, a graceful silhouette against the pearly brightness of the window.

'How long have you been there?' She was angry at first; then, seeing the look on his face, the feeling deepened to something worse than anger.

'Not long.' He came to the *chaise-longue* and looked down at her.

'Why didn't you wake me up?'

'I should have done,' he said. His eyes were very soft, too tranquil, too contented. 'But you know I love to watch you sleeping. Are you cold?'

'Frozen.'

'Then I'll attend to the fire.' He began to move away, but she caught his wrist.

'Have you been gone all night?'

His eyes slid sideways under lowered lids. Shame? 'There were certain things—'

'So you just left me to sleep on a couch again?'

'I meant to prepare a bed for you, but certain matters intervened. You must forgive me, Robyn; I am still unused to considering your needs before my own.'

'Damned right you are.' Her breathing quickened and her blood rose. He sat beside her and stroked her hair, but she folded her arms defensively.

'And now you are angry with me,' he said ruefully.

'Has she gone, your uninvited guest?'

'She's gone.'

'So you persuaded her, did you?' Her tone was so vicious that it appeared to startle even Sebastian. 'Your powers of persuasion are as impressive as ever. I hope you enjoyed it as much as she did.'

'What are you talking about?' he said quietly.

She could have screamed. Pulling away from him, she grabbed her coat off the floor as if it, too, had wronged her. 'Don't treat me like an idiot! You had her, didn't you? I wouldn't even grace it with the term "seduction".'

His lips parted; he was ready to deny it. Instead he hesitated, frowning a little. 'How did you know?'

'I just know. I saw how you were with each other; there was a bond between you, two hundred years separated or not. It's all over your face, damn it, that shameful glow.'

He seemed bemused. 'I never thought you would be jealous.'

'And you're amazed.' She buttoned her shoes, then stood up and put on her coat. 'You are absolutely amazed.'

'What are you doing?'

'Looking for my purse.' She found it on the floor under the *chaise-longue*, checked to see how much money she had. Enough. 'My God, all that cant about not wanting to share me with Harold!'

She turned and went towards the door, hurried through it and into the saloon, her footsteps ringing briskly. She was more than hurt. She felt annihilated.

Sebastian was following her. 'Robyn, don't leave.'

'No, I've had enough.'

'Where do you think you'll go?'

'Cork. Home.'

'Stop, will you?'

She halted, three-quarters of the way across the room, keeping her back to him; she did not want him to see her crying. Beside her, the crocodile skull grinned in its glass case.

He said, 'Anything that has ever been between Rasmila and myself is quite separate. I won't insult you by saying it meant nothing, but it was to do with blood, and I can't explain to a mortal—'

'And I can't understand, and I don't even want to! You're a monster. You must have taken me for such a fool.'

'Please don't leave.' His voice almost broke. He sounded desperate.

'You've got yourself; what more do you need?'

'Don't.'

Without looking back, Robyn resumed her walk to the door. She took four steps; she neither heard nor felt him move, but suddenly he seized her from behind, his arms locking across her ribs.

She gasped and struggled frantically, outraged and terrified.

'Don't go!' He turned her round in his arms, holding her with unholy strength. 'I should die if you left me!'

She almost wriggled from his grip. He thrust her up against the closed door and held her there.

'Why the hell should I stay?' she cried.

He spoke fervidly into her ear. 'This morning I came in from the outside world and the other-world and the arms of a vampire where it was bitter-cold, and I saw you lying by the fire and you were warm, you were a living fire, you were the most beautiful sight I'd ever seen, with your hair like brown flames. And I realized that you are all that matters to me, your heat and your precious life. All Rasmila wanted from me was blood. She is like ice and I could never love her, because—'

She waited for him to go on, her eyes tight shut. 'Why can't you say it?'

'I'm telling you that I cannot endure my life without you.'

'It's not enough! Let go of me!' She fought him, but he held her hard. 'What's the point, when you won't say the one thing—'

'Do you want blood from me?' he whispered.

'Say it!'

'If I do, will it make you stay?'

'Nothing else will.'

Sebastian went quiet, his mouth in her hair. She felt his grip loosening, his whole body softening. 'Have my blood, then. I love you, Robyn.'

The breath came out of her in a laugh of sheer astonishment.

'Now, will you please stay with me?' he said.

Not a struggle between them now, but an embrace. 'I'll stay,' she said. They clung together, lost to each other and ashamed of it, pinioned by the dreadful joy of surrender.

But I won, Robyn thought in bitter-sweet triumph. I've changed him, I've soured all his other victims; I made him fall in love with me and I forced him to *admit it*.

I won!

PART THREE

Sometimes the Earth Goddess cried out in the night, demanding human hearts, and then She would not be comforted until She had been given human blood to drink.

Mayan myth

I am all that has been, and is, and that will be No mortal has yet been able to lift the veil that covers me.

Inscription on the Goddess's temple at Sais

CHAPTER SEVENTEEN

VAMPIRE IN BLACK

Charlotte found it deeply unsettling to be in Cambridge again. It was four years since she'd left, and she had heard almost nothing about her family in that time. It was as if they'd ceased to exist. Rather, she'd placed them in a doll's house in her mind, where they remained frozen as she'd last known them, like vampires, reassuringly the same for ever.

It had seemed inconceivable that she would never return, but the image of doing so had been vague and couched in fantasy. The reality was at once as cold-edged as winter, and oddly banal.

How strange to see the big, greyish-cream stone house behind the high wall. To push open the gate, the wrought-iron damp and flaky under her fingers. To cross the drive, noticing how much the shrubs had grown, the different clustering of moss on the stones. Even the great trees, whose bare branches swayed above her, had subtly changed their shapes. It all looked familiar and yet strange, glass-sharp as if memory and vision were in static conflict.

She rang the doorbell. The maid answered. Dear Sally, the same as ever; tall and thin, with a vaguely worried air and untidy brown hair hanging in wisps around her spectacles.

'Miss Neville!' Sally stared at her until she was swept aside by a dark-haired woman who'd come hurrying along the hall.

'Go back to the kitchen, dear, I'll see to it.'

It took Charlotte a moment to realize that it was Anne.

The maid obeyed, bewildered, glancing back over her shoulder. Charlotte could imagine the gossip in the kitchen. Then she and Anne were alone, gazing at each other.

Charlotte saw the changes in her immediately. Still young,

attractive, warm-hearted; that had not changed. But there were fine lines around her nose and mouth, a look of maturity. She'd put on a little weight and was dressed staidly in a skirt, blouse, cardigan and long strings of pearls. A county wife.

And most clearly of all, Charlotte saw the strain that tugged at her eyes and mouth.

'You'd better come in,' Anne said at last. No display of emotion. 'You got my letter, then.'

'How did you know where to find me?'

'It was elementary,' Anne murmured, with a brief half-smile. 'I'll show you later.'

On the threshold, Charlotte hesitated. 'Is David here?'

'Not at the minute. He and Elizabeth went out for some air. They both needed a rest from the sick-room.'

So her father was still alive. She wasn't too late.

Relieved that she would not have to face David immediately, Charlotte stepped into the hall and was saddened at the way Anne quickly stepped back, keeping her distance as if Charlotte were infectious. That was why she'd sent Sally away; to protect her.

'Madeleine's here, though,' said Anne.

Her heart twisted. She didn't want to see Madeleine either, but it was unavoidable now. The worst thing of all, she thought, would be to see Henry. He'd been their laboratory assistant, much-loved by her father, nothing more to Charlotte than a comfortable acquaintance until he had declared his feelings for her. And when Karl had vanished, and she'd thought he was dead, she had married Henry, simply because nothing had mattered to her. Married him, then betrayed him and left him the minute Karl came back.

But to meet him would be merely embarrassing. Not painful.

She asked quietly, 'How is Father?' She thought of the times when she'd arrived home from an outing and her father had come into the hall to greet her, hands in the pockets of his tweed jacket, delighted to see her but gruffly annoyed that she'd ever been away. How empty the hall seemed, when he didn't appear.

'Not well.' The corners of Anne's mouth twitched down,

and she made a marked effort to control her voice. 'The doctor doesn't think he'll last much longer. Days, at most.'

For a frozen instant they stared at each other. If they'd still been friends, if Charlotte had still been human, they would have fallen into each other's arms. But Charlotte couldn't move; to frighten Anne and see her recoil would only have made it worse.

Anne turned away. Bitterness pierced them both.

'What's wrong with him?'

Anne's shoulders rose and fell. 'His heart, his lungs. He's been getting weaker and weaker for months. David says he's never been completely well since he had that influenza in 1919. I'm not sure the stuff he used to work with in the laboratory hasn't had something to do with it. My father says it's dangerous. Radium, was it?'

'Yes, radium,' Charlotte replied, her voice faint.

'Of course, losing you and Fleur didn't help.'

Charlotte said nothing. It was on the tip of her tongue to ask if she could see him straight away, but she did not.

'You may as well come into the drawing-room,' said Anne.

As she opened the door, Charlotte was arrested by the scene inside. There was her sister Madeleine on her knees on the carpet, playing with a boisterous blond toddler; or at least, trying in vain to stop him destroying a wooden train. Glancing up, the boy took one look at Charlotte and began to scream.

Charlotte stayed in the doorway. She didn't rush in exclaiming, as a human would, only watched and absorbed, as was her vampire nature. Madeleine's gaze flicked to her, registered astonishment, then went back to the toddler.

'He's been like this all afternoon, Anne,' she said, standing up. 'I can't do anything with him. I'm afraid he'll disturb Father.'

Anne bent down to pick up the wriggling child. 'I'll ask Sally to put him to bed. He just wants attention, because he knows things aren't normal.' As she passed Charlotte, she stopped. Charlotte studied the boy; even though he was red-faced and grizzling, she saw a resemblance to her brother David. But there was none of David's goodness in his eyes, only a wilful little spirit that shone out of him like blood-heat. How plump with blood – Charlotte shut the thought off, horrified at herself. 'This is my son, George. He's two and a half. Say hello to your Auntie Charlotte, George.'

The child responded with an ear-splitting bawl and turned his face into his mother's shoulder. Anne smiled tiredly. 'It's not you. Don't feel obliged to say anything nice about him; we know he's the most objectionable child in the universe. David's sure he's a changeling. But we love him. Don't we, George? Sometimes.'

She went out into the hall, calling for Sally. Charlotte remained where she was, seeing straight through Madeleine, thinking, my God, Anne had a baby and I didn't know! I didn't know.

Then she recollected herself, and went into the room. Nothing had changed. Still the Victorian clutter, the clocks ticking madly, the cosy sepia drabness.

Madeleine was smiling hesitantly, shaking her head. 'Charlotte, I can't believe it! Is it really you? Oh, look, no one's taken your coat. Let me.'

Charlotte was reluctant to take off her coat; it was like shedding a protective barrier. But she removed it and relinquished it, with her hat and gloves, into Maddy's hands.

'Isn't it lovely?' Madeleine said, admiring the coat. 'I love this swirly figured velvet. And lovely colours, russet and gold, like your hair. It does suit you . . .' Her voice seemed to give way on the last words. She half-ran out into the hall, appearing again almost immediately. She was as Charlotte remembered; all nervous energy and charm, strikingly pretty, her copper-red hair a bright, shingled cap. But Charlotte could see that she had changed. She'd lost her sharp corners, her self-centredness.

'Do sit down. I can't believe you're here.' Maddy settled on the couch, Charlotte in an armchair. 'I don't know why you had to wait until Father – oh, it's too awful, Charli. Why did you have to stay away so long?'

'You know why,' Charlotte said gently. Her sister glanced at her, looked away, looked back again. She was struggling inside. Charlotte hated to add to her pain.

'Yes, well, that's all in the past now, isn't it? I know it was awful when you left, and David and Father were angry, but I'm sure they didn't mean you to stay away for ever. You could even have brought—' She clearly couldn't say Karl's name. 'Well, you know, you could even have brought him with you. I'm sure they would have got used to the idea in the end.' Suddenly her face froze and a wild look came into her eyes. 'He hasn't come, has he?'

'No.'

A little gasp, of relief or disappointment. 'But you are still . . .'

'We're still together, yes.'

Madeleine looked as if she had no idea whether to be pleased or dismayed. She, too, had fallen under Karl's spell, but the shock of discovering that he was a vampire had almost destroyed her. Obviously she was not completely over it; she was fighting to keep her self-possession.

'But where have you been?'

'Switzerland, mostly. And America, and Austria.'

Madeleine looked stunned by this prosaic answer, as if she'd expected Charlotte to say, *Hades*. 'Switzerland? Good Lord, I went there with my husband two years ago.'

'You're married?' Something else she hadn't known. It disturbed her more every moment, to discover how much her family had changed with the passage of years, while she had stayed the same.

'Yes, to a simply wonderful man.'

'Any children?'

'Not yet. We're hoping. We're trying like mad.' There was a flicker of unease beneath the glaze of contentment, but Charlotte couldn't interpret it. 'I wish it could have happened before Father got ill.'

Charlotte took a risk. She moved to the couch and sat down beside Maddy, knowing her sister might recoil. The recollection of the way Maddy had jerked away in terror, the last time Charlotte had tried to touch her, still burned.

But Maddy didn't move. Charlotte touched her arm, then folded her hand round the tender flesh, suppressing with all her will her desire for the hot, sweet blood pulsing under the surface. As she pushed the blood-thirst away, there came instead an urge to kiss her sister on the mouth; thirst turning treacherously to lust in its refusal to be tamed. Again she controlled it. Her arm slipped around the slim, soft shoulders and Madeleine leaned into her, hungry for solace. Yet their closeness only emphasized an emptiness between them; a gap where their older sister Fleur should have been.

'I have missed you, Maddy,' she said. 'I often think about you.'

'You never wrote.'

'How could I?'

'But it's all right now . . . isn't it?' Madeleine looked up, her sweet face close to Charlotte's. She was pale with anxiety. Charlotte understood.

Maddy could not bear the knowledge that Charlotte had become a vampire. Her mind would not support it. Instead she denied it; she let herself believe that the intervening years had magically cured Charlotte — perhaps cured Karl, as well — and that she was human again. That was why she let Charlotte touch her. To convince herself it was true.

'It's not all right, really,' Charlotte said gently. 'I shouldn't have come back at all. But don't be afraid of me, Maddy. I love you more than I can say.' She cheated a little as she spoke, allowing her eyes to work their spell, calming Madeleine's fears. Let her keep the illusion. Forcing the raw truth on her would be cruel.

'What does it matter at a time like this, anyway?' Maddy said. 'We're still sisters. I'm so glad you're here.'

They were sitting like that, arms around each other, when Anne came back into the room. Seeing them, a look of grave suspicion clouded her face. Charlotte hated her for it. Don't you trust me, Anne, don't you have any faith in me at all?

A small voice added, but why should you?

'I've spoken to the nurse,' Anne said. 'You can go up and see him, if you wish.'

An unexpected wave of fear hit Charlotte. She didn't want to see her father. She wanted to remember him as he used to be. Pacing about the laboratory in his shapeless jacket, his tie askew, propounding some new theory to her and Henry, his thick white moustache tinged yellow from cigar smoke. Bluff in manner, short-tempered sometimes but not really meaning it. The kindest of men underneath. Too possessive, he'd made Charlotte suffer in many subtle ways, but he had adored her – until the day she ran away with Karl.

He'd disowned her. And she'd said such cruel things in response, things that could never be taken back.

'I'm not sure this was a good idea,' she said. 'Are you sure he wants to see me?'

'Ask him yourself,' Anne said grimly, folding her arms.

Charlotte stood up. 'You know how we parted! He said he never wanted to see me again, that I'd ceased to exist.'

'Well, you have in a way, haven't you?' Anne's lips thinned with black humour. 'Do you know, I thought it was impossible for you to turn any paler – but you've gone quite white.'

'Why are you doing this?'

'Whatever is happening now, Charlotte – you were the instigator.'

'Has he asked for me?' she said desperately.

'I think you'd better go and find out for yourself.'

Floored by Anne's obduracy, Charlotte strode out of the room and went towards the stairs. It was deathly quiet. Daylight hung like dust in the stairwell. Every move she made unleashed memories. There was the door to the study, half-open on to silence. There was the door to the cellar laboratory, where she'd spent most of her days assisting his experiments. Shut and locked now, perhaps for ever.

She mounted the stairs. She'd climbed these stairs with Karl, once . . . climbed them thousands of times without him, but always remembered that one time she'd led him to her bedroom.

She knocked lightly on the panelled door to her father's room, then let herself in. The curtains were drawn. There was a shape under the bedclothes, wisps of grey hair . . . she didn't want to look. The close, stale smells of illness hung in the air. On the near side of the bed sat a plump woman in uniform and starched white cap.

As Charlotte entered, she stood up. 'Good afternoon, madam.'

'I'm his daughter, Charlotte. How is he?'

'Resting. He's comfortable,' the nurse said confidently, telling her nothing at all. From her manner, she had been told nothing sinister about Charlotte. 'I'm pleased to meet you; I'm only sorry it's under such sad circumstances.'

'Quite, er – would you mind leaving us alone, please? I'm sure you must need a rest.'

'Well, I wouldn't say no to a cup of tea. Just call if you need me.'

When the nurse had left, Charlotte approached the bed. Her mouth was sour.

There was her father's dear face against the pillow, eyes closed, mouth open. How sunken his cheeks were. She stared at his neck, his wrists protruding from the sleeves of striped pyjamas, the narrow ribs rising and falling under the covers. How had he become so thin? He had always seemed robust. She had always known his health was delicate, but she had put it from her mind, never daring to entertain the possibility that he might die. Ever.

She remembered tiny blue specks of radium glowing in darkness, tiny flashes of light hitting a screen as her father patiently counted them. She imagined those minute particles raining into his eyes, his body. Is it radiation that's ruined his health, or grief?

The years that had frozen her in crystal had eaten him away.

She took his hand. He frowned a little in his sleep. How dry and loose the skin felt, but the hand beneath was still strong. The hand of a man who had years of life and brilliant thought left in him. He wasn't much older than Josef. But his face was grey, the face of a man closer to eighty than sixty. The wheeze of every shallow, drowning breath hurt her ears.

'Father,' she said, but he didn't hear.

She thought of another sick-bed she had attended; that of Josef's sister, Lisl. At Josef's request she had relieved Lisl's suffering, gently sucking her blood until the end came. I could do that again . . .

Or . . . could I take him now beyond death for ever? I could find Stefan and a third vampire and we could take him into the Crystal Ring, quickly, now, before it's too late.

Her head dropped. She knew she wouldn't do it. He wouldn't want it; God Almighty, it was grotesque even to think of it! And if it failed and he died – how hideous, how much worse that would be for him than dying with relative dignity. She could never bear the blame, the guilt.

No. She would do neither of those things. She would simply sit with him, the dutiful daughter.

Then, a small revelation. Anne let me come in here alone. In her heart she does trust me, after all.

'Father,' she said again. 'It's Charlotte. I'm so sorry I hurt you. You don't have to forgive me. I only want you to know that I still . . .'

His eyes opened. He blinked at her. Light seemed to gather in the pupils, and he smiled and grasped her hand. 'Oh, you came back!' he said.

Her heart sprang with relief. 'Yes, dear, I'm here.'

'It seems so long since I saw you, my darling. I'm so glad. I knew if I waited—' He broke into a spasm of coughing. She held his hand until it had subsided, then mopped his mouth with a handkerchief. Blood on the white cotton; its vivid colour and ripe scent seemed to invade her physically. She quickly threw the handkerchief down and gave him a drink of water. 'I knew if I waited you'd come back.'

He looked so joyful. He held her hand between both of his, and she thought with a rush of happiness, he's forgiven me! Not that it matters, all that matters is that he doesn't die hating me, or thinking I hate him. 'I'll stay with you now, for as long as you want me.'

'Yes, stay with me,' he said. 'Dearest Annette.'

Annette was her mother's name. She sat down suddenly in the nurse's chair as if pinned there by a lead spear, keeping hold of his hands. He thought she was not his daughter but his wife, twenty-five years dead.

Charlotte was numb. Tears burned and overflowed her eyelids.

Now it all made sense. He must have been asking Anne for Annette, not for me.

He never got over losing Mother, she thought. He always wished I was her; now he believes I am, and if it makes him happy, let him think it.

She leaned over to kiss his forehead and his lips, tasted the lingering trace of blood. He smiled. 'I won't leave you,' she said softly. 'Dearest George.'

'Where are Fleur and Charlotte?' he said. 'Will you bring them in to see me?'

He didn't mention Madeleine, because she had not existed until Annette had died giving birth to her. He'd forgotten that Fleur had died and Charlotte had left him.

'Later, dearest,' she whispered. 'When you're stronger.'

'Later. I am rather tired to have children running around.' His eyelids fluttered down, but his grasp on her hands did not weaken. 'It's so good to have you with me.' He went on talking, rambling about the old times she could not remember. His words made little sense, but he required nothing of her except her presence. Finally she lay down on the bed beside him, one arm over his wasted body, her head on his shoulder. No blood-thirst plagued her. His shallow breathing and the tap of his heart hypnotized her. She was human again, a child curled around him, his daughter.

'You know, Annette, I'm feeling a little better today,' he said suddenly, almost in his normal tone. 'I could quite fancy some eggs. Yes, eggs and toast.'

They were the last words he spoke. She felt his heart stop. She heard the last breath gurgle out of his lungs. And when it was over, she went on lying there so that he wouldn't be alone. What hurry was there to tell anyone? She stayed there, eyes wide open in the gloom, because if she moved she would break down.

She was still there when the nurse came back, ten minutes later. Then she got up calmly and said, 'He's gone.' And she didn't cry after all, though there was a strange current trying to lift her heart out of her chest.

The nurse was very quiet and businesslike as she attended to the body and pulled the sheet over his face. She uttered words of sympathy, but Charlotte barely heard her; she wandered out on to the landing like a ghost, went to the top of the stairs. Then she saw Anne with David and her Aunt Elizabeth in the hall. They'd only just come home and they had no idea . . .

So it was Charlotte's responsibility to break the news. But she couldn't break it gently, couldn't force out a euphemism such as *passed away*.

'He's dead,' she said. Their faces swivelled towards her, aghast. She started down the stairs. 'A few minutes ago. I was with him. At least someone was with him . . .

And now, she thought bitterly, they are going to think I killed him.

Elizabeth hurried straight past her up the stairs, barely giving her a glance, and muttering in a kind of anguished rage, 'Oh, I knew we shouldn't have gone out! I knew this would happen if we left him even for an hour. He might have waited!' as if George had merely been inconsiderate.

David's face, the kind and too-moral face she remembered so clearly, had lost its colour. He came straight towards Charlotte. She braced herself mentally, thinking, please don't let him be angry now, if he blames me for everything now I shall just leave, I can't stand it.

To her complete amazement, all her brother did was to throw his arms around her. He almost lifted her off her feet. 'Charlotte,' he said into her neck, muffled. Then he started to weep.

While the doctor came and went, and the family and servants comforted one another, Charlotte waited alone in the darkness of the study. How desolate it seemed, never again to be animated by her father's intellect. In the past she had often sat at that desk, in a pool of lamplight, typing out his papers and theses . . . no longer. Never again.

She had told the others how he had died, that he was happy because he thought Annette was with him. That it had been peaceful. And they'd believed her, because not to believe would have been too painful; but she saw the sorrow and confusion in their eyes. They were wondering, is she a vampire or is she still Charlotte? How odd that he died when she was with him and we were not . . . our fault or hers?

She couldn't blame them for their confusion, but it still flayed her. So she had left them to it. Separated herself from the human turmoil.

And now she sat in the static darkness, too shocked to grieve, harshly aware of the way the years had shifted under her feet.

She had been sitting at the desk one rainy night when she'd realized, with a heart-stopping thrill, that Karl was in the room with her. He had been sitting on this leather couch where she now sat alone. When he'd invited her to join him, against her better judgement, she had.

She could visualize Karl beside her now; lean, shadowy, enticing beyond reason, with tantalizing glints of red light in his hair and eyes. She could almost hear the rush of rain. That evening, under the guise of kindness, he had actually begun to seduce her. So deep she'd fallen under his enchantment by the end of their conversation, he could easily have taken full advantage of her there and then. He could have feasted on her blood – he'd told her, long afterwards, that he'd been severely tempted – yet he had held back, out of compassion, out of love.

How young, how naïve and full of hopes and neuroses she'd been. She hadn't known he was a vampire then, of course; by the time she did find out, it was too late. And ironically, it was his very kindness that had kept her fatally in love with him. If he'd been merely a charming monster, her infatuation would swiftly have died and then perhaps her family would not have been torn apart and her father and Fleur would still be alive.

In a way, she thought, I wanted to stay in the old life for ever. Yes, I felt oppressed and trapped – but that was as much by my own choice as by Father's demands. It was a shelter as well as a prison, a cocoon woven around me by my family. It was so divinely sinful to have a forbidden affair with Karl under their very noses!

It had been a time of innocence and thrilling discovery; her family going blithely about their business, while Charlotte's only real concern had been the desperate confusion she felt as she struggled not to fall in love with Karl, and failed. Never had she dreamed that it would lead to such alienation, to living on human blood, heartlessly seducing and attacking people to steal that blood, even killing them.

God, I've even done that. I was a guileless, wide-eyed girl . . . and now I'm a murderer. How did it happen?

The sheltering cocoon had been ripped open and shredded. It hadn't ended the day she'd discovered the truth about Karl, starkly horrific though that had been; nor even on the day that Ilona had torn Fleur's throat out, and David had struck Karl's head from his body. No, it had ended after Charlotte had become a vampire, and she'd come back to say goodbye; hoping for forgiveness, meeting only hostility and pain. That had marked the idyll's end.

Karl, by the magic of Kristian's dark skill, had been brought back to life, but Fleur lay in the cold ground for eternity. And Charlotte now treated her murderer like a sister. That was the ugly reality beneath the romance.

The house was dead, life and laughter extinguished. No glass in the windows, a frigid black wind blowing in . . . that was how Charlotte felt. Cold, colder. Slowly unravelling inside.

Father, she cried silently. Father.

After a couple of hours had passed, Anne came in. She closed the door, switched on the desk lamp, and stood looking at Charlotte for a moment. She looked red-eyed, exhausted. Then she sat down beside Charlotte.

'Well, it's over,' she said.

'How is everyone?' Charlotte asked.

'As you'd expect. Upset. Drinking tea and trying to pretend they're coping. I don't think David is going to forgive himself for not being there at the end.'

'David never was very good at forgiving himself for things that were not his fault.'

Anne gave her a sharp glance. 'It is strange, isn't it, that Dr Neville went so quickly after you'd gone in to see him?'

White-hot anger consumed Charlotte. She sat forward a little, the feeling coalescing in her eyes, burning. 'How dare you say that?' Anne flinched, unnerved. 'How dare you even think it? My own father! What do you think I am?'

'I don't know,' Anne said, putting up a hand as if to ward Charlotte away. 'That's just it, I don't know!'

'He was waiting for Mother, that's all. When she arrived, he could sleep. If you really think so ill of me, why did you invite me here?'

Anne's head dropped. 'You were still his daughter. And I do trust you, even though I don't know whether I should or not. I could have made a dreadful mistake.'

'You thought that if you put anyone in danger, you'd be to blame? Well, you haven't.' Charlotte's anger was cooling to sorrow. Nothing really mattered. She had sometimes dreamed of meeting Anne again in a gilded scene of reconciliation. The reality was jagged and difficult. 'I'm still myself, I still have feelings. If anything, our feelings are more intense, like knives. If you think it means nothing to me to be here – to have seen Father – and you dare to imply that I—'

Tears overcame her suddenly. Anne looked shocked, unhappy and at a loss. 'I'm sorry.'

They should have embraced and comforted each other then. Charlotte wanted it desperately. But she saw rejection in every line of Anne's body, and dared not touch her. The withholding of physical comfort hurt. But if she held Anne in her arms, she would be too aware of the thunder of her blood, sap leaping through a succulent and infinitely precious fruit.

'I'd better go,' said Charlotte.

She began to stand up, but Anne said, 'Wait, please, I want to speak to you, but it's very difficult.'

'Just talk to me as you used to. I told you, I'm still the same.'

'But you're not. That's the trouble. You should look at yourself in the mirror, Charli – if you can. You haven't aged a day, and your eyes . . . I didn't realize I'd find it this hard.'

'Neither did I.' She touched Anne's wrist; Anne jumped, so Charlotte withdrew her hand. 'How did you find me, anyway?'

Anne got up, went to the desk and opened a drawer. Returning, she placed a newspaper on Charlotte's knee, turned to an inside page. There was a photograph of a group of people at a ship's rail, smiling and waving. In the middle was Violette, with some of the *corps de ballet* girls alongside her. Just behind her, clearly recognizable despite the smudgy grey print, were Karl and Charlotte. Charlotte was smiling, a sweet-natured, carefree girl; Karl was inclining his head towards her, as if saying something into her ear. Her hand was on Violette's shoulder. 'Lenoir sails to conquer USA,' said the headline.

Charlotte gasped. This had been inevitable, she supposed. Her real shock came from realizing that she had never seen a photograph of Karl before.

'How do you think I felt when I saw that?' Anne said angrily. 'How do you think *David* felt? We managed to hide it from your father.'

'It's just a photograph, Anne. We sponsor the ballet. Help with the business side.'

Anne looked stunned, as if unable to believe that vampires could do anything so human. 'Does Miss Lenoir know what you are?'

Charlotte verged on laughter. 'Oh yes, she knows.'

Anne's question came out in a rush. '*What on earth have you been doing?*'

'I wouldn't know where to start. I can't tell you, it's too much.'

'I can't imagine seeing Karl again. The whole thing was like a bad dream.' She looked obliquely at Charlotte. 'I don't understand why sitting here talking to you is making me feel as if I'm losing my mind.'

Charlotte's guilt intensified. This was the last thing she'd wanted. 'For God's sake, don't be afraid of me. I've so wanted to talk to you. I know you're the one I upset the most, apart from Father. Elizabeth understood my reasons but she didn't care; David and Maddy cared, but they didn't understand. But you did, and you want to forgive me but you can't. If it's made you unhappy, I'm sorry.'

Anne pushed her hair back and folded her arms. 'You're not the centre of the universe, Charli. David and I are happy at Parkland, and when we've got over the Prof's death, we will be again.'

'And Maddy's happy too,' Charlotte said, to deflect Anne's sharpness.

'Is that what she told you?'

'Yes. Why?'

'She married him for his money, that's why. She wanted money to lavish on charity work to ease the guilt she feels for having such a privileged upbringing. And meanwhile she dotes on someone else. She is so besotted with this other man, or thinks she is, that she has him living with her and her husband.'

'What? Why does her husband put up with it?'

'Because he worships her. She gets away with anything. She couldn't marry this other man because he's a semi-invalid, mentally unstable, and he couldn't have provided for her. She simply looks after him, out of love.'

'Oh God,' Charlotte whispered, realizing. 'Edward.'

'Yes, Edward. Remember him? David's dearest friend, who nearly died and was fit only for a mental asylum after Karl had attacked him? He's lucky to have Maddy and us, but he'll never be really well. And you wonder at me getting upset, when David sees Karl's face in the paper, and you with him, laughing!'

Charlotte's heart shrank under the pressure of Anne's distress. *How can I defend myself, when Anne is absolutely right?* She couldn't help comparing this hostile Anne with the Anne of her daydreams, who'd been the friend she used to know: lively, sensible, confiding, forgiving. They'd kissed like sisters, and Anne had accepted Charlotte's nature and given her a sip of blood as a bond ... and although Charlotte had known the dream would never come true, nothing had prepared her for this mature, angry, harassed woman.

'It should have stayed a dream,' Charlotte murmured, 'my coming to see you.'

'Why? Do vampires feel guilty? Karl's gone, but the things he did stay with us. They almost wrecked our lives. You knew, yet you set it all aside and went with him! That's what we can't believe about you, Charli, that you could be so heartless!'

The words struck like fangs. 'I didn't mean to be heartless. But I loved Karl to the point of madness and I still do.'

'Damn it,' said Anne. 'I wasn't going to indulge in recriminations. Not at a time like this.'

'But if it wasn't a time like this, I wouldn't be here.' Charlotte's tone was gentle, cool. She was drawing away. All she wanted now was to be alone with memories of her father. 'You needn't have asked me to come. I'm grateful.'

'You're not sorry?'

'No. I'm glad I was with Father. I only wish . . .'

'Don't we all. But wishing won't bring him back.' Another bitter glance. 'And it won't bring you back either, will it?'

'No. I can't become human again.'

'Would you want to? That's the question.'

Charlotte didn't answer. 'Would you mind – would the others mind – if I came to the funeral?'

Anne's stark expression revealed that she found this an appalling prospect, although she quickly collected herself. Charlotte understood then that Anne would never accept what she'd become. Yes, she might use vampiric influence to change her friend's mind – but it would not be real. Charlotte couldn't do it.

'You don't need my permission.' There was no kindness in Anne's tone, nothing to allow them to feel better. 'It's your right.'

Dressed in black, heavily veiled, Charlotte arrived late at the chapel and sat alone at the back. She knew her presence disturbed her family, rather than comforted them; she did not want to make their grief worse.

She had spent the few intervening days on her own in Cambridge, exploring the city she had loved so dearly, avoiding anyone who might recognize her. She'd had to get away from her family, before her need for blood became fatally confused with her love for them. She telephoned Karl every day; all was quiet in Salzburg. She longed to see him, but it seemed important not to leave until her father was buried. A mourning ritual, of a sort.

The chapel was full of eminent people; fellows from Trinity, her father's colleagues from the Cavendish, many of his former students. It moved her to tears to see how well-loved and respected he had been. She wept continually and silently behind the veil. The eulogies were unbearable.

I wish Karl was here with me now, she thought. He would have held me steady against this terrible greyness that's dragging me down into itself.

As they walked to the cemetery afterwards, she recalled another burial; that of Janacek, whom she'd killed in order to free Violette. She had felt detached there, completely in command of herself. Now she felt vulnerable, as if she were made of glass; not of the same flesh as her family, but hard and fragile.

Earth fell on the coffin. David and Anne cried, leaning together. Elizabeth held Madeleine. Henry was there too; her father's assistant, virtually a son to him – and once, for a brief time, Charlotte's husband.

She did not look at him, nor he at her.

When it was over, she meant to slip away discreetly – only to find her family all around her suddenly, Maddy's hand through her arm, and David's sombre voice in her ear.

'Will you come back to the house, please, Charlotte?'

'I thought you should know,' David said, 'that Father cut you out of his will. There's nothing for you, I'm afraid.'

Charlotte felt a dart of misery run from her throat to her feet. 'It's all right, I didn't expect anything. I hadn't even thought about it.'

They were sitting at a round table in the breakfast room; David, Anne, Henry and herself, while Elizabeth and Madeleine played host to the other mourners in the drawing- and dining-rooms. Henry had aged visibly, well on course to becoming a bumbling professor in middle age. A bulky, bespectacled figure, pompous yet shy and desperately embarrassed by emotion; just as Charlotte remembered. So far he hadn't said a word to her, though it was obvious that her presence made him acutely uncomfortable.

'Why did you come back, then?' David said with sudden sharpness. Tired and distraught, he ran a hand over his fair hair. She saw a few silver strands.

'Do you think I loved Father any less, because of the decision I made? How could I not come?' She gazed at her brother, knowing the gleam of her face and eyes disturbed him. 'I know I'm making things difficult. I'm sorry. But knowing what I am, why on earth did you try to find me?'

David cleared his throat, as if he did not know how to respond. Anne glanced at him, then at Henry. Henry was studiedly not looking at Charlotte.

'About eighteen months after I left,' she went on, 'you sent a private detective called John Milner to look for us. Oh yes, he found us.'

'We know,' said David. 'Not because he told us, but because he was found wandering about in Dover without any recollection of what he was doing there. He was quite ill for a time; said he was having weird dreams, and wanted to sleep all the time so he could escape back into them. Dreams of a woman who looked like you. And there were two little marks on his neck, so faint that most people wouldn't have noticed them. So we knew, Charli, even though he couldn't tell us anything.' His tone was severe now. 'And that's why I didn't try again, until we saw the photograph. It was too dangerous.'

'But why did you try at all?'

'Because I was worried sick about you!' David exclaimed. 'Why d'you think? You're still my sister; I couldn't help thinking what that – that man might have done to you!'

'His name is Karl.' From the corner of her eye she saw Henry shudder and put a hand to his face. 'All he did was to help me become myself.'

'Oh,' said David, 'so the kind, shy sister I loved was really a demon all along?'

'David,' said Anne. She put her hand through his arm and he subsided. Anne, it seemed, had already said everything she needed to.

Charlotte, though, sat with the cruel light of revelation pouring over her. How they'd changed in such a short time. They'd had a child and there would be more; they were growing older and they would go on changing, drifting away from her. It was as if she'd stood motionless in time while they travelled without her. The gulf between them was like a grave. It terrified her.

'You're right to feel betrayed, David,' said Charlotte. 'I did wrong, but it was a case of love being stronger than reason. I can't repent. If you want me to say it was all a mistake and I'm coming home — I can't. It will never happen, so put it from your mind.'

'I see,' David said wearily. 'Just tell me one thing. Does he — does Karl treat you kindly?'

'Of course he does. He always did.'

David sighed. There was an uncomfortable silence. Their unease in her presence distressed her, but nothing could heal it; really, she was beyond hoping for healing. And she would never enchant them into accepting her. They must love or hate her of their own free will.

'I think Henry wants to say something to you,' said David.

She turned her gaze to Henry. He could barely look at her, and his voice shook as he began, 'I — I have become friendly with a very pleasant young lady. We — we want to marry.'

'How nice for you,' Charlotte said frigidly. She could imagine the woman; a prim little Methodist, approved of by Henry's mother.

'But I can't marry her, can I!' he exclaimed, slapping the table, more in bluster than clean anger. 'I'm still married to you! I want a divorce.'

A smile frosted Charlotte's mouth. This became more ghastly by the moment. Thinking she'd lost Karl for ever, she had only married Henry to keep him from walking out on her father. But Karl had come back. She felt cruel, completely a vampire. 'As far as I'm concerned, we were never truly married.'

'Well, as far as the law's concerned, we ruddy well are!' Henry turned crimson as he spoke. She felt a sudden ache in her canine teeth.

'Do you really think I am going to waste my time, sitting about in court? How can you cite Karl, when the police think he's dead? I suppose I could pretend to commit adultery in a boarding house while some private detective spies on us; David has a friend who does that sort of thing.' This dig caused her brother to blush and drop his head. 'It's ludicrous. Do what Karl and I do. Live together.'

She'd known her words would horrify him. Henry seemed close to exploding with outrage. 'This isn't Bloomsbury! It's out of the question!' He stood up suddenly. 'You are a monster, Charlotte! The Prof was never the same after you left, he simply went downhill. It should have been you in that coffin instead of him! You killed him!'

Her fingers tightened on the edge of the table, almost indenting the wood. She stared at their slender whiteness, the blue-white of the taut knuckles. 'I think we had better continue this conversation in private, don't you?'

Henry harrumphed, his back to the others. 'I suppose so.'

Anne and David looked uneasy. Charlotte said, 'Go on. It's all right.'

They left the room. The sight of Charlotte seemed to have undone all Henry's composure. Alone with her, he became rigidly correct and unapproachable, but sweat glossed his upper lip. He dabbed at it with his handkerchief, his hand trembling. From the way he kept staring at her she knew, with dismay, that his feelings for her were not dead. If anything, her vampire allure was inflaming them.

'You can say what you like now,' she said, standing up. He edged away to the window. 'Go on. I'm a monster and I killed my father?'

'You look—' he stammered. 'You look just the same.'

'What did you tell people, when I left?'

'The truth,' Henry said gruffly. He'd become even more like her father, in the years since she'd last seen him. 'That you'd left me for another man. I didn't see any point in lying.'

'That was brave. Most men would have felt too humiliated.'

He turned on her, pale with anger. 'How could I be any more humiliated than I already was?' As all his anguish came pouring out, she could only stand there and let it wash over her. 'You were sleeping with Karl while you were engaged to me! How could you? You seemed so shy, so virtuous, always Dr Neville's perfect daughter. There was no question that I would do more than kiss your cheek until we were married, but for *Karl* you would – I can't believe it, I simply can't believe what you did to me!'

His pain roused nothing in her beyond the mildest sympathy, mixed with irritation. 'Hurt your pride?'

'That is not fair! I loved you!'

Charlotte looked down. 'I did you a terrible wrong. I only married you to please my father, to please *him*, not you or myself. The woman you thought would make a quiet, un-threatening little wife wasn't me. My fault for letting you think it was. But, Henry, what did you think you were offering *me*?'

The question seemed to dumbfound him. 'A respectable marriage,' he said stiffly. 'A family.'

'But what about passion? You say you loved me, but the few times we consummated our so-called marriage, you didn't enjoy it. It was just our duty, and I must be a scarlet woman for thinking it was anything else! Everything, duty. How could you expect me to live like that?'

Henry's face coloured. 'You are a heathen, Charlotte. In a previous age you would have been burned at the stake.'

'And you would have been there, lighting the fire but not enjoying it, just doing your duty to God. I wish I could make you understand why I gave myself completely to Karl, again and again, and why I left you for him.' She was deliberately provoking him, relishing his discomfort. 'I wish I could make you feel just one moment of that passion!'

As she spoke, desire ignited beneath her heart. With excite-ment dancing through her like red feathers on a breeze, she went to Henry, pushed him down into a chair, and sat on his knee. Too stunned to stop her, he caved in beneath her as if he'd lost all his strength.

Even when she put her arms round his neck, she knew he was dying of embarrassment, not fear. He'd put the fact that she was a vampire out of his mind, because he couldn't believe it.

While he was rigid with outrage at her improper behaviour, she sensed his puritan nature warring with his secret dark impulses; with the fact that he was and always had been her slave.

Charlotte's lips found the artery beating beneath the grainy, salt-damp skin. Mouth wide, she bit down, felt the blood and salt rushing on to her eager tongue. The red starburst convulsed her. She hugged Henry to her, experiencing perfect happiness, laughing through the blood.

Henry uttered a single cry, as if a wasp had stung him. Then he was silent, passive; not touching her, not resisting. It was as if he'd found some very dark place inside himself, discovered in her bite the one thing he had always wanted . . .

It was the first exchange of genuine, unfettered passion that had ever passed between them. First and last.

Charlotte found it very easy to stop, and to slip lightly from his knee as if nothing had happened. Henry's head lolled forward. He took off his glasses, squeezed his eyes shut and pinched his forehead.

'I wish you joy of the dear little Methodist you wish to marry. She'll never do that to you. Or will she? Appearances can deceive. One day she may grow tired of making afternoon tea for Cambridge dons and develop a taste for their blood.'

Now he was staring at her as if he didn't know what had happened. He probably doesn't, Charlotte thought. His memory has already erased the unacceptable.

'What?' he murmured. 'I feel dizzy. Bit of a headache.'

'You'll be all right.' She crouched down beside him and put her hand on his leg; always she felt this easy affection for her victims. 'Henry, listen to me. Go and join the funeral feast, have some tea. When it's over, come back and I'll give you my answer.'

He revived, blinking at her. 'Answer?'

The solution was so obvious. It invaded her, with Henry's blood, like a kind of insanity. Amid the desolation of her father's death, the funeral, her family's sorrow and the twisting roots of their bitterness and unease in Charlotte's presence, it was a jewel, a cold and colourless moonstone, in its perfect setting. 'I'm going to set you free, dear.'

Charlotte waited until the guests were leaving; darkness was drawing in by then. Then she went out into the hall, joined in the goodbyes and shared the expressions of sympathy, for all the world as if she were still part of the family; the very least she could do for her father was to show his friends that his daughter had loved him. After they'd gone, she followed the others back into the drawing-room; Anne, David, Henry, Madeleine and Elizabeth, all in black. No one sat down.

Feeling very calm, Charlotte saw them as if through a lens. How distant they looked, like figures in a play. The ghastliness of what she planned to do infused her now like a cold madness. She felt as if she *were* mad; nothing else could have led her to contemplate and pursue this course.

Karl had said, be gentle with them. She tried to speak kindly, but her gentle tone could not shield them from the gleaming starkness of her words.

'I don't want to stand in the way of Henry's happiness,' she began. 'And he said he wanted to see me in a coffin. Well, so be it.'

'What on earth are you talking about?' said Anne.

'I'm thinking of Henry. A divorce would be scandalous and messy and it might sour things between him and his fiancée. But if I were dead, everything would be simple, wouldn't it?'

Henry stared at her, sweat beading on his flushed face. She thought, I shouldn't have fed on him. It's only confused him more. But it was so good!

'You can't just pretend to be dead,' said David. 'It's not that simple.'

'I'm not talking about pretending,' she said. 'I'm talking about a legitimate death certificate and a real burial. You must understand that I'm not really alive anyway. Not alive, not human.'

Henry sat down heavily on the sofa. David said hoarsely, 'For God's sake, Charli, what are you proposing?'

'The doctor pronounces me dead. You place me in a coffin and bury me. Henry's free to remarry. Well, why not?'

They looked stricken, as if this were some black joke. She

seemed to see their faces through gauze. She was travelling away from them, cutting the chains.

'Stop this,' David said.

Elizabeth said acidly, 'It sounds a perfectly good idea to me.' Madeleine's eyes were round with disbelief.

'A few conditions: have the funeral as quickly and quietly as possible. I'll pay for it, of course. And don't let the undertaker touch me. I wouldn't appreciate being embalmed.'

'How – how—' Henry stammered.

'Like this,' Charlotte said softly. She sat down beside him and composed herself, arms at her sides, head tipped back. She made her slow heartbeat stop completely. She remained like that, not breathing, not blinking, until they began to edge nervously towards her.

'Charlotte?' said Anne. She shook her arm hesitantly, then gripped her wrist. 'My God, there's no pulse! She's dead!' Anne shook her, but Charlotte was a glass-eyed rag doll in her hands. '*Charlotte!*'

Their horror was tangible. With a gasp, Madeleine backed away and ran out of the room.

Charlotte looked up at Henry's white stare, Anne's and David's consternation. Only Elizabeth's smooth, aristocratic face was blank. Then she stirred and sat up. They all started violently.

'Do you see?' she said. 'The doctor will be completely convinced I'm dead. Tell him I fell ill after the funeral, or something. When you bury me, I won't really stay in the coffin, of course. I'll vanish.'

David stood frowning, trying desperately to maintain his stiff upper lip. Eventually he said quietly, 'I can't cope with this,' and he turned and walked out after Madeleine.

Anne ran after him. 'David!'

'I refuse to have anything to do with this grotesque charade!' he called over his shoulder. Anne hesitated in the doorway, swore, then marched back to Charlotte. She clearly felt David had let her down.

'You can't mean to go through with this!'

'Why not?'

'It's too horrible! And the doctor will ask for an inquest on a young woman who dies for no reason!'

'Oh no, he won't. I'll see to that.'

'I think we should let her do it,' said Elizabeth. Her hard brown eyes met Charlotte's; enemies in truce, kindred spirits. 'For Henry's sake. I'll make all the arrangements, if the rest of you can't face it.'

Anne was shaking her head slightly, her face a mask of dismay. 'But you won't really be dead, will you?'

Charlotte spoke gently. 'No, but you can forget me then, or at least let go of me. You won't have to see me again; you can believe I am dead. Because actually I am. Un-dead.' She reached out to touch Anne's cheek. 'It's for the best.'

And Anne, for once, permitted the touch. Charlotte closed her eyes, feeling the madness rushing up around her, like a gale through a dark cathedral, like the earth walls of her father's grave. And she thought, I can't make them love me but at least they don't hate me. That will have to be enough.

CHAPTER EIGHTEEN

SWALLOWED IN
THE MIST

Alone in the library, Robyn dreamed. She seemed to be in the nursery again, with figures whispering around her. Everything had the understated malevolence of a nightmare; the light was flatly grey, the shadows frozen in heaps, while the seams of wall and floor, door and ceiling tilted at angles that filled her with terror. And in the greyness were two ghosts. One was Rasmila, the other a slender man as pale as Rasmila was dark.

They were whispering to each other with an urgency that seemed infinitely sinister, though their words made no sense.

'She is the one Lilith loves. If she comes here . . . jealousy . . . he will destroy her, he will break her wings . . . *he can do what Simon cannot.*'

Robyn was suspended in the fluid essence of the terror she'd felt when Rasmila rose out of the shadows.

She dreamed she was breaking the glass cases, tearing birds off their perches, snapping their reed-like bones and shredding their feathers, weeping bitterly because she didn't want to destroy their beauty, even if it was dead beauty—

'Robyn? Such groans!'

She started. Sebastian was there, holding her hand.

'Oh, I was having an awful dream,' she said, annoyed with herself.

'Don't dream in this house,' he said wrily. 'It might come true.'

'I'll bear that in mind.' She got up, shaking the nightmare off, wondering now if she had truly been asleep. In retrospect it seemed a waking dream, a bizarre train of thought into which she had drifted while waiting for Sebastian.

'Where have you been?' she demanded. 'I thought you told me to stay here because you had a surprise for me. That was about four hours ago!'

Sebastian only smiled enigmatically. 'Surprises like this can't be prepared in ten minutes. Come along.'

He led her upstairs to one of the main bedchambers. After the dream she didn't want to go up, but it was all right; solid and unfrightening.

Robyn remembered the room as being semi-derelict, nothing in it but a huge packing case under a sheet. Now she found the place transformed. There was a fire in the grate, which made the rose marble fireplace glow; even the ancient wallpaper took on a bloom of luxury in the light. Persian rugs had been placed over the floorboards.

The sight that stopped her breath, however, was a magnificent bed that had appeared from nowhere. A four-poster draped in lavish canopies, it looked pristine, too new to be part of its surroundings.

Robyn held the fabric between her fingers, marvelling at the embroidery. A cream background, hand-sewn with flowers and leaves in jewel colours and gilt thread. And swathes of dark blue Chinese silk, sewn with dragons, deer, horses and storks. Months, if not years of work.

'Do you approve?' Sebastian enquired.

'Wonderful . . . but where did it come from? It looks brand new, but the quality of workmanship could be from the eighteenth century.'

There was a look of great pleasure on his face. 'Did you see the packing case that was here? The bed was delivered to the house in 1735, a wedding present, but it was never used. So it is old but perfect. I never had a reason to assemble it, until now.'

'The colours are so bright!' she said. 'It's silly, but I imagined the furniture being as faded when it was new as it is now.'

'Well, it wasn't,' he said. She stared at him, struck for the first time that he remembered those times. That he could be so old, yet eternally young . . . his youth bought with stolen blood. 'It ought to be christened, don't you think?' Taking her hands, he pulled her on to the bed. 'Or whatever the infernal opposite of christening is.'

'Wait!' Robyn said, laughing. 'Fold the covers back first. It would be sacrilege to damage this beautiful embroidery.'

In the firmament of ecstasy, they allowed themselves for once to experience happiness. There was no calculation in their love-making, nothing held back. No selfishness. It was perhaps the first time they had loved each other without artifice.

Robyn was almost out of her mind with joy. She never wanted this to end; to stroke Sebastian's beautiful body and his dark hair, to have those seductive eyes endlessly on her; to have him all around her and inside her, flesh soldered to flesh. And more than that, to see that his passion was as desperate, as ravenous and blissful as hers. To have inspired such a fever in him . . .

She was grateful to Rasmila now. That experience had taught him, as nothing else could, that it was Robyn he really wanted.

Climaxing in lightning, in rains of fire, Robyn drew his head down to her shoulder. She wanted his mouth on her throat, wanted the pain. She would have given him anything. No virtue left to sacrifice, but she could give him this instead, the deeper sacrifice of her life-fluid.

Even the pain was blissful. When Sebastian lifted his head at last, he seemed overwhelmed that she'd given it so willingly. And for that look of wonder, she could forgive him anything.

'Is it over, then?' she whispered as they lay folded up together in tangled sheets. Now she felt a fatigue so heavy she thought she might never move again.

'What?'

'The war between us.'

'If you want it to be.'

'Where was it getting us?' she asked. 'Trying to ruin each other, trying to break each other's heart . . . what was the point?'

'To nourish our pride,' said Sebastian. He'd never looked more desirable than at that moment, his hair in disorder, his face coloured by her blood. 'It seems pointless now. Dry, dead, unimportant.'

'Shall we call a truce, then?'

'Only a truce, my lady?' he said. 'A peace treaty, at the very least.'

Sebastian stood watching Robyn as she slept. She was sleeping more and more as the days went by. Too pale. However careful he tried to be, each time they made love her languor deepened.

He was troubled. The emotions aroused by the mere sight of her face disturbed him. *Is it her I worship, or only her human life?*

There may be other women who are prettier, or younger, or sweeter, or more generous, he thought, *but none of them is Robyn. No,* he told himself, although he already knew it, *I need Robyn for herself. In all the faults that make her so like me, in all her magnificent warmth, she is unique. No one else will suffice. Ever.*

The knowledge made him feel agitated, dully terrified. *In loving her I've gone completely against my instincts. How has she done this? She's changed me, and in doing so she's destroyed what I was.*

She made me admit my feelings, but she has never said, 'I love you,' in return, and I have not the courage to make her.

So she has won. Yes, she can call for peace now she's won. All I can do in retaliation is to keep her here, and thus control her ... but for how long? Until she grows old? Will I still love an old woman, out of her mind because a vampire has kept her prisoner for years?

Almost in horror, he reached down and stroked her hair. Robyn pushed her head against his hand, smiling in her sleep.

No bad dreams now.

After Charlotte had left, Karl wished he could have gone with her. *She needed me,* he thought. *I have no fear of the Nevilles' wrath, and even less interest in their opinion of me. For Charlotte's sake, to show them that she deserted them, not for* a fiend who tricked and ruined her, but for someone who truly loves her – to show that we're not ashamed – I should have gone. And because of the respect I owe Dr Neville, and the affection I felt for them.

Yet here I am, putting Violette before Charlotte.

Sometimes he felt like telling Madame to go to hell. He never did, of course.

Charlotte telephoned with the news of her father's death. She would stay for the funeral, a few days. But when it was over, she called again to say she was staying a few days more.

'I can't talk about it over the telephone,' she said, sounding too calm, not herself. Karl was concerned, but she would tell him nothing. 'I won't call again. I'll explain as soon as I come home. A few days, that's all. Something I have to sort out with my family . . .'

Dr Neville's death saddened him. Karl had nothing but fond memories of his time in Cambridge and at Parkland Hall, until Kristian's wiles had caused him to betray himself. Neville had been a kindly man as well as a scientific genius; generous enough to welcome a foreigner, Karl, into his home. For which I thanked him by stealing his daughter. But he dwelled for a while on memories of the man; their long discussions of philosophy, in which Dr Neville had treated no theory as too outlandish. Even that of the Crystal Ring's existence.

Karl was in Violette's apartment, aware of every human in the house and of everyone who came and went. He could hear the dancers in the studio, the pianist starting and stopping, Violette's crisp voice giving instructions. And below them, seamstresses in the costume store, two set-designers in one of the offices, staff in the kitchen and a delivery boy at the back door. He even caught the quick warmth of cats, twining round the boy's legs for affection and treats.

All was as it should be . . .

Then Karl sensed shadows around him. Vampire presences, on the threshold between Ring and world. He looked up just as they coalesced before him.

Two angels, swathed in long hair; midnight and ice-white silk.

Karl stood up to greet them with sardonic courtesy. 'Rasmila, Fyodor; this is unexpected.'

'Is it?' said Rasmila. 'I think you knew we'd come back.' Her eyes were spheres of obsidian, lit by white comets and blue stars. Karl still found it difficult to look at her.

'Fyodor got his wish,' said Karl. 'I was removed from Simon's presence, to the relief of all. Has it helped your cause?'

Karl guessed, from the tightening of their faces, that they still hadn't found favour with Simon.

'You have no cause to speak to us sarcastically,' Fyodor said sharply. 'I can't look on you as an enemy, however hard I try. I asked Charlotte for help and she obliged; for that I am grateful.'

'It was Lilith who took us out of your way,' Karl pointed out.

'We are not Lilith's enemies, whatever you think,' said Rasmila. 'We want to help her.'

'Your use of euphemism is intriguing,' said Karl, 'but not that intriguing, so would you please explain why you're here?'

'Lilith – Violette has a particular interest in a human female, does she not? An American.'

Karl regarded them warily. How on earth could they have found out about Robyn? Only Charlotte and I knew, he thought . . . unless these creatures are omniscient, Simon's spies. Then he remembered the story Violette had related; that when she'd paid a brief visit to Robyn, Cesare had followed her. 'Where did you hear this?'

'Rumours,' said Fyodor.

'I couldn't possibly comment,' said Karl, 'on rumours.'

'You don't have to.' Rasmila came towards him; in a sari of indigo sewn with tiny mirrors, she seemed to float. 'There is someone on his way to see you. Someone very upset and desperate. When he has gone, we will come back and explain what we know – to Violette.'

The air opened and closed to receive them.

Karl could only think, grimly, that this was some plot of Simon's. Moments later, a human came running lightly up the stairs, then knocked and opened the door.

'Sir?' It was Violette's maid, Geli. 'There's a man here to see Frau Alexander. I told him she wasn't here, but he won't go away. Madame's working, I can't disturb her.'

Karl felt that Rasmila and Fyodor were not far away. Spying, without question. He must warn Violette.

'I'll see him, Geli,' he said, standing up. 'Who is it?'

'Josef Stern,' said the girl. 'He's downstairs.'

'Tell Madame anyway. If she's annoyed, tell her to shout at me, not at you.'

Karl found Josef in the small office at the front of the building. He was standing with his hat in his hands, his thick silver hair in disarray, his face lined with anxiety.

'Ah, Karl,' he said uneasily, 'forgive the intrusion. I gather Charlotte isn't here.'

'No, she isn't.' He shook Josef's hand; the greeting was fraught with unease.

'When is she expected back?'

'Not for several days. I couldn't say, exactly. Can I be of any help?'

Josef's eyebrows contracted with tension. 'I'm not sure. I really don't know what to do.'

'What is it?'

Josef hesitated, then apparently decided to trust Karl. He took a letter from his coat pocket and held it out. He seemed close to weeping; Karl wondered for a second if he'd heard about Charlotte's father and thought Charlotte did not know. But Josef said in a rush, 'It's my niece, Roberta. You met her in Boston. She's disappeared. I've just received this letter from her companion, Alice. I would have thought Alice had gone mad, if it wasn't for what I already know . . .' His voice sank on the last words.

It must take a good deal of courage, Karl thought, for him to stand in this room with me when he knows what I am.

The letter spoke of a vampire named Sebastian Pierse. The language was wild, verging on incomprehensible. Robyn had taken this vampire as her lover, shortly after the ballet had left Boston, and he had taken possession of her sanity and soul. He'd attacked Alice herself. She suspected him of murdering Robyn's other lover. Now Robyn had vanished, leaving a curt note, and Alice could only conclude that Sebastian had abducted her.

Karl absorbed all this, incredulous. *Sebastian. God help Robyn, if it's true.*

As Karl was reading the letter a second time, Violette came in, wearing her grey practice clothes.

'Herr Stern,' she said. 'What's wrong?'

Karl raised his eyebrows in enquiry; Josef nodded. Karl passed the letter to Violette.

Violette said nothing at first. But when she looked up, Karl saw her face transformed by silent, devastating fear.

'Do you know this Sebastian Pierse?' Josef asked.

'I met him once,' Karl said, 'a long time ago.'

Violette's lips parted but no sound came out. Karl had to prise the letter out of her hands.

'Who is he?' Josef cried. 'How could this have happened?'

'I have no idea,' Karl said.

'How was it possible for him to be in Boston at the same time as – as other vampires, without you knowing he was there? Or perhaps you did know, you just failed to warn us!'

'Did you warn Robyn about us?' Karl asked, and Josef subsided, looking grey. 'We did not know he was there. Vampires can usually sense each other from a distance, but a very few have no detectable aura. Sebastian, as I remember, was like that. Unless we physically saw him, he would be invisible to us.'

'And is he dangerous?'

No point in giving Josef false hope. 'Do you think I am evil?' Karl asked.

Josef's larynx rose and fell. 'Yes, I'm afraid I do.'

'You didn't trust me with your niece, but in fact I would not have laid a finger on her, out of respect for your feelings. Sebastian, unfortunately, has no such scruples. If Alice's letter is true, I cannot give you much cause for optimism.'

Josef looked as if his heart would fail. He said hoarsely, 'Can you help me find her?'

Karl groaned inwardly. Secretly he was mortified by the news and half-blamed himself – but he could not let those feelings rule him. 'I would if I could – but Robyn could be anywhere, and we have troubles of our own to deal with. I'm sorry.'

'Of course, I should have known better than to expect you to care,' Josef said bitterly. 'After all, she is only a human being. I thought Charlotte might have done, that's all—' Josef put his hand to his face, suddenly giving way to tears.

'No, you're mistaken,' Violette exclaimed with great intensity. 'I care. We'll help you find her.'

Josef's gaze caught on hers like a pike on a hook. He reddened and dropped his eyes. As if, Karl thought, he knows the nature of Violette's feelings for Robyn.

'We can make no promises,' Karl said quickly. 'I can only suggest that you write to Alice again and try to obtain some clearer information. But if we discover anything, we will let you know.'

Karl was gently but firmly bringing the meeting to an end. Looking drained, Josef retrieved the letter and made for the door. 'I would be grateful. I'm sorry to have troubled you.' He gave a crisp, Viennese bow. 'Madame, *mein Herr.*'

When he had gone, Violette began to pace round the room like a starved tigress. 'Another vampire with Robyn!' she breathed. 'I thought she was safe!' She turned on Karl, eyes blazing. 'I left her so that she would be safe! How could we possibly have missed this other vampire? How did he get to her? God, if only I'd let her come with us!'

'Violette, calm down.' Karl made no attempt to comfort her; he knew she wished Charlotte was there instead of him. 'I understand your feelings, but while we have the threat of Cesare over us, there is no chance of making a search for Robyn.'

'Do you think I don't know that? This is all I need! Who is this Sebastian?'

'I barely knew him. He came to Holdenstein once and made trouble with Kristian. Some of us thought he might side with us to depose Kristian but he would have none of it. He seemed to despise all vampires equally . . .' He thought sadly of Ilona, whom Sebastian had not despised, for a time. 'And I understand he was cruel with his victims. He liked to play before he killed them.'

'And now he's playing with Robyn.' She shuddered. Then her eyes opened wide and she cried, 'Wait, I've seen him! When I was in Robyn's room and I looked up and saw Cesare, and I fled to lead him away – another vampire followed us! I thought he was with Cesare, one of his followers, but he wasn't. He was on his own. Tallish, slim, very dark. Aloof, as if everything were beneath him and funny.'

'It could have been him,' said Karl.

'I never sensed him in Robyn's room – but what if he was there? Yes, her face . . . Someone was making her suffer. I saw it. She said, "Take away the pain." And I didn't. I failed her. Again.'

'Violette, come upstairs,' Karl said gently. 'Rasmila and Fyodor want to see you. I think it's about this.' Violette glared at him, but said nothing. 'But be careful,' Karl added. 'Anything they tell you is probably designed to trap you.'

'I'll be circumspect,' she said aridly.

They were waiting in Violette's living-room, like polarized twins; Fyodor white and silver and fragile, Rasmila a carving of rosewood and jet. She had once provoked a lethal tenderness in Karl, given him her blood only to use it against him. She still fascinated him, but she would not take him in again.

'I thought I'd seen the last of you,' Violette said, on a razor-edge. 'How dare you come in here unannounced? What do you want?'

'We want to help you,' said Rasmila.

'How?' Karl said. 'Why should she trust you?'

'Why should I trust any of you?' said the dancer. 'Karl is half on Cesare's side; he can't stand me, though he's too well-mannered to admit it. And you two have never brought me anything but misery.'

'That was in the past,' said Rasmila.

'Is it? We've had tales of woe from Simon and Fyodor. But you, Semangelof, are worse. I hate your affected passivity. You condone the lies with which women destroy themselves. You delivered me up to a man who almost raped me, and called it God's will!'

'But God's will is that—'

'Whose god?' Violette cried. 'The Catholics' god, or the Jews', or Kristian's, or that of the Hindus? They are all different beings, and I don't know which one you worship.'

'There is only one God,' Rasmila said, unmoved, 'as you should know. You must hear us. We don't hate you, we only hate what will become of the Crystal Ring if you do not give yourself up to God.'

'The Crystal Ring,' Violette said softly. She turned away and perched on the arm of a chair, her anger vanishing. 'Yes, that is my fault too.'

'Do you want to destroy vampire-kind?' asked Fyodor.

'Destroy my own children?' A thin, humourless smile curved her mouth.

'Mothers do,' said Rasmila.

'What justification have you for blaming everything on Violette?' said Karl. 'The disturbance in the Ring could be quite unconnected.'

'No,' said Violette. 'It is connected with me. I feel it.'

'But what is it?'

Rasmila's slim shoulders rose and fell. 'A mystery. I have tried to discern its nature but I cannot lift the veil. But it is death to us.'

'So, Cesare and the others are right to want me dead.' Violette's voice was low, sinister. 'Should I take my own life, to save Cesare the trouble?'

'No. Lilith cannot die. She has been here from the beginning.'

'Like the devil, I know, but what do you want me to do?'

Rasmila moved closer to Violette, with Fyodor hanging back behind her. Karl watched in apprehension. Violette could attack like lightning.

'Come with us to Simon. If we brought you in peace to him, he would accept us again,' said Rasmila, her voice a scented oil. 'If only we were together again, God would lift the veil between us. We want peace, not battle.'

'And Simon and Cesare would win, and Lilith would be in chains,' said Violette. Karl expected her to react contemptuously; instead she sounded bleak, as if she had already surrendered.

'For the good of others. Lilith may not want peace – but you do, Violette. In your heart.'

'And what shall I receive in return?'

'We shall tell you where to find Sebastian Pierse and your lover, Robyn.'

'I could find them on my own.'

'But not so swiftly. And if we warned him you were looking – never.'

Violette went ash-white. Karl, genuinely concerned for her, went to place his hand on her arm, but she shook him off. Head bent, she clasped her neck; the maiden Giselle in all her exquisite sorrow. 'I find your threats repellent – but I agree, all the same. If I find you've told me the truth, I'll do anything you want afterwards.'

Fyodor and Rasmila exchanged looks of joy, their relief a tangible radiance. Karl felt nothing but foreboding. 'You promise to come to Simon with us?'

'Yes, I promise.'

'Good. You will find them in Ireland. County Waterford, a great house called Blackwater Hall.'

Violette raised her head. Now she had the very dignified, resigned look of someone about to walk to the gallows. 'How is Robyn? No, don't tell me! I wouldn't believe anything you said.'

'We'll be watching for you,' said Fyodor. 'To see that you keep your part of the bargain.'

A rim of Crystal Ring light shone briefly round the two immortals, azure-bright against the dull lavenders of the room. They bowed, and disappeared.

'I must leave at once,' said Violette, leaping up. 'It will only take me a few minutes to change.'

'Violette, do you know what you've agreed to?'

She paused with her hand on the door of her dressing-room, blinking at Karl as if she'd almost forgotten he was there.

'No; do you? If I save Robyn's life, nothing else matters. And if I don't, I don't care anyway. They think I can make everything better by submitting Lilith's will to theirs – and who's to say they're wrong? Even you half-believe it. So don't lecture me about falling into traps!'

Not reacting, he asked, 'Would you like me to come with you?'

'No!' she flared. 'No, thank you. I would like you to watch my dancers, if you don't mind. But you don't have to. Why don't you leave? Go to Charlotte or go to hell, I don't care.'

He saw her fangs shining, indenting her lower lip. She seemed on the verge of fulfilling her threat to feed on him, transform him and destroy his soul. Karl turned cold, but he didn't move.

He said, 'Why do you drive everyone away who tries to help you?'

She seemed to master herself. 'I don't need help.'

'Or you think you don't deserve it.'

'*You* think I don't deserve it!' she flared. 'Duty to Charlotte, that's the only reason you're here!'

Karl was deeply weary of arguing with her. Hurt, she was impossible to console. He was inclined to take her at her word, and leave. 'Is duty such a foul concept to you, Madame? I have put my personal feelings aside and tried to act correctly, because I can see absolutely no point in doing otherwise.'

'I think,' she said slowly, 'that if your antipathy towards me hurt me one tiny bit, you wouldn't be able to dislike me so intensely. You're lucky, then, that I don't give a damn for your opinion, because it gives you free rein to hate me without feeling guilty.'

'I couldn't possibly compete with the loathing you feel for yourself,' said Karl.

The white fire sparked from her eyes, then died. 'Two good things have happened to me,' she said, beginning to turn away from him. 'I learned that Rachel is no longer my enemy, and my best dancer Ute came back. But I'd attacked them both. Some of my victims respond with love, like whipped dogs fawning round their master; some respond with terror and hatred. Of the two, it's the love I can't cope with. I feel such rage, Karl, and such fear. And the simple truth is that no one can help me. Not even you.'

'Well, I'm not leaving,' Karl said drily. 'Go to Robyn. I'll look after your dancers – out of love for art, if nothing else.'

The closer the time of the ceremony came, the more uneasy Pierre grew. He longed to leave. He wanted the bright lights of a city, theatre crowds, potential victims thronging around him, not a care in the world. But if he left, Violette would get him. He knew it.

I have been bad, he would think in ghastly self-mockery, and I deserve to be punished.

So instead of the life he wanted, he had Cesare the Boy Scout leader and his insufferably tedious henchmen, Simon and John; a castle full of sombre fanatics and wide-eyed gullible youths. And now there were yards of white and blood-red satin everywhere to be made into robes by the nimble-fingered Maria and her helpers. He felt he had landed in the wardrobe department of some insane theatrical company. And the nightmare was that he was trapped there.

'How can this transformation work?' he asked Cesare one day. He had actually sought Cesare out in his cell, so restless he felt. 'Three vampires to change one human; that was Kristian's way, the only way, so I was told. More vampires would be superfluous – but with fewer than three, it won't work.'

'But this will,' Cesare said, with the tranquil self-confidence that Pierre found so irritating. He sat behind his table, his hands folded. 'One vampire, one human. A necklace of power. Simon assures me that it was tried in ancient times and does work. Besides, it will not be an ordinary transformation. It will be a ceremony ordained by God.'

Cesare could go on like this for hours. Pierre groaned inwardly, thinking, I wish I'd never asked. When Ilona walked in at that point, he was pathetically grateful. She was the only source of entertainment in this wretched pile.

'You wanted to see me?' she said.

Cesare nodded, and beckoned her closer. 'I wanted to thank you for your efforts in recruiting our disciples. You have done well.'

'I brought the best I could find,' she said, with a light shrug. 'But if you don't mind me saying so, I don't see what use any of them will be against Violette. Any great lumbering mammal can be killed by a little snake.'

Cesare's manner turned glacial. Pierre loved the way she provoked him. 'You misunderstand. They are for the world *after* Violette. She will have been removed by then.'

'You're always so serious, Cesare,' she said. 'Don't you ever smile? Don't you ever think about anything but your great plans?'

Mon Dieu, she's on dangerous ground, Pierre thought. He watched in delight as she went round the table and sat on Cesare's lap. She ruffled the cropped hair, kissed his forehead, moved suggestively on his thighs. 'Why don't you relax?' she said. 'You can't always be this dull, surely.'

The leader froze. He looked revolted and furious. His hands came up to grip Ilona's arms, and he must have hurt her. She went white, and fear misted her eyes.

'We are not beasts,' he rasped. 'Humans may couple like grunting pigs; immortals do not. Blood is all we need. Carnality is a degrading sin and you, child, are no better than a whore.'

'How dare you!' Ilona exclaimed. 'How do you think I lured your beautiful young men here?'

At this, Cesare jerked her wrist to his mouth and bit into it. He ripped the flesh and fed brutally; Pierre watched in shocked amazement.

Cesare tore the wrist out of his mouth as if tearing flesh from a chicken leg. He leapt up, dumping her off his lap, then slapped her and flung her to the floor. Ilona glared up at him, her eyes spitting impotent fire.

'Get her out of my sight,' said Cesare.

Pierre helped Ilona up, and took her back to his own cell. He cradled her torn wrist as they went, licking it clean, watching the miraculous healing process. 'Well, that was one of your more spectacular efforts,' he said.

'Shut up!' Ilona barked. 'Don't speak to me!'

When they reached the cell, Simon was there, to Pierre's annoyance. Seeing him, she ran straight into his arms. Simon held her, then sat down with her on the edge of the pallet where Pierre liked to feed on his captive prey.

Matthew's head, which got about, watched from the lid of a chest. Most of the flesh was gone from it now, leaving an ash-caked skull.

'Cesare is inhuman,' she complained. 'Worse than inhuman! How dare he call me that after all I've done!'

'What did he call you?' Simon raised his gilded eyebrows at Pierre.

'I wouldn't dare to repeat it,' said Pierre.

'Oh, Ilona, you're not happy, are you?' Simon said chidingly. 'You thought helping Cesare was a game but it isn't. You can't just wrap him round your finger as you could with Kristian.'

'That's a joke,' she said. 'Kristian was completely sexless as well. I tried everything!'

'Cesare isn't Kristian. You cannot laugh at him and walk out when you feel like it.'

'Can't I?'

'I wouldn't advise it.'

'So who is in charge; you or Cesare?'

'Cesare, of course.' But he added under his breath, 'For now.'

'There's something wrong with men like that,' she said sullenly.

'Don't be angry.' Simon stroked her hair with his golden hands and kissed her face. 'Don't run away. We need you. We need you.'

Ilona let herself be consoled. Their kisses grew deeper. Pierre put his head in his hands. Couldn't bear to watch, too apathetic to leave.

If I'd known my coming here would spark Cesare's madness, he groaned inwardly, I'd have crawled back to Violette and begged her to finish the job.

★

Karl was aware of humans going about their business in the house, a few dancers lingering in the studio, their work over for the day; others in the changing room or in their rooms on the top floor. He could even pick out threads of conversation – the rehearsal pianist complaining to the ballet mistress that the piano was out of tune – and let them go again. In the kitchen, there was a bustle of activity as the cooks prepared the evening meal.

A faint noise penetrated through the murmur, growing more insistent as it came closer. Quick footsteps, someone crying.

Karl stood up. Geli rushed in without knocking, a heap of black and white fur in her arms. Seeing Karl, she stopped dead. 'Oh – isn't Madame here?' Tears were rolling down her face.

'She had to go out.'

The cat in Geli's arms hung limply, foam streaking its open mouth. 'I'm sorry, sir. It's just – I was taking some clean linen from the airing cupboard and I found Magdi—'

'Lie her on the sofa,' said Karl. Geli obeyed, but he knew the animal was dead before he touched it. 'It's too late to help her, I'm afraid. You had better take her to the caretaker and see if he will bury her.'

Geli broke into sobs again. 'Do you think she got some rat poison from outside? We've four cats, I'm worried about the others now.'

The word *poison* electrified Karl. 'When was she last fed?'

'I don't know. You'd have to ask in the kitchen, sir.'

He gathered the creature in his arms. 'Come along.' Geli followed, trusting Karl completely, as unsuspecting humans so often did.

Karl left the corpse outside, then entered the kitchen by the back door. The room was full of steam and cooking smells, which he found repellent. The staff – three cooks and four maids – turned to look at him, their faces red and shiny with the heat.

The other cats had been fed at five, one of the girls told him, but Magdi had not turned up with them. 'She had a habit of hanging around and miaowing for treats when the butcher came. I always give her a bit of sausage. She usually eats her tea as well. When she didn't turn up this evening, I thought I'd given her too much and spoiled her appetite.'

'What meat did the butcher bring today?' Karl asked.

'The usual,' said the head cook, a bony woman with grey plaits pinned round her head. '*Bockwurst*, *Bratwurst*, chicken and pork.'

'And are you cooking any of it tonight?' The cook nodded, her pink face slack with worry. A girl was placing portions of sausage and cabbage on to plates on a central table. Another was in the act of picking up two of the plates. 'Has anyone been served yet?'

'No, we're only just ready.'

'Don't serve yet. I think there is something wrong with this meat.'

The girl with the plates froze, hurriedly put them down as if they'd burned her. Karl went to the table and sliced open a *Bratwurst*. The thought of consuming this dead object was alien and vile; vampires forgot the pleasures of food at the instant of transformation. But he was capable of scientific objectivity. Under the aroma of juice and fat, he caught a false note. He touched the cut surface to his tongue; the cook yelped in protest, but he knew there was no danger of poisoning himself. A malign flavour; some metallic chemical. Presumably it would taste different to humans. Perhaps they would not have tasted it at all, but Karl knew it was poison.

'All this food must be thrown away,' he said matter-of-factly. 'Tell the dancers to go and eat in the town tonight. Madame Lenoir will reimburse them.'

The staff were in a state of consternation now. Karl knew his brisk manner was doing nothing to reassure them, but there was no time for niceties. 'Let me see the rest of the meat that was brought today.'

The head cook led him into the pantry, eager to help. He prodded chickens and slabs of meat, tasted the watery blood that oozed from the flesh. All the meat was contaminated.

'Was it brought by the usual butcher?'

'No, sir, a new boy. Never seen him before. Very handsome, fair-haired; could have been a dancer himself . . .'

How could I not have been aware of him? Karl wondered. But looking back, he knew. Tradesmen called at the house every day. Having no reason to suspect a butcher's boy of foul play, he had barely registered the visit. And if Geli had not brought the cat to me at that very minute . . .

'This must all be disposed of.'

'I don't understand,' said the cook.

'Someone wanted to make the dancers ill. I should fetch all the food yourself from the market for the time being.'

'But who would—'

'I believe I know,' Karl said, walking away.

He overtook the culprit near Ulm, half-way between Austria and the Rhineland. A young man on a motor cycle, riding along a snowy, tree-lined road in darkness. From the whispering shadow-world of Raqi'a, Karl saw him as a narrow yellowish-silver aura. From that, he knew he'd been right; it was as plain as a signature. The auras of all the young men at Schloss Holdenstein had been the same: pure, fierce, devoid of compassion.

Karl swooped. He snapped into the real world on the motor cyclist's pillion, appearing there as if from thin air, hands gripping the leather-clad shoulders in front of him.

The young man screamed, lost control of the machine and swerved off the road. Hitting the snow-banked verge, the motor cycle somersaulted. The man was flung face down into a ditch and Karl fell with him, loosing him only briefly before seizing him again.

The ditch was thick with ice and snow. A pine forest rose on their left, black and silent. Karl pulled off the man's helmet and goggles then pressed his face down in the crusted weeds, twisting one arm up behind his back. The man grunted with pain.

'Well, butcher,' said Karl, 'who sent you?'

'Sent me – to do what?' he rasped, defiant.

'To poison a houseful of innocent young men and women.'

No answer. Karl jerked the arm; the socket popped, the man shrieked. 'Was it Cesare?'

'Yes! Yes, Cesare sent me. Now will you for God's sake let me go?'

Karl turned him over and saw a handsome freckled face under straw-pale hair. It was the man on whom Cesare had so generously let him feed. He recognized Karl, but there was no stoic pride in his eyes this time. He was in fear of his life.

'I will, if you answer my questions. Are you hoping to become one of us?'

'Yes. Cesare promised!'

'Has he transformed anyone yet?'

'Not yet.' He grunted and struggled, but Karl held him down.

'If you do that, you'll get hurt,' he said mildly. 'How many of you does he plan to transform?'

'Thirty.'

Lieb Gott, Karl thought, thirty new vampires! 'When is he going to begin?'

'I can't tell you – he – *argh!*' This as Karl pressed a thumb into his throat. 'He is going to transform us all at once.'

'What? That is impossible.'

'Not for Cesare. He knows a way. I don't know how, *I don't know*, but he does. He does.'

And Karl believed him. 'When is he going to do it?'

'Soon. Very soon. Stop, stop! In two days' time. Midnight. Please, it's the truth!'

'Two days,' said Karl.

'And then I'll be like you. I'll be as strong as you, and I'll come after you and make you sorry for this!'

'That is not a very clever threat to make at this precise moment.'

'You can't defeat our leader! There'll be thirty of us to begin with, then sixty, then a hundred and twenty, then—'

'I can add up,' said Karl, feeling black pessimism descending on him. Not a beginning, but an end. 'When will he stop?'

'When he sees fit.'

'The idiot means to conquer the world – but then it would be a vampire world, not a human one. But I like the human world. I like to be a shadow in the darkness, not a daylight tyrant, an object of terror and loathing. Everyone will regret it, mortal or immortal.'

'He was right about you! You're weak. You're no use to the new order of things. Now I've answered your questions, so let me go!'

'After what you've done?' Karl said icily. 'I don't think so.'

'You promised, if I told you—'

'You should know better than to trust a vampire.'

The young man began to pull feverishly at the collar of his jacket. 'Take my blood,' he pleaded. 'You know how good it tastes. Take what you want, only let me—'

Karl looked at the tendons gleaming through the skin, the sheen of sweat, the pulse ticking madly, and felt only distaste. 'Your blood would be as polluted as the meat you delivered.'

'Please—'

Karl gripped the head at the chin and the crown. The man tried to resist, eyes bulging in terror, but he might as well have tried to shift a boulder from his chest. With a deft motion, Karl broke his neck.

If anyone from the castle comes looking for him, Karl thought, that is, if anyone cares enough even to miss him, they will take this as a warning – or a provocation.

'I have often felt pity for my victims,' he said aloud, standing over the corpse. 'But for you, none.'

Charlotte lay couched in satin like a rosy-lipped angel, but no one came to look at her. The coffin had stood in the drawing-room for three days; they were waiting now for the funeral cortège to come, the undertakers to screw down the coffin lid. Charlotte, hearing the subdued murmur of unhappy voices in another part of the house, drifted in a trance of quiet insanity.

The charade had passed off smoothly, as Charlotte had predicted. She had taken to bed in her old room; Anne had telephoned the doctor – not her own father, who would have had to be let in on the deceit and would have refused to help, but his younger partner – and asked him to come at once.

'Charlotte has been ill,' Anne told him, her voice fractured by her natural horror of lying. 'She collapsed with grief after her father's funeral and took to her bed. This morning we couldn't wake her. We didn't realize how ill she was or we would have called you earlier!'

The doctor examined Charlotte and found no sign of life. She wondered, as his hands probed her, if he found Anne's edginess suspicious. No, he would simply assume she was upset. 'The cause of death is not apparent,' he said. 'People do die of grief, but it could be anything. I'm afraid there may have to be an inquest—'

Charlotte's eyes, glass slivers under half-closed lids, caught and held his. *Sign the certificate, and leave.*

He wrote the cause of death as pneumonia, and departed hurriedly.

Anne was furious at having to tell these lies. 'My father will want to know why we didn't call him when you first fell ill, and I'll have to make up more stories. More lies! I wish you'd never started this!'

But Charlotte remained deadly calm. Anne was angry, Madeleine upset, while David had simply washed his hands of the matter, which aggrieved Anne more. Even Elizabeth was on edge. The house seemed shrouded in greyness, full of ghosts.

Charlotte hated the distress she was inflicting on them, but she couldn't stop. It was a form of madness. She had quietly lost her reason, the moment her father had died. Since then she had been fighting endlessly through thick ropes of cobweb in her mind.

Three days to the funeral. The coffin lay empty, its lid in place so that the servants did not suspect. Charlotte vanished, haunting Cambridge for victims. One night she went out to the fens; the night was chill, flatly colourless. Dropping her unconscious victim, licking the blood from her lips, she thought, I rose from a coffin tonight and I shall return to it, in the best tradition.

She shook with laughter. She was close to screaming.

Sometimes, at night when the others had gone to bed, she came back and sat in the drawing-room, staring at the coffin.

Mine, she thought. I'll never need it. If I ever die, I'll be left to rot in some forest or I'll vanish into the *Weisskalt*. No one but a vampire can know what it's like to lie in their own coffin; what it is, actually to be buried.

Once, Madeleine crept in and sat with her, as if they were holding a wake. In a way, they were; for their father, for Charlotte's lost humanity. Charlotte put her arms round Madeleine's thin shoulders and consoled her. 'It's only for Henry,' Charlotte said. 'Only for legal reasons.'

'Then why is everyone so upset?'

'They're frightened. They don't understand what I am. But you mustn't be frightened, Maddy; please don't let it give you nightmares.'

'I had enough nightmares about Karl,' Madeleine whispered. 'I'm over all that now. But they won't actually bury you, will they?'

'Of course not. David will weight the coffin with a rug or something and they'll bury that. It won't be real.'

Madeleine seemed content with that. She let Charlotte stroke her hair, while Charlotte breathed in the lovely fragrances of her shampoo and soap and perfume; forced herself to ignore the pulsing of her blood. At least she could reassure Maddy. It was too late for the others.

When Maddy left, there was silence. The clocks had wound down, now her father was no longer there to wind them.

But what would it be like, she wondered again and again, actually to be buried?

And she knew she was going to go through with it. To punish herself for the pain she'd caused her family. To atone, a very little, for Fleur's death.

She heard cars outside. It would be a very modest, un-announced affair, as befitted a fake funeral. No flowers.

Under the shroud she was wearing a dress of coffee-coloured georgette, so she could discard the shroud afterwards. They had wanted to know how she would escape. Anne had suggested that they fasten the coffin lid down with a rug inside, before the undertakers arrived. The idea of Charlotte being shut in the coffin seemed to horrify her family more than anything. But she said, 'No, I want them to see me, I want them to fasten me in. So there's no doubt in anyone's mind. We'll sew lead weights into the corners. As soon as the lid's fastened, I'll escape. I can walk through walls, I can vanish. Nothing can go wrong.'

But now the men in black were here, sliding the lid into place, turning the screws, she experienced a wild, phobic panic. Her heart, which she had stilled, began to beat madly. She nearly gave herself away; almost screamed out, 'No, don't shut me in!' Almost felled them all with heart failure.

She mastered herself. She lay like stone. Petrified.

'She hardly weighs a thing,' said someone, as her wooden cocoon swayed into the air. 'Shame, when they go so young.'

A short car journey. She was lifted and carried again, set in place. She heard the service, but sensed no one in the church beyond the minister and her immediate family: Elizabeth, David, Anne, Madeleine. No one cried. It was a drear and depressing sham, like her supposed marriage to Henry.

In the cemetery now. She was being lowered in short, jerky stages; it was like falling backwards, out of control. The priest's voice was receding. Eyes closed, she was aware of the lid barely clearing her forehead, the wooden walls confining her. She pressed her hands to them on either side as if to push them apart, to brake the downward motion.

The air turned clay-cold. Scents of soil and decay wormed their way in. When the coffin came to rest there was a terrible stillness; opening her eyes, she saw only the dim grain of wood above her nose, and thought, what if I can't enter the Crystal Ring? Faint panic. I should try, I should go now.

When the first clod of earth hit the coffin, she almost jumped out of her skin. Her mind stretched out instinctively to feel Raqi'a, touched only a blunt nothingness.

It's not there, I can't reach it, I can't escape!

Her heart, which she had halted again by the force of her will, now exploded into a wild rhythm. She pushed frantically at the sides. A vision imprinted itself on her mind as if the lid were made of glass; black walls of soil, an oblong of daylight high above, the figures in black looking down. Then one of them leaning out over her and screaming, *'You can't bury her! She's not dead! How is she going to get out?'*

Blinding insanity overcame all of them and they giggled like fiends from hell, inflicting this torture on her purely for its own sake—

No, your own mind will drive you mad. Hold still. Wait, wait until they've all gone.

No one had cried out. Nothing above but the very softest murmur of voices. Anne whispering, 'She can't still be in there, can she? She can't still be in there.'

Somehow she forced the black panic to subside, willed herself to relax. *I must see it through. To prove that I can. My punishment.*

Madness. And I had to pull my family into this madness with me, because I love them and, being a vampire, my love can only suck them dry and drive them insane.

At last she sensed the massive weight of earth pressing down above her. The supposed mourners had gone. In time, the gravediggers finished their task and they, too, left. She imagined twilight gathering between the gravestones, dew silvering the grass. And now she almost dared not try to escape, in case she really couldn't.

She relaxed, concentrated. She felt the wooden prison dissolve, felt the soil clawing at her like quicksand. She moved through it with frightening slowness, floundering through its sticky embrace, breaking free at last into the mauve, dully glittering landscape of Raqi'a's lowest circle. The gravestones and winter trees were warped ghosts of themselves.

Suddenly aware of how very, very cold she felt, she wrapped her arms around herself. A shock, to see her own form transmuted by the Ring; arms snake-slender, the shroud a mere webbing of black strands. As if she'd been so far out of her mind that she'd forgotten it would happen.

She began to walk, although she was shivering so hard that she could hardly move. She saw two human auras, one large, one small; a mother and child, placing flowers on someone's grave. As she passed, as clear as anything she heard the child's voice say, 'Mummy, that lady!'

And the mother replied, 'There's no one there, dear.'

Charlotte looked up into the firmament. She saw dark shapes moving across darkness.

All the light seemed to have bled from the skyscape. No more the heart-lifting sapphire of the void, or the dappled bronze hills rising up in magnificent layers until they became towering ships of the air. All was stormy. Worse than unwelcoming. Malevolent.

The Crystal Ring doesn't want me, she thought. She felt a rush of terror, but it was a deformed emotion, only fuelling her madness.

She was wholly unhinged now. Possessed. Something had made her act out this grisly charade of death, some black tendril of the Ring crawling into her mind and loosening the bonds of reason. Forcing herself through to the macabre end, forcing her family through it, had achieved nothing good. It had been an act of purest evil. It had only sealed her insanity.

And she'd left them without affection or reassurances. Cruel, but she couldn't help it. Something of Lilith in her.

She threw off the shroud, and watched it billow away as if it had an inimical life of its own.

She began to run, her teeth chattering. I can't go home. I'm not Charlotte any more. I can't take this gibbering shell back to Karl.

She was rising, caught on clouds and currents. She couldn't think any more. All her thoughts were streaming out of her. She was a ragged skeleton. The only way to keep the black terror at bay was to flee from it as hard as she could, to go on running, flying, running; an ice-thread lost between infinite walls of cloud.

CHAPTER NINETEEN

DEATH AND THE MAIDEN

One morning, in the winter light of dawn, Robyn realized that she was dying.

She was alone in bed, Sebastian out bringing death or nightmares to some victim in the dark. For the past two days, Robyn had been too ill to get up.

They had been making love far too often over the past weeks. She knew that Sebastian tried to take as little blood as possible – how much was that, she wondered, half a pint, a few ounces? – but even those small losses were too much for her body to support. Repeated every other night – every night, sometimes – how could her overdrawn system possibly keep up?

They'd both known, but they'd given in to their insatiable obsession anyway, pretending it couldn't happen.

She was cold. Get up and stoke the fire, she told herself. She tried to sit up but fell back, dizzy. Her head ached so severely that she almost wept with it.

She lay shivering. After a time the spasm passed and she lay still, impassive, eyes half-open. The bed canopy, the fireplace and the walls hung dimly across her vision, seeming to blur and shimmer.

She was losing her eyesight, but it didn't seem to matter.

There were ghosts in the wallpaper. They whispered to her. They peeled themselves off the wall and danced around the room.

Sebastian had not touched her since her condition had gone from weakness to actual illness. He was being solicitous but he seemed almost frightened by what was happening to her. She was too far gone to be touched by his concern. He'd sat with her constantly, except for those times when he had to go out and feed; he'd brought her endless supplies of tea, soup and food to tempt her failing appetite.

'We must build up your strength,' he would say, incongruously, like a doctor. 'Rest and eat, and you'll soon be better.'

They both wanted to believe it.

It was only this morning, without feeling any particular emotion, that Robyn realized it was too late. She hadn't been eating; she couldn't face more than a few sips of tea. Anaemia and starvation compounded each other. She had a cough, too, an infection she could not shake off.

Perhaps a blood transfusion would have saved her, but even that seemed pointless. It would only delay the inevitable.

The ghosts wove and fluttered in the walls. Robyn lay on her side, staring into the malevolent shadows, her teeth chattering. This room wished her ill, but there was nothing she could do. Only lie here in quiet despair. Sinking down into the cobweb dark.

For a while, she thought she was in her house in Boston. The bright cosiness of her own bedroom, Alice and Mary to attend to her, admirers always at the door with gifts. Showered with love, she'd given back contempt and thought it fair . . . but her needs now were as simple as a child's. To be home, Alice holding her hand.

Then she came out of the hallucination, and saw where she was. This dark, empty, freezing, Godforsaken house.

Drifting in fever-dreams, Robyn had no concept of time. At some stage she became aware of a figure in a black garment standing beside the bed.

Fear crystallized her mind to a higher state of awareness. This wasn't the fear of dying, which she'd overcome without effort, but the abstract terror of a nightmare, in which the most innocent object becomes imbued with malice.

'Oh, Robyn,' a voice murmured. The figure fell down on its knees beside her. A slight shape under a veil of black hair.

Robyn was convinced that it was Rasmila, come to impart some dreadful revelation. *You'll never see him again, I've taken him away from you.*

'Sebastian!' she cried, very faint, her voice almost gone.

'How can you call on him for help,' said the voice, 'when he's the one who brought you to this? Oh God, Robyn, I could—'

The stranger stood up and moved away. She seemed to be crying. She lit a candle on the bedside table, and as the light flared, hurting Robyn's eyes, she saw that it was Violette. The dancer looked far from gentle.

'Why are you doing this?' Violette's voice was a serpent hiss. Rage turned her face bloodless, an opal with white fires burning inside.

'What?' Robyn tried painfully to lift herself on to her elbows.

'Embracing death, like the ultimate lover! Why, why have you let him do this to you?'

A surge of adrenalin came to Robyn's aid. She sat up, head spinning. 'Because I love him.'

'Don't make me sick. Even I would never have used you like this! Love, what love has he shown you?'

'You have no right—'

Violette's hands flew down and pinioned her. 'It's not because you love him, it's because you hate yourself. Your obsession is to punish yourself.' The dancer's face was livid, terrifying in its beauty. 'Don't fight me, Robyn. I can see right through you. You think you're punishing men but really you are only hurting yourself, because in your heart you still believe everything your father and husband told you. You believe you are worthless and evil!'

Robyn was shaking uncontrollably, fighting to get enough air. Suddenly she felt very much alive, and very frightened.

'I'll cure you of this "love"!' Violette snapped. She opened her mouth. Her canines, fully extended, were thin and wet and sharp.

'Don't!' Robyn cried. All she could think about was how Sebastian would feel, when he came home and found her dead.

'Why not?'

'I can't die without seeing him one last time.'

With a moan of anger, Violette attacked.

She flung back the bedcovers and leapt on to Robyn, welding

herself against her from breasts to ankles. Violette's body in the soft black dress felt divine, almost weightless, and it also felt like a leech, sucking out Robyn's life from every pore.

The dancer's breath was hot, scentless. A veil of black hair brushed Robyn's face and its perfume was exquisite: flowers, rosin dust. She knew she would never forget that scent—

Then came the pain.

It was savage, like thick needles driving through her neck, exploding redly into her skull. She'd thought she was used to it, but this wasn't Sebastian's gentle bite, this was a Lamia in the throes of demonic rapture.

Robyn couldn't breathe. The pain sang coldly on, but the slender body against hers was warm, vibrant.

Robyn clawed at Violette's arms. She felt herself falling backwards. Falling, falling. She clung to Violette for safety, couldn't help it.

They fell together, locked, sobbing.

Light erupted between them. Searing diamond light.

As it faded, leaving Robyn in a different universe, she saw an overblown vision in crimson and black: a ghost of herself, drawn in rippling ruby light, being born from Violette's mouth.

The ghost-Robyn dropped softly to the ground, complete, but still attached by a red string that went from its throat to the dancer's lips; a grotesque umbilical cord. Violette stood facing it, her hands on its shoulders. Complete blackness surrounded them.

Violette spat out the end of the cord. Then she slid her hands over the ghost-Robyn's collarbones and, with a quick, pitiless action, snapped its neck.

Robyn felt something break and fall inside her, as if some vital organ had collapsed. Horrible, but painless.

With its head hanging at an angle, the rubescent ghost-figure seemed to collapse on itself and dissipate. Nothing left on the blackness but a great splash of blood.

'It's kinder that way,' said Violette, as if she'd wrung the neck of a bird.

And they were back on the bed, limply entangled, exhausted.

It was over. Robyn found herself staring up at the canopy, while Violette lay across her, trembling as if she'd lost her strength. 'Robyn, Robyn . . .'

'Get off me,' said Robyn. She felt unspeakably weird, as if made of hollow glass. Everything around her was shifting into unknown new shapes with the rumbling of an earth tremor . . . then she realized that it was the rumbling of her own labouring heart she could hear. She was being smothered. 'Get off!'

Violette obeyed, her hair hanging over her face. As she swept it back, Robyn saw that her expression had changed. It was sombre now, devoid of rage. Tender. Robyn, breathless and shaken, didn't know what to think or feel. The dancer's bite had changed everything, but she couldn't grasp how, or why.

'Forgive me.' Violette touched Robyn's cheekbone. 'I knew I would do this when the time was right. I almost left it too late. Only I didn't know it would be so . . . No, don't say anything!' Robyn had parted her lips to speak. 'Rest. Don't say anything until you understand.'

Violette poured water from a jug on the table, and gave Robyn the glass. Robyn drank, holding the glass tight to steady her hands. The thunder of her pulse receded. The trickle of cold water down her throat seemed to tie her back to reality. She felt . . .

'When did you last eat?' Violette asked, sitting on the edge of the bed.

The question startled her. 'Er . . . yesterday, I think. I haven't felt like eating.'

'And how do you feel now?'

Robyn shut her eyes, taking deep, tentative breaths. Her heart was beating strongly again. Her headache had gone. There was strength in her limbs. Most amazing of all, she felt clear-headed. Sebastian's feasts had always left her languid, on the edge of hallucination, but Violette's attack had scoured her like a clean, icy wind. She felt almost her normal self; the last stand of her spirit before death?

'Confused,' Robyn said shakily.

'You weren't made to be a martyr,' said Violette. She took

the glass away and placed an apple in Robyn's hand. Sebastian had left the basket of fruit for her. 'What is wrong with you, that you won't look after yourself?'

Robyn ate the apple, finding herself ravenous for its sweet juice. Violette's lovely eyes rested on her. *Is she hypnotizing me? As if she needs to.*

'What have you done to me?' Robyn asked, her voice low.

'That, you will have to find out for yourself,' Violette said gravely. 'You'll know in time.'

'How did you find me?'

'You can't hide from me.' It seemed quite natural to Robyn that Violette was clairvoyant. 'Your uncle is very worried about you.'

At that, a wave of devastation went through Robyn, shaking her almost physically out of her reverie. 'Oh, Lord. I never thought – I should have written. My God, if I died and Josef never knew why . . .'

And she began to realize what Violette had done to her.

'You are not going to die,' said the dancer. 'I won't allow it. You will eat and you will live. But ask yourself, what has Sebastian done to *you*? He's made you a victim. You were strong before you met him, weren't you? You controlled your own life. Now he controls you. This is what love brings you to!'

Robyn's mouth fell open. Her breath quickened. Yes. Yes. She was beginning to see the self-destructive insanity of her own behaviour as if looking on from outside. 'How do you know this?' she said savagely. 'I told you too much, that night in Boston!'

'It made no difference. I only had to look at you to know everything about you.'

Robyn resented Violette for turning her forcibly around and making her face what she had been doing to herself . . . Yet it came to her that her resentment proved she was capable of clear thought. That she was beginning to regain self-control, even a touch of tranquillity. To feel that her soul was stretched naked before Violette was not so much unsettling as eerily soothing. 'What about Sebastian? How much do you know about him?'

'I've never met him, but I know him through you. He cannot face the strength of his own feelings, so he walls them away. That's why he brought you here. To wall you away.'

'Oh God,' said Robyn, putting her head in her hands.

'Well?'

'Yes. Yes, I suppose that's exactly what he was doing.' Only, she thought, I was too infatuated to admit it.

She no longer feared Violette. She felt easy with her now, as if they'd been friends for a lifetime. Yet she kept seeing the vision of Violette strangling her, snapping her neck, casting her into darkness. 'You have got to tell me what you've done to me,' said Robyn, her voice raw. 'Help me understand.'

As Violette's dazzling gaze met hers, Robyn saw her as a divided entity: half goddess, half angry, passionate human. She spoke softly. 'I've changed you. I hope I have strangled the sickness in your soul so that the rest of you, the adult woman, can live. I am Lilith, the destroyer of children; destroyer of infantile needs and obsessions, if you like.'

'Are you calling my love for Sebastian – infantile?' Robyn demanded.

'No. But your need to hurt others before they hurt you, and your willingness to sacrifice your life to the first real love you've found, rather than lose him – that was a sickness.'

Robyn looked down at her own hands, lying on the beautiful embroidered silk. Now she knew how Violette – Lilith – had transformed her. She still loved Sebastian but she was no longer mad enough to die for that love. And the knowledge didn't hurt. She felt calm and self-possessed: she wanted to live out her natural life, that was all. And towards Violette, now, she felt simple tenderness. 'If I was sick, am I cured? You must be an angel.'

Violette's expressive face became bleak. 'I hate Sebastian because you loved him instead of me. That's almost human, isn't it?'

'I offered to come with you!' Robyn cried. 'If you'd let me, I would never have seen him again!'

The regret in Violette's face moved Robyn nearly to tears, but all she said was, 'If only.' She stroked Robyn's face; her fingers were achingly delicate. 'I wonder if he was sent to you by one of my enemies, to seduce you away from me?'

'Enemies? Who could hate you?'

'Almost anyone. Lilith is an evil demon, didn't you know?'

'And a paranoid one, by the sound of it,' said Robyn. Violette looked startled. 'I met Sebastian the same night I met you, at that party; how could anyone else have known? It was a coincidence, Violette. These crazy things happen.'

Violette looked down. 'I suppose you're right. I like the way you say my name. Say it again.'

'Violette. Lilith.'

The dancer breathed out softly. 'And I'm grateful to you.'

'Why?'

'For showing me that I am capable of love, when I believed I wasn't. And for proving the absolute hopelessness of it.'

'Hopeless . . . because you would do to me what Sebastian's done?'

'And because you don't share my feelings. Either way, I can't win.'

The dancer seemed close to tears. Robyn was at a loss; she had no idea what she would do if the dancer wept. 'We can be friends,' she said lamely.

'But friendship is not what I want.'

'I'm confused,' Robyn whispered. 'You assume I prefer men, but I felt nothing for men until I met Sebastian. And I felt nothing for women until I met you.'

Then she sat forward and embraced Violette. She couldn't help herself. It was the only thing to do. The dancer was so slender that she was hardly there at all, and yet she was warm and divinely firm to touch; so lovely that no one, male or female, could have resisted her. 'Lilith,' she said into the black hair in a kind of ecstasy. 'How could anyone not love you? We were lovers when you took my blood. We are lovers.'

For a few minutes, Violette held her so hard that Robyn thought her spine would break. But it was the dancer who ended the embrace. She kissed Robyn full on the lips. Electric warmth. A taste of blood and clear fluids like the sweetest nectar . . . then she drew away. 'You are so gentle, so kind, Robyn.

But to lead me into these fond delusions is cruel. Don't pity me.' Her face was composed, a formidable will-power shining behind it.

'Pity you?' Robyn gasped, astonished. 'That would be like pitying a goddess.'

'But you pity the devil a little, don't you?' Violette smiled thinly, disentangling Robyn's hair, combing it with her fingers. 'And talking of your lover, what would he say if he came back and found me sitting here – or lying beside you?'

The thought froze her. Her feelings towards Sebastian had changed but they hadn't died. 'He would want to kill you.'

'He'd have to join the queue,' Violette said tartly. 'It's rather more likely that I'd kill him.'

Robyn was horrified. 'Oh, you must leave! He could be back at any minute.'

'Do you still want to protect him, even after I've shown you the truth?'

'Of course!' she said fiercely. 'Don't you get it? I love both of you. I couldn't bear to see you fighting over me. You must go, please, Violette—'

'I'd like to break his neck,' Violette said in a chilling tone, Lilith's ruthlessness burning in her eyes.

'He could have killed me months ago, but he didn't, he spared me because he loved me. He won't hurt me. I – I've changed him, too, more than you've changed me.'

The hard light dimmed. 'Well, there is something of me in you,' Violette murmured. And then she blinked as if confused and distracted. 'In all my daughters, I suppose . . . No, I'll leave him alone – but only for your sake.'

Robyn wilted in relief. 'And my blood is in you. It's a bond, isn't it? So you'll remember that I love you, even when I'm not there. But you really must leave.'

'Yes, Robyn – but you must come with me.'

'I can't.' She added under her breath, 'Not yet.'

'You must!' Passion broke, incandescent, through the mask. 'I have not come all this way just to leave you at his mercy again!'

Robyn sat up straight, angered. 'What is this? You complain

that I'm too much in Sebastian's power — then *you* start telling me what to do! I'm not one of your pupils.'

'I want you out of danger, that's all!'

'I'm not *in* danger! Try to understand. I need to see Sebastian just once more. To say goodbye. I cannot simply walk out on him without explaining.'

They argued for several minutes: Violette was obdurate. She didn't want to understand. Eventually Robyn said lightly, 'This is our first quarrel. First of many?'

The dancer sighed, seeming to relent. 'I'm sorry. I have no right to bully you. I'm not happy about it — but if you must do this, I trust your judgement. I'd wait for you but I can't, I have to go home.'

'I must face him alone,' said Robyn. 'If I act as if I'm scared of him, I'll be treating him like a monster. I don't want to remember him as a vampire. I want to remember him as a man, my lover.'

'Enough,' said Violette. 'I understand.'

She kissed Robyn again. Overcome, Robyn could hardly bear to let her go. She grasped Violette's hand and said, 'You live in Salzburg, don't you? I'll come to you, as soon as I've left here—'

'Don't. I might not be there. I made a promise that I can't break.'

Lilith dissolved into the shadows as she spoke; her hand crumbled to dust and stars in Robyn's palm.

When Sebastian returned, Robyn was in the library with her stockinged feet on the hearth, a cup of cocoa resting on her lap. Seeing her, he rushed to her side with an unadorned delight that almost broke her heart. She was clear about what she wanted, but she was still afraid of his reaction. She'd been worried that he might suspect a change in her immediately, but he seemed oblivious; perhaps he had stopped looking at her too closely, in case he saw imminent death in her eyes.

'You're up, you're dressed,' he said, covering her face and hands with kisses. 'Are you really feeling better, beloved child?'

'Yes, much better.'

'And have you eaten anything?'

'An obscene amount,' she said. 'Fruit, porridge, eggs and bacon.'

'But this is wonderful.' He sat beside her on the *chaise-longue*. 'And there is colour in your cheeks again. If only I had a god to thank I'd be on my knees! I was so afraid that—' He stopped abruptly.

'You thought I was dying,' she said softly. 'I was. But this morning, I woke up and decided to live.' His hazel-green eyes were rapturous; she'd never seen such love there before. But she felt tranquil and distant, as she had from the prospect of death. And she saw his eyes cooling suddenly, as if he suspected a change in her. She said, 'You love me, don't you?'

'I don't know what more I can do to prove it.'

'You could prove it . . . by letting me go.'

He frowned. 'What do you mean, letting you go?'

She shook her head. Her throat began to ache. 'You're killing me, dearest. I'm not such a fool as to die for you. I love my life too much to make that sacrifice. I want to live, for myself and for you, so that you don't end up hating yourself for taking my life.'

He said nothing for several seconds. When he spoke, his voice was cold. 'So, you want to leave me?'

'I must.'

Another silence. He looked at her strangely, then lifted her chin and rested his gaze on her throat. 'You've changed,' he said. 'Why?'

'I've come to my senses, that's all.'

'No . . . someone has influenced you.' He was beginning to frighten her. 'Someone came while I wasn't here. Was it Rasmila?'

'No, no one—'

'Don't lie to me! These marks on your neck, these tiny silver-pink flowers that even a doctor would overlook, they were not made by me. Who was it?'

He was hurting her. She jerked out of his grip. 'All right! It was Violette. Don't be angry with her; she probably saved

487

my life. And she didn't influence me, she just made me see sense.'

'Made you cease to love me?' His tone was murderous. His eyes lanced straight through her.

'Sebastian!' She clasped his arm. 'Don't blame her! I don't know what I've done to inspire such love in you or in her, but she can't help that. I was dying until she came. That's where it will end if we don't stop!'

His rage diminished to brooding quietness. He stood up and paced about. 'Let us leave Violette aside. Are you telling me that you refuse to see me any more?'

'No, no.' Her confidence was returning. She felt very sure of herself. 'I'll go back to Boston. If there's still any trouble about Harold, I'll sort it out. I should never have left. I'll live in my house as before, and you can still visit me, oh, maybe two or three times a year—'

'It's not enough,' he said grimly.

'Why isn't it? It's all my body can take! Why does everything have to be so extreme with you, why is it all or nothing? If you *truly* cared—'

'You've made up your mind, obviously.'

'We could still be lovers. Not so often, that's all.' But he fell quiet, and she could find nothing else to say. She was no longer sure what she felt for him. One thing was certain; her obsessive craving for him was dead, strangled by Lilith. All that had made her vulnerable and dependent – dead.

Yet she didn't want to hurt him – assuming such a calculating, monstrous creature could be hurt. She thought, if I found he'd faked all the tenderness I thought was sincere – if he turned round now and told me he'd faked it – I couldn't blame him, but it would be unbearable. *Does* he care or not? Is he still playing games?

Robyn was calm, but she wasn't happy. I was ready to die for him; now I am not. That's all. But where the animating passion had dwelt there was a hollow sphere inside her. Has Lilith done a miraculous thing to me – or a terrible one?

When Sebastian finally spoke again, he sounded different. He was very controlled, almost impersonal. She'd never seen him like this before. His formality turned her cold. 'When do you want to leave?'

'I should go as soon as possible. Tomorrow, I suppose.'

'Do you want me to come with you?'

She thought of her intention to visit Salzburg before returning to America, but in truth she knew it was only a dream. *I might not be there,* Violette had said; and Robyn had a powerful, heart-rending feeling that she would never see Violette again.

I'm on my own now. That's the whole point.

Somehow managing to control her voice, she said, 'It's up to you. I told you, you're welcome in Boston, but if you don't want to come with me now, I'll understand.'

'Well.' He sat beside her and took her hand. He changed again, becoming gently forgiving, but she didn't trust the soft look in his eyes. His concealment of his wounded pride was too perfect. 'There is no real hurry for you to go, now, is there? Tomorrow, or the day after. Stay a little longer with me, beautiful child, for old times' sake.'

When Violette returned, and Karl told her about the would-be poisoner, he expected her to react with rage. Instead she became unnervingly quiet and composed. She sat down at a table on which a thick, white candle burned; the curtains of lavender and silver watered silk were drawn against darkness behind her. In the shimmering glow, her face was a delicate white shell, her eyes lakes of violet glass overflowing with light.

And Fyodor and Rasmila stood near by in the shadows, listening. They had come for Violette. Karl sensed their hunger; in the dark tension of the moment he felt that they were all gathered on the edge of an abyss.

'This is the end,' said Violette, staring at the candle. 'How could Cesare do this, when I've virtually surrendered to him? I had one small condition for Rasmila and Fyodor; let me finish *Witch and Maiden,* then I'll come with you. But Cesare can't wait, he must have me there *now.*'

'There is no time for you to finish the ballet,' Rasmila said softly. 'But we regret the attack. We had no hand in it.'

Karl was sitting opposite Violette, but she didn't look at him. He said, 'I doubt that Cesare knows anything about your agreement with Rasmila.'

Her dark eyebrows jerked up. 'No?'

'And Simon probably doesn't know, either. I think it was their own decision to approach you. They daredn't make promises they might not fulfil; rather, they mean to present you to Simon as a *fait accompli*. Lilith in chains. And that, they think, will make him fall on their necks in gratitude. Meanwhile, Simon and Cesare are unaware of the plan, and Cesare tries again to force you to close the company.' Karl met Fyodor's eyes. 'Is it so?'

Their expressions were rigid. They said nothing.

Violette stood up and faced them. 'Come here,' she said softly, and they came to her as if under a spell. 'Now tell me the truth!'

She was an ice-flame, a sorceress. Rasmila and Fyodor, angels or not, were in thrall to Lilith, Karl saw. He almost pitied them, struggling to master an elemental of which they were mortally afraid.

'The truth,' said Rasmila.

'Every word. What is going on?'

Rasmila looked at her companion, then turned her kohl-ringed eyes to Violette. 'Yes, we are working for Simon, out of love, to prove ourselves worthy. He left us to do as we wished. He does not yet know that you have promised to come with us – but he will. Nor have we told him where Sebastian is, or about the woman.'

'You will never tell Simon about Robyn,' Violette hissed. 'And Sebastian – is he on your side too?'

'He follows no one, but we will win him over. We must. Simon believes that he is as dangerous as – as you, Lilith.'

'Does he?' She was distracted, thoughtful. Then her gaze burned straight at Rasmila. 'And is he?'

A shadow darkened Karl's thoughts. Sebastian, icily ruthless and as strong as Kristian . . .

'Simon believes it,' Rasmila repeated, implying, *so obviously it is true.*

'Cesare doesn't,' said Fyodor, 'but Simon hates Cesare, tells him nothing.'

'Did Simon mean that Sebastian has the strength to destroy me?' Violette asked, frowning.

'Yes.' Rasmila spoke as if she wanted to lie, and couldn't. 'To overpower, weaken, imprison – not to kill.'

'As I said, to destroy. So, you lured me to Robyn in the hope that Sebastian and I would fight over her? But if that didn't work, you'd deliver me to Simon instead; either way I was caught?'

Rasmila didn't reply. Fyodor said, with a half-hearted sneer, 'Of course; what did you think? We have our quarrels and our factions, but on one point we're all agreed, even Karl, if he'd only stop being too chivalrous to admit it: Lilith is the Enemy of all. We have to do this—'

'For your own good,' Rasmila broke in with feeling, 'because you cannot live as you are, outcast, can you? We must bring you back to God!'

The dancer's crystalline face did not change. 'Can you compel me to go to Simon?'

'You know we cannot,' said Rasmila, 'but you gave your word. We did our part, we told you the truth about Robyn!'

'Do you really think I can keep my word after Cesare's execrable attack on my company?' Violette said, frosty but controlled. 'You say you didn't know but you should have done, and stopped it! The truth is that you have no influence with Cesare or Simon at all, do you? You're scrambling to get back in favour and they're using you!'

Rasmila and Fyodor stared malignly at her. Karl watched, coiled to intervene if they attacked her, but no one moved. He, too, was incredulous that they could still expect Violette to keep the bargain after what they'd admitted.

But to his astonishment, Violette said in a low voice, 'However, I did promise.'

'Yes,' said Rasmila, her eyes glittering.

Violette was very still; blank-faced, desolate. Looking into the abyss. 'What will Simon do to me?' Fear in her voice. 'No, don't tell me. I ask just one favour; give me until tomorrow afternoon to sort things out here. Then I'll come with you. If you don't trust me, stay and watch me!'

Their faces, umber and pearl, changed; they looked amazed, joyful, empowered. And sinister, like kind warders about to lead her to the execution chamber. 'No, we're needed elsewhere. We trust you. But tomorrow – you must be ready.' Solemnly the angels bowed to her and vanished.

Violette sat down again, her shoulders dropping in an outrush of tension. Karl studied her, full of the gravest misgivings.

He said, 'Do you know what you're doing?'

She stiffened. 'Do you care? You're always the devil's advocate, Karl. For all I know, you're on their side!'

'Violette, I am not.' As always, her hostility made him feel both sadder and less compassionate.

'I've decided; I am going to send all my dancers and staff away and shut up the house. It's the only way they'll be safe, until I'm out of the way. Do you agree?' It was more a challenge than a need for approval.

'It's wise, but what will you achieve by surrendering?'

'I don't know, but I can't accept the Ballet Janacek is finished. Someone must carry on after me. Ute, perhaps . . . I've been a fool, of course,' Violette said suddenly. Karl looked at her but she stared through him, her eyes burningly desolate. 'I should have seduced and flattered my way through this un-life, and had them at my feet instead of my throat . . . but it would have made me sick. Lilith can't do it. She can't lie.'

'So you're putting her out of her misery?' Karl found it impossible to pity her. He tried to be disinterested – but just for a second, something caught hard at his throat, and loosed its hold only reluctantly. 'Is there nothing I can say to persuade you not to go?'

'Nothing,' she said.

'It's the ballet, isn't it?'

'What the hell do you mean?'

'*Witch and Maiden*, Violette. You could have ended it any way you wished. Instead you chose to end it with your character's entrapment and death.'

'What else is there for me?' she hissed. 'This agony, this

hatred all around me and the thirst – I cannot endure it any longer!'

Karl, held there by her will and her terrible beauty, was utterly at a loss. Nothing he said or did would influence Violette. It was not that he wanted to control her, only to help. But she was a bird of prey, alone, impervious to advice or compassion.

Then she gave a barbed-wire smile. 'I promised to present myself to Simon. I said nothing about not ripping off Cesare's head on my way.'

'Will that solve anything?'

She leapt to her feet and shrieked, 'He killed my bloody cat, my Magdi! If I go to hell, he's coming with me!'

Her outburst took Karl aback. An explosion of simple, undefeated outrage – and she sounded so human. Wholly, heart-breakingly human.

They stared at each other. Violette looked as shocked as Karl felt. 'I suppose you're amazed that I should still care about such a thing,' she said harshly. 'So am I.'

'Well, it is the first honest anger you've shown,' said Karl. He remembered her last visit to the Schloss; vampires and mortals quaking in blind terror beneath her sweeping wings. 'If you chose to fight,' he said, 'they would stand no chance against you. And we might prevent the transformation of thirty vampires.'

'We? I don't expect your help.'

'If you go, I'm coming with you.'

'That's very noble,' Violette said. But she didn't refuse. All at once, Karl perceived her lucent glow as fragility, not strength.

'Are you afraid?' he asked softly.

'No.'

'Then why are you shaking?'

'Because Charlotte isn't here.' She clasped her arms hard across her waist, but her trembling grew worse. 'I'm not the same without her – but we can't wait for her. I won't take her into danger just to feed my strength.'

'We agree on that, at least,' Karl murmured.

'That's why I must walk in barefoot with downcast eyes, like Lila of the forest going into the cottage . . . To set Charlotte free.'

Karl closed his eyes, couldn't speak. Yes, he thought, I want Charlotte to be free of her . . . does it follow that I want Violette to sacrifice herself, that I'm prepared just to stand and watch?'

'You're afraid, aren't you?' said Violette.

He mastered himself. '*Natürlich*. I don't relish the prospect of being ripped apart and beheaded. And I'm thinking of Charlotte.'

'I'm frightened, too,' Violette said very softly, 'of Lilith. If she is the Mother of Vampires, it is in her power to destroy as well as to create her offspring. To take them all with her when she falls.'

And that, Karl thought, is what I fear.

Sebastian stood on the slope of a hill, trees massed behind him against a wild sky, a banshee wind tearing through them. Below him stood the house; cavernous, dusty, empty-eyed. Yet magnificent. His home. A casket to contain the rarest of jewels, his blood-red diamond, Robyn.

Who no longer loved him.

Remaining where he stood he entered the Crystal Ring and the wind sliced through him like a sword, like loss. The trees turned to shivering crystal; the house leaned like some distorted, anthropomorphic cartoon. And above him, seeming close enough to touch, the great mass of darkness seethed like an emanation from hell.

'Rasmila,' he whispered. His veins leapt, and the ether seemed to vibrate in response. 'Kali, Semangelof, my Cailleach; can your blood hear mine?'

They came to him through the twilight, sable and gossamer, and wound around him like cats.

'We knew you'd need us,' said Rasmila, stroking his hair, while Fyodor leaned on his shoulder. 'What can we do?'

He told them.

'And if we help, will you reward us?' Her voice was a dove's. 'Because we need you, Sebastian. You are more than Simon can ever be. We love you.'

Sebastian was barely hearing them, or feeling their feathery hands sliding over his body; in his desperation he would have agreed to anything.

'If you help me first,' he said, 'I'll sell you my soul – again.'

Surveying the probationers who stood like soldiers awaiting inspection, Cesare was overwhelmed by pride. Thirty perfect humans, ripe to receive the Crystal Ring's gift. Fit, powerful young men, all soundly drilled in the disciplines of obedience and loyalty. Men who worshipped their vampire leader as God.

There was Werner on the front row, one of Cesare's favourites. An idealist, a bright star.

Another seventeen had been eliminated after proving unworthy. Some had never recovered from John's attentions; one or two had been too wilful, threatening to run away and tell the human 'authorities' – for all the good that would have done them, Cesare thought scornfully. A few had fallen ill after vampires had fed too enthusiastically upon them; one pair had grown too fond of each other, knowing full well that all their passion should have been focused on their leader. It was to be expected that some would fall by the wayside. They were only mortal, after all. The ones who had passed were exceptional.

Cesare's pride was tempered by sad anger. One of his best men, sent to cause disruption to the ballet, had not returned. Cesare hadn't quite given up hope, but he suspected that either Karl or Violette had killed him. There had been bad news, a brief report from Simon's spies that the only fatality was a cat – but a fragment of good news, also. Charlotte was no longer with Violette.

That would weaken Lilith, Simon believed. But Cesare did not fully trust Simon. He trusted Fyodor and Rasmila even less. They are not fully committed to the cause, he thought. They lurk on the fringes, and no one ever knows what they are doing.

Ah, no trouble. While they're useful, we'll use them; afterwards, they'll be discarded.

The humans were in the centre of the chamber, immortals flanking them. Simon and John were behind his right shoulder, Pierre in the audience to Cesare's left. Everyone was waiting eagerly to hear the last speech Cesare would give before the transformation.

Cesare was deeply moved. It wouldn't take much to make him weep. Sometimes he thought, this is too much happiness for anyone to bear. I must be insane. But if he was, no one told him. They shared his insanity, loved him for it.

Standing on the dais before Kristian's high-backed chair, he began, 'Tonight you will put on the white robes of initiates while your initiators don the red robes of immortality. Consider the symbolism of the colours; the white of innocence and the red of knowledge, of blood.'

He smelled the heat of the men's excitement. How they trembled to be elevated alongside their ruthless jewel-eyed masters!

'Our father Kristian rejected the drinking of blood as a carnal act, asking that we deny our natural desires and exist only on life-auras. But I say that the appetite for blood is a gift that must be used wisely. Use it only to subjugate your prey; never indulge it for pleasure, for that way lies ruin. Carnality is a weakness of the human state, which you will soon leave behind for ever; it has no place here!' On these words he looked piercingly at Ilona, who was at the back of the chamber with the female vampires, a minority now. 'Devote all your love to your leader and to God; devote every act of feeding to God, shun the weakness of flesh, and we shall rule the world.' Cesare leaned forward, directing a steel glare at them. 'Do you think I exaggerate? Consider this: God set us above men. He set us to punish them for their sins. We have direct ordinance from God in the form of Simon. The time is coming now when He will set us to rule mankind!

'Tonight, thirty new vampires will be created. Next time, sixty, our numbers doubling each time. Think how swiftly our numbers will increase! We will inhabit new castles, creating a network of strongholds across Europe. First there will be the infiltration and undermining of human institutions, then their destruction and replacement by vampire law.' His voice rose to an ecstatic shout. He was outside himself. 'That is the work we begin here tonight. An immortal empire, ordained by God!'

The cheer that greeted these words was deafening. Cesare nodded in thanks, arms clasped across his chest, tears escaping over his lashes. He left the dais and moved among his flock. They clasped his hands, crying, laughing, as if he were their messiah.

As Cesare neared the back, however, he noticed that Ilona was not joining in wholeheartedly. Her polite clapping could have been interpreted as an insult.

Cesare loathed Ilona. She did not share his ideals. She was one of the old ones, a slave to carnality, whose only motive for helping had been hatred of another female. She'd been useful, but his new world held no role for her. After the initiation, she wouldn't survive long.

He stopped short of the female group. The women looked disappointed, especially his pet, Maria, but he ignored them. What female could be trusted, when she was irrevocably tainted with Lilith's power?

Cesare's Utopia held no place for sexuality or for death.

His ideals were nothing new; they were ancient, tried and tested. But to him, as he breathed in the charged excitement of his eager disciples, they sprang eternally fresh and new.

As he passed Pierre, returning to the dais, Pierre said rapidly, 'What if she comes again? Lilith. Aren't you afraid?'

'No such word exists here,' Cesare said icily. 'And if I hear that name mentioned again, whoever speaks it will be silenced permanently.'

Pierre glared back from sullen, cowed eyes.

'She'll come,' said Simon over Cesare's shoulder. 'She won't be able to stay away. I promise you, she'll come.'

Pierre looked down, shuddering.

There is too much of the female and the decadent in all these older vampires, Cesare thought as he mounted the dais again. They'll have to be stamped out in time.

But tonight would be for the celebration of life. Not the faintest shadow of fear touched him as he surveyed the shining faces of his acolytes; he had never felt more serene.

Then, for the first time, without arrogance, he seated himself in Kristian's dark throne.

The roar of approbation shook the walls.

Robyn had fallen asleep with her head on Sebastian's chest. When she woke to darkness, she was alone in bed.

He has gone out to feed, she thought with her eyes still closed. To suck out someone else's life so he can spare mine. How long could I have gone on, knowing that?

Well, it's all right. I shan't do it any longer. Guess that salves my conscience. She stretched and turned over in bed, feeling warm, cradled in cream and blue silk. Today I start for home. I mustn't even think about Violette. Alice will be glad to see me, at least.

But the thought made her uneasy. How can I go back to my dull old life, after knowing Sebastian?

A light moved across her eyelids. She opened her eyes to see Sebastian staring down at her, his face a carving of candlelight and shadow. She could appreciate his beauty now in a detached way, unmoved by insatiable longings and fears. Such a relief. Violette's gift.

'You startled me,' she said. 'I thought you'd gone out. What time is it?'

'Time doesn't matter here,' he said. His tone sent a flicker of panic through her. He sat on the edge of the bed and gave her a warm look that verged on a smile. 'So, you're off on your travels today.'

'I have to go.'

'No need to sound apologetic. After all, if you no longer love me, there's no point in your staying. On the other hand, maybe you never did love me, because you never said it.'

'I told you I still want to see you,' she said gently.

'Do you, now? Have your cake and eat it? But what if I

don't agree? If I said, "Leave me now and you'll never see me again," could you bear it?'

Be strong, she told herself. 'I would have to, wouldn't I?' She took his hand; his skin felt like quartz. 'I don't know what more I can say. Don't take it badly, dear, please.'

'There is nothing to take badly,' he said, 'because you are not going anywhere.'

She tried to sit up, but he held her down. At first, still confident of herself, she felt indignant. Then fear filled her in a rush. His eyes consumed her; soft, leafy, soot-fringed, they were ciphers of a single-minded and merciless will.

Her words tumbled out. 'We've discussed this, I thought you understood—'

'What is there for you to go back to?' he broke in. 'Can you resume your old life, after knowing me? I don't think so.'

Robyn flinched. 'I'll find something.'

'No, you won't.' Gripping her arms, he lifted her half out of bed. 'You forced me to admit that I love you, I love you to the exclusion of all others.' Suddenly he slammed her back against the headboard; she cried out, more in shock than pain. His fervour terrified her. 'You can't do that without taking the consequences! You can't reject me now. You've got to accept it all!'

As she gasped for breath, straining uselessly to evade him, she saw two figures at the foot of the bed. One she knew; it was Rasmila. The other was an ambiguous being with a thin face, his skin and hair shell-white. The two vampires shone with preternatural energy, their eyes bright with hunger and with an unknown, appalling intent. No trace of humanity about them. Demons.

She managed to say, 'What do they want?'

'Rasmila and Fyodor have come to help me.' His face was too close to hers, his eyes glittering.

'To do what?'

'To make you like us.'

Her heart bucked with terror. 'Why?'

'So you'll never grow old, beautiful child. So your earthly life won't matter. So we can stay together for ever.'

She could hardly take in what he'd said. The prospect filled her with absolute revulsion, with denial in every cell. She knew, with a certainty she'd never experienced before, that she must not let it happen.

'I don't want it,' she said when she could speak. 'I want to grow old and be a grand old lady. I don't want to live for ever, not at your price. I can't become some unnatural thing that drinks blood, I just can't. It wouldn't be me!'

Sebastian tightened his grip, lifting her up and out of the bed as he spoke. 'Yes, it is terrible, but you don't understand. It is also wonderful. You are coming with me into the Crystal Ring because I won't let you leave me, now or ever.'

Robyn went on fighting and protesting, but her strength was nothing against his. After the tenderness he'd shown her, she'd forgotten how physically powerful he was. Nothing tender about him now. His love was as dazzling and fierce as that of a god, and it filled her as much with awe as fear.

She was fighting for her life while he whispered into her ear, his hands numbing her arms. Realizing it was hopeless, that no amount of protest would deflect his will, she only became more frantic.

'I am going to take your blood and your life now,' he was saying, 'but you must not be afraid because the Crystal Ring will give back what we take. My friends will help you. We'll hold your hands and form the circle of un-death. You must trust us.'

'This is against my will,' she said, sobbing now. 'Never forget, you did this against my will.'

He clasped her hard, his mouth hot on her throat. She felt her ribs creak and thought they'd break. Over his shoulder she saw the other vampires drifting closer. Ghouls with staring, white-ringed eyes.

'Robyn.' Sebastian's voice was muffled, raw with emotion. 'You must love me, or I'll die.'

His pain caught a nerve deep inside her. She wanted to say, I never said I didn't. If I don't love you, why does it hurt so much that you can treat me like this? And his anguish almost won her back, despite Violette . . . if only he had given her the chance to speak.

Too late. The familiar, sensual thrust of pain obliterated her thoughts. He sucked hard and savagely, convulsing against her, strangling her.

For a time there was only the steely ache in her veins. She held him now instead of fighting, her hands locked around his back. Then a horrible greyness invaded her brain, a dust storm. She couldn't see or breathe. She was sinking. Her limbs were weightless and no longer part of her, as if made of some strange loamy substance that was floating away as all the liquid drained out of it.

She was bone-cold, shivering. Mad with fear, her mind a panicking, trapped bird. Dying.

Everything tipped sideways. Sebastian had let her go. She had a vague impression that he was holding her left hand and Rasmila her right, while Fyodor – a spectre floating before her – completed the circle. But she couldn't feel her hands. Reality had disconnected itself. Only the fear remained.

There was one last jolt, like a small but essential fire being sucked out of her.

Then darkness.

The building that housed the Ballet Janacek was empty and silent, a great desolate shell around Violette.

Only she and Karl remained there now. With bitter regret she had postponed rehearsals of *Witch and Maiden*, called everyone together, and told them that for personal reasons it was necessary to close the ballet for a few days. Rather than lie, she told them nothing, simply asked for their patience. 'Go home, take a holiday, whatever you wish,' she told them. 'All your wages and expenses will be paid. Your jobs are not in peril; bear with me.'

But she had secretly left a sealed letter with her solicitor, to be opened if she had not returned within seven days. It gave instructions for Charlotte, Ute, and her most trusted staff to run the company.

It didn't occur to Violette that they might not want to do it without her.

It had been a subdued, unhappy parting. Violette still couldn't be sure her people would be safe. She could only hope that Cesare lacked the resources or the spite to track down individuals.

They wanted to stop me dancing, and now they've got their wish, she thought. But they will pay.

That had been the morning. Now it was the afternoon, wintry and overcast, luminous with snow. Nothing to do but wait for Fyodor and Rasmila.

She kept seeing a recurring image of herself, walking barefoot and downcast between them, being presented to a triumphant Simon. Surrender, humiliation, death ... or worse, eternal life in some prison of the spirit. Out of their hair, but ever a torment to myself.

She felt the pressure of their will like ever-increasing gravity. Vampire and human, all want me dead.

No, stop this, she thought. You dragged me into this, Lilith; you can't desert me now!

But the hours dragged by, and Rasmila and Fyodor did not appear. Dusk drew in.

'I can't bear this waiting,' Violette said finally. 'Why haven't they come?'

'I wish I knew,' said Karl. 'They were so eager to have you, I'm sure they would have come by now if something had not prevented them. Perhaps Simon doesn't want you after all. He may have thought they were idiots for bringing their most dangerous enemy into the castle on the eve of the transformation.'

'What shall we do?' Karl looks so sure of himself, she thought, so calm, even if he is not.

'Fetch Charlotte and disappear,' he answered without hesitation. 'To Africa, New Zealand, wherever Stefan's gone, and hope Cesare forgets about us. I'm not a coward but I am also not stupid.'

'I know that, Karl,' she said dully. 'But it's no good. I've got to keep the promise. With or without an escort, I have to face my enemies. You don't have to—'

'I told you,' he said, with only the faintest sigh, and no recrimination, 'if you go, I'm coming with you.'

They were dressed in the simplest of clothes, for ease of movement; Violette in a loose greyish-mauve dress, Karl in white shirt and charcoal trousers. And she had stockings and plain shoes, not bare feet.

'You haven't fed enough,' Karl said as they moved through the dully grumbling storms of the Crystal Ring. 'How will you have the strength to fight Cesare if you keep yourself in this permanent state of hunger?'

I wish I were alone, she thought. Lilith is a solitary creature; I don't even want Charlotte. This is my battle and I don't need Karl here like the voice of my conscience ... but he would insist on coming. 'I'll take Cesare's blood,' she said savagely. 'I'll take Simon's. I'll take yours!'

Karl said nothing. His eyes were dark with concern.

'Don't look at me as if I were mad,' she said. 'I drink as much as I can bear to. I'm not going there to fight. One execution – then I let them have their way.'

On the banks of the Rhine, they broke from the Ring for a time to look at the undulating flank of the hill rising from the river, the ancient twisted trees with their roots wound around rocks, and at its peak the brown, turreted bulk of Schloss Holdenstein. No sign of life, no one coming or going. Yet at the sight of it, Violette felt inexplicably agitated, as if frozen fingertips were dancing over her skin. Lilith's easy rage and power had deserted her.

If I go in there, I'll never come out.

'Let me appear first,' said Karl. 'I'll create a diversion which will give you the chance to attack Cesare. Simon took me by surprise last time, but he won't again.'

'Yes,' said Violette, 'we'll do it. Come on.'

The castle, seen from the strange perspective of Raqi'a, had a curious delicacy and a strange ochre cast. Steeped in centuries of vampiric power, it seemed to exist in both worlds at once. Its walls held them like clay and honey as they passed through.

Inside, the castle was as dank and unwelcoming as she

remembered. Yet it had an overwhelmingly intense atmosphere, shimmering in the massed glow of torches, lamps and candles.

'I have never seen so much light here,' said Karl, 'nor so many vampires, since Kristian died.'

Humans everywhere. Vampires and men together, trying on robes, like friends dressing each other for a carnival in a mood of frantic, whispering excitement. They glimpsed Ilona and Pierre, assisting Maria with obvious reluctance. Violette and Karl moved through the castle like shadows, flitting in and out of the Ring, and everywhere they saw the colours of those robes; purest white and artery-blood red.

Entering the heart of the castle, they came to the inner sanctum, Cesare's room. The chamber was unlit, and from the Ring looked flattened and unreal.

Cesare was not there.

'He's not in the castle,' said Karl, 'and neither are Simon or John. I can't sense them anywhere. Can you?'

They slipped out of Raqi'a and stood in the darkness, perceiving with vampire sight the subterranean glimmer of the walls, reaching out with all their senses for life and danger.

Then Violette felt it. A great weight above them; unseen powers descending like huge, muffled figures gliding down an immeasurable distance. Figures in the other-world . . .

Karl, too, was staring upwards. She grabbed his sleeve. 'Karl—'

They leapt into Raqi'a, too late. The whole world tilted sideways. For a split second, Violette felt an uprush of coldness, disorientation, the Crystal Ring sifting down like snow; then she and Karl slammed into a wall of light.

That was how it felt. They were back in the sanctum, torches and candles blazing around them. Violette hit the floor and lay like a bird twitching its useless wings, Karl beside her. Looking up, she saw John, Simon and Cesare gazing down with reptilian, condescending smiles.

The room shook dully, like a heart beating, as she climbed to her feet. All her anger and will were dissipating. She thought, what am I doing here? What did I think I could achieve?

Karl stood up beside her and held her arm protectively. Normally she hated to be touched, but this time she barely noticed.

Now they surrounded her, their faces full of contempt; Simon the gilded sun-god, Cesare a choirboy with the steely eyes of a general, John a scarred mass of hatred. They'd accumulated massive powers, she realized, absorbing them from the walls of the Schloss and from their own ambition, from the blood of luscious youths and from the darkening thought-patterns of the Ring. They had fed each other with self-importance.

All Lilith's strength seemed to wither before theirs. I knew this was a mistake, Violette thought. Without Charlotte . . . did they know? I can't kill Cesare – but I can't submit to them, either! It's the same as with Lancelyn. I thought I could but I can't . . .

Her most powerful instinct was to flee. She felt fragile and defenceless, as she once had in the hands of Senoy, Sansenoy and Semangelof. And Lilith's talent was to flee, not to stand and fight.

'There is no need for violence,' said Karl. 'We entered peacefully.'

'But where are Fyodor and Rasmila?' said Simon. 'They were meant to accompany Lilith.'

'We haven't seen them,' said Karl.

Simon's godlike face tightened and Violette thought he would attack Karl. 'Have you not?'

'No. We waited; they failed to keep the appointment,' Karl said sardonically. 'Do you think we killed them? Does this mean you actually cared about them after all? And I thought your affections were purely expedient.'

'Far from it,' Simon said thinly.

'Why are you here, Karl?' said Cesare. 'There may be unsettled scores between us but you are no longer of any importance to us. It's *her* we must deal with.' He pointed at

Violette but didn't grace her with a glance. Trying to reduce her to an object.

'I am here to witness precisely what it is you want of her,' said Karl. 'After all, only Sebastian can vanquish her; isn't that what you believe?'

'An unproved theory, Karl,' Simon replied. 'Samael and Lilith are equal but the same, destructive; whereas we represent the forces of the Right Hand Path, the holy wrath of God. What do you think? Would you give your life to save Lilith? I don't know why you are bothering. She hates you. She corrupts your wife, mutilates your friends and despises your daughter. What reason have you to make noble sacrifices for her?'

'Simply to stop the madness of creating a race of vampires,' said Karl.

'You could have created the world in your shape, Karl,' said Simon. 'You had your chance, and turned it down.'

'If I'd agreed,' Karl said coolly, 'I would without doubt have been as mad as John by now.'

'Not you,' said Simon, 'my love.'

'So you're using Cesare instead, despite the fact that you loathe him?' Violette said contemptuously. 'Are these God's instructions? You couldn't control me, so now you try to do it through Cesare. An angel of God? You're no more than fodder for anyone who calls on your name, as you were for Lancelyn!' She glared at them, but they only looked back with bland arrogance; John with the insouciant danger of red-hot iron. 'You're all poison.'

'No,' Simon replied. 'You are the snake, Lilith, the venomous serpent in our garden of immortality.'

Cesare stepped forward. He came so close that his metallic eyes almost hypnotized her. 'We don't want your darkness and destructiveness. We want a bright, golden future and the dominion over mankind that is rightfully ours.'

All she had to do was to seize him and stab her fangs into his neck. But she found herself turning to stone. Why can't I move? Why am I frightened instead of angry?

'Leave her alone,' Karl said harshly. 'You've made your point.'

Too late, she realized that Cesare's approach had been a distraction. Someone moved behind her. Then John's hands clamped on her shoulders, while Cesare grabbed and pinioned her flailing arms.

All the boundless strength, with which she'd once terrified them, deserted her.

She saw Karl leap at Cesare, fangs extended, fingers clawing at the leader's throat. Saw Simon lash out and knock him aside, so violently that Karl collapsed with a grunt. Saw the angel swoop down after him and pin him down, burying his face in Karl's throat.

But Violette was being borne down to the flagstones. In shifting his grip, Cesare released her momentarily and she slashed John's face with her nails. Then Simon loomed over her and pressed her legs to the floor while Cesare and John held her arms. John was hurting her, as if there were a ton of invisible muscle within his small, bunched form.

I killed Matthew as a cat kills to protect her kittens, can't you see?

Karl was silent. She couldn't even turn her head to see what had happened to him.

Simon-Senoy was staring intently at her, his fingers like vices on her knees. The conquering warrior. And she knew, with the greatest horror she'd ever experienced, that he intended to rape her.

'You should have let Lancelyn do this.' He was pushing her legs apart as he spoke. 'But you were too proud. You'd destroy a man rather than let him invade your so-perfect body. You'll be damned for your pride, Lilith. I want the wisdom you denied to Lancelyn.' His tone was sneering. 'Let me break the veil and enter the sanctum of the Black Goddess. Then you won't mind doing the same for Cesare, and John, and Pierre, and all the others, all those virile young mortals.'

Her revulsion hung fluttering on the edge of madness. It had been so easy to stop Lancelyn. But this was no weak-kneed, sweating human. This was a ruthless, heartless intelligence whose strongest desire was to humiliate her.

Simon moved a hand to her thighs, pushing up her dress as far as her stocking-tops. With her free leg she kicked out with all her might, caught him in the chest, then spun away into the Crystal Ring, twisting as she went so they couldn't keep hold of her. The chamber turned dark and distorted like the depths of a lake. Violette soared up towards the light, with their demonic hands catching at her, clawing, wounding. But she evaded them and flew.

They were pursuing her. How many times had this happened, Lilith flying from her three pursuers? They seemed very close, barely a few inches behind her; she felt their fingers tangling in the webs of her hair. She glanced back in panic. Cesare's form in the Ring was dusty-grey, John's black as a bull. Simon glowed, no longer angelically golden but the baleful orange of hot coal.

Losing Fyodor and Rasmila had diminished him; lust for power had corrupted him.

No, she thought. Losing *me* diminished him and he'll never forgive me.

The skyscape swivelled past in a blur. Directionless, she strove for freedom, swimming through a hostile ocean.

'Run, Lilith,' said Simon. 'Flee as if the devil were on your tail.'

They were laughing at her.

Then she knew. They were letting her escape. Worse; they were driving her.

The substance of the Ring thickened about her. She floundered through sand and slush. Straining to look up, she saw the vast midnight fortress ahead of her, the hellish accretion that had begun to afflict the other-world from the moment of her creation. It had grown. It hung across the sky, a rootless mountain with forests flowing from its skirts. And they were forcing her towards it.

All choice taken from her, she found herself stumbling into a nightmare forest. The pseudo-trees were close-set, carbonized spikes that shifted and re-formed and murmured all around her. Hard pain radiated from them. They terrified her, but she was forced to run between them, like the dryad Lila in the ballet, pursued by hunters. Her tormentors drove her like the wolves of hell.

Violette found herself running on all fours now, a wolf

herself. She was climbing a slope through the forest, a black slope that ran with blood – but when she bent to lap at it, it tasted of nothing, like glass. She cursed God as she ran, but she didn't weep. These monsters would never make her weep.

They ran her to ground against the wall of the fortress. Her back was pressed to the basalt wall; the three wolf-demons panted around her, their eyes red embers.

'This is the end,' said Cesare. 'Surrender!'

'Never.'

'You must,' said Simon. 'This is your place of exile. You have nowhere else to go.'

Following his gaze, she looked upwards over her shoulder at the fortress towering up and up out of her sight.

'Yes,' said Cesare. 'Go inside. You created it, Lilith. It is fitting that it should be your prison.'

'We never wanted to destroy you,' Simon added with mocking sweetness, 'only to contain you. What will it be? Rape or exile?'

Pressing herself back against the wall, she felt it softening beneath her. She glared into their arrogant faces, projecting all the impotent fury and hatred she felt. It couldn't hurt them, but they couldn't take it away from her. If she chose the prison, she would be alone for ever – but at least her spirit would be intact.

'Exile,' she whispered.

'So be it,' said Simon.

John nodded, not with glee, only with satisfaction at the rightness of it. He said, very faint, 'Now Matthew can rest.'

'Go then,' said Cesare. 'Go inside and reap the harvest of your nature.'

Violette gave up, and the wall drank her into herself. She dissolved through it as if falling slowly into a lake of ink, welcoming the utter blackness as if it were a lover, her other-self, the black hag of death.

Robyn seemed to be moving . . . yes, *rising*. There was light above her. Colours of incredible beauty, stormy heliotrope and amber fire.

All her fear had gone. She no longer even remembered being afraid. She knew the three beautiful demons were with her, even though she couldn't see them; there was only the light, and a wonderful sense of anticipation.

Something I meant to do ... oh, to tell Alice and Josef I'm sorry ... to tell them I'm quite all right ...

The thought faded, and ceased to matter.

Every earthly concern relinquished its hold on her.

And now she saw the swirling blackness coming towards her, like angel wings or a great cloak. It was Violette! It was the beautiful dark Mother winging her way across the sky to save her.

Robyn turned over in the sea of fire and lay along Sebastian's body, her arms around him, her head on his shoulder. She couldn't see him but she knew he was there. No more conflict between them, only perfect tenderness and peace. Nothing to do but wait for Violette. She was close now, her silky black feathers all around Robyn, filling her world.

She smiled and let go of her last breath.

Fell into the kind darkness of Lilith's wings.

Sebastian did not feel the Crystal Ring's chill as they drew Robyn into it. He was on fire with her blood and her life-essence, wildly determined, fiercely excited.

They formed the enchanted circle; three immortals sharing their strength to draw a mortal, on the very point of death, into the other-realm. The Crystal Ring flowing like blood to fill flat veins and dessicated cells with bright energies, dark hungers. The miraculous change from human to vampire.

Robyn's body hung between them, bluish-white. Her hair drifted like sea-wrack. He watched for the change, for whiteness to blush into rose and down through the deepest reds to ruby-starred ebony. He waited. He was aware of energy flowing from Rasmila's hand to his, a tingling current that would channel life into the initiate's body ...

Arctic bitterness zinged on his face.

He felt the current flow from his hand to Robyn's, and stop.

The Ring held her but it did not enter her. Her form should have been a sponge in water but it was a stone, smooth and impervious.

And all of this seemed to take place slowly but in fact it was very brief; Sebastian's disbelief as he realized that nothing was happening – and then the electric shock between his hand and hers, driving them apart.

In panic he tried to seize her again, but she slipped through his fingers like melting ice. Then she vanished. Winked out of the Ring as if she'd never been there.

Rasmila stared at him across the gap where she'd been. Ghastly, the knowing look in her eyes.

Sebastian dived back to earth. He found Robyn beside the bed, where he'd taken her life. She lay on her side, one arm flung out on the rug, the other folded across her breasts, her legs softly bent. He fell to his knees beside her.

A second later, Fyodor and Rasmila reappeared.

'Help me!' he cried, seizing Robyn's limp wrist. 'Form the circle again!'

They looked gravely at him. Then they obeyed with maddening slowness. 'Hurry, goddamn it!'

But the moment was lost. Robyn remained tethered to the world, slipping out of their hands like soaped marble every time they tried to take her. The Crystal Ring would not accept her.

Dimly, Sebastian realized that he was acting hysterically. It dawned on him also that Fyodor and Rasmila were only helping him in order to prove that it was hopeless.

He lay over Robyn's body, kissing her waxy cheeks, trying to will the life back into her. She was so white, so heavy. He had done this to her. He began to weep bitterly, his tears running over her closed eyelids into her open mouth.

'What did we do wrong?' he cried. He glared up at the others. 'You – you betrayed me, you bastards!'

Rasmila pressed her hand to his wrist. 'Sebastian,' she said calmly, 'we did nothing wrong. Sometimes the transformation does not work. You knew that before we began.'

'But why?' He kept staring at Robyn, touching her, sobbing uncontrollably. 'Why?'

'Many reasons,' said Fyodor. 'She told you it was against her will. I've never known anyone resist the transformation by will alone, but . . .' He shrugged. 'There are some the Crystal Ring won't accept.'

'It's Violette's fault,' Sebastian said, his voice hoarse. 'She turned Robyn against me.'

'More than that,' said Fyodor, leaning against a bedpost. 'The changes she has caused in the Crystal Ring might have prevented—'

Sebastian leapt up and seized the thin material of Fyodor's shirt. Fyodor winced, turning his blanched face away. 'Is that what it comes to?'

Rasmila tugged at his arm. 'What, Sebastian?'

'You made this go wrong, to make sure you'd set me against Violette! Killed Robyn, so you could use me!'

'No, no,' she said soothingly. She went on pulling at him until he let Fyodor go. 'We did not, I swear. Lilith is already ours; we had no reason to harm Robyn!'

But they didn't care, he knew. He wanted to rip them apart for their indifference. And suddenly he understood. 'It was you who told Violette where to find Robyn! Was that the bargain you made with her? Jesus Christ! Nothing matters to you, does it? You act but you don't feel. You are reptiles, not angels. God forbid I should ever become like you!'

'Every pain and every loss you suffer will make you a little more like us,' Fyodor replied.

'Get out,' said Sebastian. He got up and thrust a poker into the embers of the fire.

'You don't mean this, it is the grief speaking,' said Rasmila. 'We warned you about Lilith. We tried to help you. If this is Lilith's fault, don't blame us!'

'And she's going to pay for it,' Sebastian said grimly. 'But on my terms, not yours. Now get out of here before I kill you.'

'Don't send us away; we are forsaking Simon for you!' Rasmila persisted, her tone musical, soothing. 'We will take Lilith to Simon, and when he is overcome by our dedication and he begs us to return, then we shall laugh and tell him it's too late, we belong to you instead. How beautiful our revenge will be! You promised us that we three would be together, a trinity more powerful than ever we were with Simon—'

'I lied. I used you.'

'But we love you!' she cried, pawing at him. 'We can still—'

Sebastian spun round and drove the poker, red-hot and smoking, into Rasmila's breastbone. She fell backwards, uttering a shriek, the most hideous he'd ever heard, but he bore down with such violence that the poker went straight through her ribcage and into the floorboards beneath her. She lay there, pinned, shrieking.

Sebastian grabbed a firescreen, a heavy sheet of brass with embossed patterns and thick, blunt edges. Fyodor flung himself at Sebastian, clawing at him wildly and screaming curses in Russian. Ignoring him as if he were a twittering bird, Sebastian slammed the metal screen down on Rasmila's throat and saw her head roll aside in a gout of crimson ichor.

Her eyes gleamed up at him. Comets and blue stars, dying. She had meant . . . something to him.

Sebastian uttered a single sob. And then he saw Fyodor fleeing past his shoulder and out through the door.

Racing after him, Sebastian caught him within six paces. They ran two steps in the Crystal Ring, then jerked back to the real world.

When Fyodor twisted round to fight, Sebastian shoved him backwards into one of the big windows. Glass shattered and rained on the courtyard below; the angel's thin back caught hard across the window-ledge. Sebastian heard, almost felt, the dull crunch as the spine broke; curses rose to screams. Crazed, Sebastian shook the screaming vampire; broke his neck against the window-frame, slit his throat on broken glass, dropped him head first so that his skull smashed on to the cobblestones thirty feet below.

Blood oozed, like yolk from a diseased egg, red into the silver hair.

Sebastian stared down at the angel's corpse, shaken. I have killed my own gods, he thought. So much energy, so much rage, and none of it has brought Robyn back to life.

Calmer now, he returned to the room, lifted Robyn's body

on to the bed and sat beside her for a long time, stroking her face and talking to her.

'Well, and if you weren't dead, I'd murder you. Look what you have done to me. I wanted no one's company but my own, until I met you. Then you worked on me and turned me against my own nature until I couldn't exist without you – and then you go and leave me. That is cruelty, Robyn. I thought I was the master but you've surpassed me on every count. I see you're smiling a little there in your sleep. And you never once told me you loved me. You never surrendered. I have to admire you for that. So you won after all, and I have to concede defeat for the first time in my life – but I'm a bad loser, beautiful child. A very bad loser.'

CHAPTER TWENTY

HIEROSGAMOS

As Simon bore Karl to the floor and sank hooked fangs into his neck for a second time, their minds touched.

To Karl, Simon seemed a red-gold entity, a lion-god of ancient power who believed himself omniscient and yet did not fully know *himself*. Always seeking wholeness through others, never finding it. Forever feeding, discarding the drained husks – Fyodor and Rasmila, Cesare some time in the future, Karl and Charlotte if he could – but afterwards, always, still hungry.

Clamped in the red embrace, Karl felt Simon's emptiness but he could find no sympathy for his ravening self-obsession. Even to be the chosen of God was not enough for Simon.

'I thank God,' Karl whispered into the blond hair, 'that I am not like you.'

The words fell like drops of acid into milk, curdling love to blazing hatred. Simon raised his head, fangs slicked with Karl's blood, his eyes wheels of metal, sparkling.

'Don't think love will save you. You had your chance; you are nothing to me now.'

Karl waited, rigid, for him to feed again. Instead, Simon made to stand up; but as he did so he wrenched Karl's left arm so hard that Karl collapsed in agony. Simon threw him aside, walked away.

The pain, as the torn muscles began to heal themselves, was so searing that Karl could barely move. Struggling against it, he turned his head to see Violette being held down by Cesare and John; and Simon poising himself above her hips in the ultimate, arrogant expression of conquest.

Her head was back as she strained to avoid Simon's mouth, her own mouth open and her fangs extended. Karl willed her to strike, but she seemed unable to defend herself against the imminent violation, as if Raqi'a had withdrawn its fickle strength from her and poured it all into Cesare's trinity. Her naked grief burned into Karl's soul. However little fondness he felt for her, her plight at that instant filled him with empathic rage. And he thought fervently, this obscene behaviour is for humans, for brutes. We are immortal, we should be above it!

With a surge of will, Karl defied the pain and dragged himself to his feet. He looked around for a weapon to use against Simon, anything, even a lit torch – too late. Violette vanished into Raqi'a, and the other three dived after her.

Simon hadn't weakened Karl; he'd only taken a few mouthfuls, a token of superior strength. Trying to ignore the explosions of fire running from his shoulder to his wrist, Karl plunged into the Crystal Ring.

He saw streaks of darkness against the firmament; Violette a ragged arrow, the other three on her heels, close enough to catch her. Yet they did not. They were letting her flee, and the fuliginous mountain above them seemed to draw her like a magnet.

Karl saw a strange forest, saw it swallow Violette and her pursuers. Seconds behind them, he plunged after them, becoming a wolf running silently between the trunks of weird obsidian trees. The surface beneath him was slick yet solid as rock, sheened with ruby redness. Glacial air enveloped him. The silence sang.

What is this place, he thought, what has happened to Raqi'a?

He was losing all sense of time. The pursuit seemed an eternal event, a myth, taking place on the mountainscape of a dream.

He saw Cesare, Simon and John – three demons, grey, iron-red, dusty black – catching Violette at the base of the coal-black wall. She lay against it like a crucified figure; he could barely make her out, a gleaming moth of jet, pinned. They were talking, but he couldn't hear the words until he was almost upon them.

Then he heard Violette say, 'Exile' and Cesare's cold words, 'Go inside . . .'

Karl made a desperate effort to catch up. But when he reached them, only moments later, Violette had gone.

Cesare and his comrades turned to look at him. They appeared dangerous and grimly self-satisfied, victorious knights still itching to engage in holy war.

They must have hoped I'd follow them, Karl thought. That's why Simon did not disable me completely.

'Always the hero,' Simon said, laughing at him. 'Why are you so frantic to protect the witch? She's never treated you with anything but scorn. She would have been the end of all if we hadn't contained her.'

Karl ignored his taunts. 'Where is she?'

'In the darkness, where she belongs.' Simon waved a dully radiant hand at the wall. 'Will you go after her?'

'What is this place?'

Simon smiled, as if he knew but wouldn't tell. 'Her prison. She brought death into the immortal realm; now she's trapped within it. Fitting, isn't it?'

'You cannot do what you are planning.' Karl spoke quietly, gazing straight at Cesare. 'You can't overrun the world with vampires. Mankind can't support us. We are meant to be solitary, unseen predators, not a brazen army. We are Lilith's children – not yours.'

'Sentimentality keeps you trapped in the decadent past,' Cesare replied. 'The world is changing, and you can't stop it. You owe us your life – for murdering Kristian, for defying both Simon and me – but you're not worth executing. You are pernicious, but weak. The Crystal Ring, under God's will, favours its chosen ones. Who are you to argue with it? We've brought vampires back to God; that's how we defeated Lilith! We are going back to Schloss Holdenstein now and you have a choice; come back with us as our prisoner, or go freely after Lilith.'

Karl knew, hopelessly, that Cesare was right. He couldn't defeat them, and he couldn't leave Violette to face the darkness alone.

'Go,' Simon said venomously. 'Then I can have Charlotte to

myself.' Karl looked stonily at him and Simon added, 'What shall I do – send her to you instead?'

Karl thought of Charlotte, coming home to find the dancers gone and no sign of him or Violette, searching, never finding them . . . but Charlotte seemed so far away. Besides, he knew she wouldn't want him to desert Violette. She would do the same herself, he thought despairingly.

'Go on, then,' Simon said, flourishing a hand. 'Follow her. I said you'd go to hell with Lilith; am I not a prophet?'

Not gracing him with an answer, Karl touched the wall. It was hard as granite, yet it seemed to liquefy under his fingers. Dread chilled him, froze his heart; whatever lay beyond, he knew he could never go back.

Gathering himself, Karl walked forward into sable nothingness.

For several long moments, he was held like a fly in molasses. Then the substance relinquished him. There was space around him, but the darkness was so intense that even vampire sight could not penetrate it.

He walked slowly forward, blind. His arm throbbed, but the pain was tolerable now, the injury almost healed. Concern for Violette inured him to it; that, and fascinated terror.

Suddenly he saw faint white flames ahead of him. Violette's face and hands! He had the impression she'd been standing with her back to him, her hair covering her shoulders, then turned round.

'Violette!'

Relieved, Karl hurried to her. The surface beneath his feet felt hard but yielding, like wood; odd illusion. As he faced Violette, her eyes were enormous, swimming in light and fear.

And the realization hit them both at once.

'My God,' she exclaimed, 'we're back in human form! But we're in the Crystal Ring, aren't we?'

'We were,' said Karl. 'Now I don't know where we are.'

Then she was suddenly furious. 'Why did you follow me? I didn't expect it, I didn't want it!'

'It was this, or go back as Cesare's prisoner!' he said harshly, patience swept away, his voice a razor-cut of antipathy. But the emotion receded and he said more gently, 'Because if I were you, I would rather not be here alone. Are you all right?'

'I don't know,' she said briskly. 'I'm cold, exhausted, upset and frightened. Other than that, I'm perfectly all right.'

Karl thought, I should have learned by now that it's hopeless trying to show her any concern. 'Then we had better try to find a way out.'

'There isn't one.' A tremor came into her voice. 'That's the point, there is no way out for me. Nothingness for ever. Exile, starvation, but never death. That's why I'm scared, Karl. I don't know why you had to walk into it after me. That must have delighted Cesare! Why is it I can hurt someone like Pierre, who was nothing to me, yet I can't lay a finger on a bastard like Cesare? But it's too late to rage about it now . . .'

Karl looked around. Blackness, in every direction. Terror plucked at him with insistent fingers, whispering inarticulately inside his skull. He perceived their prison as an infinite construction, groaning under its own weight and inconceivable age. An oubliette of all human malice and nightmares.

'I suppose this is what I wanted,' she half-whispered, 'to be out of harm's way . . . but where has all this hatred come from? My hatred and theirs.'

'I wish I had an answer,' said Karl.

'If Josef's right and it's only in my own mind – why does everyone else see me as Lilith too? They believe I am Death. They think they have destroyed Death, but how can they have done? It's ludicrous, but they need to believe it because they hate me simply for existing, and I don't know why.'

Her words sent a chill through him. Irrational, but nothing here held logic.

'Nevertheless, we can't give up yet,' he said firmly. 'We must search for a way out.'

He moved away from her, hoping to find the outside wall, but Violette remained where she was. Karl looked back. 'We must stay together. It's too easy to lose each other in this darkness.' Short of manhandling her, however, he couldn't force her to do anything. His instinct not to touch her equalled her loathing of being touched.

'No, wait,' she said. Her face floated like an opal on a dark mirror. 'Not that way. We must go further in and upwards.'

Turning, she began to walk directly away from him. Karl had to follow, or lose sight of her. And in doing so, it seemed to him that he became the servant of the dark goddess that possessed her.

Although Karl couldn't see the walls around them, he could sense them. It was something in the subtle movement and pressure of the air. He felt they were in a cold, haunted room, with a high ceiling and corridors leading from every corner. Then his hand, stretched out in front of him, made contact with an object at waist height. An edge, a flat surface. It felt rough and dusty under his fingertips, not quite real. A table, an altar?

Violette was moving ahead of him, and he lost sight of her as if she had walked behind a screen. Hurrying after her – relieved to see the glimmer of her arms again – he felt the walls and ceiling close in. They were in a tunnel. There was a stench of stone and mildew, like a deserted house.

He reached out and touched a wall. How strange it felt, rubbery and gelid, brick-solid yet soft as cobwebs, all at once. He searched for a door, found none.

Then the tunnel gave on to a square void in which a cold draught sank from above. And Violette began very slowly to climb unseen stairs.

Karl groped for a handrail in the blackness, and found one. The treads felt solid beneath his feet.

'Whenever anyone tries to pin Lilith down,' Violette said, 'she flees. Gilgamesh drives her out of the willow tree. Adam drives her out of the garden and she flees to a desolate place . . . This is desolate enough, isn't it? But it isn't the desert.'

'What desert?' Karl asked.

'When Charlotte transformed me, I found myself in the most beautiful red desert. Sand like dried blood, rocks like rubies. I imagined it, I suppose. But I belonged there. It was as pure as fire. The only place I've ever belonged. That is Lilith's home, the wilderness among the wolves and the owls . . .

The stairs bent at a right angle and ran up to a landing. There Violette stopped, touching something in the darkness. Karl went to her side and felt panelling under his hands.

'A door,' she said. She found the handle, and the door swung open without sound.

A huge chamber lay beyond. The blackness no longer seemed absolute; Karl could make out the faintest shapes sketched in dust. Chairs and sofas, perhaps, the hint of a fireplace at the far end, the frames of paintings on the walls.

'I've been here before,' said Violette, catching her breath.

They walked on together. The darkness weighed on Karl like fear; he felt he'd gone blind and would never see clearly again. Strange objects everywhere, tauntingly impossible to identify. Angular silhouettes; furniture, cabinets? Demon heads, with curling animal horns.

A sense of implacable eternity. The unseen faces in the portraits were those of all his victims, staring at him in blank accusation.

You'll go to hell with Lilith.

In a sudden fever, Karl went to the wall on his right. He found an alcove, felt some web-sticky fabric that could have been a curtain. Behind it was a smooth surface, a little grainy, like rock crystal. A window?

He struck the surface with his fist as if to break the glass and touch the outside world. The blow jarred his good arm, re-igniting pain in his left shoulder. No glass, no window. Only the nightmare stuff of their prison.

'What are you doing?' Violette sounded anxious.

'Just exploring.' Controlling the fear, he went back to her.

'I know this place,' she repeated. 'I've made this journey before . . .'

'So, where are we?'

She led the way across the chamber to another door. Beyond was another cavernous room, more strange shapes insinuated on the inky air. He touched the curly, carved backs of chairs, traced the shapes of candlesticks on a sideboard. Everything he touched seemed to radiate sighing evil . . . like the ancient tunnel where Kristian had met his death.

'It's where Robyn . . .' Her voice faltered. 'It's like the house where I found Robyn.'

'But it isn't,' Karl said. 'It can't be, can it?'

Another room, and another. Doors everywhere, but none to the outside. A long, bare corridor. He could see Violette's face and arms, her hair a raven shadow against their whiteness, but everything else remained obscure.

More stairs. Violette ascended like a sleepwalker, slow but sure of her purpose. Karl said, 'You seem to know where you're going.'

She stopped and glanced back at him. 'This is my journey, Karl. You don't have to come.'

'But I will, if you've no objection.'

'Only you could still sound sardonic, in this place.'

'But where is this journey leading you?'

'I've no idea,' Violette said with a shiver.

Night lay all around them and above. The house was infinite and labyrinthine. We can never escape, Karl realized, because we are walking through Lilith's mind.

At the top of the stairs there were more corridors, endless bare rooms. And then they opened a door and saw a rocking horse formed of dust on the darkness, glaring at them from black wooden orbs; dolls' houses, toys, prams, the debris of a hundred lost childhoods all heaped up like ash.

The nursery, for no clear reason, filled Karl with terror. Violette's face mirrored his fear. Her hand hovered near his arm, as if she were on the point of wanting physical comfort.

She caught her breath sharply; he thought she was going to weep. Such grief in this room. Ghosts crying soundlessly for lost children.

But she only said, 'We must go on. This is the way through.'

Another door led out of the nursery to a narrow passageway. Violette led him on like a candle-flame, until they reached a small lobby. The air seemed warmer here, but it gave Karl no hope; it was a warmth that spoke of airlessness, suffocation, the end of all things.

Over Violette's shoulder Karl saw an arched doorway, and beyond it a room so immense that he could sense neither walls nor ceiling. But there was a hint of light. A pewter glow sifted down from above as if through a high cupola, but only the light itself could be seen, like dusty blades of moonlight, illuminating nothing.

Another mystery. He felt they were moving towards the heart of the maze, where some fearful revelation was waiting to unleash itself.

Violette stopped in the doorway, pressing herself against the frame as if for support.

'Karl,' she said, 'I have to go on.'

He thought she was asking him to stay behind. Her eyes were black with fear, pupils huge within a ring of lapis. And the colour of her irises was infinitely lovely for being the only colour he could see. 'Alone?'

'It's your choice. But if you come with me . . . you can't go back.' Her breath quickened, as if a tiny lightning fork had stabbed her. 'I want you to come with me.'

'As you wish.' He spoke impersonally, but the midnight air seemed to echo with warnings. This threshold was a point of no return, like a cliff-edge. If he crossed it, something would happen that could never be undone.

Violette took his hand. Touched him voluntarily, for the first time; touched him in reassurance, not conflict. And Karl was so startled, so strangely transfixed by the web of mystery that throbbed softly all around him, that he went with her.

They walked into the centre of the chamber, where the phantom light coalesced into a blurred pool on the floor. The doorway vanished in darkness behind them. Facing each other in the spotlit heart of nothingness, Karl and Violette were the only creatures who existed in all the universe.

'It's here,' she said faintly. 'Here is the place where it ends. There is nowhere else to go . . . except into each other.'

The eerie look on her face unnerved him completely. He

tried to remain emotionless. He had nothing to give her but impartial companionship.

'What do you mean?'

'Don't speak to me like Josef.' Her voice shook a little. 'I mean that where we go is irrelevant now. It's what we do that matters.' He said nothing, unable to believe what she was implying. 'Oh God, do I have to spell it out? You must make love to me.'

Karl froze. An inner chill seized his heart and crawled along his limbs. Pure denial. She moved as if to touch him; he caught her wrists and stopped her. 'You are not yourself. You don't mean it.'

'I do,' she said, 'We *must*.'

'Why?'

She stared at him like a wild creature, with no desire in her eyes. 'To open the gates. So that I can become myself. How can I understand my fear if I don't face it?'

'But how would you ever live with yourself – or forgive me – if it was as bad as you feared?' He added softly, more to challenge the assumption than to accept it, 'Besides, you hate me.'

'That's irrelevant.'

'You loathe all men. I saw how you were when Simon was about to violate you, and I know how you felt about Lancelyn. It almost killed you! And I simply could not bear to inflict that depth of revulsion and misery on you.'

He hoped his words would deter her, but she persisted. 'That's why it must be you, Karl. You're the only one I can trust not to use me.'

'*Mein Gott*.' He released her wrists and turned away, for once in his life at a loss. She only moved round to face him again. He really thought she had lost her mind.

'Am I so disgusting to you?' she said.

'You know you are beautiful. You don't need flattery to convince you of it.'

'Beauty? What has that to do with desire? You've always been so cold to me, Karl, so indifferent. I never caught you looking lustfully at me behind Charlotte's back.'

'I hardly think you would have appreciated it if I had. You should know by now that a vampire's desires are neither simplistic nor random.'

'So you cannot possibly . . .'

Her agitation distressed him. Whatever he did now, he could not win. His only defence was reason.

'What would Charlotte say to this?' He spoke in the calm certainty of resisting her. Even as a human he had hated the tawdry heartlessness of coupling without love. That feminine sensibility drew women to him, not knowing they were presenting him with the temptation of their blood rather than their sexuality. But Charlotte, who had woken every possible desire in him, was his soul's companion and he wanted no one else. 'What would I achieve, by hurting both of you? Charlotte is your friend. Don't ask me to betray her.'

'I am not asking for betrayal, I'm asking for transformation. Charlotte would understand.'

'Transformation?'

'It's what Lancelyn tried to do but couldn't because he was the wrong one. Not a prosaic act, Karl, but sacred magic, the alchemical wedding, *Hierosgamos*.'

She began to shed her clothes as she spoke. Her dress, shoes, silk stockings and undergarments of ivory satin. She stood naked before him, her velvet-black hair slipping over her shoulders. Her body was white, slim, long-limbed, the perfectly honed dancer's body in which she had received her reluctant immortality; wonderfully sensual, Karl saw, despite himself. Heart-stopping, the lines of her neck and shoulders and her small, rounded breasts tipped with coral. The curve of her hips outlined an alluring symmetry; the dark jewel of her navel and the shadowy triangle of hair between her flexuous thighs.

Perfectly artless, she seemed, with her flower-pale skin, eyes innocent as violets and the flowing fall of her hair. Karl could not understand how he had ever thought her too perfect to be desirable. The ice in his limbs liquefied. His heart was a crucible, bringing burning tears to his eyes. He wanted her. Oh God, he did, after all.

She came to him, slid her hands over his chest, and began to unbutton his shirt. He stood absolutely still, though the feel of her flesh pressed against his clothed body was unbearably arousing.

He said, 'I cannot do this if you are going to hate it.'

'Vanity, Karl.' She slid his shirt off and cast it away, outside the pool of light. And she bit his chest with her front teeth, not hard enough to draw blood, just hard enough to hurt. His hands came up to enfold her back. Her skin felt smooth as cream over the firm muscles. 'It would hurt your ego not to please me, that's all.'

'Violette.' His control was becoming precarious. Heat prickled a path from his heart to the bitter-sweet pressure at his loins. Unable to look at her, he lowered his head and felt his hair brush hers. 'Stop this now, or I will not be able to stop.'

'Good. I don't want you to stop.' Her fingers, slim and warm, plucked at the buttons of his trousers. 'Will you please help me?'

Karl made himself meet her eyes, and was shocked by the depth of fear there. His arms went round her and he held her hard against him, pressing his lips to her neck. 'Don't be afraid,' he whispered.

She stiffened and pulled back, as if she were losing her nerve. 'Listen to me with your conscience; this is nothing to do with your love for Charlotte or with infidelity. It's completely separate. Now I am going to lie down. You wouldn't walk away and leave me there in humiliation, would you?'

He could have done that. It was his only chance to escape, the moment she lay down in the small lake of light. But he could not. She looked so vulnerable, stretched out like a moon-bleached lily on obsidian. Like a sacrifice. The black void thrummed all around him with the pressure of its unvoiced designs; he felt caught up in a dream, a sacred rite.

He quickly finished undressing and lay down beside her. The floor was cold but Violette felt warm. The heat of her flank against him was delicious. He recalled Josef's description of Lilith as a seductive witch whose embraces brought disaster. It was Lilith who lay before him now, offering an act of magical transformation; or threatening the death of love between him and Charlotte. No one Lilith attacked was ever the same again. She'd turned on Lancelyn before he could consummate the act, drained him and left him insane. Karl knew she would take his blood; it was inevitable. She was leading him towards the very act he had dreaded.

Then he knew; Simon had only threatened rape, because he had not actually dared to go through with it. Unguessable darkness waited, and yet Karl still could not hold back.

His hand travelled over her from neck to thigh, gentle as feathers. Her wide eyes flicked to his face; her tongue was poised between her parted lips. He cared with a passion as powerful as lust that she should not find this hateful. But as he rose up over her and kissed her, Violette went rigid. Shivering violently, she turned her face away and said, 'Just do it.'

He stopped. Lilith was also Violette, forcing herself with every mote of her formidable will to walk through a nightmare. He couldn't comprehend what it cost her, to put herself at his mercy like this. She was all will-power and defiance. But behind the glaze was a frightened, human girl, whose dread filled him with sorrow.

'No,' he said. 'You are still expecting me to violate you, and I won't. Come here.' He sat her up with her back to him, and began to stroke her shoulders. She remained tense under his hands. 'Unless you can bear me to touch you, there is no point. Has no man ever treated you with tenderness?'

'Never.'

'Then life has been cruel to you, but we are not all cruel.'

She spoke in a low voice. 'I hated and feared my father, but I didn't *want* to hate him. I danced on Janacek's grave, but it gave me no pleasure to feel like that. I drank Lancelyn's blood, but I didn't want to! They all forced me to fear them against my will. I can't forgive that. I believe some part of me even wanted to love them. So why, why, if they couldn't treat me kindly, if they could only bully and abuse me, why couldn't they leave me alone?'

'Control,' said Karl. 'Possession. And I agree with you, it isn't love.'

'I don't need you to love me,' she said. 'You despise me, so don't pretend. I'd rather have honesty.'

'Look at me.' She did so, over her shoulder. As if she'd slid over the apex of her fear, she leaned into him; his hands glided over her long, flat stomach. The tension between them became formidable; their words ran together like the heat and rhythm of sex. 'I have never hated you,' he said. 'All I feel for you at this moment is tenderness. All I will show you is tenderness. If you can read the truth in people's faces, you must believe me.'

'I thought I could bear it with Lancelyn, but at the last moment I couldn't, because like all men he was only thinking of himself.'

'That is the mistake they make, but I learned a long time ago always to put my lover before myself. That isn't pride, Violette. It is simply the way things should be.'

'Your hands feel nice,' she said. 'Gentle.'

'When we become vampires, the fact that we are male or female loses its meaning. We change. Our desires become the same. We are outside the human race but we grow ever closer to one another. So, can you see nothing feminine in me? Nothing you can forgive?'

She almost smiled. 'Don't ask too much of me.'

'But how can there be transformation, unless we both lose ourselves to the pleasure and the darkness?'

'Oh,' she whispered, her eyes dazzlingly intense. 'Oh, you do understand.'

'And you will be in control, so there's nothing to fear.' Karl turned her and lifted her, so that she was sitting on his thighs with her legs around his waist.

Of her own accord, she slid forward, clasped her hands behind his neck, and kissed him. The kiss electrified him. And after a moment, her tongue came questing hesitantly into his mouth. Desire surged, a sword of crimson heat, a weight drawing him breathless towards the edge of a chasm. He half-thought of Charlotte, but he could not stop, could not wait.

Karl reached down to the moist folds hidden within the soft hair between her thighs, stroked her there. She caught her breath. Ending the kiss, she rose up so that she could guide him.

Now he was poised against the tender portal. She lowered herself, easing towards him until he felt the tight flesh yield; and she slid on to him, and he was inside her.

Violette gasped. Her eyes were glazed sapphires, blank but for the faintest etching of anxiety. He clasped her head and made her look at him.

And something changed, something new flowed between their eyes. A rueful kind of acceptance; he could not define it. But with it came an intense mutual wave of compassion. Suddenly they were sharing this with a tenderness as intense as grief.

They sat still. Enveloped in the fiery sanctum that he was the first to breech, Karl was suspended between a sense of peace and the heavenly ache of need. The moment was golden, wrapped in sorcery.

Words from another time, unspooling a filament of dread. *Those who dare to unveil the Black Goddess receive wisdom, or madness, or death . . .*

Violette's arms glided up and over his back. Karl dropped his head and they clung together hard, almost weeping, both overwhelmed. It was as if mortal enemies clung together in a shipwreck. The only survivors.

As they embraced, she began to move tentatively against him. If somehow he could feel nothing, if he could let the act be solely hers, perhaps that would absolve him . . . but it was impossible. Trails of exquisite fire were licking his loins, his abdomen, spreading upwards to tantalize his throat and the tips of his fangs.

Violette only stared at him, her hands resting on his back. She showed no emotion, no discomfort; only a detached curiosity, as if she were thinking, so this is the mystery.

The sensations were burning now, excruciatingly sweet, building by degrees as Karl forced himself to hold back and let her have her way. Her warmth and her subtle perfumes wove around him. Her presence engaged all his senses.

Violette. She was lovely, so lovely.

Then something happened. She gasped, her face tautened and flushed, her gliding movements grew stronger and more insistent. It was as if she'd discovered her own capacity for pleasure, and was completely amazed by it.

Blue-black energy ignited around them, softly sparkling. Their tension became incandescent. Karl experienced a slippage of consciousness, as if he were entering Violette's mind, and she his. They undulated together in a dark, infernal realm, serpents swaying to a primal drumbeat.

She pushed him back suddenly, making him lie flat. Kneeling astride him, hands on his shoulders, she thrust down on to him with increasing intensity. Her face was savagely hungry.

Karl closed his eyes. In an agony of need and pleasure he surrendered, letting her sweep him past the point of no return and towards the fire . . .

He became Violette. Her emotions crowded into him; the dread that had preceded this, the instinct that nevertheless forced her on to the dark path – and then a softening, an inchoate trust of Karl's gentleness, enabling her to follow the path to its end for the first time.

Then the sudden, devastating surge of lust, ambushing her. She'd expected a mechanical act. Not this. Wonderful beyond description.

But behind it all rose her true self, Lilith. Hungry and sure and accurate in her flight as a horned owl.

Now the anguish of bliss held them both, too much to bear. Karl opened his eyes, and although they were inside each other in every cell, he saw her above him. Saw her eyelids fall shut, her face contort. Then her whole body spasmed and she cried out, her head falling back to expose her long throat.

Her rapture brought him to the edge. He felt himself tipping over, all sensations converging to a searing fire-tipped arrow of release as perfect as pain.

It seemed to go on for ever, unwinding into the darkness.

He seized her arms, only half-aware of what he was doing, to drag her down towards him – but she was already swooping down, her lips drawn back, her slender sharp fangs fully extended. The pain as she struck was as violent as a second orgasm. Somehow, quite out of his mind now, Karl twisted his face into her neck and found the vein.

Her blood was a wave of light; indigo, garnet-red, sharp as silver, intoxicating as a honeyed libation. Karl's pleasure surged again and it wouldn't stop. Lilith caught him up, flung him spiralling into the realm of visions.

In the ring of blood-crystal, toothed serpents mated.

They were equals, their joy and love untainted by subjugation. A woman and a man, entwining like bejewelled snakes. The goddess and her consort.

Rain falling. Wheat ripening. Red rain ... blood spilled upon the earth, running in rivulets between the furrows.

Blood gushing from the mother-goddess as she laboured to deliver new life. The blood of the consort, the sacrificed king, flowing out in emulation of her magic.

Rain washing the blood into the earth. Saplings springing up, becoming a dense forest as if time were flowing at manic speed.

And then, a woman running through the forest, pursued by faceless figures. Her hair was wild, her face wrought with fear, anger and terrible knowledge.

They caught her. They burned her alive.

Karl writhed, feeling the flames on his skin, sharing her agony.

Lilith's rage flared brighter than the flames. She burst out of the fire and soared up towards the sky like a meteor.

Never again. I'll hide in the darkness. I'll come to you in your nightmares. Deny me, reject me, use all your power to destroy me, I will still be waiting for you at the end of all. No man, however righteous, has yet escaped the judgement of the Crone, the black goddess of death ...

The vision ended.

Violette collapsed on Karl's chest, breaking the circle of blood. Her hair spilled over his arms. He put his arms around her and held her, but he felt cold.

Presently she looked up at him with grave wonder in her eyes. 'This isn't finished,' she said.

'I know.'

'We've lifted the veil, but we're still on the threshold. We need the courage to go inside ... to look full on the face of the Black Goddess. We need light.'

Karl sat up, lifting her up with him. He hadn't died, and he was not sure that he had received wisdom ... Suddenly he realized that he could see, and that the room had changed. Although still dark, it had taken on definite features and dimensions. He felt a soft carpet beneath him, and he saw the bulky shadows of a wardrobe, a dresser, chairs, a large bed. A hint of Regency elegance and lush fabrics; the resemblance to the guest room he had occupied at Parkland Hall was uncanny. The room where he had first seduced Charlotte ... but that was impossible.

So, he thought, does this mean I've gone mad?

'We should find somewhere more comfortable to talk,' he said.

'Talk?' Violette blinked at him. Her eyes were magnificent. 'You always want to talk, but it will do us no good now.'

Yet she did as he suggested. As she rose and went to the bed, Karl watched the pale curves of her hips and buttocks, and wanted her again. He closed his eyes briefly. He felt tender towards her, but how could he express it, without betraying Charlotte further? Besides, Violette was showing him no affection, and seemed to expect none from him.

He thought, where can this lead? Of course, if we can't escape this place and we never see Charlotte again, it is academic. But if we do ... Too late to go back now. We have not merely lifted the veil but rent it, and it can never be repaired.

'We need ...' Violette said under her breath, pulling back the bedcovers. Karl went to her, and lay down beside her on the clean white sheets. A blade of pewter light fell through the curtains, but he had no desire to see what lay outside; the earth, the Crystal Ring, or limbo. He still feared that Violette would regret what they'd done and loathe him for it, but when he put his arms round her she relaxed against his body, seeming quite at ease.

'Give me your blood again,' she said. He lacked the will to object, or to feed on her in turn. He simply lay still as she lapped softly at his throat, untroubled by the lancing pain. Too late now, he thought, caressing her wondrous hair.

Has she changed me? I don't know ... but nothing can be the same after this.

Karl still felt the visions of blood, flight and rejection crawling across the back of his mind, a pressure that must be released before the spell would break. But what more was there to do? He had encountered the goddess of death. Now he lay with her in his arms and he was not afraid. All he wanted to do was to sink into her rose-red core again and if he died there, if he went mad, he didn't care.

Violette raised her head. 'We need light,' she said again.

He kissed his own blood from her lips.

'Wait,' she whispered. 'We need Charlotte.'

A profound sense of ceremony permeated the castle. Werner felt immensely proud, excited and nervous, like a soldier going into battle; he saw the same look in the eyes of the young men all around him.

The meeting chamber was ablaze with torch-flames. The air was hot, golden, smoky, sweltering with the heat of mortal excitement. Ten minutes to midnight; the transformation was imminent. Soon Werner and his comrades would no longer be novices but initiates, steeped in the mysteries of the Crystal Ring.

Werner thought of his mother. John had tried to stamp her out of him, but he still kept a small shrine for her in his mind. If only she could see me now, how proud she would be!

It did not occur to him that she might, in fact, have been horrified. He saw nothing but perfection in immortals.

The vampires, all dressed in scarlet satin, looked awesomely beautiful; fallen angels in cardinals' robes. The humans were in white. Empty vessels to be filled, Cesare had said.

Gathered in two separate groups, they waited for Cesare to enter. Werner's eyes were moist, his breath shallow. No one said a word. It seemed to him that the vampires' thirst pressed on the air as heavily as the novices' apprehension.

There was a stir. The Leader, at last! Cesare entered, flanked by Simon and John, all three in red. They came in without ceremony, yet their presence generated a bow-wave of power; solid, certain, absolute.

A cheer flowed up as Cesare seated himself in the black throne.

Werner saw him as a vessel of pure light, a prophet, a Christ figure, a god. Such love shone from his hands and his silver eyes!

Werner was overwhelmed. Under such leadership, he thought, I shall want for nothing. I shall never stumble and fall. This is the first day of the future, a new world, for ever and ever, Amen. The moisture in his eyes gathered and spilled over as Cesare raised his hands for silence and began to speak. Simon and John, standing on either side of him, were smiling as Werner had never seen them smile before.

'Some news, my friends, before we begin,' Cesare said. 'For too long, our brotherhood has laboured in the shadow of the Enemy, Lilith. Lives have been lost in the fight against her. However, tonight . . . it is my joy to inform you that the threat has been removed. Lilith came here tonight, as was predicted; John, Simon and I overpowered her, bound her and destroyed her. She gave herself up to us because she knew' – Cesare had to shout over the exuberant swell of voices, but he was laughing – '*she knew* that her time is over! God was with us because we have done His will. *All* of you have helped to defeat the Enemy through your devotion to God! And now the future is ours.'

An explosion of cheering; Werner shouted himself almost hoarse. How terrible that day had been when Lilith came; no one would ever forget it. This news was almost unbelievable, the end of a nightmare!

With a gesture, the Leader silenced them, changing the mood to one of solemnity.

'I understand, but you must conserve your energy, my friends,' he said. 'Never before in history has our gift been bestowed on mortals in such numbers, or with such openness and love. All of you stand here now because you have proved worthy to enter the Crystal Ring. Well, there's nothing more to say. The time is here. I hand you to Simon. You have an abyss to cross – but God will be with you and I will be waiting on the other side.'

Utter silence. Suddenly Werner was very scared. He looked at the man next to him but his eyes were fixed ahead. Each of them was alone.

Simon stepped off the dais and came among the humans, who flocked around him in a circle. He was like a winged archangel and yet he was so warm, so kind!

'Put your trust in God,' he said, as if he knew they needed reassurance. 'Each of you will be paired with an immortal who will take your blood and your life. You have nothing to fear, because you will receive it back, and more. Then we shall form one great circle, a rosary, if you will excuse the analogy, that will generate a flow of power and lift you into the Crystal Ring. So simple I have nothing more to say but this: God be with you.'

Werner was trembling as the vampires, who had been allocated their partners in advance, began to move among the humans. The leaders themselves were taking part. Werner prayed to be paired with Simon or Cesare – but not John, please God, anyone but John!

Instead, he found himself looking into Ilona's eyes.

A thrill went through him. He hadn't been allowed to speak to her for weeks! How perfect that it should be Ilona!

Werner smiled, but her darkly burning eyes looked straight through him. He was puzzled, thinking, doesn't she know it's me, doesn't it mean anything to her? It must! But he dared not speak.

She placed her hands on his shoulders. Around them, other couples were doing the same, as if they were about to begin a bizarre, courtly dance. Her lips, satin cushions in which two daggers nestled, were as red as her robe; Werner's pulse drummed so hard that he thought he would faint. Excitement as much as fear.

Then, at some unheard signal, Ilona struck.

A violent shock of coldness and pain. Werner had anticipated pleasure; receiving none, he was stricken. He felt as if he were locked in a cage with bars of freezing iron, and Ilona was a winter sky looming over him, or a crone, pushing his cage under the surface of an icy black flood.

He felt her lips on his neck, taut with the urgency of her thirst. Her slender body was hard against his; no consideration in her mind beyond her own need.

Werner was choking, drowning. Dizzy to the point of faintness. Then, with a hideous sense of disconnection, he found himself floating near the ceiling, watching everything that was taking place.

He saw his comrades, each in the same lethal embrace; saw their faces turning bluish-white or bruise-purple, their eyes closing, mouths opening. Some fought, some were passive, some responded like passionate lovers. All were dying.

Then, as one, each vampire released his or her partner and joined hands, both with their own victim and the one nearest, until one great circle was formed; red, white, red, white, like rubies and pearls on a necklace. The vampires pressed shoulder to shoulder, to keep the wilting men on their feet between them. Werner could see himself, pressed between Ilona and Pierre! Oh, and the lucky soul with Cesare and Simon.

He felt no emotion. Only curiosity.

An invisible string was tugging at him. With a rush, he was back in his own body again. Still alive, barely. His vision was a mosaic of colours and faces. His heart and brain felt ready to explode. The hands that held him were like stone.

Then emotion rushed back. Wildest panic, blackest terror. *Mother, help me, what am I doing here, I didn't mean to—*

Ilona sucked out what little of his energy remained.

The chamber swirled and vanished.

And the visible world rolled back to reveal the fires, the writhing smoke-clouds and the livid red chasms of hell.

Chapter Twenty-one

THE CHALICE OF CRYSTAL TEARS

Charlotte raced through the Crystal Ring, so far out of herself that it was as if she'd ceased to exist. Her madness was not a prison of agony, like that of mortals. It was a shedding of the self.

She soared between towering mountains, arms outstretched, rising away from the earth. Raqi'a flowed around her, lava and blue flame. It flowed *through* her. A dazzling light drew her upwards; she was nearing the *Weisskalt* but she was beyond fear. Even the cold could not touch her.

Faint doubts played a counterpoint to her mania. But the *Weisskalt* is death. Am I like a human, throwing herself from a cliff in the crazed belief she can fly?

Charlotte couldn't stop.

She ceased to be aware of her body's dimensions. Her skin was no longer a membrane to separate her from the Crystal Ring; the Ring flowed freely into her, until she felt that she encompassed the whole firmament within herself.

This is what Simon has done to me, she thought.

Or am I doing it to myself? Simon's voice: *We'll be angels together, Charlotte; oh yes, it is going to happen to you . . . If it happened to you, you'd know . . .* And her own words: *. . . you forget who you are. You lose your sanity. You become just a cipher for the Crystal Ring . . .*

Dear God, it's happening.

Heart-stopping, wondrous, terrifying. And she had no power to resist.

The snowy blaze of the sun drew her towards its heart, and its searing light, too, was inseparable from her self. It filled the sky; it was the veil between her and the ineffable light of heaven.

Charlotte arced high above the electric white plain of the *Weisskalt*. She was a comet with a tail of glittering ice-dust, and the cold was only a dew sifting over her.

She pierced the veil. Blinding radiance possessed her.

This was what Simon had called God. She understood now. Knowledge came, as it must have done to him; a cool, clear, purposeful voice. *You cannot change what you have done. It is past. There are others who need you now; there is knowledge to be discovered. Seek it. Your only purpose now is to unlock the truth.*

A revelation, but not of God. To Charlotte, the light revealed a billion presences, not one.

There could be no god in the light because it had no prejudices and no chosen ones, no judgements to make. It was itself; purest energy, the impartial fire of wisdom, *life*.

She saw stars, planets, galaxies whirling out in the void. She had touched the edge of the universe.

The brilliance, mercifully, began to fade. Passing the apex of her flight she curved downwards, out of the *Weisskalt* and into a sea of storms. As she fell she saw that her demon-form had changed from dark to bright. Her limbs and body were glistening alabaster, webbed with rainbows of opal and palest gold.

Yet all this seemed quite natural. As if in a dream, Charlotte found herself acting and feeling without analysing. Out of her mind, but fearless.

Now she was being drawn downwards.

She saw a mass of darkness floating in the skyscape below her, the amorphous fortress that she dreaded. No surprise to see it now, or to feel herself being pulled towards it. One moment it was a bud, the next a vast sable blossom filling the skyscape. Each petal became a mountain soaring above her as she dropped into blackness.

The fall ended. She had passed from absolute light to absolute darkness. And now she was afraid.

Angel, goddess, cipher; whatever she had become, she was afraid.

Black walls enclosed her. Although she could see nothing, she felt a profound change in the atmosphere. This was not the Crystal Ring, and yet it was . . .

A wash of light appeared from somewhere ahead. Charlotte saw that she was in a corridor; soft carpet beneath her feet, paintings on papered walls.

Instinct made her look down at herself. She was in human form again! Two selves at once; the immortal and the innocent girl, walking along this corridor to an encounter with Karl that would leave her changed for ever . . .

Karl was waiting for her, she knew. The knowledge filled her with anxiety and delicious excitement.

A door stood ajar, and through the gap fell the glow that had drawn her. She pushed open the door, and there was Karl, caught in the evocative flicker of a candle. He stood naked before her, his body a long white flame on the darkness. A lean, beautiful sculpture, exquisitely lit and shadowed.

Still as if dreaming, Charlotte's mind asked no conscious questions. Their meeting seemed inevitable and perfect. At the sight of him she experienced an intense thrill of anticipation. Yet, as she reached him, it was as if they'd never met before. His gaze, travelling over her, absorbing her, was dark, reflective, sad, fiery, alluring, all at once. And Charlotte knew that if she had changed, so had he. They were strangers to one another, and yet there was a deeper recognition between them. No need for words.

Karl held out his hand and led her into the room. She could make out detail and lovely soft hues in the shadows; damask, brocade, Regency furniture. She caught her breath. It was so like the bedrooms at Parkland Hall . . . exactly like Karl's room, where they had seduced each other that first, magical time.

This could not be Parkland, but the goddess inside her, who was part of the strange magic, accepted it.

Charlotte saw a bed with its covers in disorder. On it lay a lily-pale figure, Violette. With a languid hand she brushed her raven hair out of her eyes and looked up at Charlotte.

That was the moment at which the dream began to twist and darken. Charlotte felt incredulous, fearful, confused. Karl would never betray me but . . .

Violette in my place? Violette and *Karl*?

Looking enquiringly into their faces, she saw no guilt in their eyes, no apology; only dark intelligence. Tender, seductive invitation.

And she knew that Violette had fed from Karl. His unnatural flesh had erased the scars, but a single spot of blood remained on his collarbone like a birthmark. More than that, it was in his face, that haunted look. Of course she had fed.

So Lilith has finally had her way, Charlotte thought, in a state of weirdly calm horror. All her threats . . . '*How strong is your love, if it can't survive my bite? I'll take you away from Karl . . . and you'll never see me coming.*'

And Charlotte hadn't seen. Violette had got to Karl first. Charlotte's fear of losing him was agony at times, and often she'd wanted that agony to end. To detach herself from love. Not to care. But in reality to lose the feeling would be infinitely worse, it would be hell, but it was too late now; if Lilith had drawn Karl down into Hades, Charlotte had no choice but to follow.

Without a word, Karl drew Charlotte towards the bed. Violette stretched out her arms and said, 'Charlotte.' Her tone was raw with need. 'We've been waiting for you.'

Karl kissed Charlotte's neck from behind and began to undress her. He lifted the coffee-coloured dress over her head and threw it aside, and with it she shed the lingering horror of the burial. Karl and Violette no longer seemed like the people she loved, but strangers with hidden, sinister intentions.

Even through her fear, she was wildly excited. The power inside her asked no questions but simply drifted with it, accepting, welcoming.

Naked, Charlotte lay down on the bed between Violette and Karl. Their hands flowed lovingly over her, their hair brushed her skin. The beauty of it made her weep.

She bathed in memories like fire. Ah, the first time, when

she'd come to Karl's room in innocence, and suddenly found she couldn't leave until their relationship had passed from friendship to fire. That imperative passion, heating the air between them. Both of them knowing it was wrong, but knowing, deliciously, that they couldn't stop. And the breathless miracle; no longer to behave as decorous strangers, but to discard all propriety and lie mouth on mouth, flesh on flesh, melting into each other, sated and insatiable.

They were living it again. But how strange, how wonderful that Violette was here with them, that they could all share this without jealousy or guilt.

Nothing can be wrong in this, she thought, when my whole life has been leading towards this point. Charlotte was sinking in ecstasy. Karl inside her, offering her his throat . . . Violette's mouth and hands travelling over her. Incandescent pleasure.

Charlotte's lips found Violette's neck. She bit down. First taste of her blood for such a long time. The wine of purest love. Charlotte cried out through the blood. More than love, this was sorcery.

And then came the moment that Charlotte had dreaded; Lilith's devastating, transformative bite. Her words again, *I'll come back for you and Karl. I'll do it. I'll take you away from Karl and you won't care . . .*

No, in her bliss Charlotte had forgotten the threat. She'd been trapped, seduced into it, but it had to happen, there was nowhere else to go.

Nowhere else to go . . . except into each other.

'Do it, Violette,' she whispered. 'If you've taken Karl, you can't leave me behind. I know you've always wanted to . . .'

Writhing against Charlotte in her own bliss, Violette's sharp canines stabbed into her throat. Charlotte gasped. She could feel Karl's hands on her shoulders, his body pressed to her back, his legs entwined with hers; Violette's arms round her waist with her hands resting on Karl's flanks. The three of them spiralling outwards on the crest of enchantment to a different level of consciousness.

A single, slow heartbeat. Their faces, their crystalline eyes floating close to hers. And in their eyes – amber jewels, violet jewels – visions floating, layers of mist peeling away to reveal forgotten histories.

Karl and Violette were hovering on the edge of truth, but seeing only darkness in it they hesitated. They had lifted the veil but they had not entered the shrine.

They waited for me, Charlotte thought in joyous amazement. They needed me and they waited for me!

Charlotte understood. In losing her mind to Raqi'a, she had absorbed the persona of a goddess, just as Violette had become Lilith, and Simon had become Senoy. Charlotte was Isis, empowerer, light-bringer, interpreter.

I'm ready. Don't be afraid.

Clasping each other, they became a thorned circle; Violette feeding on Charlotte, Charlotte on Karl, he on Violette. And then they gave themselves up to the darkness and let Lilith have her way.

Terror, falling, great wings beating like a storm.

Warm darkness surrounded them. They were travelling down into the earth. And Lilith became Persephone, leading them through the warrens of the underworld, down to the primal womb that was also a tomb. Karl and Charlotte became the god and goddess who must descend before they can rise again.

Whatever ancient power Simon had drawn from mankind's collective subconscious, Charlotte had found something older by far; history's deepest secrets, concealed for thousands of years. The wisdom of Isis was a cool diamond on her forehead.

She saw serpents dancing in a circle of fire; Lilith and her consort, Samael. She saw men within a forest clearing, cutting themselves so that their blood ran on to the ground. She saw Lilith as a seductive witch and as a terrified woman fleeing through a forest . . .

And then all the visions came, a million images caught in drops of blood raining down—

Lilith lives in the night, haunting dreams because no one will suffer her to show her face in daylight. She is in exile but she will not submit to it; despite every attempt to suppress her, her fiery rage echoes on

*down the aeons. She is the Black Goddess of sexuality and wisdom,
terrifying to men – but why is she feared, why rejected?*

And the cool diamond poured light into the shadows of
Lilith's soul.

Goddess and god, Charlotte and Karl walked the passages of
the underworld; Charlotte like Kore, walking of her own free
will into the darkness. Karl, like Osiris descending after his
attempt to fly free of the earth has brought destruction; now he
must abandon himself to the source of all things. For that he
had sacrificed his blood. It flowed into the mouth of Violette-
Lilith-Persephone, queen of the underworld.

*They feed on the fruit of Persephone. The pomegranate bleeds, its
red crystals bursting on their tongues. The tears of life.*

*The fruit of Persephone changes them, makes them one with the
darkness for ever. But they understand the darkness now. They drink
its beauty. They meet Lilith-Persephone not as destroyer or ruler, but
as friend, healer, lover.*

The chamber that contained them was the fruiting head of a
poppy, life-in-death. Scarlet petals flamed around them.

Then the ruby-red lushness of the vision faded softly away.
They were in the darkened room again, wrapped around each
other, their blood wholly mingled from their mutual feasting.
Drops lay scattered like garnets on their throats and breasts; how
beautiful it feels, Charlotte thought, to be touched in absolute
love.

Violette looked exhausted, and the ends of her hair were
plastered to her breasts as if by sweat or blood. Charlotte felt
almost too drained to move. She looked at Karl. He was
dishevelled, his eyes drowsy.

They lay gazing at each other, shipwrecked on the far side of
their journey, at peace, metamorphosed. But after a time,
Violette sat up and looked down at Charlotte.

'Tell me what you learned,' Violette said quietly. 'I need to
be sure we all made the same interpretations.'

With an effort, Charlotte sat up and leaned on her drawn-up
knees, her hair trailing down over her thighs. 'Lilith isn't evil,'
she began. 'She never was. Men demonized her as a scapegoat

for their own fears. Thousands of years ago, before they created God in their own image, there was a Goddess. She was all-powerful, like a mother to a child; she created life from the blood of her womb as men never could, she could give nourishment or withhold it, create or destroy. She was the first holy trinity, Maiden, Mother, and Crone, but one based in the reality of birth, life and death, or spring, harvest and winter. The cycles of nature.'

Violette was nodding, her eyes closed and her face a composed mask of relief. 'Yes,' she said, 'but men turned against nature.'

'Because the Goddess, the female, was too powerful,' Charlotte went on. 'Men envied her magic. They could only emulate the shedding of her sacred blood by cutting or sacrificing themselves. Lilith – any woman – represented not only sexuality but wisdom, prophecy, knowledge, beginning and end. The Goddess contained everything, good or bad, and she was embodied in women. Men feared her, they feared dissolving into her, whether in sex or in death, so they began to associate her purely with death, the enemy. Isn't this what we all learned? They saw the Great Mother only as the destroyer, Kali, the black crone.'

'And of course they had to plan their escape from death,' Karl said drily, resting his hand on Charlotte's hip. 'They needed a god to offer them eternal life, a linear existence of life, judgement, heaven. As this god is a spirit, uncontaminated by death and decay, they also needed to invent our friend, the devil. This is always what I've felt to be the truth—'

'But you didn't see the other side, until now!' Violette broke in fervently. 'In elevating the male, men disempowered the female, twisting all that's sacred in menstruation, sex and birth to seem filthy and bestial. Spirit was split from nature. Men were "spiritual" beings, women mere flesh, like beasts. And all their natural gifts of sexuality and wisdom came from the devil and must be reviled!'

'Lost. Wasted,' Charlotte said bitterly. Tears flowed down her face. She felt anguish at the madness of it all – yet a weird consolation in knowing they were all three in accord at last.

'Did they mean to cripple the world by diabolizing half the human race?'

Karl exhaled. He sounded weary and deeply saddened. 'All religions have taught men to hate women. The church has never been about anything but power. God's name is used to sanction any atrocity, yet death is mysteriously not his fault! They blame it instead on the disobedience of Eve.'

'Yes, when Lilith-as-serpent told her, "Rediscover the wisdom of the Goddess before it is lost for ever!"' said Violette. 'But it was too late. The Goddess herself had already been split in two. Eve the mother, who submitted meekly to punishment and slavery, and Lilith the witch, who would submit to no one, not even to God. She's everything women are not meant to be!'

'Lilith personifies the rejected Goddess,' said Charlotte, to reassure Violette she understood. 'That's what the vision told me. Her flight into the desert symbolizes the end of matriarchy.'

Violette seemed sure of herself now. Her eyes were alight with conviction. 'The Holy Grail was the lost cauldron of the Goddess, the womb of rebirth. What were the alchemists searching for in the touchstone, the holy *graal*, the stone that carries the power of transformation, like the veiled stone that is Cybele – if not Her?' Violette leaned towards them, her face passionate. 'God provides a fantasy of life after death; the Goddess reveals the inescapable truth that everything dies and decays – even us, one day. That's why she was rejected.'

Suddenly she leapt off the bed and paced about in a blaze of fury, her black hair rippling. 'How dare they, how *dare* they make me into a demon! But why are women so feared if we didn't once have true power? The Goddess never required men to be subjugated; all are equal in her eyes. Perhaps she should have been less trusting. This God of theirs – if he's real, with his plagues and floods and eternal damnation, he's infinitely worse than the devil! I curse him!'

Karl had propped himself on one elbow to watch her. Turning to glare at him, Violette said, 'Have you something to say in God's defence? Surely it meant something, what we've been through?'

'I don't know what Lucifer's crime was, beyond challenging God's arrogance – like Lilith,' Karl said, looking steadily back at her. 'I've no sympathy with Simon, Cesare and their kind. And Kristian represented the ultimate denial of flesh; he was a vampire, yet he refused to feed on human blood. Now I know why. He abhorred the blood ritual for the same reason that some men began to reject women. Fear. I was afraid of you, Violette, but I've walked through the darkness with you. You don't need to ask.'

And as they looked at each other, Charlotte felt a thrill run through her from head to foot. But it was not jealousy.

'The truth is this,' said Violette. 'No god, no power in heaven or earth, can rescind the cyclic law. The Goddess's blackness is the blackness at the beginning and the end of life. The infinite void. The darkness is terrible but mankind – and immortals – must learn to face it. They cannot live by rejecting Lilith!'

Her anger spent, Violette came back to the bed and rested her head on Charlotte's shoulder. 'Now I know who Lilith is, I'm not ashamed. I don't have to fight her any more.'

'But she's still in you?' asked Charlotte.

'Always.'

'I don't know how I found you here,' Charlotte said thoughtfully. 'When I left my family I felt I'd gone insane. I felt transparent . . . I think that's why the Crystal Ring entered me. It wasn't good, it wasn't evil, and it certainly wasn't God. It was what I've always suspected: the ebb and flow of mankind's subconscious having its way with us. But we don't have to be helpless vessels for it; we can take what we need, and filter out the destructive side, if only we're aware of what's happening. Something in me must have known that you needed light.'

'Who was she?' Violette asked softly. 'The one who entered you.'

'Like Lilith, she has many names. Such as Isis.'

'Only the Goddess herself!'

'I'm no goddess,' said Charlotte, 'but I think I finally understand why we're driven to drink blood. Blood used to be seen as the source of life and wisdom; women gave it in childbirth, men in sacrifice. The sacrifices ceased but the memory remains in the Crystal Ring. That's why it creates vampires! The ancient reverence for blood.'

'You mean mortals still need to offer their blood to deities?' Karl said ironically.

'More than that,' Charlotte went on, excited by the revelation. 'I don't think there *were* any vampires until God had replaced the Goddess. I believe we evolved slowly, after men started demanding eternal life. After they suppressed the memory of the blood rites until there was nothing left but the chalice of wine at the altar.'

'The chalice,' said Violette. 'All that's left of the dark womb from which we issue and to which we all return.'

'But we're not gods,' Karl said gravely, 'and we should be wary of even thinking it, or we'll become as deranged as Simon. It is my opinion that the Crystal Ring had a deeply perverse sense of humour.'

'And now we know,' Violette sighed. 'If I was insane, it was because I was divided against myself. But now I'm whole.' She smiled coolly. 'I may still seem mad, but be assured, I know exactly what I'm doing. And now I think that we should try to go home.' She stood back, looking at Karl and Charlotte. 'Well, has Lilith's bite cured you of being slaves to each other?'

Charlotte looked at Karl, and knew, with a rush of joy, that nothing had changed. His lovely eyes, fixed softly on hers, held sadness and wisdom – and more warmth than she had seen there for a long time.

'I don't think so,' she said.

'No,' Karl said emphatically.

'No,' said Violette, 'because it wasn't meant to. The transformation was to destroy fear, not love.'

Charlotte smiled. 'I needed it to bring me back to earth. I *was* quite out of my mind when I walked in here.'

'And where, precisely, is here?' Karl asked.

'Wherever it is, it can't hold us now,' said Violette. 'But before we leave . . .' She held out her arms to them. They stood up and went into her embrace. As they did so, Charlotte saw that either the room or her perception had changed; it was not luxurious after all but threadbare, damp and neglected. Not Parkland Hall.

'Now I know I was right to reject Lancelyn,' Violette went on. 'He could never have shown me the truth. It had to be you, Charlotte ... and you, Karl.' She stroked his face, shoulder, his long lean arm. 'I needed you to stop me being afraid.'

'Of what?' He looked at Violette, ironically, tenderly.

'Of God, of men, of myself. You've taught me that men are not gods or demons. They are only human ... Even immortals are only human.' Violette's face flickered towards a smile, then turned grave. She was still the Black Goddess, covered in a veil so bright that no mortal could look upon it. She slid closer to them, her arms enfolding Charlotte's shoulders and Karl's waist. 'The wisdom concealed by the Goddess's veil is knowledge of the future. Do you dare to look?'

Charlotte recoiled inwardly – but Lilith would not be denied. One last trial, before the underworld would relinquish them.

'Hold me tight,' Violette said. 'Don't let me bear it alone.'

They held each other, and the visions came.

The relentless march of patriarchy.

The dark concretion in the Crystal Ring, they saw, was not of Lilith's making; rather, it was a concentration of mankind's thought-energy, an evil movement growing under a glaze of fervid ambition. *A new future, a new pure race, enemies annihilated.* Cesare's words but not his voice. Trembling, Charlotte saw an endless flow of images; she tried to keep them out, and could not.

She saw pavements glittering with broken glass. Innocent people taken away in the depths of the night. Armies on the move, families being driven on to trains like cattle, smoke and flames rising. Cities in ruins. The sky aflame. Untold suffering.

She was looking at a world in which vampires were no longer needed, because men could create far greater horrors of their own.

It was this embryonic corruption that had bred the darkness in the Ring; a grim flow from the minds of power-mad men and their followers. And Cesare was merely caught on the edge of it, a mouse riding on the hem of an emperor's robe.

Violette broke the link and the visions vanished. They stood speechless for a long time, bodies pressed together. And then Charlotte felt the change that Lilith had wrought in her, and heard it in Karl's voice; a new strength, the ability to watch this human folly as if they truly were outside it.

He spoke calmly, with a sardonic note that drew them back from the brink of despair. 'If Lilith's bite has taught me something that Kristian, for all his words, never could, it is that vampires are not going to change anything, that we are not *meant* to change anything.'

'And we are at the mercy of humans,' said Charlotte. 'I always thought so.'

'I know what this place is now,' said Violette, looking around at the dilapidated walls and ceiling, deep in shadow, 'and it can't hold us. It's the heart of remembering and forgetting. This is where men are shedding all their ancient memories in their pursuit of power and conquest. And it's where we had to come to remember.'

'But Simon didn't know that, when he sent you in here,' said Karl. 'He had no idea. He was blind, as are mortals.'

Charlotte said, 'Is it too late to make them see?'

'We can't stop the tide,' said Karl.

'And now they need no more of us,' Charlotte whispered. 'They can create enough nightmares of their own.'

Werner tried to hang on to his dreams of glory through his horror. Impossible. But, with all his might, he tried.

Clouds of fire, streaked with crimson, swarmed across his vision. He was flayed, boneless, silver-raw with fear. He'd expected heaven and found hell.

So cold now. Shivering. Helpless. His hands were numb and he couldn't feel Ilona or Pierre holding him, or even move his head to look at them. The circle hung in the void, the ruby vampires darkening to jet, the humans remaining pearl-white.

Their hair and garments floated. Empty vessels, waiting for the rain of life to fill them . . .

Werner heard a drumbeat from a great distance. No, not drums. Marching feet. An army, bearing down in legions. Thousands of booted feet advancing, shaking the infernal skyscape, making the whole world tremble. Magnificence beyond his wildest hopes—

Precisely and deliberately, Ilona let go of his hand.

He didn't realize what had happened until he found himself tilting backwards, like a corpse in water. He saw her hand and his, with feet of air between them. Caught a glimpse of her face. Purest evil in her searing eyes and her thin, malevolent smile.

Betrayal.

He saw the others, dead-white, floating like driftwood. Dried up, waiting for the stream of light – but it stayed outside them, cruelly caressing them but refusing to enter. He felt Pierre jerk his arm, as if in shock. Then, one by one, the humans began to wink out of the Ring.

Werner saw the immortals staring at each other in apparent consternation. Their alarm was infectious. Unmanned by terror, he began to scream soundlessly.

The unseen army was trampling him underfoot.

Hysteria twisted through him and he sobbed for mercy. As the marching feet passed over him and away, leaving him crushed in their ruthless wake, he glimpsed the amorphous shape of the future.

Horror and pain ground him to nothing. He could not even cry out for Cesare. When the castle walls congealed around him once more, no glory awaited. All the promises were broken. Lying untended on the flagstones, Werner slipped into oblivion.

As they dressed, Violette became acutely aware of how real the room felt. It no longer threatened to metamorphose around them. It was shabby, cold and haunted – but obstinately solid. This was not the Crystal Ring.

Charlotte slipped into her soft pale-brown dress and Karl buttoned it for her, his eyes tender. Watching them, Violette could hardly believe she'd ever had such a violent desire to tear them apart.

I'm glad, she thought. I never wanted them to be unhappy.

Lilith, too, had changed. She was less cynical, more tolerant. Just a little.

When Karl and Charlotte turned to her, she smiled. No guilt, no regret. Warmth flowed between the three of them, the delicious bond of shared secrets. Sweetest of transformations.

Outside the room, they found a narrow corridor with a high ceiling and bare, flaking walls.

'This is the real world, without question,' said Karl. 'How did we come to be here?'

'I don't know, but I know where we are,' said Violette. She felt all Lilith's calm strength upended in turmoil. 'It's the house where I found Robyn. It really is. If she's here, this time I'm going to take her with me. And if she has left, I'll find her!'

Dull grey light filtered through windows along one side. Looking out, Violette saw a courtyard with crumbling yellowish walls.

'Oh God,' she breathed.

'What is it?' said Karl over her shoulder. Then he and Charlotte saw what Violette had seen. The long, thin white corpse of a vampire, sprawled like a broken crane-fly on the flagstones. The head was still attached, but only by ribbons of flesh; the skull was crushed, the spine obviously severed.

'That is Fyodor,' said Karl.

Without speaking they walked the length of the corridor, the dust-caked floorboards creaking under their feet. Although Violette could feel no other presences in the house, human or vampire, as they turned a corner she was stopped in her tracks by a wave of dread.

'What is it?' Charlotte asked.

'Don't you feel something?' Not waiting for confirmation, Violette went on.

The next corner angled on to a wider corridor that ran past

the master bedrooms. Violette recognized it. Her step slowed; the corridor seemed endless. In the wintry light, she saw, at the far end, the doorway to Robyn's bedroom standing ajar.

She had no sense of Robyn's presence. Robyn must have left, she thought . . . so why does the atmosphere feel so wrong? I perceive no one and yet I'm sure there's someone here . . .

Violette went on, the others a little behind her. But when they reached the door, Karl said, 'Let me go in first.'

She let him. Charlotte placed a gentle hand on Violette's shoulder-blade. Violette quailed for a moment, thinking, I can't go in; then, what's the matter with me? I must!

With Charlotte beside her, Violette entered.

The curtains were drawn, the only light coming from a dying fire and an oil lamp. An odd shadow like a discarded coat near the fireplace, but Violette barely glanced at it. She took in the canopied four-poster, draped in lavishly embroidered silk of cream and dark blue; saw Karl in silhouette inside the doorway, and another figure beside the bed. It was a vampire she'd seen once before, tall and dark-haired with a softly luminous beauty about him. His hands were folded and his head bowed, as if he were standing beside a death bed.

The vampire said softly, 'Don't come in. Please don't.'

The plea was half-hearted. Nothing was going to stop Violette now. She walked past Karl and looked down at what lay on the covers.

Then she fell apart. Her composure, her very soul disintegrated, and she flung herself down at the foot of the bed and screamed, '*NO!*'

She knew Robyn was dead, without studying the pallid face or touching her stone-cold hands. Robyn gave out no life-aura. That's why I was so sure she'd escaped, Violette thought, anguished. It never occurred to me – I daredn't think – oh, Goddess, why didn't I stay with her?

Grief held her in its heavy net. No one spoke, no one touched Violette as she remained on the floor, clinging to the bedcover, crushing its delicate fabric in her knotted hands. She was glad they left her alone. She couldn't have stood sympathy.

Her shock was so extreme that she couldn't speak or move. *Robyn Robyn Robyn* . . . She could only stare at the body that had once been replete with luxuriant life; turn her gaze from the waxen mask to the dispassionate face of the vampire who stood beside Robyn.

Sebastian.

In a cat-like leap, Violette flung herself clean over the corner of the bed and seized him. His expression flashed into rage; madness swam in his eyes.

'You killed her!' Violette screamed. She was Lilith and she was going to kill him, tear his neck open and snap his spine as she'd done to Matthew a lifetime ago—

But he was strong. He fought back, gripping her wrists, straining to reach her throat. Grief weakened her and strengthened him.

'No, *you* killed her!' he roared. 'You turned her against me!'

His fingernails tore like scalpels into her throat and chest. She lunged, slit his cheek with her fangs – then someone grabbed her from behind. Charlotte was trying to pull her off, while Karl got between them and began to force Sebastian backwards. For a few moments Violette and Sebastian went on fighting like maddened dogs. Then they were dragged apart, struggling to reach each other across a space magnetized by their hatred.

Two crazed demons, feral and blood-dappled. Lilith and Samael.

'Stop!' Charlotte yelled. 'This is what they wanted! *This is what Simon, Rasmila and Fyodor wanted!*'

The words sliced the air between them, a bright sword. Violette froze. But she and Sebastian went on pouring arctic loathing upon each other.

In the silence, from the corner of her eye, she saw that the shape near the fireplace was the body of a vampire, its severed head gazing at the ceiling from a pool of blood.

Rasmila. Violette felt nothing; she had nothing left.

'What happened to Robyn?' Karl asked, his voice icy calm.

'What do you think?' Sebastian snarled. He bit into Karl's restraining arm, but Karl only flinched and held on.

Violette hissed, 'Murderer!'

'No!' Sebastian said furiously. 'We tried to transform her but it failed. The Crystal Ring refused to accept her—'

'So you blamed Rasmila and Fyodor,' said Charlotte. She sounded as if she were weeping, but her hands on Violette's arms were hard. 'Was it their fault?'

Sebastian pointed a bone-pale finger at Violette. His rage was like Lilith's; heartless, implacable. 'It was *her* fault! She came here and poisoned Robyn against me.'

'I made her see the truth, that's all,' Violette retorted. But inside she was stricken, thinking, if I hadn't, would she still have been alive?

'Truth? What the hell is that? She knew she'd die if I didn't transform her. That's why I did it, so she wouldn't die!'

'But *you killed her*! She died because she didn't want to be like you!'

'If that is so, it's still as I said. *Your fault.*' Sebastian made another lunge; Karl hung on to him with deathly strength.

'No,' said Charlotte. 'There's a disruption in the Crystal Ring. That may have prevented her transformation. It doesn't always work, anyway; you must know that! It's no one's fault.'

Sebastian, motionless in Karl's grip, said, 'If there is any disruption, Violette is the cause of it.'

'If anyone is the cause,' Karl said bitterly, 'it's Cesare and Simon and mortals like them. They're the ones who have corrupted the Ring – not Lilith.'

'Cesare,' Sebastian said flatly. Violette saw the light in his greenish-hazel eyes go dull, like claws drawn in, hatred redirected. He was hanging from wires of grief, like her, but that induced no sympathy in her. It only made her hate him more.

Violette put a hand to her throat, to stop the scream that threatened to tear her mind out of her body.

'I did not kill her,' Sebastian said quietly. 'I wanted her to live.'

'So did I,' Violette whispered.

'Come away from here,' Charlotte said into her ear. 'Come on.'

She began to coax Violette away. Violette resisted, then gave in, letting herself be drawn slowly towards the door. But the scene branded itself on her mind; Karl in shadow against the wall, Sebastian's hatred and grief searing into her, Rasmila's pitiful corpse lying ignored.

And Robyn on the bed with all the dear, precious life bled out of her. Never to stir or speak or smile again.

'All my power,' Violette said faintly, 'all my power, and I can do nothing to help her. What use is it, when I cannot bring a single soul back to life?'

CHAPTER TWENTY-TWO

WHITE TO CONTAGION, PRESCIENT TO FIRE

Torn from the Crystal Ring, Cesare pitched forward on to cold stone, dragged down by the corpses who still gripped his hands.

He couldn't open his eyes. He knew what he'd see. Couldn't bear it.

He could hear voices around him, groaning, crying. Death was a leaden grey emanation in the air.

Cesare looked. He saw heaps of blood-splashed white satin in a deformed circle round the meeting chamber; between them, vampires in red rising unsteadily to their feet as if they'd partaken of an exhausting ritual slaughter. Cesare, also, rose and stood swaying, seeing everything as if through water. Nothing seemed real.

This could not, *could not* be real.

With a scream, Cesare fell to his knees.

His heart was broken. All these young men who should have stood before him in proud splendour! – instead lying drained and lifeless, mouths open, faces blue. And he almost despised them, because they weren't immortals, they were only dead humans. They'd let him down. *Someone* had let him down. But he wept bitterly, too, because they had been so beautiful and so full of hope. They hadn't deserved *this*!

All round the chamber, his followers were crying out in disbelief, shaking the humans as if to force them back to life. A few lay weeping on their partners' breasts.

Four of his flock came rushing towards Cesare and fell on him as if they'd lost their minds. 'Father, what are we to do?'

Cesare pushed them away and climbed to his feet. 'Don't

touch me!' Tears of rage and grief began to flow down his face. 'Stay here. Be calm. This isn't the end! We'll start again!'

And the vampires looked at him as if he were crazed.

'It is the end,' said a voice. Cesare turned and saw Simon, standing like a statue amid the devastation, unmoved.

'You told me this would work!' Cesare raged.

'It should have worked,' Simon said without emotion. 'Nothing went wrong, but—'

John was coming towards them, a hunched figure, one outstretched arm trembling with tension. 'It was her,' he said. 'She broke the circle!'

John was pointing at Ilona. She stared defiantly back at them, hands on hips, her eyes like blood-drops. And Cesare knew. His anguish was magnesium fire flashing through him. *Never, never should I have trusted her!*

All Cesare could say was, 'Take her away.'

John strode to Ilona and seized her. Pierre, in a rare burst of chivalry, tried to protect her, but John only shoved him aside. Ilona let herself be led out of the chamber without protesting or trying to escape; only looking back at Cesare with a cold smile.

'You had to blame her,' Simon said scornfully. Cesare turned to him, burning with suspicion.

'So, you care more about her than you care about *this*?' He swung round and snapped at his followers, 'Don't stand there doing nothing! Lay the bodies out in some dignity. Attend to it!'

They obeyed slowly, giving Cesare brooding looks. Bitter, he turned back to Simon and lowered his voice. 'They think I've let them down. But we'll try again!'

'I don't think so,' Simon said woodenly. 'I could have told you that it was a mistake, trying to make so many vampires, but you would not have believed me until it was proved. So here it is; proof. It's no one's fault but yours, Cesare. You are useless.'

Cesare stared at him, utterly incredulous. For a moment he felt like a child, betrayed and abandoned by God, and he howled with inward rage. But the flame of self-belief came to his rescue and he *saw*.

There is something wrong with Simon, he thought. Not with me. Simon's topaz eyes were empty and coldly mad.

'We had better have this discussion in private,' said Cesare.

'No, let them hear,' said Simon. 'You are finished. You were never more than a poor substitute for a leader. When Ilona said you were my last choice, she was exactly right. Fifth best, tenth-rate.'

'I was right never to trust you,' Cesare said, enraged, disgusted. 'You were using me!'

'Yes, of course! It wasn't you I wanted, it was Karl and Charlotte! I needed to absorb power from you to win them.'

'A vampire who preys on vampires? Is that all you are?'

'All?' said Simon. 'Don't you know why I needed such power? Power is light, illumination to uncover the hidden wisdom of God! But all you cared about was your earthly empire. You're a creature of clay, Cesare, blind as a mole!'

Cesare didn't understand. He didn't want to. He was too wrapped up in righteous grief to care what Simon thought. 'Liar,' he said. 'Traitor. I'll go on without you. I don't need you!'

'Blind, Cesare.' Simon's voice was hollow. 'Or you would have seen, while we were in the Crystal Ring, that we are all finished.'

In a copse on the long green flank of a hill, out of sight of the house, Charlotte held Violette and kissed her dry cheeks. Violette was ashen, but Charlotte knew she didn't really want sympathy. She wanted Robyn. And Charlotte thought, how am I going to tell Josef?

'You should have let me kill Sebastian,' said Violette.

'Perhaps, but it won't bring Robyn back,' said Karl. Sebastian had let them leave the house without argument.

'How wonderful.' Violette's tone was softly bitter. 'I know all about taking life but nothing about giving it back. I'm certain Robyn didn't want to become like us. She let herself die, rather than let it happen. Goddess, why could I not also have died?'

'Don't,' said Charlotte, anguished.

'The Crystal Ring decides,' said Karl, 'as arbitrarily as nature.'

'We should go home,' Charlotte murmured.

Violette seemed to master herself, and clasped their hands. What had passed between them could never be forgotten or lost; it had changed them for all time. Magic encircled them, shadowy with grim wisdom and loss; yet it was still magic.

'Oh no,' said Violette, with a demonic and utterly chilling smile. 'We have unfinished business at Schloss Holdenstein.'

Charlotte had been prepared for a battle. Instead they found the castle lying in deathly stillness.

As they walked along the corridor that led to the heart of the castle, the hush was pricked by soft voices, moans. A scent of dead blood and human exudations met them, but no sign of human life.

Entering the meeting chamber unhindered, they found carnage.

Human corpses everywhere. Thirty young men in white lay like scythed lilies, leopard-spotted with blood, bathed in dying torchlight. All of them drained of blood, cheated of eternal life.

Suddenly there was a weight in Charlotte's chest. Mingled with relief she felt sorrow for the waste of life, for the betrayal.

There were about thirty vampires in the chamber, all Cesare's flock. Some were dragging the corpses into rows, others sitting dazed on the floor as if they'd emerged alive from a disaster. Pierre was with a group at the back of the chamber, talking quietly among themselves. Charlotte saw one yellow-haired male vampire clinging to a corpse and weeping steadily. She thought of Robyn and tears came to her throat.

Cesare and Simon were near the ebony throne, engaged in a quiet but rancorous argument.

Karl, Charlotte and Violette entered very softly. For a moment, no one took any notice. Simon saw them first but barely reacted; he only gazed flatly at them and stopped responding to Cesare's words. After a few seconds Cesare froze, and turned to see what Simon was staring at.

Cesare staggered backwards, tripped on the dais and rescued

himself on the arm of the throne. His face coloured horribly, like those of the dead mortals. 'How did they get out? You told me they'd never escape!'

'A misjudgement,' Simon said dully.

'What? You came to me from God and you—'

'Can't you understand?' Simon said viciously. '*They* are the new leaders, not you. That's why we can't contain or destroy them! They are the future!'

'If only,' said Karl. Cesare looked so betrayed, so heart-broken, that Charlotte sincerely pitied him.

Violette walked to the centre of the chamber and looked around as if she were alone. This time she came not as a storm but a self-contained entity, yet everyone stared and drew away, as if they had seen her die and rise again from the underworld.

But that's what we did, Charlotte thought. And she realized, it's not just Violette they fear, it's all of us! She saw Pierre among the others, eyes wild, his face like wax.

'Well, which of you shall it be first?' Violette said conver-sationally. She was a goddess of ice-crystal, her hair the night sky, her eyes arctic violet-blue. 'Simon?'

Simon walked to her as if he couldn't resist, didn't care. What's wrong with him? Charlotte thought, chilled. His eyes! They're like glass, *dead*.

'Your friends were killed,' said Lilith, taking his hand.

'Friends?'

'Fyodor, Rasmila. By Sebastian. Do you care?'

Simon only frowned a little, like a man who had lost his memory. 'How did you escape?' he asked.

'Let me show you.'

'Yes. Show me what I already know.'

No one moved as Violette stood on tiptoe to press her lips to Simon's throat. Simon stood like a gilded figurine, steeped in the blood-red stain of his robe. Her long, sinewy arms went around his shoulders, the widow's veil of her hair half-covering them both. Simon's sculptural face became immobile, his eyes hooded, his lips parted. A frown indented the smooth skin between his eyebrows.

Cesare clung to the throne, aghast.

In the silence, Karl said, 'Where's Ilona?'

Pierre rushed forward and tugged at Karl's arm, clearly desperate to escape Lilith. 'I'll take you.'

Charlotte watched them stride out through the archway. Then she looked at Cesare. His countenance darkened and he came towards her, lips parting to reveal his fangs.

'Don't touch me,' Charlotte said, putting up her hand. Cesare stopped. She thought, I have power over him; have I become like Lilith in some way? Isis, gold and white light.

'This will never be forgotten or forgiven,' he said. 'God will be your judge.'

'It's not our fault the transformation failed,' she said angrily. 'We weren't here! This is all a lie! Fanaticism is a human disease; we should know better.'

'We failed because we were betrayed!'

'No, you failed because the Crystal Ring has more sense than you.' Charlotte walked past him and went to look at the bodies. The other vampires watched her expectantly, as if waiting for her to continue. 'Well?' she said. 'You were there, didn't you feel what was happening? The Crystal Ring itself won't allow so many immortals to be created. Something worse than you is coming, Cesare. The world has no place for you and your empire. It can conjure its own nightmares without your help.'

'Liar!' said Cesare, frantic, helpless.

'We've seen the future,' said Charlotte. 'No more vampires.'

There was a sound behind her, the rustle of a robe. When she glanced round, Cesare had disappeared.

Charlotte looked at the others. 'Do you still love him? Still believe in him?'

No one responded. The yellow-haired vampire, who was clinging to his dead friend, looked up at her with piercing black eyes, but said nothing. Sighing, Charlotte gazed with sad detachment at the corpses. Trying, like Karl, not to turn away in horror. I have been sealed in a coffin and buried and I'm still alive . . .

One of the bodies twitched.

She bent down beside it and felt a pulse, a weak life-aura. His face was drained, his breathing shallow – but he was alive. Unchanged, still human.

'What's your name?' Charlotte asked in German.

The man's eyes fluttered, trying to focus.

'Werner. Am I in hell?'

'More or less.' She knew, urgently, that she must get him out of the castle before one of the others decided to stamp out his tenuous life. 'Get up,' she said, holding his arm. 'I'll help you.'

He was a well-built youth, but she had the strength to half-carry him along narrow twisting corridors until she found the door, under a deep archway, that opened to the outside. Like the others, he was handsome, not very bright; he'd worshipped Cesare's dogma, and yet, for some reason, Charlotte wanted him to live.

She dragged open the door and thrust Werner out on to the hillside. He stood blinking at her, utterly confounded.

'Go on!' said Charlotte. 'It's a miracle you're alive! Just go!'

The youth went, stumbling, into the darkness.

Then the stench hit her.

The warmth of other humans, steaming from below. The sourness of sweat and excrement. Charlotte ran down a spiral stair, wrenched open a locked cell door, and saw three dozen pairs of eyes blaring through the dark in terror and supplication.

She gasped, holding her throat. She knew what they were. Victims, held ready to feed Cesare's new-fledged race of immortals.

'You're free,' Charlotte said, almost losing her voice. She pointed, 'Up the steps. The door is open. Come on!'

'What happened?' Karl asked as Pierre led him to a passageway lined with iron doors. Kristian had used to lock up recalcitrant disciples here; Karl himself had been imprisoned here more than once. He shuddered, thinking, if John has harmed Ilona, he'll think I am Kristian, come back from the dead.

'It all went wrong,' Pierre said with a shrug. 'John and Cesare blamed Ilona for breaking the circle.'

'Insanity to transform them all at once.'

'Simon swore it would work. Maybe he knew it wouldn't. He's just admitted that he's been using Cesare; they've had a glorious argument. And what now?'

'You tell me,' said Karl.

Pierre caught Karl's elbow. Their eyes met; Pierre looked exhausted and frightened for his life. 'My friend, you are the one who brought Lilith here again. I don't know what the hell you are playing at! Since I came here I have thought about nothing but how to escape her . . .'

Feeling no sympathy, Karl said coldly, 'Have you considered facing her instead?'

They came to a cell in which Karl sensed two immortals. The door was open. Inside, between the lightless walls, Karl saw Ilona facing the doorway, the grotesque figure of John confronting her.

'Daughter of Lilith,' John was saying; his voice was the whisper of an inquisitor, a torturer. 'You betrayed us. You are a serpent.'

Ilona smiled at him. 'Flatterer,' she said.

She was unhurt, Karl saw in relief; she and John were like wolves circling, each waiting for the other to attack first.

'Shameless whore,' said John.

'You couldn't afford me.'

'Witch!'

'And you are scared to death of witches, aren't you?'

Karl walked in and seized John's arm so hard that he exclaimed in pain. He glared redly at Karl, all his hellish strength and rage seething behind his deformed visage. But he'd lost the spark of courage. His jaw dropped, he seemed to mouth, *But you are* – and then he vanished into Raqi'a.

Karl looked at Ilona. 'Are you all right?'

'I hate you,' she said, her head tilted to one side, her mouth sulky. 'I was enjoying that.'

Then she ran into Karl's arms.

As they returned through the thin corridors and stairways, Karl asked, 'Did you really sabotage the transformation?'

'Oh, yes,' said Ilona. 'I broke the circle and I did it on

purpose. Also I did not quite kill my partner, so he would be a block to the energy.'

'Why?' Karl said in astonishment.

'Because I'm Lilith's daughter.' She smiled thinly. 'I have my pride; I never thought that anyone could break my spirit, until I met her, and I wouldn't admit she'd done it until I found myself being used by Cesare. Yes, I know he was using me, but I was too busy hating Violette to care.'

'What changed your mind?'

'Realizing the perfect insanity of what Cesare was doing. My God, to think I was helping that half-wit to become a tyrant, just to revenge myself on her! But then I came to see that Violette acts as she does because she's exactly like me, *nicht wahr*?'

Karl and Pierre shared a look of ironic surprise over Ilona's head.

Ilona went on, 'I couldn't face what she'd done to me. She makes you look at yourself and it's not a pretty sight.' She grinned at Pierre, who looked sulky. 'I thought I was being clever, not giving in to her. But my idiocy lay in coming to Cesare, instead of forcing myself to face it. Still, it didn't take me so very long to come to my senses.'

When they returned to the main chamber, there was no sign of Cesare, Simon, Violette or Charlotte. The vampires in scarlet lingered restively, as if waiting for something to happen.

Karl saw a vampire he knew, Maria. She was standing passively, head bowed and dark gold hair escaping the hood of her robe. 'Where are Cesare and the others?' he asked.

'They left separately,' she replied, not looking at him. 'First Cesare, then Charlotte. And when Lilith let Simon go, he walked away, speaking to no one. Then Lilith vanished. But they are still in the castle, I believe.'

'Why don't you leave?'

'Where would we go? Only Cesare can protect us from Lilith.'

'We are waiting,' one of the others said acerbically, 'for Cesare to tell us what we are to do now!'

'Why do you need anyone to tell you?' Karl said, exasperated.

'We need answers!'

Turning away, Karl began to move through the grisly scene of devastation, compelled to look at every corpse. Such young faces, once plump with radiant health and idealism; now drained, empty, collapsed in on themselves, the features distorted and coloured with the random ugliness of bruises. Life cared what it looked like; death did not. He looked at their slack mouths and half-open eyes, their out-flung hands. They had died before their neck wounds could heal, so the holes were still ragged. Their chests were dabbled with dried blood. Blood-coloured maps stained their virginal robes. Not just their own, but the blood of their comrades, which had spurted from torn arteries. No survivors.

He saw visions of the past and the future; thousands of young men felled in their prime to fulfil the evil dreams of idealogues . . .

A small group of vampires was huddled in a corner, weeping. One had collapsed over a corpse as if all his hopes lay dead within it.

Some of them believed in this, Karl thought. Some of them cared, which makes it even worse.

Ilona and Pierre were watching him, though he was only half-aware of them. Suddenly, although he'd been too preoccupied to notice her coming back into the chamber, Charlotte was touching his arm. 'Karl? Don't brood on this. It isn't your responsibility!'

'Where have you been?' he asked.

'One of them was alive. I set him free. And some others, captive prey—'

'One,' Karl said flatly. 'Did Cesare tell them what a risk this was? Did he tell them they were gambling with their lives?'

'They wouldn't have stopped, even if he had,' said Ilona.

'I wonder if he will give them a decent burial,' Karl said with black sarcasm.

'Should I feel guilty?' Ilona asked.

Karl shook his head. 'No. If Cesare had succeeded, it would have been a disaster of a different order. And the transformation would probably have failed without your intervention anyway.'

'Oh, don't tell me that! At least I tried!'

'I'm sure Cesare blames you, anyway,' said Charlotte.

'Oh, he must have someone to blame.' Ilona laughed. 'Yes, as long as he thinks that *I* had the power to ruin him, I am vindicated! By the way, you won't tell Violette any of this, will you? I don't want her thinking she's won me over. My pride won't allow it.'

'She'll know,' Charlotte said.

Pierre broke in, 'And you are just going to let her run amok? Your worship of Madame's artistic talents seems to have completely blinded you to the fact that she's insane. She tried to kill me!'

'Pity she failed,' said Ilona.

'You're a perfect bitch.'

'At least I'm perfect. There is always one who can't or won't see the truth beneath the surface.'

Karl gave Pierre a cold look. 'Violette has made mistakes. Which of us hasn't?'

'Pierre's trouble is that he's always lived with the illusion that he's strong and pitiless.' Ilona went to Pierre and leaned on his shoulder. He looked sour. 'Imagine how dreadful it was for him to be brought face to face with his own weakness – or with the fact that he actually regretted his first victim being his mother, after all.'

'Ilona, shut up!' Pierre said savagely. 'Violette did nothing to change me. She's a fake, an evil fake like Kristian. Do me the courtesy of letting me hate her, without patronizing me as if I'm a sad misguided fool. What's brought about *your* change of heart, Karl? Did she offer you something more than her blood?' He glanced at Charlotte, and sneered. 'You really should restrict your appetites to blood alone, my friends. Otherwise you start acting like sentimental humans.'

'Heaven forbid,' Karl said drily.

'Don't be miserable, Pierre,' said Charlotte. 'You're still alive. Just be thankful Lilith hasn't taken revenge on you for helping Cesare.'

'I didn't help him,' Pierre retorted. 'And I hope she tears his eyes out.'

Ilona came to Karl and laid her hands on his chest, tilting her face up to his. 'Father,' she said quietly, 'I don't want you to regret transforming me for the rest of your life. It would once have killed me to admit this, but I can say it now. I'm not sorry. Tormenting you was fun, but even such amusements pall in the end. You don't regret it . . . do you?'

Her need to know was almost childlike.

'No,' Karl said heavily. 'Even knowing what would happen, I would do it again tomorrow.'

Smiling, she bowed her head on to her chest. And still Karl did not know how much this change of heart was genuine, how much another manipulation. Unable to speak, he rested his head on Ilona's hair, his eyes closed. But his hands remained at his sides.

Cesare knelt in the inner sanctum, praying. All the doors were closed, all the candles lit. He was terrified, but he was determined not to flee.

The sword lay before him. A heavy, sharp broadsword that had hung on the wall in one of Kristian's rooms.

To see Simon lose his mind then give himself up to Lilith without pride or defiance had unhinged Cesare. She won't take me like that! Dear God, have mercy on your servant, forgive me for my sins and failures, only lend me your strength against the Enemy! I kneel before you, the last bastion against the dark, and I swear that I will stand and fight to my last breath—

He felt the air change. Felt a hand on his shoulder, like a long slim claw.

It was her. Lilith.

'You're mine,' she said, as piercingly dispassionate as a cobra. He couldn't look at her. He knelt under her claw, dying of fear. 'Let me kiss you, as I kissed Simon. I know how you love the kisses of women. Let me enter your soul and show you the truth.'

Cesare scrambled to his feet, grabbed the sword, and ran, flinging back the doors in his path. He stayed on earth because to face her in the Crystal Ring would have been even worse.

Lilith smiled and came quite slowly after him, a snow-maiden in blood-spattered lavender silk; an owl gliding towards her frantic, earth-bound prey.

Simon had known the truth before Violette came to him and pressed her icy lips to his flesh. That was why he had not tried to evade her. Lilith's lash of fire, painfully revealing as it was, became almost a formality.

He'd known, in the moment that the mass transformation had failed. The Crystal Ring had wrecked their ambition as a hostile sea swallows a ship. The veil of light had ripped to reveal, not the face of a god who would lift his élite to a perfect heaven, but the dark and blindingly beautiful face of the death-dealing Crone, who never discriminated between male and female, Brahmin and Untouchable, saved and damned.

Reality.

Live ten thousand years, Simon. The fantasies and ambitions of your tiny soul will still be no more and no less to me than the life of an ant.

The Crystal Ring had made him an angel, a dual being of flesh and omniscience with a calling to unite vampire-kind under God. Just as abruptly, it had torn his status away. And he couldn't bear it. The simple pleasures of earth, of love and blood and flesh, were not enough for him. It was not enough to be a vampire. He needed the absolute, the eternal. The linear process of birth, life, elevation to heaven – not the cyclic process of death and decay to give new life to others.

Simon needed to be a god.

He'd come so close! And then to find it was all illusion, that the God in whom he'd put absolute faith was only an exudation of the human psyche within the Crystal Ring – that was unbearable.

When Lilith had finished with him, and his soul hung tattered, exposed to the winds of disillusion, and as raw as the wound she'd made, Simon quietly left the chamber and climbed the twisting stairs towards the highest castle balcony.

He thought of the *Weisskalt* but it was not final enough. To him, it would be no more than a light sleep.

On his way, he took a hand-scythe from a wall and tested its sharpness. He also found a length of rope.

Reaching the balcony, Simon loosened a block of stone with his bare hands. It took time, but the mortar was old and his fingers were hard as steel. At last he lifted it out of the waist-high wall and placed it to one side. He gouged channels in the blocks on either side, working feverishly, his glassy nails crumbling the stone like cheese. Then he placed the scythe across the gap so that it rested, blade upwards, in the grooves he'd made.

He tied one end of the rope round the loose block, parcelling it so that it could not slip free. Having placed the block on top of the wall, he tied the other end of the rope into a noose which he slipped over his head and tightened under his chin.

Simon worked as single-mindedly at this as he had at everything. He thought of nothing else. He felt no fear.

He did not know that the weightless feeling in his chest was overwhelming grief. He had no awareness of Rasmila and Fyodor as beloved presences in his mind, calling him.

Kneeling down, Simon bent forward and rested his neck in the curve of the scythe. The edge nicked his skin but he welcomed the pain and the silver-sharp pressure of the steel. Below, the wall fell sheer into the steep hillside.

Simon pushed the block off the wall. He saw it falling with the rope rippling behind it. When it reached its full extent, the block jerked and dragged Simon's head down with it. The blade slid swiftly through the structures of his neck with a whispered *crunch*. The stone went on falling.

Yet his consciousness persisted. He felt the stump of his neck as a circle of acid fire, saw the trees rushing up to meet him as he hurtled down through space. One second of annihilating horror—

Then, like a flame, he expired into the kindly oblivion of Lilith's wings.

*

Cesare seemed more enraged than terrified, yet he went on fleeing from Violette. She followed him along the tortuous corridors of the Schloss, kicked off her shoes and ran barefoot. Lighter and faster than him, she could have caught him at any time she chose, but she let him stay just ahead. Teasing him.

He made no attempt to enter the Ring. Perhaps he thought it would be worse there; perhaps the castle gave him an illusion of security.

She ran him to ground in the meeting chamber. A crowd of vampires, Karl and Charlotte among them, stared and gasped, transfixed, but Violette took no notice. She thought, Cesare must have come back here thinking there's safety in numbers, that his acolytes will protect him.

But in the centre of the chamber, in front of Kristian's throne – it had never truly been Cesare's – he stopped and faced her, brandishing the sword.

The others bore witness, but Violette ignored them. Audiences did not distract her.

'Mortal weapons against Lilith?' said Violette, sweetly poisonous, aiming at Cesare all her grief over Robyn's death. His greed, she felt, had killed Robyn. He was part of the despotic, militaristic wave that was deforming the Crystal Ring. 'You'll never touch me with it,' she said. 'Lay it aside.'

She stepped towards him. The blade wavered at her throat. She gazed along its length to Cesare's face; he had the look of a schoolboy, debauched by premature knowledge and power. Strangely innocent, though. His pale grey eyes were awash with tears of pain. Only evil in that he was passionately deluded.

'But these delusions are infectious,' she said aloud. 'They will oppress and slaughter millions.'

'You are filth, you don't deserve to live!' Cesare exploded. 'Whore, impure female, witch, hag—' A stream of insults washed over her and faded. The sword shook in his hands. Suddenly he took a step back and cried impotently, 'If Kristian were still alive—'

'Oh, I should have liked to have met Kristian! He was worth a hundred of you. That's what they say, although it isn't saying much.'

Violette grasped the sword and wrenched it out of his hands. The blade cut her palms, but she barely noticed the pain. She flung the weapon down behind her. Cesare let out a short scream. He seemed petrified by her eyes, racked with horror because he knew it was almost over.

'Let me alone,' he said, his voice trembling. 'I'll go away. I'll live like a monk, anything you say, only don't—'

'I'm not going to kill you – yet.'

'I know!' he cried in anguish. 'But I'd rather die than be infected with your evil!'

'Poor Cesare,' she said softly. 'How hideous it will be to live without the comfort of your fond illusions. But I can't spare you.'

She reached for him, quite languidly. The spell broke; he span round and made for the side wall of the chamber, arms outstretched as if to launch himself into Raqi'a.

Pursuing him, Violette saw a dark shape suddenly materializing between Cesare and the wall. She stopped in her tracks. And then a great weight brought her down from behind.

Flattened by the pain of impact, she couldn't fight back at first. A hard, leathery body pressed her down, thin hands gripped her like talons. She smelled damp mustiness and stale blood. Then a dry mouth came scraping over the back of her neck, fangs pricking the skin, sending a wave of cold revulsion over her.

She twisted furiously, and from the corner of her eye saw John above her. The sneering demon face, the veined bulb of his head, his eyes like hot embers pouring hatred over her. Soulless eyes, as rabid as the mediaeval, devil-obsessed age from which he'd sprung.

'You are dead, serpent-witch,' John whispered. And his fangs sank into her neck. The precise pain froze her to the spot, as if the sheer force of John's hatred had equalled Lilith's power. Her fingers clawed at the floor, trying to claw her way into the Ring—

The pain leapt to a crescendo of hot agony, but the weight was abruptly gone. Through a crimson mosaic, Violette saw shapes moving in front of her, felt movement behind. Someone had pulled John off her, and his fangs had ripped holes in her tender flesh.

Her vision cleared, her agility returned. With one hand pressed to the wound, she leapt to her feet, crouching ready for another attack. And she saw Karl, standing above her, his eyes full of amber fire; saw the sword in his hand, the blade glistening with blood. And John lay at her feet, his head severed.

As she watched, Karl struck again, and the head rolled into two grisly halves.

Violette straightened up. Karl dropped the sword and embraced her. No word was spoken. He turned her, holding her against his side with one arm round her shoulders, and Violette saw what was happening to Cesare.

She'd seen a shape appear, a split-second before John's attack. That shape was Sebastian. Unable to stop, Cesare's momentum had carried him straight into Sebastian's arms.

And now the dark vampire was feeding on Cesare, the pair side-on to Violette and Karl. As they watched, Sebastian lifted his head, his lips peeled back from long wolf-teeth that were slicked with blood. Holding Cesare at arm's length, he stretched out his other hand, fingers hooked like talons, and ripped Cesare's robe. Then he thrust his hand into Cesare's stomach, straight through the flesh, plunging deep into the internal structures.

Cesare hung there as if flattened against a sheet of glass. His silent agony throbbed in the air. Violette couldn't move, could only stare as Sebastian worked his hand deeper in Cesare's body, up beneath the rib-cage. Blood oozed like the juice of red grapes around his wrist. Cesare's eyes strained in their sockets and his mouth hung open, but no sound came out.

Sebastian grasped something, twisted and wrenched it. There was a sucking, snapping noise. Then Sebastian held a trophy aloft: Cesare's heart, filling his palm like a pulsating, glistening strawberry.

Cesare hit the floor like a felled tree. Undying, he writhed, clutching at the bloody pit in his abdomen, spreading his own blood everywhere.

A sound rose from his throat, a whine that was the worst noise Violette had ever heard. But Lilith, the dispassionate witness, held her motionless.

Sebastian crouched down over Cesare, brandishing the heart. 'This is what you've done to me,' he said in a low voice. 'How does it feel?'

Cesare plainly had no idea what Sebastian was talking about. He tried to shake his head.

'How long do you think it will take you to die,' Sebastian said, 'while I tear you apart, piece by piece? A long time, you bastard. Everything starts to heal and regenerate, doesn't it, ready for me to rip it out again and again. We could have quite a little family of your hearts here. It could take for ever.'

Cesare's whine rose in pitch. He began to sob, an animal sound.

'I wouldn't waste my time.' Sebastian squeezed the heart, making gelatinous maroon drops fall on to Cesare's face, then flung it away.

Cesare's sobs became words, hoarse, distorted, but vicious. 'Fool, Sebastian. You have all eternity in front of you but you live in the past, thinking of nothing but yourself! At least I thought of the future. At least I thought of all vampire-kind, not just my own narrow life!'

Leaning down, Sebastian bit hard into Cesare's trachea; not drinking, but gashing a deep wound.

Suddenly finding her voice, Violette said, 'Leave him!'

Her tone was commanding but Sebastian ignored her. He seized Cesare's head, snapped his neck. Then he went on biting, tearing through the fibres and vessels until he reached the spinal column itself.

Leaving Karl, Violette ran forward and seized Sebastian's arm, but it was like clutching granite. She couldn't stop him.

She heard the rasping crunch as his teeth closed through bone and nerve fibre. The head moved as if the neck were lengthening, then rolled aside. Cesare was dead. His eyes contemplated oblivion with the same impervious fanaticism they'd shown in life.

Violette dropped down to face Sebastian across the gore-soaked body. They crouched like two black-haired harpies squabbling over the kill.

'Why?' she said.

He met her gaze. His face was colourless, hag-ridden. 'To avenge Robyn.'

'So you had to blame someone.'

'Yes!'

'Why did you have to kill him?'

'Holy Mother of God, the sister of mercy! What's made you go soft?'

'I haven't,' she hissed. 'Don't you see what you've done? He died with his illusions intact! My punishment would have been far worse than yours. His physical pain could never have compared with the horror of finding his whole life was a lie! And you've taken that from me!'

'So you are as bad as me,' he said. 'So don't lecture me, madam. Just go back where you belong. Go to hell!'

Sebastian straightened up, glared hostilely at the others. 'If any of you wish to take issue with me over this,' he said, his tone thinly dangerous, 'you are welcome.'

No one moved. Someone shouted, 'We don't want another Kristian. We won't accept you!'

'I am not offering,' Sebastian replied. 'And all of you, too, can go to hell.'

Sebastian turned his back on them and vanished. An uprush of voices like soft flame released the tension. Violette put her fingers to her temples and pushed them into her hair, not realizing she had Cesare's and her own blood all over her.

The other vampires were gathering, staring at the bodies of John and Cesare. Staring at *her*. Charlotte came and stroked her arm, unspeaking, her eyes sombre.

The acolyte of Cesare's who had spoken out – the male vampire with yellow hair and black eyes, who earlier had been weeping bitterly – said, 'We don't want revenge. I lost a human friend whom I loved today. Cesare let us down; he led us on with false promises and he broke them. We've come to the conclusion that those who try to rule us have had their day.

They demand sacrifices and reward us with betrayal! We've had enough. Lilith – I don't know how I should address you – Lilith, no one wants to avenge Cesare – but we don't want you in his place!'

'Good,' Violette said fervently. 'I am not setting myself up as queen of vampires. I am not your Enemy, whatever Cesare told you. I have acted harshly at times, but I've done nothing that was undeserved. If you approach me in friendship, not in fear, I won't harm you. But the truth hurts – and some find me too honest.'

She sounded cold, she knew, and she looked like an ice-witch; ebony, snow and blood. But she could put no warmth into her manner.

It was Charlotte who redeemed her, bringing the light and the warmth, as she had when they'd entwined with Karl. Resting a hand on Violette's shoulder, she said, 'You don't understand who Lilith is, or what she represents. She will teach us to face the darkness without fear. Don't drive her out. That's the mistake men have made for thousands of years and will go on making. But we don't have to be like them. Let her in, welcome her. Listen to her.'

Another of the vampires said, 'Is this a new theology to replace Kristian's?'

'No, it's not doctrine.' Charlotte's words were impassioned. Violette sensed the others warming to her, perceiving her as sincere, generous-hearted, unthreatening. 'We've seen something of the future. The Ring, which is not God but the subconscious of mankind, will let us create no more vampires. They don't need any more of us, because their minds are set on a future that will bring more horrors than ever we could. The disturbances in the Ring are being caused by thought-movements on earth. Not by Lilith. By man. It's a wave, it can't be stopped.'

There was an electrified hush.

'My God,' said Pierre, 'does this mean we'll die?'

'No, I believe we'll live. But there will be no more of us, for a time, at least. So we must face this darkness together, not at each other's throats! In the Crystal Ring we have the power to be anything; angels, gods, monsters. But be careful; the trans-forming energy is born from the fears and desires of humanity. The Ring is a sentience without consciousness or conscience; it can use us, consume us and spit us out. And if we go too far—' She paused, smiling a little. 'If we go too far, Lilith is the power that says, "Enough."

'I want to say something else. We're not human; we don't need leaders, we can each rule ourselves. It's hopeless to cling to the past. You must leave this castle. It's destroying you. The pain of your victims has soaked into the walls, and one day it will come back to claim you. It's an illusion that humans are at our mercy, because in reality, we are at theirs. But in recom-pense we have these wonderful gifts! Don't squander them on false prophets. Don't waste them. That's all.'

Silence. Charlotte looked at Violette and shrugged, as if to say, 'What's the use?'

Then the black-eyed vampire came forward. He kissed Charlotte's hand and bowed to her, paid the same respect to Violette, then inclined his head to Karl. After him, one by one, all the others followed suit. Even Ilona, though she did so with an edge of irony. All except Pierre, who remained obstinately apart, staring at Violette with hollow eyes.

Second to last came Maria, handmaiden first to Kristian, then to Cesare. Instead of bowing she threw back her hood and offered her throat to Violette. She looked like a saint in scarlet.

And Violette-Lilith took her; a sharp embrace, a few passion-ate mouthfuls, just as she'd taken Ute so long ago. 'Now you know,' Lilith whispered, putting Maria away from her, 'that you need never be a slave again.'

Maria walked blankly away without speaking and followed the others who were now leaving the chamber. She was dazed but she would recover, Violette knew, and *see*.

Only Pierre and Ilona remained with them now. Charlotte put a hand to her forehead and released an astonished laugh. 'They listened to me!'

'Yes,' said Karl, kissing her. 'They listened.'

Then Pierre came forward at last. He came reluctantly and stopped two feet from Violette, not touching her.

'Well?' she said.

'You will be the death of me!' Pierre exclaimed. 'After all you've done to me, Violette, I fear that I am still hopelessly in love with you. Humiliating, is it not? I don't want to stop being terrified of you, ever. It's heaven within hell.'

Alone, Karl went to look for Simon. Simon had slipped away unseen and there was no sense of his presence in the Schloss, yet Karl, driven by some strange instinct, needed to know what had become of him.

Exploring the upper levels of the castle, Karl came out on to the highest balcony overlooking the Rhine. The stars were very bright. In their implicit light he saw the body; blood-red satin loosely contouring a magnificent golden form, the sinewy neck reduced to a crude stump.

Karl saw the scythe wedged across a gap in the wall, the blade smeared with blood. He knew then that Simon must have taken his own life. Not easy for a vampire to decapitate himself, but not impossible. Karl groaned inwardly.

Some could cope with the truth that Lilith revealed; some could not. Karl felt sad, despite the hostility between them. Given time, he thought, perhaps we could have become friends . . . perhaps not. The most elevated fall the hardest.

Karl took a step towards the body, halted. It seemed to him that two translucent figures were twined around Simon, sobbing out their grief; one dark, like ultramarine and umber mixed, one albino. His breath caught and he thought, do vampires have ghosts? Or can these 'angels' never truly die?

He moved, and the figures vanished. A trick of the starlight.

He looked over the balcony, down into the tangle of trees and bushes and rocks. He sensed someone moving down there. And he thought, dear God, the head!

Karl launched himself over the balcony and jumped.

Plunging downwards, he went into Raqi'a so that branches and rocks did not tear him to pieces. He landed in undergrowth with the hillside rearing above him, trees weaving spider-webs of frost down to the edge of the Rhine. There was a sprinkling of snow over everything but the river was a black sword. Karl began to search urgently through the bushes for Simon's head.

Again, he saw the two shadows.

They were drifting towards him, it seemed, between great rocks which were nuggets of silver in the phantom light. Then Karl saw, lying in his path and theirs, a rock unlike the others. It was cuboid, dull, tied up with rope.

Karl dashed towards it, determined to reach it first. He followed the snake of rope with his eyes, saw the head at the other end, flawless as pale gold marble, lying in a frosty drift of leaves.

Karl lifted the big square stone and dropped it on to Simon's perfect visage. The skull crunched like an egg. He pushed the stone aside with his foot and saw the crushed mass of white, gold and crimson; a ghastly mosaic. Karl sighed, feeling horrified, relieved and drained.

When he looked up, there were no grief-stricken shades of Fyodor and Rasmila watching him in recrimination. There was only a human. A youth, Ilona's protégé, the only survivor. His face was colourless and he was gaping at Karl as if he were immersed in a nightmare.

'It's essential to destroy the skull,' Karl said, feeling he must reassure the youth by explaining. 'Otherwise we can come back to life.'

The young man only went on staring as if Karl were insane; which, in that moment, Karl felt that he was.

Werner could not take his eyes off the vampire or the crushed head of Simon. He was dizzy, he couldn't think, there were weird gaps in his memory. He couldn't believe he was alive; more likely he was dead and in some insane other-world; a rippling world of spun silver where madmen thought severed heads could come back to life.

The vampire, tall and mahogany-haired, shook his head as if mortally tired, and vanished into thin air.

Werner was alone. I am ill, he thought, shivering. Must get

help. But he was lost and it had taken him for ever to come this far from the castle.

Then they came. A train of women and children and a few men, down the steep path he'd taken from the Schloss. Not strong golden youths, these, but dark-skinned gypsies, the kind of imperfect lowly mortals that Cesare had taught his flock to despise.

But Werner could not despise them. Their piteous state and their suffering floored him with overwhelming empathy and anger. It filled his chest, stopped his breath. Who could have done this to these poor souls?

The answer came. *I could have done it.*

I'm going home, he thought, wiping his eyes, feeling only sick revulsion at the memory of Cesare. I was spared! On my mother's name I swear I'll never fall under the spell of such a dictator again. I shall fight dictators, with all that's left of my life!

Violette had been given no chance to say goodbye to Robyn. So, after they left Schloss Holdenstein, she slipped away from her friends and returned to Ireland alone.

In Raqi'a, the inky fortress still seethed. It would grow worse, she knew, before it began to dissipate.

But here was the house of sorrow, cupped in lovely green hills. A mansion of ghosts, silver-yellow, like old bone.

The bedroom lay in darkness. Violette's preternatural vision did not register the rich embroidery of the bed-curtains; the only colour she saw was Robyn's hair, richest brown, like wood from the tree of life. The face, though, was no longer Robyn's. It was sunken and discoloured and the jaw had dropped. Her hands, folded on her chest, seemed to have shrunk.

But I am the funerary priestess, Violette thought. I see the dying through death and beyond. This holds no horror for me. Robyn's body will nourish the earth and the wheel of life turns.

Violette walked from one side of the bed to the other, taking in every detail, forcing herself to accept it. She was trembling. Her emotions were so extreme that she could not define them as mere grief.

Rasmila's body, which had been near the fireplace, had gone. But she took this in without interest.

'Could we have been anything, my dear?' she whispered. 'Or was I just dreaming, torturing myself with dreams?'

She found a pair of scissors in the bedside cabinet and cut off a lock of Robyn's hair. As she replaced the scissors and put the skein in her pocket, she became aware of another vampire in the room.

Sebastian. She turned to see him standing just inside the door, an immaculate dark figure, like a clergyman who'd never lifted a finger in rage.

'What are you doing here?' he asked quietly.

He was the last person she'd wanted to see. She had hoped he would not be here. But now he was, she lacked the energy for another fight.

'I'll have to tell her Uncle Josef where she is,' Violette said tonelessly. 'Then he can come and fetch her.'

She expected him to object, but he said, 'That's only right. It's a shell, after all. It isn't Robyn.'

'I expect he'll have to notify the police, but that's nothing to do with us.'

'I buried what was left of Fyodor and Rasmila,' said Sebastian. 'No one will be looking for them.'

'No,' Violette said indifferently.

She meant to say a final goodbye to Robyn, and leave. But as she stood there, a great weight seemed to hit her below the ribs. Unable to help herself, she sank down on her knees, clawing at the side of the bed, and began to sob uncontrollably.

A few minutes passed, though time lost clear dimensions. Then she felt Sebastian slide down behind her. Folding his arms around her, he held her tight, his forehead resting on her shoulder-blade. And she didn't mind. She was glad.

They remained like that for a long time, weeping together.

'Simon is dead, too,' Violette said eventually. 'He killed himself. I didn't shed a single tear for him.'

'He was one of my creators,' said Sebastian. 'It should be like losing a father, but I don't feel anything. Why did he do it?'

'I showed him the truth. He didn't like it.'

'Truth?'

'That he and people like him create God out of their denial of death. That all the old beliefs which accepted death had to be taken over or diabolized, in order to destroy them. All out of fear . . .'

'Oh, Violette.' She felt his breath on her neck; it was as warm and consoling as his arms. 'I could have told you that. We didn't all lose the old religion. I am part of this country, after all. Last century the supposedly Christian folk of County Waterford worshipped at a well with a figure described by some writer as looking "like the pictures of Callee, the Black Goddess of Hindostan". They can't erase our memories of the Dark Mother so easily. But I murdered Rasmila and Fyodor in my rage. My own creators. What have I done? Destroyed two treacherous vampires, or slaughtered gods? Surely I'll be punished.'

'I think,' said Violette, 'that we are being punished enough. Rasmila was part of me; an aspect of Lilith in some way. But she didn't know me, she couldn't see past Simon's illusions. I only wish that I'd had the chance to make her *see*. She could have borne the knowledge.'

'Can you bear this?' he said softly, looking at Robyn.

'Sometimes I can,' she said, 'and sometimes I cannot.'

'Well, I can't,' he murmured.

'Do you still blame me?'

'No,' Sebastian said heavily. 'Not you, not Cesare. Only myself. And now there's nothing for me but to place myself in the *Weisskalt*.'

His words shocked her. She hadn't realized – or been able to admit – the depth of his grief. 'Why?'

'I blamed Robyn a little, too. She changed me. I was as evil as it's possible to be, I was the devil incarnate, and I was perfectly content. Then along came Robyn and I fell for her like an idiot. Oh, Lilith, I don't need you to make me look at myself; she's done a fine job of wrecking all my self-delusions. How can I live with myself now? How can I live without *her*?'

Violette folded her hands over his. 'Don't.'

'How did Simon do it, by the way? We can come back from the *Weisskalt*. I'd like something final.'

'Stop this!' She turned her head to look at him. 'Don't think of it.'

'Why not?' he said dully.

'Too many of us have gone. If I can live, so can you.'

And she felt him yield to her. 'As you wish, Madame.' They were quiet for a time. She exhaled, leaning back into him, the noose of pain easing.

Sebastian said, 'Rasmila once told me you hated men. Couldn't stand them touching you.'

'I don't mind this. It feels comforting. It was another sort of fear, the opposite of Cesare's, I suppose. I had to overcome it.'

'Well, at least I've been of some use,' he said.

'Oh, it wasn't you.' Violette was past caring what she said to him. There was nothing between them but tenderness, shared grief. No hostility, no secrets. 'It was Karl. I let him make love to me. No, I didn't let him, I persuaded him into an act of magical transfiguration.'

'He needed persuading? The man must be made of ice.'

She half-smiled. 'So am I, so we were well-matched.'

'No, you're very far from that. Oh, but why Karl?'

'What?'

'You should have waited for me.' His tone was dry; he sounded only partly serious. 'Weren't we married once? Lilith and Samael.'

'I don't think so.'

'Lilith was the bride of Samael, the devil. King and queen of hell. Have you quite forgotten me, my dear? You're not the only one who has felt the timeless weight of other lives.'

Something dark shifted within her. 'What do you remember?' she asked.

'Silhouettes. Serpents. Black vines with red flowers. And the fire and the drums . . . not memories, only *knowledge*.'

'The Crystal Ring playing games with our minds.'

'Ah, but such wickedly dark and rich games,' he said. 'And the same with both of us . . .'

'Sebastian,' she said coolly, 'you must understand that it was a single event with Karl. It was a sacred act, not an expression of desire. I only love women. I'm not sure there can be anyone after Robyn, but my feelings haven't changed.'

'And you must understand,' he said, his tone equally cool, 'that I also want no one after Robyn. Do you really imagine I thought you could replace her?'

'No, that's not what I thought,' she said. Too sad to argue. How eerie this felt; comforting yet bleak, skeletal.

'Whatever was between us is in the past.'

'Perhaps we weren't husband and wife,' Violette said gently, 'but brother and sister. That endures.'

'Then stay, just for a little while, dear sister,' said Sebastian. 'Not to weep alone. That's the most we can ask for.'

They were at home in Switzerland, within a circle of red–gold firelight; Karl in an armchair beside the fire, Charlotte curled on his knee with her head on his shoulder.

'Have you changed?' Karl asked. 'Am I to share you with some overexcitable deity?'

He spoke lightly, but now they were alone there was a filament of anxiety between them; their mutual inability to take each other for granted.

'No,' said Charlotte. 'I'm just me. A little older and wiser, that's all. And you?'

'You must understand,' Karl said, very quietly, 'that Violette and I . . . I wish it had not happened. It was not love, it was not even lust.'

'Dearest, you don't have to explain. I was there; I joined in, if you remember. It was sorcery.'

Karl half-smiled, as if unable to stop himself. 'Well, you have my word that it will not happen again.'

'No, I suppose it won't,' Charlotte said, rather sadly. 'We have no reason to feel guilty; in the Goddess's eyes sex is sacred, not a sin. All the same . . . I want you to myself. Always.'

'And so do I,' said Karl. 'The danger was that I'd lose *you* to Violette . . .'

'You won't.' She met his gaze. 'But must she be alone for ever? I wonder if the effect of Lilith's embrace was to make us even further removed from humanity. I should feel guilty about what I inflicted on my family. I never gave Anne visible proof that I had left the coffin. For all they know I am still in the ground. I meant to give them love and gave them nightmares instead, yet I can't bring myself to agonize about it.'

'Perhaps you have realized the pointlessness of agonizing. And I should be horrified at your rashness in doing what you did, but . . . I think I have grown rather used to you, *Liebling*.'

Charlotte stared at him, indignant. 'So you expect me to behave badly?'

'But you are never dull,' Karl said, his lips curved. 'Write to Anne.'

'Yes.' They were silent for a time, gazing tranquilly into the fire. Presently she said, 'Then there are things we can't even talk about. The sharing of victims.'

His eyes slid towards her under his long lashes; amber shadows and points of blood-red light. 'We can talk about it if you wish.'

'I think I'm less human than you, Karl. After we'd taken prey together I only remembered how beautiful it was, but you hated yourself.'

'It was a singularly hateful thing to do. Would you prefer me to glory in it?'

'No, but . . . we are vampires. You are such a gentleman and you expect me to be a lady; if a human came to our door and offered himself to us this minute, you would very politely send him away. I love you for that, but . . . I don't want you to torment yourself. We're vampires.'

'Whom Lilith has made a little crueller,' Karl said softly.

'No, more accepting of our natures.' Charlotte gave up, leaning her head on his chest, one hand in his hair. Still hopeless to speak of it, it seemed. 'Violette is talking of leaving Salzburg and finding new premises in Switzerland or England. She wants the company to have its own theatre and ballet school. I'm so glad. I thought she'd give up after Robyn.'

'She's too strong,' said Karl.

As he spoke, someone knocked at the front door. Karl and

Charlotte looked at each other, surprised; then she slipped off his knee and followed him along the hall to the door.

Karl stood in the doorway, an elegant silhouette against the deep dusky-blue of mountains, forest and sky. Facing him, on the wooden porch, were Stefan and Niklas, blond hair vivid as moonlight. And between them stood a human; a male of about twenty-five with curly black hair and rosy cheeks, slightly drunk, happy and friendly and completely innocent of what his new friends actually were.

'We couldn't stay away,' Stefan said apologetically. 'I felt so dreadful for deserting you, and I couldn't help thinking of what we might be missing, and, what is worse, I was bored.'

'Your timing is immaculate,' Karl said sardonically. 'It's all over.'

'Oh,' said Stefan, looking, Charlotte thought, more relieved than disappointed. 'Well, then you can tell us all about it.' He placed a fond hand on the human's shoulder. 'We brought . . . refreshments.'

Karl and the young man regarded each other. Then the man's smile vanished, and his pink face turned deathly white.

'Come in,' said Karl.

FLAME TO ICE

By its opening night in Vienna, Violette had given *Witch and Maiden* a very different ending. The dark spirit Lila, rejected by Siegfried in favour of the pure Anna, curses them and abducts their children. As her curse unwinds, Siegfried repents and lies dying of love for Lila. In desperation, Anna goes to Lila and asks how she can lift the curse. Lila replies that instead of rejecting her, she and Siegfried must invite her in and accept her. The two women – Violette and Ute – dance an exquisite duet; at the end, by a stunning special effect, the two become one; Lila-Anna, danced by Violette in a wonderful costume of black, white and gold. Siegfried comes back to life, the children are restored, the divided goddess becomes whole.

The ballet was magical; unsurpassed, Charlotte thought, even by Violette's previous creations. The audience responded ecstatically. *Witch and Maiden* was from its first moment a new classic.

Charlotte had hoped Josef would come to the ballet; he had been sent an invitation. But he did not appear. Afterwards, Charlotte slipped away from the post-show party – leaving Violette among her rapturous well-wishers – and went to his apartment.

She found Josef sitting at his desk in shirt-sleeves. There was a pen in his hand, a blank writing pad before him, but he was gazing at nothing. There were crumpled balls of paper all around him. Seeing her, he gave a slight start and almost smiled. Not quite. His face was calm but his eyes were dark, half-dead. He looked older.

'You didn't come,' she said softly. 'You missed a wonderful evening.'

'I didn't feel like enjoying myself.'

'Was it tactless of me to invite you? I didn't know what to do for the best. I thought it might take your mind off—'

'Nothing can do that. Not even time.' Exhaling heavily, he put down his pen. 'I was trying to write to you. Hopeless.'

She went to his chair and knelt down beside him. 'Why?'

'To tell you what happened about Robyn. To say – oh God, I don't know what. I can't find the words.'

'Tell me now.'

His fine-boned, strong face looked beautiful in the glow of his desk lamp; silver hair and eyebrows dewed with light. 'It was just as you'd expect. I informed the police that I'd been told – anonymously – where she might be. They found her. There was a post-mortem, then the body was returned to Boston for burial. Now the Irish and American police wish to question one Sebastian Pierse about her murder. And I should like to kill him with my bare hands—' He stopped, raw pain suffusing his face, then fading. 'They'll never find him, *natürlich*.'

'Of course not,' Charlotte said under her breath.

'And her death is my fault.'

'No!' She grasped his arms. 'Don't you dare say that! How could you possibly be responsible?'

'Because I befriended vampires, Charlotte.' He looked candidly at her. 'I failed to protect her from them. This is the result, and it was bound to happen, and I should have prevented it – but I didn't.'

'That's nonsense,' she said vehemently. 'It was a coincidence that she met Sebastian. There was no dark plot behind it. We didn't know him, we didn't even know he was there! You couldn't have prevented it.'

'But would she have succumbed to him, if she had not first been enchanted by you, Violette and Karl? You left her wanting something desperately – and, God, I should know how she felt! Now I cannot help thinking that this is some sort of punishment.'

'For what?'

'For my arrogance. Thinking that you and I could be friends. How can it possibly be? It is against nature, against God. There was bound to be retribution.'

'You don't believe that.' She felt unutterably distressed.

'Intellectually, it is of course a nonsense,' he said, his voice very dry. 'But I cannot persuade my heart of it. I am too exhausted to try. I was writing also to suggest that we should not see each other again.'

'I see.' She stood up and walked slowly around the study. Rows of books. Silver-framed photographs of Robyn, in all her radiance. 'Perhaps you're right. I've caused you nothing but distress.'

Silence. He rested his head on his hands.

'But before I go,' she said, 'I have something to tell you. Violette has achieved the wholeness you said she needed to find—'

'Individuation.'

'But to find it involved taking apart everything we believed and looking at it from the inside. You should do it too, Josef. Do you remember telling me that the Adam and Eve story was based on a misinterpretation of an earlier myth? I've never forgotten that—'

'Charlotte, please. I haven't the energy to discuss theology.'

'I'm sorry.' She paused. 'All that was leading to something important. A warning.'

He stirred tiredly. 'What warning?'

'Within the next few years, I don't know exactly when, Austria will become a dangerous place for you. You'll have to leave.'

At that he straightened up, more indignant than alarmed. 'Leave my home? Whatever for? Will vampires come to take revenge on me?'

'Not vampires. Men. Violette saw the future and it is very ugly. I can't tell you any more. But unless you leave and go somewhere safe like England or Switzerland, your life will be in danger.'

Josef's only reaction was another sigh. 'I don't know why. I have offended no one.'

'But millions of people who have offended no one will be persecuted, all the same,' she said quietly. 'It has happened countless times in the past. It's bound to happen again.'

'A tragedy for those others,' he said, his head bowed. 'But a threat to my own life fails to wake any trepidation in my soul, I'm afraid. It doesn't matter so very much.'

'Josef!' She flew to him, dismayed. 'I'm serious. You won't feel this grief for ever. You'll want to live. I want you to live.'

He looked up and took her hand, smiling. 'Well, I am being very selfish, thinking only of myself. I didn't notice how sad you look. What is wrong, Charlotte? Not just pity for an old man?'

A touch of his usual spirit and humour lit his eyes. With one unconscious, natural movement, she was sitting on his knee, her arms around his neck.

'My father's dead,' she said. 'It made him ill, my leaving. So I have been blaming myself as well.'

'Oh, God, poor Dr Neville,' Josef said into her hair. 'I didn't know! He was a good friend, many years ago; it didn't occur to me that I'd never see him again. I am so sorry.'

His sympathy was unforced; he didn't stop to wonder whether a vampire would care about her mortal family. In that moment she felt hopelessly and completely human.

'You've lost a niece who was your daughter in spirit,' she said, 'and I've lost my father. I miss him.'

They held and comforted each other, quite off their guard. And the inevitable happened. Charlotte felt the soft, lined skin of Josef's throat under her lips, and she bit down. It was an act of desperation and tenderness, not thirst; a need to purge her feelings, to connect with another being. The luscious flow of blood was a lightning strike.

Then she realized what she was doing, and began to pull away, horrified.

Josef fought her, straining to keep her teeth in the vein. He wanted her to carry on. But Charlotte won. Gasping, she pulled back, fighting off his hands.

'No, I won't! I said I wanted you to live and I meant it. If you want to die, it's not going to be by my hand!'

'But there is no other way I wish to die, Charlotte.' He spoke intensely, gripping her arms. 'Don't forget that. When my time comes, you had better be there. It would be kind, not cruel, can't you see that?'

She nodded. 'Yes. I know.'

He released her. His voice dropped. 'To bring this love to me and then to take it away – that is the real cruelty.'

She kissed his forehead. 'Forgive me,' she said, but he was like stone to her touch.

When Charlotte returned to the party, she decided to say nothing of her meeting with Josef. Violette's bite had given her the gift of detachment, at least. She could experience sorrow without being crushed by it; she could remember that all grief eases with time.

The party, held in an opulent state-room in a hotel near the theatre, was almost over. Violette must have dismissed all her human colleagues and the hotel staff. Only vampires remained: Karl and Ilona, Pierre, Violette, Stefan and Niklas, a handful from Schloss Holdenstein. How elegant and lovely they looked in their evening clothes; their opalescent skin, their lustrous hair and eyes gleaming in the diamond light of chandeliers. Charlotte felt a rush of dreadful excitement, knowing she belonged with them.

Then, to her shock, she saw Sebastian. He hadn't been at the ballet – or had he? He might have been in the audience unseen, a shadow. And Charlotte thought, thank goodness Josef didn't come after all!

As she crossed the room, Karl turned to her with the warmest look she had ever seen. He'd missed her; her reappearance brought light to his eyes. To know she was so wanted made her weak with happiness.

Yet the same feeling enlivened the whole room. There was a sense of unity between the vampires that she had never felt before.

'Is this a truce?' Charlotte said as she went to Karl's side.

Ilona gave a wry grin. 'Us against the world, dear,' she said.

'It would seem foolish to go on arguing amongst ourselves,

in a world that has decided it will support no more of us,' said Stefan.

'A truce,' said Violette. She seemed gentler, less aloof yet more vivid; radiantly graceful in her strength. 'One that will last, I hope.'

'We should drink a toast,' Stefan remarked. There was a murmur of laughter, then a pause. A change of mood.

'Well, why not?' Ilona said. And she went to Stefan, put her arms round him, and bit into his neck. That initiated the chain, a languid, magical ritual that seemed to Charlotte like a dream. She and Karl exchanged sips of blood with passionate tenderness, kissed with the blood still on their tongues; then Stefan was pulling her away, Violette embracing Karl. And they all passed from one to another, giving and receiving sips of life fluid as if in a slow-motion dance. It was the most extraordinary experience of Charlotte's life. An unholy, absorbing, loving, utterly enchanted sacrament.

At the end, she somehow found herself between Ilona and Violette. They clung to her and covered her with kisses; she almost died for joy.

That we can do such ghastly things, she thought ... She looked across the room to see Karl with Sebastian, two tall, darkly beautiful figures, fatally alluring to their prey. Such appalling, unconscionable things, all of us, and yet we still love each other so deeply. What can it mean, this miracle?

Karl and Sebastian were the last to meet. They exchanged a look of mutual reluctance to taste each other's blood. Yet they did it anyway, and when it was over, the tension between them had vanished.

'So,' said Karl, 'you chose not to follow Simon's path?'

Sebastian shrugged. He was self-contained, yet there was a ghost-like quality to him, a lack of vitality. 'Violette asked me not to. Who am I to argue?'

'She can be very persuasive.'

'So I heard,' Sebastian said drily. 'You must understand, there is nothing between us. Only our love for Robyn.'

'That is a stronger bond than many.'

Sebastian's eyes held a brief look of abstraction. Then he seemed to collect himself. 'Could you live, if you lost Charlotte?'

'I don't know,' Karl replied honestly. It was something he could not contemplate.

'You'd live for the blood.' Sebastian's voice sank harshly on the words. 'There is nothing else.'

'Then why are you here?'

Sebastian made no reply. Karl looked at Charlotte, an enchanting tawny-haired sylph; he watched her with Violette and Ilona. He found the affection with which they hugged and caressed one another spellbinding. And he had the strangest feeling that it should have been Robyn with Charlotte and Violette. It was as if they were the goddess trinity of his vision, and that Robyn was the rightful third member. Instead, Ilona had taken her place. This was not wrong, yet Karl felt, all the same, that they had lost something. Robyn had been taken, not just from Sebastian, but from all of them.

Strange to realize that he no longer resented Violette. He loved her, in a way. Loved them all.

Violette detached herself from her companions and spoke.

'Whatever the future holds, we can't change it. Sebastian was right when he said that our purpose is a selfish one; to live for the blood-hunt, to bring pleasures and nightmares to individuals. Not to change the world. The Crystal Ring itself won't let us do it. That's why Cesare's ambitions failed; to make way for something worse. I fear we have drunk to a very dark future.

'Everything men do is in denial of death. They think they can destroy death and live for ever. But no man can kill death, no mortal can escape Lilith. That's why they invented God to destroy me. But a few, just a few take the risk of embracing me and accepting my kiss.'

'And we become immortal?' said Pierre.

'You live a little longer,' said Violette. 'That's all.'

'But we will live,' Sebastian broke in. Karl saw his gaze lock with Violette's, her lips curving as if he'd taken the words out of her mouth. 'Just when he needs the Mother-of-all most, mankind turns his back on her . . . but she will come anyway, dressed for battle like the Morríghan, and take her revenge for being rejected. Then we shall feast like vultures on their folly.'

As he spoke, a ghastly vision struck Karl; cold mist drifting over the mud and trenches of a battlefield, and himself, moving from one dying man to another, as if by taking the last of their blood, by immersing himself in their suffering, he could somehow understand why it had happened. Bridge the chasm. Be reconciled to his guilt. But never again, Karl thought. I will never let human folly torment me like that again.

'And when it's over,' said Chárlotte, 'we will still be here.'

Karl had meant to complete the last task alone, then decided that he would prefer company. He seemed to have less taste for being alone of late. So, he thought, even immortals can change – as if I did not already know it.

Besides, he did not want to deprive his friends of witnessing this purging act.

So one night he took Charlotte, Violette, Ilona, Pierre, Stefan and Niklas on their last visit to Schloss Holdenstein. In the chamber where the corpses of the young men still lay, they made a funeral pyre with branches; they went through every room, dousing the walls and furniture with petrol. The six vampires who still huddled there, the remnants of Cesare's flock, tried to stop them; Karl and the others brushed them aside. Eventually the six acolytes fled.

And then came the glory of the conflagration. Karl stood on the river bank, his arm around Charlotte's waist, their friends grouped around them. The Rhine flowed behind them. Above, on top of the ridge, the castle floated in plumes of gold and apricot fire. Great bubbles of flame and smoke surged through the doors and windows, crackling and roaring towards heaven.

The walls were turning black. Heat cracked the stone. The balconies began to crumble, and the roofs collapsed with a *whoosh* like soft thunder. The smell of roasting meat filled the air, and was swallowed by smoke and heat.

In an uprush of scarlet flame, in columns of firefly sparks, Schloss Holdenstein shrank to a weightless black skeleton and died, taking its ghosts with it.

No one wept. Charlotte embraced Karl, transfixed; Violette leaned on Charlotte, Ilona clung to Karl's other arm.

After a while Charlotte said, 'All the visions we saw, all the lost secrets of the Goddess – no one would believe us. Particularly not men. No church, no political or religious body could afford to believe it or to let it become common knowledge. There is too much power at stake. How could they ever give up their power by admitting it was based on lies? So the secrets will remain hidden, except to a few. Such a loss. They'll stay hidden for ever.'

'Always in the twilight,' said Violette. 'Like us.'

Sebastian watched the fire from a distance, but he had no desire to join the others. That should have been Blackwater Hall aflame, he thought. But it means so little to me now that I lacked even the will to finish what I started before Simon came. Let it rot. It's not my house any more.

After a time he turned away and entered the Crystal Ring.

We will live, he had said to the others, but even then the words had tasted flat in his mouth. People all around him, vampires and humans, teeming crowds of people to provide him with an endless fountain of blood until the end of time . . . but none of them was Robyn, none of them would ever, ever be Robyn.

It is not just the loss of her, Sebastian thought as he rose through the cloudy mountains, the dark manifestation of men's folly still seething above him. It is not knowing whether she ever really loved me. That's what I can't bear. And now I'll never know.

I am alive and you are dead, beautiful child, but you won. You spoiled my pleasure in being a vampire. You taught me to love and you tore it away. Oh yes, you won a victory so complete that you might as well have annihilated me and held victory celebrations on my grave.

But was it what you wanted? Robyn, does your soul look down on me now with pity or with heartless glee?

If only you had given me an answer. I cannot live for ever without an answer.

Lilith, my sister, I'm sorry – but I cannot.

So he left it all behind. Sebastian passed from flame to ice, to the *Weisskalt*'s dazzling eternal winter; embraced the very extremity of the solitude that he had always held so dear.

All Pan Books are available at your local bookshop or newsagent, or can be ordered direct from the publisher. Indicate the number of copies required and fill in the form below.

Send to: Macmillan General Books C.S.
                Book Service By Post
                PO Box 29, Douglas I-O-M
                IM99 1BQ

or phone: 01624 675137, quoting title, author and credit card number.

or fax: 01624 670923, quoting title, author, and credit card number.

or Internet: http://www.bookpost.co.uk

Please enclose a remittance* to the value of the cover price plus 75 pence per book for post and packing. Overseas customers please allow £1.00 per copy for post and packing.

*Payment may be made in sterling by UK personal cheque, Eurocheque, postal order, sterling draft or international money order, made payable to Book Service By Post.

Alternatively by Access/Visa/MasterCard

Card No.   ☐☐☐☐ ☐☐☐☐ ☐☐☐☐ ☐☐☐☐ ☐☐☐☐

Expiry Date   ☐☐☐☐ ☐☐☐☐ ☐☐☐☐ ☐☐☐☐ ☐☐☐☐

Signature   _____

Applicable only in the UK and BFPO addresses.

While every effort is made to keep prices low, it is sometimes necessary to increase prices at short notice. Pan Books reserve the right to show on covers and charge new retail prices which may differ from those advertised in the text or elsewhere.

NAME AND ADDRESS IN BLOCK CAPITAL LETTERS PLEASE

Name _____

Address _____

_____

_____

_____

8/95

Please allow 28 days for delivery.
Please tick box if you do not wish to receive any additional information. ☐